THE DARK
REMAINS

D1440470

ALSO BY MARK ANTHONY

Beyond the Pale
The Keep of Fire
Blood of Mystery

THE DARK REMAINS

Book Three of THE LAST RUNE

Mark Anthony

EARTHLIGHT

SIMON & SCHUSTER

London • New York • Sydney • Tokyo • Singapore • Toronto • Dublin

A VIACOM COMPANY

First published in Great Britain by Earthlight, 2001
An imprint of Simon & Schuster UK Ltd
A Viacom Company

This paperback edition published in 2002

1 3 5 7 9 10 8 6 4 2

Simon & Schuster UK Ltd
Africa House
64–78 Kingsway
London WC2B 6AH

www.simonsays.co.uk

Simon & Schuster Australia
Sydney

A CIP catalogue record for this book is available from the British Library

ISBN 0-671-02885-5

Typeset in Bembo by SX Composing DTP, Rayleigh, Essex
Printed and bound in Great Britain by Omnia Books Ltd, Glasgow

For Trey R. Barker and LuAnn Salz—
Thanks for Providence and Dark Redemption

And for the Millennium Gang—
Kathy Kirby and Stan Kirby
Christie Golden and Michael Georges
and Raven Moore—
Three a.m. will never look quite the same

THE DOMINIONS
and surrounding lands
Leagues

0   25   50

THE WINTER SEA

Ur-Torin

THE ICEWOLD

TORINGARTH

Fal Imbri

IMBRIFALE

The Rune Gate

Fal Threndur
(Ironfang Mountains)

SHADOWSDEEP

Gravenfist Keep

THE BARRENS

River Fellgrim

(MALACHOR)

EMBARR

Keloior

Barrsunder

River Serpent's Tail

The Winter Wood

Spardis

River Farwander

EREDANE

White Tower

Fal Erenn
(Dawning Fells)

PERRIDON

THE WILD COAST

Erendel

Galt

Western Wood

GALT

Gray Tower

Fal Sinfath
(Gloaming Fells)

Gloaming Wood

Ar-Tolor

THE DAWN SEA

Calavere

River Dimduom

Black Tower

Borelga

CALAVAN

TOLORIA

The Queen's Way

The Great

River Kelduorn

Gendarra

THE FREE CITIES

Whitestone Peaks

BRELEGOND

Mountains of the Shroud

To Torras

THE SUMMER SEA

With Fellring sword of Elfin art,
Ulther smote the Pale King's heart.

*And farewell words too often part
All their small and paling hearts.*

PART ONE:
HIGH COVEN

1.

It was in the final, burnished days of summer—when cool mornings gave way to languid afternoons under hazy skies, when the wheat bowed in the fields, shafts heavy with fruit, and all the land was still as if drinking in one last, long draught of gold—that the Mournish came to Ar-tolor.

Through the window of her chamber, Aryn watched the line of wagons creep along the road that led to the castle. At this distance the wagons were smaller than toys, but the young woman's blue eyes were sharp, and she could make out many of the fantastical shapes into which they had been wrought.

There were swans with high, curving prows and snowy wings folded against their sides, and snails painted pink with small round windows set into their spiraled shells. A lion crouched low to the road, as if ready to pounce on a hart crowned by tree-branch antlers, while an emerald frog bounced behind. More wagons rolled into view: tortoises, fish cresting carved blue waves, lizards, tawny hares, and a dozen other creatures that Aryn had never seen before, except perhaps coiled along the edges of pages in old books.

One by one the wagons vanished beneath the green curve of the hill, and the road was empty again. But even at that moment, Aryn knew the wagons were coming to halt in the field outside the village, opening painted doors to release the spicy scent of incense, the cool *clink* of silver, and the undulating rhythms of music.

The young woman turned from the window, her sapphire eyes bright. "Let's go see the Mournish!"

Lirith, who sat in a chair on the other side of the small sitting room, did not look up from her embroidery. "And then let's get tossed in the dungeon and make the acquaintance of a few dozen rats. For you know as I do, sister, that Queen Ivalaine has made it plain she wishes no one in her court to associate with the wandering folk. Their entertainments are for villagers and farmers."

Annoyed, but not surprised, Aryn indulged herself in a particularly noxious frown.

"And what a fine baroness you'll make after your face freezes that way, sister," Lirith mused, her dark eyes still focused on the embroidery hoop in her lap. "Even bold dukes and proud knights will quail before you."

"As well they should," Aryn said. Although she smoothed her features and made a quick glance at a silver mirror on the wall nearby to be sure she hadn't done permanent damage.

"I saw that," Lirith said.

Rather than reply, Aryn gazed back out the window. The most interesting sight she saw now was a flock of sheep dotting the side of a distant hill like flowers. She amused herself for a few moments, imagining plucking tiny sheep from the grass, weaving them into a squirming, bleating chain, and placing them around her neck. Then she considered the smell, and that fancy passed.

"I'm bored," she said, not caring how petulant she sounded. She *felt* petulant.

"All the better reason for you to stay and work on your embroidery."

Aryn scowled at the black-haired witch. "I know perfectly well that you loathe embroidery, Lirith."

"Indeed. And my loathing keeps me well occupied, so that I do not become bored. Now sew. Sister Tressa will be here soon, and she'll expect to see some progress."

Aryn turned from the window, pulled close the wooden stand that held her embroidery hoop steady for her, and did her best to pretend that sewing unicorns was really more fascinating than buying packets of sugared nuts, laughing at performing monkeys, and watching men who swallowed knives and burning brands.

Yrsaia knows, you should be more grateful for your boredom, Aryn of Elsandry, she scolded herself. *Where are Grace and Goodman Travis and Lord Beltan now? Sitting in a comfortable chair in a safe castle with a cup of sweet wine at hand?*

She sighed, and Lirith looked up, an expression of concern on her face.

"I am certain they are well, sister. It is to their homeland they have journeyed. And no one has power to heal as does Lady Grace. I imagine Sir Beltan is telling bawdy jokes and drinking ale even as we speak."

Aryn wished she had such a good imagination.

It had been a month since they had begged their leave of Queen Inara and set out from Castle Spardis. They had left the seat of Perridon in good order. The young queen had rescinded all of the usurper Dakarreth's proclamations, and with the help of the Spider Aldeth—who was making a steady recovery from his injury—had cemented her position as regent to her infant son, Prince Perseth. While there would continue to be plots

against the queen—this was Perridon, after all—Aryn
expected Inara to rule long and well.

After only a day of traveling they had bid farewell to
Melia and Falken, for the bard and the lady intended to
journey north to find their friend Tome—who, like
Melia, was a former god. Aryn would have liked to see
the golden-eyed old man again; he had the power to
make her laugh no matter the sorrow she felt.
However, Inara had already sent a messenger to
Ivalaine. Aryn and Lirith were expected in Ar-tolor,
and Durge had agreed to escort them there.

Although Lirith was her friend and teacher, and
Durge was good—if sober—company, the ride across
Perridon and Toloria seemed lonely. Grace and Travis
had returned with Beltan to their world in hopes of
healing the knight's old wound. Melia and Falken had
their own journeys. Even Tira was gone.

Except that wasn't true, was it? For sometimes,
when Aryn woke in the gray dawn, she glimpsed a star
as red as fire low in the southern sky. She still didn't
understand what had happened in Spardis, when
Travis gave Tira the Stone of Fire. But Melia said the
red-haired girl was a goddess now, and Melia should
know. Aryn supposed that, in a way, Tira would
always be with them.

They had reached Ar-tolor with little event, and
Aryn had been more glad than she expected to see its
seven spires soaring over fields of jade. Queen Ivalaine
had welcomed them with a rare smile, and at once
dispatched a man to Calavere to inform King Boreas
that Aryn would be visiting at the court of Ar-tolor for
a time.

"You shall resume your instruction with Sister
Lirith at once," Ivalaine told her that first day in the
castle, and Aryn had not disagreed.

The weeks since had passed pleasantly—walking the castle grounds, sewing under Tressa's attention, reaching out with the Touch to grasp the magic of the Weirding as Lirith whispered calm instructions in her ear. And if at times it all seemed dull compared to their desperate journey east to the Keep of Fire, Aryn knew she should be grateful for that dullness.

With the Necromancer Dakarreth's scourge of fire ended, the land had recovered more quickly than she had believed possible. Crops had been hastily resown, flourishing under golden sun and gentle rain. Now Keldath was nearly over, and there would be a good— if late—harvest this year. It seemed a wonder, but perhaps there was a lesson in it; perhaps she should never underestimate the power of life.

Then don't underestimate Beltan's life. Or Grace's or Travis's. They're going to be fine. So you might as well stop worrying.

However, Aryn might as easily prevent the stars from spinning in the night sky. And she knew it gnawed at Lirith and Durge as much as it did her. They all feared for the others, who were beyond their reach now.

Which was precisely why a diversion like the Mournish caravan was in order.

A knock sounded at the chamber door. Aryn bit her lip. She had hardly sewn three stitches all morning. What would she tell Tressa? The queen's counselor seemed to have a vastly inflated notion of the importance of sewing.

The door opened. It was not Tressa who stepped into the room, but rather a short, deep-chested man with drooping mustaches and somber brown eyes.

Lirith rose from her seat. "Good morrow, Lord Durge."

He nodded to her. "My lady."

Aryn thought about it for less than a moment, then leaped to her feet.

"Durge, we're going to see the Mournish."

Lirith glared at her, but Aryn ignored the look. It was a mean trick, but she had learned a bit about tactics from her days as ward to King Boreas of Calavan. When blocked on one front, advance on another.

Durge's perpetual frown deepened. "That is a perilous idea, my lady. The Mournish are a queer folk. They make no homes save the wagons they travel in, and it is said the music of their flutes can drive a man to wildness."

Aryn groaned. That was hardly the response she had hoped for.

Lirith folded her arms over the bodice of her rust-colored gown and glanced at Durge. "She has it in her head to go down and see the wandering folk, even though Ivalaine has forbidden it."

"She didn't forbid it," Aryn countered. "Not precisely, anyway. Ivalaine merely *discouraged* us from going. Besides, I'm weary of moping about this castle. I think we all are. It would do us good to get some fresh air." She held her breath, looking from knight to witch.

Durge stroked his mustaches and gazed at Lirith. "I believe she means to go no matter what we say, my lady."

Lirith sighed. "Aren't chains an option?"

"A temptation, to be sure, but I fear not. It is best if you and I accompany her to see that she does not fall into trouble."

If she had possessed two good hands instead of one, Aryn would have clapped. "Now that's the sensible Durge I know." She stepped forward and kissed his craggy cheek.

The knight blinked, his expression bewildered, and Lirith's brow furrowed with displeasure. Aryn didn't care if she had been too familiar. For the first time in days she felt her spirits lift. The others would see that she was right—this was exactly what they needed.

2.

Sunlight drenched the world like warm rain from the cobalt sky as baroness, countess, and knight passed through a colonnade of trees and stepped onto the village green.

It had been a simple feat to slip from the castle. Too simple for Lirith's taste. Was it merely chance they had not come upon Lady Tressa or another member of the queen's court on their way through Ar-tolor's busy halls? Or had luck received some degree of assistance in the matter?

Lirith cast a glance at Aryn as they walked. She still didn't know what the young woman had done over two months ago, when in secret they followed after Grace and Durge as the pair set off from Calavere. Tagging along had been a foolish plan, and Lirith had agreed to it only because she had been certain King Boreas's knights would ride forth to retrieve them before they had gone a league from the castle. Only somehow Aryn had misdirected the king and his men. Lirith didn't know how, but there was one thing of which she was certain: Aryn had used a spell of some kind to achieve their escape.

Yet despite Aryn's rashness, Lirith was grateful—if not precisely glad—that she and Aryn had followed after the others. The road had been arduous, filled with fire and death, but there had been purpose to it. For if they had not stolen away from Calavere that day, there was so much Lirith would never have witnessed: Grace's courage against the burning plague, Goodman Travis's wisdom before the Necromancer, the girl Tira's mysterious and wondrous transformation. And there was more she would never have known. . . .

I miss all your questions, Daynen.

A sigh escaped her lips, as it always did when she thought of the sightless boy who had given his life to save Tira at the bridge over the River Darkwine. For so many years she had prayed to Sia to grant her a child, and she had drunk an ocean of infusions and simples to quicken her womb. However, no amount of prayers or herbs would ever cause seed to grow in the soil of a salted field; she knew that now. But perhaps Sia had heard her pleas after all, for Daynen—however briefly she had known him—had seemed a son to her. She would never forget him.

"Come on, Lirith!" Aryn said, tugging on her arm.

Lirith let the young woman pull her across the grass while Durge trotted behind them, clad in a heavy gray tunic despite the brilliance of the late-summer afternoon. Already people from the town wandered uncertainly onto the green, as if fearful of yet compelled by the fantastical wagons. As the trio passed, the townsfolk cast startled glances at Aryn, eyeing her pale, lovely face and azure gown—no doubt surprised to see a member of the queen's court there. As well they should be. Lirith hoped it was only the townsfolk who saw them.

The three reached the edge of the circle of wagons. Now that they were close, Lirith could see the vehicles were more than a little roadworn: wood cracked, gilt peeled, and dust flecked sun-faded paint. Yet somehow this only added to their patina of mystery.

Although they had wandered for time out of mind, it was said the Mournish came from the south. And indeed the appearance of their wagons had been a more frequent—if far from regular—sight in Lirith's childhood home in southern Toloria. Still, she had not seen the Mournish up close since her girlhood. The scent of spices, candles, and roasted meat reached her nose, and memories flooded her.

"Listen!" Aryn said, coming to a halt. Lilting music drifted on the air, blowing back and forth with the breeze. The young woman shut her eyes and swayed like a slender tree. "It's so beautiful."

Lirith drew in a breath, letting fresh air clear the memories from her mind. "Well, are you feeling wild yet, Sir Durge?"

He seemed to consider her words, then gave a solemn nod. "Perhaps just a bit, now that you mention it."

Lirith gaped at the stone-faced knight. Had the Embarran made a joke, or was it merely a happy accident? Either way, she laughed. Perhaps Aryn's impulses had proved beneficial once again—perhaps visiting the Mournish was not such a bad idea after all.

"All right," she said, engaging Aryn's good left arm and Durge's iron-hard right, "I believe there are some spice pies with our names on them."

It did not take them long to find the pies. They paid a copper coin apiece to a toothless woman clad in orange and yellow, then sat in leafy shade. There they bit into bubbled crusts to release warm juices that dribbled down their chins. When the spice pies were gone, Aryn and Lirith laughed as Durge diligently licked each of his fingers.

After that, the three wandered from wagon to

wagon, and at each one a new and enticing aroma
drew them on. There were plates of sugared nuts,
sizzling bits of meat on sticks, and small cups fashioned
ingeniously of leaves, filled with honeyed wine as gold
as the sun, but cool against the tongue as evening dew.

And not all of the wagons contained food. Many
were open to reveal black cloths piled with silver rings,
bright scarves that fluttered on the air like butterflies,
knives of blue steel, polished stones, rugs woven with
swirling colors, tin whistles, and boxes of wood carved
like the Mournish wagons themselves into the forms of
animals and birds.

At one wagon—this one shaped like a crouching
rat—an old man beckoned them closer with a bony
finger. They peered into the gloom within the wagon,
and only as their eyes adjusted did they make out the
glass jars that lined wooden shelves. The jars were filled
with yellowish fluid, and things floated inside them. At
first Lirith couldn't tell what they were, then a jolt of
horror surged through her. One jar was filled with
eyeballs, another with snakes, and one with the half-
formed fetus of a pig, its clearly visible spine ending not
in one head but two.

Displaying a rotten grin, the old man reached out
and brushed Aryn's left arm with something dark, dry,
and shriveled: a monkey's paw. The baroness screamed
and darted from the wagon, bumping into a rickety
wooden stage where a monkey—this one quite alive—
danced in time to a drum. The stage tilted, and the
spindly creature leaped for Aryn, eliciting another
shriek. She heaved the monkey back at its owner, who
caught it as he shouted at her in a hot and musical
tongue.

Lirith and Durge grasped the baroness's shoulders
and quickly steered her away. As they walked, Aryn

collapsed against them in breathless, trembling laughter, tears streaming from her eyes. Lirith couldn't help joining in, and even Durge's craggy cheek seemed to twitch. At last the three of them came to a halt beside a tree, away from the circle of wagons. Heavy light infused the air, and the leaves whispered soft, green secrets above; the day was waning. Aryn's laughter dwindled, and she let out a breath as she leaned against the smooth bark of the tree.

"I feel sticky," she said.

Lirith nodded in agreement. Durge said nothing, but his mustaches stuck out at odd angles.

"It's nearly sunset," Lirith said. "We should get back to the castle. The queen will notice if we're not at supper."

Durge held a hand to his stomach and winced. "Please, my lady. May I beg that you do not mention the word 'supper' again this evening?"

Lirith gave the knight a wry smile. "I told you not to go back for another spice pie."

"And no doubt I shall pay for my folly, my lady. Do I need the lash of your tongue to punish me as well?"

Lirith smiled sweetly.

Aryn stepped away from the tree. "Can we walk slowly back to the castle? It's been such a fine day."

The two women started back across the green arm in arm as Durge lumbered none too swiftly behind them.

"Now here is a sight," said a voice as deep and rich as a bronze bell. "There walks the moon and the sun arm in arm. And look—a gloomy cloud follows behind them."

The three came to a halt, searching. It took Lirith a moment to see the hulking shape nestled in the deepening shade between two trees. Then she made out the ridged spine, the sinuous neck, the folded bat wings. Aryn gasped beside her, and out of the corner of her eye she saw Durge grope in vain for the greatsword that was not strapped to his back.

For a heartbeat, Lirith was transported to the high, windswept bowl of stone where they had encountered the dragon Sfithrisir.

And here are two Daughters of Sia, both doomed to betray their sisters and their mistress. . . .

But how could such a terrible and ancient creature be here, in a well-tended grove beneath the queen's castle of Ar-tolor?

A shadow moved between the trees: the shape of man. "Good sisters? Good brother? Is something amiss?"

It was the thrumming voice again—the warm voice of a man, not the dry hiss of a dragon. Realization drained through Lirith, leaving her trembling. How could she have been so foolish? It was not a real dragon before them, but rather a Mournish wagon carved in the shape of one. Now that she peered closer, she could see the craft's spoked wheels, its circular windows, and the peeling, painted scales of the dragon's neck. Yet they had not seen this wagon before. Why was it set apart from all the others?

The man stepped closer, still awaiting an answer.

Lirith swallowed. "It was nothing, sir. A shadow of the past, that is all, and soon gone."

The man paused, and it seemed he stiffened. Then he said softly, "I have found in my travels it is usually best not to dismiss what one glimpses in shadows."

Before Lirith could speak again, a cracked voice drifted through the wagon's window.

"Sareth, who is it out there? I cannot see them, blast my failing eyes. I should give them to Mirgeth and his jars for all the good they do me."

"It is . . . two beautiful ladies and a stern knight, al-Mama."

"Well, bring them here where I can look at them. I will see their fates for them."

"This way," the man said, gesturing to the wagon. "Al-Mama does not like to be kept waiting. She says at her age there is no time for patience."

He turned and started toward the wagon. Lirith glanced at Aryn and Durge, but they only shrugged. It seemed there was nothing else to do save follow.

3.

The Mournish man walked swiftly—although there
was a peculiar cadence to his gait—and in moments
they reached the wagon. Smoke and the scent of
lemons rose on the purple air. Bits of copper hung
from the eaves of the wagon, filling the grove with
chiming music.

The man turned toward them.

"What did you mean?" Lirith said before he could
speak. "Back there, when you said, 'there goes the sun
and the moon'?"

The man smiled, his teeth white in the premature
gloom beneath the trees. "It is simple enough, *beshala*.
You are as brilliant as the sun and your sister as
luminous as the moon."

Durge cleared his throat. "And what was this speech
about clouds?"

The man clapped the knight's shoulder. "It is no
insult I meant you, good brother. For the cloud grants
the sun and moon a chance to rest when he lies over
them."

Even in the dimness, Durge's blush was plain to see.
"I have not . . . that is, I do not lie over . . . I mean to
say . . ."

The man laughed—a sound as joyous as the chimes,
but octaves lower, thrumming in Lirith's chest.

Curious for a reason she could not name, she studied him.

The Mournish man's skin was the color of burnt sugar, and his eyes were as dark as old copper coins. Short as it was, his black hair was thick and curling, and his pointed beard was glossy with oil. He wore only a pair of blue, billowing pants in the style of the Mournish, and a red vest open to expose a flat chest. A dozen short, thin scars marked each of his forearms. The scars were precisely lined in parallel, which made Lirith suppose they had some ritual meaning. He smelled of sweat and strong spices. It was not an unpleasant scent.

The man's laughter faded, and his eyes narrowed, as if he noticed Lirith's attention. She quickly looked away.

"Where are they, Sareth?" came the cracked voice from inside the wagon. "It is almost time for my tea."

Sareth grinned again. "My al-Mama will see you now."

He pulled a handle near the dragon's tail, and a door swung open. Beyond was smoke and dim, golden light. Sareth unfolded a set of wooden steps, then climbed into the wagon. It was only as he did this that Lirith finally noticed his leg.

Sareth's loose pants ended just below his knees. On the right, his bare calf and foot were well shaped. However, on the left, there was no leg beneath the knee, but instead an ornately carved shaft of wood ending in a bronze cap. The peg leg drummed against the wooden steps as Sareth climbed inside.

"Come," he said to the three below.

Lifting the hem of her gown, Lirith started up the steps, followed by Aryn and Durge. She couldn't imagine there would be room for them all inside the wagon. But there was—barely. Light emanated from a single oil lamp, but Lirith couldn't see the walls or ceiling, for everywhere hung jars, pots, bundles, and bunches of dried herbs. Sareth gestured for them to sit on three small stools while he stood near the door, blocking the waning daylight.

"A silver coin each it will cost you," came the same cracked voice they had heard before, louder now.

Only then did Lirith realize that what she had taken for a bundle of rags against the far wall was in fact a woman.

She was ancient. Her body was lost in the tangled mass of rugs and blankets that covered the bench, but the arm she stretched forth was as thin and withered as a stick. Her head bobbed on a long, crooked neck, and her scalp bore only wisps of gray hair. However, amid the countless wrinkles of her face, her eyes were bright and warm as harvest moons. Bracelets clattered around her bony wrist, and large rings hung from her ears.

Before Lirith could respond, Durge held out three silver coins. The old woman snatched them from his hand and bit each coin with what appeared to be her only tooth. Then she grunted, spirited the coins to someplace deep within the mass of rags, and turned her large eyes on the visitors.

"You are marked with power," the old woman rasped, thrusting a long finger toward Aryn.

Aryn started. "What . . . what do you mean?"

"Your arm," the woman said.

Aryn lifted her hand to clutch her withered right arm, but the appendage rested as always in a linen sling, hidden beneath a fold of her gown.

"Always the balance seeks something in return when a great gift is given," the crone said in her harsh voice. "Beautiful I was, until I discovered my *shes'thar*."

Durge frowned at Sareth. "Her *shes'thar*?"

"She means her magic."

Now Durge cast his somber gaze on Aryn, but what he thought he did not say.

"My cards, Sareth," the old woman barked.

"They are next to you, al-Mama," he said gently.

"Well of course they are." The old woman snatched up a deck of cards from a small shelf. Another birdlike hand appeared from the rags, and she shuffled the cards with deft motions. "Each of you must draw a card from the *T'hot* deck."

She fanned the cards out before her. The backs of the cards were faded, their corners worn, but silver symbols still gleamed against midnight-blue ink. Lirith exchanged looks with Aryn and Durge, then reached. Her fingertips seemed to tingle as she brushed one of the cards; she drew it. The others followed suit.

"You," the old woman said with a nod to Durge. "Show me what you have drawn."

Durge turned over his card, revealing a drawing that was at once dusky and radiant. It depicted a man with dark hair and eyes, standing by a pool of water that reflected the moon hanging in the slate-blue sky.

No, not just a man, Lirith. Look at the sword in his hand, and his armor. He's a knight—a knight with a moon emblazoned on his shield.

The old woman took the card, running a yellowed fingernail over its surface. "The Knight of Moons. A man of war you are—trustworthy and strong. Yet you are ruled by the heart. And so full of sorrow! You believe you fight alone, but that is not so. For see? She smiles upon you always, although you know it not."

The crone pointed to the drawing of the moon. Painted in the circle was the face of a woman, her lips curved in a soft smile.

"But who is she?" the old woman muttered.

"Someone gone, or someone yet to come? My magic cannot say."

Durge grunted. "I do not believe in magic, madam."

The crone looked up. "And yet magic shall be the death of you," she said flatly, burying the card back in the deck.

"Al-Mama!" Sareth said in a chiding voice.

The old woman shrugged. "I do not make their fates, Sareth. I but speak them. Now you." She pointed to Aryn.

Trembling slightly, Aryn held out her card.

"Hah!" the old woman said, as if something she guessed had now been confirmed. "The Eight of Blades."

On the card, a beautiful but solemn woman in a blue dress rode on a white horse across sun-dappled fields, a sword in her left hand. In the distance behind her rose a castle with seven towers, each crowned by a sword.

Aryn gasped. "But I've seen this before!"

Lirith glanced at the baroness. What did she mean?

The old woman nodded as she took the card. "As I said before, you have great power. See how the woman rides so proudly? All love her beauty even as they fear her sword. Yet there is always a price to wielding power. For see? She does not notice the poor man in the grass who is trampled beneath the hooves of her horse."

Lirith stiffened. There—she could just make out the face in the long grass beneath the horse, eyes shut as if sleeping.

Aryn shook her head. "I don't understand."

"You have forgotten about one who bore pain for you."

"But who is it?"

The old woman slipped the card back into the deck. "That is for you to remember, child."

Even before the crone gazed at her, Lirith knew it was her turn. After Durge's and Aryn's tellings, she was not so certain she wanted to see the card she had drawn, but she didn't have a choice. She turned it over.

Lightning slashed across a black sky behind a barren landscape as gray as ash. White shapes stained red scattered the ground. Perched on a twisted tree was a dark form, its eyes like hard beads.

A hiss escaped the old woman. "The Raven . . ."

"What does it foretell?" Lirith said, surprised at the calmness in her voice.

"The raven scavenges on the fields of the dead." The old woman's hand shook as she took the card. "Fields poisoned with spilled blood, where nothing will ever grow again."

The dimness closed around Lirith, and the stifling air pressed against her so that she could not breathe. She blinked, and it seemed the images on the *T'hot* card moved. Sinuous lightning slithered across the black-ink sky. The bird opened the cruel hook of its mouth as if laughing.

Lirith swayed on her stool, but a strong hand gripped her shoulder. She blinked, and the images on the card were motionless again. She looked up to thank Durge for steadying her—

—and froze. It wasn't Durge who stood above her, but Sareth.

"Are you well, *beshala*?"

She licked her lips. "It's nothing. I just need some air."

"I will help you outside."

Aryn and Durge looked concerned as the Mournish man helped her stand.

"You flee your fate," came the old woman's voice behind her. "Yet you cannot escape it, for it lies within you."

Lirith stiffened, then stepped from the wagon into the gray-green air of the grove. She turned toward Sareth. His eyes were filled with such a strange softness that she almost gasped aloud. Why should he act this way for a stranger?

"I must apologize for my al-Mama," he said, his deep voice husky.

Lirith forced her chin up, meeting his eyes. "Why? Are her tellings not true?"

His cheeks darkened, but he did not reply.

"Your leg," Lirith murmured before she could stop herself. "Was that the price you paid for your *shes'thar*?"

His smile returned, but it was fiercer now, sharper. "No, *beshala*. That was the price I paid for my pride."

Lirith opened her mouth, but before she could answer Durge and Aryn stepped from the wagon. Aryn's face was pale, and Lirith did not fail to notice the way Durge hovered close to her.

"We should get back to the castle," he said.

Aryn lifted her hand to her chest. "I don't feel well."

Lirith took the woman's hand. "Do not fear, sister. You have only eaten too many sweets, that's all. The feeling will soon pass."

She led Aryn from the grove as Durge followed three paces behind. Only after a moment did she remember to look over her shoulder, to bid Sareth farewell. But the grove was empty, save for the now-shut wagon and the soft music of chimes.

Lirith turned her face forward. Together the three walked back toward the castle in the fading light of sunset, their shadows stretching out before them.

4.

They arrived at the castle just as the gates were closing. The land in all directions was steeped in twilight, but the last few rays of sunlight still fell upon Ar-tolor: a golden island in a deep, purple sea.

"Your Highness," said a guardsman clad in black and green, stepping from a side gate to bow to Aryn. He turned and bowed to Lirith. "My lady. It is well you are here. We have scoured the castle for you."

Alarm rose in Aryn's chest, and she glanced at Lirith.

"What is it?" Lirith said.

"Queen Ivalaine wishes to see you both. We have been searching for you all afternoon, my lady."

Durge stepped forward. "If the ladies' absence has caused trouble, then you may lay the blame for it upon me. It was I who accompanied them from the castle."

Aryn grimaced. That wasn't right. It wasn't because of Durge they had gone to see the Mournish; it had been her idea.

"Why does the queen want us?" she said before she could consider the wisdom of the words.

The guardsman started to make a crude gesture with his left hand. Then, as if remembering in whose company he stood, he hastily changed the motion and straightened the yellow sash slung over his shoulder instead. "It is not my place to suppose the mind of Her

Good Majesty." His voice was overloud, as if he believed it might be overhead.

"Of course," Lirith said. "Thank you for this service, guardsman. We shall attend the queen at once."

Aryn felt a firm tug on her left arm as Lirith pulled her through the gate.

"What is it?" Aryn whispered. "Do you think she knows that we went to see the Mournish?"

"Don't be foolish, sister. Ivalaine doesn't have a magic mirror. There's no way she could know where we went. If she is displeased with us, then it is merely for answering late to her summons. So let us make haste."

Aryn swallowed, wishing she could be as confident, but she said nothing more as they hurried through the castle. Unlike the dark, smoky corridors of Calavere, the vaulted halls of Ar-tolor were airy, lined with slender arches and rows of high windows that let in the silver-gray twilight.

"My ladies," said a rumbling voice behind them.

The two women skidded to a halt, then turned to gaze into somber brown eyes. Aryn winced. They had completely forgotten about Durge.

"If my assistance is no longer needed, I believe I shall retire."

"Of course, Durge," Aryn said breathlessly.

The Embarran gave a stiff nod, then started to turn away.

"My lord," Lirith said, halting him with a touch. "Thank you for accompanying us today."

He nodded, then disengaged his arm and walked down the corridor, his sooty form melding with the gloom.

Inwardly, Aryn groaned. Why hadn't she thought to thank Durge? After all, she was the one who had dragged him to see the Mournish against his advice.

Now, if they got into trouble, it was likely the blame would fall on him. How could she be so cruel and forgetful?

But perhaps it was not so unusual after all.

You have forgotten about one who bore pain for you. . . .

It was true, there were those who had suffered for her sake, but Aryn had not forgotten them. She would never forget dear Garf, who had died trying to protect her from a mad bear. Or the brave and broken Sir Meridar, who had sacrificed himself to save Tira and Daynen, and to prove himself worthy in Aryn's eyes. And certainly she would never forget Leothan.

A chill stole through her, as it always did when she thought of last Midwinter's Eve, when the handsome nobleman she had fancied had drawn her into a side chamber and kissed her. For a moment it had seemed all her dreams had come true. Until he had forced himself against her, revealing himself as an ironheart. Then had come the fury, and along with it a power she had never known she had, flowing from her and turning Leothan's brain to jelly. She had always believed evil was something that dwelled in the hearts of others; never until that moment had she known it resided within her own as well.

No, she would never forget that night—*could* never forget it. More likely the old Mournish woman was simply daft.

Then what of the card, Aryn? It was just the same as the vision you saw when Ivalaine bade you look into the water that day in Calavere. How could the old woman have known about that?

Before she could think of an answer, she felt a hand on her shoulder.

"Come sister," Lirith said. "The queen is expecting us."

As servants lit torches, filling the passages with warm light, the two women hastened through the castle.

High, bubbling laughter rang out.

Aryn and Lirith skidded to a halt as a gangly form clad in yellow and green sprang from an alcove, turned a flip in midair, and landed before them with a chiming of silver bells.

"Master Tharkis!" Aryn gasped.

The scrawny man flashed rotten teeth in a grin, spread his arms, and bowed so low his pointed chin touched the floor. "Two evening birds, one brown and one blue, fly to their lady's nest." He straightened, and a sly light crept into his permanently crossed blue eyes. "But will they flap or will they sing when they must take her test?"

Lirith recovered quickly, drawing herself erect. "Fool, we have no time for this. The queen awaits us."

The man laughed, dancing a caper in place, the bells on his parti-colored cap bobbing.

> *"Awaits us, our fates us—*
> *Berates us, for late's us."*

Color touched Lirith's dusky cheeks, and she opened her mouth for a reply. However, Aryn spoke first, affecting an exaggerated frown.

"Is that the best rhyme you can forge, Master Tharkis? I'm afraid it's not much of a poem."

The fool scuttled forward. His bony knees protruded from faded green hose, and his pointed shoes were scuffed and muddied. He tangled thin fingers, his wayward eyes bright. "And does my sweet spinstress, in so short a time, fancy she'd weave a cleverer rhyme?"

Aryn drew herself up. "I believe I could. In fact, I

wager I can make a better poem out of your name than
you can of mine."

Lirith scowled at her, but Aryn ignored the look.
Tharkis clapped his hands and grinned again.

"A game! A game!" He turned another flip in place.
"How a fool loves a game. Pray, my lady, make a verse
of my name."

Aryn drew in a breath. Ar-tolor's court fool had a
tendency to interpose himself in one's way at the most
inopportune times, and playing his game seemed like
the swiftest way past him. Only now she wasn't so
certain it had been a good idea. She frowned in
concentration. Then, as if by magic, the words came to
her, and she spoke them in a laughing voice:

> *"Where hides Master Tharkis?*
> *That I cannot tell—*
> *But the sound that you do hark is*
> *The chiming of his bell.*
> *So swifter than a lark is*
> *The mischief he'd best quell—*
> *For nothing else so dark is*
> *The deepest dungeon cell."*

Aryn couldn't suppress a satisfied smile as Lirith
gaped at her. It wasn't a bad little poem, if she did say
so herself.

Evidently Tharkis agreed, for the fool sputtered,
pawing at his jangling cap so that strands of lank hair
escaped.

"Come now, Fool," Aryn said. "It is your turn in
the game."

"Must I beg it on my knees? A moment, spinstress—
a moment please!"

Tharkis turned toward the alcove, back hunched,

and muttered under his breath. Aryn didn't waste the chance. With the way clear before them, she grabbed Lirith's hand and dashed down the corridor.

They had already turned a corner when they heard a shrill howl of dismay behind them. The sound spurred them on, feet pounding on stone, until at last they were forced to stop and sag against a wall, gasping for breath and laughing.

Aryn wiped tears from her eyes. "Was he truly king once, as the stories say? It's so hard to believe when I see him."

Lirith smoothed the tight, black coils of her hair. "Indeed he was, sister. For many years Tharkis ruled the Dominion of Toloria. But one day while out hunting he fell from his horse and struck his head against a stone. When he awoke again he was like this. I fear his brain was addled without repair."

Aryn had heard the tale. King Tharkis had neither wife nor heir, and after his mishap Toloria was torn by strife as various barons vied for the throne. Had it not been for Ivalaine—a distant cousin of Tharkis who, within days of reaching the age of eighteen, managed to unite all the barons—the Dominion might have been sundered forever.

"So Tharkis truly is mad, then," Aryn said. "Yet it seems cruel to keep him like this. A man who was king should not be the court fool."

"And would it be less cruel to lock him high in a tower where none might see him? This is who he is now. And I think, after a fashion, he enjoys it."

Lirith was right, of course. All the same, there was something very wrong about Tharkis. The less Aryn encountered him, the better.

"Come," Lirith said, "the queen awaits us."

"In order to *berates* us," Aryn said with a grin.

A guardsman bowed to them as they approached the door to the queen's chamber.

"You may enter, my ladies," he said.

Aryn and Lirith exchanged quick looks, their mirth vanishing as they stepped through the door.

"Such disobedience is not to be tolerated," said a voice as clear and hard as diamonds.

Aryn froze. Was the queen not even going to greet them before chastising them? A hasty apology rose in her throat, but before she could open her mouth a voice spoke sharply in her mind.

Quiet, sister. Do not confess your crime when you have not been asked. It is not to us the queen speaks.

Aryn bit her tongue. She still hadn't gotten used to Lirith's ability to speak without words. It was not a skill Aryn had mastered herself. However, her shock was replaced by relief as she saw that Lirith was right.

The queen's antechamber was a spacious room, lined on one side by high windows that caught the reflection of the rising moon in a hundred small panes. Queen Ivalaine stood in the center of the chamber, towering over a slight young man who hung his head, his long, black hair concealing his visage. Beside him, her expression at once stern and motherly, stood Lady Tressa, the queen's plump, pretty, red-haired counselor. It was the young man who had been the focus of the queen's hard words.

"You were forbidden to enter the stables again," the queen continued, her words precise as arrows, "yet you did so today, and by your pranks caused such agitation among the horses that one broke her halter and escaped. And in regaining her, one of the stableboys fell and broke his arm."

"So I'm to blame for clumsy stableboys?" the young man said without raising his head. He was clad all in black, from tunic to boots.

The queen went visibly rigid. "It is not blame that matters to nobility, Lord Teravian. It is responsibility. Your actions gave cause to this injury. Will you not accept fault?"

The young man did not reply.

"Then I have no choice but to take the fault upon myself," Ivalaine said, "for you are my responsibility. This is what it means to be a ruler. Lady Tressa, see to it that the stableboy and his family are duly compensated from my treasury."

Tressa nodded, then bent to make a note on a parchment resting on a small table.

Ivalaine shook her head. "What shall I tell your father of this?"

Now the young man looked up, his hair falling back from the pale oval of his face. His features were fine, almost pretty, his eyes like emeralds beneath raven brows.

"And why tell King Boreas anything?" he said, a sneer twisting the soft line of his mouth. "I know he sent me here so he could forget about me."

"You know nothing," the queen said, her visage so icy that the young man took a step back, as if rethinking his insolence.

"May I go now, Your Majesty?" he said finally.

"I think you had best."

The young man gave a curt bow, then turned and—with the litheness of a dancer—moved to the door. He did not even glance at Aryn and Lirith as he departed.

Aryn watched him go. She remembered Teravian well from her first years in Calavere. Back then, King Boreas's only son had been a sullen, ill-tempered boy four years her younger. He had little to do with Aryn aside from occasionally tormenting her with pranks, such as the time he filled one of her bed pillows with wriggling mice.

Then, two years ago, Boreas had sent Teravian to Ar-tolor. It was the custom for royal children to be fostered at a foreign court; this was one way alliances between Dominions were forged and maintained. Aryn remembered that Teravian had thrown fits the day he learned he was to be sent away, but she had heard little of him since that time.

A few days after their arrival in Ar-tolor, she had sought Teravian out, to greet him as a cousin. However, when she came upon him in the castle's orchard, he had not come down from the top of a wall where he sat, and he had said nothing to her, save to laugh when she slipped on a rotten apple. It seemed Teravian had changed little during his years in Ar-tolor save to grow a bit taller and more cruel. Sometimes Aryn wondered how he could truly be the son of a man as good and brave as King Boreas.

The queen lifted a slender hand. "Where have I gone amiss, Tressa?"

The red-haired woman smiled, although it was a mournful expression. "He is a boy fighting a hard battle to become a man. One need not look for other reasons."

"And yet there is another reason, is there not?"

Tressa said nothing, and Aryn wondered what the queen meant. However, Ivalaine spoke before she could.

"Come closer, sisters. Do not think I have not seen you standing there."

The two women hurried forward and curtsied.

It was often said that Ivalaine was the most beautiful woman in all of Falengarth. Her hair was like flax, her form slender and proud, her eyes the color of violets touched by frost. Yet Aryn knew there was one even more beautiful than the queen, someone who was a world away.

I miss you so much, Grace.

Once again she hoped Grace and the others were well.

"It is good of you to come, sisters."

"We hastened here as soon as we received your message, Your Majesty," Lirith said.

Ivalaine's eyes glittered as she studied the dark-skinned witch. "So you did."

Silence filled the chamber, and a mad urge to start babbling about all they had done that day rose inside Aryn. Fortunately, Tressa spoke before she could give voice to her compulsion.

"Would you like some wine, my child?"

Aryn nodded, then had to force herself not to snatch the cup from the witch's hand and gulp it down in one draught. The wine was cool and clear as rain. Aryn took small sips and felt her nerves grow steadier.

"It is late," the queen said, "and I have much yet to do before sleep, so I will be direct. I have called a High Coven to meet here in Ar-tolor at the next dark of the moon."

Aryn frowned. She had never heard of a High Coven before. However, by the sudden brilliance in her eyes, Lirith had. The dark-haired witch gripped her goblet in both hands.

"May I ask, sister, are we to be part of it?"

Ivalaine nodded. "It is my great hope that both you and your sister Aryn will choose to attend."

"It is the first High Coven to be called in seven years," Tressa said, beaming. "All our sisters shall be there."

Lirith's smoky lips curved in one of her mysterious smiles.

An unnamable excitement filled Aryn, and she couldn't restrain herself any longer. "But what *is* a High Coven?"

Tressa laughed softly. "Why, it's a wondrous thing, my child. Witches from all the seven Dominions—and from beyond—are journeying to Ar-tolor even now. We shall all come together beneath the stars to weave a common web."

"And what is to be discussed?" Lirith said.

Ivalaine moved to a silver basin that rested on a pedestal, her gown rustling like the wings of a bird. "Matters of great importance."

"But what are they?" Aryn asked.

The queen did not turn around. "I believe that is enough for you to know at present. You will learn more at the coven."

Lirith glanced at Aryn. Both knew when a meeting with the queen was over. Questions burned inside Aryn, but they would have to wait. They set their cups down, nodded to Tressa, then moved to leave the chamber.

"One more thing, sisters," Ivalaine said, halting them at the door. "You have yet to tell me if you enjoyed your visit to the Mournish caravan."

Aryn went stiff, and Lirith sucked in a sharp breath. Ivalaine still gazed into the basin of water, and a jolt of realization coursed through Aryn. The queen had no enchanted mirror, but she had other means to see things. Aryn recalled that day when Ivalaine halted her and Grace in the corridors of Calavere and bid them to gaze into a basin just like this. It was there, in the water, that Aryn had seen the vision of herself riding a white horse, sword in hand, before a castle with seven towers.

Now the queen did look up, turning piercing eyes

upon the two women. "It is said the magics of the Mournish are like dark seeds that can grow only into thorned flowers. You would do well to remember that. Sisters."

Aryn and Lirith could only nod. Together they stepped through the door, into the passage beyond, leaving the queen to her work.

5.

"Going so soon this time, are you, my lord?" the woman said in a sleepy voice, burrowing deeper beneath the bedcovers.

Durge only grunted as he sat up. He swung his legs over the edge of the bed. The stone floor was cool against his bare feet. He drew in deep breaths as sweat dried on his naked back. Dawn was still an hour away, and steely air drifted through the window along with the soft, lonely call of a dove.

He shut his eyes, remembering. Ever were the doves her favorite. He would laugh at her when she threw grain on the ground for them in the morning. But as night fell, she would open all the windows of the manor and let their music fill the house. Back then he had never understood; he had thought it the most forlorn sound he had ever heard. Why had it taken him so many years to realize just how beautiful it was?

"Shall I expect you again this eventide, my lord?"

Durge opened his eyes. "You should never expect me."

He stood, took his breeches from a chair, and pulled them on. Behind him, he heard Lesa sigh and roll over in bed.

He had found her not long after their arrival in Artolor. Lesa was a townswoman who worked sometimes as a maid to one of the queen's ladies-in-waiting. Her husband had died a year ago, but she had been left barren by the difficult birth of her second child and so no man in the town would have her for a wife. She was plain and dull, but good-hearted enough, and kind to her children on the few times he had seen her with them. Durge had liked that. Besides, she needed coin for bread as he needed a mistress. It worked well enough.

Durge cinched the waist of his breeches, then straightened. As he did, he caught a glimpse of himself in the murky depths of a bronze mirror. The mirror was short, so that he could not see above his shoulders, and for a moment it was like seeing a ghost.

With his face hidden, he did not look so different than he remembered looking in younger days. His arms were still hard, the thick hair on his chest still dark, and his belly had not gone to pudding as with many men his age. It was his hands that gave it away. They were rough, big-knuckled, etched with lines and scars. The hands of an old man.

He shrugged his gray tunic on over his head, belted it into place, then turned around. Lesa was sitting up in bed now, her snarled brown hair falling about her shoulders, watching him with small eyes. Her face was lined and battered beyond her years by a hard life, but her breasts were small and well shaped.

She hugged her arms around her knees beneath the covers. "When will you make me your lady, my lord?"

"I shall never make you my lady," he said, and pulled his boots on.

She laughed and patted the bed beside her. "I'm your lady here, I am. So solemn you seem. But you're bold enough when you press yourself to me. Is that not enough for you?"

Durge laid three silver coins on a small table. "Buy some shoes for your children. I saw them barefoot in the town commons." He moved to the door.

"I will, my lord," she said. "Buy some shoes that is. Jorus bless you."

Durge said nothing as he stepped through the door and shut it behind him.

The castle was quiet; most of Ar-tolor was still abed. He trod the passages back toward his chamber, but he did not hurry. This was one of his rare moments to himself, and it was proper to savor it. Over the last two decades, Durge had grown accustomed to being alone, and he did not find it a burden. There was so much that could be heard—so much that could be seen and felt—only in the stillness of solitude.

Not that he regretted the time he had spent with Aryn and Lirith. Above all else, a knight must have purpose. But then, that was part of his present difficulty, wasn't it?

A knight needs someone to serve, but what need have they of your service here, Durge of Stonebreak?

He knew with the solidity of stone that it was time for him to leave, to go back to Embarr. Yesterday evening, upon their return to the castle, Aryn and Lirith had dashed off without a backward glance at Durge. But then, what use were somber knights when brilliant queens requested one's attention?

Left to himself, Durge might have worked on his alchemical studies, but he had been unable to procure the proper supplies and equipment here. As far as he could tell, engineers and men of logic were as rare in Toloria as witches and blades of grass were common. So instead he had gone to Lesa. After the day's events, he might rather have occupied his mind with his research, but it was good to occupy one's body as well, lest one or the other grow weak from neglect.

He paused before a window, gazing at the world beyond the glass. A fine mist rose from the ground, and all things—hills, sky, trees—were cast in shades of gray. Sometimes Durge preferred it this way: a world without color, filled only with shadows. Or was it simply that this was all he knew?

No, there *had* been color in his world once. In his mind, he pictured a beautiful young woman with eyes as brown and warm as honey. Only then the color of the woman's eyes changed, so that they were no longer brown but a vivid sapphire blue.

And you are an old man, Durge of Stonebreak.

But that wasn't true, either. For he didn't always feel old. Sometimes, when Lady Aryn was near, he almost felt young again, full of hope and vigor. But that was a foolish fancy, and he knew it.

Strong as stone, you present yourself, Sir Knight, a remembered voice hissed in his mind, *and yet your heart is tender and weak with feelings for another . . . if only you were young and handsome enough to deserve her.*

It was cruel, but dragons spoke truth. Was that not what Falken had said? The ancient creature called Sfithrisir knew his heart better than he did.

As did another . . .

Somehow, in the Barrens, when he and Lirith huddled out of the soundless fury of the storm while Falken ventured into the ruin that had once been the Keep of Fire, the witch had touched his hand, and she had come close to him. Perilously close. He had seen his past play out while she watched, as if performed by actors on a stage, and all the deepest secrets of his heart had been laid bare.

In the time since, he and Lirith had never discussed that moment. However, he could see the knowledge in her eyes each time she and Aryn were near. Which was all the more reason why it was best that he return to Embarr. Aryn could never know of his feelings—*would* never know. She had burdens enough to bear without having a love she could never return placed upon her.

If only Durge could find a way to take his leave of the baroness without causing her harm. In her innocence, it seemed she had grown fond of his care and protection. It was a fondness Durge knew must not be mistaken for something deeper. All the same, to leave her might cause her distress, and that was something he could not do.

With a sigh—and no answer to his dilemma—the knight turned from the window.

As he did, he nearly collided with a trio of young women. Durge did not know any of them by name, although he recognized them as ladies of the queen's court. What had caused them to rise before the dawn? Then he noticed their wind-snarled hair, the dirt on their hands and cheeks, and the bits of dry grass and twigs that clung to their gowns, and he was certain they had not just risen but instead were only now going to their beds.

He nodded to them, and the young women burst into giggles. They bent their heads, whispering as they glanced at the knight, and despite himself he felt his cheeks grow hot. This brought more peals of mirth. Then, clutching each other, the three ran down the hall.

Durge glowered. He appreciated women of strength. His noble mistress, Lady Grace, was a woman of power. But of this—these idle games of spells and mischief—he did not approve. Would that Aryn not become such as these women. Although he doubted that would happen. Her teacher, the Lady Lirith, was not given to frivolity, and for that Durge respected her.

All the same, Durge wondered if perhaps Sir Beltan wasn't onto something. There were too many women in this castle with too many secrets, all watching and waiting. It was like the card he had drawn from the crone's deck: the woman gazing down from the moon, beautiful but watching.

He had been right about the Mournish; they were indeed a queer folk. Going to them had been unwise, for the old woman's words had seemed to upset both Aryn and Lirith.

And what of her words to you, Durge of Stonebreak?

But it was more trickery, that was all. In these last months Durge had seen wonders, yes, but they had been wrought by the hands of gods, not men. He did not believe in such human magic.

And yet magic shall be the death of you. . . .

An icy breath of air coiled around Durge, and he shivered as the hairs on the back of his neck stood on end. Had the window behind him swung open? If so, this was a wind out of the depths of winter, not the gentle days of late summer. He turned back toward the window to shut it and for the second time that morning saw a ghost.

Man of logic though he was, he knew at once those shades were more than a mirror's tricks of light and shadow. They stood before the window—which was still tightly shut—as colorless and translucent as the mist beyond. She was a maid of twenty, lovely if far from perfect, with an overlarge chin and wide eyes, her hair the stuff of shadows. Before her stood a tiny child, his mouth a pretty bud. His hair was as light as hers was dark. They had never known where he had gotten it, for both of them had hair of brown.

Durge's heart had stopped beating. This was a stillness akin to death. The two seemed neither sad nor happy. They only stared forward, their expressions without emotion. Did they even see him? Then her eyes met his, and there was pale recognition in them. She opened her mouth, but no sound issued forth.

Durge staggered back. It felt as if the blood had been drained from his veins by a cold knife.

"Go away," he croaked. "I am an old man now. Will you not let me be free?"

Tears coursed down his cheeks, steaming in the frigid air. Now the woman's expression seemed sorrowful. She reached for him, but at that moment the rising sun broke through the mist outside. Its light pierced the substance of the ghosts, and in an instant they were gone.

6.

Lirith woke with a gasp.

She sat up in bed, her nightgown damp and clammy with sweat. Something had awakened her—but what was it? She saw only mundane objects in the colorless light that filtered through the narrow window: a chair, a table, the wardrobe. Quickly, she shut her eyes, gazing with another sort of vision.

At once she saw the shimmering web of magic that wove itself over and among all things, brilliant with color where all had been dull gray before. The warmth of the Weirding flooded her, filling her with reassurance. Everything was as it should be.

Perhaps it was only her dream that disturbed her. Why it had come to her, she didn't know. It had been so long since she had thought of that place, that time. Yet she could smell the heavy smoke of incense, hear the clink of beads and harsh laughter drifting on steamy air as if she were still there.

Dance, my dark one. Dance if you ever hope to be free. What a beautiful thing you are, as lovely as the night itself. Yes, you see it now—this is the only way. . . .

Despite the comforting tendrils of the Weirding that coiled around her, Lirith shivered. What had made her think of things so long and far ago? But perhaps it was not such a mystery.

You flee your fate. Yet you cannot escape it, for it lies within you.

Lirith could still see the drawing of the barren battlefield on the card, and the black shape of the Raven. But the old woman was wrong. Lirith *had* escaped her fate. She had escaped it the day she fled Gulthas's house seven years ago. Maybe Durge and the queen were right; maybe the magics of the Mournish were nothing more than tricks and illusions intended to poison.

And what of him, sister? Is that a trick as well—the way he keeps stealing into your thoughts?

Without even meaning to, she concentrated, forming the threads of the Weirding into a glowing shape before her: a man with black hair, deep, mysterious eyes, and one leg. So easy it would have been to extend the threads of the Weirding, to mold them into a new leg so that in her vision he would be perfect. However, she did not.

Late last night as she lay in bed, after their meeting with Queen Ivalaine, she had conjured a similar vision, although in this one he had worn no vest, no billowing trousers of blue. It was a bit of foolishness, more to be expected of a young witch just learning to shape the Weirding than of a lady full grown and past her seven-and-twentieth year. All the same, Lirith had brought the vision close to her, touching herself as she imagined him entering her.

As she should have expected, it had been like touching cold clay rather than warm flesh.

A breath escaped her, and she let the image before her unravel. There was no use in thinking of him or his deep, chiming laugh. In a few days, Sareth would leave Ar-tolor with his people to wander the world again. Such was his fate. And the old woman had been right about one thing—nothing and no one could bring life to a land so long barren. Such was hers.

It was time to rise; Lirith could feel the sun breaking through the mist outside, filling the land with new life, if not all who dwelled upon it. She started to let go of the Weirding.

That was when she saw it. Her vision of Sareth had blinded her, but now that her sight was clear there was no mistaking it. It seethed on the edge of her vision like a knot of gray serpents: a tangle in the threads of the Weirding.

Warm reassurance became watery horror. Always in Lirith's experience, when she used the Touch to glimpse them, the threads of Weirding wove smoothly among one another in a web as faultless as a spider's. Now, as she watched, another strand of gossamer was pulled into the snarl, its light dimming to the color of ashes. How could this be? How could there be a tangle in the very web of life? She opened her mouth to scream—

—and a sharp rapping noise fractured the air.

Lirith clamped her mouth shut. In an instant the Weirding vanished, replaced by mundane sight. Gold light spilled through the chamber's window: dawn.

Again came the sound. Someone was knocking at the door. Lirith threw back the covers and tumbled from the bed. She could think later about what she had witnessed—perhaps she could discuss it with Ivalaine and Tressa—but not now, when she felt so cold and empty.

Lirith staggered to the chamber door and jerked it open. Only when she saw the wide eyes of the guardsman did she realize she still wore only her nightgown of loose gauze. Never had she cared for the craft of illusion, but there were times when it was necessary. Lirith spun a quick thread around herself. The guard shook his head, then his expression relaxed. Lirith knew he now saw her clad in a pretty gown of russet and blue, and that he believed it was what she had been wearing all along. It was easy to make people see what they expected.

"My lady," the guardsman said, "they are asking for you. Will you come?"

Lirith sagged against the doorframe as if struck a blow. Once again, words spoken long ago sounded afresh in her mind.

They are asking for you, Lisenne, shouting for you. It is you they want to see over all the others. Listen to their voices! Will you not dance for them?

"My lady?"

"Who asks for me?" she managed to croak.

"Did you not see them ride up to the gate? Lord Falken Blackhand and Lady Melindora Nightsilver. They are here, in Ar-tolor." The young man grinned. "My grandmother used to tell me tales of them when I sat at her knee. But they were just stories, or so I believed. I never thought I would see those two with my own eyes. And it is said you know them, my lady."

Now the guardsman blushed, evidently embarrassed by his outburst. Lirith absorbed his words. Melia and Falken were in Ar-tolor? It would be good to see the bard and the lady, of course. She had grown fond of them both, despite their unusual natures. But why were they here? Last she knew, they had been journeying in search of their friend—and Melia's kindred—Tome.

"They are going even now to the great hall to beg hospitality of the queen. Are you coming, my lady?"

"I'll be there in a moment." Lirith did not want to meet Lady Melia in an imaginary gown. Something told her the amber-eyed woman would see through any enchantments she might hope to spin.

Lirith shut the door and turned around. Her mind was clearing, like the mist in the morning light. Tricks and illusions, that was all. However, as she reached into the wardrobe for her gown, she could not help glancing again at the corner of the room. This time she saw only empty air.

Minutes later, Lirith stepped into Ar-tolor's airy great hall. A small group of people stood before the dais on which rested the queen's throne. Ivalaine was nowhere to be seen.

"There you are!" Aryn said, holding up the hem of her yellow gown as she rushed forward. "We've been waiting for you. Where have you been all this time?"

Lirith managed a wry smile. "Getting dressed."

Ignoring Aryn's puzzled look, she moved to Falken and Melia, who stood with Durge. Both appeared little changed since the last time she had seen them— although that was to be expected. For Falken had been born in the kingdom of Malachor, which fell centuries ago, and he was over seven hundred years old. And Melia was older yet, a goddess of Tarras who had forsaken her celestial realm to walk the world in a more limited, human form.

Falken was clad in his usual travel-worn garb: fawn tunic, scuffed boots, and a cloak the color of deep water. His silver-shot hair was as shaggy as ever, and his lined mien as wolfish. Melia had traded her blue kirtle for a simple shift the color of moonlight. Otherwise the small, regal woman looked as she always had: her coppery skin flawless, her hair falling in a blue-black wave down her back.

Falken grinned as Lirith drew near. "I hope you'll indulge an old bard," he said, enfolding her in lean arms. "It's not every century I get to hug a beautiful countess."

Lirith laughed and returned the embrace with equal force. The dark stubble of his beard scratched against her cheek, but she didn't care; he smelled like a forest. He was a strange being, this immortal bard, but he was good as well. Lirith knew that without doubt—no matter what the tales told. She would not believe an entire kingdom had been doomed by his hand alone.

"You look well, dear," Melia said, gliding forward.

Lirith did not pretend for a moment that Melia would embrace her as Falken had. Not that Melia didn't care for her. But there was a distance to the onetime goddess that made her as cool, as radiant, and as unreachable as her namesake. Only Falken seemed able to bridge that gulf—and perhaps Sir Beltan and Goodman Travis to a lesser extent. Lirith gave the woman a rigid nod.

At this, Melia halted, then moved back a half step and nodded in return, her amber eyes filled with an expression that seemed almost . . . sad. A pang of regret filled Lirith's chest.

She concealed the awkwardness of the moment with a question. "Where is the queen?"

"I fear you are too late, my lady," Durge said.

Aryn frowned at the knight. "Ivalaine hasn't passed away, Durge. She's only at breakfast."

"We were about to find some breakfast ourselves," Falken said, slinging the battered wooden case that held his lute over his shoulder. "Will you join us, Lirith?"

She nodded, then took his arm when he proffered it.

"Falken," Aryn said as they moved toward a side door, "you still haven't told us why you've come to Ar-tolor. I thought you were going to travel for a while with Tome."

The bard shrugged. "Tome decided he'd rather rest. But then, he *is* over two thousand years old, so we didn't argue the point. Besides, when we heard a High Coven was being called, we decided to come here instead."

Lirith froze. "But Queen Ivalaine has only just called for the coven."

"Yes, dear," Melia said. "We know."

Once again Lirith studied the amber-eyed woman. While no longer truly a goddess, Melia's powers were still mysterious and vast. The Witches had always respected her . . . but they were wary of her as well. Melia was of the new religions of Tarras, not the ancient worship of Sia.

Then again, it seems that those who shun the name Sia rise most quickly among the Witches these days, is that not so Sister Lirith?

The furrows in Durge's brow deepened. "I have not heard of this High Coven. What is it?"

Lirith opened her mouth, wondering what she should tell the knight, but before she could speak, another voice—cracked and high-pitched—answered for her.

> *"My good, glum knight, don't you know?*
> *It's where sewers spin and spinners sew.*
> *Weaving secrets to and fro—*
> *So let's to the High Coven go."*

By the time Lirith caught a flash of green and yellow, he was already scrambling down a tapestry like a great, gangly spider. He must have been hiding up among the beams of the hall, listening to everything they said.

"Begone with you," Durge rumbled, his hand

moving to the knife at his hip as the fool scuttled toward them.

Falken laid a hand on Durge's arm. "No, he was king in this hall once. Let him stay."

Tharkis spread bony arms and bowed, the bells of his cap jangling dissonantly. "No wish to bother, no wish to harm. A poem I would speak, our great guests to charm."

Durge did not look like he was in the mood for poems. "Speak it, knave, and then away with you."

Tharkis bowed so low his pointed boots touched his brow. However, the moment Durge glanced away, the fool performed a caper, miming with uncanny verisimilitude the act of drawing a sword and falling upon it. Lirith swallowed a giggle, and Aryn clamped a hand to her mouth.

Durge snapped back around. "Whatever your history may be, Fool, your antics are not appreciated here."

"Oh, I don't know," Melia said, moving past the glowering Embarran. "I believe I rather like him. Speak your poem for us, Master Tharkis. Please."

The fool leaped to his feat, then spoke shrill words in a fractured rhyme:

> "The wolf said to the moon one day,
> 'I think I can no longer stay
> Upon this path so long I've run—
> It always ends where it's begun.'

> "The moon said to the wolf one night,
> 'Come with me, and we'll take flight.
> We'll eat of suns and drink of stars—
> All we've dreamed will here be ours.'

"But though as much as he did try,
The wolf could never leap so high.
Nor could the moon descend so deep—
I've heard it said they both yet weep."

Throughout the verse, the smile on Melia's face gradually faded. When Tharkis finished speaking, she looked away. Falken glanced at her and sighed. Lirith didn't understand why, but the poem had seemed to sadden the two.

"Your rhyme makes for a poor welcome, Fool," she said.

"Did I say welcome?" A sly gleam entered Tharkis's crossed eyes. "Perhaps I meant farewell. One's so like the other, it's often hard to tell."

"Or perhaps you're simply a bad poet," Aryn said. "After all, I bested you once."

Tharkis scurried toward the baroness, his rubbery limbs tangling and untangling as he moved. "But we have not finished our game yet, my sweet. I'll speak you your poem when next we do meet."

Before Aryn could reply, the fool sprang backward in a series of flips. Then, with a chiming of bells, he scampered through a door and was gone.

There was a long silence, broken when Durge cleared his throat.

"I have been thinking," the knight said seemingly to no one in particular. "Lord Falken and Lady Melia can offer both better company and better protection than I. Perhaps now that they are here it is time I return to Stonebreak. It has been long since I have seen personally to the affairs of my manor."

Aryn's blue eyes went wide. "Oh, Durge, you mustn't even make a jest of leaving!" She rushed forward and grasped his left hand with hers. "I am certain your reeve can look after your manor well enough. Please—you must promise me that you will stay with us."

The Embarran hesitated, then nodded, clasping rough fingers around her smooth hand for a moment. "As you wish, my lady."

Aryn beamed, but Durge's careworn face appeared more deeply lined than ever. Lirith didn't need to steal his thoughts as she had in the Barrens to know that this gesture had cost him. Lirith wished she had never learned of the knight's feelings for Aryn. And sometimes she wished she could tell the young woman. Perhaps there was a chance. . . .

But no, that was foolish. Durge was over twice Aryn's age. And while such marriages happened often enough, they were arranged for land, money, and alliance, not for love. Durge would never make his feelings plain to Aryn. And Lirith had sworn she would never tell.

Yet it was more than this that seemed to weigh on him; Durge seemed grimmer than ever today. Had something happened to him? Or was it that, after the tangle she had glimpsed that morning, nothing seemed quite right.

"Come on," Falken said. "The queen granted us her hospitality, and I'm ready to take advantage of it. Let's get breakfast."

7.

The next day, witches began to arrive at Ar-tolor.

Aryn first suspected something was happening as she sat in her chamber, taking breakfast. A tingling danced along her spine, and—compelled for a reason she could not name—she set down her spoon, rose, and moved to the window. In the bailey below, a rider clad in a green cloak and hood sat upon a black horse. A guardsman reached out to help the rider dismount, but instead the traveler looked up and the hood slipped back, revealing a cascade of gold hair. The rider was a woman past her middle years, but still possessed of a powerful beauty.

Evidently the guardsman was as surprised as Aryn, for he stepped back. The woman on the horse turned her head, as if searching. Then her gaze locked on the window through which Aryn watched, and a smile touched her lips. For a moment Aryn gazed into sea-green eyes. Then, with a gasp, she hurried from the window. It seemed like the woman in the bailey had seen her watching. But that was impossible.

After breakfast, Aryn went in search of Lady Tressa, for there was much to do before the dark of the moon and the start of the coven, which—from what scant knowledge Aryn had been able to glean—was to span four days. She was near the entry gallery of the castle when she caught a scent like nightflowers. This was odd not because it was midday, but because for all its beauty—and like all castles Aryn had ever been in—Ar-tolor smelled more like a privy than a garden. She turned in time to see a tall, slender figure all in black vanish between two columns. Aryn hurried after but found nothing save a scattering of white, fragrant petals upon the stone floor.

It was after midday when Aryn finally finished counting all the candles stored in the castle's cellar. It seemed an odd task, but that was what Tressa had bid her do and so she had. Aryn walked down a corridor, trying her best to brush the dust and spiderwebs from her gown. Working in the cellar had been grimier than she had imagined.

"Mind if I have some of that cobweb, deary?"

Aryn looked up to see an ancient woman clad in a shapeless brown frock. There was little hair left on the woman's knobby head, but her blue eyes were bright in her wrinkled face.

Aryn shrugged. "No, not at all. Here you are." She handed the other a gauzy, gray ball.

The old woman gave a cackle—she was quite toothless—and spirited the cobweb into a pocket. "Thank you, deary." She hobbled past.

After several steps, Aryn stopped and blinked. She glanced back over her shoulder, but the old woman was already out of sight. Aryn turned and hurried to Lirith's chamber. She found the dark-eyed woman inside, grinding something with mortar and pestle. It smelled fresh but bitter.

"Something peculiar is going on in this castle," Aryn said, shutting the door behind her.

Lirith did not look up from her work, but she smiled mysteriously. "Five witches have arrived since dawn, last I spoke to Tressa."

"I knew it!" Aryn flopped into a chair. "I *knew* they had to be witches. Each of them was strange in her own way." A thought occurred to her. "But how can they be arriving at the castle when Ivalaine only announced the High Coven last night?"

"You mean she only told us about the High Coven last night. For all we know, she might have sent out messages weeks ago."

A thrill coursed through Aryn, and she sat up straight in the chair. "Yes, but what sort of messages?"

Lirith crumbled a few dried leaves into the mortar and said nothing. That was answer enough for Aryn. Ivalaine *had* sent out a message about the coven, but not one written with ink on paper. And perhaps that was why Melia and Falken were here; perhaps Lady Melia had overheard.

Then why didn't you hear it, Aryn? Or Lirith?

But maybe the message had not been intended for them. And Aryn's ability to speak across the Weirding was limited at best, although she certainly intended to improve. And Lirith was going to help her whether she wanted to or not.

A sigh caught Aryn's attention. The pestle lay motionless in Lirith's hand; the witch stared into space.

"Are you well, sister?" Aryn said, excitement replaced by concern.

Lirith smiled, but the expression seemed fragile somehow. "Lady Tressa is looking for you. I believe she has another task for you to start."

Those next days passed swiftly. As it turned out, Lady Tressa had many more tasks for both of them before the coven began. They helped to air out dozens of the castle's spare chambers, and they spent long afternoons venturing into the groves that dotted the land near Ar-tolor, searching for goldleaf, moonbell, and other herbs Tressa bade them find—all of which could be ground into a heady incense, good for purifying air and clearing vision.

However, there were other tasks that made little sense to Aryn. They burned three candles—one to a stump, one halfway, and one just for a moment—before extinguishing them and wrapping them in red-linen cloths. They drew water from the castle well in the blackest hour of the night, although Aryn could hardly see how it would differ from water drawn in daylight. Wet was wet. As she discovered when, in her bleariness, she spilled a chill bucket on herself.

"At least that woke you up," Lirith said with a laugh, then lowered the bucket back into the well.

Most inexplicable of all, with the help of Ivalaine's ladies-in-waiting, Tressa bade them sew three robes. The first was white and woven from the wool of lambs. The second was brilliant green, colored with fresh rushes. And the third was dark as smoke, dyed with ashes. What were the robes for?

Tressa smiled when Aryn asked this. "Why, she has three faces, and so she wears three robes: one for her waking, one for her fullness, and one for her waning."

"But who is she?" Aryn asked, more perplexed then ever.

Tressa's smile only deepened.

"All right, Lirith," Aryn demanded that night at supper in the great hall, speaking low under her breath, for the queen sat only a few places away. "What is this High Coven really all about?"

"You will see," Lirith said, and took a sip from her wine.

Aryn started to groan—it was a typically enigmatic answer—then her eyes narrowed. "You don't actually know, do you?"

Lirith did not meet her gaze. "I have . . . an idea."

Aryn wasn't certain what it was: luck, instinct, or some unspoken message translated across the threads of the Weirding. All the same, she knew the word on Lirith's mind.

"Runebreaker," she whispered.

Now Lirith did look at her, eyes sharp, face hard. "You will not speak that word again, sister. Not unless it is spoken to you first. Do you understand me?"

Aryn had never heard Lirith speak so harshly before. She gave a jerking nod, then finished her supper in silence.

As the moon waned to a sliver, more witches arrived in Ar-tolor. Some came openly under the bright light of noon, while others drifted into the castle with the purple air of twilight. And sometimes Aryn would awake in the deep of the night, move to her window, and see dim shapes gliding across the bailey, bending heads close in silent speech. Soon the very stones of the keep seemed to echo with whispers, and the castle's servants and guardsmen walked with the quick-footed nervousness of mice who know a cat's afoot, looking always over their shoulders.

Finally Aryn counted the days, thinking that if the High Coven did not begin soon she would burst with questions. Some relief did come in her time with Melia and Falken. They told her stories of the great lost kingdom of Malachor, and of the city of Tarras when it was still the shining heart of a vast empire. But though interesting, the stories were only diversions. It was not the past that interested Aryn, but what was to happen in mere days.

It was the morning of the day the High Coven was to begin that she woke to find the Mournish had left Ar-tolor. Sometime during the night they had folded up bright awnings, packed their fantastic wagons, and rolled away down the road, wandering to their next destination.

After breakfast—which Aryn could barely swallow for her excitement—she and Lirith walked down to the commons below the castle, for Tressa had said all was ready for the coven. They walked among tall trees, which swayed back and forth, murmuring a tired song. Summer was passing. Keldath, the gold month, was over. It was Revendath, and the wheat in the field fell before the blades of scythes.

It was easy to make out the yellowed places on the grass where the Mournish wagons had stood. At one of these, Lirith knelt and plucked something from the withered grass. It gleamed in the dappled light: one of the cheap bronze charms the Mournish sold to ward away sickness, to ease pain, or to bring love. This one was shaped like a spider. Aryn wondered what effect it was supposed to have.

"I wish we could have seen them again. The Mournish."

"It is well we did not," Lirith said flatly.

Startled, Aryn glanced at her friend. Lirith seemed to gaze into a far-off place.

"What is it, sister?" Aryn said, touching her hand.

Lirith drew a deep breath, then smiled. "It's nothing. Really."

Aryn nodded; she thought maybe she understood. The old woman's words had affected all of them. Once again Aryn thought of the image she had glimpsed in Ivalaine's ewer and again on the old woman's card. But what did it mean? Of all the castles Aryn knew, only Ar-tolor had seven towers. And Ivalaine was mistress here.

"We should return to the castle," Lirith said. "This

evening we will have far more on our minds than the Mournish."

Aryn nodded, and they started back the way they had come. But she did not fail to notice that Lirith carefully coiled up the spider necklace and slipped it into the pocket of her gown.

8.

The remainder of that day seemed to drag on for an eternity. Aryn tried to occupy herself with embroidery, but the thread seemed determined to tangle and knot. Lirith had told her the first meeting of the coven would be a welcoming incant, in which all the witches might greet one another. The real work of the High Coven would come in the days that followed. Aryn wasn't entirely certain when things were to start, but instinct told her it would not be until the sun slipped beneath the horizon, leaving other, deeper powers to steal over the world.

Just as the music of doves drifted through the window, a soft knock came at the door of her chamber. Outside was a woman Aryn had never seen before. She was exceedingly tall and thin, curved like a tree; her brown hair was cropped close to her head in a man's style. The woman wore a simple robe of light green, and a similar robe hung over her arm.

"It is time," the woman said before Aryn could speak. She held out the spare robe. "I am Nayla, your guide. Don this, then follow me."

Minutes later Aryn moved through the dim corridors of Ar-tolor, treading after Nayla along with several more young women. One by one they had gone to the chambers of the others, waited as each donned the spare green robe the witch always seemed able to produce, then continued on their way in silence.

As they walked, Aryn glanced at the young women to either side of her. Most were pale and pretty, while one was dark and lustrous like Lirith. All of them looked lovely in the simple green shifts, their shapely arms left bare by the garments' half sleeves. Aryn tried to ignore her own withered right arm that flopped out the end of its sleeve. Even as a small girl she remembered being aware of the need to keep her arm concealed. Now that it was in plain view, she felt strangely naked.

A tingle danced across Aryn's neck. She turned to see one of the young women staring at her. No, not at *her*, but at her arm. The other quickly looked away, but it was too late; Aryn had seen the horror in her expression. After that, Aryn kept her own gaze fixed rigidly ahead.

They reached a crossing of ways and came upon another group of women in green shifts. All of them wore wide-eyed expressions. They were even younger than the witches of Aryn's group; the eldest couldn't have been more than fifteen, and the youngest was surely not beyond her twelfth winter. Could she truly be a witch at so young an age?

As if sensing eyes upon her, the girl looked up, a knowing expression on her face, her lips curving in a smile. Aryn looked hastily away.

It was only when Nayla nodded to the woman leading the second group that Aryn realized the other was in fact Lirith. The dark-eyed witch looked elegant in her green robe, her black hair tumbling behind her in tight ringlets. Aryn opened her mouth to say something, but a slight shake of Lirith's head stilled her question.

Not just yet, sister, Aryn thought a voice whispered in her mind. *Follow now, speak later.*

Lirith nodded in return to the tall witch, then without exchanging words the two led the way down a corridor. The others trailed after in a single group.

It was only when they stepped through a door into cool, purple air, and Aryn breathed in the perfume of evening flowers, that she realized what their destination must be. They left the stone walls of the castle behind, walking down winding paths deeper into Ar-tolor's gardens.

The gardens of Ar-tolor were both larger and wilder than Calavere's, with its neat paths and well-tended hedge maze that Aryn had played in so much as a girl she could navigate it with her eyes closed. Here, the walkways tangled back on themselves, leading at every turn to unexpected grottoes, shaded fountains spilling over mossy stones, and thickets where gods peered from leafy shrines with serene marble eyes.

They passed through an arch of moss-covered stone Aryn never recalled seeing in all her garden wanderings and stepped into a great space beyond.

It was like a temple all of green. Ancient trees formed twin colonnades, their trunks like columns arching into slender beams overhead. Flowering vines wove among the branches, completing the walls and vaulted dome. Silver moonlight tinged with emerald filtered down from above, and fallen petals glowed on the ground. Leaves stirred on the night breeze like the whispers of many voices. Then Aryn shivered, and she knew it was more than just the leaves that were whispering.

The garden was filled with witches.

All of them wore the same light green robes, and in the dimness the garments melded with the shadows of the trees, so that it was impossible to be certain how many there were. But Aryn was certain it was tenscore if it was one. A thrill rose in her chest.

Oh, Grace. I wish you could be here for this. It's so marvelous—I never knew there were so many like us. You'd see that you're not alone, that you're never alone.

At the far end of the grove, marble steps led up to a circular rostrum. On the rostrum were seven pedestals, and atop each one shone a globe of light. At first Aryn wondered if they were glass balls filled with fireflies, but that was absurd. How could they be kept alive? Besides, it was too late in the year, and the light the globes gave off was not yellow but greenish like the leaf-filtered moonlight.

"What can it be?" Aryn murmured.

She felt eyes upon her and looked up into Lirith's midnight gaze.

It is called witchfire, sister. Bright to look at, but cool to the touch.

Witchfire? Lirith had never spoken of such a thing before. But then, there were so many things Aryn had yet to learn. She opened her mouth to say more, but at that moment the tall witch who had led her group spoke.

"This way."

Nayla guided Aryn and her companions toward the middle of the grove, while Lirith led her group to one side. They passed by other small clusters of women, and when they halted again Aryn saw that there was an order to the placement of the green-robed witches. The youngest were gathered on the right as one faced the rostrum. Aryn's group was to their left, while in the middle of the grove were witches who were more of an age with Lirith and Grace. Beyond were witches of greater maturity, many beautiful still, but their hair graying, their faces lined with wisdom. And nearly lost in the shadows on the far left side were the eldest of the witches: the hags and crones, backs hunched, limbs gnarled, jaws toothless.

As she turned back, a flash of white caught Aryn's eye. She glanced in that direction, then gasped. For a moment she thought the young woman was clad in the snowy petals that still drifted down from above, for she seemed to shine in the green gloaming. Then Aryn blinked, and she understood: It was a white robe the other wore—the very same garment she and Lirith had helped to weave only days ago.

"Isn't she beautiful?" one of the witches of Aryn's group—the one who had stared at her arm earlier—now whispered in her ear, her brown eyes shining.

Aryn nodded. As a girl, she had gazed into mirrors and had tried to picture what she might be like when she was grown: dark, slender, radiant, and whole. However, as she grew older, Aryn had never seen that beautiful young woman reflected back at her. Until now.

The young witch in white might have been Aryn's sister. Her hair was dark as shadows, her eyes blue gems, her skin smooth as ivory. Yet there were realms of difference between them, for the other carried herself proud and straight, gazing on everything around her with an assured expression—two well-shaped arms folded across the white robe.

"Who is she?"

Now the young woman with brown eyes laughed; it was a mocking sound. "Why, don't you know anything? Cirynn is to be the Maiden for this coven."

The Maiden? Aryn started to ask. However, at that moment, a clear sound rang out over the garden. Three of the very youngest witches stood on the steps of the rostrum, each holding a silver bell of a different size. Three disparate tones blended together, shimmering on the night air.

As the tone faded, the girls left the rostrum and returned to their group. Obviously the first meeting of the coven was about to begin, for other witches hurried through the gathering, making their way to their places.

"Pardon me, deary," a cracked voice said. "These old bones are sharp, and I'd hate to poke you with them."

Startled, Aryn turned around to see a hunched form. She breathed a sigh, recognizing the ancient witch she had given the cobweb to the other day. The crone looked just the same—head balding and knobby, hands twisted like roots, red-rimmed eyes like bright buttons lost in masses of wrinkles—except now she wore a robe of ash gray. Once again Aryn recognized her own handiwork: This was the gray robe she and Lirith had helped sew.

"What is it, deary? You look as if you've got a bird in your mouth trying to fly out."

Aryn remembered herself. "I'm sorry," she gasped. "Please, come through."

The crone grinned—displaying bare gums—and hobbled past, disappearing into a shadow near the foot of the rostrum. Next to Aryn, the young witch with brown eyes shuddered.

"She's positively awful." The young woman glanced at the left side of the grove. "They're all awful."

Aryn shrugged. "They're just old. We'll all be old someday, if we're lucky to live so long."

The other made an exaggerated grimace. "I should never want to live so long if it means I'll look like that.

I don't know why we let them come. All they do is mutter about Sia and the old days when nobody cares."

"But everyone should care," Aryn said. "Maybe they aren't young anymore, but they *are* wise. And beauty isn't everything."

The young woman's brown eyes narrowed to slits. "I suppose someone like you would say that."

Aryn's face stung. She opened her mouth, but before she could speak, the young woman with brown eyes bolted from their group and hurried to the knot of young women clustered around Cirynn. She whispered something in Cirynn's ear, and Aryn felt blue eyes upon her. As Aryn watched, Cirynn smiled, then twisted her right arm into an unnatural position, drawing it halfway up the sleeve of her white robe as she curled her fingers inward. Those gathered around her clasped hands to mouths, failing utterly to stifle their laughter.

Still Aryn stared, turned to ice. The grove dimmed, and the laughter of the young women transmuted, growing higher in pitch, echoing in her mind until it phased into something else—the singsong rhymes of children.

> *Little Lady Aryn,*
> *What is she wearin'*
> *Under that dress of blue?*
> *A dead bird wing,*
> *Such an ugly thing.*
> *She'd fly if she had two.*

Shut up, Aryn wanted to shout at them. *Shut up, all of you!* But her voice was too small, a little girl's voice. She couldn't speak, and she had no wings to let her fly from this place. All she could do was run—run and hide somewhere they wouldn't be able to find her.

"Sister, are you well?"

Aryn staggered, then a cool hand touched her good arm, steadying her. The images of the past faded, and a figure came into focus before her.

The woman clearly belonged with the witches who stood in the center of the grove—that must have been where she was moving when Aryn stumbled against her. She was beautiful, although not in the pale and perfect manner of Cirynn. Rather, her beauty seemed to radiate from within, its brightness independent of its housing, like the light of a lamp.

Her skin was the color of almonds, her cheeks high, and her nose small and flat across the bridge. Her dark eyes tilted at the corners, and fine lines radiated from them, lending her a sage look. A single streak of frost marked jet hair. Some years ago, Aryn had met a countess who possessed this same exotic look; she had hailed from the eastern reaches of Eredane. Perhaps this witch did as well?

"Sister?"

"I'm fine—really. Thank you." However, as Aryn spoke, her eyes flickered toward Cirynn's group.

Her glance was not lost on the other. The witch nodded, a knowing look in her eyes. "You must not heed them, sister. They doubt their own beauty and so must belittle that of others. When they grow older, they will learn that beauty is found rather than given. As shall you." She paused. "But then, you are old beyond your years, are you not?"

The witch lifted a hand and pressed it to Aryn's cheek. Aryn closed her eyes; it was, strangely, a comforting gesture.

"Sia bless you," a voice murmured in her ear.

The warmth against her cheek vanished. Aryn

opened her eyes to see the witch already moving away.

"But what's your name?" she said, more to herself than the other, for she dared not shout. All the same, an answer came back, whispering in her mind.

You may call me Sister Mirda.

Then the other was lost in the crowd. Before Aryn could wonder more, motion caught her eye. From the shadows, three figures stepped onto the rostrum: one clad in white, one clad in jade green, and the other in gray.

"I am Her dawn," said the young woman in white. It was Cirynn. Only she seemed graver now, more poised and less proud. Perhaps Aryn had misjudged her.

"I am Her day," said the woman in green, and Aryn gasped, for only as the witch spoke did she realize it was Queen Ivalaine, regal beyond all others.

"And I," croaked a rough voice, "am Her twilight."

The hag in gray whom Aryn had spoken to earlier hobbled into place next to Ivalaine and Cirynn. Aryn wondered what her name was.

She is called Senrael, said a soundless voice in Aryn's mind. *She is to be Crone at this High Coven, just as Ivalaine is Matron and Cirynn is Maiden.*

Aryn glanced around, searching, then saw Lirith standing not far to her left. She wanted to send words back to Lirith, but she had no idea how to do it. However, Lirith seemed to anticipate her question.

She has three faces, and so three women stand for Her. It is how it has ever been.

Aryn wanted to know more, but on the rostrum Ivalaine spoke again, her graceful arms spread wide.

"In Her name, let the circle be closed, and let this coven be called."

At these words, a tingling coursed through Aryn. By

the intake of breath around her, others felt it as well.
There was power in the air.

"In whose name do you mean, Matron?" a voice
called out.

All turned their heads, searching for the speaker.
Then Aryn saw her, standing near the center of the
gathering, close to the rostrum. It was hard to make her
out, for her back was mostly to Aryn, but she was tall
and carried herself proudly. Her hair was flax touched
with hints of fire, coiled high upon her head, and she
wore many fine bands of gold about her wrists and
throat—the only jewelry Aryn had seen upon any of
the witches that night.

"What do you mean, Sister Liendra?" Ivalaine said,
as if this interruption were all part of the ceremony.

The witch who had spoken stepped forward. Her
voice was clear and sharp, like glass. "You say you call
the witches to this coven in Her name. Do you mean
the name *Yrsaia*? Or the name *Sia*?" With this last
word, her voice edged into a sneer.

On the rostrum, Senrael's wizened visage wrinkled
in a frown, while Cirynn shifted from foot to foot and
chewed her lower lip. Whispers ran through the
crowd.

"And does it matter which name it is?" Ivalaine said,
her features tranquil as a deep ocean.

Aryn couldn't see Liendra's face, but somehow she
knew the witch was smiling.

"I believe it does matter. To many of us, at least. We
would know what our Matron believes before the
circle of this coven is bound."

More whispers rose from the witches, along with
some nods. Above it all, Ivalaine stood without
motion. Only when silence fell again did she speak.

"Then this is your answer," Ivalaine said, her words

cool and precise. "Even as all women are one, so are all goddesses."

Murmurs of assent rippled through the gathered women. Aryn let out her breath and only then realized she had been holding it. It was like Lirith had once said; it seemed as if some of the witches did not like the name *Sia* anymore, that they believed she was a goddess followed by only hags and hedgewives. But it wasn't so for all of them, was it? Aryn could still hear Mirda's soft words. *Sia bless you.* Certainly Mirda was no hag.

Once again silvery bells rang out. Aryn shivered and turned her face forward. Lirith had said this first meeting was to be only a welcoming, that the real work of the coven would not come until later. All the same, instinct told her something was about to happen. Something marvelous.

"The moon is full in Her darkness," Senrael rasped in her ancient voice.

"From darkness will Her light be reborn," Cirynn said, her voice only slightly unsteady.

Ivalaine took Senrael's hand in her left and Cirynn's in her right. Then Cirynn and Senrael joined hands— one smooth, one withered—closing the circle: Maiden to Matron to Crone, round and round.

"Now let us all weave together as one," Ivalaine said in a chantlike voice, "so that our circle may never be broken."

And Aryn forgot everything as two hundred shimmering threads coiled around her.

9.

Lirith was dreaming again, but she didn't care. The dream was far too beautiful to resist, so she let herself sink into vibrant swirls of color, let them draw her on.

She was on the common green beneath the castle again, strolling among the Mournish wagons, gazing at their fantastical shapes. Then she saw him—Sareth—standing beside a gilded wagon carved like a lion. He was more handsome than she remembered, clad only in his vest and billowing trousers. With a look he beckoned her.

As she drew near he held out his hand. On his palm lay a spider charm like the one she had found. Except this one was not bronze but gold. She reached out to take it, but before she could it started to move, scurrying across his hand as if it were a living thing. Even as she watched, she saw tiny, gold pincers sink into his flesh, and a drop of blood welled forth, glittering like a small ruby.

Sareth screamed. A hole appeared in his hand where the spider had bitten him. As Lirith watched in horror, the hole spread outward. His entire hand vanished into nothingness, then his wrist, his elbow, and his shoulder. Then his scream ceased as, in a heartbeat, the remainder of Sareth's body blinked out of being. Only the wooden peg of his false leg remained, clattering to the ground.

Lirith turned to flee, but from the shadows of the trees to either side gray threads sprang forth and spun around her, tangling her limbs, muffling her cries. She was caught in a web—a great, tangled web—and the more she struggled against it the more tightly it held her.

The wagons vanished as everything went dark. The only sound was a faint clicking that grew rapidly louder. Straining against the web, she turned her head, then saw them: gold spiders. Hundreds of them—no, thousands. All scuttled toward the center of the web where she lay entangled.

But there was something more, something lurking in the dimness beyond the golden spiders. It was gigantic, its terrible bulk weighting down the very web that supported them all. From the shadows it stared at her with eyes like black voids while ichor drooled from its open maw. It was hungry, this thing, so terribly hungry, and Lirith knew with perfect certainty that no matter what it consumed, it would never be sated. She tried to scream again, but this time sticky globs of web filled her mouth, choking her.

Then Lirith felt the first sharp pricks of pain.

10.

Lirith sat up in bed, clutching a hand to her throat.

Breathe, sister. It was merely a dream, nothing more.

With conscious effort, she forced her lungs to function, drawing air into her body and moving it out again in shuddering breaths. She reached beneath her nightgown and pulled out the bronze spider that hung from a cord around her neck. She stared at the Mournish charm; it lay still and lifeless on her palm.

Lirith slipped from her bed, shivering as the dream-sweat dried from her skin. The chamber's window glowed with colorless light. It was not yet dawn; yet she knew further sleep was impossible after the dream. It had been horrible. Although, in some ways, it was better than the others she had been having. The dreams of the past. The dreams of dancing.

But what did all of it mean? She had never been prone to nightmares. Why, of late, had she been possessed of so many?

One thing is certain, sister. No more maddok *before bedtime for you.*

Or was there something else to it? She had not seen the tangle in the Weirding again since that morning after visiting the Mournish. Perhaps it had simply been her imagination. She had listened, but she had not heard any of the witches in the castle mention seeing such a thing.

But it *hadn't* been her imagination. She could still feel the sickness that had filled her at the sight of the abomination. No amount of *maddok* was enough to induce that. She wished Grace Beckett were there; somehow Lirith knew her friend would have understood. Except Grace was far beyond her reach now. Perhaps if she glimpsed the tangle in the Weirding again she would know better how to find it, and she would be able to show another. Perhaps Tressa, or Ivalaine.

Lirith hesitated, then before she lost her nerve she closed her eyes and reached out with the Touch.

A loud thump shattered the predawn air.

Lirith gasped, the shining threads slipping from imaginary fingers as her eyes fluttered open. This time she remembered to throw a robe over her nightgown before she answered the door. However, it was not one of the castle's guardsmen.

"Sister Lirith," the girl said in a serious and slightly lisping voice, "Mistress Tressa wishes to see you."

The girl could not have yet passed her twelfth winter. A novitiate then; she would not be able to glimpse the Weirding until after her first blood. Sometimes Lirith envied the young ones, like this girl, who would learn to use the Touch from the first moment possible. When Lirith was twelve winters old, she had not yet even heard of the Witches.

Sulath blast you, you little grackle. Couldn't you have waited another year? Now there'll be no work from you tonight, nor tomorrow I warrant.

I'm sorry, Gulthas.

Sorry! The little bird is sorry? Well don't that fill my coffers. Now you listen here, grackle. You're going to have to

watch yourself now. No bastards are made at my house—
that's what I promise all my lords. Minya will show you how
to clean that mess up, and how to keep anything from taking
root in you. She's too old and worthless to do anything else.

"Sister Lirith?"

The shadows vanished, and the room snapped back
into focus. Lirith pressed an unconscious hand to her
abdomen, as if she could still feel the warmth of the
sparks that had once dwelled there, however briefly.

"I will be there at once," she said.

Minutes later, clad in her favorite gown of russet, she
hurried through the corridors of Ar-tolor. What did
Sister Tressa want of her? Perhaps she wished to discuss
the happenings at the opening of the High Coven last
night.

It had not gone as Lirith might have guessed.

She knew there was growing discord among the
Witches. It had been many years since village hags who
spoke the name Sia were burned upon piles of sticks or
pelted with stones—but not so many that such things
had been forgotten. Some in the Witches wished to
distance themselves from those old images, and nor
could Lirith entirely blame them. Yet the Crone was a
facet of who the Witches were. She was old and ugly,
but She was wise as well, and subtle in Her power. If
they dismissed Her, they would lose much.

However, Lirith knew that not all believed as she
did. What she had not guessed was that such
individuals would speak openly on the first night of the
High Coven. And who was this golden-haired witch
named Liendra? Lirith had never heard of her before,
although she had caught a few whispered rumors last
night—how Liendra hailed from Borelga in
Brelegond, where she had come into the Witches only
a few years ago, the daughter of a minor noble house,

and had quickly risen to a role in the triumvirate of the Borelgan Coven.

Still, despite the dissension among the Witches, when Ivalaine had called for them to weave as one, Lirith had felt all the women come together, binding their threads into one great, shimmering web. Perhaps their differences could be overcome. Not that Lirith had been able truly to immerse herself in the weaving. She had barely Touched the Weirding at all since the morning she had glimpsed the seething tangle of threads. She could only hope Ivalaine had not noticed that her strand had been missing from the web.

She reached Tressa's chamber to find a lady-in-waiting outside the door. The young woman quickly ushered Lirith inside, then departed. Tressa's chamber was much like the woman who dwelled within it: motherly and comforting. Crimson carpets softened the floor, and pillows seemed to strew every available flat surface.

The queen's advisor stood near the arched window. Next to her was another woman. With a jolt, Lirith realized it was Aryn. The young baroness's blue gown was slightly askew.

"Thank you for coming so early, sister," Tressa said. She wore a simple robe of green, and her red hair was bound in a tight knot at her neck.

"Of course, sister." Lirith's gaze flickered to Aryn. The young woman gave a slight shrug; evidently she had no idea what this was about either.

"I saw that look, sisters," Tressa said in musical tones.

Both Lirith and Aryn winced. However, Tressa smiled to show she was not displeased.

"Well, I don't suppose I can blame you. Curiosity is hardly a crime in our circle, now is it? And I'm certain you both wonder why I've called you here at this hour."

"What is it, sister?" Lirith asked.

Tressa's smile faded. "There's been an incident."

Lirith listened with increasing interest as Tressa described what had happened.

It seemed, earlier that morning, a novitiate had been dispatched to wake Sister Cirynn, for it was customary for the one chosen as Maiden to greet the dawn on each day of the High Coven. However, Cirynn had not been in her bed. A quick search of the castle—no doubt with the assistance of the Touch—had revealed the young woman's location: the barracks room of some of the queen's guardsmen. Tressa had found Cirynn fast asleep, wearing a smile upon her face. As were several of the guards.

Tressa heaved a deep sigh. "It seemed our Maiden is a maiden no longer, and likely has not been one for some time. Which means we must find a replacement at once."

Lirith felt her chest tighten. "But Sister Tressa, I—"

The red-haired witch lifted a hand. "Of course, dear one. A Matron you would be. But there was another I was thinking of."

Of course—how could she have been so stupid? Lirith gave an emphatic nod. "I quite agree, Sister Tressa."

"And is she ready, then? You are her teacher, Sister Lirith. That is why I summoned you here."

Lirith thought carefully—this was not a decision to make lightly—but then she nodded again. "There is much she has yet to learn, and her command is not so deep as her ability. But she is ready for this. You could not choose better than Sister Aryn."

Lirith couldn't help smiling at the effect these words

produced. Were it not attached to her face, Aryn would have had to pick her jaw up from the carpet.

"There, there, child," Tressa said, taking her hand. "You needn't make such a fuss. It's a simple enough role, you'll see. You'll be a lovely Maiden. And you *are* a maiden, are you not?"

Aryn's face blazed bright red as she fumbled for words.

"Very well, that's answer enough," Tressa said, patting her glowing cheek.

Lirith moved to the young baroness and embraced her. "Sia be with you, sister. I am so pleased."

Aryn let out a small gasp as she returned the embrace with her left arm, but she seemed unable to utter any words.

"All right, then," Tressa said. "We must be off, Sister Aryn. There is much to teach you before the coven meets again."

"Good luck," Lirith said, releasing the young woman.

Aryn gave her hand one last squeeze. "Thank you," she said at last, blue eyes shining. "For everything."

Lirith only nodded as Tressa bustled the young woman from the room. The door shut, and Lirith sighed, alone again.

Now what? There was little for her to do until that evening, when the witches in the castle would meet in smaller circles and covens. It was in three days that the High Coven would reach its climax, when the Witches charted their future course as one. In the meantime, the witches in the castle would meet in smaller groups, exchanging simples, spells . . . and whispers.

Lirith was to meet with a group of witches her own age that evening. She looked forward to it, for there would be seven of them, one hailing from each of the seven Dominions. But what could she do until then? She could think of nothing . . . unless she tried once more to use the Touch.

She started to shut her eyes.

"I knew she'd forget me," a sullen voice said.

Lirith's eyes popped open. So she was not alone after all.

He slouched in a corner, half-sunk into a pile of pillows, his bloodred tunic merging with the crimson fabric. Long, black hair half concealed the pale oval of his face.

"Lord Teravian!" Lirith said.

The young man sat up, cross-legged on the pillows. "You were about to cast a spell, weren't you? Your kind are always casting spells. So did I ruin it?"

Lirith drew in a breath, her composure quickly returning, and took a step toward him. "It was nothing, my lord. You needn't apologize."

A smirk touched his mouth. "I didn't apologize. I think it's funny when you make mistakes. It's like seeing a spider get caught in its own web."

Lirith forced her visage to remain smooth. Aryn was right; Teravian was a frustrating boy. He hardly seemed related to the blustering but good-hearted king of Calavan. Boreas was a solid bull of a man; his son seemed more like a shadow—slight, dark, and ephemeral. Still, Teravian was King Boreas's heir and Queen Ivalaine's ward. Lirith knew she must treat him with respect.

"We have never properly met, my lord," Lirith said. "I am the countess of—"

"I know who you are, Lirith of Arafel," Teravian said in a bored voice. He flicked his hair back over a thin shoulder. "I know everyone in this grotty castle. It's not like there's anything else to do."

Lirith sighed. *So much for that line of polite conversation.*

Teravian stood and walked to the window. Unlike so many young men of sixteen winters, Boreas's son was anything but awkward. He moved with lean, catlike grace, leaning on the stone sill, gazing through rippled glass at the bright world beyond. Lirith supposed there was nothing to do but ask her leave. She took a step forward—then was surprised as her lips uttered a different question.

"Why are you here in Lady Tressa's chamber, my lord?"

He kept his back to her. "Are you a dolt? I was being punished, of course. It's not like they talk to me for any other reason."

Lirith ignored his insult. "What were you being punished for?"

He turned, his green eyes piercing beneath the sharp, black line of his eyebrows. They nearly joined above his nose, but the effect was striking rather than homely.

"You're full of questions, aren't you? *Sister.* Why should you care?"

Lirith said nothing; she knew he would speak if she waited. It did not take long.

"I'm being punished for stealing bread from a breadmonger in the bailey." His voice was defiant, although his shoulders crunched inward.

"Why did you steal bread? Does not Ivalaine feed you all the bread you wish?"

Teravian clenched his hands into fists. "You're just like they are! You'd rather believe some horrid little peasant instead of me. But I don't care what you think. I didn't do it—I didn't steal his grotty bread."

"I believe you."

Teravian opened his mouth, then snapped it shut

again, as if only just hearing what she had said. His eyes narrowed.

"Why do you believe me?"

"Did you speak a lie?"

"No. I told you I didn't do it."

"Then that is why I believe you."

Instead of replying, Teravian flopped back down on the heap of pillows. He picked one up, fidgeting with the tasseled fringe, not looking at her.

"I'm sure you can go now," Lirith said.

"No, I can't. Tressa never dismissed me. She was just getting into it about the breadmonger when she learned about some grotty maiden who was having a roll with a few guardsmen. It sounds to me like the maiden was just trying to have a little fun. But I suppose that's a crime in this castle. The news put Tressa all in a spin, and she forgot about me. People always forget about me."

Lirith arched an eyebrow. "And why do you suppose that is?"

Teravian seemed to think about this, then he looked up at her. "Don't people always forget the things they don't like?"

Lirith pressed her lips together. How could she deny the truth of that? She wasn't certain why—he was without doubt a self-centered, brattish young man—but she felt a desire to comfort him. Maybe it was that, in a small way, he reminded her of Daynen: a slight youth lost in a world of shadow.

"You're wrong," he said before she could speak. "Talking to Ivalaine about it won't make it any better. She won't believe me, either."

Lirith stiffened. "How did you know what I was going to say?"

These were the first words she had spoken that truly

seemed to affect him. He blinked, his lips going slack. "I don't know. I suppose . . . I just know things sometimes."

Lirith studied him. Were he female, she would have probed, tested. But he was male—it couldn't be. Yet she knew, on rare occasions, that there were men with some scant shred of talent.

His expression sharpened into a frown. "Quit looking at me like that."

"Like what?"

"All hard and wondering. She's always looking at me that way, like I'm something she's got in a jar."

"Whom do you mean?"

Teravian stood. "Can I go now? If you say I can go, then I can blame you if Tressa gets angry at me."

Lirith took a step back, then nodded. "You may go."

He brushed past her, leaving without another look. Lirith started to turn, to at least say good-bye, then froze as something caught her eye.

It was the pillow Teravian had been idly playing with. Somehow he must have pulled apart one of its seams, for spilling out of it was a mass of yarn. The tangled knot of threads seemed to seethe and expand even as she watched, and a sickness filled her. But it was an accident. He couldn't have done it on purpose. Could he?

I just know things sometimes. . . .

Lirith clasped a hand to her mouth and hurried from the chamber.

11

"Do you have any sense at all of what they're up to, Melia?" Falken said, pacing back and forth before the sun-filled window of Ar-tolor's library.

"Just a moment, Falken," the amber-eyed lady murmured, not looking up from the wood-covered book open on the table before her. "I'm just getting to the good part."

Durge craned his neck, attempting to peer surreptitiously over Lady Melia's shoulder. He was curious what a person like Melia—who was so terribly wise—would choose to read.

"Don't even bother trying, Durge," Falken said with a snort. "It's not as if she's reading something interesting. I'm afraid it's one of those newfangled romances the bards here in Ar-tolor have taken to penning."

Durge frowned. "Romances? How could one compose an entire book about romances?"

"I'm not really sure," Falken said. "But as far as I can tell, they're all about long-haired knights in white armor who sing songs about flowers and slay dragons in order to win the hearts of wan maidens who don't seem to do anything but pine about having to marry some rich king."

Durge stroked his drooping mustaches. "These

knights and maidens you describe sound demented."

"Oh, they are," Falken went on, grinning wolfishly now. "They're always spouting poems about how gold and jewels mean nothing, how love is stronger than a thousand swords, and other positively absurd ideas. All I want to know is whatever happened to good stories—you know, ones where the dragon eats the suitor and the maiden forgets about him, marries a wealthy baron, gets fat, and has lots of kids?"

Durge nodded in approval. "I like that story."

"Of course you do. Who wouldn't? But these romances"—Falken waved his hand at an entire shelf of books with ornate gold writing on their spines—"as far as I can tell, they contain nothing of any importance."

"And what would you know about what is or isn't important to a woman, dear?" Melia said pleasantly, her eyes still on the book. "The last time I counted, it had been a century since you had good fortune with a lady. Or has it been two?"

Falken clenched his hands into fists, sputtered something completely unintelligible, then turned and stamped back to the window.

Melia sighed, shut the book, and clasped it to her chest. "Now this," she said, "is a how a man should behave."

"My lady . . ." Durge began. It was time to quit discussing modern literature and find out why Melia and Falken had called him there.

"Of course, dear," Melia said, handing him the book. "You may borrow it. But don't get any blood or food on it. And pay particular attention to page seventy-four. Only use more flower petals."

Durge accepted the book in fumbling hands. He flipped through the stiff parchment pages, but the few words and pictures he glimpsed were far more strange and mysterious than anything he had ever read in one of his tomes concerning the alchemical arts. The knight hastily set the book on a stack of others the moment Melia turned her back.

"Oh, quit sulking, Falken," she said.

He didn't turn away from the window. "It hasn't been *that* long since I got lucky."

"Of course, dear. I forgot to count the one-eyed fishwife in Gendarra."

Falken turned, thrust his shoulders back, and snapped his gray tunic straight. "And thank you very much."

Durge's eyes bulged, but he stifled any urge to ask for further explanation.

"Now, to answer your question, Falken," Melia said, folding her arms across the bodice of her silver-white kirtle. "I suppose I have as much of an idea of what they're up to as you. For years they have whispered of his coming. And last Midwinter he was revealed."

Falken rubbed his chin with his black-gloved hand. "Who would have thought they'd actually turn out to be right?"

"No, Falken," Melia said, her tone stern. "Do not dismiss the power of the Witches simply because you do not comprehend it. Their magic is different than that of your runes, but it is every bit as old. The name *Sia* has been spoken in the lands of Falengarth as long as that of Olrig Lore Thief."

"And both have been spoken longer than any of the names of the New Gods of Tarras, in case you had forgotten."

Melia's eyes flashed molten gold, and Durge took a step back, even though he was not the focus of her ire.

"I have hardly forgotten, Falken. The magic of Sia is ancient, and it is alien to me—although in some ways it does not disturb me as does the magic of runes, and often I wonder why that might be. All the same, I've heard it said there are some in the Witches who no longer speak the name *Sia*, but that of my sister, Yrsaia the Huntress—who is, if it had slipped your mind in your heathen ways, one of the New Gods."

Falken laughed. "Just because I haven't discarded the Old Gods for every new mystery cult that comes along doesn't mean I'm a heathen."

"No, I suppose it doesn't." Melia ran small fingers over the spines of a shelf of books. "But sometimes it seems you have difficulty accepting anything that is new, Falken. Yet the world grows newer every day."

The bard grunted, and when he spoke his voice was gruff. "I will not argue the point with you. But there is one thing you must concede. Any power the Witches have comes not from Yrsaia, no matter what name they speak."

Melia hesitated, then nodded. "It is true. My sister tells me that she has not heard any prayers from these Witches."

"That's because it's a front. Sia makes people think of toothless hags casting curses, so they pick a fresh, pretty, and popular goddess as their mascot. But deep down they're still the same old Witches. Some things *don't* change, Melia."

There was a silence, and at last Durge cleared his throat. "I do not pretend to understand what you both speak, but are not Ladies Aryn and Lirith witches? And certainly my mistress, Lady Grace, must be called a witch as well. Do you accuse them of some misdoing? If this is the case, then with all respect, I must take offense."

Falken let out a deep, musical laugh. "Don't get your greatsword just yet, Sir Knight. I don't think duty will require you to lop our heads off. Of course our three good ladies have done no wrong. But it *is* because you know them so well that we asked you here this morning."

"Certainly we don't mean to say the Witches are evil, dear," Melia said. "Strange as they are, many of them are healers and do great good. But there is . . . something more."

At these words the small hairs of Durge's neck prickled. But that was foolish; he was a man of logic, not superstition. "May I ask that you speak plainly, Lady Melia?"

The small woman drew in a breath, then glanced at Falken. The bard's face was grim now.

"For many years the Witches have foretold the coming of a man," Falken said. "One whom they keep watch for."

Durge shrugged. "Why is it our place to be concerned with one whom the Witches seek?"

Melia locked her eyes upon him. "Because the one whom the Witches seek is Travis Wilder."

A short while later, Durge walked down a lonely corridor, away from the castle's library. That morning he had donned only a gray tunic of light cloth against the summer day, but now he felt as cold and heavy as if he had strapped on his chain mail in the blue depths of winter.

For a quarter hour, he had listened as Melia and Falken spoke in low voices of the one called Runebreaker. But it wasn't only the Witches who watched for him. Once before Durge had heard the name *Runebreaker*. The ancient dragon Sfithrisir, whom they had encountered in a high, barren valley of the Fal Erenn, had also referred to Goodman Travis as Runebreaker. When Durge had pointed this out, both Melia and Falken had given him tight-lipped nods.

Yet in all of this, Durge could find no logic. Why would witches and dragons have such great interest in Goodman Travis? Durge knew that Travis had certain . . . abilities. However, it was also true that these abilities seemed largely tied to the three Great Stones—the Imsari—none of which was in Travis's possession any longer. What was more, Travis was no longer even on Eldh.

It is true, Melia had said when Durge spoke these facts. *But if Travis were ever to return to Eldh, he might be in grave peril.*

But why? Durge had asked. *What do they seek him for?*

However, Melia and Falken had only exchanged solemn looks; if they had any notion why the Witches sought Runebreaker, they had not voiced it.

It's important that you let us know if you hear anything, Durge, Falken had said. *It might help us protect Travis.*

Durge's mustaches had bristled. *I will not spy upon my mistresses.*

We're not asking you to spy, Durge, Melia had said. Then the diminutive lady had done a thing that had shocked him. She had gripped his hand, and she had looked up into his eyes with what could only have been described as a pleading expression. *But you will listen, won't you? Promise me, Durge.*

Who was he to deny this woman anything? He had nodded.

I will listen, my lady. On my sword, I promise it.

However, as Durge walked through the castle back to his chamber, he knew he would never hear anything of use to Melia and Falken. He had promised Lady Aryn he would remain in Ar-tolor, and remain he would. But he had said nothing about being near. Instead he would remain at a distance—a safe and proper distance.

It was better this way: to be present, but not to be seen. Just like the two ghosts he had glimpsed that foggy morning. They were sad reminders, yes, but they had no true power to affect or harm. They were merely shades of what had once been.

And you should be a shade as well, Durge of Stonebreak.

He flexed his fingers, feeling the joints of his knuckles grind together. Maybe, before too long, he would be. He pressed on alone through dust and gloom. This corridor was seldom trod—which was exactly his reason for choosing it.

A faint sound reached Durge's ear—a soft scrabbling—and he came to a halt. He peered into the dimness, but though his eyes remained sharp, he could not make out a thing. Still, instinct told him he was not alone. His rough hand slipped to the knife at his belt.

"Show yourself, shadow," he said.

A faint noise drifted on the air—like mirth, or perhaps like a song—and the hairs on Durge's arms stood up. Was it the ghosts again, returning to remind him of what never could change? He took a step backward. As he did, something dropped down from the rafters and landed with a *plop* before him, looking like nothing so much as a great, gangly spider—a spider clad in green, with jangling bells on his cap and pointed shoes.

Durge let out his breath and let go of the knife. In a way he had been right; it had indeed been a ghost stalking him, only this was the still-living kind.

"Out of my way, Fool," he rumbled.

Tharkis hopped from foot to foot, tapping the tips of his spindly fingers together, his perpetually crossed eyes looking at Durge in alternation.

"Where are you going, dreary old knight?
Do you not have a dragon to fight?
Did the beast hear you sneaking
From your bones and joints creaking,
And spread its wings and take flight?

"Or is there another reason you're here?
More than a beast—a thing that you fear.
Can eyes of blue and hair black as night
Be harder to bear than a dragon's bite?
Yes, flee from what you hold dear."

Durge felt anger set fire to his veins, but he clenched his jaw and forced his blood to cool. It was Master Tharkis's game to get a rise out of others, and Durge did not intend to hand him a victory. A king he might have been, but Durge knew things changed—that people changed. All Tharkis was at present was a nuisance.

"I said out of my way, Fool. Do not think I won't remove you from my path if need be."

Tharkis trembled in mock apprehension, the bells of his costume jingling. "Oh, dread knight, please spare me do—for news of your quarry I bring to you."

Durge frowned. He knew it was dangerous even to listen to the fool's words—they were crafted to baffle and befuddle—but all the same the question escaped him.

"What quarry do you mean?"

Tharkis grinned, displaying rotten teeth. "The spiders of course—the weavers of webs. Has the moon lady not sent you to follow their threads?"

"What do you know of that? Were you there in the library, listening to us?" Durge advanced, fist raised. "Tell me, Fool, or I'll throttle it out of you."

Tharkis scampered back a step. "No, no, fearsome knight, I heard not a thing. There's no need for Fool's poor neck to wring. But I know things, I do—I cannot say how. They come to me sometimes. They come to me now."

Durge lowered his fist. Something about the fool altered even as he watched; the mad grin faded from Tharkis's lips, and his wandering eyes grew distant.

"What do you mean, Fool? How do you know things?"

Tharkis pressed his thin body against the stone wall. "I think . . . I think it is part of what was done to me." He licked his lips, whispering now. "There's so much—it's all right there. I can see everything. The eyes . . . the eyes are in the trees, and the shadows are reaching out for me. I fall, and my horse runs, and I run . . . but the shadows are too swift. They have me."

Durge stared at the fool. Only dimly did it register on him that Tharkis was no longer speaking in verse.

The fool coiled his bony arms around his skull. "There's too much, too much. I can see everything that happened, but it's all in pieces, like a thousand broken mirrors I can't put back together. Only the rhymes . . . only the rhymes make sense. Only they fit together. The shadows are in my head. . . ."

Tharkis went stiff, his mouth opening and closing like a fish on dry land. Durge hesitated, then reached out for him.

A bony hand batted him back. The fool sprang away in a neat flip. His crossed eyes were bright again, and his grin had returned, splitting his gaunt face from side to side.

"You can't catch me, my doddering knight, for on my feet I'm far too light."

The fool had changed for a moment—he had

seemed more like a small, frightened child than a mad prankster. But whatever had happened, the moment was gone, and Durge had had quite enough.

"And under my feet you'll be pressed, Fool, if you don't move—*now!*"

Durge barreled forward, and Tharkis was forced to jump into the air and turn a somersault to avoid being trampled. There came a dissonant chiming as the fool landed behind him, but Durge kept moving. Tharkis's shrill voice called out behind him.

> *"A spider spins a shimm'ring web,*
> *And seeks to catch us with her thread.*
> *But all her plans can come to naught*
> *If in her own web she is caught.*
>
> *"Who's the spider, who's the fly?*
> *This riddle answer as you spy:*
> *If a spider can be captured,*
> *Who then spins the web that traps her?"*

The words faded on the dusty air, but Durge did not turn to reply. Instead he shut his ears to ghosts and madness, and strode away down the corridor.

12.

In all the activity of the three days between the first
meeting of the High Coven and Prime Incant—when
the Witches would weave a new Pattern to last them
until their next meeting—Lirith was almost able to
forget about the dreams. And the tangle she had
glimpsed in the Weirding.

This was only the second High Coven she had
attended since her entry into the Witches. The first had
been seven years ago, held in the castle of Baron
Darthus in southern Toloria—where it was said that
the old baron knew quite well his young wife was a
witch, and that he was more than pleased by the fact,
given the simples she brewed which had brought new
vigor to his loins. That had been in the spring of
Lirith's twentieth winter, and only months after she
had fled the Free City of Corantha, walked on bare,
bloody feet to Toloria, and never looked back.

At that High Coven she had been more a mouse
than a novitiate: small, brown, and wide-eyed, pressed
into corners while she watched those of greater
strength and cunning prowl around her. But she had
paid attention, and she had learned.

It was less than a year later when she caught the eye
of Lord Berend of Arafel, one of Baron Darthus's
counts. Six months later they were wed—despite

Lirith's lack of history and the protests of Berend's sister, who fancied herself countess and did not care for competition.

When Berend died just over a year later, it was whispered—and mostly by Berend's sister—that it was a potion concocted by Lirith that had done the trick. However, while it was true that Lirith had used some small charms to gain Berend's notice, it was not by magic that he had loved her, and not by magic that he had died. While Lirith could not say she had truly returned Berend's love, she had felt affection for the count, and she had never been cruel to him.

After Berend's death, his sister had petitioned Queen Ivalaine for possession of the estate, but the queen had refused and Lirith remained countess. After the count's sister followed her brother to the grave the following winter—there had ever been weak hearts in that lineage—no one seemed to recall that Lirith had not been born to the position. She had ruled for several years, and her subjects had cared for her.

Then, two years ago, when Queen Ivalaine summoned her to Ar-tolor, Lirith had gone willingly. She had left care of the estate to Berend's nephew, and so the count's sister finally got what she had wished for—only she had not lived long enough to enjoy it, as happened often with those who were consumed by desire.

In the time since, Lirith had thought little of Count Berend or their estate in southern Toloria. This was where she belonged. In Ar-tolor, in the service of the Witch Queen, attending a High Coven.

And this time Lirith did not hide in corners. Instead, she sought out those witches of most interest to her, to speak about herb lore or the art of scrying, or ways to Touch the Weirding and weave it in new patterns. It was no chance that many whom she went to were the eldest of the Witches: the crones and hags. It was they who held the deepest knowledge and the most ancient secrets. However, it was not lost on Lirith that she was one of the few younger witches to seek out and speak with her elders.

"But I don't *want* to know what they know," Nonna, a witch from the Dominion of Brelegond, said to Lirith in a whining voice. "They're all so *ugly*."

This was the first evening after the High Coven began, at the meeting of the small coven to which Lirith had been assigned, which contained seven witches her own age, one from each of the seven Dominions.

Lursa, a solemn-eyed witch from Embarr, let out a sigh. "I fear no one told me it was a requirement of wisdom to be pretty. I suppose I shall have to color my lips and comb my hair before I can learn another spell."

Unexpected laughter escaped Lirith. She winked at Lursa, and the plain-faced witch gave a shy smile in return. However, some of the other women shifted uncomfortably; not everyone disagreed with Nonna.

"It was the hags they took first," one of the witches said in a quiet voice.

The other six turned to gaze at the speaker. Her name was Adalyn, and she came from the Dominion of Eredane. Earlier that evening, they had listened to Adalyn's bone-chilling tale: how she had escaped from Eredane just after last Midwinter, and how black knights who served a nameless baron had begun riding across the land, murdering all witches, runespeakers, and priests—or anyone who was accused of being one.

"I think they were they easiest to see and catch," Adalyn went on. "The ancient ones, the crones. Soon it seemed as if any old woman who muttered under her breath or who owned a cat was put to fire. At first we were silent; it was not we who were burning. But soon they came after anyone who was rumored to be a witch. Many of my coven sisters were . . . not able to flee as I did. Maybe if we had stood against the black knights earlier, when they took the old ones, we might have put a stop to it."

After that, there was no more talk about hags. But Lirith saw the hard light in the eyes of Nonna and some of the others, and she knew Adalyn's tale had only strengthened their dislike of the elder ones.

The next two days brought more meetings and more witches. Lirith greeted all with interest. While most of the time was focused on the exchange of learning, there was also no lack of discussion about how the Pattern would be designed at Prime Incant. Many spoke of Yrsaia, and how her name should be woven into the pattern alongside Sia's—or perhaps, some boldly stated, atop it. Others held that the time was coming when the Witches would no longer just watch the Warriors of Vathris but would begin to work actively against them.

These rumors troubled Lirith, but not so much as a few whispered fragments she caught.

. . . that he is already among us . . .

. . . to stand against him, we must . . .

. . . but I say the end is closer than we . . .

Always the whispers abruptly ceased when Lirith drew close. But she knew the whispers started up again as soon as she was out of earshot, and she knew what at least one of them would be.

It is said she traveled with him. . . .

On the second day of the coven, just as silver twilight fell, Lirith strolled along one of the castle's high battlements, taking a rare moment to herself to consider all she had learned. Insects hummed drowsily, singing the summer away.

She was just about to return inside when motion below caught her eye. A small side door of the castle opened, and a figure clad in a drab brown cloak and hood stumbled out—a woman by her slender form. The woman looked back over her shoulder as if at the one who had pushed her, but the door slammed shut. She stumbled forward. Then, as if sensing eyes upon her, she looked up, and the hood of her cloak fell back. Even in the dim light, Lirith could make out the pale oval of her face, framed by dark curls.

Below, Cirynn searched back and forth, but Lirith stepped into a shadow. At last the young woman who had been Maiden lowered her gaze. She stumbled down the path that led from the castle, weaving left and right, as if she did not know where she was going.

Lirith didn't know how—perhaps it was simply experience—but somehow she knew exactly where Cirynn was heading, even if the scheming young woman did not know herself. She sighed. Lirith, of all people, knew what a brutal and hardening place a brothel could be.

Sia watch over her, she prayed silently, then turned and stepped back into the castle.

The next morning, just after dawn, Lirith rose and went in search of Aryn—of whom she had not seen so much as an eyelash in the last two days. She found the baroness just leaving Tressa's chamber.

"Our new Maiden is doing wonderfully," the red-haired witch said with a motherly smile. "She will be thoroughly prepared for her role tomorrow evening."

"I am pleased to hear it," Lirith said.

When the door shut behind them, leaving the two

alone in the corridor, Lirith grinned and squeezed Aryn's hand.

"You're marvelous," she said.

Aryn gave a nervous laugh. "I don't know about that. But I *have* managed to keep my head from exploding, despite all the things Sister Tressa has stuffed into it. I had no idea there were so many rules to follow just to be a Maiden."

Lirith nodded. "I've heard it's much simpler to be Crone. But then, by the time you've made it to that age, I don't think you want a lot of younger witches telling you what to do."

"I should think not," Aryn said.

They walked for a time past sun-dappled windows. Lirith spoke of what she had done at the coven, and Aryn described the things she had learned in her studies. At last they made their farewells in the castle's entry hall. However, just as they began to part ways, a woman stepped through the main doors of the castle.

She was a witch, that much was certain, although Lirith could not recall seeing her at the coven. And she was certainly striking enough to remember. Her dark eyes were slightly tilted, and her midnight hair marked by a single lock of pearl. The witch passed the two women, her multicolored robe fluttering like the wings of a butterfly.

"Good morrow, sister," the witch said, nodding to Aryn. Then she moved through an archway and was gone.

Lirith looked at the baroness. "Who was that?"

"Her name is Sister Mirda."

Lirith had not heard the name before. "Is she one of Liendra's group?"

"No, I don't think so. At the first meeting of the coven, she wished for Sia to bless me."

Lirith considered this. Surely no one from Liendra's faction would impart such a blessing. However, Lirith knew the great majority of the witches in the Dominions by name if not by sight. Only she had never heard the name Mirda before.

"Maybe she's a friend of Ivalaine's," Aryn said with a shrug.

Lirith sighed. "Sometimes I'm not sure Ivalaine has any true friends among the Witches. Many respect her, of course. But she has made it her place to stay a step removed from the others, to be a source of unity when there is dissension."

"Do you think she can remain that way? She tries to balance herself among all views, but Liendra is not the only one who wants to know what Ivalaine believes."

Lirith could not disagree. But as for what Ivalaine truly thought—that was a mystery that would have to wait.

Kissing Lirith quickly on the cheek, Aryn turned and dashed down a corridor, looking like nothing so much as a dark-haired girl, although this coming winter would be her twentieth. Lirith smiled, then turned to make her own way through the castle.

This time it came utterly without warning. She had not even been using the Touch, but it was there all the same, undulating in the corner of the entry hall: a tangled mass of threads. Lirith's mouth opened to scream, but no air passed into or out of her lungs. Even as she watched, the seething knot seemed to reach out hungrily, drawing more shimmering threads into itself. They dimmed to dull gray as they merged with the tangle. Then Lirith felt the first few tugs on her being. Memories flooded her. Once before she had been pulled like this toward a destination that would devour her.

Dance, my little grackle. Ah, but you are not so little anymore, and you can hide your beauty no longer. Come dance, and they will shower you with gold. Dance!

A moan escaped her lips, and Lirith began to sway back and forth. The seething of the knot quickened, as if excited by her movements. A gray thread spun out, reaching for her.

"My lady?"

The far corner of the hall was empty; the tangle was gone. Before Lirith stood a serving maid—barely more than a girl—a fearful look on her dirt-smudged face.

"Forgive me, my lady, but are you ill? Should I send for the queen's men?"

Lirith found her voice. "No, I'm fine. Thank you."

The serving maid ducked her head, then scurried from the hall.

Lirith glanced once more at the corner, but she knew that even if she used the Touch she would not see it again.

But it's still there, I can feel it. And it's growing.

Yet what did it mean?

A thought struck her. There was one who might know—one who was older and wiser than any witch in this castle. Lirith picked up the hem of her gown and ran from the hall.

13.

Melia was not in her chamber.

"I'm sorry, Lirith," Falken said, looking up from his lute. "I'm afraid she was in one of her moods today. When she left, I didn't ask where she was going."

Melia couldn't have gone far in an hour; at least so Lirith assumed. However, Melia had powers she couldn't hope to understand. And that was precisely why Lirith needed to find her.

"Thank you, Falken," she said breathlessly.

Falken opened his mouth to reply, but before the bard could speak Lirith turned and dashed back down the passageway.

In no particular order, she tried the great hall, the baths, the library—even the privy—all with no luck. After that, she ventured outside. However, there was no sign of Lady Melia in the bailey, the orchard, or the stables. At last Lirith was forced to halt, leaning against a stone wall near Ar-tolor's north tower. She had run out of both castle and breath, all with no sign of the amber-eyed lady. She would simply have to talk to Melia later.

And how much larger will it grow in the meantime?

She considered going to Ivalaine, to tell her what she had seen, but something held her back. Certainly if any other witches had glimpsed the tangle, Lirith would have heard whispers. That meant she was likely the only one who had seen it. In which case Ivalaine might simply declare her mad or ill and remove her from the coven. That Lirith could not allow.

It would just have to wait until she saw Melia again. Then, if the lady could not help her, Lirith would go to Ivalaine. Drawing a breath into her lungs, Lirith started back toward the main keep of the castle. But as she heard the faint sound of singing, she realized there was one place she had not looked.

The shrine was small and shadowed; it was little more than a wooden shack, really, leaning against the outside wall of the castle. But then, the mysteries of Mandu the Everdying had never been terribly popular in the Dominions, and certainly not in Toloria. Most of the mystery cults offered its followers salvation and the promise of joy after death. However, the cult of the Everdying God promised nothing to those who followed its mysteries—no final peace nor golden land of promise. Instead it offered only the story of its godhead: Mandu, who was born, who grew, and who was slain by treachery again and again, as inexorably as day was stolen by night.

But while the cult of Mandu might not have been popular in Toloria, Lirith knew that would not matter to *her*. They were her brothers and sisters, were they not? Lirith stepped forward, into the shadow of the little shrine.

Inside, Melia was dancing.

Lirith froze. The singing was clearer now; it was Melia whom she had heard outside. The lady's voice was rich and bright as burnished copper, rising and falling in a wordless melody that reminded Lirith, in a way, of the undulating music of the Mournish.

As she sang, Melia moved in a slow circle, holding

her arms in elegant curves. Her head was tilted back so that her onyx hair spilled down the back of her white kirtle, and her eyes were closed in rapture. On the stone altar stood an ivory likeness of Mandu, arms at his side, one foot forward. He gazed ahead with blind, serene eyes, a knowing smile on his lips.

"Melia?" Lirith gasped.

At once the small woman staggered, her eyes fluttering open. Lirith rushed forward, grasping Melia before she could fall. The lady was as light as a bird against her.

"Sister?" she whispered, her voice tiny and forlorn. "Sister, is it you? I do not think I can bear it. I know now that it was he who made the river run red with the blood of our people. I would rather die than wed such a monster."

For a horrible moment Melia's face was a mask of confusion, her amber eyes wide with fear. Then Melia stiffened. Gently, but forcefully, she disentangled herself from Lirith's grasp.

"Lirith," she said, her regal face stern. "What is the meaning of this?"

Lirith fought to keep from reeling. "You were dancing, Melia. You nearly fell. I . . . I caught you."

Melia frowned. "Dancing? I have not danced in more than two thousand years. Not since . . ."

Her voice trailed off as she followed Lirith's gaze to her bare feet and the gold rings on her toes.

Melia's ire melted. She glanced over her shoulder at the altar. "I had come to speak to my brother. Mandu was ever the most sensitive of the Nindari, and I have been hearing such strange news from the south. I wished to know what he thought of it all. Only I must have lost myself in the past for a moment." Her gaze grew sharp once more. "But I am quite well now,

Lady Lirith. Is there something you wish of me?"

Lirith winced at Melia's formal manner. But it was her own fault; she was the one who had chosen to greet the lady so coldly when she arrived at Ar-tolor. Now she regretted that action. What cause did she have to be so mistrustful of Melia?

You know perfectly well the cause, Lirith. She and Falken are agents of Runebreaker, are they not?

Lirith forced this thought from her mind; right then there was a more immediate question to answer. Before she lost her nerve, she explained in clipped words about the tangle she had twice glimpsed in the Weirding.

When Lirith finished, Melia folded her arms and paced before the altar. "Can this possibly be related to the whispers we have been hearing?" she murmured, although Lirith had the sense Melia was speaking not to her but to the statue of Mandu.

She answered nonetheless. "What whispers do you mean?"

Melia glanced up, as if she had already forgotten Lirith was there. "I'm not entirely certain I can put them into words. They aren't really whispers in the sense you think." She cast a fond glance back at the altar. "Words are limiting things. Yet most of what I have heard has, at its heart, the same matter. Of late, some among the New Gods of Tarras have sensed a change."

"A change?"

Melia sighed. "How can I explain it any better? It's as if . . . you're sitting in a lovely garden at noon, dozing in the warmth, when suddenly a cloud passes before the sun. Nothing in the garden itself is different than it was a moment ago, and yet the entire nature of the place is altered."

Lirith thought she understood. "So you're saying the city of Tarras is like that garden?"

Melia nodded. "Many of the New Gods are uneasy, although none can really say why."

The words startled Lirith. She had not thought it possible for a god to be afraid. But were not the gods simply reflections of the people who followed them? More powerful and beautiful and sublime by far—but reflections all the same? And certainly people feared things which they could not name.

Lirith nodded to the figure on the altar. "What does he think? Is this shadow in the garden the same as the knot I have seen in the Weirding?"

Melia sighed. "I fear Mandu speaks little anymore. With each circle he completes, he grows more perfect— and, I think, more distant. And I'm afraid I know little enough of the Witches and the Weirding to be able to tell you what this tangle is. Yet it seems to me there must be a connection somehow. Why else would you see a change in your web even as we have seen in ours?"

Lirith felt a bit of the tightness leave her chest. Melia's words weren't exactly an answer, but it was a relief to know she wasn't the only one in the castle who had sensed something strange.

"Do not worry, Lady Lirith," Melia said. "I shall be happy to tell you any more I might learn."

Lirith winced—not because the amber-eyed lady seemed to have read her mind, but rather at the coolness in her voice. Once more Lirith rued her foolishness in the great hall.

Before her courage fled her, she lifted the hem of her gown and stepped forward. "You must forgive me, Melia. I did not mean to be so cold to you before. I know you and Falken both work to great good in the world. It's just . . ."

Melia's visage softened. "Of course, dear. And I forgot how difficult it must be for you right now. I doubt the names Falken and Melia are fondly spoken in your circles."

Lirith gave her head an emphatic shake. "But they don't—"

Melia raised a slender hand. "No, dear, there is no need to speak of it further."

Warmth filled Lirith. She knew she should resist, but she could not help herself as she rushed forward and caught the small woman in an embrace. However, Melia did not push her away, but instead returned the gesture with equal fierceness.

"We women of mystery must stick together, dear."

At last the two women stepped apart. As they did, Melia cocked her head. "Where did you get that necklace, dear?"

Puzzled, Lirith glanced down. The spider charm rested against the bodice of her gown; it must have slipped out when she rushed forward.

"It's just a trinket of the Mournish. It doesn't mean anything." Lirith felt her cheeks flush, for these words weren't entirely true. It reminded her of *him*, did it not?

Melia tapped her jaw with a finger. "I believe you are wrong, dear. In my experience, the Mournish make no meaningless trinkets. Everything they craft, however simple, has a purpose and a power. And of all the symbols they fashion, the spider is among the strongest—and the most secret."

"You sound as if you know them."

"I know *of* them. In all the centuries I have walked upon Eldh, I have been among them countless times. Yet I cannot say I truly know the Mournish. I'm not certain anyone who is outside their clans does. And they have never accepted outsiders."

Lirith turned away, toward the door of the shrine, and clutched the spider charm. "Is that so?"

"What is it, dear? Is something wrong?"

Lirith opened her mouth and knew she would not be able to stop herself from telling Melia everything: the card, the dreams, Sareth. However, at that moment two silhouettes appeared in the door of the shrine.

"Melia, there you are," Falken said. The bard glanced at Durge beside him. "You were right—I don't know why I didn't think to look in the shrines first."

The Embarran nodded. "It seemed the logical choice."

Falken moved to the amber-eyed lady. "Are you all right? You were acting a bit peculiar this morning, and then I couldn't find you."

"It's gallant of you to worry about me," Melia said, "but I'm quite fine now."

She smiled at Lirith, and Lirith smiled back.

Falken groaned. "Don't tell me she's been giving you lessons."

"Lessons?" Lirith said in her most mysterious voice. "Concerning what?"

"That!" the bard said. "One beautiful woman who speaks in knowing riddles is quite enough. We don't need another."

"Come, Falken," Melia said, taking the bard's arm. "Let's go back to our chamber. You can rant to your heart's content there."

The bard gave a snort, then stamped from the shrine, Melia in tow.

"They care for each other deeply," a solemn voice said after a moment.

Lirith had almost forgotten Durge; the knight's gray

tunic blended with the gloom. But it was what he said that startled her most, for it seemed a tender expression for the usually stern knight. But then, Lirith knew the truth locked beneath his armored exterior.

"I think we can never understand what they have endured together," she said.

Durge only nodded. In the dimness his craggy face seemed more somber than ever. But it wasn't just the gray light. These last days the air of grimness the knight wore had become more like a mantle of sorrow. Lirith had first noticed it the morning Melia and Falken arrived at Ar-tolor. She had seen Durge little since that day, but each time he had seemed sadder.

"What is it, Durge?" she said. "Has something happened?" She reached a hand toward him.

The knight's brown eyes went wide and he shrank from her touch. Her fingers curled in, and she drew her arm back. Then Durge took a half step toward her, as if realizing what he had done.

"My lady . . ."

"No, Durge, I don't blame you. Not after what I did to you in the Barrens. You're wise to keep your distance."

There was silence for a long minute.

"Have you told her?" Durge asked.

"I have not," Lirith said. "I gave you my word. I will never tell her."

Durge nodded. "That is well, my lady."

Without further words, the knight turned and left the shrine. Lirith sighed and gazed into Mandu's empty eyes, searching for solace. But the god only smiled, waiting for his inevitable death.

14.

Purple twilight gathered outside the window as Aryn paced back and forth in her chamber, chanting under her breath, her snow-white robe rustling softly.

"Snuff out the candle, ring the bell, then speak the incantation. Snuff out the candle, ring the bell, then speak—"

She froze and looked up, her blue eyes wide. "Or is it ring the bell, speak the incantation, *then* snuff out the candle?"

Her head buzzed as if her brains had been replaced by a swarm of moths. No thought would hold still for her long enough to grasp it.

Dread filled her. What would happen if she were to perform the ritual incorrectly? Would the entire Pattern unravel? She wasn't certain, but there was one effect she knew she could count on: If she did not act out her role as Maiden perfectly, Tressa would change her into a gnat.

Aryn drew in a deep breath.

Concentrate, sister. You can do this. Remember, everyone will be watching.

Panic surged in her chest.

All right—so don't remember that. Just think of your last lesson with Tressa, then. Everything went perfectly.

A shred of calm crept into Aryn's mind, and the

fluttering eased. Of course, that was it. How could she have been such a goose? It was bell, candle, and *then*—

A knock sounded on the door, shattering her thoughts. A second knock spurred her into motion. She hurried to the door and opened it.

"Well, it's about time, deary. These old bones aren't getting any younger just standing here."

Aryn gulped. The coven hadn't even started, and she was already making mistakes. "I'm so sorry, Sister Senrael. I didn't mean to trouble you."

The old woman laughed. "Well, of course not, deary. Not a precious thing like you. There isn't a cruel bone in your body. But fear not. Sia willing, you'll get to be old and disagreeable like me one day."

You're wrong, Aryn wanted to say. *I once killed a man with my magic. Is that not cruel?* However, no words came out.

"Come along, deary. The moon will rise soon. We must be ready by then."

The old woman's ash-gray robe swished as she turned and hobbled down the corridor. Aryn hurried after, heart pounding.

Will I have to make decisions about what goes into the Pattern? she had asked Tressa nervously that morning.

Only so much as any witch does, the red-haired woman had said. *All threads are woven into the Pattern. The Maiden, the Matron, and the Crone are there simply to help, just as the shuttle helps pass a thread through the warp when you weave. But it is the threads themselves that determine the Pattern.*

After her meeting with Tressa, Aryn had gone in search of Lirith, to see if her friend had any wise words to guide her. However, she had not been able to find Lirith anywhere in the castle.

You'll see her at the High Coven, she had told herself. Yet for some reason Lirith's absence troubled her.

"A pox on it all!" Senrael said, stopping so suddenly that Aryn nearly ran into her.

"What is it?" the baroness said, hoping she was not included in the rather wide scope of the old witch's curse.

"I knew I shouldn't have had that last cup of *maddok*," Senrael grumbled. "Now I need to make a stop at the privy. You'd best hurry along to the garden and find the queen. I'll be right behind you."

The old woman vanished through a door. Aryn would rather have just waited, but one didn't disagree with one's elders. And it wasn't as if she didn't know the way to the gardens. With a sigh, she started down the corridor.

"Well, if it isn't our new Maiden," a cooing voice said.

"Maiden?" answered another high, clear voice. "More like *half* a Maiden, I should say."

Fear drove a cold spike through Aryn, halting her. She turned, searching for the source of the voices.

"What? Can't you see us?"

A shadow that had draped a nearby archway vanished like a cloth unraveling. Beyond was a knot of six young women in green robes. They stepped through, and Aryn recognized some of them as the witches who had stood with Cirynn at the first meeting of the High Coven.

"Look at her gape," a golden-haired young woman said with a laugh. "You'd think she'd never seen a shadow spell before."

Aryn managed to find her voice. "I have seen spells."

Immediately she winced at the words; her voice trembled like a little girl's.

"Of course you have. *Deary*."

The other witches laughed at these words, spoken by a brown-eyed witch. Aryn knew her. It was she who had abandoned Aryn's group to go stand with Cirynn. Since that night, Aryn had learned her name; it was Belira.

"That robe doesn't really suit you," Belira said, drifting forward while the others watched with keen gazes, smiles curling their lips. "But then, it was made for another, was it not?"

Aryn felt herself shrink inside the robe, like a turtle drawing into its shell. The white garment was heavier than the green robe she had worn previously, but it still did not cover her withered arm. She tried to move down the corridor, but Belira interposed herself.

"Why are you doing this?" Aryn gasped before she could stop herself.

Belira's eyes narrowed to slits. "I'll make it plain for you. We liked Cirynn, and we don't like you. Understand?"

Aryn shook her head; she could not speak.

The golden-haired witch stepped forward. "What a simpleton she is. One arm and half a wit. How on Eldh did she get to be Maiden and not one of us?"

"Ivalaine chose me," Aryn managed at last.

Belira curled her lip, and the expression marred what little prettiness her face held. "Yes, Ivalaine. But that only brings up another question—why is *she* Matron and not Liendra? Everyone knows Sister Liendra speaks for all the Witches."

Aryn felt some of her fear transform into anger. Who were these young women to think they knew so much?

"You're wrong, Sister Belira. Liendra doesn't speak for everyone—she doesn't speak for me. Now let me pass."

She tried to take a step forward, but the others closed in around her in a circle. Aryn felt her lungs grow tight. She seemed to shrink, until she was a small child again, jeering faces whirling around her in a blur as remembered voices rose and fell like the harsh calls of birds.

> *Little Lady Aryn,*
> *What is she wearin'* . . .

No, she would never feel that way again. Never. She had vowed it on Midwinter's Eve when she slew Leothan with her magic. For so long after that night, she had regretted her action, had believed it made her evil. But she had been wrong; she was not the evil one. It was the others—the ones that laughed and jeered, the ones that treated people like objects to be used, scorned, and discarded. All her life, others had looked at Aryn like she was a monster just because of her arm; but she knew now that she wasn't the monster.

They were.

Leothan had been an ironheart, a thing no longer human. And while no lumps of metal resided in the breasts of these young women, they were every bit as heartless. Aryn needed to endure such cruelty no longer. Not theirs, not anyone's. Not when she had the power to stop it. She would show them what it meant to cast a spell.

Both fear and anger melted from Aryn. Instead a calm possessed her, like the stillness before a storm. She stood straight, then gazed at Belira with clear eyes.

"I must go, sisters," she said, her words cool and polished as marble. "The High Coven is about to begin. I must ask that you let me pass."

Belira glanced at her companions, who nodded encouragement, then turned toward Aryn with a smirk. "Make us."

"Very well, if that is what you wish."

Belira frowned. Clearly these had not been the words

she was expecting. The others shifted behind her. Belira opened her mouth, but before she could speak, Aryn lifted a hand—not the left hand, but the right: small, pale, and twisted as a broken dove.

It was so simple; she didn't even need to shut her eyes. Aryn reached out with the Touch and clasped six shimmering threads in an imagined hand. Then she pinched the threads, squeezing them tight.

As one, the six young women around her gasped and stumbled back, hands fluttering up to clutch their throats. Their eyes bulged in their faces as their mouths opened and closed in silent, airless spasms.

The young witches spun away from Aryn like drunken dancers. After a few moments blue tinged their lips. So easy—it would be so easy to squeeze their threads until they snapped, to end their breathing forever . . .

Stop it, Aryn. If you harm them, then you'll be just like they are.

She stared at her withered hand. No—she would not let them make her into a monster.

Aryn lowered her hand, releasing the threads, and the young women staggered, drawing ragged breaths. A few dropped to their knees, gulping in air, and others sobbed as they hung on to one another. Of them, only Belira stood still. She gazed at Aryn, holding her throat, her brown eyes filled with terror. And hatred.

Aryn didn't care. She had neither need nor desire to win the affection of witches such as these. Unlike her own, their bodies were perfect and whole; but their spirits were more twisted than any limb of flesh could ever be.

Her white robe whispering softly, she strode past the young witches.

"I will see you at the High Coven. Sisters."

15.

Lirith hastily smoothed the wrinkles from her green robe, then finger-combed the worst of the snarls from her black, coiled hair. A quick glance in a bronze mirror confirmed that the results were acceptable. The gray air of twilight crept through the window; it was almost time for the High Coven to begin.

How she had nearly overslept, Lirith didn't know. Her head had been throbbing all day, and she had lain on her bed just to rest her eyes. However, somehow she had drifted into sleep—and into another dream of Sareth. This one had been murkier than the last. They had both been naked, and he had been making love to her. Only she felt a terrible coldness, and when she looked at him she saw that Sareth was no longer a living man, but a statue of dull stone. The coldness spread through her, and she tried to scream, but her tongue was already stone.

Thankfully she had awakened then. In some ways this dream had been worse than the one of the golden spiders. The thought of spending eternity like that—alive, aware, but utterly numb and frozen—made her flesh crawl.

Lirith left her chamber and hurried through the castle. Servants and petty nobles looked up with wide eyes and scrambled to get out of her way. She couldn't blame them; she had a feeling she looked like a mad hag at the moment. It was Ivalaine's wish that the witches move discreetly in Ar-tolor, so as not to alarm the castle folk. However, she had no time for anything but the most direct route to the gardens. She was lucky she had not been assigned a group of novitiates to guide to the coven that night. She picked up the hem of her robe and quickened her pace.

"It doesn't matter if you run, you know," a sibilant voice said. "You're still going to be late."

Lirith skidded to a halt. A slender silhouette stood against a fading window.

"Teravian," she said. "I didn't see you there."

"Why should you see me? No one else ever does."

Lirith hesitated. She should have been at the coven by now. But, as before, there was something about Teravian—a sadness, maybe—that compelled her to speak.

"Perhaps you should consider wearing less black," she said.

The young man blinked. "I didn't know witches could be funny."

"Oh, I'm a very peculiar witch. You probably shouldn't even be talking to me. No doubt it's causing all sorts of irreparable damage."

Now his lips curled into a smirk. "Good."

Lirith's gaze moved to the window; the first stars were just beginning to appear.

"It's all right. I know you've got your little meeting to go to, so you might as well leave. *She* always leaves me."

All traces of the smile fled his expression; his face was a pale, grim oval floating in the gloom. Lirith thought about it only a moment, then moved closer to him and laid her hands on his shoulders. He was slight for a young man of sixteen winters, and they were very nearly the same height, so that she could gaze into his green eyes.

"Listen to me, Lord Teravian. You must believe me when I tell you that I know what it is to be left behind. But in the years since, I have learned something I very much wish I had known at the time, and that I will tell you now. Although others may abandon you, you must never abandon yourself. Do you understand?"

He said nothing, but it seemed his gaze grew thoughtful. Lirith would have to hope it was enough. She let go of his shoulders.

"I must go now—to my little meeting, as you call it. But I will come speak to you again. I promise."

He shook his head, not gazing at her, but into the shadows still. "No, you're wrong. You'll be going soon."

A cool breath touched Lirith's skin. "What do you mean?"

Teravian only shrugged, then the young prince turned and walked down the corridor, his black hair and clothes melding with the darkness.

Minutes later, Lirith stepped, breathless, through a braided arch of branches and into the tree-lined temple deep in the gardens of Ar-tolor. Globes of witchfire hung from high branches, filling the glen with green light. Through the moving screen of leaves above, Lirith just caught the silver crescent of the horned moon, sinking toward the invisible horizon.

Two hundred witches—the youngest on the right, the eldest on the left—faced the marble rostrum at the far end of the temple. It looked as if Lirith was the last to arrive. On the rostrum stood three figures, one clad in white, one clad in green, and one in ash-gray. The woman in green was speaking.

"—and in our weaving, a common Pattern shall come into being." Ivalaine's voice rose on the air. "A Pattern into which all threads shall be bound, and which shall serve as our guide in the coming moons. So in the name of *all* goddesses, let our threads be spun together this night."

Lirith breathed a sigh. She had missed the coven's opening incant, but the weaving had not yet begun. That was a blessing from Sia. Surely Ivalaine would not have failed to notice if Lirith's thread had been missing from the Pattern. And it was more than that. The Pattern was what bound all the Witches together, what elevated them from a disparate band of hedgewives and village healers into a union of true power. Lirith did not wish to be left out of that circle.

On the rostrum, Ivalaine nodded to Aryn and Senrael, and the two stepped forward. Aryn carried a small bundle wrapped in black cloth, and Senrael held a silver bowl in gnarled hands. Together, Maiden, Matron, and Crone would speak the High Incant before the Pattern was woven. Doing her best to avoid notice, Lirith started moving through the crowd as quickly as she could.

"Do not think we fail to see what you are doing," a hard voice rang out.

Lirith went rigid. Had her tardiness been noticed? However, none of the witches gazed at her; all of them stared forward, their expressions ones of shock—and interest.

A tall witch, sharply elegant in her green robe, had stepped close to the rostrum. She was half-turned to the side, as if she addressed the gathering as much as the queen. Lirith could just make out the proud angle of her cheekbones. Her red-gold hair was woven with green gems.

As she had at the last meeting, Ivalaine appeared unshaken by the interruption. Her icy eyes were tinted by the light of the witchfire, turning them the color of a cold, clear ocean. "I do not understand, Sister Liendra. What I am doing is what has always been done. I am calling for the Pattern to be woven."

"Yes, the Pattern." Liendra lifted a slender hand. "You seem almost in a hurry to get to it. Are you so afraid to let us speak before the weaving begins?"

Whispers coursed through the gathering, like a wind through a grove of trees.

Ivalaine spread her hands. "And what is there to speak of before the weaving, Sister Liendra? Will not all threads—and all voices—be bound into the fabric of the Pattern?"

"That is true," Liendra said. Now the witch gave up all pretense of speaking to Ivalaine and turned to face the gathering. "And yet, there are some matters that might be uttered before the weaving . . . matters which, if voiced, could well color some of those threads before they are woven into the Pattern." Liendra turned again toward the rostrum. "Is that not what you seek to avoid in your haste, Matron?"

"I beg you speak these matters, sister," Ivalaine said. "There is nothing to be feared in words."

The queen's voice was cool and even as always, but Lirith noticed that she stood stiffly, and that a note of color had touched her milky cheeks.

"I would not be so certain of that," Liendra said, her words rising with the incense on the still air. "But I will defer to your desire for speed; indeed, I would see the Pattern woven quickly as well. And so I will ask but one question. Why have *they* been allowed into the castle while our High Coven proceeds?"

"And who is it you speak of, sister?"

By the renewed hiss of whispering that filled the grove, all knew exactly who Liendra spoke of. However, the witch voiced the names anyway, her lip curling just slightly.

"I speak of Melindora Nightsilver and Falken Blackhand. Their reputation for meddling is well known, as is the company they keep. For what other reason can they have come here but to spy on us? It would have been wiser to turn them away."

"Forgive me, sister," Ivalaine said, her voice honed to a knife edge. "I did not know you were unfamiliar with the laws of hospitality that hold sway in these Dominions. I will explain them to you. When folk who have done no wrong beg hospitality, it must be granted."

Liendra winced under the force of Ivalaine's words. If anyone had forgotten that Ivalaine was queen as well as Matron, they remembered it at that moment. A witch might question Ivalaine's decisions as Matron, but never her decisions as ruler of Ar-tolor. However, Liendra smoothed her robe and spoke again.

"You say you must grant hospitality to those who have done no wrong?" Even from a distance Lirith could glimpse the dangerous smile on Liendra's face. "But did not the bard Falken, by his own hand, bring about the fall of Malachor? All the tales say it is so, and he has never denied it. I would say the murder of an entire kingdom might count as *doing wrong*."

Ivalaine opened her mouth to reply, but Liendra was swifter. "No, Matron, you are wise in your decision to rebuke me. Indeed, I have delayed the weaving of the Pattern far too long. Please forgive me."

With a nod to the queen, Liendra returned to her position near the center of the gathering. On the rostrum, anger glinted in Ivalaine's eyes. While

Liendra's words had sounded contrite, they had cut more deeply than any accusation. Cool needles pricked at Lirith's flesh. It was difficult to express in words, but at that moment she sensed a change in the tenor of the Witches. It was subtle, yet fundamental, like a shift in the direction of a wind. Something had just happened.

Before Lirith could consider it further, Aryn and Senrael moved forward to join Ivalaine. They would perform the High Incant now. Lirith took the chance to hurry to her place.

By the time she stood with a group of witches her own age, the High Incant had begun. With twisted hands, Senrael sprinkled water from her silver bowl. Aryn had unwrapped her bundle and from it had taken three candles, which she now placed on an altar. One candle was tall, one half-burnt, and the last a mere stump. With a flaming brand produced seemingly from nowhere, Ivalaine lit the candles.

Lirith held her breath as she watched the High Incant. Usually a young witch had weeks to prepare for her role as Maiden; Aryn had had days. However, Tressa seemed to have done her work well. Aryn made no mistakes as she moved through the prescribed steps of the incant.

Yet it's more than that, sister.

Never had Lirith seen the baroness so confident before. Her bearing was straight, even regal, and her voice was clear and strong. Usually Aryn went to great lengths to keep her withered right arm concealed, but not tonight. A few of the younger witches uttered mocking whispers, but the girls were quickly hushed by their companions.

Lirith smiled. She did not know the source of Aryn's newfound assurance, but she was glad for it.

The High Incant was nearly over. On the rostrum,

Aryn rang a small silver bell. She snuffed out the tallest candle, and at the same time Ivalaine extinguished the middle candle and Senrael the shortest. Then the three spoke in unison, their voices melding into one.

"Let the Pattern be woven."

It began in an instant. All were anxious to see what shape the Pattern would take. The air around Lirith tingled with magic. She shut her eyes, and she could see them: two hundred shimmering threads spinning in all directions. For a moment she hesitated—would it be there, lurking in the corners? But she saw no sign of the tangle, and she let the glittering threads draw her in.

That was when the voices began. At first they were faint and fragmentary, the shards of whispers.

. . . but can you . . . yes, I . . . let me come to . . . so many, and so beautiful . . . I am here . . .

Lirith knew many of the voices belonged to the younger witches, entranced by the mystery of what was happening. But gradually, as the initial wonder quieted, older and stronger voices began to speak, each spun by a glowing thread.

It is said . . . I have seen the signs of . . . and Sia has ever been our . . . can it be that the time is close at . . . and the Hammer will strike against the Anvil, while all is caught . . . it is the Huntress that . . . but who are we to . . .

So far there had been only chaos in the movement of the threads, but all at once—as if of their own will—several strands joined, braiding themselves together. At the same moment, like the sounding of a horn, a voice rang out.

He has come!

A thrill coursed through Lirith. Before she could form the word with her mind, a hundred other threads whispered it.

Runebreaker.

Now the voices grew louder, coming more swiftly and from all directions. Often one voice spoke alone, but with each passing moment more and more threads bound with the others, and disparate voices were merged as one.

I have seen . . . we have seen him. The rune of peace, broken under his hand. It is said . . . the gray men themselves did turn against him. He can only . . . devastation. But I . . . and I . . . and we believe it must be so. Our seers foretold it . . . yes, we have seen it again. By his hand all the world . . .

A dozen threads wove together at once, and now the sound was like a chorus of trumpets.

Runebreaker will destroy Eldh!

Fear tinged Lirith's exhilaration. She pulled her own thread back, keeping it separate from the others, then searched for Aryn's thread, wondering if she should speak to her. But she could not see the young woman's strand in the undulating tempest of the Pattern.

And what did it matter? The Witches had made up their minds that Travis Wilder was their enemy; that much was already clear from the Pattern. Lirith let her strand be pulled back into the weaving. The mass of threads was still largely chaotic, but not everywhere; in places, the strands had fallen into place, binding together as more witches began to speak of like mind.

Questions careened in all directions, and answers as well.

What of the men of the bull?

The followers of Vathris have always craved blood.

But would they seek the destruction of all the world?

Surely he is their Hammer, the one who they speak will bring about the Final Battle.

Yes, so we have heard. They believe that when they fight

this Final Battle they will lose, but that they will die glorious deaths, and afterward they will dwell with their god for all eternity. Madness, it is madness.

But what of the Anvil?

Against the Anvil the Hammer strikes, and all are caught between. What else can it mean? They seek to crush all that is alive.

But who is this one?

We do now know. We know him only. But the Anvil cannot be far from the Hammer.

We must stop them!

In large places the threads of the Pattern had aligned themselves. The voices that spoke out against Runebreaker, and the ones called Hammer and Anvil, were nearly deafening now. But suddenly, from the shadowy edge of the weaving, came other voices: coarse and rough, but deep with wisdom.

It is not Sia's way to do harm to others, even those who would harm us.

Yes, those who do wrong will work their own ends. An evil thread has a way of turning back on the spinner.

We must not let ourselves be caught in their folly. If the Warriors seek blood, then it is their own blood they will find. And if Runebreaker desires to destroy the world, it is his own destruction he will meet. That is Sia's way.

These words were like a balm to Lirith's spirit, as cool and sustaining as a draught of water from a deep well. However, even as these voices spoke, others rose up, overwhelming them.

Sia dwells only in the past. We must think of what is to come. Those who cannot move forward must be left behind.

It is Yrsaia who stands for us now. If Sia is not dead, then she is dying.

We are not some band of hags cackling over toads in a cauldron.

With these words, a great swell rose in the weaving. A number of threads—the dimmest ones, and the oldest—were pushed to the very fringes of the Pattern. They were not gone, but they had been relegated to the edge—from which they might later be easily plucked without damaging the rest of the garment. Weak protests arose but were quickly strangled.

Sorrow filled Lirith. This was a mistake; they should not forget the old ones. However, the Pattern was beginning to take shape, and there was no resisting it. Thread after thread fell into place.

We must seek out Runebreaker.

Yes, he cannot escape us, no matter where he has gone.

We will stop him before he can cause more harm.

He will never destroy the world, for we will destroy him first, and the Warriors as well.

RUNEBREAKER MUST BE SLAIN!

These last words rumbled with the force of thunder. More and more threads flocked to the center. At the very heart of the Pattern shone a brilliant green thread around which nearly all the others were woven. It was Liendra's strand—Lirith was sure of it. But where was Ivalaine's?

Few single strands remained. Lirith's was one of them, and there was Aryn's bright blue strand, not far from a pearly thread that, after a moment, Lirith sensed to be Ivalaine's. So there was hope yet; not all felt Liendra's burning thirst for murder. Then, even as she watched, Ivalaine's thread shuddered and moved to the center; the queen's strand was lost in the Pattern.

Despair filled Lirith. There was no point in resisting so many voices. Ivalaine had no choice—not if she wished to remain Matron—nor did the rest of them. Although she hated what it was becoming, the Pattern would be woven, and Lirith could either be part of it or be nothing. She started to spin her thread out toward the center of the Pattern.

Caution, sisters. There is peril even in doing good.

Lirith halted. This voice was low and gentle, yet filled with a quiet strength that somehow cut across the shrillness.

If we go to war, then are we not warriors? If we destroy, then are we not destroyers? If we are to be the healers and the preservers of the world, then let us heal and preserve. Let us seek this Runebreaker, yes, and let us watch him, that we might find a way from preventing his fate from coming to pass. But let us do no harm with our own hands.

Whose voice was this? Lirith didn't know, but the words filled her with a shard of new belief. She sensed anger and resistance from the center of the Pattern, but the few remaining threads aligned themselves with the new voice. Lirith hurried to do the same, and as she let her thread bind with the others she sensed Aryn there as well.

They were not many; they formed barely a scrap of cloth compared to the great tapestry that was the Pattern. But now that they were bound as one, their threads could not be denied. The resistance from the center ceased, and the new strand was woven into the Pattern. Around her, a single voice spoke in grand, resonating unison, and only as it sounded did Lirith realize her own voice was part of it.

By our hands Runebreaker will not die. But we will seek him, and we will capture and hold him. We will not let him harm himself or the world.

There was a chime, like the ringing of a bell. Lirith's eyes flew open. Once again she stood in the garden, two hundred witches around her. All wore looks of awe that Lirith knew mirrored her own.

On the rostrum, Ivalaine set down the silver bell.

For a moment the queen seemed to sway on her feet. What had it cost her when she joined the Pattern and Liendra's strand? However, before Lirith could wonder more, Ivalaine's face grew hard, as if hewn of marble. She drew herself up and spoke in a crystalline voice.

"The Pattern is complete."

Immediately, witches began to leave the gardens, their green robes merging with the shadows between the trees, leaving only moonbeams in their wake. Many of the witches would depart Ar-tolor that night, and nearly all would be gone by tomorrow's sunset, journeying back to their homelands. How long would it be until they all wove together again? Yet that was the purpose of the Pattern—to bind them all together even when they were apart.

"Lirith! There you are!"

She looked up and saw a flash of white moving through the remains of the gathering. Lirith rushed forward, and they met in the center.

"Aryn."

She embraced the young woman, holding her tightly. Aryn returned the gesture with no less fierceness for her one arm. At last they pulled back.

"You were beautiful tonight," Lirith said. "No, radiant. I was glad to see it, although I must say you were not so confident when last I saw you. What happened?"

Aryn shrugged, smiling. "I decided to be myself. Just like you told me to do."

Lirith squeezed the baroness's left hand. She started to say more, then halted as a tall form with fiery gold hair passed nearby. Lirith felt the warmth drain from her, and Aryn stiffened. Liendra walked at a stately pace from the garden, surrounded by a tight knot of witches. She kept her gaze fixed forward, as if unaware of the attention she was receiving, although her smug smile betrayed the illusion.

Suddenly, as if she sensed eyes upon her, Liendra turned her head. Green eyes sparkled in Lirith's and Aryn's direction, and the smile on her lips deepened. Then Liendra walked from the garden.

Aryn drew in a hissing breath as if to speak. However, her words sounded not in Lirith's ears, but in her mind.

She's absolutely awful. Look at how smug she is. You'd think she was queen of this place.

The delivery of these words startled Lirith more than their content. When and how had Aryn mastered the art of speaking along the Weirding? Lirith had yet to work with her at the skill.

Lirith spun a quick thread, answering the young woman.

She is not queen. But remember—it was Liendra's thread at the very center of the Pattern. I don't know who she is or where she came from, but the Witches seem more than ready to follow her lead.

Not all the Witches, a warm voice said.

The voice was not Aryn's, but by the baroness's wide blue eyes she had heard it as clearly as Lirith.

Do not forget, the voice continued, *there were some threads who did not align themselves with the heart of the Pattern. Not all witches think the same as Sister Liendra.*

For a moment Lirith wondered if it was Ivalaine who was speaking, but there was no sign of the queen. Besides, the voice was different than Ivalaine's. Softer, smokier, yet powerful in its way. Then the thinning crowd parted, and Lirith saw a witch whose jet hair was marked by a single streak of ice-white.

"Sister Mirda," Aryn whispered.

Lirith nodded, and she knew why the woman's serene voice sounded so familiar.

"It was you," she murmured. "You were the one who reminded us that the Witches must do no harm. And it was your thread that changed the Pattern."

The hint of a smile touched Mirda's lips. "May Sia guide you both on your journey," she said. Then she turned and moved through the garden, green robe fluttering, and was gone.

Aryn frowned, her expression puzzled. "What was that supposed to mean? What journey was she talking about?"

Lirith thought of the young prince Teravian and the look of sorrow on his face.

You'll be going soon. . . .

"Come on," she said, taking Aryn's arm. "I think I need a strong cup of *maddok*."

16.

"Do you require anything else, my lady?"

Aryn did not turn from the polished silver mirror as she adjusted her gown.

"No, Elthre. Thank you."

In the mirror's reflection she saw the serving maid curtsy, then slip from the room. Aryn smiled—Elthre was a sweet girl, if timid—then concentrated, using practiced motions of her left hand to fasten the buckles and tie the straps of the gown. It was just after dawn, but she had awakened over an hour ago, her body still light and tingling with the magic of the Pattern. She had talked to Lirith until well after midnight, but since waking Aryn had thought of a hundred other questions she wanted to ask the dark-eyed witch.

In her mind, Aryn saw again the weaving of the Pattern, and how the last remaining threads—hers and Lirith's among them—bonded with the strand that spoke in calm, immutable words. There was no doubt that the strand had been Sister Mirda's. But who was this wise, serene witch? And where had she come from? No one Aryn asked seemed to know, nor did Lirith. Yet it was Mirda who had prevented all the witches from flocking to Liendra's thread.

Except most did, Aryn. Even Ivalaine joined with the heart of the Pattern in the end.

But certainly Ivalaine had had no choice, not if she wished to remain Matron. And this way, perhaps Ivalaine could have some influence over Liendra's faction. At least that was what Aryn hoped. However, she had seen neither Tressa nor the queen since the coven.

Nor had she seen Senrael. It was wrong how the old ones had been dismissed. Their voices were rough, but they carried such wisdom. Beauty had little to do with true power. But the crones had been shunted to the fringes of the Pattern, and if Mirda had not spoken the Witches might have vowed to do anything—even shed blood—to destroy Runebreaker. As it was, Aryn was glad Travis Wilder was a world away. And while she would like to have seen him, she hoped he would never leave his home again. For his sake. And perhaps for Eldh's.

Aryn decided to forgo breakfast and head right for Lirith's chamber. She could only hope Lirith was awake. But at that moment, Aryn couldn't imagine sleeping.

Besides there's always maddok. *If you bring a pot to her room, Lirith won't be able to resist getting out of bed to drink it. She's a bee to honey for the stuff.*

She finished adjusting her gown, then started to draw an extra fold of cloth over her right arm. It was a completely instinctual motion, one she had made every day for as long as she could remember.

All at once, she hesitated. Slowly, Aryn pushed the fold of cloth back over her shoulder, leaving her right arm exposed in its linen sling.

She stared at her reflection. In her mind she had never pictured herself with her withered arm; always she imagined it concealed. But now that she gazed at the pale, twisted shape, she could not envision it any other way. It was strange, yes, but it was *her*.

A warmth filled her, almost like giddiness. Always before she had dreaded people seeing her arm, but now she almost looked forward to it. Let them stare, let them mock her as Belira had. It would only make her stronger. Smiling, she adjusted her arm in its sling, then moved to the door.

Sister, can you hear me?

The voice sounded faintly but clearly in Aryn's mind.

Aryn, if you can hear me, you must come at once to Lady Melia's chamber.

It was Lirith. Aryn gathered her will and tried to answer. Last night, before the coven, she had finally discovered how to speak across the Weirding at will. Like so many things, it was easier than she had thought. It was as if the ability had been there all along, only concealed. Just like her arm. However, there was so much yet to learn, and she was still clumsy at the skill. She could not glimpse Lirith's thread; it was too far away.

I'm coming! she called, even though she knew Lirith could not hear her. Aryn dashed from the room. What could have caused terror to sharpen Lirith's usually calm voice? Perhaps Melia had fallen ill again; Lirith had mentioned that the lady had been acting in a peculiar manner of late.

Aryn was nearly to Melia and Falken's room when a spindly form sprang from an alcove, landing before her in a twisted knot. She let out a muffled cry. The thing untangled long, bony limbs, stretching upward into the shape of a man. Bells chimed like the sound of laughter.

"Master Tharkis," Aryn breathed, only half-relieved. This was not a distraction she needed. "What do you want?"

"What?" the fool said. "Have you forgotten, sweet. We yet have our contest of poems to complete."

She lifted her left hand to her chest. "What do you mean?"

He prowled toward her on pointed boots; dust and cobwebs clung to his motley. Where had he been lurking to get so filthy? "A rhyme you spoke, for my name. Now for your own I'll do the same."

There was something odd about his voice. It was quieter than usual, more sibilant. A sly light glinted in his crossed eyes. Aryn could only watch as he spread his arms and spoke in a low, singsong voice:

> "Sweet Lady Aryn
> Must marry a baron,
> But none shall take her as wife.
> Blessed with one arm,
> And power to harm—
> The price of her love is a life.
>
> "Her beautiful sisters
> All have dismissed her,
> But one day they'll sorrow the deed.
> With a sword in her hand,
> She'll ride 'cross the land—
> And trample them all 'neath her steed."

Aryn's blood turned to ice. Had the fool seen what she had done to Belira and the others? But the last part of his rhyme was even more troubling; it reminded her of the card she had drawn from the old Mournish woman's deck. But there was no way the fool could possibly have known about that . . . was there?

Tharkis grinned, displaying pointed, yellow teeth. "I can see I have won by the look in your eyes. And now, my sweet, you must grant me a prize."

The fool sidled close to her, and a sour scent filled her nostrils. His grin spread, stretching his face into a grotesque mask of lumps and furrows. Bells jangled, then were muffled by blue cloth as he pressed himself against her.

Anger rose inside Aryn: pure, white, and hot.

"Get away from me, dog," she said in a voice she barely recognized as her own. As if of its own volition, her right arm rose from the sling.

Tharkis sprang back. The fool's grin was gone, and his expression was one of terror. His eyes were no longer crossed and seemed to gaze right through her.

"Don't speak like that, sweet," he said, his words hoarse and trembling. "All hard and cold your voice is. It sounds like hers, it does. And your eyes, so sharp. They pierce me just like hers do."

Aryn forgot her anger. Tharkis cowered now, hugging himself, and made small whimpering sounds.

"Whom do you speak of?" she said.

"The shadow in the trees!" All traces of rhyme had vanished from his voice. "The one with many eyes. She sees everything. I cannot hide . . . even when I sleep she finds me. But she is not the only one who sees." Laughter fell from his mouth like pieces of broken glass. "I have seen things as well."

Aryn hesitated, then reached out her left hand. "It's all right, Master Tharkis. It's just—"

She halted as his wild eyes locked on hers. "She will come for you, too. You cannot escape. She spins a web for the spinners . . . and in it she will catch them all."

A shiver crept up Aryn's back. "Who are you talking about? Who is she trying to catch?"

"She will . . . she sees, but she is not alive. Watch for her, spinner. Her web closes in on us even now. And she will eat all who are captured in it." He clutched shaking hands to his head and squeezed. "She thinks I . . . don't remember. But sometimes I almost do. I almost . . . it's in the trees . . . I must ride. Not fast enough . . . it comes. Obey me, for I am the king. Oh, by all the gods, it comes. . . ."

Tharkis was shaking violently, snot running down his face. In his eyes was a look of stark and empty terror. Yet his words seemed strangely lucid. She opened her mouth, unsure what she should say.

"Aryn?" a voice called from down the corridor. "Aryn, is that you?"

Like a puppet jerked by the strings, Tharkis leaped to his feet. His eyes were crossed once more. "Fear the one alive and dead," he hissed, "for you cannot escape her web."

With weird speed, the fool scrambled up the wall, then vanished in the shadow between two rafters above. Aryn craned her neck, searching the ceiling, but she knew it was no use; she would not find him.

"Aryn, there you are! I thought I sensed your thread."

A silhouette moved toward her, then resolved into Lirith. Her ebon face was paler than usual, as if dusted by ashes.

"Did you hear my call, sister?"

"I did."

"I thought you had, but I wasn't certain. You must come at once."

"What's happened?"

"I don't think I can explain." Lirith took Aryn's left hand. "Come, you will see."

Thoughts of Tharkis vanished from Aryn's mind as Lirith pulled her down the corridor. They reached the door of Melia and Falken's chamber and slipped through. Aryn didn't know what she had expected to see, but certainly it had not been this.

Durge pressed himself against the far wall, as if trying to retreat into solid stone, his brown eyes wide. Falken knelt not far from the door, gazing upward, an expression of sorrow on his weathered face. In the very center of the room, Melia was weeping. Wails of grief escaped her, rising and falling with the cadence of a chant. She tore at her blue-black hair, and tears streamed from her amber eyes. However, it was not this that made Aryn stare, her breath caught in her lungs. Rather, it was the fact that Melia floated in midair.

The small woman hovered in the center of the room, several feet above the floor, curled in a tight ball. She spun slowly as she wept, bobbing up and down as if tossed on a stormswept sea. She seemed oblivious to the others in her grief.

At last air rushed into Aryn's lungs. She must have stumbled, for Lirith caught her arm, then Falken was there, steadying her. Durge edged around the room to join them.

"She's in mourning," Falken said, his voice quiet, in answer to Aryn's unspoken question. "I'm not certain how long it's going to last."

Aryn shook her head. "Mourning? For whom?"

"For one of her brothers."

Fear shot through Aryn, and she clutched the bard's arm. "Is it Tome?"

Although she had met him only once, it had been more than enough to grow fond of the gentle old man with golden eyes. Like Melia, Tome was one of the Nine who had forsaken godhood long ago to walk the face of Eldh and work against the Pale King's Necromancers. In the time since, most of the Nine had grown weary and had faded from the world.

"No, it is not Tome," Falken said. "It is a god of Tarras she weeps for."

Aryn fought for understanding. "But Mandu is the Everdying. Will he not simply rise again?"

"It's not Mandu either," Lirith said in a clipped voice.

Aryn looked to the witch, then to Falken. At last the bard spoke in a grim voice.

"A god is dead."

Aryn listened in growing shock as Falken told her what he had already explained to Lirith and Durge. That morning, just before dawn, Melia had awakened with a scream, and Falken had rushed to her side. *He is gone!* she had cried. *I can feel it—like a wound filled with nothing!* Before she was consumed by her grief, Falken had managed to get a few words from her. The god's name was Ondo, and he was a minor deity of Tarras— not one of the Seven who were worshiped in the Dominions. Ondo had been revered primarily by the Tarrasian guild of goldsmiths.

"I still don't understand," Durge said, stroking his mustaches repeatedly. "To be sure, I know scant of the ways of gods, and what I do know holds little logic. Yet I have heard the gods are immortal. So how then can a god die?"

Falken opened his mouth, but it was another who answered.

"Because he was murdered."

As one, they turned and stared. Melia stretched her legs downward, until her small, bare feet touched the carpet. Her coppery cheeks were still stained by tears, and her hair was wild with snarls, but her eyes shone with a fierce light.

"I have spoken with my brothers and sisters in the

south," she said. "And they tell me that Ondo was murdered. More than murdered. There is no trace left of him. He has been utterly destroyed." Now sorrow returned to her visage, mingled with fury. "Poor Ondo. He was far from perfection, but he harmed no one. He wished only to play with his gold."

Aryn still struggled to comprehend. "But who would have the power to murder a god?"

Melia clenched a hand. "That is what I intend to find out. Ever has there been competition and plotting among the gods of Tarras. Some gain in position, others lose—that has always been the way. But never, in all the eons since the founding of Tarras, has one god directly harmed another. And it is not just the gods. Worshipers have been murdered as well, and not only those of Ondo. Blood flows in the temples of Tarras." Melia hugged her fist to her chest, her eyes growing distant with thought. "Yet if there is a pattern to it all, none of us can see it. All my brothers and sisters are afraid."

Aryn had never imagined that a god could be afraid. But then, she had never imagined that a god could be killed, either.

Lirith tightened her arms over the bodice of her gown. "None of this makes sense. How can everything just unravel like this?"

Aryn glanced at her. There seemed more to the witch's words than just a comment on Melia's news. Was there something else Lirith knew?

Melia smoothed her hair back over her shoulders. "One thing is certain—something has changed in Tarras. And I intend to find out what it is."

"What do you mean?" Falken said, raising an eyebrow.

Melia regarded the bard, her expression resolute. "I

leave for Tarras at once. If you would come with me, Falken, I should be glad."

The bard opened his mouth to answer, but at that moment a shrill scream sounded—muffled but distinct—through the chamber's door.

The five exchanged startled glances, then they were moving. Durge led the way, flinging open the door and charging down the corridor even as a second scream rang out. The others ran after, hard pressed to keep up with the Embarran's sturdy legs. The corridor widened into a larger space—the castle's lesser hall, where some of the smaller feasts and revels were held.

The source of the screams was plain to see. Elthre the serving maid crouched in the center of the hall, hands to her cheeks, a tray of smashed crockery on the floor. She gazed up, her eyes circles of horror. A gasp escaped Lirith, and Falken let out a low oath.

A gangly form clad in green dangled from one of the hall's high galleries, bells jangling dissonantly as he swung back and forth.

Lirith moved to the serving maid to comfort her. Aryn clamped a hand to her mouth, lest she scream like Elthre had. A length of cloth had been wrapped around Master Tharkis's neck—one of the dozen green-and-yellow banners of Toloria that hung from the hall's galleries—and it was by this he had been hanged. His bony limbs jutted at odd angles, and his teeth were bared in what seemed a mad grin, as if he had been frozen in the act of one last jest. However, the illusion was dispelled by the crimson streams that still seeped from the two empty pits where his crossed eyes had been.

A sigh escaped Melia. "Poor Tharkis. This was not the end he deserved. But how can this be?"

"It is clear enough from the evidence," Durge

rumbled. "The fool could stand his madness no longer. He gouged out his own eyes and hanged himself from the gallery."

Aryn shuddered. She remembered what Tharkis had said to her only minutes ago, about the eyes who saw everything.

I have seen things as well . . .

Tharkis had seemed so terrified. At the time she hadn't understood. Maybe now it made sense. She started to speak, knowing she had to tell the others of her encounter, but Falken spoke first.

"Are you so certain of your judgment, Durge?"

The knight scowled. "What do you mean?"

Falken pointed upward with his black-gloved hand. "If Tharkis plucked out his own eyes, why is there no blood on his hands?"

17.

The moon sailed through a sea of silver clouds. Below, deep green shadows filled the garden, and a cool wind slipped among the branches, like a voice whispering forgotten secrets. Midnight had come and gone.

The wind faded, and for a time the garden was still. Then the shadows parted, and a figure stepped through. Pale moonlight washed her red–gold hair to steel as she turned her head from side to side, searching. She hugged her heavy cape around her. While the days were warm still, the nights were already growing chilly. But then, she knew it was not only the night that made her shiver, but also the one she sought.

"Show yourself, blast you," she muttered. "Must you play these games, even now?"

A patch of darkness separated itself from a tree and drifted forward. The woman clutched a hand to her breast, a gasp frozen in her lungs.

"What is the matter, sister?" a shimmering voice said. "Did I startle you?"

Anger replaced fear as the woman regained her breath. "Of course you startled me, Shemal, as was surely your intent."

The shadow drifted closer, resolving itself into a slender, feminine figure. Here and there a shard of ice-white skin glinted in the moonlight, but for the most

part the night cloaked her. A fragment of a mouth
turned upward in a smile.

"Why be so cross with me, dearest? Did not all go
exactly as I said it would?"

The woman tightened her fingers on her cape. "I
still do not see why she should remain Matron."

"Tut, tut," the other clucked. "Do not be too
greedy too quickly, sister. A greater change takes
greater time. Now what of the others—that shambling
corpse of a bard and the amber-eyed bitch from the
south?"

The woman smiled despite her anger. "They are
leaving Ar-tolor. I understand she has received ill news
from Tarras. She leaves on the morrow, and he will go
with her."

"Excellent," the shadow said. "I do loathe it when
she is near, for I must take care she does not sense my
presence. Limited as she is, she has abilities that must
not be underestimated. It is well they are leaving. Yet
they must be watched."

"How?"

"Are not two of your sisters their companions?"

The golden-haired woman curled her lip. "Yes, but
they can hardly be trusted. They were among those
who came last to the Pattern."

"And yet come to it they did," the other snapped,
"and they are bound to the Pattern even as you are. It
is they who must go, for they are close to Melindora
Nightsilver and Falken Blackhand. And to *him* as
well."

She breathed the word without thinking.
"Runebreaker."

The other was staring at her from the darkness; she
caught a glint of a hard, colorless eye. She shivered
again. How she hated this damp air.

"I do not understand," the woman said. "If they are close to him, will not they betray us for him in the end?"

Cruel laughter drifted on the air. "It seems you have much yet to learn, sister. One cannot betray those whom one despises. One can only betray those whom one loves."

The woman nodded, although she was less than convinced. All the same, she could see no other way. "And how am I to assure they accompany Nightsilver and Blackhand?"

"Bid your dear Matron send them. She cannot refuse your advice—not now."

The woman smiled. It was true. Ivalaine would have to listen to her; the Pattern required it. There was only one last, small matter. "What of the boy?" she said.

She could not see, but somehow she sensed a smile within the shadows. "Concern yourself not with the boy. I will watch over him myself. And when the time is right, I shall make myself known to him."

"And then what?"

"And then he will lead us in our battle against the Warriors of Vathris, and with him before us we will crush them all." A slender hand clenched into a fist. "So is his destiny—a male witch, first in a century, full-blooded in his power as any of your sisters. More so, in fact, save one. And I do not mean you, sister."

The woman winced, then let the slight pass. It was not from her ability with the Touch that her power and position came, she knew that well enough and had accepted it. Warmth replaced the coldness in her. It was happening then. After so many years of whispers and promises, of waiting on the edges while others stood in the center, it was truly happening.

"I will leave you then," the woman said, only too

happy to be done with this conversation. She knew she needed Shemal, but she did not like her. From the first, she had always come in shadows.

"Wait," the other said. "There is something else. I have felt something . . . strange of late. A weakness in the fabric that binds all things together. Have you sensed it?"

The woman frowned, shaking her head.

"But I am foolish to have asked you," the other said. "Of course, your power is far too weak. Yet if you learn anything, you will tell me."

"Of course," she said, but once again annoyance rose in her. Why must Shemal always mock her ability with the Touch? That one-armed runt was said to be the strongest of them all, and what good did it do her, the pathetic little thing? There were other, better sorts of power.

The air was paling to silver. The darkness receded; it was nearly dawn.

"I must go now," the one cloaked in shadows said.

"When will we speak again?"

"Soon."

There was a faint rustling, then the woman knew she was alone. She turned and walked from the garden. By the time she reached the entrance of the main keep, the sun was just cresting the horizon. A guardsman nodded to her as she approached the doors.

"Good morning, my lady," he said. "Were you out for an early stroll? It's a beautiful morning—full of promise."

A smile touched her lips. "Yes," Liendra said as she stepped through the castle doors. "It is."

PART TWO:
RETURN

18.

Dr. Grace Beckett drifted like a ghost through the antiseptic corridors of Denver Memorial Hospital and prayed to the gods of another world that no one would recognize her. If anyone saw her—anyone who remembered her face, or the events of last October—then this would be over in an instant.

She tugged at the too-short white coat she had pilfered from the Emergency Department locker room, hoping it covered her shabby jeans and thrift-store sweater. Maybe tall and bony worked for supermodels and actresses, but right now Grace wanted to do anything but stand out. She had found a broken stethoscope tossed on a shelf and looped it over her neck. It would do as long as no one asked her for a consult on a rattling lung.

She punched a red button and slipped through a pair of stainless-steel doors as they *whooshed* open, into a pastel peach hallway. The sound of respirators whirred on the air like the wingbeats of vultures. *Hold on, Beltan. I'm coming.* But the words were pointless. Even if she could have sent them along the spindly, sooty tatters of the Weirding that existed in this city, he couldn't possibly have heard them.

A pair of smooth-faced young men in khakis and short white coats appeared from around a corner.

Grace stiffened, then relaxed. First-year interns—their too-tight neckties were dead giveaways. No doubt both of them were fresh out of medical school that spring. Which meant they were new enough not to know all the residents at the hospital yet.

They fumbled their hellos. Grace gave them a clipped nod in return—no intern would believe a friendly smile from a resident they didn't know—then pushed on past. Only as she turned a corner did she let herself breathe again.

This is idiotic, Doctor. You know there's been no change in his condition—Travis was here just this morning. Beltan is still in a coma, and all you're going to accomplish with this stunt is to get yourself caught. What are you going to tell Travis when you have to use your one phone call at the Denver police station to talk to him?

Then again, the police weren't the only ones looking for her.

She kept moving. It had been nearly a year since she had last set foot in this place, since the night she had slain the dead man with the iron heart and had fled into darkness and another world. Yet it was easier than she might have guessed to slip back into her old rhythms. She strode with cool purpose through the halls, keeping her gaze high and distant, as if this were a dominion and she its ruler. More people passed by— nurses, technicians, janitors, medical students—but none of them gave her more than a cursory glance.

And why should they have recognized her? The Keep of Fire had changed her, just as surely as the girl Tira had been changed when she closed her small hands around the Great Stone Krondisar. Certainly Grace was not the same person who had haunted these sterile hallways, healing the wounds of others while she ignored her own.

As if this thought were an invitation, the shadow that dwelled on the edges of her vision rushed to the foreground. Its dark folds surrounded Grace, suffocating her. She stumbled, clutching for a wall she could no longer see as memories oozed forth. Once again she smelled the dusty air of the shed, the sharp reek of blood. Once again she was ten years old.

In the name of God Almighty, what have you done to her, Grace Beckett?

But I was trying to help her. Ellen used the wire on herself, Mrs. Murtaugh. She said she had to get it out—she said Mr. Holiday put something in her.

You are a wicked liar, Grace Beckett. And you are a murderess. Surely the fires of Hell will burn you for what you have done to Ellen Nickel.

No, you don't—

You must pray, pray on your knees here in her blood, and beg God for repentance.

But I was trying to help her, Mrs. Murtaugh! We have to take her to the hospital. Maybe she'll be all right. Please, you have to listen to—

No, try none of your spells on me, you Jezebel. I know you have given your soul to Satan. I have heard you utter your chants to him—at night, and in no tongue spoken by good Christians. Now take this wire in your hand. Take it! Use it on yourself as you did upon Ellen Nickel. And pray that you have enough blood in you to win your salvation. . . .

Crimson light flashed, and pain pierced Grace through to the center, bright, sharp, and—

With a sound like gushing water, the shadow receded. Grace blinked against the fluorescent glare, relieved to see the hallway was empty. At Castle Spardis, Beltan had been dying, his old wound reopened by the Necromancer. In order to use the Touch to sustain the knight while they journeyed to

Earth, Grace had had no choice but to accept the shadow attached to the thread of her own life, the shadow that for so many years she had pretended didn't exist. And now that the door had finally been opened, she could not shut it again.

There was never any logic to the shadow's coming; it seemed anything could trigger a regression. Some were brief, as this one had been. Others were . . . not. All of them left her sweating and shaking, feeling as if she had been cut with scissors from a sheet of stiff, white paper. So far she had managed to keep her episodes concealed from Travis; there was enough for him to worry about with Beltan's condition. However, she wondered how much longer that could last.

She still didn't remember everything that had happened to her at the Beckett-Strange Home for Children—there was so much, and the shadow was so deep—but it seemed almost every day new details came to her. Just when she thought there couldn't possibly be more to remember, the shadow was there and she was a child again: five years old, a pale nine, thirteen with flames dancing around her.

She forced her mind to focus on deciphering the hospital's inscrutable room-numbering scheme. Even when she had worked here it had made no sense. Then she saw the etched plastic plate: CA-423. That was the number Travis had given to her. She pushed through the door and into the room beyond.

Machines and monitors hissed and beeped, filling the cold, white space with their drone like a chorus of electronic monks. A thick-waisted nurse stood beside the bed, her salt-and-pepper hair neatly bound at her neck, checking the drip on an IV. She looked up, her expression curious but not surprised.

Grace hesitated, then breezed into the room. During her time in the Dominions, she had discovered that if you acted as if you belonged in a place, people invariably assumed you did.

"Can I help you, Doctor?"

"I doubt it," Grace said. She made a quick glance at the chart by the bed. "Dr. . . . Chandra mentioned he had a persistent vegetative case in here. I'm doing a study."

The nurse frowned. "A study? Which department is funding it?"

Indignation rose in Grace, so strong it startled her. Who was this woman to question her authority? She started to open her mouth to speak outraged words.

Stop it, Grace. No one thinks you're a duchess here. You can't just dismiss someone with a wave of your hand.

True, she was no noble. But she *was* a doctor, and in this place, that meant more than a jeweled crown.

She gave the nurse a stiff, impersonal smile. "Why don't you leave us for a minute?"

The nurse stared at her for a heartbeat, then in one swift motion folded her aluminum clipboard and sailed from the room—no doubt off to the lounge to warn the other nurses that there was a skinny new witch of a doctor to watch out for. She wouldn't be entirely wrong. Forgetting the nurse, Grace approached the bed.

She had not seen Beltan since the day she and Travis had touched the half-coins together in Spardis, leaving Eldh behind. A heartbeat later, they had blinked as the silver light dimmed around them and had found themselves next to a Dumpster not twenty feet from the ED entrance. Travis had run inside for help, and seconds had passed, each one an agony. The Weirding was present on Earth—Grace had sensed it at once now that she knew how to look for it—but it was crowded, noisy, and dirty. And thin, so terribly thin, a silk cloth worn into a filthy rag. The thread of Beltan's life had begun to slip through her fingers. She couldn't hold on.

Then, thankfully, in a rush of commotion and light, the ED personnel were there. In the confusion, Travis slipped away and pulled Grace with him. She had wanted to stay, to make sure they could stabilize him, to warn them he had never had a tetanus shot or inoculation in his life, but Travis had pulled harder. It was too dangerous for them there. She had cast one last glance back at Beltan, pale as a ghost on the bare asphalt, then they had run into the dry Denver night.

The days that followed had seemed peculiarly unreal, as if it were Earth, not Eldh, that was the foreign world. Again and again Grace reached out with the Touch, but she was like a fresh amputee groping for a phantom limb. For instead of a shimmering web of gossamer spanning between every living thing, all she found were faint echoes of magic.

Then there was the shadow, leaping out to consume her without warning. And when she was not failing to use the Touch, or caught in the shadow of the past, she spent her time thinking of Tira—the fragile, mute, red-haired girl who had turned out to be so much stronger than any of them. But while Tira was gone, she was far from lost. It was Grace who felt lost.

If it hadn't been for Travis, she didn't know what would have happened to her. He seemed to adjust to life back on Earth far more quickly than she, as if he really belonged here. It had been his idea to sell three gold Eldhish coins—their faces deliberately scratched—at an East Colfax pawnshop. With the money they had gotten food, then had hopped a bus west down Colfax, past peeling storefronts and spastic neon signs. At the Blue Sky Motel they took a room that looked as if it hadn't been updated since the carefree, shaggy, burnt umber days of 1965. The TV was so old Grace had expected it to show *I Love Lucy* when she flicked it on. Instead, a faint column of smoke drifted up as several cockroaches wriggled out the ventilation holes in the back. In a way, it was every bit as entertaining.

The next morning, Travis had left while Grace lay on the bed, staring at the sagging ceiling and trying in vain to Touch the Weirding. He returned at noon with bagels and a fake social security card.

"Say hello to Hector Thorkenblat," he had said, holding up his new card.

She had wrinkled her nose. "That doesn't sound so much like a name as something you have to clean up."

A few days later, once they felt more confident that his face wouldn't be remembered from the night of their arrival, Travis had taken his new card down to Denver Memorial and gotten Hector a job as a night janitor. And that was how they had learned that Beltan was alive but in a coma.

Since he had started working at the hospital, Travis had been checking on Beltan every few days. Grace knew Beltan was getting the best care this world had to offer—which was considerably more than the last. All the same, she had to see him, to touch him for herself. Even here, there were things she could sense that no electronic monitor could detect.

Grace gripped the metal railing of the bed. It had been more than two months, and she knew what happened to long-term coma cases. All the same, a gasp escaped her.

"Oh, Beltan . . ."

In her memory she saw him tall and strong, clad in chain mail and holding his sword, a fierce grin on his face. The man on the bed bore little resemblance to that memory.

He looked old. The limbs that protruded from the hospital gown were white and thin, as if his sharp-edged bones had been stretched impossibly long. Beneath the gown, his muscles had atrophied, and the hands that rested at his sides looked like bundles of sticks.

Her eyes moved past the IV tubes and monitor leads—he was not on a respirator at least—to his face. They had let his scruffy beard grow. It seemed dull, brownish rather than gold, and it took her a moment to find the homely, cheerful face she knew beneath. She would have given anything to see one of his brilliant smiles, but he was motionless save for the steady rise and fall of his chest.

Grace pushed aside the gown and let her fingers dance along the mass of pink scar tissue on Beltan's left side. She shut her eyes and concentrated. It was dim and murky—like a blurry X-ray with no backlighting rather than a computer-colored, three-dimensional scan—but Queen Ivalaine had been right. Even on Earth, Grace had the talent.

His old wound had healed well—far better than it ever had on Eldh. Abdominal surgery and antibiotics still had an edge on magic. However, his blood loss had been catastrophic, and it was this that had induced the coma. The doctors could repair his body, reinfuse his veins with blood, but no amount of surgery had the power to wake him.

Maybe he needs some magic after all, Grace.

She replaced the gown, then laid a hand on the high expanse of his forehead. There were more lines on his brow than she remembered. For some reason she felt like singing to him, which was very undoctorlike. Then again, didn't research suggest that familiar voices could help coma patients to wake from unconsciousness? Words came to her lips, so old she had all but forgotten them.

> *"And farewell words too often part*
> *All their small and paling hearts.*
> *The fragile glade and river lain,*
> *Beneath the hush of silent rain."*

She touched the angular metal pendant beneath her shirt. The song was a thing of her childhood, like the necklace. But where had it come from? Certainly no one at the orphanage had sung it to her. And there was no doubt in her mind that the words were wrong. She must have heard it as a small girl and, like children so often do, transformed strange sounds into familiar words. All the same, the song was comforting. To her, at least, if not to Beltan. She began to murmur the words again.

His eyelids twitched.

Grace drew in a hiss of air. *It's just an autonomic reflex, Doctor. Don't read more into it than there is.* All the same she pressed her hand against his brow and shut her eyes.

Beltan?

It was hard. The threads of the Weirding were so faint around her, like filaments of cobweb. They fell apart as she grasped them.

Beltan, can you hear me? I'm here, Grace. And Travis has been coming to see you every night.

She held her breath, straining to listen. There was only gray silence. Then, just as she started to let go, she heard it. It was far less than a word—a shard of a thought—but she had heard it.

Grace's eyes snapped open. It was Beltan. He had made the sound in her mind, she was certain. His face was motionless once more, but there could be no doubt about what she had heard. She gripped his hand. Hard. "Come on, Beltan. You've got to come back to us. Please try. For me—for Travis."

Grace knew that if he didn't wake soon, they would move him to a state institution. This was a public hospital; they couldn't turn people away, but they wouldn't let a John Doe occupy a bed indefinitely. Yet that was far from her sole worry.

It was only a matter of time until Duratek found them.

In a way, Grace was surprised the three of them hadn't already been apprehended. Almost daily she or Travis saw one of the sleek, black vehicles driving down a city street—slowly, as if searching. No doubt Duratek believed that if either Grace or Travis ever came back, they would come here, to Denver. And they were right.

Grace had no idea how they were supposed to do it, but somehow she and Travis had to get back to Eldh. And they had to take Beltan with them. She was certain Duratek would be more than interested to get their hands on a native of the world they sought to rape and conquer.

Only now Beltan was close to waking. If they could just get him somewhere safe while he finished his recovery, they could start searching for a way back. However, it wasn't as if she could ask the police for help. To them, Grace was the woman who had handcuffed one of their detectives and threatened him at gunpoint. No matter that Janson had been an ironheart; the police didn't know that. So where could they go for protection?

But you've known all along, Grace.

She reached into the pocket of her jeans and pulled out a business card. It was more gray than white now, smudged and torn, but she could still read it:

THE SEEKERS
1-800-555-8294

She had kept the card with her for so long, ever since that night in late October when Hadrian Farr had given it to her. Who else could she go to for help if not them?

You should ask Travis.

But even as she thought this, she headed for the door and the nearest pay phone.

19.

Deirdre Falling Hawk sat in a corner of the dim Soho pub, staring at the glass of clear green liquid on the table before her. On a plate next to the glass was a cube of sugar and a silver spoon. Although they were hard to make out in the gloom of the pub, there were words etched into the surface of the spoon: *Drink and Forget.*

If only it were really that simple. But wasn't that why she was here? The board that hung outside the peeling door of the pub read Crumbe's Cupboard. And the occasional tourist or businessman who stumbled inside found only sticky tables, warm glasses of Bass Ale, and cold fish and chips. But from her visits to London, Deirdre knew that to the locals this place was known as The Sign of the Green Fairy. And they came here for something else.

Quickly, as if afraid she might change her mind, she placed the sugar cube on the spoon and lowered it into the glass. Then she raised the glass and took a long sip of the green liquid. It was sweet and powerfully bitter. The licorice-like taste of anise coated her tongue, and the pungent esters of wormwood rose in her head, an emerald mist to shroud her brain.

As Deirdre lowered the glass, an old-fashioned lithograph on the opposite wall caught her eye. It depicted a young man in Victorian suit coat and cravat, sitting at a table and scribbling madly with a quill pen on a paper before him. Behind him, tangling slender fingers through the writer's hair, was a woman clad in a flowing gown. No, not just a woman. Wings of gossamer sprouted from her back, and her gown trailed away in a comet's tail of leaves and stars. A fairy, then. Her eyes were closed, and the smile on her inhumanly beautiful face was both serene and cruel.

Deirdre didn't know who the man in the picture was supposed to be. Wilde, or perhaps Tennyson. It didn't matter. They had all drunk absinthe, hadn't they? Half the artists of the time had been addicted to the bitter green liqueur. They had drunk it for inspiration, to gain artistic vision. And then after that, when the visions faded, they had kept on drinking, trying to forget their commercial failures, their debtors, their persecution. Their demons.

She clenched her jaw, then downed the rest of the absinthe.

Deirdre leaned back, letting her head hit the wall behind her. Why had she come to London? She hated London. For the last three months she had been trying to forget the past. But the past was everywhere in this city, a thing constantly on display.

Not that anyone seemed to see it. Slack-eyed tourists shuffled through the Tower of London in pink-plastic sandals and Anne Boleyn T-shirts like blood had never flowed over those stones. Hansom cabs bearing giddy brides and grooms clattered down cobblestone streets where thousands of corpses had once sprawled, dead from plague and alive with flies. Cheerful gardens covered plots blasted bare of buildings and people in the Blitz. Around every corner, down every lane, from the gray Thames to Hyde Park to the slowly melting obelisk of Cleopatra's Needle, history lingered like smoke. Didn't anyone else see it?

Or was that the point? The past weighed so heavily on this place that it would crush people if they let it. Maybe there were really only two things anyone could do in London; maybe that was the reason she had come here. To drink. And forget.

Just over two months ago, the spontaneous immolations plaguing two continents had ceased as suddenly as they had begun. And, not long after that, so had Deirdre's desire to be a Seeker.

How could she have been so blind to their arrogance? They thought they knew so much, that their eyes were open to mysteries that mundane people never dreamed existed. But what had their musty files, their secret surveillance networks, their vast rooms of computers revealed to them? Nothing that those same mundane people hadn't been able to read in the morning newspaper: People were burning, and no one had the slightest fucking clue why.

There had been ripples of panic for a time. People had begun to mutter that the turning of the millennium had been only a test run, that this was the real beginning of the end. True, most of them had been cultists, tabloid devotees, militia members. Then again, some were suburbanites, avid churchgoers, telephone salesmen. In the United States, where the majority of the immolations had occurred, the government had quietly mobilized a portion of the National Guard.

Then, just when the ripples had been ready to coalesce into a tidal wave of outright fear—just when the graphs compiled by the Centers for Disease Control predicted that the number burnt was about to leap from the hundreds to the thousands—the immolations had ceased.

For a moment the world had stood still, like a ball balanced on the edge of a chasm. Then all of humanity had let out a collective sigh, and the ball had rolled back. In a week, the news had returned to the usual parade of wars, political scandals, and celebrity-lifestyle pieces. Sure, there was the occasional businessman-turned-cultist who walked around with a placard, face stained with ashes. And most days there was a small article tucked in the back of the newspaper's A section, telling how a remote Brazilian rain forest settlement had just been discovered, burnt to the ground, or how tests had shown that the DNA of one American burn victim demonstrated affinities with some Mediterranean populations—an incongruity given the victim's Asian ancestry. However, all in all, it seemed the world was only too happy to forget what had happened.

So why can't you, Deirdre Falling Hawk?

For a time she had. Working on Black Death 2.0 had left her no time to eat, to sleep—to think. Theories ricocheting across the Internet had blamed the deaths on a government-engineered chemical-warfare agent, or an alien virus, or the wrath of God. But from their own tests, the Seekers had confirmed their early suspicions. Compound residues found with several of the burn victims had chemical signatures identical to those recovered from sites of confirmed Class One Encounters. Without doubt, the plague was otherworldly in origin. Nor was there doubt about which world it had come from. AU-3. The world called Eldh. Grace Beckett and Travis Wilder's world.

Although the Castle County coroner had presumed Travis dead in the explosion at the Mine Shaft Saloon, the Seekers' analyses had shown otherwise. Remains of four separate individuals were found in the ruin of the Mine Shaft. None of the samples had matched Travis's

DNA—which they had on file thanks to a small skin sample he had never noticed Deirdre taking.

It was just one of the many ways she had used him. And while the madness of the new Black Death had occupied her, now there was nothing to keep the memories from creeping back—memories of what she had done to her friend.

So, is that your shadow self, Deirdre? The one that can lie?

She would never forget the sound of his voice when he spoke those words. It had been so soft, yet it had damned her more surely than a ringing chorus of anger. He had thought her a friend, and she had deceived him, manipulated him for her own ends. No matter the reason, how right it had seemed at the time. Deirdre had never believed the end justified the means; at least she had always thought so. Yet in order to serve the Seekers, she had betrayed her friend. And for that she would never forgive them.

Not long after the immolations ceased, she had simply stopped showing up at the Manhattan Charterhouse where Hadrian Farr had been directing their research. She had ignored the phone calls, the e-mails, the pager beeps. Damn the Seekers, but couldn't they ever do anything in person? Then, without really thinking about it, she had gotten on a plane and had put an ocean behind her. At first she had thought she was going to Ireland. The years when, as a girl, she had lived with her grandmother outside of Cork, listening to old songs and first learning to play music, still lingered in her mind. But the plane had touched down at Heathrow, and the muted grays of London had shrouded her in a soft dullness that, if she didn't think about it too much, could almost be mistaken for comfort.

Deirdre clutched the empty absinthe glass, willing it to fill again, to help her forget if not forgive. All hail

Our Green Lady of Oblivion. But the glass remained empty.

"Hello, sweetie," said a woman with a mop of orange hair as she slid onto the bench next to Deirdre.

She was long and lanky, curved as a willow, her limbs seal-sleek in clinging black vinyl. The face she turned toward Deirdre was stark white, and her eyes were lost amid dark circles of kohl. It was hard to tell through the smoky, clove-scented air of the pub, but beneath the garish makeup her features might have been exquisite.

The woman coiled a thin arm around Deirdre's neck. "You look dangerous *and* yummy."

Deirdre did not smile. "Just the first one."

The woman's eyes narrowed. There was a listlessness to them, a dullness, yet a hunger as well. She bit a lip colored the deep purple of a bruise. "That'll do."

The woman shifted closer, vinyl creaking. Deirdre felt her heat through the plastic. In a way she was tempted. It might not be such a bad thing to lose herself with another—a different sort of oblivion. Her work with the Seekers had left little time to take a lover. It had been a while since she had been with a man—or a woman. However, there was something about the haziness in the other's eyes, the languor of her motions, that sickened Deirdre even as she envied it.

"I'm not in the mood," she said.

"Then I'll help you get into it, sweetie."

The woman pushed something onto the table, then lifted a strangely long hand to uncover a pair of purple pills, each marked with a white lightning bolt. So that was the source of the haze in the other's eyes.

The woman took one of the pills between thumb

and finger and slowly, as if it were something delectable, took it between her lips. She nudged the other pill. "Now you, sweetie."

"I don't touch Electria."

The woman frowned at Deirdre's empty glass. "What? You'll drink that nasty old shit, but you won't take something new and clean? What's wrong with you?"

Where should I start? However, at that moment a gigantic, bald-headed man clad in tight black-leather pants made an angry gesture at the woman.

"Get back over here, Glinda."

The orange-haired woman flicked her eyes at the man. The muscles of his arms were hugely swollen, and his clean-shaven chest was shirtless and massive beneath an open leather vest. A goatee framed a thin, angry mouth.

"I said get over here."

"But I *want* her, Leo," the woman said.

The man bared silver teeth. "I'll tell you what you want." He shook a small, plastic bottle. "Now come on."

The woman hesitated. She started to rise from the bench. Then, in what seemed a furtive motion, she leaned close and licked Deirdre's ear, probing with a warm, moist tongue.

"Save me," the woman whispered.

Before Deirdre could respond, the woman gripped her hand, then slid from the booth and sauntered over to the bald man. She leaned her head on the expansive slope of his shoulder and ran her hands over the mountains and valleys of his chest. Yet the entire time her eyes were on Deirdre. The man grimaced, adjusting his crotch, then led Glinda away, into the back of the pub and darkness.

Deirdre almost considered going after them. *Save*

me, Glinda had said. But from what? That hulk of a man? The Electria? However, as she started to rise, she realized there was something in her hand—the hand the woman had squeezed. At first she thought it was simply a British pound coin. But it was silver and too large, about the size of three American quarters stacked together. The drawings on it were unrecognizable in the gloom. She started to bend closer to make them out.

"So they were right," said a smooth, masculine voice. "You *are* here. I had thought surely they must be mistaken."

Deirdre closed her hand on the coin, then looked up. "What? You're actually admitting the Seekers can make mistakes?"

Hadrian Farr sat across from her and folded his hands on the table. "All the time, I'm afraid," he said with a crooked-toothed smile.

Deirdre winced. Farr's smile was so damned charming; she hated it. It was that smile that had lured her into his bed the night they met in Glasgow three years ago. It was that smile that had enchanted her the next morning over tea as he spoke of the mysteries the Seekers sought to understand. The expression was so secret, so inviting, like he was just about to tell you the deepest wonders of the universe. Only he never did.

"What do you want?" she said.

"I think you can rather imagine."

Deirdre did not answer. Farr leaned across the table, darkly handsome as always: square jaw clean-shaven, lips full, eyes deep-set and well spaced. His faded jeans and black T-shirt accented his slender but muscular frame. She wondered when he found the time to work out. Wasn't he always busy harassing otherworldly travelers?

"You've not come to a Charterhouse in over a month, Deirdre. You have not responded to our missives, you have ignored our summons. Have you forgotten the Vow?"

Deirdre fingered her empty glass. "No, but let's give it a few more minutes and see."

Farr frowned. "I would have thought better of you, Deirdre. You know there's no magic in absinthe. It's just a cheap trick. And, until recently, quite illegal."

Deirdre laughed, a sound every bit as bitter as the absinthe had been. "So is bugging people."

She tucked the odd coin into the pocket of her jeans, pulled out something else, and shoved it across the table toward Farr. It was a small transistor, smashed, glittering in a stray beam of light.

Farr grimaced. So he was capable of a real reaction.

"That was hardly my idea," he said. "I think you know me well enough to see the truth in that."

Deirdre looked away, into the darkness. "I don't know what I know anymore."

Farr reached out and took her hand. She was suddenly too weary to resist. The absinthe, of course.

"Listen to me, Deirdre. We need you. *I* need you."

Still she did not look at him. "I doubt I can help you. In case you'd forgotten, he doesn't like me any more than he does the Seekers. You saw to that."

"Damn it, Deirdre, I'm not talking about Travis Wilder. I'm talking about you. You're one of the bloody best the Seekers have ever had. We need you more than ever now."

At last Deirdre turned her gaze to him. "When I first met you, Hadrian, I thought I would do anything to understand the mysteries you talked about, that I would pay any price. But the price was too high, after all. I lost a friend."

"Did you?"

"What do you mean? That I didn't betray Travis?"

"No, I mean maybe he wasn't really your friend. Friends don't just turn their backs and run away. They forgive us our mistakes."

Deirdre shook her head. *You're wrong*, she wanted to say. But her lips couldn't form the words. Maybe she didn't really believe them.

"Please, Deirdre. You don't have to make a decision now. Just come back to the Charterhouse with me. An hour, that's all I'm asking. Then you can go if you want, and we'll leave you alone. On the Book, I swear it."

The short hairs on the back of Deirdre's neck prickled. Why was Farr making an offer like this? It was hardly his style. Then, in a bright flash that cut through the green mist shrouding her brain, she understood.

"Something's happened," she said, sitting up straight. "What is it? Tell me."

Farr drew in a deep breath, then nodded.

"She's called," he said.

20.

Even in the cement-covered heart of the city, Travis Wilder could always tell when the wind was about to blow.

He turned his back just as a gritty blast of air hurtled down Sixteenth Street, its force magnified as it squeezed between the narrow glass and stone canyons of downtown Denver. Two women in power skirts and tennis shoes were blown into a street fountain gone mad, and shrieked as water frothed around them. Several teenagers huddled together, trying in vain to keep the dust out of their fresh piercings. And a legless man held up shaking hands and laughed without teeth as pieces of trash whirled and danced around his wheelchair like bright paper fairies.

As suddenly as it had come, the wind ceased. The fountain returned to the confines of its circle, releasing the two women. Paper settled back to the sidewalk, lifeless trash once more. Travis started walking again. He had been down this street a dozen times before, and each time he had seen no sign of them. All the same, he knew he had to keep searching. What else was he supposed to do?

Motion flickered on the edge of his vision: a tall, pale figure clad all in black striding down the street on long, lanky legs. Sudden hope surged in his chest, and he turned. At the same moment the figure halted and faced him. The breath held hostage in his lungs was released as he understood.

Travis approached the plate-glass window. Even after two months, he still didn't recognize the man reflected in the window's surface. He was tall and almost lean, with shoulders far broader than Travis had ever pictured. The other was clad all in black despite the brilliant late-September day: jeans, T-shirt, trench coat. The skin of his hands and face was smooth and powder-pale, and his eyes were hidden by dark glasses. His head was shaven clean, and a short red-brown goatee framed the solemn line of his mouth.

You've been looking for him so long you're starting to look like him, Travis. Brother Cy.

Not that Travis had much choice in the way he looked. His new skin—burnt and reborn in the hot flames of Krondisar—was still soft and exquisitely sensitive. He was forced to keep it covered and protected, hence the black thrift-store coat even on fine days like this.

His eyes were the same story. That first day he and Grace had returned to Earth, he had discovered he no longer needed his glasses. It was still possible to wear the old gunfighter's spectacles, but everything was warped and strange-looking through them. These days he kept them in his pocket as a memento of Jack Graystone—as if he needed another reminder besides the secret rune that marked the palm of his right hand.

Like his skin, his new eyes were highly reactive; bright light hurt them, although he found he could see shockingly well at night. He had bought a pair of wraparound sunglasses for three bucks from a street vendor and never took them off from dawn to dusk, and sometimes not even then.

As for his bald head—that had been his own choice. His hair had begun to grow back not long after their return, and over most of his body it had come in as he remembered it, if a bit redder than before. However, the shocking, flame-colored curls that had sprouted on his crown had nothing in common with his old, sandy brown hair.

It was too much for Travis—too strong a reminder of what had happened to him—so he had taken a razor and shaved it off. At least his skull wasn't a moonscape of ridges and craters; that was one difference between him and Brother Cy.

The goatee had come a few weeks later. He had never worn one before in his life, but something told him he had never worn this *body* before, so the change seemed appropriate. And as for the silver rings dangling from each of his ears—well, Travis had had a hard time explaining them to Grace when she asked.

In some of the neighborhoods I've been searching, people stare if you don't *have a piercing, Grace.*

She had accepted his explanation, but he wasn't certain he had been entirely honest with her. Not that he truly understood the reason he had let the muscular, nose-pierced young man at the tattoo parlor talk him into it.

It doesn't matter if you want them, man, he had said, running his hands over Travis's smooth head. *You* need *them.*

Maybe the man had been right. The Stone of Fire had destroyed Travis, then had forged him anew. And even though he was still a man—neither god nor monster by choice—he wasn't sure he was entirely the *same* man. He still had Travis Wilder's name. He still had his thoughts, his memories, his fears. And he still had the magical symbol branded deep into the flesh of his right palm. All the same, instinct told Travis that every atom in his body was utterly new. Somehow, looking different made the mystery of that change easier to bear.

Travis had taken his hat off when he sensed the wind coming. Now he pulled it from the pocket of his trench coat—the same pocket he had found it in after buying the coat for four bucks at a thrift store on South Broadway. The hat was black, shapeless, and vaguely beretlike. Grace said it looked like a bad toupee or a dead cat, depending on how she squinted. Travis liked it.

As he settled the hat on his head, he caught a glimpse of mountains behind his image in the window. They hovered in the gap between two buildings like gray ghosts on the horizon. For a moment he wished he could go back there, to the mountains, to Castle City. Wasn't that where they had always helped him decide what he was supposed to do—Brother Cy, Sister Mirrim, and the dark Child Samanda?

But the strange trio wasn't there anymore. It had been risky, maybe even stupid, to let anyone know that he was alive and on Earth, but a few nights ago Travis had picked up the phone and dialed information.

What city please? the recorded voice droned.

He had hesitated, then said the words. *Castle City.*

What listing?

That was harder. He had thought about Jace Windom, but she was a deputy. Wouldn't she have to report any conversation with Travis to Sheriff Dominguez? After all, twice now he had vanished from the scene of a fire in which others had died.

Davis or Mitchell Burke-Favor, he said before he really thought about it.

One moment please.

Davis and Mitchell had always come to the Mine Shaft Saloon every Friday to dance to the country music on the jukebox. They were close enough friends that they would help him, but not so close they would be compelled to come find him. Besides, their ranch was just south of town, not far from the Castle Heights Cemetery. If anyone might have seen Brother Cy there, it would be them.

This time it was a real operator that spoke. She gave him the number. He hung up, then dialed. The phone rang twice, then a deep, twanging voice answered. *Hello, you've got Mitchell.*

Travis's throat had nearly closed. Finally he managed to speak.

Mitchell, it's me.

A silence, filled only with the hiss of distance. Then, *Travis? Travis Wilder?*

Their conversation had been short, but surprisingly not awkward. Although he had every right to do so, Mitchell had not asked where Travis had gone, what had happened to him, or where he was calling from. Instead he listened to Travis's questions, then answered in a deep, melodious voice that made Travis think of a cowboy poet he had once heard on the radio. Unfortunately, Mitchell didn't have much to tell. He hadn't seen a tall man in black around town. And no, the revival tent that had popped up last October had not reappeared. Travis ran out of questions.

There's a grave for you, Travis. Up on the hill in Castle Heights.

I know, he said simply. It was enough.

Be well, Travis. We'll sure miss you.

Travis didn't know what else to say. He settled for, *Give Davis my best.* It was Mitchell who hung up first, leaving Travis with the lonely sound of static in his hand.

While he was glad he had made the call, it had only confirmed what Travis's instincts had already told him. Brother Cy wasn't there anymore, in the mountains. But he had to be somewhere. That was why Travis had spent these last weeks searching for him here, in the city.

Besides, even if Brother Cy was still in Castle City, you couldn't go back there, Travis. It's too dangerous. That's the first place they'd be looking.

As if that thought had somehow been a cue, Travis watched in the window's reflection as a sleek, black SUV approached along a cross street, moving toward the corner where he stood. The traffic light changed, and the vehicle stopped as pedestrians crossed in front of it. Through the flickering screen of their legs, Travis made out the license plate: DRATEK33.

"Don't be an idiot, Travis," he muttered under his breath. "They've got a multinational corporation to run. Not every one of their cars can be looking for you and Grace."

In what he hoped was a casual motion, he turned from the window and crossed the street with a cluster of walkers. Only after a half a block did he let himself turn and look back at the intersection. The light had changed; the vehicle was nowhere in sight.

Travis shoved his hands in his pockets. He knew he should keep going; it was hours before he had to be at the hospital for the janitorial night shift. But he was tired of walking, tired of searching. He bought a cup of coffee from a street vendor, then hopped the free shuttle down to the end of Sixteenth Street. He crossed the pedestrian bridge high above the railroad tracks, then descended to a green park beside the Platte River. He sat in the middle of a bank of cement steps and watched the waters of the Platte rush by, as thin and brown as the coffee in his paper cup. He took a sip. It wasn't *maddok*, but he felt a faint tingle of jittery energy seep through his veins.

He set the cup on the step, then drew a small piece of bone on a string from beneath his black T-shirt. It seemed so long ago and so far away—the day he had pulled the bone from the witch Grisla's bag near the half-ruined fortress of Kelcior. He could still hear the hag's rasping words.

I wouldn't have thought you would draw that one. One line for Birth, one line for Breath, and one more for Death, which comes to us all.

At the time he hadn't understood what the rune had meant—much to Grisla's disgust. It was only later, when he stood in the frozen depths of Shadowsdeep— when Beltan lay dying in the blood-soaked snow, and the Rune Gate opened to release the armies of the Pale King—that Travis had finally understood the meaning of the rune. It was hope. While there was life, there was always hope.

Travis tightened his hand around the rune. Beltan had nearly given his life so Travis could learn that lesson. Travis was not going to give up on him now.

Wake up, Beltan. Please. You've got to wake up so we can get out of here.

Travis and Grace didn't talk about it much anymore; they didn't need to. Both of them knew they had to get Beltan out of this city before Duratek found them. He started to pick up his coffee again, then halted as a billboard across the river caught his eye. He should have been surprised, but he wasn't. They were everywhere; he knew that now.

On the billboard, a man, a woman, and a girl all smiled with imbecilic joy as the girl released a dove into a sky that was far too blue to be beautiful. In that sky, sharp as a sickle, hung an oversize crescent moon that merged into the capital D of their logo. *Duratek. Worlds of Possibility*.

Travis winced. He knew all too well what the billboard really meant. Once, one of their agents had told him that the meeting of Eldh and Earth was inevitable, and that Duratek's mission was only to manage the convergence, to make sure it happened the right way. Travis knew that was a lie. Their real mission was to get to Eldh before anyone else, to conquer its peoples, to pollute its rivers, and to strip its lands of trees and minerals. And Travis was going to do anything he could to keep them from getting what they wanted.

But even if—even *when* Beltan woke up, how were they going to get back to Eldh? The silver half-coins seemed to work only in one direction: from Eldh to Earth. Despite all of his and Grace's experiments, the coins appeared to have no power on Earth. That was why he spent his days searching for Brother Cy.

"Where are you, Cy?" he murmured. "*What* are you?" But the words were lost on a gust of air.

He let his gaze wander. Across the river, a huge, skeletal shape forged of metal girders rose into the sky. Then the wind unfurled the banner that hung from the side of the construction:

COMING SOON TO DENVER!
THE STEEL CATHEDRAL
Everything you seek is just around the
corner . . .

So it was one of those gigantic new megachurches. Bigger is better, wasn't that the philosophy today no matter what you were selling? If only the words on the banner were right, if only what he sought really was just around the corner. But whether he found Brother Cy or not, they still couldn't go anywhere until Beltan woke up. And although Travis refused to give up hope, there was no telling when that would be.

Almost every night, usually after 2:00 A.M. when at last things grew still and silent, he would put down his mop and make his way to Beltan's room. Each time he was struck by how frail the knight looked beneath the tangle of tubes and wires. Beltan had always said he was Travis's protector, but Travis knew it was the other way around now. Yet somehow it was a comforting feeling. He could stand this, being the strong one.

For a time each night—a few minutes, maybe longer—he would watch the blond man for any signs of motion, however small. He knew that Beltan loved him. That was what the knight had tried to tell him once in Perridon, although Travis had been unable to hear, for he had just turned the rune of fire back on Master Eriaun, and his ears had roared with the sound of flames. It wasn't until Beltan lay dying in Castle Spardis, when he kissed Travis with bloodied lips, that Travis finally understood.

What it meant was another question. Night after night Travis stood above Beltan, trying to imagine how someone could actually love him, and trying to imagine if he could love another, trying to feel if it was even possible. Then, finally, in what might have been an act of desperation, Travis had bent down and had pressed his lips against Beltan's.

It had been so easy he had almost laughed. There was no lightning strike, no grand revelation, no resistance or sudden awakening. It was just flesh to flesh. Why had he expected anything else? In all his late-night reveries, he had been so busy wondering if he *could* love Beltan that he had forgotten to ask himself the simple question if he *did*. And as for the answer, well—

Like a dark bird, something fluttered on the edge of Travis's vision. He looked up.

The woman stood no more than thirty feet away across the park, in the center of a bare expanse of concrete. She was tall and lithe, her body clad in tight-fitting black leather, her legs apart and high-heeled boots planted firmly. Short, dark hair was smoothed sleekly against her head, and she wore a solemn expression on the bronze oval of her face. She stood without the slightest motion, gazing at him with gold eyes.

Travis started to draw in a breath. *Who are you?* he wanted to say. However, before the sound left his lips, the air around the woman rippled and folded, and she was gone.

21.

Mitchell Sheridan Burke-Favor sat up in bed and stared into the stone-colored light between night and morning, waiting for the alarm beside the bed to go off.

It wouldn't be long now. Life on the ranch started well before dawn, no matter the time of year. The hired hands would be showing up soon, clattering into the kitchen, wanting breakfast. Then there were horses to feed and saddle, cattle to be moved between pastures and watered, and miles of fence to mend. The earlier they started, the earlier they'd be done.

Not that Mitchell would have minded a few more minutes of sleep. God knew he was tired enough. While the years seemed to be getting shorter, somehow each workday seemed to be stretching out longer. But weary as he was, he was damned if he could sleep an entire night anymore. He was always thinking about the price of cattle, how many they'd have to sell to make it through the winter, and the cost of hay. But then, didn't they say folk slept less the older they got?

We're not young men anymore, Mitchell. There are no kids running around to remind you, so you can almost forget about it. But we're not thirty, and we haven't been in a whole herd of years.

Motion in the bed beside him. Mitchell turned and let his eyes ride over the planes of Davis's body stretched out beneath the sheet, as sharp and windswept as the high plains. Sleep had smoothed out the lines carved by years of wind and sun, but Mitchell knew they would return the moment Davis woke up and smiled.

All the same, with his thick wheat-brown hair, Davis didn't look all that different than when they had first met twenty-five years ago. Davis had been working the amateur rodeo circuit then, and Mitchell had been an announcer at the fairgrounds in Billings, Montana. Davis had lasted only four seconds on the bull. Even before he hit the ground, Mitchell had known their life together was going to last a whole lot longer.

While Davis was leaner than ever, Mitchell had gotten bulkier with time. A few years back his size 32 Wranglers had quietly given way to 34's. Then, last month, after some serious complaining on the part of his waistline, he had broken down and bought his first pair of size 36's down at McKay's General Store. He was still strong, though—the ranch work saw to that—and his thick, black handlebar mustache did a good job of hiding the creases around his mouth. And as for his balding head—well, only God and Davis ever saw him with his hat off.

Besides, there were other ways of staying young. That was why he and Davis had taken up two-stepping a decade ago. They had gotten good enough to win a few prizes at the national competition in San Francisco a while back. When you were dancing, it was impossible to feel old.

Except now there was nowhere in town to dance anymore.

Mitchell sighed, and he knew it was not thoughts of horses, cattle, and fences that had kept him awake. Where the hell had Travis Wilder called from?

Mitchell hadn't asked when the phone rang two nights ago. You never asked a man where he was from or where he was going; that was the cowboy code. If he told you of his own free will, you just nodded, and that was all. But Travis hadn't said where he was, or where he had been. All the same, the question had bucked and kicked in Mitchell, and it had been all he could do to rein it in.

No one knew who had dug the grave for Travis up in Castle Heights Cemetery. Some in town had said it must have been the new grave-digger who had come with the strange heat of summer and left just as suddenly. Mitchell couldn't say, as he had never seen the man. The summer had left little time for anything outside the ranch; the heat had come close to taking a terrible toll on the animals, and had it gone on much longer it would have.

Yet while no one had known for sure who had dug Travis's grave, everyone assumed that whatever was left of him was buried in it. The destruction of the Mine Shaft had been all but complete. A natural gas explosion, the Castle County fire marshal had determined. He had gone through all the old buildings along Elk Street and found a dozen other leaks in antique pipes and boilers. In a way it was a wonder it hadn't happened sooner. But then why had it happened at the Mine Shaft? Everyone still remembered the fire at the Magician's Attic a few years back, when Jack Graystone had died and Travis Wilder vanished for the first time. Now the Mine Shaft had burned, and Max Bayfield and several unidentified people had burned with it.

But not, as Mitchell learned two nights ago, Travis Wilder.

Through the window—open a crack for air despite the chill mountain night—drifted the sound of tires against gravel. Mitchell sat up in bed. Had some of the hired hands shown up already?

Outside, a vehicle door shut: solid, heavy, well oiled. Another followed, and a shiver rode across Mitchell's chest. Neither of those had sounded like the doors of a rusted-out pickup truck, and he was pretty sure none of the hired hands had been in the market for a brand-new car. He sure as horseshit wasn't paying them enough.

Mitchell stood up from the bed. Cold air slapped his bare backside. Swiftly, he pulled on the pair of jeans slung over a chair. He fumbled on the nightstand, then his hand came back with a pair of glasses rimmed with silver wire. Davis said they made him look handsome and smart. Mitchell knew they made him look old, but damn if he could shoot a target at ten paces without them.

The sound of footsteps crunched closer. Mitchell cocked his head, counting. Just two. Those weren't bad odds. He moved to the window, parted the checkered curtain a fraction, and peered into the steely predawn. They were just visible around the front corner of the house: the sleek, black curves of two SUVs parked in the dirt driveway. Two men in dark suits paused, gazing at the horizon with eyes concealed by heavy sunglasses, as if even the pale glow of first light was too much for them. Then they turned and continued toward the house.

A rustling in the bed behind him, and a sleepy voice. "What is it, Mitchell?"

Mitchell turned from the window and spoke

through clenched teeth. "Get your gun, Davis."

Two minutes later they stepped out the door of the ranch house onto the broad front porch. The last winds of night fled, as if fearing the coming of the sun. On the other side of the porch railing stood two men in black. The wind seemed to have no power over their stiff hair and heavy suits. Mitchell shivered, and one of the men—his hair coal-black, his features smooth and indeterminately Asian—smiled. It seemed a dead expression, his eyes hidden behind the thick sunglasses.

"We would have waited," the man said, "for you gentlemen to attire yourselves."

On his way to the door, Mitchell had stopped to slap his Stetson on his head, but other than the blue jeans that was it. Davis had pulled on a white tank top and a pair of battered khakis. Both of them were barefoot.

"No, no—they are cowboys," the other man said with a smile that was equally empty. He was tall and Nordic, his hair so blond it shone bone-white in the dawn. "I have seen this in the movies. They are only naked if they do not have their guns. Is that not right, boys?"

On reflex, Mitchell tightened his grip around his rifle, but Davis gave a laugh and twirled his revolver around his finger like a dime-store gunfighter. He always had been the showman.

"Why don't you little dogies jus' git along home?" Davis said in a grotesque Western drawl.

The air lightened a fraction, and the crescent moons painted on the doors of the vehicles glowed as if lit from within. The Asian man stepped closer.

"Of course. We are only too happy to . . . *oblige*. Is that not the word you Western people use? But before we go, please oblige us by letting us ask a question or two."

Davis tucked the revolver into the waist of his khakis and laughed, leaning on the railing. "It's your nickel," he said. "But I sure hope you're not expecting a cup of coffee while we have our little chat."

Davis could laugh at anything. Once, while camping, a hungry black bear had stuck its head into their tent, snuffling around for food. Davis had let out a guffaw, then slapped the bear on the nose. Stunned, the beast had wandered away. But Mitchell hadn't laughed then, and he didn't laugh now. There was something about these men—even without being able to see their eyes—that made them look hungry. But maybe it was just that he knew a wolf when he saw one.

Mitchell raised his rifle. "I told your kind once to pack up their tricks and never come back. I meant it."

Despite the rifle leveled at his chest, the dark-haired man stepped closer. "You misunderstood our company representatives, Mr. Favor. Ranching is a hard business—harder than ever these days, as I know you are aware. Were you not recently forced to take out a second mortgage on your property because of low cattle prices?"

Mitchell stiffened. How the hell did they know that?

The man spread his hands. "You see, we only wished to help."

Davis snorted, his grin gone. "You mean like you helped Onica McKay?"

When Mitchell had gone to McKay's General Store to buy his jeans, Onica had seemed oddly quiet as she rang up the sale. It was only a few days later, talking to one of the ranch hands, that they learned she had been unable to keep up her contracted payments, and that Duratek had assumed ownership of the store. Onica was now a minimum-wage employee at the business her great-grandfather had started. That was the kind of help Duratek offered.

The man gave a heavy sigh. "No one is sadder than we are when one of our arrangements does not work out. But a contract is a contract. I am sure, as businessmen, you must understand."

Mitchell had had enough of this. "I told you I would never sign one of your contracts. Now—"

The pale-haired man lifted a hand. "No, no, Mr. Favor. It is not a contract with you we seek. We have had a chance to check the numbers on your little operation here. Our earlier offer was made in error and has been withdrawn. It is another contract we are interested in."

"Please tell us," the Asian man said. "Do you know a Mr. Travis Wilder? He was, until recently, proprietor of the Mine Shaft Saloon in Castle City."

"What do you want with Travis?" Mitchell said, then winced. A glance from Davis told him what he had already realized; he had just told these men that he indeed knew Travis.

"You see," the dark man said, "like Ms. McKay, Mr. Wilder signed a contract with us. However, some months ago he grew delinquent in meeting his contractual obligations. Then, conveniently, the Mine Shaft burned, and Mr. Wilder disappeared."

"Died, you mean," Davis said. The revolver was back in his hand.

The Nordic man shrugged. "That is one explanation. I doubt it is the true one."

"You see," the other continued, "we have reason to believe Mr. Wilder is not dead, that he arranged the destruction of the Mine Shaft in order to evade his financial responsibilities to our corporation."

"That's a lie," Mitchell spat.

All the same, the words shook him. What if it were true? After all, Travis *was* alive. What if Travis had signed a contract with Duratek? Was that the reason he had not said where he was calling from?

The others must have noticed his reaction.

"Do you know something, Mr. Favor?" the black-haired man asked. "If you do, you should tell us now. You see, we can easily get a summons for a deposition. I am certain you know it is a crime to lie under oath. And you seem to be a lawful man, Mr. Favor."

The other's voice was calm and reasonable. And things were precarious on the ranch right now. There was no way they could afford a lawyer. And that fact was, Travis's behavior *was* strange. He started to open his mouth.

The click of a revolver's barrel stopped him. Davis had leveled his gun at the two men; the hammer was cocked.

"Here's a little lesson in the law," Davis said. "You two are trespassing."

Mitchell nodded. He had been about to give himself to these wolves, but whatever power their smooth words had on him evaporated. He pumped the rifle and sighted along its length.

"On the count of three, Davis."

"One," Davis said.

The dark-haired man held out a hand. "Davis, Mitchell—you must listen to me."

Mitchell adjusted his grip on the rifle. "That's Mr. and Mr. Burke-Favor to you."

"Two," Davis said.

"It is not wise to—"

"Three."

In perfect unison, two fingers pulled, two peals of thunder sounded. The men in dark suits ducked as bullets flew scant inches above their heads.

"Just in case you're wondering," Davis said, his grin back at full strength, "we weren't really trying to hit you. That time. Mitchell?"

They lowered the aim of their guns.

The men in black started to back away. The pale one clenched a fist, his mouth twisting in a knot of rage. "You are both going to regret this."

Despite the tightness in his gut, Mitchell found himself grinning as madly as Davis.

"Bullshit I will," he said.

This time the gunshots sent the two men running. They heaved open the doors of their SUVs and scrambled inside. Engines roared, and the two vehicles bounced off down the rutted road, columns of dust rising into the sky behind them.

Mitchell lowered his rifle. Davis was watching him, eyes clear and bright as the new morning sky.

"I'll get breakfast started," Davis said, and headed inside.

By the time the sun had fully risen, the hired hands had shown up, gathering in the ranch house's rambling kitchen. There were just three today—although during calving, or when they were tagging and branding, there could be as many as a dozen. Davis served ham and eggs while Mitchell brewed several pots of hot, strong coffee. Occasionally, some of the men joked that real cowboy coffee was made from mud and water, not French roast. Then again, every one of them took a minimum of three refills.

While they ate, Davis flicked on a small television on the counter to catch the weather report on the Denver morning news. Mitchell would rather have listened to KCCR, the low-power Castle County radio station. He volunteered there one night a week, reading news and local advertisements just to keep his voice in practice. However, the hired men seemed to have formed a cult of worship around Anna Ferraro, the doe-eyed Channel 4 morning news anchor, so TV it was. They drooled into their eggs while they watched.

"It's my turn to clean up," Davis said when Mitchell started to wash out the frying pan.

Mitchell knew better than to argue. "I'll get the boys going on the north fence line."

The hired hands had already wandered outside, finishing their coffee. Mitchell helped them load the fence-mending equipment in the pickup, described what part of the fence to get started on, then told them he'd meet them later. There was room enough in the truck for him, but Mitchell felt like riding out to the fence line. Sometimes it was nice to forget cars, power tools, mortgages, and stock reports. When Mitchell rode across the ranch, letting the power lines slip out of view behind him, it wasn't hard to imagine this was Colorado a hundred years ago. The wind and the sagebrush hadn't changed.

But the world had. While things might have been less complicated a hundred years ago, they had been harder as well. What place would the world have held for him and Davis? All the same, there was a peace in riding. He sent the boys on their way, then turned and headed back into the ranch house for some sunscreen. Davis wouldn't let him outside without it these days. Another concession to modernity, but cancer wasn't pleasant in any century.

Mitchell stepped back into the house's main room. Through the open door to the kitchen he could hear the clink of dishes and the low drone of the television. He spotted the sunscreen on the mantel above the room's gigantic sandstone fireplace. The fireplace was dark and empty now, but winter wasn't far off. Mitchell looked forward to those days, when there wasn't much work to do outside. He would sit by the fire, mending a saddle, while Davis set up his computer on the coffee table and worked on his newest book. He had published two romantic Western novels with a small California publisher, and was working on his third. They weren't great literature, but they had what Davis liked to call hot bull-on-bull action. All Mitchell knew was that, when he read the unbound pages sitting there on the floor, it wasn't always the roaring fire that made him sweat.

The sound of clanking dishes floating through the kitchen door ceased. A second later came the sound of Davis's voice, not loud, but hard and sharp.

"Mitchell, get in here."

Had a prairie rattler gotten into the house? It wouldn't be the first time. Mitchell dropped the sunscreen and covered the distance to the kitchen in long, swift strides.

Davis stood by the counter, a dish towel in his hands. "Look," he said.

Mitchell followed his gaze. Anna Ferraro's voice trilled over video showing a half-constructed building. Given the river and the tall buildings in the background, it had to be near downtown Denver. Mitchell drew closer.

". . . that work on the Steel Cathedral is proceeding ahead of schedule. With miles of reinforced girders and tempered glass, it will be one of the largest enclosed spaces in the state of Colorado when it opens next year. As you can see, in this footage taken yesterday, the building—which is meant to mirror the Rocky Mountains—is beginning to take shape. And, like a mountain, its designers are hoping that the Steel

Cathedral will help bring people closer to—"

"There," Davis said. "There he is again."

The camera pulled back, revealing a park near the construction site. The park was nearly empty: a woman pushing a baby stroller, a pair of rollerbladers, that was it.

No, there was one other figure. He was tall, clad all in black with a shapeless hat on his head. There was nothing remarkable about him, save for the heavy attire on a fine day. Then, almost as if he sensed the camera, the man turned around.

Mitchell drew in a sharp breath.

It can't be him. Damn it, he doesn't look the same at all.

But despite the changes, there could be no doubt about it. The man in black was Travis Wilder.

The video ended, and Anna Ferraro's blankly smiling face filled the screen again. Mitchell switched off the TV and looked up. Davis's expression was unusually grim.

"If we saw this and recognized him, then you have to bet others in town did as well."

Mitchell sighed. Davis didn't need to say any more. If Duratek had come to their ranch asking about Travis, then they would be asking others as well. Travis was in danger, but this was out of their league. They needed help, and there was only one place Mitchell knew to get it.

"Call the sheriff," he said, and Davis reached for the phone.

22.

"Good morning, Mitchell," Castle County Sheriff's Deputy Jacine Fidelia Windom said into the chunky black receiver.

As always she spoke with crisp inflection. Jace did everything in her life with precision. Her honey-brown hair was cut in a short, even line just above her shoulders, and her khaki uniform was as neat and sharp-creased as a newly unfolded road map. Even her features had a preciseness about them: small but not delicate, regularly spaced in the oval of her face.

The main room of the county sheriff's building was quiet. Jace had come in early to catch up on paperwork. There was something satisfying about the act of stamping papers, sorting copies into appropriate piles, and filing each in the exact place it belonged. Where there was order there was reason, comfort, and safety; without it the world would be an endless, churning ocean of chaos.

When she came in, she had found Deputy Morris Coulter clutching a cup of coffee in big hands and muttering to himself in a clearly failing effort to stay awake for the remaining hour of his shift. Jace had relieved him, then poured a cup of the coffee Morris had brewed and sat down to work. She figured she had more than an hour to herself before Sheriff Dominguez came in. Fifteen minutes later, the phone rang.

"What can I help you with, Mitchell?" she said, picking up a pen in a small hand just in case. It behooved one to stay a step ahead in life.

She listened carefully to the deep, musical, slightly twanging voice on the other end of the line. It wasn't often that she spoke to Davis or Mitchell Burke-Favor as the two were occupied most of the time by their ranch south of town, although she did listen to Mitchell's radio show if she happened to be at the sheriff's station on a Wednesday night. As long as she had known them, the two men had run a good operation. They were polite to their neighbors and kept their hired hands in line. Castle County could use a few more citizens like that.

She adjusted the phone in the crook of her shoulder and wrote in a blocky shorthand on the pad of paper. "So two men came to your ranch early this morning?"

Affirmation from the other end of the line.

"Did you know them prior to their coming?"

Hesitation, then a negative.

"And can you describe these men to me, Mitchell?"

Jace started to jot down notes as the voice on the other end continued. Then, carefully, she set down the pen and pushed the pad of paper away from her.

"I see. And did these men from Duratek tell you what it was they wanted?"

Jace only heard two words before Mitchell's voice was drowned out by a roaring that seemed to rush through the wire and into her ear.

Travis Wilder.

Jace knew that sound. It was the roar of the ocean she dreamed about at night—the great, roiling sea that was neither solid nor liquid, neither dark nor light. The dream had first come to her as a girl in sixth grade, precisely one year after the day she wheeled her pink bicycle into the garage, had noticed an oddly swaying shadow, and had looked up into the swollen, violet face of her father.

She had still been standing there—clutching the handlebars of her bike, gazing at her strong, handsome father, who had hanged himself from the rafters at the age of thirty-six in a place where he knew his daughter would be the first to find him—when the door to the garage opened and she heard her mother's scream.

For most of her life Jace had had the dream rarely, only after a particularly unsettling day. And those were rare enough—for her entire adult life, from junior college to truck driving to law enforcement, had been an ordered series of steps as easy to manage as the files on her desk.

Then things had changed, and all her logic, all her preparation, was nothing against what would be. For the last two months, the dream had come to her nearly every night. Ever since Maximilian Bayfield perished in the blaze that consumed the Mine Shaft Saloon. Ever since Travis Wilder had vanished.

She still had the newspaper clipping from last June, the first one to bear a headline about the new Black Death. That Max had had the disease there could be no doubt; all the symptoms had been evident. But the newspapers had been wrong on one account. It was not a plague of "unknown origin." Jace knew exactly where it had come from.

I was just wondering if you'd seen Max today, Travis had said to her that day at the Mosquito Café. The last day she had seen him. The last day of Maximilian's life.

Marriage and kids had been next on the checklist of Jace's life, and Maximilian had been healthy, cute if not handsome, smart for certain, and—perhaps most

importantly—gentle of nature. Love was one thing
Jace was pretty sure had been removed from her list
that day in the garage, but she had cared for
Maximilian. And she had been able to do nothing for
him.

It doesn't make a lot of sense, does it, Jace? Travis had
said.

He had seemed so genuinely concerned. For a
moment her heart had softened. Then she had steeled
herself. Whatever he might feel, this was his fault. The
John Doe who had been immolated at the saloon was
the carrier who had brought the plague to Castle City.
It was because of the man's touch that Maximilian had
fallen sick. And the madman in black had come here
looking for Travis. While Jace didn't know the true
cause of the sickness, she did know that it had come
with Travis Wilder.

Nothing makes much sense these days, she had said to
Travis that day in the café. And she had not seen Travis
Wilder or Maximilian Bayfield again.

The roaring in her ears phased back into words.
Deputy Windom? It was Mitchell's tinny voice coming
through the phone. *Deputy Windom, are you still there?*

A spasm coursed through Jace. She sat up straight in
the chair.

"Yes," she said. "Yes, I'm here, Mitchell."

Even as she spoke, her mind raced, fitting together
the pieces of what Mitchell Burke-Favor had said.
Then, like the papers on her desk, everything fell into
place. Wherever he had gone, Travis Wilder was back.
And she knew where he was.

A pause on the line, and a hiss of static. He was
waiting for an answer. She licked her lips.

"I'll give your report to the sheriff, Mitchell." Lies
were not so difficult if one spoke them with the

authority of truth. "Don't worry. We'll keep an eye out for these men and make certain they don't harass anyone else. Of course. And you're welcome. Tell Davis hello for me."

Jace hung up the phone. The hand unit seemed made of lead rather than plastic as she settled it back into its cradle. She waited a second or two—for what, she didn't know; for the last echoes of the roaring to fade from her ears, perhaps—then looked up at the two men who stood in the doorway.

She wasn't certain exactly when in the course of her conversation she had become aware of them, only that before she hung up she had known. They had a way of impinging on the senses slowly. It was as if they were so used to watching unnoticed from the shadows that it required special effort to make their presence felt.

"I told you they wouldn't help you," she said.

One of the men—the dark one with almond eyes—shrugged as he slipped sunglasses into his coat pocket. "Nor did we expect them to, Deputy Windom, for we trust your opinions. We have found your descriptions of the local population most insightful."

Jace let her gaze slide past them. Somehow it was easier not to watch them when they spoke. "Then why did you go to Davis and Mitchell's ranch?"

Now the other one laughed: a raw, brash sound. "Sometimes when a man does not wish to help you, he cannot prevent himself from doing so. It is interesting that Mr. Burke-Favor has called you, no? I wonder what the old cowboy had to say."

Jace did not like the blond one. He was big and broad-shouldered, but somehow pale and sickly despite his size, as if too many years under the Arctic sun had left him forever deformed, like a gangly, wax-white bean plant she had once grown in a dark closet as a school science experiment.

Jace clutched the edge of the desk. These men always talked in innuendo and gray shades of truth. She hated that about them. And now, because of these men, she had taken to uttering lies and performing acts of subterfuge herself.

"I don't like this," she said through clenched teeth. "A report made to a law enforcement officer is confidential until it is officially released."

The dark one approached. With a graceful motion of his hand he took her words and set them aside. "There are greater issues at hand here, Deputy Windom, than bureaucratic regulations. I believed you understood this."

The pale one started to speak, but the other lifted a hand, silencing him. So Jace's judgment was correct. Despite the big one's bluster, it was the small, slender man who was the commander.

The dark one sat on the corner of her desk. The black fabric of his suit made soft, sensual sounds as he moved. He smelled like her gun after she had just polished it.

"Your duty is to protect the public, is it not, Deputy Windom? Now here is a man whom you know to be a danger to all who come in contact with him. A man who we are interested in for our own reasons—for knowledge he has wrongfully withheld from us, and for the death of three of our operatives. And this is all in addition to the deaths of at least two citizens of this town. If you have decided to stop assisting us, I cannot hope to understand your decision, but I would expect at least for you to inform us."

Rage flared up inside Jace, then just as quickly died. She felt the first, queasy hints of the world yawing beneath her. She knew that if she shut her eyes she would see it: the dim, oily ocean, swirling.

She disliked these men, but she needed them. In the days after Maximilian's death, nothing had made sense to her. She had drifted, a castaway on the gray sea, and she had nearly drowned. Then, unasked for, they had come, and their words had been a life preserver. Madness had surrounded Travis Wilder. But the men from Duratek had offered reason, explanation, and logic. With nothing left to save her from sinking, Jace had grabbed on for dear life.

The chair seemed to rock gently beneath her. No, she could not let go yet. If Travis Wilder was not a murderer, then he was certainly a bringer of death and madness, of that there could be no doubt.

She shut her eyes, and for a second it was there: leaden waves roiling beneath a sky that was a mirror, so that it was impossible to know which way was up and which was down.

You shouldn't have done that, Daddy, she whispered without sound. *You shouldn't have done that.*

Jace opened her eyes. "I know where he is."

The man before her smiled. "So you do, Deputy Windom. So you do."

23.

Six hours after her conversation with Hadrian Farr, Deirdre Falling Hawk packed her one battered duffel bag, signed out of the dreary East End efficiency flat she had been renting by the week, and checked into the Savoy Hotel.

The desk clerk eyed her T-shirt and scuffed leather jacket with polite disdain. However, when he swiped the credit card Farr had given her and glanced down at the card reader's glowing display, his eyes bulged and a small, squeaking sound escaped him. After that the mousy fellow nearly tangled his arms together in an effort to serve her. He clapped for two bellhops to bear her bag ahead, then asked if she would prefer flowers or champagne in her room.

"Both," Deirdre said with a smile.

For all their faults, that was one good thing about the Seekers: They had a positively magical credit rating. Deirdre didn't know where the organization got its money. Rumors spoke of warehouses stuffed with Renaissance treasures and chests full of Roman coins. However, she suspected the more likely story was that, over the centuries, the Seekers had invested in various international financial concerns. There was nothing like five hundred years of compound interest to fatten a bank account.

Whatever the source of their money, one thing was certain: the Seekers were fabulously wealthy. And Farr had told her to take a room anywhere she wanted, as long as it was near the Charterhouse. They were flying nonstop to Denver in the morning to meet with Dr. Grace Beckett and Travis Wilder, and they did not want to be late.

Why are you doing this, Deirdre? she asked herself in the elevator. *You said you would never have anything to do with the Seekers again.*

There was only one answer, and it wasn't that this was her chance to tell Travis she was sorry. Whatever their faults, whatever their machinations, the Seekers knew things, had access to things that no others could possibly show her. Knowing what she did—that there were indeed worlds other than Earth—how could she blind her eyes to them?

She had made no apologies to Farr for her earlier behavior, but she had taken his credit card, and she had agreed to meet him at the Charterhouse at 8.00 A.M. Now a lightness filled her, and a wild energy, as when she rode her motorcycle too fast through twisting canyons. There were answers waiting for her on the other side of that ocean, answers to mysteries she had dreamed about since girlhood. And while it was not her reason for going, she would apologize to Travis Wilder all the same. Whatever he might believe of her, she would always hold him as a friend.

The two bellhops showed her to her room, and Deirdre tipped them generously from the wad of notes Farr had given her. They shut the door, leaving her alone. There was a massive bed, an ornate sofa and chairs, and a marble fireplace with a gas fire burning. The champagne and flowers had arrived ahead of her, arranged on a table before a window that had a view of

Westminster Abbey, Big Ben, and the Thames.

Not bad.

Deirdre kicked off her boots, unzipped her duffel bag, and pulled out the file folder Farr had given her earlier. She headed for the bed, detouring along the way to grab the bottle of champagne from the ice bucket, and flopped on the king-size mattress.

For the next hour she drank champagne and flipped through papers. She hadn't talked long with Farr at the Sign of the Green Fairy. He had said he had matters to attend to before their departure, and that he would brief her further on the plane to Denver.

There wasn't much in the folder, and she had seen most of it before. There were photographs of Travis and Dr. Beckett, and of various locations in Castle City. There was the drawing of a sword taken from a half-burned journal found at the ruins of James Sarsin's London bookshop in 1883, and a photograph of Dr. Beckett's necklace, which could be nothing but a fragment of the very sword depicted in Sarsin's journal. Of course, Sarsin was one and the same with Jack Graystone, Travis's antique dealer friend who had persisted for many centuries in London and then in Colorado. How his case—one of the most celebrated in the history of the Seekers—was connected to Grace Beckett was still an enigma. But perhaps that would be answered soon.

Deirdre skimmed through the rest of the folder. There were schematics of the Mine Shaft Saloon, chemical analyses of samples taken from burn stains on the floor, and also from soil samples taken at the Beckett-Strange Home for Children. Only at the end of the file was there something new to her: the transcript of Farr's conversation with Dr. Beckett, recorded yesterday.

Champagne bottle propped between her legs, Deirdre sat cross-legged and scanned through the transcript. Certain words stood out. *We're back*. And then later, *We're all in Denver*.

We, she kept saying. But exactly who was Beckett referring to? Travis Wilder certainly. But her words seemed to imply the presence of another. One didn't usually say *we're all* when talking about just two people. Then, near the end, her eyes met words that caused a thrill to well up insider her, like the bubbles in the champagne bottle.

We're not alone—we have a friend. He's in the hospital, in a coma. A question from Farr. Then, *Yes, he's from Eldh*.

Deirdre read the words again, heart racing. If this were true, it had enormous implications for their studies of the alternate universe. It was almost unimaginable what they could learn of the otherworldly culture and biology from direct study of an indigenous.

Deirdre read through the rest of the transcript. The last sentence struck her.

Please help us.

Beckett had called the Seekers to ask for help. But to help with what?

She shut the folder and laid it aside. Suddenly the taste of champagne was sour in her mouth. She set the bottle on the nightstand, dug into the pocket of her jeans, and pulled out something round, silver, and heavy.

Save me. That was what the woman Glinda had said earlier that day, when she slipped the coin into Deirdre's hand at the absinthe bar in Soho. However, her plea was just as mysterious as Dr. Beckett's. Save her from what?

Deirdre turned the coin over in her hands. In the light, she could make out the symbols. On one side was a pair of shoes with little bows on them. On the other side were the letters *SD*. She didn't know what it meant.

But maybe someone else would.

It was already getting late; she knew she should go to bed. Then again, she would have nine hours to sleep on the flight to Denver. And something told her time was running out for Glinda.

Deirdre stood, wishing as her head swam that she hadn't drunk so much of the champagne. She blinked to clear her vision, then pulled on her boots and grabbed her jacket. At the door she hesitated, casting one last glance back at her expensive suite. Something told her she wouldn't be getting the Seekers' money's worth out of it.

She tried the desk clerk and the concierge, but neither of them had seen anything similar to the coin before. Her best chance was back at the Sign of the Green Fairy. She headed through a side entrance, onto a narrow street. Outside stood one of the hotel's maintenance workers, smoking a cigarette. He was young—rail-thin, pale, and stoop-shouldered, but somehow pretty for it all. His hair was bleached stark white, and tattoos of dragons raced up his arms, disappearing beneath rolled-up white shirtsleeves.

"Hey, American girl," the young man said. "Nice jacket."

"Thanks." Deirdre started past, then on a hunch she turned back. In a way he reminded her of Glinda, at once tough and far too fragile for this world. She showed him the coin.

His lip curled up in a sneer. "No bloody thanks, girl. That's not really my scene." Belatedly he seemed to rethink his words. "But hey, I suppose if it works for you, then that's . . . well, that's that."

"What is it?" Deirdre said, meeting his bleary eyes.

"You don't know? Bugger. I thought you were making a proposition." He took a long draught on his cigarette. "It's a token. It'll get you a free drink over at SD."

"SD?"

"Surrender Dorothy. You know, over in Brixton. I was going to say, you really don't look like part of that scene. You haven't got any glitter on you." He tossed his cigarette into the gutter and sighed. "Shit, I'm out of fags. Want to come with me and buy a pack? I know a room in the hotel we can do it in. I'm pierced, if you like that."

Deirdre grinned. She pulled a pack of cigarettes from her jacket pocket and tossed it to him. "Sorry. You'll have to make do with this."

He caught the cigarettes in fumbling hands as she walked away. By the time she looked back over her shoulder, he was leaning against the wall, smoking again.

She caught a cab to Brixton. Deirdre paid the driver and stepped out, letting go of the handle barely in time to keep her arm from being ripped off as the vehicle sped away.

The street was deserted, but distant shouts echoed off sooty facades, and here and there shadows huddled in the alcoves of doorways, the cherry-red tips of cigarettes hovering before them like fireflies. Deirdre scanned the dim storefronts and at first saw nothing. It was only on her third or fourth pass that she saw a small, emerald neon sign she was certain had not been there a moment ago. It formed two letters: *SD*. Beneath it, also in neon, was outlined a pair of red shoes. Deirdre headed for the sign. There was a narrow, unmarked door. She opened it and slipped inside.

The doorman was an achondroplastic dwarf clad in black leather. He perched on a barstool behind a podium, his head shaved and a pointed blond beard on his chin. His eyes were a brilliant, handsome blue. He couldn't have been more than twenty-two or twenty-three. After looking her up and down, he bared large, white teeth in a grin.

"We're full," he said.

Deirdre eyed the empty hallway behind him. It was all black except for the floor, which was painted a scuffed yellow. The shimmering sounds of electronic dance music pulsed from beyond.

Deirdre matched his grin. "I don't think so."

"Oh, yes, we're not taking anyone else tonight," the doorman said. "You'll have to come back tomorrow."

"How much?" Deirdre said with a sigh. "Five pounds? Ten?"

The doorman only shook his head.

Deirdre leaned on the podium. "Listen—this is important. I'm looking for someone I met earlier today. Her name is Glinda. I need to know if she's here. She gave me this."

Deirdre set the drink token on the podium. As she did, the doorman's eyes widened.

"Ash and blood! Why didn't you tell me you were looking for Glinda?" He snatched the coin up, tucked it into a pocket, and hopped down from his stool. "This way." He grabbed the hem of her coat and tugged. "Come on—this way."

The hallway was longer than Deirdre would have guessed. The painted black walls were disorienting, receding into darkness so that the glowing yellow floor seemed a path leading across a lightless plain. Then the dull throbbing expanded into a rhythmic storm of sound. Fractured shards of a rainbow alighted on her skin, then flitted past, like fireflies whirling through the smoke-heavy air.

"There she is."

The doorman pointed to a murky corner, past the glowing dance floor where a dozen spindly figures clad in sequins, feathers, and bright plastic undulated. Deirdre caught a flash of orange hair and the glint of haunted violet eyes.

The doorman turned and disappeared back down the hallway. Deirdre made her way across the club. Tinsel dangled from the invisible ceiling, and television screens hovered at odd angles, flashing images in jewel-like colors. Figures lounged in foggy alcoves and dim corners: some small and stout like the doorman, others long and slender, draped languorously on shabby chaises. She felt curious gazes touch upon her before slipping past.

Glinda was curled up on a ratty purple sofa shaped like a half moon. Her willow-switch arms were folded on the back of the sofa, her mop of orange hair resting upon them. Violet eyes stared at the flickering lights, as empty as the small plastic bottle lying upended on the sofa cushion beside her.

Deirdre swore softly. She picked up the bottle and sat on the sofa. "How many, Glinda? How many did you take?"

Deirdre pressed a hand to her forehead, then squeezed her shoulder and shook her. Glinda's flesh was cold and stiff as clay beneath the creaking black vinyl. In small amounts, Electria could induce euphoria and a sense of well-being. In large doses it could depress the heart rate, lower the core body temperature, until coma and death resulted.

"Glinda, you've got to tell me how—"

She halted. The other's eyes gazed at her, hazed with a fog like that drifting over the dance floor, yet somehow piercing all the same. Deep purple lips parted in a smile.

"You came." Glinda's voice was a soft croak. "Moon and stars, you came. But you're too late, sweetie. You're too late."

Deirdre smoothed tangled orange hair back from her face. "It's not too late, Glinda. Just tell me how many pills you took. I'll get you to the hospital."

Glinda sat up straight. "No," she spat. "Needle-stabbers. Blood-lickers. No, you won't take me there. They're all the same. Poke and prod, turn you inside out. What makes you tick, sweetie? What runs in your veins, sweetie? Spread yourself and give us another look inside, will you?" A shudder wracked her too-thin body. "Leo took me there once. I won't go again."

Deirdre cursed herself; she couldn't save Glinda by driving her away. She took the other's hands, folded them together, and pressed them between her own; they were cold as sticks.

"All right, I won't take you there. Promise. And I won't let Leo take you, either."

At this Glinda laughed, a sound like a broken silver bell. "He can't take me, sweetie."

"What do you mean?"

"Leo's dead. He thought he could bargain with them, that he could get a good price for me. Stupid Leo. I told him they take whatever they want, only he never listened. He hurt me sometimes, and he used me. But he didn't deserve that. No one deserves that."

Deirdre tightened her grip on Glinda's hands, but somehow she felt the other slipping away. "Who,

Glinda? Who was Leo trying to bargain with? Why do they want you? I have . . . friends who can help us."

Slowly, as if with terrible sorrow, Glinda shook her head. "No, sweetie. I told you, it's too late. They don't need me anymore. They don't need . . . us."

Carefully, she disentangled her fingers from Deirdre's, then pressed them against her belly. Only then did Deirdre notice the faintest swelling in the center of her willowy body.

Glinda sighed. "Arion told me tonight."

"Arion?"

"The doorman. Everyone's whispering about it. No one knows how, but they've gotten themselves a pureblood. They don't need any of us now."

Deirdre tried to comprehend the other's words. "I don't understand, Glinda. Please, help me."

But Glinda wasn't looking at her anymore. Instead she gazed up at something over Deirdre's head. A dreaminess stole across her face, like the peace just before sleep.

"She's so beautiful," Glinda murmured. "So beautiful, and so pure. If only I could have been more like her."

Deirdre turned, craning her neck, and finally she understood. *Of course—Surrender Dorothy. Where else could she have taken her name?*

On a nearby television screen, a scene played out in vivid Technicolor: reds, greens, yellows, and blues all as lush and juicy as they had been the better part of a century ago when first revealed to a drab, black-and-white world. Dorothy Gale stood before a fallen farmhouse surrounded by Munchkins as a bright bubble of light danced toward her, shimmering and expanding until it became a woman clad all in gauzy, glittering white.

Deirdre turned back toward Glinda. "It's not too late. You can come with me . . . with us. Whoever it is who wanted you, if they don't need you anymore, they'll let you go."

"You're wrong, sweetie. They don't let anything go."

A calmness filled Glinda's eyes, and it sickened Deirdre. They couldn't give up without a fight. She opened her mouth, but Glinda shook her head, and suddenly Deirdre found that words had fled her. She worked her tongue, but she could make no sound.

"Hush, sweetie. It's all right." Glinda's voice was like cool water. "You came for me, and that's all that matters. Sometimes just by wanting to save someone, you do."

Deirdre shook her head and felt the warm wetness of tears against her cheeks.

"Here, sweetie." Glinda pulled a silver ring from a slender finger, then pressed it into Deirdre's hand. "This came from my mother. I won't . . . I won't be able to give it to my daughter. You keep it instead, so that we live on. At least a little bit."

No, Deirdre tried to say. *I don't want it.* But she closed her hand around the ring. Glinda leaned forward and pressed her purple lips to Deirdre's, kissing her deeply, lingeringly.

Deirdre's eyes went wide, for in that moment the murky nightclub around her vanished. Instead, she and Glinda sat on a flat, moss-covered stone in the middle of a misty forest glade where moonbeams stole between silver trees like ghosts. The only music there was the chiming of water tumbling over polished stones. All around her, like bits of gossamer, tiny beings with ugly faces floated on the air with butterfly wings.

Deirdre pulled away from Glinda's kiss.

"Where——?"

But at that moment the forest vanished, replaced again by the nightclub and the throbbing pulse of electronic music.

Glinda curled up on the couch, drawing her long limbs inward until she was small as a girl. Deirdre began to reach for her, but a stubby hand on her arm stopped her.

"They're coming," Arion said. "You have to go."

She shook her head, beyond words now.

The doorman pulled her arm. "Sticks and stones, come on! If they find you here, they'll spill your blood. They have no love in their hearts for your kind—if they even have hearts at all."

Deirdre stumbled to her feet. The doorman pulled her toward the back of the nightclub. Deirdre glanced over her shoulder, but the sofa was empty, save for a single twig bearing two silver-green leaves resting on one cushion.

Arion tugged again, and she stumbled through an opening. The pulsing music ceased with the sound of a shutting door. One by one, the night sounds of London drifted to her ears: laughter, footsteps, the distant wail of a siren. She stood on the edge of an empty lane, beneath the flickering orange haze of a lone streetlamp. At last she turned around, and she was only slightly surprised to see a blank brick wall behind her.

24.

Dr. Rohan Chandra, third-year resident at Denver Memorial Hospital, specialist in cranial neurology, and at thirty-four years old already the author of five scientific papers discussing the cause, consequence, and reversal of long-term comatose states, had forgotten something.

He stood before his open locker in the residents' lounge, quite frozen, overcoat pulled halfway onto his slender, well-shaped frame, caught in the act of thought. Several times a day his coworkers at the hospital found him in similar poses: a pen and chart forgotten in his hands, or cafeteria food suspended on a fork between plate and mouth, his brown eyes distant, his lips open and contemplative, his body as still and articulated as a many-limbed statue of Krishna.

At home, his wife Devi had grown accustomed to this habit. Theirs was an arranged marriage, crafted with care and attention by their parents living in India, although both Rohan and Devi had come to the United States for university. Because their union was arranged, they had worked to discover love, and when they did find it, like a yellow flower they had never noticed unfurling between them, it was all the more mysterious, powerful, and sweet.

Devi was an electrical engineer at a computer chip

manufacturing firm—although these last months she had remained home to care for their infant son, Mahesh—and so she placed everything in terms of circuits and transistors.

"You're preemptively multitasking," she told him one day. This was after she found him in the bathroom, clad only in his boxers, toothbrush jutting from his mouth, staring into space while toothpaste quietly foamed and bubbled down his chin. After he woke from his spell—she knew never to disturb him until he did—he had frantically scribbled down an idea that had led to a paper published in the *Journal of the American Medical Association*.

She had nodded. "It makes sense. You're giving fewer processor clock cycles to nonessential tasks like tooth brushing in order to divert power to the execution of more critical, computationally intensive calculations."

"I love you as well, dearest," he had said. Then he had kissed her foamily, deeply, and he had quickened even as she let her simple house wrap slip to the floor. Exactly forty weeks later—Devi prided herself on her ability for accuracy—Mahesh was born: brown, squirming, and perfect.

Chandra's eyes fluttered shut, then open again, and he knew what it was he had forgotten. He shrugged off his coat and placed it back in the locker. Devi was expecting him, and he longed to play with Mahesh, to bounce that compact little bundle of life on his stomach, toss him in the air, and bring him down to kiss like a living jewel. But there was a good chance the unidentified patient in Room CA-423 was a candidate for his new study, and Chandra had wanted to observe the comatose man again today, only he had been too busy until now.

He shut the locker. Devi would forgive his lateness. As long as he stopped for mango ice cream on the way home.

With soft, swift steps Chandra made his way through the corridors of Denver Memorial. As a child smaller than most other children, he had gained the habit of moving without attracting notice. As a man smaller than most, it was a habit he unconsciously maintained. Sometimes Devi would look all over the house for him, only to find him sitting, absorbed in a medical book, in the very room she had begun her search.

As he turned the corner into the C wing corridor, his eyes caught motion ahead. A door opened, and a man wearing a black overcoat stepped out. The man shut the door behind him; even this far away, it seemed a quiet action. In a single glance, Chandra counted the doors between his position and the man, then added the number to that engraved on the door plaque to his left. The final result: CA-423.

The man started to move away down the corridor, quickly, silently.

"Hello?" Chandra called out.

The man hesitated but did not look back. Chandra walked toward him. Since his arrival at the hospital, the identity of the patient in CA-423 remained unknown. Did the other know him? Or was it merely a janitor, on his way home for the evening, remembering he had left something in the room as he had cleaned it?

"Hello there," Chandra called again. "Do stop for a moment, please."

The man hesitated, then continued walking away down the corridor. Chandra started after him—

—then halted.

In the space between two moments, the other disappeared from sight. It was as if he had moved around a corner. Except that wasn't a possibility, for the corridor was long and without bend. Rather, it was as if the white air had quivered and folded, concealing the man from view.

For long seconds Chandra stared motionless, body forgotten, his brain devoted to thought, searching for an explanation. Then he saw the dark place in the hallway. One long segment of fluorescent lighting was burnt out, casting a ten-foot length of the hallway into shadow. Beyond there was an opening that led to an intersecting corridor. Clad as he was in black, the man might easily have seemed to vanish into the relative dimness, only to pass through the opening before Chandra's eyes could adjust to the stark difference in contrast. He started into motion again and stepped through the door of room CA-423.

The gentle whir of machines filled the clean, antiseptic air. It had been several days since Chandra had last come to observe the patient. The changes were subtle but immediate.

The level of spontaneous muscular activity was certainly an order of magnitude higher. There: a slight curling of the fingers in the right hand, followed almost immediately by the small but perceptible twitch of a cheek. With a thumb, Chandra raised one of the eyelids. Immediately the pupil constricted, highly reactive to the overhead light.

Chandra released the eyelid and nodded, satisfied. His earlier beliefs appeared correct. After weeks in a deep coma, the patient was close once more to consciousness. Whether he would cross the veil remained to be seen; sometimes such victims surfaced briefly, only to sink deeper and not return. However, Chandra's newest study focused on the use of combination drug therapy to enhance the recovery process. Certainly this man seemed a good candidate for the research. Chandra would speak to the hospital administration tomorrow.

Chandra leaned over the rail of the bed. "Soon, my friend, you shall be able to tell us your name."

The man remained motionless. Once again, Chandra wondered who he was. He was a tall man, certainly a full foot taller than Chandra if he were to stand, and before the atrophying of his muscles he had been powerful as well. Clearly he had led a rough life. When taking his history, a nurse had cataloged over a dozen significant scars on his body. And there was the wound that had nearly cost him his life, a gash in his side that had pierced the body wall. The wound was well healed now, his veins filled with blood again. What remained was to see if his brain would forgive his body for the trauma.

"You are a fighter, aren't you, my friend?" Chandra murmured.

It wasn't only the scars. Certainly there was a wildness to him, even in unconsciousness: a fierceness to the sharp features, a freedom to the long hair tumbling back from his brow. He seemed a fallen warrior, lying in his funeral boat as the waves carried him from the shore. Except he was not dead. Not yet.

"Nor will you be. If you are a fighter, then fight, my friend. Tomorrow I will help you in your battle."

The clock on the wall ticked the seconds away. Chandra sighed. Time to pick up the mango ice cream, to kiss Devi's sweet, sticky lips after she ate it straight from the carton, and to raise Mahesh cooing in his arms.

It was only as he started to turn from the bed that he noticed it, draped over the IV stand beside the bed. At first he took it for a piece of gauze. It was only as his fingers pierced its fabric that he understood. He pulled his hand back and stared at the gossamer shreds. It was a spiderweb, dense and glittering. He went still, thinking, but before he could arrive at a conclusion there was a faint *plop* as something small fell from the ceiling above and landed on his arm.

The thing was about as large as a quarter, its surface a dull, burnished gold marked by a crimson diamond in the center. Then, even as he watched, the thing stretched forth eight slender, golden legs and scurried down the length of his arm. It moved with a mindless precision that seemed more mechanical than organic, scuttling over the cloth ridges and valleys of his white lab coat.

Fascinated, he watched. Two tiny eyes glinted like rubies. Then the gold spider crawled over the cuff of his coat sleeve and onto the back of his hand. He could actually see its gold pincers extend forth, could observe them sink easily into his flesh, piercing skin, reaching for moving blood.

The pain was instant and agonizing, like fire. With a cry, Chandra flung his hand aside. There was a gold flash, and a skittering sound against the polished floor. Chandra turned and moved toward the door, but already his muscles were stiffening to cold clay as the poison moved through his body, carried rapidly by the increased blood flow and heart rate that accompanied fear and the rush of adrenaline.

He tried to cry out for help, but his vocal cords were already paralyzed, and the sound was a hoarse croak. A neurotoxin then, like that of the pit vipers that had haunted the edges of his childhood village in India. He had once seen a playmate of his struck by a snake not twenty feet away, and the boy had been dead by the time Chandra had run to him.

The floor rushed up to meet his left cheek, striking it with a curiously dull and muffled sound. A convulsion turned his face upward. The pain was fading. Chandra's last vision was of the face of the clock on the wall, as distorted as a timepiece in a painting by Dalí. Even then, his mind was able to achieve a clarity apart from his physical being, to crystallize itself in thought.

Time of death: 7:09 P.M. Cause: heart failure from a rapidly acting neurotoxin of unknown origin.

A weak muscle spasm passed through him, then came one final meditation.

Kiss Mahesh for me, dearest.

And for the first time since his birth, Dr. Rohan Chandra's thoughts were silent.

25.

Somehow, Grace expected Travis to be angry when he stepped into their musty motel room, pale and tired from his night's work at the hospital, and she told him she had telephoned the Seekers. Instead, a haggard grin crossed his face. "So what took you so long?"

She crossed her arms inside her preposterously baggy thrift-store sweater. "Do you mean to say that all this time I've been agonizing over whether or not I should contact the Seekers and how quickly you were going to eviscerate me if I did, you've been expecting me to call them?"

He sat on the corner of the opposite bed, mattress springs mewling like a nest of baby mice. "Pretty much."

Grace let out a groan. Nothing like torturing oneself for days on end for absolutely no reason whatsoever. She glared at the cardboard box and pair of Styrofoam cups strategically positioned on the nightstand. "If I had known you were going to be this easy, I wouldn't have bothered getting coffee and King Donut to soften you up."

"On the contrary, Grace, you chose wisely." He flipped up the lid, grabbed a powdered jelly, and took a big, squishy bite. "If the Seekers are coming to town, we're going to need all the energy we can get."

She popped the lid on her coffee and took a deep swig. A reflexive grimace crossed her face.

He cocked his head. "What is it?"

Grace laughed, gazing down at the oily surface of the brown liquid in the cup. "It's nothing, really. It's just that on Eldh I always found myself wishing for real coffee. And now that I'm here . . ."

"You wish it were *maddok*."

Her smile faded, but she concealed it by raising the cup and taking another sip of the coffee. It was hot and bitter, and it burned her tongue.

"You miss Eldh, don't you, Grace?"

His voice was soft, his gray eyes concerned. Sometimes this new seriousness of his startled her. Since she first met him, Travis had been funny and complaining and charming in a fumbling way. And, when both worlds had needed it most, impossibly brave. But since Castle Spardis, where he confronted the Necromancer Dakarreth in the fires of the Great Stone Krondisar, he had changed.

It was subtle. Had they not been through so much together, she might not have noticed it. However, there was something to Travis now that had never been there before. She could call it depth, perhaps. Or strength of character. Or even wisdom. It was hard to diagnose it precisely.

"I do miss it," Grace said. "It's hard to explain. For so many years I tried to make a place for myself here in Denver, a place where I could survive. And I did. But on Eldh, I did more than just survive. There, it felt like . . ."

"You belonged," he finished quietly.

She nodded.

"We'll get back, Grace. I don't know how, but we'll find a way. We have to." He warmed his hands around his coffee. "I'm not sure where I belong anymore, if I even belong anywhere. But you need to be there, and so does Beltan."

Grace sucked in a breath. Yes, that was it—that was the peculiar aura around Travis these days. He had given up everything he was, everything he had ever been, to save Eldh. Maybe now he was a man who had nothing left of himself that he feared losing. There was a peace in such freedom, and a purity, but a terrible sorrow as well.

An urge filled Grace to touch his arm, to say something comforting, but she held herself until it passed. Over the improbable course of this last year, she had learned she could still care for others, that the heart she had thought long ago excised still beat within her. But it was yet a fragile organ, and she did not believe it would ever be completely whole.

"So, did you check on Beltan last night?" she said, opting for brisk instead of sympathetic.

He crammed the remains of the jelly donut into his mouth. "I couldn't get to his room. Something happened on the fourth floor of the hospital before I got in, but I don't know what it was. There were security guards posted at the doors, and they weren't letting anyone through."

A sour taste rose in Grace's throat. The coffee was cheap stuff. She should have sprung for Starbucks; they still had several gold coins they could sell on East Colfax for money. She forced the bile back down her gullet. This was strange news, but it would be foolish to believe it had something to do with her and Travis. Not everything in Denver revolved around them. As of yesterday morning, when she had dared to venture into Denver Memorial, Beltan had still not awakened. Nothing had changed. Travis could check on him again tonight.

"Come on," Travis said, holding out a donut. His grin was back now, and his silver earrings glinted. "You need to build up your strength if you're going to talk to the Seekers. Everything they say is a riddle wrapped in the *New York Times* crossword puzzle translated into ancient Greek. So eat."

He tossed the donut into the air. She caught it in an easy motion and took a big, shockingly sweet bite.

Fifteen minutes later they walked down West Colfax, the mountains and a cool autumnal breeze at their backs. A cluster of glass-and-steel skyscrapers rose before them, looking strangely alien. Shouldn't they have been made of gray stone, their crenellated parapets crowned with bright, snapping banners? But Calavere was a world away. These were a different sort of castle.

They could have taken the No. 16 bus to Civic Center Park. They were to meet Hadrian Farr and Deirdre Falling Hawk at the Denver Art Museum, which stood on the south side of the park. But they still had over an hour until their appointed time. The day was lovely, and it was only a couple of miles to the museum, so they had decided to hoof it.

Or maybe it was just that neither of them had quite gotten reaccustomed to cars and buses. The hard, shiny vehicles roared past them down Colfax, seeming to hurtle past at an outrageous speed Grace supposed was all of thirty-five miles per hour. She relished the solid feel of the sidewalk beneath her boots of Eldhish leather.

Grace wasn't entirely certain when she noticed the police car. It impinged on her awareness slowly, like a gathering shadow, until suddenly she turned her head. The patrol car drove not thirty feet behind them. She snapped back around, clutching her cup.

"White or black," Travis said through clenched teeth.

He didn't need to say more. *White* meant a police car. Of concern, but not immediately dangerous. Grace was still wanted in this town for assaulting an officer, but not every cruiser would be looking for her. As for black—that meant *them*. And from what Travis had told her, she would much rather have a long conversation with the police than a chat with one of the friendly representatives of Duratek.

"White," she said.

They kept walking. Grace was aware of a pale blur as the patrol car drove past, but she did not glance in its direction. She breathed a sigh as the vehicle rolled down the street ahead of them—

—then her breath ceased as the vehicle slowed and halted. Through the dim rectangle of the rear window she saw the driver look back over his shoulder. She caught the faint sparks of his eyes with her own. The car's reverse lights blinked on, and her heart stuttered.

Grace clutched Travis's arm. "What do we do?"

"I don't know. If we run, we might as well hold up a big sign that says Fugitives 'R' Us."

Motionless, she watched the car back up toward them. What would she say when they questioned her? *You can't detain me, Officer. I'm a citizen of another world.* Something told her there were no Calavaner embassies in Denver.

A blaring noise vibrated through her body. She managed to crane her neck in time to see a delivery truck hurtling east down Colfax. Brakes hissed and squealed as the truck slowed, coming to a stop mere inches before colliding with the police car. The truck's door flew open, and the meaty driver clambered out, his face puffy and red as he strode toward the patrol vehicle, arms waving.

"Now," Travis said. "While he's distracted."

A row of brick-and-glass storefronts lined the block, a shopette that had no doubt seemed sleek and modern in 1964 but was now squat and drab, part of an architectural experiment that had ended, not only in failure, but in ugliness. Travis pulled Grace toward the nearest doorway.

The sound of chimes floated on the air as the door shut behind them, along with the sound of water bubbling over stone. A faint haze of smoke drifted on the air, rich and mossy on the tongue. A tree branch arched overhead, its gold leaves glinting in the faint light.

A small gasp escaped Grace. Once before she had walked into a room only to discover a forest instead. It had been in Castle Calavere, when she and Travis had gone to speak with Trifkin Mossberry and his troupe of actors. Through some magic of the Little People, their room had seemed at once a castle chamber and a greenwood glade. Was there a similar magic at work here?

"Hello," a husky voice said. "Can I help you find something?"

Smoke swirled, and before them stood a tall, lean, dark-skinned woman. From her clingy red minidress sprouted slender, beautifully muscled arms and impossibly long legs that Grace knew hordes of Paris runway models would gladly sell what little remained of their souls in order to possess. White platform shoes made her nearly as tall as Travis, and the fantastically sculpted black coiffure that crowned her head was clearly not meant to be anything but a wig. She was, in a word, gorgeous.

"Incense? Herbs? Candles?" She lifted a hand tipped by wonderfully unnatural press-on nails, gesturing to the crowded shelves all around. "If you need a little magic, you've come to the right place. Just tell Marji what you need."

How about getting us off this world? Grace glanced back through the door, but the glass was obscured by sunfaded posters, and she couldn't see the police car she knew was parked on the other side. Was he still occupied with the truck driver?

She turned back. "We need . . . that is, we wanted . . ." Grace felt her eyes bulging. Had she always been such a terrible liar?

Travis rescued her. "Candles," he said. "We need candles." He pointed to a nearby shelf. "Those red ones look good."

The woman—Marji—raised a precisely tweezed eyebrow, then sauntered to the shelf. She picked up one of the red tapers. "These? You're sure?"

"Yes, those are the ones I want."

Marji's smoky lips curved in a smile as she slipped her fingers up and down the length of the candle. "Honey, you light these in a ritual to make a man do your bidding, if you know what I mean."

Travis returned Marji's smile. "I know. I'll take five of them."

Marji laughed—a delicious, throaty sound—and fanned herself with a hand. "Well, it's nice to see you're so modest, honey. But are you sure you don't want ten? That way you can get the whole team at once."

Travis rubbed a hand over his shaved head. "Let's stay with five. I'm only human, after all."

It was fleeting, but Grace noticed his grimace as he said these words. She wasn't the only one, for the shadow of a frown touched Marji's face.

"Of course you are, honey. Aren't we all?" She took

five of the candles, set them on the Formica counter, and wrapped them in purple tissue. When she was done, she turned toward Grace. "And what can I get for you, queen?"

Grace took a step backward. "Why did you call me that?"

Marji shrugged, raising her arms—an elegant motion, like ribbons in water. "You're pretty as a queen, honey, that's all. Maybe you'd like a Valkyrie charm bracelet." She reached into the case beneath the counter and pulled out a slender silver chain. Tiny charms dangled from it, making a faint but audible music, like the sound of falling snow. "I see that you like them."

"Like what?"

"Runes." Marji brushed the charms with a finger. "Like the ones on your necklace, honey. Although, as I like to say, I'm a girl who knows her *futhark*, and those aren't Viking runes you're wearing. Do you know where that writing comes from? It isn't Minoan, is it?"

Grace clutched a hand around her necklace. It must have slipped out when they dashed inside. "It's nothing," she said, tucking the pendant back beneath her sweater. "And I'll take the bracelet. It's perfect."

Marji wrapped it up. She totaled the items, and Travis paid her in cash. She handed him the paper sack.

"Thank you, miss."

"You're welcome, honey."

Travis started to move from the counter, then glanced at Grace. Neither was certain if it was safe to go outside yet. Hindu tapestries and Egyptian camel rugs draped the store's windows; she couldn't see outside.

Marji crossed her arms and leaned on the counter. "All right, you two. Now why don't you tell me why it was you really came in here? And I am not going to believe that you came running in like Bonnie and Clyde on the lam because you needed candles and some pretty new jewelry." She placed hands on her hips. "And call me Marji. I haven't been *Miss* since Bobby Farrell caught me behind the bleachers."

Travis opened his mouth, but Grace was stunned to find herself speaking. She was pathetic at lying, but it turned out she was pretty good when it came to the truth.

"There's a police car out front. We came in here to get away."

Marji gazed at Grace with gentle brown eyes lined thickly in mascara. Then she came around the counter and placed one of her long, beautiful hands on Grace's. "I know what it's like, honey. To not want to be seen."

Grace studied the other, then nodded. Of course. "I suppose you do," she said.

Marji lifted Grace's hand and gently turned it over. With a red fingernail she traced the lines on Grace's palm.

"What are you doing?"

"Relax, honey. I'm a professional. Besides, you don't want to go outside just yet, do you? Now take a breath and let your sister Marjoram do her work."

Sister. The word was a comfort to Grace. Marji's touch was warm and light as a hummingbird against her skin.

Marji gave an appreciative murmur. "Well, I've never seen such a strong lifeline, honey. Here, it was cut just after its beginning, and then again not so long after that, but each time it just kept going. And there's another happening yet to come that will try to take you, but your life is too strong to stop."

Grace bit her lip. Maybe Marji wasn't a professional. She had always felt her grasp on life was tenuous at best.

"Now, your headline is sharp and deep, so you're a total brainiac. I think we all knew that to begin with. And as for your heartline . . ."

A soft gasp escaped Marji's lips.

Grace went rigid. "What is it?"

Gently, Marji pressed Grace's hand shut.

"It's broken," she said.

Grace pulled her hand back, held it against her chest, and nodded. Maybe Marji knew what she was talking about after all.

"It doesn't have to stay that way, honey," Marji said, her words soft and husky. "The lines on our hands don't lie, but they can change even as we do."

Grace gave a bitter smile. Then again, didn't they say you could never trick fate?

"How about Travis?" she said to change the subject. It was not as if Marji's words had revealed anything she didn't already know. "What's his hand say?"

Marji reached out and took Travis's hand. As she did, her eyes widened, and she made a cooing sound. "Honey, I've never felt such a soft hand. It's like a baby's. You have to tell me how you do it."

Travis let out a soft laugh. "It's a secret."

Grace nodded; she supposed it was at that.

Marji cocked her head, regarding him, then turned his hand over. She looked up, shock in her wide brown eyes. "But you don't have any lines on your hand. Not one. I've never seen anything like it."

Travis drew his hand back. "It was fire."

Marji curled a long hand beneath her chin, but something in her expression did not look convinced.

Grace cleared her throat. "I think . . . I think we

should go now. We don't want you to get in trouble if the police come in here looking for us."

Now Marji laughed, waving a hand. "Please, honey. I know how to deal with the police. I beguile the boys and befriend the girls." She spread her arms wide, then hugged herself. "To know Marji is to love her, no?"

Grace could only laugh in agreement.

Marji beckoned with a long finger. "This way, you two. Follow Marji. You can take the back door to make sure no prying eyes see you leave."

They followed as she parted a beaded curtain. Beyond was a space even more crowded than the store outside. Sagging shelves were lined with sweet-dusty bundles of sage, brass candlesticks, polished pieces of hematite, lacquered boxes, packages of incense, and jars filled with a hundred different kinds of herbs. Grace would have liked to stop and study some of the herbs, to smell them, taste them, probe them with the Weirding to see how they compared to the plant species she had worked with on Eldh. However, Travis tugged her arm, pulling her onward.

They reached a door. Marji opened it a crack, peered through, then pushed it wider. Beyond was an alley littered with empty boxes and broken pallets.

"Now, I know you both have important things to do," Marji said. "No—no need to explain. I see it in your eyes. But you come back to Marji if you can. You're a special lady, queen. Those are some witchy green eyes you have."

She squeezed Grace's hand. Grace squeezed back.

"And you." Marji ran a hand over Travis's head. "You're pretty cute for a bald white guy."

Travis only grinned.

"You take care of yourself, honey. Both of you."

Grace and Travis nodded. Sometimes words weren't

enough. Then they stepped into the alley. Behind them, the door shut and locked with a *click*.

Travis sighed. "I get so used to running from people who want to use us for their own ends, sometimes I forget there are people who will help us and not expect anything in return." He shoved his hands in his pockets. "We owe her."

"Him, you mean."

Travis frowned, and Grace laughed. Maybe the new Travis was still a little clueless after all.

"Marji's a man, Travis. Well, genetically, at least. I suppose, in all the ways that count, she's a woman. Except no woman I know could have pulled off that ensemble."

Travis stared into the wind. Grace wondered what he was thinking. Before she could ask, he shrugged his shoulders and smiled.

"Well, what's the point of being alive if you can't choose what you're going to be?"

It sounded good, coming from his lips. But sometimes Grace knew you didn't have a choice, that life decided for you, and that no matter how much you wanted something, you could never have it back once it was taken from you. She glimpsed it: the shadow that always followed her, just one step behind.

"Come on," she said. "It's not polite to keep members of mysterious international organizations waiting."

26.

The Denver Art Museum loomed on the edge of Civic Center Park, just south of downtown. Travis knew the museum was considered a masterpiece of neogothic architecture, but to him it looked more like a castle seen through a fun-house mirror: big and hulking but distorted, containing none of the original grandeur. Only after a minute did he realize that both he and Grace stood before the museum's glass doors, unmoving.

Travis could understand his own hesitation. After all, his last conversation with the Seekers had been anything but cordial. He had been furious with Deirdre Falling Hawk, accusing her and the Seekers of manipulating him. It wasn't until he returned to Eldh and encountered the ancient, wise, and vastly cruel dragon Sfithrisir that he realized what a weapon the truth could be. Sometimes lies were the only thing that made the hard realities of life bearable, and the Seekers had known that.

But why was Grace hesitating? The Seekers had helped her escape an ironheart at the Denver police station not three blocks from this museum. And certainly Grace's analytical mind was a good match for the Seekers.

"There's something wrong," she said.

He looked around but saw only a scattering of tourists, skateboarding teenagers, street people, and one group of schoolchildren led by a harried teacher. "What is it, Grace?"

Her eyes were closed. "I don't know. I can't really use the Touch here. The Weirding is so faint. But I feel something—a shadow, a presence. Like something watching." She sighed and opened her eyes. "I'm sure I'm mistaken."

Travis wasn't so certain. He didn't really understand Grace's abilities, but she was a scientist, and he had seldom heard her advance a theory she didn't have evidence to back up.

"Come on," she said. "There's no use waiting around. If there is something, it will show itself."

The interior of the museum was more comforting than the exterior. A maze of high walls soared upward to the random window slits that made so much more sense when viewed from this side. The two of them wandered past abstract canvases and sculptures of steel and glass. Farr had only said that he would meet them on the first floor of the museum. Travis wasn't concerned. Knowing the Seekers, Deirdre and Hadrian would find them first.

"What is *that*?" Grace said, stopping before the entrance to a dim alcove. Inside, clear tubes dangled from the ceiling, each one holding a naked plastic doll. Scattered on the floor were books, video games, and movie posters. Red ribbons tangled over them like fire. Or blood. A card on the wall read:

Protecting Our Children
A. Becker

"It's an installation," Travis said.

Grace snorted. "I thought you installed plumbing, not art."

Travis couldn't disagree with that. But something about the art installation compelled him, drawing him inward as Grace moved on. It seemed to be saying that, in trying to protect others from harm, we could simply end up isolating them. But what was the alternative? To let them drop down into the blood and fire below?

Travis didn't have an answer. He moved on, and a painting caught his eye. Its realism stood out among all the abstracts surrounding it, but it wasn't this that beckoned him closer.

The painting was all in purples and greens. It showed a farmhouse standing on a lonely plain with only a single tree for company, crooked limbs bowing achingly toward the house. An empty path led to the front door. From the upstairs window a pair of haunted eyes peered outward, and a pair of small, white hands pressed against the glass. The card by the painting read, *Coming Home.*

Travis shut his eyes. He could see it again, half-lost in the deep, hazy twilight that came only to the moist fields of the Midwest: the farmhouse where he had grown up. Would it look like this if he were to go home? Had she been there all this time, waiting for him to return? Alice.

It was his fault. As a kid, reading had been especially hard for him, and he had mixed up the numbers on the label on her medicine bottle. He had given her too many pills. Far too many. But even as she took them, she had forgiven him. *I love you, Travis.* Then she had shut her eyes, and she had never opened them again. And it was a strange fact of life that sometimes forgiveness was harder to bear than the most bitter accusation. He lifted a hand toward the painting.

"Travis?"

He turned toward the sound of the wine-rich voice behind him, knowing in that moment there was a purity and beauty to forgiveness that outweighed any hurt, any pain, any regret. He stepped forward, lifted his hands to her cheeks, and kissed her deeply, lingeringly, on the lips. At last he stepped back, and he was amused to see that this time it was her smoky green eyes that bore the look of complete astonishment.

"It's good to see you, Deirdre Falling Hawk," he said, and he meant it with all his heart.

Slowly, tenderly, a small smile crept across the arched bow of her lips. "What happened to your hair?"

Travis ran a hand over his bald head and laughed.

They found Grace and Hadrian Farr already embroiled in quiet conversation, sitting on a bench beneath a hulking iron sculpture that reminded Travis of the dragon Sfithrisir, stretching vast wings whose outlines blurred with the very air so that they were maddening to gaze upon.

Grace looked up as Travis and Deirdre approached. Her face was hard and bloodless, and Travis stopped in his tracks. He glanced at Deirdre, whose expression was grim, then back to Grace and Farr.

"He's gone," Grace said before he could speak.

Perhaps there was enough of her Weirding left in this place for her to Touch and speak to him, or perhaps it was simply the instinct that comes with urgency and closeness. Either way, when Travis spoke the word, a numbness filled him: the coldness of truth.

"Beltan."

27

Minutes later they sat in the comfortably upholstered interior of a black limousine as the streets of Denver moved like shades beyond the tinted windows. On the other side of the driver's partition, a silhouette piloted the vehicle with skilled, anonymous assurance.

Travis sat next to Deirdre, his hand resting on top of hers in what had begun as an unconscious motion only to continue in an active desire to hold on to something real, solid. On the seat opposite sat Grace and Hadrian Farr. The Seeker was as handsome and elegantly disheveled as Travis remembered, the strong line of his jaw shadowed by a day's worth of stubble, the sleeves of his white shirt rolled up, his chinos rumpled but well tailored. He was twilight next to Grace's bright afternoon, dark and sensual where she was chiseled and regal. It was hard not to notice that they looked striking together.

Farr and Deirdre explained what they knew. It was precious little. Upon their arrival that morning, they had gone to Denver Memorial to confirm that the hospital was secure.

"And just to see him," Deirdre said, eyes shining. "To look at someone born on a world other than Earth."

Despite the tightness in his chest, Travis laughed.

"You know, they put their breeches on one leg at a time just like we do." All the same, he understood her.

However, instead of Beltan, the Seekers had found a crime scene. Travis and Grace listened in silence as the two Seekers described what had happened last night— and what had been kept from the hospital staff until that morning, not long after Travis's shift had ended.

Just after 7:00 P.M., a resident and a nurse ran to Room CA-423 in answer to a heart-monitor alarm. However, when they entered the room, they did not find what they expected: the coma patient seizing, or perhaps dead. Instead, the patient's bed had been empty. IV tubes and monitor leads had been torn out. Only as they came around the bed had they seen the other in the room: the real code blue.

"He was a third-year resident at the hospital," Farr said, flipping through a file folder. "His name was . . . his name was Dr. Rohan Chandra."

Grace nodded. "I knew him. Not well, of course." A sigh escaped her, but she seemed completely unaware of it. "I suppose I didn't know anyone at the hospital well. But he was a smart man, a bit more interested in research than in patient care, but he was always kind."

Travis's head throbbed. "I don't understand. What does this doctor have to do with Beltan?"

"Actually, nothing." Deirdre turned so she could face Travis, her black-leather jacket creaking. "As far as we can tell, Dr. Chandra had the misfortune to be in the wrong place at the wrong time."

"You mean he got in the way," Travis said, and a sickness filled him. "He got in the way of the people who took Beltan, and they disposed of him."

"What was the cause of death?" Grace said, her haunted eyes belying the clinical tone of her question.

Farr took a photograph from the folder and handed it to her. It showed a swollen lump on the doctor's forearm, marked by a pair of tiny holes.

Grace frowned, tucking a lock of ash-blond hair behind one ear. "I don't understand. This looks like some sort of insect bite. Maybe a spider."

Farr took the photograph and returned it to the file. "Your diagnosis is correct, Dr. Beckett. The initial autopsy performed this morning suggests that the spider bite introduced a highly potent neurotoxin into Dr. Chandra's bloodstream. He was dead within ten seconds of being bitten."

"No." Grace crossed her arms over her sweater, even though it was warm in the vehicle. "That's not possible. I remember reading about this in my toxicology class in med school. The venom of some spiders can be fatal, but none of them can kill a man that quickly. Not even a small man like Chandra."

Farr slipped the folder back into a briefcase. "Your old professor may need to revise his course curriculum, Dr. Beckett." He opened a small cabinet set into the side of the limousine. "Can I offer anyone some gin?"

Travis hated gin. He nodded. Farr handed him a glass, then made another drink for Grace, but she held it in her hand without seeming to notice its weight or coldness. Travis raised his own glass, held his breath, and drank.

"So who did it?" Grace said. "Who took him?"

Farr met her eyes. "There is only one organization I know of who would use murder to gain an otherworldly specimen."

Grace turned on him, speaking with a sudden vehemence that shocked them all.

"He's not a specimen, Mr. Farr. He's a man. His name is Beltan of Calavan. He's a knight of a royal house. He likes to drink beer and tell bad jokes, and he is kind and strong and courageous. He doesn't deserve to be treated like a lab rat. Not by anyone."

And what's more, I love him, Travis almost said. But he had never uttered those words aloud. And if anyone should ever hear them for the first time, it should be Beltan.

Farr regarded Grace for a silent moment, then gave a crisp nod. "Of course. You must forgive me, Dr. Beckett. Sometimes I can be impersonal with regard to people I do not know. The mind of a scientist. I think you can understand."

Grace looked out the window and said nothing.

"So it was Duratek," Travis said, more to himself than to the others. "But how did they know Beltan was at the hospital? As far as we know, they don't even know we're in Denver."

"They do now, Travis," Deirdre said, her eyes serious above high cheekbones. "At least, we have to assume they do. We don't dare underestimate them."

"The police," Grace murmured. She turned back from the window and met the questioning stares of the Seekers. "I think the police are looking for me. A patrol car nearly stopped us this morning, on our way to the museum."

Farr rubbed his chin. "That would fit. Duratek often works in association with law enforcement. On the surface, at least, they appear law-abiding."

A bitter smile twisted Grace's lips. "While I, on the other hand, am a dangerous criminal."

"I know this might be difficult for you to believe, Dr. Beckett," Farr said, "but it is actually a good sign that the police are searching for you. It means Duratek knows you're in the city, but not your exact location. The hospital is one place where they might expect to find you. That could explain why they discovered your friend."

Grace pressed a hand to her forehead. "Of course— I was an idiot to go. I checked on Beltan myself yesterday morning, and then that night he's abducted. I didn't think anyone recognized me, but someone must have seen me enter his room."

"Duratek does have a way of making people recall things," Farr said, his expression grim.

Grace reached a hand toward Travis, then started to pull it away. "I'm so sorry, Travis. I . . ."

He caught her hand before she could withdraw it. "It's not your fault, Grace. None of this is your fault. Besides, it could have been me that someone at the hospital recognized."

"No, I don't think so." It was Deirdre who spoke, her voice low and thoughtful. "You're different, Travis. I don't think anyone would recognize you if they didn't know you well. It's almost like you're . . ."

"Like I'm a whole new person." But he had no more words beyond that.

Finally Grace drew in a breath. "I still don't understand how Duratek could use a spider to murder Dr. Chandra. It seems awfully risky. After all, you can't tell the thing whom to bite. Have they used spiders before?"

Farr leaned back. "To our knowledge they have not."

Travis felt gentle pressure as the shadowy world slowed outside the windows. He peered through the smoky glass. They were just two blocks from the Blue Sky Motel, where he and Grace had been staying.

"Now what?" he said.

Farr sat up straight. "Now you and Grace must remain hidden while Deirdre and I work to discover where Duratek has taken your friend."

Travis opened his mouth to protest, but Deirdre spoke first.

"It's better this way, Travis. It's too dangerous for you and Grace to be moving about the city right now. It's quite possible that Duratek is using Beltan as a lure to get you and Grace."

Grace looked at him. "She's right, Travis."

Farr rolled down the window a few inches and gazed at the litter-strewn street. "Do you know if anyone has followed you to your motel?"

Travis shrugged. "I doubt we'd be sitting here with you now if someone had."

"Good point," Farr conceded, as the window whirred shut. "Then I suppose this is as good a place as any for you to remain. We'll be posting a pair of operatives to keep watch. We'll call you with descriptions so you won't be alarmed when you see them. Also, we'll arrange for your meals to be brought to you, so you don't need to leave your room."

"This is starting to sound suspiciously like prison."

"On the contrary, Mr. Wilder," Farr said in his smooth, accentless voice, "you can leave any time you wish. Just remember what is waiting for you if you do."

Travis clenched his hands. What use was freedom with choices like that?

"It's best if you walk back to your room from here," Deirdre said. "I have a feeling most patrons of the Blue Sky don't get dropped off by limousines. We'll watch to make sure you get there."

"Thank you," Grace said. "Both of you."

Her eyes glowed green-gold as she regarded the Seekers. It almost seemed she was enjoying herself. But even on Eldh, Grace had always been better at spying and secret plots. All Travis wanted to do was find Beltan and get back to Eldh. He opened the limousine door.

Deirdre touched his arm. "May the wind guide you, Travis."

He nodded, then stepped out of the vehicle. Grace followed him, and the door shut. The limousine rolled away, as long and sleek as a serpent, then disappeared around a corner.

"They'll find him," Grace said, her voice resonating with belief.

Travis said nothing so she wouldn't hear the doubt in his own. They turned to walk back to the motel.

Motion caught the corner of Travis's eye. A fragment of shadow seemed to detach itself from the space between two buildings and glide toward them. He almost thought he saw two glints of gold. Then the air rippled, and the shadow was gone.

Grace touched his shoulder. "What is it, Travis?"

He gazed a moment longer into empty air, then turned away. "It's nothing," he said.

28.

Three days later, Deirdre looked up from the glowing screen of a sleek, silver notebook computer as the door of their suite at the Brown Palace Hotel opened and Hadrian Farr stepped through. He looked haggard and shockingly thin, wearing the same wrinkled clothes as when he had departed just twenty-four hours earlier.

"You look like hell," she observed, then returned her gaze to the computer screen. She had just connected to the Seekers' main computer system in London to view the results of the analysis she had initiated her last morning in London. The Seeker labs had just completed it. Crimson words scrolled across the screen.

REPORT FOR:	D. FALLING HAWK / SA-9774U
REQUESTED ANALYSIS:	PARTIAL MITOCHONDRIAL SEQUENCE —CROSS-POPULATION COMPARISON WITH PHYLOGENETIC TREE
SUBJECT:	CODE NAME—GLINDA

"I go to London and come back to Denver in the space of a day, and that's all the welcome I get?" Farr threw his leather satchel on the sofa, tossed a much-worried newspaper on the table, and moved to the room's minibar. He pulled out a miniature bottle of scotch and twisted the cap.

"You know, those little things are perversely expensive," Deirdre said, her eyes still on the screen. She clicked a button, and a progress bar appeared: *Downloading . . .*

Farr snorted. "Good. It's on the Seekers." He drained the bottle in one draught, grabbed another, and flopped into a chair, scowling at her. Farr was one of those men who looked dangerously handsome when he scowled.

"Aren't you even going to ask me how it went?" he said.

She watched the progress bar: 32% complete. "I already know how it went."

"What do you mean, you already know? I just got off the bloody plane."

"Yes, after a nine-hour flight. In the meantime I used this fascinating little invention called the telephone. Have you heard about it?" 74% complete. "Anyway, Sasha told me everything. Congratulations. It looks like we're still in business."

Farr grunted, then struggled to open the second bottle. He gave up, tossed it down beside him. "By God, I hate hotel rooms."

"Well, right now your hatred is costing the Seekers four hundred American a night. So be sure to make the very most of it."

Data started to stream across the screen: small bars, each representing specific genetic loci. Hundreds of them. Thousands. Deirdre watched them go by, letting her eyes drift out of focus as if she might somehow see patterns if she did.

"Anyway," Deirdre said, "I fail to see what you're

so upset about. They approved your invocation of the Ninth Desideratum, didn't they?"

Farr had left Denver yesterday morning for a whirlwind trip to London. Deirdre had urged him to make his case via electronic means, but he had insisted on going in person. Which made little sense, for as far as she knew no one had ever talked to the Philosophers directly, not even Farr. The leaders of the Seekers were always in communication, but they remained out of view, veiled in secrecy and anonymity. So it had been throughout the five-hundred-year history of the Seekers.

However, Farr had thought it best to return to London. Perhaps, if nothing else, it demonstrated his commitment to the cause. And evidently it had worked. Despite their direct violation of the Third Desideratum—*A Seeker watches but does not interfere*—there would be no reprimand from the Philosophers.

Not that Deirdre believed she and Farr had done anything wrong in coming to Denver. After all, it was Grace Beckett who had called them, not the reverse. However, the Nine Desiderata were not written in shades of gray. The intention of the Third Desideratum was to forbid Seekers from interacting directly with otherworldly subjects, so as to prevent any contamination of their behavior.

Fortunately, Seeker agents tended to be a clever and resourceful lot, and as a result it was nearly four centuries ago that one of them, Marius Lucius Albrecht, first invoked in his defense the Ninth Desideratum: *Above all else, a Seeker must let no other being come to harm.*

Albrecht had been faced with expulsion from the Seekers for contacting—and some stories said falling in love with—a woman who had otherworldly connections. However, he demonstrated that she had been in peril for her life, and that he had no choice but to intervene.

Above all else . . .

Albrecht claimed those three words meant the Ninth superseded all other Desiderata and, after long deliberation, the Philosophers agreed. Albrecht was not expelled, and he went on to become the most celebrated Seeker agent in the organization's history. It was said he would certainly have become a Philosopher himself were it not for his death at the age of thirty-seven.

Of course, Deirdre had heard it whispered often enough among her fellow agents that Hadrian Farr was the next Marius Lucius Albrecht incarnate. So perhaps it was only fitting that he invoked the Ninth Desideratum himself—for the third time in his career. And certainly there was no doubt that Grace Beckett and Travis Wilder were in danger. As was their otherworldly friend, the one they called Beltan. The Philosophers had had no choice but to grant Farr a dispensation.

Deirdre stood and walked over to Farr. "I don't understand why you're upset, Hadrian. The Philosophers agreed with you."

"Yes, they did. Except I'm not entirely certain that they should have." He leaned toward her, elbows on knees. "These are the Philosophers, Deirdre. The dread, all-powerful, maddeningly inflexible, and mysterious Philosophers. By God, they should have put up something of a fight, don't you think? Instead they granted my dispensation with barely a moment's thought. For all their mumbo jumbo about history and the weightiness of duties, they seem perfectly willing to send one Seeker, one journeymen, and a bit of muscle to counter Duratek in what is clearly the most important case of this century."

"Maybe they have confidence in us," Deirdre said with a shrug.

"Well, I'm not certain I do." He rummaged in the seat cushion beside him, retrieved the second liquor bottle, and finally managed to struggle the cap off. He downed half the contents.

Deirdre frowned. "So breaking the Third Desideratum isn't enough. Now you're going after Number Six. *A Seeker shall not allow his judgment to be compromised.*"

"Oh, and you're a fine one to quote from the Book. And don't tell me that was crème de menthe I found you drinking in Soho."

She affected her most pious look, learned in imitation of her devoutly Catholic great-aunt during one of her summers in Ireland. "I was on a break from the Seekers at the time."

He laughed: a rich, booming sound that completely startled Deirdre. In her experience, Farr had always been unfailingly—sometimes exasperatingly—composed no matter the circumstance. She had never before heard him utter a sound containing the ring of desperation.

"No, Deirdre. Don't you see? There's no such thing as a break from the Seekers. It's not a social club you attend when the whim strikes. It's a holy marriage with no hope of annulment. Until death do us part." He raised the bottle and downed the remaining liquid.

Deirdre watched him drink. The fact was, his words *did* disturb her. Why were the Philosophers willing to invest so much faith in two people when so much was at stake? She didn't understand. But then, there was much the Philosophers did and said that she failed to understand. They had purpose and knowledge unknown to the rest of the Seekers.

Behind her, the computer let out a soothing electronic tone. She returned to the table. The data had finished streaming, and the summary report filled the screen. Deirdre scrolled through the rows of information. As she did, her sense of unease grew.

"This doesn't make sense," she murmured.

A rustling of linen behind her. Farr.

"What have you got there, Deirdre?" His voice was low and measured again; the Hadrian she knew.

"I don't know," she said honestly. "I really don't know."

She hadn't told Farr about her encounter with Glinda that last night in London. It was hard enough to understand herself why she had gone looking for the woman, let alone explain it to another. A dozen times Deirdre had replayed the conversation at Surrender Dorothy, but still she could not fathom what it meant. Only Glinda's sorrow had been achingly clear—as was the cool, green forest Deirdre had glimpsed when they kissed.

The silver ring Glinda had given her at their parting was an intriguing artifact; Deirdre had performed several remote searches in the Seekers' databases, but so far she had found no match for the symbols engraved on the inside surface of the ring. On a hunch she had even tried a pattern match with runes known to have originated on AU-3—the runes on Grace Beckett's necklace. There were no similarities. The writing on the ring was spidery and flowing, unlike the angular runes of the world called Eldh.

However, the ring had more than just writing with which to tell a story. Deirdre had wrapped it in plastic and had couriered it to the Seeker laboratories. There had been enough skin cells on the ring for them to do DNA sequencing. But the sample must have been contaminated somehow, because the report she was reading could not be correct. She scrolled again to the words at the bottom of the file:

ANALYSIS INTERRRUPTED: ERROR—MITOCHONDRIAL
SEQUENCE INCOMPLETE—
BAD OR MISSING DATA
IN SAMPLE—HUMAN DNA
INTERRUPTED BY
RANDOM BASE PAIRS.

CONCLUSION: UNABLE TO COMPLETE
PHYLOGENETIC
ANALYSIS—SAMPLE
RELATED TO NO KNOWN
HUMAN POPULATIONS.

Farr leaned against the table and bent closer to the computer screen. "What is this, Deirdre?"

"It's a DNA sequence."

"I can see that. I mean where did you get it?"

Deirdre shook her head. "It doesn't matter. The sample is contaminated. The analysis is worthless."

"No, I don't think that's true. May I?"

She glanced up at him, puzzled by the soft intensity of his words, but before she could answer he took the computer and slid it toward him.

"You're connected to the main system in London, right?"

Farr opened a new session window and typed in his authorization. A menu Deirdre had never seen before appeared, its cryptic options beyond her understanding. Farr selected one, and a list of files appeared.

He clicked, and columns of short, alternating bars filled the screen. Another DNA sequence.

"There," Farr said. "Look."

He pointed to a portion of the sequence. Deirdre took the computer back. She resized the windows and positioned them side by side. One by one she compared rows. The pattern was identical.

"I don't understand." Her breath fogged against the screen. "Where did you get this sample?"

"I didn't get it. It's from a relic contained in the vaults beneath the London Charterhouse. In 1817, the Seekers acquired a crystal phial purported to contain the blood of St. Joan."

"St. Joan?"

"Yes, Joan of Arc—the girl who led the French to battle and who was burned at the stake as a heretic. According to the elderly Franciscan monk from whom the relic was obtained, the blood was collected by a faithful friar, taken from one of St. Joan's wounds while she was imprisoned, and preserved in the phial of crystal. It was several years ago that I obtained permission from the Philosophers to open the phial and have a sample of the blood sequenced. I was performing a study on genetic anomalies in individuals with extra-Earthly experiences."

"You're saying Joan of Arc had otherworldly connections?"

He shrugged. "She spoke to God, didn't she?"

Deirdre didn't know how to answer that. But if Farr was correct, then whatever St. Joan had possessed that set her apart from other humans Glinda possessed as well. As did, perhaps, her unborn child. Deirdre closed her eyes, picturing Glinda's lovely, fragile face.

No one knows how, but they've gotten themselves a pureblood. They don't need any of us now. . . .

But what did it mean? Who had Glinda been talking about? She opened her eyes and started to reach again for the computer, then froze, her eyes locked on the front page of the battered London *Times* Farr had thrown on the desk when he entered. A buzzing filled her ears.

"Where did you get this sample, Deirdre?" Farr said, his voice low, excited. "I had thought my analysis at an end years ago, but once again you've opened a door for me. We should dispatch a Seeker to keep watch on this Glinda subject immediately. Where can we find her?"

Deirdre licked her lips. "You won't find her."

"What do you mean?"

Deirdre hardly heard him. It was amazing how one could mourn the loss of something one had never really had. Once again she read the headline:

BRIXTON FIRE REMAINS A MYSTERY
Death Toll Reaches 13

She touched the paper, running her hand over a photo showing the burned-out shells of several storefronts. The destruction had been nearly complete. Newsprint smeared under her fingers like a haze of smoke.

A soft oath behind her. "I'm so sorry, Deirdre. It looks as though someone got there first."

Yes, someone. But who? Images flashed in Deirdre's mind: purple pills, a white lightning bolt, an empty bottle. With the discipline of spirit taught to her by her shaman grandfather, Deirdre acknowledged her sorrow, then set it aside to be lived fully later, when the time was appropriate. Now she kindled a fire from anger. It was time to take action.

She shut the lid of the computer and stood, then

turned to see Farr watching her with an expression that was both curious and—despite his drinking—utterly sober.

"Yes?" he said simply.

"How about we see what our good friends at Duratek Corporation are up to?"

He arched a single eyebrow. "Do you mean to tell me you know where they are holding the subject from AU-3?"

She grabbed her black-leather jacket from a chair and pulled it on. "Let's say I have a pretty good hunch. This morning I managed to follow one of their vehicles for a while. And unless they're opening their new corporate headquarters in an industrial building next door to the dog-food factory, I think we just might be on to something."

"And why didn't you tell me about this earlier?"

She zipped her jacket up and grinned: a feral, humorless expression. "You were on a plane, Farr. Remember?"

29.

Beltan of Calavan, bastard son of King Beldreas, knight errant, captain in the Order of Malachor, and onetime Knight Protector to Lady Melindora Nightsilver, was running.

He ran through an empty dominion, over flat, gray plains beneath a flat, gray sky. It was impossible to tell if it was night or day; the very air was gray, like everything else in this place, and there were no shadows. Nor was there sound, save for that of his own breath. Even his feet made no noise as they trod upon soft, colorless grass. He was naked.

Beltan did not know where he had run from, or where in this shadowless dominion he was running to. He only knew that he could not remain still; that if he ceased to move there would be nothing to prevent him from fading into the grayness all around until he was gone altogether.

Sometimes as he ran he recalled stories told to him as a child, spoken by grizzled warriors who sat in the warmth of the fire in Calavere's great hall, their fighting days long done—waiting now for the one final battle which they could only lose. Some were missing eyes, others fingers, arms, legs. They laughed and said that a lost limb went on ahead of a warrior and that it would be waiting for him when he got to Vathranan,

the great hall of the god Vathris Bullslayer that lay
beyond the marches of the world, so that the dead
might fight beside the living in the Final Battle. But
sometimes, in hoarse voices, they also spoke of
Sindanan, the Gray Land where cowards and traitors
went after death, and the hands of the old men shook
as they said these things, so that they spilled their beer
on the hot stones of the hearth where it hissed into
steam and vanished.

Perhaps this was the Gray Land the warriors had
spoken of. Perhaps Sindanan was also the place where
bastards who murdered their own fathers went when
they died.

With his left hand, Beltan gripped his side as he ran.
It seemed an instinctive motion. Hadn't there used to
be pain? He looked down, but there was no wound in
his flesh. Instead, the skin was smooth and pale,
without blemish. Yet there had been a gash there
before, he was sure of it, its ragged edges yawning open
and closed as he ran like a laughing mouth. How long
ago had he last seen it? He didn't know. Time had
faded like everything in this place.

When Beltan glimpsed the shadow some distance
ahead and to one side, he could not comprehend what
it was. He almost turned his face away and ran on.
There were no shadows in this land; there was
nothing. Only the love men held in their hearts for
cowards, traitors, and bastards: a cold, empty cup.

The shadow moved, raising long, gangling arms
above the small blot of its head.

For the first time he could remember, Beltan slowed
his pace, then came to a halt. Gray grass whispered
around him, stroking his bare shins, and a great
drowsiness fell over him. *Lie down*, the grass seemed to
whisper. *Let us grow over you, and in you, and we shall be*

you, and you us. Come, lie down.

His knees grew weak; he could feel them buckle.

The shadow gestured again; the motion seemed more urgent now. Then a queer thought struck Beltan, and his legs went rigid. Perhaps it was *his* shadow beckoning him. After all, he had yet to glimpse it in this land. But that didn't seem right. The shadow was hunched and crooked, its arms too long for its body, its head too small. Beltan looked down; his own body was lean, tall, and straight. He looked up again.

The shadow was gone.

A muted sensation of dread filled him. Since he had been in this place, Beltan had run in only one direction. Now, with great effort, he turned from his path and ran in the direction of the shadow.

It was impossible to tell if he was going the right way. Everything looked the same. Was he too far to the left? He considered turning, then thought better of it. Right—it was to the right he needed to go.

Had he altered in his course three steps sooner, he would never have found the door. Instead, as he turned, his left hand grazed against something hard and solid. He halted, then reached a hand out, searching through gray air, until at last his fingers found it: smooth, dense.

The door was the exact color of the air. Even right upon the thing, it was difficult to see against the grayness all around. He only knew it was a door by touch: frame, hinges, latch. It stood alone on the empty plain.

Beltan gripped the latch, then paused. What lay beyond the door? What if it was only the same colorless landscape on the other side? But the shadow was there no longer. It had to have passed through the door.

Still he hesitated. Was this not the place he belonged? He did not remember how he knew, only that he did. He had murdered his own father through deceit, stabbing him when his back was turned. What could there possibly be beyond the door for one such as he?

But there *was* something. He couldn't remember what it was, although it seemed there was a face, a voice, a name. A man. Yes, there was a man beyond the door, his eyes as gray as this land, but not empty, and not cold. The man was searching—searching for him.

Beltan let out a wordless cry. The sound rose as it issued forth from him, a great, bullish bellow, until it was like a wind that roared across the Gray Land. The grass bent down; the air trembled. He tore open the door, then flung himself through.

30.

At first Beltan thought he was still in the Gray Land. For a while he drifted; perhaps he had fallen down in the grass and was even then fading away. But the light around him was tinged scarlet, not gray, and there was sound: a rhythmic *whir*, as of the beating of great wings. Then shadows appeared against the light, and he knew he was no longer in Sindanan, but somewhere else.

Only after a time did he realize that the echoing sound he heard was a voice. One of the shadows was speaking.

". . . at this, Doctor. There's a three hundred percent increase in both the Alpha and Theta ranges compared to yesterday. And he's demonstrating significant rapid eye movement. He's entered a dream state."

The man's voice was oddly harsh, and the words it spoke were strange and guttural. Beltan felt he shouldn't have been able to understand the words, except somehow he did.

The shadows shifted, and another voice answered, a woman's, speaking the same hard, unlovely words as the first. "I'm not entirely surprised. Our tests have shown the effects of the alternate blood serum on the neurological system as well as the gross tissue level. And human physiology is not so very different than that of chimpanzees. He had entered a lighter coma stage as it was. I expected he would begin to wake up once the treatment was administered."

"Then do you think we should speak in front of him, Doctor? What if he can hear us?"

Laughter. A pretty sound, unlike the language. "Oh, he can hear us all right. He's close now, very close. But he won't be able to understand a word we're speaking. Which is unfortunate, as we so very much wish to talk with him."

"But the linguists will work with him. I've heard they already have a vocabulary of over three hundred words."

"Well, soon it will be much more than that."

The voices ceased then, and the shadows drifted away, leaving only the ruddy light. Beltan began to drift again, then jerked himself back.

No, you can't go back to the Gray Land. By Vathris, don't be such a piteous weakling, Beltan of Calavan. She said you're close. Close to what? To waking? But you are awake. So open your bloody eyes already. . . .

The effort the act required was staggering, more agonizing than any battle he had ever fought. With a moist, parting sound, his eyelids rolled open. Crimson light bled to white.

At first he could see nothing, and he wondered if he was blind. Then he realized he was staring upward into some kind of lamp. It was terribly bright, its light far more intense than any torch or oil lamp he had ever seen before. It was more like the magical lights he had sometimes witnessed Melia conjure, although this light was stabbing and harsh, with none of the shimmering beauty of enchantment.

He turned his head slightly—this act again a brutal war only barely won—and the light dimmed, receding to the corner of his vision. Gradually, his smarting eyes adjusted, and he found he could see.

Beltan lay in a white room. Walls, floor, ceiling: Everything was white. It was difficult to look at. Every surface was strange to him: sharp, smooth, and too bright for his eyes. He was forced to squint, and a feeling of nausea came over him. Everything was too square, too regular. It made him feel trapped.

He *was* trapped. Beltan tried to sit upright, but he could not. It was more than mere weakness. Something held him down, pressing him to the odd, angled bed in which he lay. He craned his neck, shut his eyes against a wave of dizziness, then opened them again.

He was naked, that much had been real. The bed beneath him was made of steel, and he was strapped to it with lengths of a shiny cloth he did not recognize. Either he was very weak, or the cloth was far stronger than it looked. Or perhaps both. His body was thin, his ribs showing plainly, the ends of his bones jutting beneath his skin. He looked like an old man.

Tubes sprang forth from the flesh of his arms like worms. The tubes were clear like glass, but obviously flexible in nature, so they could not be glass after all. The tubes coiled above him, leading to bladders that hung from a steel rack, and which contained various liquids, most clear, but one pale green, like emeralds in water.

He studied the bladders and thought he understood. The liquids dripped down the tubes and flowed into his veins. This was unlike the tube they had placed in his phallus, which was obviously intended to collect his piss. Beltan was not one to necessarily assume magic in things he did not understand, but it was hard not to wonder if he wasn't being held by some kind of wizard.

Being tied down to the steel bed made him think of dead knights he had helped to carry off countless battlefields, strapped to their shields. But he wasn't dead—although it seemed to him he should be. He glanced down at his left side. Shouldn't there have been a wound there?

A spasm passed through him, the memory of pain. Yes, he was beginning to remember. He had been in Spardis, in the baths, seeking to waylay Dakarreth. Only the Necromancer had been too powerful for him, had forced him down and dug impossibly strong fingers into his side, opening his old wound. Blood had poured forth like warm water on the tiles.

However, the wound was gone now; Beltan searched with his eyes, but he saw only a pale scar snaking across his skin. He felt a cool tingling dance across his flesh.

He wasn't entirely certain, but he thought he must have awakened again in the baths, but Dakarreth had no longer been there. Instead there had been others bending over him, only it was hard to remember who they were. One had leaned toward him. Beltan remembered laughing, then lifting his head up to press his lips against the other's. . . .

I just wanted to tell you that I'm not sorry after all.

I don't understand, Beltan. Not sorry for what?

For this.

He drew in a sharp breath. Travis. Travis Wilder had been there, and so had Lady Grace and the others. But where were they now? He had to find them, to tell them he was all right.

And what will you say to Travis when you face him, Beltan? He has not heard the call of the bull—he told you as much. The only reason you kissed him was because you thought you were dying, and you thought you would never have to explain the deed to him. Now here you are, alive. Even when you're dead you're a thick-skulled dimwit, Beltan of Calavan.

He would have to worry about finding a way to beg

Travis's forgiveness for his misdeed later. Right now he had to try to understand where he was and what was happening to him. He could yet end up dead.

A grunting noise reached Beltan's ears, rising above the sourceless *whir* that droned on the air. The sound came again, along with a metallic rattling. With effort, he turned his head to the right.

It took his numb mind a long moment to understand what he was looking at. Bright metal wires wove back and forth over the frame of a large box raised several feet off the floor. Only when he saw the shadow moving inside did he understand it was a cage.

The thing inside crept to the edge and slipped long, dark, wrinkled fingers through the holes in the wire. The creature was large—nearly as large as a man. It was shaped like a man as well, but oddly distorted. The creature was short-legged and barrel-chested; its head was small and its face jutting. Black, wispy hair covered the creature's naked body.

Sour dread spilled into Beltan's empty stomach. Was the thing in the cage a *feydrim*? In some ways it reminded him of the gray, twisted beasts he had fought off at the Rune Gate last Midwinter's Eve. But the *feydrim* had been fanged and feral, monsters created by the foul magic of the Pale King. Instead, this creature gazed at him with brown eyes that seemed somehow sad and even knowing.

The creature in the cage spread its long, gangly arms. Beltan sucked in a sharp breath. Yes, he knew that gesture. It was the same one the shadow had made to him in the Gray Land, the shadow that had led him to the door. It was a gesture of welcome.

The animal watched Beltan, waiting. What did it want of him? It was difficult because of his immobility, but Beltan managed to nod toward the creature.

"Hello," he said, almost surprised he was able to make a sound, although it was as rasping as the call of a vulture.

The thing stood up in the cage. There were two slots at the top, places where food could be dropped into the cage. The animal threaded its curled hands through the slots and stretched its long arms outward. The undersides had been shaved of hair. It was easy to see the white, convoluted scars traveling up and down the creature's arms.

It seemed the thing was trying to tell him something, as it had in the dream. But what? Then he looked down at his own body and saw the scars left by a score of different wounds he had received in his years as a knight.

He looked back up into sorrowful, intelligent eyes. So manlike this thing, but not a man. And not a monster, either. He remembered the strange words the voices had spoken above him, thinking him asleep.

Our tests have shown the effects . . . not so very different than that of chimpanzees. . . .

Beltan studied the scars on the creature's outstretched arms. Some of the wounds were still fresh, their edges sewn together with black thread. Yes, certainly they had done their experiments on this creature, this *chin-pasi*, as they called it. Beltan struggled against his restraints, but to no effect. Would they be performing experiments on him as well?

The *chin-pasi* drew its arms back into the cage and sat down. It no longer looked at Beltan. Instead it seemed to stare at one of the walls. Beltan followed its gaze.

The wall was covered with paintings of bones.

He frowned, studying the paintings. The bones seemed to glow against their dark backgrounds, and only after a moment did he realize it was one of the bright white lamps, set into the wall, shining through the paintings.

Beltan had seen enough bones in his life to recognize many of the images. In the middle of the wall was a thighbone, then a hipbone, hands, ribs, and a skull. They looked to be the bones of a tall man.

A shiver crept along Beltan's naked skin. He looked down at his left hand, strapped next to him. The last joint of the littlest finger was crooked, broken and never reset when he was twelve winters old. He looked back up at the glowing image of the skeleton hand. The littlest finger was also crooked, bent at the last joint.

The bones in the paintings were his own bones. But how could one paint a man's bones, down to the smallest detail, when they were still in his body? He could see faint outlines around the bones, like the hazy ghosts of flesh. Again, he disliked assuming magic was at work, but it was difficult to see how else these images could have been made. Perhaps if Melia were there, she would have been able to explain it to him.

Or not Melia, but Lady Grace. Except he wasn't quite certain why he thought this. Only that, for some reason, he felt Grace would understand.

His eyes moved farther along the wall. More bone paintings, glowing like the first, showing hands, skulls, hips. But these bones were shaped differently than his own. One of the skulls was low, its snout protruding, and the hands below it were long and curled. Surely those bones belonged to the *chin-pasi* in the cage. It still stared at the wall. Was the thing clever enough to recognize its own bones as Beltan had?

His eyes moved to the last set of bone-paintings. Again, a chill swaddled him. One painting showed a skull that was high, delicate, and pointed, like the shell of an egg. The eye sockets were huge and tilted, the jaw tiny. Was it a child's skull? But it was far too large. Beneath the skull was the image of a hand. The finger bones were long, even longer than the *chin-pasi*'s, straight, and terribly slender, like the twigs of a willow. Beltan did not know what creature these bones belonged to, but one thing was certain: It was neither man nor *chin-pasi*.

A metallic *chunk* echoed on the cold air. Beltan turned his head in time to see a steel door open. A figure stepped through: small, slender. A woman. She wore some kind of breeches, like a man, and a thin white coat. Perched on her nose were a pair of spectacles like the ones Travis wore, only these had black frames instead of wire.

"Well, you're awake," she said with a smile.

He recognized her voice. She was one of the two shadows who had spoken over him earlier, the one called *doctor*. Hadn't Lady Grace once used the word to describe herself? But that had been a word from her world. . . .

Beltan stiffened. The doctor hurried to the side of his bed. She laid a hand on his brow; it was cold. "No, don't worry. There's no cause for alarm. We won't harm you, we only want to learn about you, that's all." She sighed. "But why am I bothering to tell you that? You can't understand me."

But he *could* understand her. And if they did not mean to harm him, why was he strapped down like a prisoner? He swallowed. It was hard to force the words out, but he did, one by one.

"Let . . . me . . . go."

Beltan knew there was something strange about the words even as he uttered them. They sounded harsh and guttural, just as her words had, and not only because of his dry throat.

The woman stumbled back from the bed, mouth open, eyes wide, and reached up to keep her spectacles from tumbling off her nose. Yes, she had understood him. He strained against his bonds; the shiny material creaked. So there was some muscle left in him yet. He spoke again through clenched teeth.

"I said . . . let me go."

Fear blossomed on the woman's face. She scrambled for a device clipped to her belt, pulled it off, and held it to her mouth. "I need security in Lab Four. Repeat, security in Lab Four. Now!"

Beltan knew what those words meant. Guards were coming. He pulled against the restraints, feeling a strength he knew he should by no right possess. Now his entire body tingled, as if he had rolled in snow. Across the room, the *chin-pasi* let out a screeching sound and beat against the walls of its cage.

The woman grabbed something from a shelf and stripped paper off of it: a kind of tube with a needle on the end. Using both hands to control her shaking, she slipped the needle into one of the tubes that led into Beltan's arm.

Instantly the world grew hazy and dull. Once before a woman had stolen his manhood with a poison spell. Lady Kyrene. Not again.

"What have . . . you done to me . . . witch?"

His words were barely a whisper. She lowered the needle and stepped back, watching him, but he glimpsed all this as through a veil. The screaming of the *chin-pasi* faded away.

Help me, Travis.

But he knew he didn't manage to speak these words aloud. Instead the world went not gray but black and, after that, Beltan knew no more.

31.

After their conversation with Deirdre Falling Hawk and Hadrian Farr at the museum, Grace and Travis kept to their musty, dilapidated room at the Blue Sky Motel, curtains drawn, waiting for the Seekers to contact them. However, by the third day, Grace was ready to break down the door and bolt, no matter if a whole army of Duratek agents was waiting with chains and shackles on the other side.

"There's nothing on TV," Travis said in a voice that encroached dangerously on a whine.

They had convinced the manager to replace their TV with one that worked—albeit nominally, and only so long as green was one's favorite color since that was the only one it displayed.

Grace didn't look up from her book of crossword puzzles. They had had this same conversation on pretty much an hourly basis. "Change to a different channel."

"You know perfectly well there isn't a different channel. This is the only one we get."

"Then get a mirror and watch this one backwards."

This won a snort. "You know, that might be an improvement. Have you seen this guy? His name is Sage Carson. He's supposed to be some sort of televangelist, but I think he's really a robot. His hair looks like a vinyl replica of the state of Kentucky."

"What's wrong with Kentucky?"

"Nothing. Except when it's on your head."

Grace clutched the pen in her hand. She cared for Travis a great deal, had even risked her own life to save him, but she was going to kill him very soon. However, she would make it quick and painless. Nothing said love like a swift jab to the medulla oblongata.

Travis turned off the TV, flopped onto the other bed, and stared at Grace. "I thought you hated crossword puzzles."

"I do. They're a complete waste of time."

"So would you care to explain why you're doing an entire book of them?"

"Because right now wasting time is exactly what we're supposed to be doing."

He grunted at that, then leaned on an elbow and picked at a battered cardboard box of donuts. "You know, we're not prisoners. We can leave here if we want."

"Sure. And we'll just tell our bulky friends outside the motel that we're stepping out to buy them each a neck, since as far as I can tell neither of them seems to possess one."

As promised, Farr had stationed a pair of operatives to keep watch on their room. Grace pegged them as former football players or professional wrestlers. Their expensive Italian suits strained across their shoulders, and both of them looked as if they could crush subcompact cars with their bare hands. Neither of them seemed anatomically capable of smiling.

Every few hours one of them—either Stewart or Erics, who could only be told apart because Stewart was gigantic while Erics was merely huge—knocked on the room's door to verify that everything was all right. Grace had tried to engage them in conversation a few times, but to no avail. Evidently language skills had not been part of the job description when the Seekers hired them. A few times a day they brought food and beverages. However, Travis had made the mistake of saying they liked King Donut, and so at least twice a day that was what they got.

Holding a donut in his mouth, Travis moved to the window and peered out a narrow gap between plaid curtains. He bit off half the donut, swallowed. "They may be big, but I bet they're slow. I say we can outrun them."

"And then what?"

"I don't know." Travis ran a hand over his freshly shaved head. "Aren't you getting tired of waiting here? We could just find Beltan ourselves."

Grace looked up at him, and he winced.

"You know, I think that evil eye of yours actually works."

"I *am* a witch. Then again, what you're feeling might have something to do with the fact that that's your fourth donut in the last half hour."

He slumped against the wall and tossed the donut into the waste-basket. "I know, Grace. I know we can't go out. It's just that he . . . I mean, they could be doing anything to him."

Grace set down the crossword puzzle book. It was more than mere boredom eating at him, at both of them. "I'm worried about him, too, Travis. No, not worried—terrified. But the Seekers have resources far beyond our means. And as long as Duratek is looking for us, and as long as the police are looking for me, it's not safe to go out there."

"Maybe it's not safe for us to look for him, Grace." He turned his gray eyes on her—that unsettling seriousness again. "But what if it's *right*? Both of us have . . . abilities that the Seekers don't."

Grace hugged her knees to her chest. It was true. They both had learned so much since they had last set foot on Earth. But this wasn't Eldh, and while there were still a few shreds of magic left on this world, as far as Grace could tell they were exactly that: a thin, polluted trickle that had once been a great, primeval river. Magic was not going to help them, not here.

"I'm going to get some ice," she said, grabbing a cracked plastic bucket from the nightstand. "We could both use a drink."

Travis nodded. "I'll get the bottle."

Grace stepped onto the second-floor walkway, and the door of dented, orange-painted steel closed behind her with a heavy *chunk*. No wonder fugitives always picked motels to hide in. Metal doors.

The day had surrendered. Thick, purple air settled over the cars in the parking lot below. Above, fluorescent lights flickered spastically, filling the air with a sick light and a humming drone. A few late, lazy flies spiraled toward the glow. Somewhere out of sight children laughed, splashing in chlorine-rich water, while a woman called out in the wordless, angry, universal tongue of mothers. Motel twilight.

Bucket in hand, Grace moved along the walkway. At once she felt attention upon her, and she didn't need to look back to know one of the Seeker operatives watched her through the tinted glass of the black sedan in the parking lot. Stewart—he usually staked out the front of the motel. Right then he was probably soiling his expensive, too-tight Armani suit and talking hotly on the radio to Erics stationed on the other side of the motel. Grace knew she wasn't supposed to leave the room. But she was only going to the ice machine. Besides, the boys needed a little excitement once in a while.

She rounded a corner and found the ice machine lurking in a dim alcove, gurgling and rattling like an old man in a rusted iron lung. Grace positioned the bucket and pushed the lever. After several minutes and an inordinate amount of raucous groaning, the bucket had collected exactly six milky ice cubes. Good enough. Gripping the bucket to her chest, Grace headed back along the walkway.

The sounds of splashing had ceased. The pool was closed, the mother victorious, the children dragged back inside, roughly toweled, set down on vibrating beds to eat hamburgers from a paper bag and watch TV. Traffic whirred beyond the motel's overgrown privacy fence, and a crescent moon glowed like a half-shut eye.

Grace turned the corner, and the back of her neck prickled: the sensation of being watched again. She glanced down at the parking lot—

—and her forehead tightened in a frown. It was nearly dark now, but in the light drizzled by a single streetlamp she could see that the door of the black sedan hung open. So Stewart hadn't been content to just sit and watch her. An indignation rose within her. Didn't they know what she had been through, what she had survived? Who were they to watch her like this?

By force of will, her anger cooled. *They're just doing their jobs, Grace. Why don't you make it a little easier for them by getting back to your room?*

Cinder-block walls and painted doors slipped by.

She was nearly there when she heard it: a low, snuffling-grunting sound. It reminded her of a dog, its nose stuck in something ripe. The sound emanated from the mouth of a dim passage that cut through this block of rooms, leading to a set of stairs on the back side of the motel. She paused before the opening, peered inside.

The first thing she saw were the shoes, toes up, their polished leather outlines glowing in the green light of an EXIT sign. They were large shoes, expensive-looking. She cocked her head, trying to understand what it was she was seeing. Then the fluorescent bulb overhead let out a staccato burst of light, and in the momentary strobe Grace saw everything.

The Seeker operative—Stewart, given his size—lay on his back, big hands splayed against the cement. A pool of blood slowly crept outward, and something spindly and hairy crouched over him, eating loudly out of the wet pit where his face had been.

A foul scent washed over Grace, metallic but sweet. The ice bucket slipped from numb fingers and clattered to the walkway. One cube slid toward the creature, coming to a rest next to its long foot. It let out a snort and looked up, its short, wrinkled muzzle dripping. Bits of tissue flecked the matted black hair that covered its torso. For a moment Grace gazed into pale eyes that were far too large for the low, pointed head into which they were set. Then the thing blinked—a dull expression, sated—and bent back over its prey, cradling the dead man's head in long, curving arms as it feasted.

32.

Doors blurred past Grace with horrible slowness as she ran—three, four, five. Her fingers fumbled against the knob, then she was inside. She pulled the door shut, scrabbled like an animal for the dead bolt, slid it into place, then stumbled back. The edge of the bed caught her behind the knees, and she fell onto it.

Travis stepped from the bathroom, two chipped glasses in his hands, each filled halfway with scotch. "Did you get the ice?"

She looked up at him, licked her lips. "I think we're in trouble."

He stared at her. Then he set down the glasses, moved to the window, peered out.

"What's going on?"

"I don't know." Her hands twisted the cigarette-burned bedspread into knots. "There's something out there. A thing. It's . . . it's eating Stewart."

He turned around, the blood draining from his face. "Did you say *eating* him?"

Grace gave a stiff nod.

"Shit, that's bad."

That was an understatement on any world. He moved to the bed, sat, and put his arm around her. It was stronger than she would have guessed, harder.

"What is it, Grace? What's out there?"

It was difficult to breathe. She forced herself to fill her lungs slowly, knowing she was hyperventilating. Adrenaline buzzed in her brain, screaming at her in an ancient, wordless tongue to flee. But there was nowhere to go. *Be a scientist, Grace. Don't feel—just describe.*

"I don't know what it was. It was big, almost as big as me. Thin, elongated limbs, and fur. No, not fur— hair. Long, black hair on its body."

"Was it a *feydrim*?"

Grace thought of the gray, spindly creature that had once attacked her in her chamber in Calavere. In a way, there was a similarity between the *feydrim* and this creature. Both appeared twisted, malformed. But this thing was different. Stronger, more brutish. And its eyes: tilted, clever.

"No, it wasn't a *feydrim*. It was . . . something else. Simian in a way. What do we do?"

"The radio. Get the radio."

Grace grabbed the slim walkie-talkie off the nightstand. She pressed a button, held the unit to her ear. "Erics," she hissed. "Erics, can you hear me?" Static popped and crackled. "Erics, come in. We need you." Still no answer. Grace threw down the radio. "Where the hell is he?"

"There," Travis said.

He was peering through the gap in the curtains again. Grace hurried next to him.

"Look," Travis said. "Down in the parking lot."

It took her eyes a long moment to find what he was seeing: a bulky, broad-shouldered form stood beside Stewart's black sedan. Then the form looked up, and she saw his face in a stray beam from the streetlamp. Erics. His head moved from side to side. He was searching—for Stewart, no doubt.

Up here, Grace wanted to scream. She started to push aside the curtain, to wave frantically to him.

She halted in mid-action. From the darkness beyond the streetlamp, shadows appeared. There were two of them this time. They hunched low to the asphalt, using both arms and legs to propel themselves forward in a swift lope. Erics saw them, reached inside his suit coat, drew out a gun.

He was too slow. The first of the creatures struck him, and the gun flew from his hand. Erics was a large and phenomenally strong man; the thing threw him backward into the open door of the car like a small child. It clambered in after him. The second creature followed. Grace couldn't see through the tinted windows, but she knew what was happening all the same. For a moment Erics's flailing legs stuck out of the car door, then they were drawn inside. The car rocked violently.

Grace felt sour vomit rise in her throat. The car grew still. The struggle was over; they were feeding.

"The Seekers," she said. "We've got to call the Seekers."

Travis was already reaching for the phone. He cradled the receiver next to his ear and started to dial. Then, quietly, he put the phone back down.

"It's dead."

So, there would be no calling the Seekers. And the radios were short-range only, designed to reach the receivers in Stewart's and Erics's cars. They were on their own.

But who had cut the phone lines to the hotel? The creatures out there seemed clever, yes, but in a hungry, animal sort of way. Were they intelligent enough to know the threat of phones, to open a metal box, to pull the right wires? Somehow she doubted it.

"I think they have help," she said. "I think whoever sent them is here as well."

Travis nodded. "Maybe they—"

Both ceased motion, speech. It was faint but audible: the slap of long, naked feet against cement. The sound stopped. Then came a low *whuffling*. It was outside their door.

The curtain. It was parted an inch, and the lamp on the nightstand was on. Grace wanted to reach for the curtain, to jerk it shut, but Travis held her with frightened eyes. The *whuffling* grew louder. There was a wet snort—

—then the footpads again, moving away, until at last they were gone.

Grace forced her lungs to expel air. It didn't know which room they were hiding in.

"We have to get out of here," Travis said. "It's only a matter of time until they figure out which room we're in."

Grace wanted to disagree but couldn't. Whatever those things were, they would keep searching until they found what they had come for. She pictured the way the creatures had dragged Erics into the car. A door would pose no barrier to them. But out there, she and Travis would be exposed. In the dark, their human eyes would be no match for the large, pale orbs of the creatures.

Travis swore. "I just wish we knew how many of them are out there."

But there was a way. Before she could lose what remained of her nerve, Grace shut her eyes. She tensed, then reached out with the Touch.

Instantly it was there: the shadow. Memories clawed at her, demanding that she relive them again and again. Owls flew through the darkness, their cries melding with sounds of despair. White hands reached from the gloom, and the old fear flooded her. But there was a new danger, one more present—if not less potent. She let the memory of flames come, as it always did in the end, let it burn the visions of the orphanage away. Then the shadow was behind her—not gone; it would never be gone—but she could see beyond it.

The Weirding was weak here, so woefully forlorn and weak. She had only a moment, no more, to grasp the threads, then it all fell apart in her hands.

It was enough. Grace's eyes flew open.

"They're everywhere. All around the motel. I can feel them . . . like wounds in the night."

But there was more. She had felt something else. Another presence. *Or was it presences, Grace?* They were different than the dark blots she knew to be the creatures, gleaming gold, but she had only glimpsed them—it?—fleetingly, if at all. She tried to reach the Weirding again, but it was no use. The shadow blocked her way now, it would not be brushed aside so easily this time.

Travis's voice was ragged, the hope draining from his face. "How many, Grace?"

"I can't be sure. I was only able to touch the Weirding for a moment. But I'd say five, six. Maybe more."

He nodded, the set of his jaw grim. She knew the conclusion he had made; she had reached it herself. That time in her room in Calavere, working together, she and Travis had just barely managed to kill a single *feydrim*. What hope did they have against a half dozen creatures that were as strong and as bloodthirsty?

Grace raised a hand. "Travis, what about your—"

"It's no use, Grace. Not here." He crossed his arms

over his black T-shirt. "I think this world has forgotten the meaning of runes."

Silence. Shouldn't there have been the sounds of voices coming through the thin walls, the noise of cars in the parking lot? Travis paced to the window.

"It's so still. I don't see anything moving out there."

"Maybe they've left," Grace said. "Maybe this is our chance, before they come back."

In a minute they were ready. Travis dug his stiletto from a drawer and gripped it in his right hand. Grace drew her own knife out of the sheath in her boot; the blade seemed pitifully small, but she would take it over nothing. She tightened her damp fingers around the hilt. Their plan was simple; it was all their fevered brains could come up with. Make it to the parking lot and get Erics's gun. If they made it that far, they could recalculate. They pressed themselves against the door, listening. Nothing. Travis reached for the knob, started to turn it.

Crimson light welled forth, staining the air like blood. Grace stared.

"Your knife, Travis. It's glowing."

The red gem set into the hilt of his dagger shone with a fiery, pulsing light. He opened his mouth to speak.

Whatever words he uttered were drowned out by the sound of shattering glass as the room's window exploded inward. The thing hurtled inside, a coiled ball of fury. It landed on the nearest bed, turned, and unfurled itself. Large, colorless eyes blinked once, then focused. It ducked its pointed head, almost as if bowing to them, then its mouth yawned open, baring teeth as jagged as the broken glass still tumbling to the carpet. Talons extended from curved fingers and toes, shredding the mattress.

Grace pressed against the warmth beside her. "Travis . . ."

He started to lift his stiletto, but there was no point. With a shrill, eerily human shriek, the creature stretched out its arms and sprang.

The air in front of Grace blurred, folded. Something gold flashed, and the creature's trajectory abruptly changed. It flew sideways, long arms flailing wildly, then screamed as it struck the wall. The creature's body broke cheap paneling and splintered wood as it hurtled into the adjacent room.

Air rippled like water, and a woman stood in what had been empty space a half second before. She was tall and golden-eyed. Her hair was dark, close-cropped, and her sinuous body was covered in sleek black leather.

Before either Grace or Travis could speak, the woman lifted her arms, ready. The creature roared through the gap in the wall, back into the room. Large splinters of wood protruded from its flesh, and blood matted its fur. However, the thing seemed not to notice. Shrieking, it lunged for the woman.

Long arms closed on thin air. She was gone.

No, not gone.

The creature jerked its snout around. The woman in black stood behind it now. A smile slashed across her fierce, beautiful face, and a spiked boot kicked out, contacting the thing's face.

A wet, crunching sound. Grace knew the sound of shattering bones when she heard it.

Silent this time, the creature sailed back through the open window. Then there came the wet thud of something striking the pavement below.

Once again the air blurred, and now the woman stood before Travis and Grace, regarding them with solemn gold eyes.

How the hell did you do that? Grace wanted to say. But it was Travis who spoke first.

"You." His voice was barely a croak. "I've seen you before, watching me. Who are you?"

The woman rested her hands against her hips. She wasn't even sweating.

"I'm your only hope," she said.

33

"Now what?"

Grace peered past the shredded remains of the curtain, into the night outside. Chill autumn air poured through the broken window, but Travis hardly felt it. He was already numb as he gazed at the woman who stood in the center of the room, legs apart, stance ready. She was sharply beautiful, her gold eyes set above proud, coppery cheekbones. But it was not her beauty that held Travis's gaze. She carried no gun, no knife. All the same, she was deadly. And she had been following him.

"You cannot stay here," the woman said. "The others will have heard the sound of battle, and the scent of blood will lead them. You must follow me." Her English was perfect, yet richly stilted, as if studied too well and practiced too carefully.

Grace turned from the window. "Why should we follow you?" Her tone was not accusing. She was simply a scientist, looking for facts on which to base a conclusion.

The woman knelt, touched a pool of blood soaking into the shag carpet, and stood again, her hand now wet and red.

"Because if you stay here, in five minutes this is all that will remain of you."

Grace nodded and said nothing. The woman moved for the door, her motions sleek, prowling.

"No." Travis was surprised at the metal in his voice. "That's not good enough. How are we supposed to trust you? You've been following me for days, spying on me, and now you just pop into view like some black-leather Barbara Eden and expect us to follow. We don't even know who you are."

"My name is Vani. Now you know." Then the door opened, and she was gone into the night.

Grace started after her.

"What do you think you're doing?" Travis said.

She met his gaze, her expression hard. "Trying my damnedest to stay alive."

Grace stepped out the door. Travis glanced at the stiletto still clutched in his hand. The gem in the hilt was dimmer than before, but a faint, bloody light still shone deep in its heart. He swore softly, then followed the others outside.

He saw Grace standing not far away, at the head of the staircase that led down to the parking lot. Someone had switched off the fluorescent lights above the walkway, and the motel was silent, except for—somewhere—the muffled barking of a dog. There was no sign of Vani.

"Where is she?" he whispered.

Grace gazed into the gloom. "I don't know. She was here a second ago, and then . . ."

Great. She had led them into danger, exposed them, then ditched them. Maybe saving them back in the room had all been part of her plot to get them out here.

"You know, I really don't think I—"

—*like her much*, Travis was going to say. Instead, his words ended in a hiss as the air beside him undulated. She stepped from between two folds of shadow, her garb blending seamlessly with the night.

"Where were you?" he demanded. "And how did you—?"

She held up a hand, silencing him with a sharp motion. "You must not question me, Travis Wilder. There is no time for it. These stairs are not safe. This way." She moved along the second-floor walkway.

Travis frowned at Grace. "Congenial, isn't she?"

"I wouldn't put it exactly like that." A grin cut across Grace's visage, thin but wry in the cast-off cityglow. "Then again, nice girls don't kick hairy mutant ass like she does. I'm sticking with her."

Travis couldn't argue with that logic. He reached out, found Grace's hand, and her fingers curled around his. Together they moved along the walkway, following the half-blurred shadow they knew to be Vani.

They caught up with her in the dim breezeway that cut from the front to the back of the motel. Something lumpy lay on the floor, half-blocking the passage. Only as Vani stepped lightly over the thing did he realize it was a man. His face was completely gone, but Travis recognized the blond crew cut, the big hands. Stewart.

He swore softly, too stunned to be sick. Grace tugged his hand. Together they edged around the corpse, trying not to slip in the slowly congealing blood.

They halted at the head of another staircase. It led down to a narrow parking area behind the motel, lit only by secondhand neon from the twenty-four-hour restaurant on the other side of the back fence. Vani halted, gazing with eyes that seemed to glow faintly in the darkness.

"What are we doing?" Travis croaked.

"We will move swiftly toward your Seeker's

vehicle. There, near the fence, do you see it? You must remain close to me at all moments."

"Do you know the Seekers then?" Grace asked.

"I have watched them, yes."

"And do they know about you?"

"I should think not."

Again Travis frowned, studying their strange savior. She was a haughty one, that was certain. But if she was not a friend of the Seekers, then who was she allied with? Duratek?

No—he couldn't say why, but he knew that wasn't the case. She was perilous, yes. And she wasn't telling them the whole truth. But she had said she was their only hope, and right now Travis believed it. He wished he could pull out his gunfighter's spectacles and look at her. Sometimes with the spectacles on, if he squinted just right, he could see coronas of light around people: auras that reflected who and what they were.

There was no time. Vani had already started down the stairs. Keeping close, he and Grace descended.

They reached the parking lot; the night was still. Travis felt a frantic impulse to scream, swallowed it. He would almost have preferred it if the things just showed themselves. It was better to see death coming than to wait for it to leap out of the darkness, invisible and snarling.

Grace gasped, her eyes fluttering open. Travis had not seen her shut them.

"There are five of them," she whispered. "They're all around us, moving fast. I can't get a fix on them. And there's . . . something else. I couldn't quite see it, but I felt it. A presence. Watching."

Vani nodded. "I feel the other as well. That is why they are not so easily frightened—their master is here. This will not be as simple as I thought."

Travis groaned. "So what do you propose we do?"

Vani turned toward him, then her face went hard. "Run. Run for the vehicle as fast as you can and get inside. Now!"

With that last word she pushed Travis and Grace. They stumbled in the direction of the car—

—just as a black streak screamed out of the night.

Travis felt hot talons graze the back of his neck. Then Vani was there, moving so swiftly her arms and legs seemed to blur. Blows rained on the creature; black spheres of blood spun and glittered on the air. Shrieking, the thing reached out, but Vani was gone. Then the air behind it warped, buckled. Vani leaped off the asphalt as easily as if climbing a staircase and kicked out with both boots. The creature flew forward, limbs flailing, into a wall. Cinder blocks cracked. The thing crumpled to the ground, motionless.

"Travis!"

The scream pierced the dull membrane shrouding his brain. Grace pulled his arm. He gripped her hand, and they careened across the parking lot toward the car.

The darkness boiled around them, but Travis kept his eyes focused on the car. From the corner of his vision he saw a snarling maw lunge toward Grace, fangs gleaming, then it jerked back and fell behind, as if it had struck an obsidian wall.

Time slowed, the parking lot stretched, Erics's car receded. Each footfall was like slow thunder. A paw shot from the side and clutched at Travis's throat, squeezing. Then the night tore apart, and a pair of strong hands reached from the gap, pulling the creature back into darkness. Snarls turned to inhuman screams, then ended with the sound of breaking bones.

Time dilated, snapped back. In one dizzying rush the car grew to fill Travis's vision. They had made it. He started to reach for the door handle.

The air above the car wrinkled like cellophane, then grew smooth again. With a fluttering of jet cloth, a figure landed lightly on top of the car. Travis gazed up into a serene, gold face.

The figure crouched, wrapped all in black—trench coat, gloves, cowl. Set into the cowl was not a human face, but a mask: gleaming and burnished as the death mask of a pharaoh, smiling with strange peace as it gazed upon what no other could possibly see. The figure lifted a gloved hand and made a gentle, caressing motion.

A gold needle of agony plunged into Travis. His heart shuddered in his chest, faltered. He tried to speak, but only a soft gurgle escaped his lips along with a foam of saliva. The figure squeezed its fingers together. As it did, Travis's heart slowed. . . .

Grace lashed out with her dagger. The figure moved its hand aside, easily avoiding the strike. However, the movement interrupted the spell. Travis was free. In one motion he reached for his own knife, jerked it from his belt, and thrust it forward.

His action was stiff, clumsy; the other should have dodged the blow without effort. Instead, it was as if flesh and blade were drawn to one another. There was a blinding flash of crimson, followed by a mind-flaying scream. Travis shut his eyes, blinded. When he opened them again, the masked figure was gone.

He jerked his head to look at Grace. Her eyes were wide.

"Where . . . ?" she started to say, but then the air melted, resolidified, and Vani was there.

"Get inside. Now."

They did not argue. Travis ripped open the door. He and Grace fell into the backseat; she groped for the door and slammed it shut behind them. Vani was already in the front seat. Engine roared, tires wailed against pavement, and the car leaped into swift motion.

There was a wet thump as the vehicle struck something. A shadow spun past the tinted windows. The car made a violent turn, throwing Travis against Grace. By the time they managed to untangle their limbs and sit upright, streetlights and glowing signs flashed by. They were driving west down Colfax, the motel already a dim spark of neon behind them. Vani piloted the car with precise movements that nonetheless seemed too conscious.

She's a good driver, but she has to think about it. She can't have been driving very long.

"The one in the mask," Grace said, clutching the back of the passenger seat. "Who was that man?"

The rearview mirror framed Vani's unsettling gold eyes.

"Not man. Sorcerer. It was he whom you sensed earlier, Grace Beckett. He was the master of the *gorleths.*" She spoke this last word like a curse.

"Gorleths?" Travis said in a croak. His throat ached, and his heart fluttered in his chest.

Vani did not take her eyes from the street. "It means, the Mouths Which Hunger. His kind often create such slaves to do their bidding, although I have not seen the likes of these before. They are new, I think. And had I known he was present, and not just his minions, I might have thought again about what I was doing. However, the sorcerer did not like the sting of your knife, Travis Wilder. It is well you had it."

On reflex, he glanced down at the stiletto. To his surprise, the gem in the hilt still flickered red. Motion caught his eye: a glint of gold. It scuttled across the back of the passenger seat, toward Grace's arm. A spider of gold. Fascinated, he watched as it wriggled closer. . . .

The car did not veer even slightly as Vani lashed out a hand and crushed the spider. She flicked the crumpled bit of gold out the open window.

Grace blinked, her expression startled. "What was that?"

"Death," Vani said.

Travis glanced again at his stiletto; the gem in the hilt was dark, quiescent. The danger had passed. For the moment, at least.

Sirens cried out. Flashing lights approached, then whizzed past them. So the police were finally coming. However, Travis didn't need Vani to tell him that no matter how hard the officers searched, they would find no sign of the *gorleths* or the one in the gold mask.

"Where are you taking us?" Grace said, her face frightened, yet resolute.

"Somewhere you will be safe."

"And then?"

"We must free your companion, the knight. They cannot be allowed to hold him."

Next to Travis, Grace went stiff. He felt his heart lurch again, but this time it was beating too swiftly.

"Beltan?" Grace whispered. "You know where Beltan is?"

"I do."

Travis studied her reflection in the rearview mirror. In a way, her eyes were as gold and serene as the sorcerer's mask. But there was a life to them the mask had not held. He drew a deep breath.

"You're from Eldh, aren't you, Vani?"

Travis did not take his eyes off Vani's in the mirror. At last she nodded.

"Why have you been following me? And why did you help us tonight?"

For a moment it seemed sorrow crept into the reflection of her eyes. Then the glare of passing headlights blinded Travis, and by the time his vision cleared she had turned the mirror so that all he could see was darkness.

"Because," Vani said softly, "it is my fate to return with you to Eldh."

PART THREE:
TANGLED WEBS

34.

Lirith stood at the prow of the *Fate Runner* and watched a hundred domes of gold rise into the shimmering air, growing larger with each splash of spray against her cheeks.

The sea was a silver plate, beaten and dimpled by the relentless hammer of the sun. Chalky cliffs soared toward the lapis sky, their summits crowned with precisely spaced colonnades of slender *ithaya* trees that transmuted the brilliant light through yellow leaves. The wind was steady off the Summer Sea, and the sleek, two-masted ship that had borne them from the Free City of Gendarra streaked like a dolphin past towering twin obelisks hewn of the same white stones as the cliffs, into the encircling arms of an azure bay and toward the oldest city in all of Falengarth.

"There she is," said a voice as rough as a gull's behind her.

She turned from the railing, then smiled, the wind unfurling her hair behind her like sails. "Captain Magard."

The captain of the *Fate Runner* was not an old man—certainly he was no more than ten years Lirith's senior—but life on the sea had taken its toll. His powerful shoulders were hunched from years of gripping the tiller, and his coarse hands bore something less than the usual complement of fingers. However, Magard's billowing red shirt and trousers were every bit as bold as the stories he had a habit of telling.

Lirith turned again to face the swiftly growing city. Birds drifted among the domes like flecks of white down. She could see that Tarras rose up in a series of concentric circles, each walled in buff stone, to a cluster of fabulous spires at the summit.

Magard laughed, as it seemed he did at everything, and gestured to the massive obelisks even now slipping past them to either side. "No matter how many times I sail into Meron's Gate, I never tire of this sight."

Lirith agreed. She had never seen anything like them in her life. The obelisks stood upon the ends of two rocky prominences that reached from the shore, encircling the bay of Tarras. They were surely twice as high as the tallest towers in the Dominions, yet as slender as needles, their pale stone carved with words and symbols softened by vast centuries of salt and wind. There was space enough for a score of ships to sail through Meron's Gate without any risk of collision, and the obelisks seemed to hold up the sky.

"Meron was the son of Taron, First Emperor of Tarras," Magard said. "The stories say he raised the obelisks as a monument to his father's victories. At least, that's what the official stories say."

Lirith arched an eyebrow. "And what of the unofficial stories, Captain?"

"They say Meron raised the obelisks not to his father's conquests in battle, but rather to his own conquests in the bedroom. From what we know of Meron, this was a shape he rather fancied."

"But Captain Magard, these obelisks are enormous."

"Well, historians say Meron always did have a high opinion of himself."

She clapped a hand to her mouth to keep from guffawing like a sailor.

"I'd better get below," Magard said, stepping back from the rail. "We'll be dropping sails and rowing into port soon." The captain started away from the prow, then stopped and looked back. "So this is your first journey to Tarras?"

"It is."

His black eyes shone. "Then heed my advice and take care, my girl. This is an old city—so old it has forgotten a thousand things other places will never learn. It is said the springs in Tarras flow not with water, but with wine strong enough to warm the coldest spirit, and bitter enough to poison the purest heart."

Lirith thought about his words. Certainly Tarras was an ancient city, and one long into its decline. Once, the Tarrasian Empire had spanned most of Falengarth, the greatest power on Eldh. But over the centuries, under the rule of weak, cruel, and petty emperors, the Tarrasian Empire had retreated, its borders moving ever southward, leaving the northlands first to tribes of barbarians, then later to the seven Dominions. Now the empire—such as it was—consisted of little more than Tarras itself, along with a group of smaller cities clustered along the shores of the Summer Sea.

Yet even so far into its ebb, it was said Tarras was still the greatest city in all the world. And looking at the myriad domes, spires, and soaring bridges, Lirith could believe it.

The captain disappeared belowdecks, and Lirith turned toward the prow. The city was close now; she could smell the scent of spices on the warm, drowsy air. People moved on the docks, men and women dressed in flowing clothes of subtle, jewel-like hues. It was strange and marvelous how, in just the space of a fortnight, she could travel to an entirely new world.

They had departed Ar-tolor at dawn the day after Melia learned of Ondo's death. And the day after they found Tharkis, mad fool and onetime king of Toloria, hanging by his neck from a rafter, his crossed eyes gouged out.

The murder of Tharkis had unsettled everyone in the castle. Most said that Tharkis had finally uttered one too many taunts, and that some knight or lord had finally taken out his wrath upon him. However, there were other whispers in the castle as well, ones that said it was not a knight or lord who had slain the fool, but rather a woman. After all, could it be coincidence that Tharkis had met his gruesome end even as the witches who had secretly journeyed to Ar-tolor were just as secretly departing?

Lirith knew no witches had murdered Tharkis, that this was simply the fear of the common people speaking. And yet . . . It seemed to her there was a kernel of truth to what the rumors said. For some reason Lirith felt a woman's touch in this terrible deed. But whose? And why?

Aryn had been the last to see Tharkis alive, and later that day, the baroness had told Lirith of her encounter with the fool. Listening over a thread of the Weirding, Lirith had heard Tharkis's words even as Aryn recalled them.

She sees everything. I cannot hide . . . even when I sleep she finds me. But she is not the only one who sees. I have seen things as well.

And then, stranger yet, his final words. *Fear the one alive and dead, for you cannot escape her web.*

But how could one be both alive and dead? And why would this woman want Tharkis murdered?

Unfortunately, all of this only added up to Master Tharkis's final and most puzzling riddle. And by that evening, both Lirith and Aryn had known they had more pressing concerns to worry about.

Ivalaine had summoned them well after dark, as the horned moon sank toward the western horizon.

I have a burden I must place upon you, the queen had said as they entered her chamber, *one which brings me no joy in the giving, and yet which I must give all the same. For I am bound to the Pattern, and even as I must lay this task upon you, so must both of you accept it.*

Lirith did not know what it had cost Ivalaine to join the center of the Pattern, but perhaps the price she had paid was even dearer than Lirith had guessed. The queen did not look at them as she spoke, and both her words and motions seemed stiff, like one who was half-frozen. Tressa stood in the corner of the chamber, her lips pressed in a tight line, but the red-haired witch said nothing.

What is this task you must give us? Lirith had finally dared.

Ivalaine's answer had, in one crystalline moment, utterly changed Lirith's and Aryn's lives forever.

Lady Melia is to journey to Tarras with the bard Falken Blackhand. You will accompany them. As you travel, you will keep watch upon them and learn what you can of the one called Travis Wilder, whom the Witches have named Runebreaker. If he returns to them . . .

The queen had fallen still. Her slender shoulders were hunched, her left hand clenched into a fist.

Yes, Your Majesty?

Now Ivalaine did look at them, and her expression was not one of anger or steely resolve as Lirith might have guessed. Instead, her eyes shone with an icy light that stopped Lirith's heart, a light that altered her vision of the queen of Toloria. It was the light of fear.

If that should happen, then you will send word to me at once.

With that the audience was over, and Tressa was guiding them to the door with gentle but insistent motions.

May Sia bless you, Lirith had said as they stepped into the corridor.

Tressa gazed back into the chamber, at the slender silhouette that stood before the night-darkened windows.

May Sia bless us all, she whispered.

Then the door shut, leaving Aryn and Lirith alone. The two women exchanged looks, and in that moment a conversation took place. Neither knew exactly what Ivalaine's words—or the fear in her eyes—portended. But the Pattern was clear, and they had their task.

As they walked to Melia and Falken's chamber, Lirith formulated an argument in her mind, a compelling reason why they should accompany the two on their journey south. She needn't have bothered.

Dear ones, Melia said at once, embracing them both, *it would please me if you would travel with us.*

Thank you, Falken told them at the door, after they had all agreed to meet in the bailey at dawn. The bard's wolfish face was haggard. *One road-worn bard isn't exactly ideal company at a time like this. It will be good for Melia to have two bright, beautiful ladies along—and two friends she cares for.*

These words left Lirith and Aryn speechless. *But don't you see?* Lirith had wanted to shout. *We're betraying you both, and Travis as well!* But she only met the bard's eyes and nodded.

On their way back through the castle, they stopped by Durge's room. As Aryn's guardian, he had to be informed of their decision.

I will begin readying my things at once, the knight had said.

Can't you even question us, Durge? Lirith had wanted to say, but she knew it was no use. Durge trusted them even as Melia and Falken did.

It's better this way, Aryn had said across the Weirding as they walked from Durge's room.

How do you mean?

Lirith still didn't know when the baroness had learned to speak without words, but it was both a comfort and a convenience; Aryn's voice was strong and clear in her mind.

It's like Ivalaine said . . . the Pattern is set. No matter what we do, the Witches are going to search for Travis. Don't you think it's better if we're the ones who find him—his friends who care for him?

Lirith knew the young woman was right. Ivalaine had not forbidden them to talk to Travis, to warn him, to tell him to return to his home and never come back to Eldh. That was the thread Sister Mirda had risked everything in order to weave into the Pattern.

Besides, Lirith knew it was possible they would never see Travis again. Or Grace or Beltan, for that matter. But the thought was bitter comfort.

It was only the next morning, as they mounted their horses in the bailey of Ar-tolor amid the rising mists of dawn, that Lirith looked up, saw a pale face gazing down at her through a high window, and realized that she had broken her promise after all.

How Teravian had known she would be leaving Ar-tolor was a question Lirith had pondered with every passing league. Perhaps he had overheard Ivalaine and

Tressa talking about the plan to send Aryn and Lirith south with Melia. After all, Teravian had a way of watching without being seen.

But of course that didn't make sense. Lirith had spoken to Teravian the final night of the High Coven, hours before Melia learned of the murdered god. Difficult as it was to believe, there could be only one answer.

Teravian has the Sight.

True, the talent was not unheard of in men; Lirith knew the boy Daynen had possessed some fragment of it, for he had seen in the blinding light of the sun the moment of his death, and the vision had proved true. However, the talent was rare in males, and any vestiges of the Sight were lost upon entering manhood. But Teravian was over sixteen winters, a man in body if not in mind, and if his words were to be believed, this was not the first time he had seen things.

But what did it mean? Lirith was not certain, but she had a feeling there was more to Queen Ivalaine's willingness to foster Teravian than simple courtesy to her ally King Boreas of Calavan.

Although they were journeying from the mystery of one murder to that of another, somehow Lirith felt her spirits lift as they left Ar-tolor and set off on the road to Tarras. The gold afternoon of summer had given way to the copper evening of autumn, and while the days were warm they never quite lost the crispness of dawn before purple dusk settled over the land.

They talked little as they rode south through Toloria, and although the silence was tinged with the sorrow of Melia's loss, it was also peaceful in its way. It was through well-populated lands that they rode. All the same, by unspoken agreement, they eschewed manors and inns in favor of camping each evening in some well-tended copse of trees, or a few times in a *talathrin,* one of the old Tarrasian Way Circles. The weather was too mild, too glorious, to be wasted on the indoors.

Curled next to Aryn in warm blankets on the ground, Lirith would wake before the sun to hear Melia's soft prayers and the gentle clatter of Falken making breakfast. Soon after would come a faint chiming, then Durge was there in his mail shirt, kneeling beside them, telling them it was time to rise. The rich fragrance of *maddok* would draw Lirith from the makeshift bed, and she would sit by the fire and curl her fingers around a hot clay cup while Falken served them pan-fried bread. Then they would break camp, mount the horses, and ride once more across the burnished landscape.

It was strange, but Lirith could not remember a time in her life when she had been happier.

After eight uneventful days they reached the Free City of Gendarra. This was a large, dirty, noisy, and exhilarating port city situated on an estuary of the Summer Sea, at the mouths of the Rivers Kelduorn and Dimduorn.

Lirith was grateful fate had not taken them to the Free City of Corantha. She had not stood within that city's walls since the day she fled north to Toloria to begin her life anew. For all her changes since then, she was not certain she would ever have the power to set foot within those walls again. Fortunately, the sea at Corantha was rough this time of year, and so they had made for Gendarra instead.

The Free Cities were a league of loosely allied city-states that, two centuries earlier, had overthrown their ruling lords in favor of a government controlled largely by merchants. Rather than a count or duke, each city was governed by a mayor who was elected by representatives of the various merchant guilds. As a result, the Free Cities were prosperous and busy—but not always so orderly and stable as the castle keeps of the Dominions. Although she had spent nine years of her life in one, Lirith had always thought the name *Free Cities* was a bit misleading. While you could buy anything you wanted there, everything had a price.

As Falken learned when he went to the docks to book passage for them on a ship to Tarras.

I was robbed! the bard had exclaimed upon entering the inn where they were staying. *The captain might as well have turned me upside down and shaken the gold out of my pockets.*

Yes, that's terribly upsetting, dear, Melia had said. *But you did get us a nice ship, didn't you?*

In fact, Falken had gotten them a very nice ship. Captain Magard's trade centered on jewels, spices, and other precious but compact commodities, which meant his vessel was neither smelly nor crowded. Falken's gold bought them three tiny cabins, one for Melia, one for Durge and the bard, and one for Aryn and Lirith.

It was a good thing Melia had her own room, for as it turned out the amber-eyed lady was not at all good at crossing the water. Lirith wasn't certain why, but for some reason this pleased her. Nobody, not even a former goddess, should be perfect. However, Falken—who spent much of his day running buckets to and from Melia's room—looked considerably less happy with the situation.

Lirith had never been on a ship before; she loved it. While Aryn and Durge were not in such dire straits as Melia, both seemed to prefer keeping belowdecks. Not Lirith. She spent almost all of her waking hours basking in the sun and spray, watching sleek dolphins race alongside the ship, or gazing at the night stars while Captain Magard told her which were most useful for navigating across the open sea.

Not that the *Fate Runner* was ever far from shore. Often Lirith caught glimpses to starboard of rocky cliffs or green lines of trees and, once, of pale peaks merging with a distant line of clouds. Then that morning, their fifth at sea, she scrambled up a ladder onto the deck to see a glint of sun on gold directly before them, and with a queer note of sadness she knew their journey to be over.

35.

By the time the *Fate Runner* was secured at the dock, the others had appeared on deck. Durge staggered under a heavy load of bags and bundles; they had sold Queen Ivalaine's horses in Gendarra, and apparently the knight believed it his duty to replace them single-handedly. Lirith hurried to take a pair of bags from him. Aryn seemed to wince, then rushed to do the same.

Falken guided Melia toward the gangplank, where Captain Magard oversaw the unloading of his cargo. There was still a greenish tint to the lady's usually coppery skin, but the sight of land seemed to have vastly improved her condition.

"Thank you, Captain," she said, "for a journey I shall not soon be able to forget."

Magard grinned and bowed low. "If I could have stilled the sea for you, great lady, I would have."

She smiled and gave his rough cheek a pat. "Do keep working on it, dear."

The docks of Tarras were crowded, filled with colors and smells at once vivid and rancorous. Passersby jostled against Durge, so that the knight spun in circles, fighting to keep hold of his many burdens. The city soared above them, and Lirith could see now that it was built upon a hill. A pinnacle of white rock soared upward near its center, a striking contrast to the smooth towers and gilded domes that surrounded it.

Lirith started toward the others. Suddenly the glare of the sun went thin and cold, and the din of the crowd receded to a muffled roar like the voice of the sea. A dread spilled through her, chill as water from the bottom of a frozen ocean.

The figure stood across the dock, twenty paces away, beyond a screen of people. Everything seemed to move with a strange slowness. The figure was already turning away, black robe billowing on the heavy air, but she caught a spark of gold in the shadow of the robe's cowl. He had been watching them, just like before.

No, that wasn't quite right. Several times on their journey south, in one of the towns or cities through which they passed, Lirith had felt a tingling along the Weirding, and she had turned just in time to glimpse a flutter of dark cloth just vanishing around a corner or into a doorway. It was never much—never enough to be certain, but Lirith had a feeling they were being watched as they journeyed.

Yet while those incidents had left her curious and unsettled, none had filled her with the cold fear she felt now. The planks of the dock seemed to yaw beneath her, as if she still stood on the deck of the ship. Nor had she ever seen the glimmer of gold before.

"Lirith?"

The crowd knotted before her, then thinned again, and the figure in the black robe was gone.

"Lirith, are you well?" It was Falken, his faded eyes concerned.

"It's nothing," she said, licking her lips. "A moment of dizziness, that's all. It has passed."

Falken nodded, then returned to Melia.

That is not all it was, Lirith.

She looked up as the voice spoke in her mind. Aryn's brilliant blue eyes were locked on her.

You saw something, didn't you? Just now. What was it?

There was no point in telling anything but the truth; lies were impossible to speak across the Weirding. *I don't know, Aryn. Maybe I saw something. I can't be sure. But it's not—*

Before Lirith could say more, Melia spoke. It was obvious the lady was feeling well again; her amber eyes shone as brilliantly as the gold domes of the city. But then, Melia had just come home.

"Well, don't just stand there," she said. "We need to go to the Second Circle. I would speak with Orsith at once."

There was no time to ask who Orsith was or why they might want to talk to him. Melia started off along the dock, weaving smoothly among the tangles of people, and the others had to hurry in order to keep up with her.

36.

Aryn marveled as they ascended through the outer circles of Tarras, craning her head in an attempt to see everything at once. Only a year ago she had greeted the idea of stepping outside the walls of the castle with no small amount of trepidation. But since then she had learned there was a whole world out there she had never imagined, and while it was sometimes terrifying, it was wondrous as well.

She had savored every moment of their journey south, and not only for the sight of new lands. For she had been exploring in a different way. As they rode through Toloria, she had used her time to practice reaching out and weaving the threads of the Weirding. Often she spoke with Lirith about the Touch, but she was not afraid to experiment on her own. After all, she had learned to speak across the Weirding without help. And Lirith seemed impressed with her rapid progress.

It is as if you have suddenly found a key to your talent, sister, Lirith said over the Weirding as they sat by the fire one evening, making a lesson of sensing and identifying every living thing within twenty paces.

Except it was more like the key had been there all along, gripped in her twisted right hand, only Aryn had never let herself open her fingers to see it.

Always the balance seeks something in return when a great

gift is given, the old Mournish woman had told her.

Belira and the others had jeered at her because of her arm, but they were silly girls, unaware that there was so much more to being a witch than what appeared on the surface. Aryn no longer feared them. Nor was she angry. Rather, she felt sorry for them, and she hoped one day they might learn what she had—that the key to power was not wanting something you didn't have. Instead, it was daring to see what was already yours.

One day, excited, she had tried to explain these things to Lirith over the Weirding. Except an image had formed in her mind: a proud woman in blue, holding a sword as she rode from a castle with seven towers, a crumpled form in the grass beneath her.

You have forgotten about one who bore pain for you. . . .

Hastily, Aryn had broken the thread that spanned between her and Lirith. The dark-haired witch had given her a puzzled look as the thread was severed, but Aryn had mumbled a hasty excuse about being weary and had gone to bed.

But who had the old Mournish woman been talking about? Surely she was not so cruel as the old woman had said.

Or was she? A fragment of a singsong rhyme echoed in her mind.

> *Her beautiful sisters*
> *All have dismissed her,*
> *But one day they'll sorrow the deed.*
> *With a sword in her hand,*
> *She'll ride 'cross the land—*
> *And trample them all 'neath her steed.*

In a way the fool's poem reminded her of the dragon's words. Sfithrisir had said she and Lirith were both doomed to betray the Witches. Was that what the fool Tharkis had been trying to tell her as well?

But Aryn would never harm any of her sisters. Not even Belira. The fool and the dragon were wrong. Certainly one had been mad and the other wicked. All the same, these thoughts had hung over her all the way south, the one dark cloud marring the otherwise brilliant journey.

Now, as they walked through the ancient, thronging streets of Tarras, Aryn pushed such troubles from her mind. There was too much to see to dwell on riddles told by fortune-tellers, fools, and dragons.

From the docks, they walked through a triumphal arch of white stone that was no less than thrice the size of the main gates of Calavere, into the Fifth Circle of the city. It was the largest of the city's five circles, and—according to Falken—the place where the laborers and common folk dwelled. While the main avenue they walked was wide, spotlessly clean, and lined by columnlike *ithaya* trees, to either side she could see the mouths of dusty lanes too narrow for the sun to reach. Filthy faces stared out from the shadowed openings. Aryn was glad when they passed through another arch and into the Fourth Circle.

The main avenue was steeper there, climbing rapidly past larger, well-kept homes and businesses. Honeysuckle climbed up iron gates, filling the air with a sweet scent, and everywhere the sound of fountains chimed on the air. The Fourth Circle was the home to the city's merchants and craft guilds. Clearly the merchants had good standing in this city, given the beauty of their dwellings. But, Falken explained, the tiers of Tarras were arranged so that those farthest in and highest up belonged to the classes with the greatest power.

Soon they passed into the Third Circle, which belonged to the Tarrasian military. They passed blank walls with infrequent doors, each portal guarded by a pair of soldiers. The Tarrasian soldiers were dressed in peculiar fashion compared to the knights of the Dominions. Their chests were covered by leather jerkins and breastplates of beaten bronze, and bronze helmets adorned their heads, but they wore only short kilts, leaving their legs bare, and sandals on their feet. Still, by the hard expressions on their faces, Aryn did not doubt that these were skilled men of battle. For all its decline from greatness, it seemed Tarras had not entirely forgotten how to make war.

Aryn was glad when they passed through another archway into the Second Circle.

"This is as far as we're going to go for now," Falken said. "Unless any of you besides Melia happens to be close personal friends with the emperor and simply forgot to mention it. Only his guests, his servants, and members of his court are allowed into the First Circle."

"We shall concern ourselves with Emperor Ephesian later," Melia said. "At the moment, this is precisely where we need to be. The Holy Circle of Tarras."

Aryn gazed around and saw white-stone shrines and domed temples in all directions. Men and women moved along the quiet streets, wearing flowing robes of myriad hues, and Aryn knew at once they were priests and priestesses of the temples.

Some wore crimson, their heads shaved. Others had carefully curled their hair in oiled ringlets and wore sashes of gold over emerald robes. Yellow, azure, flame orange—all colors were represented. If the priests and priestesses of Tarras were so varied a group, Aryn could only imagine what the gods themselves were like. She knew there were more mystery cults in Tarras than the seven known in the Dominions, but just how many she had never imagined until now.

Durge cleared his throat in a nervous rumble. "Melia, may I ask exactly how many gods there are in this city?"

"Don't worry, Durge," Falken said, faded eyes twinkling. "The Second Circle is also home to the Tarrasian university, where the greatest scholars, mathematicians, and engineers in the world are said to be gathered."

Durge raised his eyebrows at this. "I believe I should like to see this *university*, as you call it."

"Oh, you will," Falken said with a wink. "But first—"

"My brothers, my sisters," said a soft voice, "is this truly to be our home? It is so much more beautiful than I could ever have imagined."

Melia swayed back and forth, her arms folded about herself, a beatific smile upon her lips.

Aryn saw Falken and Lirith exchange looks. It was like the incident Lirith had described, when she found Melia dancing in the shrine of Mandu. Melia had not had another such spell on their journey, although there had been peculiar moments. Melia seemed to speak of the past a great deal, and her visage would grow dreamy when she did. However, Aryn had simply assumed it was because they were traveling to Melia's home. Now, it seemed as if Melia was not even there.

No, that's not it, Aryn. It's as if we're the ones who aren't here, as if Melia really is seeing Tarras as it was long ago, when she first came to this place.

Gently, Falken touched Melia's shoulder.

"Dear one," he whispered.

For a heartbeat Melia went stiff, then she turned and

glared at the others. "Well, don't just stand there and gawk. We're going this way."

With that, Melia led the way down a side lane paved with white stone. There was nothing for the others to do save follow.

As they went, Aryn noticed one dome that rose above all others in the Second Circle, and which rivaled the dome of the emperor's palace that loomed above them in the First. This dome was not gold, like so many in the city, but was rather painted blue so that it seemed to merge with the sky. Aryn wondered which god was honored by this temple, which was so much grander than the others. However, it was not toward this dome that they walked.

When they stopped, it was before a temple that, while lovely, was far smaller and plainer than those around it. Its columns and cornices were unadorned, and it was without windows. A narrow door was the only opening.

Melia regarded the others, her amber eyes now sharp and clear. "It is best that you empty your minds of petty thoughts and wants before you enter here. There is no room for fear, anger, or desire in the realm of Mandu. It is because he seeks nothing that he is ever dying. And it is because he seeks nothing that he is ever reborn."

"Perhaps he should seek to build a few more windows in order to save on candles," Durge muttered, but a glare from Melia caused the knight to clamp his mouth shut. Aryn had to resist the urge to hug the practical knight. Instead, they followed Melia through the door and into the temple beyond.

37

Evidently Mandu the Everdying was little more
popular in Tarras than in the Dominions. The main
space of the temple bore only a handful of worshipers.
There was not much furniture—a few wooden
benches where one might kneel in prayer, a bare
marble altar, and, in the dim nave of the temple, carved
of milky stone, a likeness of the god as tall as two men,
gazing forward with serene, empty eyes.

A priest rushed toward them, tugging at his ill-fitting
white robe to keep it from falling off his skinny
shoulders. He was a young man, with a homely but
cheerful face and a large, crooked nose.

"Your Holiness, Melindora! So the vision Mandu
sent my master was true—you have come."

Melia glided forward. "Tell me, acolyte, do you
make it a habit of doubting the power of Mandu and
the wisdom of your master?"

The young man's eyes bulged. "Never, Your
Holiness! Of course Mandu is all-powerful and my
master is most wise. I only meant to say—"

"—that you are going to bring wine for your weary
guests who have traveled far, then lead them to see
Orsith at once," Melia finished for him.

The young priest gaped at her.

"Wine," Melia prompted with a pleasant smile. "Then Orsith."

Aryn forced herself not to laugh; the young man was clearly having a bad enough time as it was. Yet she could see the mirth in Melia's amber eyes. It was clear the lady was not angry.

All the same, the priest acted as if his god had appeared before him in a blaze of wrath and glory. And perhaps that wasn't so far off the mark, for Melia had once been a goddess herself—a fact of which the young man seemed quite aware. He hastily brought them wine, slopping some of it on the floor and wiping it up with the hem of his robe.

Only as she drank did Aryn realize she was indeed terribly thirsty; she wondered why she hadn't noticed it sooner. Her eyes flickered to Mandu's peaceful stone visage, but before she could wonder more the young priest beckoned them toward a door.

"This way, Your Holiness. He is waiting for you."

When they stepped through the door, they found themselves standing in an utterly empty room. It was difficult to tell how large the space was, for floor, walls, and ceiling were all white. There seemed to be no distinct way to define where one plane ended and another began, and the light was a silvery glow that emanated from nowhere and everywhere at once.

"Welcome," a dry, warm voice said.

Aryn looked up and saw the room was not entirely empty. An old man floated in midair in the center of the room, cross-legged, hands on knees. His robe, hair, and flowing beard were all the same silver-white as the stone walls. However, his wrinkled cheeks were a dark, coppery color, and his small eyes were as brown as nuts.

Melia stepped forward, beaming. "Orsith. It is a joy to see you again."

The old man smiled; it was one of the sweetest expressions Aryn had ever seen.

"My dearest, the joy is mine. But you must forgive me that I do not come down to greet you more warmly. I am in the second day of a Stillness, and I have yet one more day to remain here. Even speaking is a bit of a violation, but I suspect Mandu will forgive me under the circumstances."

"Oh, I'll see to that," Melia said. "And don't worry, I shall come to you."

With that the small woman rose into the air, until she sat cross-legged like Orsith, hovering a few feet from him.

Falken let out a snort. "Show-off."

Lirith moved closer, wonder on her dusky face. "Forgive me, Orsith, but may I ask how you do it?"

"Do what, lovely one?"

"Float without touching the floor."

The old man shrugged bony shoulders. "I'm afraid I haven't the faintest idea. I simply sit as still as I can and think about nothing at all, and after I while I notice that the floor has quite fallen away from me."

Lirith smiled and nodded, as if this meant something to her, but Durge frowned, furrows digging into his forehead.

"And where are we to sit?" the knight grumbled.

Orsith smiled. "Why, you may sit anywhere, my serious fellow."

"But there is nowhere to sit," Durge said.

Orsith cocked his head. "Well, that's odd. And here I was thinking there was *everywhere* to sit."

Aryn laughed, then sat cross-legged on the floor.

"Yes, that's it, my dear," Orsith said. "And what striking eyes you have. Have you seen the blue pearls in the emperor's palace? There are no more than a dozen in the world. But drab pebbles they seem compared to your eyes. The emperor will have to throw them out the moment he sees you."

Aryn gasped. She felt Lirith squeeze her hand as the witch sat down beside her. Falken followed suit, then finally Durge. The Embarran's knees creaked alarmingly.

"Orsith," Melia said, "there is much to talk about. It has been so long since I have seen you."

"I believe my beard was considerably shorter and blacker the last time you were in Tarras."

Sorrow flickered across Melia's face. "So it was, Orsith. But we will have to speak about the passing years another time. Right now you must tell me everything you know about poor Ondo."

Now the humor in Orsith's expression was replaced by gravity. "I fear it will take little enough time to tell you what we have learned. Usually Mandu prefers to remain apart from the arguments and rivalries of the other gods, but even He has been forced to become involved by what has happened. I have been sending good Landus—the acolyte who brought you to me— out into the city to be my ears and eyes. But all Landus has heard is what I have heard in my heart, and what you no doubt have heard as well—the clamor of all the gods and their followers speaking at once."

Melia nodded. "Yes, I've heard it, like the roar of the ocean."

"It seems each temple has accused all the others of spying, plotting, and dissembling," Orsith went on. "Which, of course, is not so very far from the truth. This is Tarras, after all. Yet for all their machinations, it seems none of the temples knows who committed this monstrous deed. And it is not only Ondo who has been taken from us. Seven priests and priestesses, all from different temples, have been slain. Nor is there any pattern to these awful deeds. For all we can tell, the slayings are utterly at random."

"No offense, Orsith," Falken said, "but haven't there always been strong rivalries among the various temples?"

"There have. Although Mandu has rarely taken part in such activities, it is hardly uncommon for the gods to forge schemes, create alliances, and break them again in an effort to gain more followers or greater standing in the city. And I fear that a few of the less scrupulous temples have resorted to foul methods on occasion. This is not the first time the blood of priests has been spilled. But never, in all the two-thousand-year history of Tarras, has there been anything such as this. A god is no more."

Melia clenched her small hands into fists. "But what is the Etherion doing about it?"

"Sadly, they are doing little," Orsith said. "Save to argue and cast accusations."

"The Etherion?" Aryn said. "What's that?"

Falken answered her. "It's the combined assembly of the temples of Tarras. It's where the priests of all the temples meet to discuss important matters. Or to bicker, as the case may be. Did you see the great blue dome on the way here? That's the Dome of the Etherion."

"I seldom leave the temple anymore," Orsith said, "yet I did go to the Etherion three days ago, to the most recent assembly. However, nothing was accomplished, save the flinging of rumors and intimations. It seemed as if every priest was shouting that this was all a plot hatched by some rival god to steal worshipers or prestige from his own."

Durge let out a snort. "These gods and priests of

yours sound like a bunch of children quarreling in the castle bailey."

"You're not far off there," Falken muttered.

"Why do the gods not band together rather than fling mud at one another?" Durge went on. "Surely together they could find the perpetrator of this crime."

"A fair question, good soldier," Orsith said, "but I doubt the answer to it will please you. You see, for all the anger and accusations in the Etherion, there was a stronger, deeper current I felt while I was there, flowing through all who were present. It was fear."

Lirith nodded. "Of course. If whoever did this has the power to slay a god, what's to stop him from killing again?"

Now Aryn understood. "The other gods must be afraid that if they try to find the murderer, then they might be the next victim. And if the gods are afraid, the priests must be terrified."

Orsith nodded. "There is truth in what you say, my dears, although it is not quite so simple. The history of alliances and rivalries among the gods of Tarras is a vast and turbulent ocean, and mortals can do no more than skim along its surface and hope they are not pulled beneath."

Melia chewed her lip. "Even to us nonmortals, it's not always that much clearer. I had hoped the Etherion might work together to find Ondo's murderer, but I confess I feared it would not happen."

"Was anyone mad at Ondo?" Falken said.

"Oh, many of the gods were angry at Ondo," Orsith said. "He was not the most powerful, yet he was the patron of the guild of goldsmiths. That meant all the working of gold into jewelry and ornaments was under his control. And many gods favor gold for the adornment of their priests and temples."

Falken scratched his chin with his gloved hand, but if he thought this information important he did not say.

"Well," Melia said, her eyes shining hotly, "if the Etherion cannot be made to take action, then I shall simply have to appeal to another power in this. I will request an audience with Emperor Ephesian."

Orsith shook his head. "And you will be refused, dearest. Yes, even one such as you. The emperor has closed the gates of the palace out of mourning for Ondo."

"Out of a desperate desire to hide is more like it," Falken said. "I'm sure the emperor is shaking in his bed even as we speak, wondering if he's going to be the next to go. The Ephesians were always cowards."

Orsith nodded. "Alas, it seems that is a trait all nineteen have had in common."

"Nineteen?" Durge said. "You mean there have been that many of them?"

"Indeed," Orsith said, "the current Ephesian is the nineteenth of that name to hold the scepter. It has been a long dynasty."

"But why hasn't the dynasty been overthrown? Why put up with nineteen weak and cowardly emperors?"

"Because," Orsith said, "it is better than nineteen strong and cruel ones."

Once again Durge was at a loss to answer.

"Now what?" Falken said, gazing at Melia.

She bobbed gently in the air, arms folded. "I don't know. We'll have to find a place to stay. I need time to think."

With that, Melia drifted gracefully downward, her feet alighting softly on the floor. However, getting Durge upright was a less elegant task and required a solid tug on Falken's part. At last the knight stood, his expression a mixture of indignation and embarrassment that was somehow quite charming. Aryn kissed his craggy cheek, much to his further chagrin. They bid Orsith farewell with a promise to return soon, leaving him to float in the air.

"So where to?" Falken said to Melia as they paused at the main door of the temple.

"Perhaps good Landus could recommend a respectable hostel where we might stay."

The young priest, who had guided them back to the door, bobbed his head. "Of course, Your Holiness. All the hostels are in the Fourth Circle. I believe you might find the House of Nine Fountains to your liking."

"No!" the small woman cried out, her body going rigid.

Aryn stared at her, as did the others. The lady's face had drained utterly of blood.

Landus gulped. "Forgive me if I have offended, Your Holiness. If that hostel is not to your liking, then—"

Falken pushed the young priest aside. "What is it, Melia? What's wrong?" The bard gripped her shoulders. For a terrible moment she was as a statue, then she slumped against Falken, clutching his tunic and sobbing.

"It's Geb," she said in a choking voice.

Aryn had never heard the name before. "Geb?"

"The Rat God," Landus said. "The god of thieves and beggars. But—"

"What is it?" Falken said.

However, even as Melia spoke the words, Aryn knew what had just happened.

"He's dead," Melia said, her voice quavering. "Geb has been murdered!"

38.

Durge did not like Tarras.

The knight could not deny that it was a large city, or that it was ancient, and he supposed it must be called magnificent. Its five encircling walls were high and thick, and their design would afford excellent defenses—for if invaders breached one barrier they would have four more between them and the center of the city. In addition, the city's military appeared disciplined and well trained, and its markets were prosperous and filled with exotic goods. Even the climate was favorable: warm yet not sweltering, with cooling breezes off the sea.

However, as they made their way back toward the Fourth Circle, Durge knew he would trade it all for his manor of cold, gray stone on the windswept moors of Embarr. There was something *wrong* about this city, with its multitudinous cults and bickering gods, its spice-heavy air, its crowded streets and dim grottoes. He wasn't certain exactly what it was, but he could see it in the walls, which for all their ponderous strength were covered with a fine web of cracks, patched and repatched countless times over the centuries. And he could see it in the eyes of the people who passed them on the street: a deep yet somehow hollow look. This was a weary city.

*No, not weary. Bored. It has dwelled here too long in the
hot sun; it has seen again and again everything time has to
offer. This city is bored, and its people as well.*

Durge knew this was a perilous thing. When men
were bored, they would commit rash and foolish acts
to experience, even for a moment, some new
sensation. He had seen men drink and wench
themselves to death out of boredom; and he had seen
them go to war and kill for the same reason.

And if an entire city was bored?

"Are you well enough to keep walking, Melia?"
Falken said once more, as they passed through an
archway back into the teeming streets of the Fourth
Circle. "Lirith and I can go ahead to the hostel and
send a litter back for you."

Melia's regal visage was hard. "I told you I will not
ride in a litter, Falken. What comfort will soft cushions
give me now that two of my brothers are no more? I
will walk to the hostel on my own feet."

They turned onto a side street that was made nearly
a tunnel by buildings that leaned together overhead.
The sun did not reach there—just the blue-white glow
of used light, reflected again and again from high
above. Only as his eyes adjusted from glare to gloom
did Durge see them: a gray woman holding a child,
drifting toward them.

Durge stumbled, and he was certain his heart had
stopped beating. How could they be here in this hot,
foreign city so far from the frozen plains of Embarr?

"Durge?"

A hand on his wrist. He knew it was only the
warmth of human flesh, but it felt like a hot brand.

"Durge, are you all right?"

It was Lirith. He looked at her, and she must have
seen the fear in his gaze, for she snatched her hand

back, a look of horror blossoming in her own dark
eyes. But his fear was not for her and her witch's touch.
He looked back down the street.

The ice melted in his chest; blood and breath
returned.

They were close now, woman and child, close
enough that he could see they were not ghosts. The
woman wore a robe of pale gauze that fluttered around
her like mist, and her skin was rich and dark beneath
the ashes that stained her cheeks and brow. The infant
wrapped in swaddling cloth in her arms was as dark as
she, its tiny face marked with ashes as her own. The
woman bent her head over her child, humming a soft
song as she passed.

I am well, my lady, Durge started to say, but at that
moment Melia moved toward the woman in gray.

"I do not recognize your robes," Melia said in gentle
tones. "May I ask whose cult you follow?"

The woman looked up from her infant and smiled.
"It is no wonder you do not recognize my garb,
mistress. The one I follow is new in this city. She is
named Tira, who is called the Child of Fire."

Durge heard both Lirith and Aryn gasp beside him.
Even he felt a twinge deep inside, and had it not been
so many years since such feelings had been lost to him,
he might have thought it to be joy. As a rule he placed
little stock in gods, but then seldom had he journeyed
with one. And there had been something about the
girl, a peace that was strange but compelling as well.

"Of course, I should have known," Melia murmured.

The woman in gray misunderstood this answer. "Do
not trouble yourself that you did not know, mistress.
Yet I think soon many in this city shall know Her, and
when they do they shall follow Her. For She went into
the flames that we might all be transformed."

Melia's gaze grew sharp. "Transformed? Into what?"

"Why, into ourselves."

With that, the woman held her child close to her breast and moved down the street, her gray garb fading into the cool dimness. They were not ghosts. However, as Durge had learned these last few weeks, one did not need to see ghosts to be haunted. He wondered if he would ever see Embarr again.

A heavy breath escaped him, and he was belatedly glad that the others seemed not to hear it, their attention on Melia. The lady continued down the street, Falken beside her, and while sorrow still veiled her, it seemed a faint smile touched the corners of her mouth.

"It's Tira," Aryn whispered, eyes shining. "She really is a goddess."

Lirith nodded. "I had wondered if this might come to pass, if a mystery cult might form around her. Only I had not believed it could happen so swiftly. Do you see how Melia's mood has lightened? Gods have been slain, but here is a new goddess born."

Durge did not understand the first thing concerning the workings of gods and goddesses. If he could not heat a substance in a crucible, or drop it in a vial of acid in order to observe its properties, then it was beyond him. All the same, Lirith's words heartened him for a reason he could not name.

The House of Nine Fountains was situated on the east side of the city, not far from the wall of the Third Circle, on a slight prominence that afforded a view of the sea.

Falken had said the Fourth Circle was inhabited by the merchant class of Tarras, and to a great degree the hostel reflected that. It was large and comfortably appointed, if not particularly luxurious. The walls were white and clean but mostly unadorned, and the mosaics that covered the floors were simple in design but pleasing to the eye. The hostel was a square building of several stories, built around a roofless courtyard in the center. In the courtyard were a number of bubbling fountains from which the hostel evidently took its name.

The hostel was run by a woman named Vil, her black hair streaked with gray but her face still smooth and lovely. This surprised Durge, for in the Dominions it was not usual for a woman to own a business, except if it were a brewery—for the making of beer was women's work. However, this was a strange land, and its customs were bound to be just as strange.

Besides, Vil seemed to run a prosperous and efficient establishment. In fact, the more Durge thought about it, the more it made sense. Would he not rather stay in a house kept by a woman than a man? This might explain the poor state of inns and taverns in Embarr. Perhaps some of the peculiar customs in this city were not so bad.

While most of the guests at the hostel appeared to be merchants visiting from one of the cities near Tarras, it was clear from the rooms Vil led them to that, from time to time, the hostel also accommodated more important—or at least wealthier—guests. The floors were covered with blue tile. Large windows opened onto the courtyard below, and sheer curtains billowed in the breeze.

The sound of water reached Durge's ears; it was coming from a bronze basin set into a marble stand. A small pipe protruded from the wall, and water bubbled from it into the basin. Yet the basin seemed never to overflow. Durge moved to it.

"But where does the water come from?" he muttered. "And where does it go?"

Falken laughed. "Behold the magic of plumbing, my friend."

Durge shook his head. Plumbing? He had never heard of this particular magic before. But then, to his eyes it looked more like the art of an engineer than the craft of a wizard. Even as he looked, he saw a small hole near the rim of the basin through which water drained. There must be a pipe to take water out of the building even as there was one to bring it in.

"Is it to your liking, mistress?" said the proprietress of the hostel.

Melia moved to the window and drew in a deep breath. "It's wonderful, Madam Vil."

Falken handed the proprietress several coins. She bowed and departed.

There were three sleeping rooms off the main sitting area, one for Melia, one for Aryn and Lirith, and one for the men. There was also, Durge discovered, a room that contained a tub for bathing with more of the ingenious plumbing to bring water to it, and even a kind of chamberpot that cleansed and emptied itself with water from a small cistern above. Durge had never seen such a thing before, and he tipped the cistern into the pot and watched the water drain away several times until Melia clucked her tongue and told him not to waste water, that it came many miles from the mountains to the north. After this, Durge sat and tried to imagine a way in which fresh water could be brought over many leagues from mountains to a city by the sea.

"So, we're here," Falken said. "Now what?"

The bard was eating olives from a bowl brought by a servant, and Lirith and Aryn sat near a window, sharing an orange. Durge had eaten olives before, and he had once tasted an orange in the Dominions, but these things were rare there, delicacies to be savored by nobles. Yet he had seen common folk hawking them on the streets on their way to the hostel.

Melia sat in a chair, a fluffy black kitten curled up on her lap. Durge didn't know where the kitten had come from; he supposed it lived at the hostel and had simply wandered into their rooms. It looked uncannily like the kitten that had journeyed with them to Perridon earlier that year, but Durge knew that was impossible. That cat would have nearly reached its full size in the intervening months.

"I don't know what to do," Melia said. "I really don't know."

These words stunned Durge. They had journeyed to Tarras at Melia's behest; he had simply assumed that, once here, she would have a plan for how she would solve the mystery of the murdered god. Or gods, as the matter now stood. However, she gazed out a window, absently petting the kitten. He saw Aryn and Lirith exchange glances; clearly the two were as shocked as he.

To his further astonishment, Durge found himself standing. But this silence was useless; someone had to take action. "We must use logic to find the murderer."

Falken let out a snort. "This is a city full of gods we're talking about, Durge, not one of your alchemical potions. Believe me, logic doesn't apply."

Durge would not accept that; logic *always* applied. The gods were mysterious and powerful, yes. But while they were much more than human, there were still rules they had to abide by, as evidenced by the machinations for followers and status that Melia and Falken had described.

He cleared his throat. "Melia, will you tell me of the gods Ondo and Geb?"

"What does it matter? They are gone now."

Durge did his best to speak gently, although he did not know if he succeeded in the attempt. "It does matter, my lady. If we could come to know these gods, then we might understand why it was that someone would wish to harm them. From what I have been able to observe, it seems both Ondo and Geb were minor deities."

Now Melia looked up, eyes blazing. "That doesn't mean they deserved to be slain!"

Durge winced. Melia's face was nearly as ashen as the woman in gray they had encountered earlier. But the damage was already done; there was no point in stopping. This was a puzzle, and Durge was good at puzzles. There had to be a pattern here—he had only to find it.

"I did not mean to imply that the death of these gods is of no importance, my lady. On the contrary, that one might slay a god is deeply troubling, for it suggests a murderer with both great power and cruelty. What I meant to ask was simply this: Why was it these two *particular* gods who were slain?"

Falken looked up. "You mean you think Ondo and Geb were chosen for a reason?"

Durge shrugged. "A killer must choose his victim somehow, must he not?"

"It doesn't make sense," Aryn said. "It must take abilities we can't even imagine to slay a god. If you're that powerful, why not start with one of the most important, like Vathris or Jorus?"

The young woman stood before the window now, her good arm folded over the withered one. She had changed into a lighter gown of blue fabric, and Durge could see a soft radiance through the material, as well as the curves of a slender figure. He averted his eyes—

but not quite as hastily as proper decorum might have required.

Aryn tapped her cheek. "I suppose I can imagine why Ondo might be a target; he did control the goldsmiths in the city, and it sounds as if the gods covet gold as much as people do. But what use would there be in killing Geb? I can't imagine many people would miss him, except for the thieves and beggars who worshiped him. And I doubt those groups have much standing in this city."

Like a sharp sword, it pierced him. "But that's it, my lady. You've put the arrow in the eye of the target."

Aryn's blue eyes went wide. "I have?"

"As you said, my lady, few in the city will miss the Rat God. Present company excepted, of course," he added quickly, as ire ignited in Melia's eyes. "And from what Orsith told us in the temple of Mandu, Ondo was not particularly well loved by the other temples."

Melia glared at him. "What are you getting at, Durge?"

"I see it now," Lirith said. "If you attacked one of the most popular gods, then certainly all the other gods would band together to hunt you down, no matter how afraid they were. But if it's the least-loved gods who are slain, the despised and the envied, then what is there to unite the gods? The killer need not fear a hunt. Which means—"

Lirith's words ended in gasp, and Durge gave a grim nod.

"There is nothing to keep the murderer from killing again," he finished.

Now Melia rose, her small hands clenched into fists. The kitten jumped to the floor with a yowl of protest. "No, the gods would not be so callous. This is madness!"

Falken laid a hand on her shoulder. "Is it, Melia?"

Slowly she sank back into her chair. A sigh escaped her.

"Forgive me, Durge," she said quietly. "It's just that you spoke a truth I did not wish to hear. I suppose in a way I knew it myself. I do love all my brothers and sisters, but even I must admit their love for one another is not so universal. You are right—there are those who are likely not filled with sorrow at the news of Ondo's demise. Or Geb's."

The kitten settled again on her lap, and she stroked its fur with slender fingers.

"But this leaves us exactly where we started," Aryn said. "What do we do now?"

Melia looked up, and Falken raised his head, his gaze expectant. Both Aryn and Lirith were silent. All at once Durge realized that everyone was looking at him. A jolt of fear coursed through him—followed by a peculiarly warm sensation.

"We must find out who stands to gain the most from the deaths of Ondo and Geb," he said. "If we do that, then logic dictates we will have found the murderer."

"And then what do we do?" Melia murmured.

But that was a question to which Durge had no answer.

"Come on," Falken said, his gruff voice breaking the silence. "We have work to do."

39.

Lirith walked through the Fourth Circle of Tarras and tried not to feel that this was the place she had been searching for all her life.

You are being foolish, sister. You no more belong in Tarras than you do in ancient Malachor. It is merely that it reminds you of Corantha, that is all.

Certainly the Free Cities had much in common with Tarras. So many things—white sun on white walls, the yellow, perfumed blooms of *lindara* vines, the songs of women as they carried their burdens from market—reminded her of the streets of Corantha, but without . . . those things she would not care to dwell upon.

And if you think Tarras lacks for brothels, sister, then think again. There are decadences bought and sold in the light of day in this city that even in Corantha are hidden in the fastness of night, if they can be found there at all.

It was true, but even that thought could not weigh down the sensation that buoyed her heart. Every large city she knew of—yes, even cold, craggy Barrsunder in Embarr—had its equivalent of the Street of Scarves.

All the same, it was only the Street of Scarves in Corantha that held pain for her—the street on which she had found herself at the age of eleven, a lost and desperate child, her parents murdered before her eyes by thieves. But her mother had always wanted to see a great city, and her father had never denied his beloved anything. They had packed the wagon, had journeyed from their little home in the green hills of southern Toloria. And after that first night in the city, when the family made a wrong turn down a shadowed street and moonlight glinted off cold steel, Lirith never saw any of them again.

The parents were left to bleed and die in the gutter, but everything was for sale in the Free Cities, and the child had been more valuable to the thieves alive. Screaming, they had taken her . . . and had sold her to Gulthas.

There had been no ravens on the Street of Scarves as on the card she had drawn from the deck of Sareth's grandmother, but all the same it had been like a battle-field from which she could not escape. Except in the end she *had* escaped it, and nothing would ever make her go back there. For years Gulthas had paid her less than he charged her for her keep, making sure she could never save enough money to buy her freedom from servitude.

However, he never knew of the coins she earned working magic tricks in the street and which she kept hidden in a hole in the wall. On her twentieth birthday she had presented him with a sack of gold which held exactly the price the city laws decreed for the servitude of one woman. Gulthas had exploded in rage, but she had been ready for that, and she had fled Corantha to the north—to freedom and her future.

And what of the old woman's card, sister? Did she not say that you could never escape your fate?

Lirith could not think of that now. She bought a small packet of sugared *lindara* petals from a vendor and let them melt on her tongue as she made her way down a lane lined with tall sunleaf trees.

She was searching for the guild house of the goldsmiths, and she had to be getting close. According to a traveling merchant she had spoken to at the hostel, the guild house was located on the Street of Flames. So far Lirith had found a Street of Smoke, a Street of Torches, and a Street of Many Colors. This last had nothing to do with flames, but she had liked the name so had walked down that lane anyway. Banners had hung above every doorway and were strung over the street, each one of a different hue, bedazzling her eyes. It was the street occupied by the city's cloth dyers.

The others had their tasks as well—and Lirith had been grateful for Durge's display of good, solid, Embarran logic at the hostel. The death of a god was a completely incomprehensible thing, but treating it as if it were something mundane and usual, something that could be studied and understood, had removed the sense of paralysis that had bound them all. Maybe there was no point to it—maybe they would never truly understand the mystery at work here—but at least now it *felt* like they were doing something about it.

So while Lirith had been charged with seeking out the guild of the goldsmiths, Durge was to accompany Aryn back to the narrower and more crowded streets of the Fifth Circle in order to speak to the priests of the god Geb. Lirith had thought it interesting that the Rat God's temple was not in the Second Circle with the other holy houses, but rather in the district inhabited by the downtrodden folk who followed him. Perhaps Durge had been onto something; it was not likely many of the gods cared for Geb. It was his and Aryn's mission to discover if the priests of Geb knew any reason why another might want their god destroyed. Lirith was to do the same with the goldsmiths.

In turn, Melia and Falken had ascended toward the

center of the city to request an audience with the emperor. It was not likely they would be granted entry, given Orsith's words earlier, but Melia had insisted.

Ephesian cannot refuse us, she had said. *Not now that a second god has been murdered. Is this how he wishes to begin the dynasty of his name, with such chaos in the city?*

All of them had stared at Melia as she spoke those words. Her cheeks had glowed hotly, and her eyes had seemed too bright, like beads of spun glass.

At last Falken had laid a gentle hand on her shoulder. *Melia, it's the nineteenth Ephesian in the dynasty we're going to see, not the first.*

For a moment the small woman had gone rigid, her eyes staring but seeming not to see. Then she had frowned at Falken.

I know that, she had snapped. *Do you think I'm an idiot?*

Before anyone could say anything more, she had sailed through the door of their room. Falken had followed after her, but not before casting a worried look back at Lirith. Melia's spells seemed to be increasing in frequency. But what did they mean? Why was Melia getting so caught up in the web of the past?

And what about you, sister? Why can you not stop thinking of Corantha, and of dancing for Gulthas?

The air was warm, and sweat beaded on her brow. Even her summer gown, tailored as it was for the cooler climes of the Dominions, was heavy and hot here. She wished she was dressed as those around her, in bright, loose, flowing fabric. She settled for unlacing her bodice partway; in the Dominions this might have been improper, but in Tarras she doubted anyone would notice.

She almost passed through the Street of Flames without knowing it. Her throat had grown dry, and she was thinking of trying to find a vendor who sold iced wine. However, the lane she walked down was unusually empty, and its only decorations were dark cloths that draped the tops of marble columns at either end of the street.

Just as she was leaving the street, a breeze—sharp with the scent of the ocean—rushed down the lane, momentarily lifting one of the black cloths and revealing what lay beneath: a curving, coiling shape carved of stone, gilded with gleaming gold.

Of course, you dolt. This is the first street you've come to that wasn't crowded. You should have known it would be like this. After all, they're in mourning.

The wind ceased, and the black cloth settled again over the gilded stone carving of the flame. Her thirst forgotten, Lirith turned back down the street. There were a score of workshops, although all of them were dark and silent. She chose a large door near the center of the street. It was painted green and adorned with a golden hand—the sigil of the god Ondo, she guessed. She raised her own hand to knock.

"Go away!" said a muffled voice from the other side.

Lirith snatched her hand back. In the center of the hand was a small hole. So that was how they had seen her.

"Hello," she said, trying to direct her voice at the peephole. "If you have a moment, I would speak with you."

A snort. "You mean you would kill us and swindle us out of our gold."

Lirith frowned. If the owner of the muffled voice was at all representative of his guild, then these goldsmiths were a suspicious lot. Then again, having one's god murdered no doubt did little for one's sense of security.

"That is not so," Lirith said. "It would be quite impossible to swindle you out of your gold *after* I'd killed you."

"Oh, well then, in that case . . ."

There was the *click* of a lock being turned, then the door swung inward a few inches. Beyond was a dim space and an exceptionally tiny and wizened old man in a yellow robe.

Lirith nodded. "Thank you."

"Wait just a moment, girl." A few wisps of white hair fluttered above the old man's head. "You weren't mocking me just now, were you? I think perhaps you were."

"Of course not," Lirith lied hastily. "I was merely trying to reassure you, that's all. I'm completely harmless. See?" She spread her arms, showing her empty hands.

"Humph. Well, you're certainly skinny enough. And you dress strangely. Are you a beggar, then? Don't think we're inclined to be generous with our gold just because your god was done in, too. You'll not get anything from us!"

"You mean you know about Geb?"

"Geb, Shmeb! What does the Rat God matter when Ondo the Golden is no more?" The old man passed a withered hand before his eyes. "No more gold for the domes of Tarras. Dull and drab they shall be forevermore, like our hearts."

Sympathy crept into Lirith's breast. This poor man—he had lost everything that mattered to him, and she was teasing him. She reached out to touch his arm.

He batted her hand away with a stinging *smack*!

"Get that thing away from me, girl! The gods know when it's been washed last. Probably never. Can't you beggars ever ask for soap? Always so greedy for gold, you are. But you'd do well to make yourself presentable. Maybe then someone would take you as an apprentice so you could earn an honest living. Of course, no doubt you're stupid and have no talents.

But certainly the dyers would take you to stir their vats. That doesn't require a shred of wit or skill. You'd be perfect for it."

Any sympathy Lirith had felt for the other evaporated like water in the sun. She tried to speak, but she could find no words, and only by clamping her arms at her sides did she prevent herself from throttling the old fellow right there.

"What?" he sneered. "Have you lost your tongue? Well, I suggest you go look for it somewhere else. We have no use for peculiar-looking, slack-mouthed dim-wits here. Now leave me to my woe and suffering!"

The door slammed, coming to a halt a hairbreadth from Lirith's nose.

She spent another hour on the Street of Flames, but with little more luck. With the help of the Touch, she sensed which workshops were populated, then knocked on those doors. However, the conversations that ensued were, if possible, even less pleasant than the first. While all of the goldsmiths were bereft at the loss of their god, to a one they were haughty, insulting, and mean. If Ondo had been anything like those who followed him, Lirith could imagine that the other gods would be only too glad to be rid of him.

Weary, longing to return to the cool quiet of the hostel, she forced herself to try one last door. A pretty woman no older than herself answered, and for a moment hope rose within her.

It was as quickly crushed as the woman launched into a caustic tirade that made the greetings of her fellow guildsmen seem warm in comparison.

"How dare you come at a time like this, seeking treasures from us?" the woman shrieked.

"But I'm not seeking treasure," Lirith said, "I simply wanted to—"

"I demand to know who you follow. Is it Imai? Jorus? Ah, I see." She jabbed a finger at Lirith's chest. "It's Sif that you follow. Well, you might as well leave. You'll never get your precious gold amulets, not now. Until we are granted a new god by the Etherion, the goldsmiths aren't making jewelry for any of the temples. And we'll never make anything for those who would plot to steal from us! Bronze is all you'll ever get."

This time Lirith was ready for it. She stepped back, narrowly avoiding the door as it slammed shut. Her good mood gone, she left the Street of Flames and started back toward the hostel.

At the first vendor she came upon, Lirith bought a cup of wine. Or tried to anyway. For after she handed the man a coin, he tipped a clay jug, spilling wine on the street, then handed her a wooden cup with a smile and a nod.

"Excuse me," Lirith said, gazing at the empty cup, "but doesn't one usually get the cup first and *then* the wine?"

The vendor slapped his forehead. "Forgive me, mistress. I can't seem to do anything right today. I keep mixing everything up, I do. Why, just after I came back from temple, I tried to fill my pitcher when it was already full. I spilled wine all over a lady's feet. She wasn't happy about that."

"I imagine not," Lirith said. She held the cup out.

This time the fellow got the order of things right. Lirith accepted his apologies—and the cup, which he told her to keep for her trouble—but she hardly tasted the sweet liquid as she drank. She did not want to have to tell the others that she had learned nothing from the goldsmiths.

Or had she? Something that last woman had said seemed important. She had mentioned something about Sif, about thinking that was who Lirith followed.

Was Sif a god? And if so, why had the other thought
Lirith to be one of Sif's followers?

She remembered the way the woman had pointed at
her and looked down. Revealed by the unlacing of her
bodice, the bronze spider amulet glowed dully in the
sunlight.

Bronze is all you'll ever get. . . .

Yes, that was important, she was sure of it. But what
did it mean? Lirith closed her fingers around the
Mournish amulet as she turned down another street.
She would ask Melia about this Sif as soon as she got
back to—

A scream escaped her, half-strangled by terror.
There, beyond an archway, she saw it: a writhing mass
that filled an entire courtyard. Even as she watched,
more bright threads were pulled toward it. The threads
dimmed to gray, becoming part of the tangle. Lirith
felt the first tugs on her being; her feet skittered along
stone, toward the archway.

It was bigger here, far bigger than it had ever been
in Ar-tolor. And it was growing. Even as she looked it
shuddered, then expanded. The courtyard couldn't
contain it. It spilled onto the street, gray tendrils probing. It wouldn't stop until it found and consumed her,
until it consumed all of the Weirding and every living
thing that was part of it.

Sickness flooded her. The cup fell from her hand.
She bent forward to spill what wine she had drunk
onto the pavement.

That action saved her life. Something hissed just
over her head, like an insect, and there was a flash of
silver. She jerked her head up. A slender knife quivered
in the trunk of an ornamental tree only an arm's length
away. Already the bark of the tree was turning black
where the knife had pierced it.

Poison.

She turned, searching with her eyes; she did not dare use the Touch, not now. The tangle still seethed on the corner of her vision. If she tried to touch the Weirding, it would drag her in for certain.

There—a flash of gold. A figure clad all in black stood in the dimness of an alley. It was him, the one she had seen at the docks. Then she saw the figure lift another knife. There was no time to turn, to run.

At least the tangle will not be able to consume you if you are already dead, sister.

It was small consolation. The figure in black tensed to throw—

—then snapped his head around. Again Lirith caught a glint of gold deep in the cowl. The figure stood motionless, as if listening. Then, like a shadow before the dawn, he spun around. There was a flutter of black, then the alley was empty.

Lirith lifted a hand to her throat, quite stunned to discover she was still alive. Surely the figure in the alley had possessed the necessary desire and skill to murder her. Why had he fled so suddenly? It was as if he had seen something coming toward him.

She looked around but saw nothing that might grant her a clue. The tangle had disappeared, and the court-yard beyond the arch was empty. Lirith hesitated, then reached out with the Touch. She sensed life all around, whole and beautiful: people, trees, birds in the air. That was all.

No, that wasn't true. For a fleeting moment she felt something else: a presence, watching her. But that was not the thing that shocked her most. For a delicious warmth rose within her, flooding her veins like rich, heady wine.

Then the presence was gone, and the feeling spilled out of Lirith, leaving her an empty husk.

40.

Aryn spun one more time, reveling in the soft swish of fabric around her. It was foolish, she knew, and more becoming of a girl than a woman grown, but there was something about her new garb that simply required spinning.

"By the Swiftest Arrow of Yrsaia," she said, "I thought I would never be clean again. I had imagined that the thieves and beggars in this city might have to dwell in the sewers. But I never thought Geb's temples would be there as well."

"Well, he *was* the Rat God," said Lirith, who sat before a window in their room at the hostel. "I believe they prefer those sorts of places."

Aryn shuddered, wondering if any amount of perfume would be enough to make her forget the smell. At first, in the Fifth Circle, when she and Durge had asked folk where they might find the Rat God, she had thought their answers to be mocking insults at the god's expense. However, before long it became clear it was no jest.

They had entered the sewers through the mouth of a pipe tall enough for them to walk upright next to one another. An old woman had told them to follow the rat once inside. Aryn had wondered how a rat could possibly lead them, then Durge had pointed to scratches on the wall: a triangular shape with two dots. Clearly it was meant to represent the face of a rat. Beneath had been an arrow; they had followed, carrying a torch Durge had bought from a vendor.

As far as Aryn could tell, the sewers ran for leagues beneath Tarras. Many of the tunnels were obviously ancient and unused, and those were not so terrible to tread, aside from being musty and littered with broken tiles that were treacherous underfoot. A few times she reached out with the Touch, and she sensed the threads of many lives not far down tunnels that branched to either side. And she sensed eyes watching them out of the dark as well. After a while she stopped reaching out to the Weirding.

It was when they were forced to traverse a newer— and still actively used—section of the sewers that their trek turned more nightmarish. They waded through dark water that came up to their knees, so that Aryn's gown floated out around her. It was not the only thing floating in the water. And things swam in it as well. More than once she saw sleek, wriggling forms fleeing the circle of light cast by Durge's torch. The stench was fierce and relentless, so that breathing was torture.

When Aryn dared to cast a thread out to the Weirding, she sensed no human lives nearby, only the rats in the water. She supposed those who dwelled beneath Tarras and knew its ways had no need of symbols to find the temple of Geb. The signs were for visitors only, and no doubt by intention led through the most unpleasant ways. Aryn was certain none of the followers of Geb frequented this tunnel themselves.

At last the passage ended, and they had trod dryer ways, soon coming upon a cavernous, echoing space that could only be the temple of Geb. Tiled columns rose to a vaulted ceiling that was lost in shadow despite the flickering light of hundreds of candles. Weathered boards and crates were arranged into makeshift benches before a rude altar atop which stood a wooden likeness of Geb: a thin man with the head of a rat.

Unfortunately, their journey to the temple proved to be far from worth the smell and trouble. Few of Geb's followers were in the temple. Most had fled deep into the sewers, fearing hunts and reprisals now that their god was no more; that was why Aryn had sensed so many lives hidden in the tunnels. Without a god to protect them, there was nothing to stop others from doing what they wished with the city's outcasts. Sympathy blossomed in her heart. These people had little enough to begin with; now even that had been taken from them.

My lady, Durge had said in a hoarse whisper, *I think it is best if we leave now. I do not believe we are . . . wanted here.*

Sympathy had drained from Aryn, replaced by dread. Quickly she reached out with the Touch. Yes, there were eyes upon them again. Angry, suspicious eyes. She grabbed Durge's hand, and together they hurried back the way they had come.

By the time they reached the streets of Tarras, they were so filthy and reeking that people scrambled to get out of their way. Aryn knew her gown was ruined, and the only other garment she had was far too heavy for the warm climate of Tarras. What was she going to do?

Despair turned to elation when they stepped into their room at the hostel and discovered that Melia had bought new clothes for all of them.

I had a feeling you might be needing these, she had said, her small nose wrinkling.

Aryn had soaked for at least an hour in the marble tub in the bathing chamber, sprinkling flower petals and scented oils in the deliciously warm water. Now she felt fresh and light in the dress Melia had bought for her: a gauzy confection of sky-blue fabric that, for all the manner in which it flowed about her, was surprisingly modest and simple to move in. Lirith wore a similar dress of bright yellow, a striking contrast to her dark skin.

Aryn's spinning did not go unnoticed.

"I believe that gown suits you, sister," Lirith said.

Aryn curtsied low. "Why, thank you, sister. And may I say that you look lovely in yours."

Lirith smiled, but the expression was fleeting, and she turned her head to gaze out the window. Was something wrong?

Before Aryn could ask, the door to the bathing chamber opened, and Durge stepped out. At least she *thought* it was Durge.

The knight had shed his customary heavy gray tunic and instead wore the new attire Melia had bought for him: a pair of billowing, sea-green pants that were gathered at the waist and ankles, and an open vest of dark purple. He tucked a dagger into a black-leather belt slanted across his hips. However, it was not really his clothes that made Aryn stare.

She had never seen quite so much of Durge before. His bare arms were chiseled like those of a statue, and the thick, dark hair of his chest swirled in circular patterns. She could count the muscles of his stomach as if they were precisely lined paving stones in a Tarrasian road.

Durge frowned, apparently noticing Aryn's attention. "Is something amiss, my lady? I suppose I've managed to get these trousers all wrong and look the fool for it. I fear I couldn't tell which was meant to be the front and which the back."

He had trimmed his mustaches and shaved his cheeks, and his wet, brown hair was slicked back from his brow. The soft glow of late afternoon through the curtains softened the crags and valleys of his face.

"Durge," Aryn breathed, "you're so . . . that is, I mean, you look . . . ."

Melia drifted forward. The lady still wore a white kirtle, but it seemed lighter than before, almost translucent, and trimmed with fine silver thread.

"I believe Aryn means to say that you look very manly, Durge."

He glowered as he plucked at his gauzy pants. "That is passing strange, my lady, for I do not feel particularly manly at the moment."

"Just trust me on this one, dear." She squeezed his arm, and her eyebrows rose. "Falken, perhaps you should grow muscles like this."

The bard snorted and strummed a sour note on his lute. "Only if I can get them drinking ale."

Falken also wore new clothes courtesy of Melia: pants like those Durge wore, only soft gray in color, and a loose-fitting shirt of azure cloth belted at the waist. While more slender than Durge, Falken was in fact lean and wiry. He had shaved as well, and he looked striking in his new clothes, if still a bit wolfish and wild around the edges. However, the bard only held Aryn's attention for a moment.

What is it, sister? spoke a voice in her mind.

Aryn realized she was staring at Durge again.

It's nothing, she spun the words back across the Weirding.

She started to feel a question return to her, but she hastily snatched back her thread and turned toward a sideboard to pour herself a glass of wine. However, as she sipped the cool liquid, she wondered. Why had she been gawking so rudely at Durge?

Or course—she was simply surprised to see a man of Durge's advanced years looking so hale. After all, he was past his fifth-and-fortieth winter now. Yet she knew his greatsword weighed half as much as she did; no doubt swinging it kept him in good form. And she was glad for the fact, for Durge was her friend, and she wished him to remain well and hearty for many years to come. Satisfied with her explanation, Aryn downed the rest of her wine.

"So were you granted an audience with the emperor?" Lirith asked. Melia's kitten had sprung up into her lap and was playing with a corner of cloth from her gown.

Melia let out a sound that might have been any number of different words, none of them particularly pleasant.

"You can take that as a *no*," Falken said. "How about some of that wine, Aryn?"

She hastily poured two cups for the bard and lady.

Durge started to sit, seemed to get momentarily tangled in his pants, then hastily stood again. "I find it puzzling that Emperor Ephesian would turn you away, Melia, given your . . . er, your stature here in Tarras."

"Ephesian would never turn me away," the lady said. "He wouldn't dare! He knows what I did to his great-grandfather, Ephesian Sixteen."

Aryn gulped. "And what was that?"

Melia's lips coiled in a smug smile. "Let's just say he never sat on his throne again without using an extra cushion."

"I don't understand," Lirith said. "If Ephesian respects you, Melia, why weren't you granted an audience?"

Falken answered. "Because that little wart in expensive clothes—excuse me, I mean the Minister of Gates—wouldn't even let us into the First Circle. Nor would he relay our message to the emperor."

"But Melia," Aryn said, "couldn't you have just, you know, *tampered* with the minister?"

"I'm afraid that's frowned upon here in Tarras, dear. A god tends to get touchy when you meddle with one of his followers. There's such competition for disciples in the city that everyone gets a bit possessive. And the Minister of the Gates wore the emblem of Misar."

"Misar?" Durge rumbled. "Who is that?"

Melia let out a pained sigh. "The god of bureaucrats. So believe me when I tell you Misar is a stickler for rules. Much as I would have liked doing so, I couldn't try anything to influence that horrid little man."

"So now what?" Lirith asked.

"Now I must see if I can find other means of getting a message to Ephesian. If I can, then . . ."

Melia's words faltered, and she lifted a hand to her brow.

Falken moved to her side. "The headache again?"

She gave a shallow nod. "Do not fear. I am certain it will pass as quickly as the others."

Aryn gave Lirith a concerned glance. Since when had Melia been getting headaches?

Falken helped Melia into a chair, then looked up at the others. "I would be pleased to hear that the rest of you had better luck than we did."

Unfortunately, they had not. Together, Aryn and Durge related their foul and fruitless trek into the sewers beneath the Fifth Circle.

"All of the followers of Geb are in hiding," Aryn said in finish to their tale. "They're afraid they'll be killed now that they're without a god. I suppose I can't blame them. But we didn't find anything at all helpful."

"I did find this," Durge said. He tossed a gold coin into the air and caught it again. "I saw it as we made our way through one of the more malodorous passages. Although I confess, it seems odd to find money in a sewer. Nor does it do us any good."

"Odd indeed," Falken said. "May I see that, Durge?"

The knight handed him the coin. Falken turned it over in his hand. "It's blank—there's no imprint on either side."

Durge nodded. "I imagine it has been worn smooth by time. Most likely it has lain there for centuries."

"Maybe." Falken handed the coin back to Durge.

"What about you, Lirith?" Aryn said. "What did you learn from the goldsmiths?"

Lirith pushed the kitten from her lap and stood. "That if Ondo is anything like his followers, then nearly everyone in the city would have motivation for murder."

They listened as Lirith recounted her numerous unpleasant conversations on the Street of Flames. When her words trailed off, she looked once more out the window. She gripped her gown, knotting the fabric in clenched hands.

Aryn moved to the witch. "What is it, Lirith? Something's wrong, something you haven't told us."

At last Lirith turned back, her dark eyes grim. "I was attacked on my way back here."

They all listened with growing horror as Lirith told how a man in a black robe—a man she she had glimpsed as they disembarked from the *Fate Runner*—had thrown a knife at her before fleeing.

"I don't know why he ran," Lirith said, gazing at her

hands. "Surely he meant to kill me, but for some reason he fled before he could throw his second knife."

Aryn knelt beside her and placed her good hand atop Lirith's.

Melia moved toward them, her expression grave. "Did you not . . . sense anything, dear?"

Lirith sighed. "I believe I did sense another presence, but I couldn't be sure. You see, there was . . . something else I saw in the Weirding just before I was attacked."

Aryn felt Lirith's flesh go cold beneath her hand.

"What is it, sister?" she gasped.

Lirith looked up, her eyes haunted, and Melia nodded.

"You've seen it again, haven't you?" Melia said.

Aryn gripped tighter. "What does she mean, Lirith? What did you see?"

Lirith licked her lips, then spoke words that made Aryn's breath cease in her lungs.

"I have seen a tangle. A tangle in the threads of the Weirding."

41.

Two days later, Durge awoke to cool silver light.

At first he could not tell whether it was late or early. Darkness never seemed to fall in this city, not completely; even in the deep of night, the white buildings reflected the light of the moon, the stars, and numberless torches, imparting a paleness to the air so unlike the inky, impenetrable nights that fell upon the Dominions. Durge did not like the eerie citylight; it made him think of ghosts.

But they are not here, Durge of Stonebreak. Nor are they anywhere save beneath the hard soil of Embarr, and well over a score of years buried at that.

However, if that was so, why had he seen them so clearly in Ar-tolor? Maere and little Durnem, looking just as he remembered, except blanched of all color, all life. And so sad; he had never remembered her looking so sorrowful, even when he told her the king had ordered him on patrol of the northern borders, that he would be gone all the summer and the autumn—but no more—and that he would return to her with the first snow.

Promise me one thing, she had said, pressing her hands to his cheeks. *All the king's knights are so somber, as if the price to win their swords was their smiles. Promise me that you won't come back grim like them.*

It had seemed such an odd request, but never had he refused her anything.

I swear it by my heart, Maere.

However, he did not return with the first snow. A large band of wildmen had moved south with the coming of winter. It was Falken Blackhand who had warned Embarr's king, and that was how Durge first met the ancient bard. Durge's patrol was given the task of sending the wildmen fleeing back north. It wasn't until Midwinter's Day that he finally returned to his manor at Stonebreak. And he found two fresh graves waiting for him, one large, one small.

Bless them, Yirga, the reeve's wife, had said in answer to his numb silence. *The fever took not one but both. I think the gods did not wish mother and child to be apart. It is a mercy, it is. Oh, bless them, bless them.*

Durge had said nothing, but he knew Yirga was wrong, that the gods knew nothing of mercy. He had knelt beside their graves as soft snow fell, and for the last time in his life Durge had wept. He wept long and bitterly, pounding at the frozen soil until his bare hands ran bloody, as if he were burying his own heart there with them.

And, for all these years, he thought he had. Maere had made him promise not to become grim, but she had broken her part of that vow by leaving him. So Durge had become a good and solemn knight in service to King Sorrin of Embarr, and he had put aside joy, love, and other such frivolous things. That was, until . . .

Durge shut his eyes and once again saw the way Aryn had stared at him two days ago. Memories of ice and sorrow melted under the heat of a fire so long banked he thought it had gone utterly to ashes. But there was yet a spark.

He sat up in bed, sweating. This had to cease at once. Aryn had stared at him because he looked a fool, that was all. One so young and fair could never find him worthy of attention.

True, there were men who turned their gazes from Aryn due to the condition of her arm; but they were not fit to marry dogs, let alone a woman of high station. And there were other men who, like Durge, thought nothing about her arm, except that perhaps because of it she had found a quiet strength to match her beauty.

"Foolishness and fancy," he whispered under his mustaches. "What is wrong with you, Durge of Stonebreak? These days if you are not drifting in thoughts of the past, then you are picturing futures that can never be."

Perhaps the same malady afflicted him as Lady Melia. Several times again over the last two days she had become caught in reveries of long ago. Durge could see that Falken was worried, but the bard seemed not to know what to do. Nor did Melia seem aware of her behavior, which was perhaps the strangest fact of all. For Durge had never known another—man or woman—who appeared as assured and in control of her faculties as Lady Melia.

The light had brightened a fraction. Early then, not late. Morning was coming, still an hour away across the sea, but he knew he might as well rise. He stood and clothed himself in his new trousers and vest, grudgingly admitting the garb was practical for the climate. Only as he moved to the door did he notice that Falken's bed was empty. He stepped into the larger room beyond.

"Good morning, dear." Melia stood beside a table, using a silver pitcher to fill a pair of cups with a pink liquid. "Would you like some *margra* juice?"

Durge had absolutely no idea how to answer that question, as he had never heard of *margra* juice before, but he did not wish to insult the lady. He nodded and accepted a cup.

"You're up early," Falken said. The bard sat in a chair, strumming a soft tune on his lute.

"As are you," Durge said. As he often did, he marveled at the way the lute seemed a part of Falken's body. Sometimes it was as if the bard spoke with the mellow tones of the instrument as much as with his own voice.

"I'm glad you're up and ready," Melia said. "I learned during the night that a meeting of the Etherion has been called. It will commence at dawn."

Durge frowned. "My lady, surely I would have heard if a messenger came to our rooms during the night, yet I heard no such thing."

Melia only smiled and poured herself a cup of juice. Durge knew it was best not to press for further explanation. Much as he favored reason, he knew it did not always apply where Melia was concerned. He settled for drinking his juice. It was cool and sweet, and the cup was empty before he knew it.

"More?" Melia said, and Durge nodded. It seemed he liked *margra* juice after all.

They reached the gate of the Second Circle just as sunlight touched the highest domes in the city, setting them ablaze.

"We'd better hurry," Falken said, eyeing the sky. "Didn't you say the Etherion assembled at dawn? We don't want to be late."

"Actually," the lady said, "we do." She walked at a stately pace through the archway.

Durge glanced at Aryn and Lirith, but they shrugged; neither knew what Melia was talking about.

The ladies had arisen and dressed hastily, yet both looked lovely. They had coiled their hair high atop their heads, as was the fashion for women in this city. Of course, as pale as she was, Aryn would never be mistaken for anything but a woman of the northlands. However, with her dark, burnished skin, Lirith could easily have passed for a high lady of Tarras.

Falken groaned. "Please, Melia. It's far too early in the morning to be enigmatic."

"But it's really very simple," she said. "Only the priests and priestesses of the lesser temples will arrive at the Etherion precisely at dawn. To arrive late signifies that one is so confident or all-knowing that one does not fear missing anything important. And the later one arrives—"

"—then the more important one is?" Aryn said tentatively.

Melia laughed. "Well, at least the more important they *believe* they are, dear. And sometimes, in Tarras, that's all that matters."

This made no sense whatsoever to Durge. "I do not see how someone can be important merely by believing that he is. If I believe I have armor when I do not, it will hardly prevent a man from sticking a sword in my belly."

Melia patted his cheek. "You might be surprised, dear."

They were not alone as they passed through the airy streets of the Fourth Circle. Men and women clad in robes of myriad hues moved toward the blue dome that towered above all others.

As they went, Aryn and Lirith bowed their heads toward one another. Their lips did not move, yet all the same Durge had the feeling they were speaking. Their first evening in the city, when Lirith told them of the magic tangle she had seen, Durge had not had the faintest idea what she was talking about. However, Aryn had blanched as if a cold wind had struck her, and Melia and Falken had given knowing nods.

In the time since, Lirith had been far more subdued than usual, speaking little, and then usually with Aryn. Durge's knowledge of witches was scant, yet logic did tell him one thing: It seemed far beyond coincidence that Lirith's tangle should be greater here in Tarras, the city where gods were being murdered. Certainly the two had to be connected; as for how, that was leagues beyond Durge.

What concerned him more—because he might actually do something about it—was the man who had made an attempt on Lirith's life. Why had he been spying on them at the docks? And why did he want to harm one of their number? Durge didn't know. Yet all the same, he found himself wishing his greatsword wasn't back at the hostel.

Be watchful, Durge of Stonebreak. Sure as the sun must set, there is danger ahead of you this—

His thoughts were shattered by the high, clear sound of a child crying.

Durge glanced up; the others had moved slightly ahead. They did not seem to hear the child's cries. He shuddered. Was it the ghosts again, only no longer silent?

He turned, then breathed a sigh as he saw the source of the wailing. It was no ethereal child, but a mundane boy of perhaps four or five winters. He stood on the side of the street, black hair tousled, tears streaming down his round face. Had he lost track of his parents? As he cried, the boy flapped his arms, his hands lost inside long, dangling sleeves.

Durge frowned. It wasn't just the sleeves that were

too long. The blue robe the boy wore was far too large for him, slipping half over his shoulders and pooling around him like water on the street. The robe was clearly intended for a grown man. In fact, it looked like the robe some of the priests they had passed earlier had worn. But then why was this weeping boy wearing it? He gazed around himself with large, bewildered eyes, then his flood of tears gushed anew.

There was something odd about the child and his too-large robe. Durge started toward him.

"Durge!" a voice called behind him. "Come on!"

He jerked his head around. It was Aryn. The others were some way ahead of him now. She motioned for him to hurry.

Durge glanced back. A woman had approached the boy now and was speaking to him in a consoling voice, no doubt asking him if he knew the name of the street he lived on. Satisfied, Durge hurried after the others.

However, it was some time before the sound of the child's grief faded completely from his ears.

42.

The light of the sun was just creeping over the wall of the First Circle below when they passed between two towering pillars of white marble into the Etherion.

They moved along a broad hallway. Then the walls fell away to either side, and Durge stumbled to a halt, gripping a stone balustrade for support. For all their skill, he knew the engineers of Embarr could never have constructed the likes of what he saw before him.

The space beneath the dome of the Etherion was vast—so impossibly vast an entire castle might have fit within, leaving room to spare. So far was it from the place they stood to the opposite side that the moisture on the air was visible as a faint haze. The dome soared above their heads, as blue as it was on the outside, so that it seemed they were looking at a vivid sky. Round windows were cut near the base of the dome, and golden sunlight rained down. Birds flitted back and forth across the lofty heights.

The Etherion formed a great circle, and its walls were lined with colonnades of marble veined with crimson. Durge counted seven levels or tiers, each supported by a row of columns, and between each pair of columns was a kind of alcove in which onlookers could gather. The alcoves in the bottom tiers were small and cramped, providing only standing room, while those in the topmost tiers were large and open, appointed with chaises where priests or priestesses might recline while watching the proceedings. Evidently higher meant more important in the Etherion just as in Tarras itself.

"Look at Durge," Aryn said with a smile. "A bird could fly into his mouth. I believe he's struck with awe."

Falken laughed. "More likely he's trying to figure out how the Tarrasian engineers built this place."

"I imagine they had some help in the matter," Lirith said, casting her dark gaze toward Melia.

"Come," Melia said. "My alcove is this way."

Durge managed to wrest his attention from the marvel of the Etherion. "*Your* alcove, Melia?"

She shrugged. "Well, I suppose I would have to share it with Tome, if he were here. After all, it was reserved for the Nine of us. Although it was always a bit cramped if all of us showed up at once."

Melia's alcove was located on the sixth tier up, only one below the highest, on the side opposite the great archway that led into and out of the domed space. The alcove was large and furnished with comfortable chairs and tables of polished wood. However, all were covered with a thick layer of dust. How long had it been since Melia had last been to Tarras? Before Durge could ask, the small woman flicked her hand, and the dust was gone. Had he only imagined it then?

Deeming it best not to inquire, Durge sat with the others, although he chose a seat nearer the alcove's door than the balcony overlooking the Etherion. Should anyone enter, Durge did not wish to be caught unawares.

After a few moments, someone did enter: a servant bearing a pitcher of wine and five cups. Another servant brought a bowl of some pale green fruit Durge did not recognize.

"Melia," Aryn said, "are you going to address the Etherion?"

"I don't think so, dear. At least not today." She handed the young baroness a cup of wine. "I'm afraid I'm something of an outsider these days. It's my intention simply to listen and find out what the various temples believe. And who knows? Perhaps those who plotted against Ondo and Geb will stumble in their speaking and reveal themselves, as the guilty so often do."

Durge considered that a slim chance, although he did not say so. One who slew gods could not be an amateur.

Only about half of the Etherion's alcoves were filled; the others were empty. No doubt many priests feared to leave their temples with the murderer still at large in the city. After all, it was not only gods that had been slain.

"It looks as if the discourse is about to begin," Melia said. "Let's listen."

She moved to a gilded horn, shaped like a kind of trumpet, that protruded from the wall, and removed a cover that capped its mouth.

From his position near the door, Durge craned his neck so he could see over the balustrade. The white floor of the Etherion, far below, was empty save for a dais of creamy stone, triangular in shape. Three figures stood upon the dais, as did a pedestal topped by a gold orb. In addition, a trio of gold horns—similar to the one on the wall of Melia's alcove—protruded from the pedestal. Again Durge wondered what they could be for. If they were trumpets, then they were facing the wrong way, for their larger ends faced outward.

"Who are those people?" Aryn whispered to Melia.

"They are the three Voices of the Etherion," Melia said quietly. "They are selected anew each year to lead the discourse. One is selected by the temples of the two lowest tiers, one by the two highest tiers, and the other by those in the middle. Thus are all the temples represented."

Aryn opened her mouth to ask more, but at that moment one of the three on the dais raised a hand and spoke. He was a tall priest, with shaggy black hair and, even from a distance, black eyes that glinted fiercely.

"I said the Etherion will come to order!"

Durge would have thought the man's voice would be lost in the vastness beneath the dome, but somehow it seemed to come booming into the alcove. Despite the force with which his words were spoken, priests and priestesses continued to speak with one another and to move between the various alcoves and tiers, holding spontaneous meetings.

Falken let out a snort. "I'm not sure coming to order is something the Etherion knows how to do."

Melia's expression was pained, but she did not argue.

Durge watched the proceedings with a mixture of interest and disdain. It was clear the bard was correct; this was no orderly moot, but more a great, chaotic melee in which words were the weapons of choice.

The tall, shaggy-haired priest on the dais, Durge soon learned, was named Medris, and he represented the temple of Zeth, who was clearly one of the most powerful and important gods of Tarras, for the emperor followed his mysteries.

The woman who stood on the dais was Vanhera. She was nearly as tall and proud as Medris, but she was cool silver to his hot iron. As he listened, Durge learned that she was the high priestess of the temple of

Yrsaia the Huntress, a fact which made Aryn gasp when it was revealed. Durge knew Yrsaia was one of the more important goddesses in the Dominions, but here Vanhera represented only the middle tiers of the Etherion.

The third priest on the dais, representing the lowest tiers, was an emaciated man in a drab brown robe, yet he seemed somehow more compelling than those who stood beside him. He was Lyderus, priest of the temple of Gol, who, from what Durge could gather, was the god of a group of ascetic hermits. He supposed that explained Lyderus's gaunt visage.

Durge knew the gods themselves were not present in the Etherion, only their priests, but there was a power on the air he could not deny. It felt like the air on the moors of Embarr just before a storm swept out of the north with thunder and lightning. Wherever they were, the gods were watching.

"The circle is open," Medris said, his voice again booming into the alcove. "Who would address the Etherion?"

All around, flags of different colors were unfurled and draped from various balconies.

Medris scanned the flags, then nodded. "The Etherion recognizes the right of the temple of Vathris Bullslayer to speak."

He laid his hand on the golden orb that topped the pedestal before him. There was a faint whirring, like the sound of wings, and something rose from the shadows below. As far as Durge could tell, it was a huge crystal set into an ornate wood frame. It was like a window, but with no walls around it, and made with glass so thick that things seen through it were distorted. Attached to the frame were two more of the gilded horns.

The crystal was supported by some sort of mechanical frame of wood and iron, with multiple joints, gears, and pulleys that Durge could not fathom at this distance. The crystal began to rise toward the highest tier.

"Halt!" Lyderus said on the dais, the gaunt priest's voice sharp and thin as a knife, but ringing into the alcove as Medris's had.

Lyderus moved to the center of the dais. "The records shows that at the last assembly of the Etherion, the final speech was made by the temple of Vathris of the first tier. Precedence must be granted to a temple of another tier, if one would speak. The Etherion will hear the temple of Ondo."

Medris glared at Lyderus, his rage clear even at a distance. Both he and Lyderus looked to Vanhera, who stood apart from them on the dais. She glanced to one side, and Durge saw a hollow behind the dais he had not noticed before. In it a scribe wrote furiously in a book. The scribe flipped back a page, then nodded to Vanhera.

"The record is as Lyderus describes," she said, her voice filling the Etherion. "The temple of Ondo will speak."

Medris gave a poisonous scowl, but he stepped away from the pedestal. Lyderus placed his hand on the golden orb. At once the crystal began to move again, the mechanical arms carrying it down to the third tier, then moving it halfway around the Etherion. At last Durge realized the movements of the crystal corresponded to the motions of Lyderus's fingers upon the orb; somehow he was using it to control the crystal.

The crystal came to a halt before the alcove whose priests had unfurled a golden flag. The purpose of the crystal became clear, for one of the priests stepped toward it, and the crystal enlarged the image of his face, so that it filled the entire frame, ensuring that all in the Etherion might plainly see his expressions. The priest spoke, leaning toward one of the golden horns, and his voice rang out in Melia's alcove.

Durge began to understand. The horns on the frame of the crystal were like those the three Voices spoke into on the dais. Somehow the horns carried the voice of the one who spoke into them, redoubled it, and brought it through other horns into each of the alcoves in the Etherion. It was a trick, like that of the crystal. However, he had never known light and sound could be manipulated as if they were wood or metal. The Tarrasians were indeed great engineers. Or at least, they had been when the Etherion was built over a millennium ago.

The priest of Ondo was speaking in a shrill voice, his pinched face filling the crystal. Lirith was right; they seemed a rude lot.

"This is an outrage! How could another temple dare try to speak before us—we, the followers of Ondo, who are bereft of our god? By what precedent would the temple of Vathris usurp our right to be heard? Unless, perhaps, it was their god who did this ugly and violent deed!" Spit flecked the crystal, magnified a dozen times over. "All know how Vathris Bullslayer craves the taste of blood!"

A roar went up from many of the alcoves, loudest of all from that belonging to the temple of Vathris, where a red flag waved angrily.

"Now will the temple of Vathris speak," Medris said.

Lyderus started to protest, but Vanhera shook her head. Medris gripped the orb, and the crystal whirred up and across the Etherion to the highest tier.

"Lies and more lies!" roared a burly priest. His thick neck puffed out in rage, nearly splitting the collar of his crimson robe. "Everything that the temple of Ondo speaks is known to be a lie. It was so before their god perished, and nothing has changed since. Who here wasn't promised gold, never to receive it?"

Shouts and catcalls echoed around the Etherion. Scores of flags waved in agreement. In their alcove, the priests of Ondo quailed.

Falken let out a soft whistle. "Ondo really didn't make many friends in the Etherion, did he?"

Melia glared at him. "He didn't deserve to die."

"I'm not saying he did."

She leaned back in her chair and sighed. "I suppose it's true. Ondo always was a bit on the selfish side. But he was not a bad god."

"It's all right, Melia," Falken said. "We'll find the guilty ones."

However, Durge was not nearly so confident as the bard. The morning wore on, and many more of the temples spoke. It seemed that flags were always waving, and the crystal always flitting back and forth across the Etherion as Medris, Vanhera, and Lyderus wrestled for control of the golden orb below.

Yet for all the speeches that were made, and for all the angry words flung back and forth, things only seemed more muddled by the time the Etherion disbanded for the day. The temple of Ondo had accused a dozen more temples of conspiring in the murder of their god—even temples that had lost priests and priestesses to the murderer themselves. No one spoke for the Rat God, and the followers of Geb were nowhere to be seen.

Even before the discourse ended, priests and priestesses were streaming from their alcoves into the broad halls that ringed the Etherion. The only thing that Durge had learned for certain was that none of the temples seemed to have any idea what was going on in the city, and that all of them were deathly afraid. He was fairly certain none of the temples present had conspired in the murders. It wasn't much, but he supposed it was something.

The others rose from their chairs to depart the alcove. Durge opened the door and stepped through first, to be sure the way was safe. The great, curving corridor was crowded. Priests and priestesses hurried past, robes fluttering, on their way out of the Etherion.

Something caught Durge's eyes. Twenty paces away, a trio of priests moved quickly down the corridor. They moved opposite the flow of the other priests and priestesses, away from the entrance of the Etherion. The three priests wore robes of dark gray crisscrossed by pearlescent threads. Durge did not recall seeing any gray robes in the Etherion, or any gray flags waving. Who were these priests? The three moved hastily to an opening that led to a set of stairs, their hooded heads moving back and forth as if they did not wish to be seen. Then they ducked into the opening and were gone.

The others stepped into the hallway. Durge turned to ask Melia about the three priests in gray, but before he could she breezed down the corridor.

"This way," she said. "I would speak with Orsith."

They came upon the old priest not far from his alcove, holding on to the arm of young Landus for support. This surprised Durge, for Orsith had seemed so free and graceful as he drifted in the air at the temple of Mandu. But now, forced to move by more mundane means, he walked slowly, his back hunched, his fingers as thin as twigs on Landus's arm.

Durge saw Melia's eyes grow bright with sorrow, and somehow he knew what she had just realized: that this trip to Tarras was the last she was likely to make in Orsith's lifetime. What must it be like for a being such as Melia or Falken, both of whom must have left so many they cared about behind them? The thought left his heart heavy and cold. Who was he to dread ghosts?

"Dearest one," Orsith said, a smile lighting up his face. "I thought I saw you across the Etherion, although I confess my eyes are not what they once were. Only Mandu appears clear to me now. And good, sturdy Landus here, for he is ever at my side. A fine priest of Mandu he will make one day."

The young acolyte bowed his head, but his smile was still clear for all to see.

"I wanted to ask you what you thought of the discourse today," Melia said. "I'm afraid it was not as illuminating as I had hoped."

"And yet you mustn't cease hoping, dearest," Orsith said. "For it is all we have in the end."

Melia opened her mouth, but what she was going to say Durge never knew, for at that moment a peal of thunder rang out in the corridor. Again the thunder came, and again. Only it couldn't be thunder, not here inside a building, however vast it was. And the sound was strangely sharp.

Screams echoed down the corridor, and people came running from the direction of the sound, robes clutched up around their ankles. Durge exchanged looks with the others, then they dashed down the corridor against the flow of fleeing priests and priestesses, leaving Orsith and Landus behind.

The corridor curved to the left, following the circle of the Etherion. Durge pushed his way past a tangle of priests in orange robes who were falling over one another in an effort to escape. Then he came to a halt, the others beside him.

Three forms lay sprawled on the white-marble floor of the corridor. Blood pooled around their bodies, as crimson as their robes. One stared upward, a corpulent man, his eyes bulging, his face a dead mask of astonishment. Durge recognized him; he was the priest of Vathris Bullslayer who had addressed the Etherion earlier that morning. By their robes, the other two were priests of the warrior god as well. All of them had been struck dead. Falken moved to the fallen priests; Durge followed. Acrid smoke hung on the air.

Durge and Falken both knelt to examine one of the priests. There was a small rent in the man's robe. Falken tore the garment aside. The hole was not only in the cloth of his robe. A single small, red pit marked the center of the man's chest; it was from this that the blood flowed. The hole looked not unlike an arrow wound to Durge. However, there was no sign of whatever it was that had pierced the priest.

Falken stood, his hand red with blood. "I don't understand. What kind of magic could do this?"

Durge did not know, but as he knelt beside the fallen priest, he realized that they had learned one thing this day after all.

Even the Etherion was not safe.

43.

Lirith made her way through the crowded, dusty streets of the Fifth Circle, past countless merchants selling silver rings, rugs, ripe fruits, veils, and roasted meat. This was the outer circle of Tarras, where the poor, the forgotten, the outcasts dwelled. Again she shut her eyes, casting a thread out to the shimmering web of the Weirding.

Where are you, sisters? You must be here—you have to be. Show me how to find you.

However, the only answer was silence and the faint hum of life that coursed ceaselessly along the Weirding.

She opened her eyes and saw an old man sitting on a carpet on the street, selling mysteries of wood. These were tiny idols, representations of the New Gods a follower of one of the mystery cults might keep in a pocket or knotted in a scarf. Lirith recognized some of them: a crude wooden bull with a needle in its side for Vathris Bullslayer, a man with the face of a horse for Jorus Stormrunner. There were far more she did not know: a goddess with four arms and a serene, painted smile; a god with snowy wings sprouting from his shoulders; and another god with the legs and horns of a goat, a leering grin, and a monstrous phallus.

Lirith moved past the seller of mysteries. Perhaps she

was wrong; perhaps they were not here. Perhaps the New Gods had driven Her away from this place.

But you know that's not true, sister. Sia is everywhere, even in this city where the New Gods hold court.

She moved on. Faces of a dozen different hues passed by, some as dark as her own, some darker yet. It had been some time since Lirith had seen others of similar complexion to herself. There had been a few in Corantha, fewer yet in the Dominions. Was she kin to any of these people?

But she would never know. Nor would she ever be able to ask her parents about her heritage. All she knew was that Toloria had not always been their home, that they had traveled there from somewhere else before Lirith was born. And that was all she would ever know.

She came to a grimy plaza where rag-clad children ran from red-faced vendors and women filled clay vessels from a murky fountain. On one side of the plaza, a number of men and women sat on the cobblestones, leaning against a wall. At first Lirith thought they were laborers taking a midday break. Then she drew closer and knew that was not so.

Their eyes were neither open nor closed; instead they were dull, unseeing. Their limbs were sticks inside filthy clothes, and flies crawled across their sun-darkened faces. Each of them smiled with purple-stained lips, as if gazing upon some blissful scene. In their limp hands rested crude wooden cups.

Strangely compelled, Lirith reached out to the Weirding, searching for the threads of these people. She snatched her mind back as nausea flooded her. She had seen the threads of the men and women; they were dark and shriveled.

"Care for a cup, mistress?" a hoarse voice said.

A man stood before her. He might have been

comely once, but rot had taken his teeth, and the flesh of his face seemed oddly slack, as if it barely hung on to his skull. A sweet scent rose from him. Decay. His lips were stained a dark purple, like those of the others.

"What?" she choked.

"It is a new potion, mistress, like nothing you have tried before." He held a small wooden cup toward her. "Some call it the Elixir of the Past. Imbibe it, and all your fondest memories will appear before you as if they had never faded. You can live the past again and again."

Sickness rose in Lirith. Live the past over and over? "No," she said, gagging.

She pushed aside the man. However, he seemed not to notice her as he turned to offer his cup to another passerby. This man surrendered a coin and took the cup. Swallowing bile, Lirith fled the plaza, leaving the shriveled, empty people to their visions of the past.

At last the sickness in her subsided, and she tried another street. The afternoon was drawing on; she had been searching the city all day. No doubt the others would wonder where she was, for she had told Aryn she was merely going for a walk.

Where would you go in this city, sister? That is where you should seek them.

Even as she thought this, she saw a narrow arch in a stone wall. Beyond was a dim, green-gold space. As if drawn, she moved to the arch.

There was an iron gate, and through the bars she saw a garden. It was cool and shaded, a grotto of emerald flecked with copper. She pushed on the gate, but it did not move. It must have been locked.

She glanced down. It *was* locked, but not by wood or metal. Instead, living vines coiled around the bars, holding the gate shut. Yet that made little sense. The gate would have to remain shut for days for the vines to grow over it so extensively, but the garden beyond looked carefully tended.

Then she understood. The gate was indeed locked, but only to those who did not possess the right key. Lirith slipped her fingers through the gate and brushed the vines. It was a simple spell; she didn't even need to shut her eyes. In her mind she touched the threads that belonged to the plants and unwove them.

The vines fell away from the bars.

Lirith pushed, and the gate swung inward. She stepped into the grotto beyond. There was a rustling behind her, and she did not need to look to know that the vines had coiled back over the bars. She made her way down a narrow path, past braided walls of fruit trees and curtains of flowers.

The voices were faint at first, so that she thought them merely the murmuring of unseen fountains. Then she heard faint whispers in her mind, and she knew she was not alone.

Who is this one?

A trespasser. A follower of the New Ones.

No, daughters, she knew the spell. She wove it with great skill.

She hails from the north then.

But her face is dark as dusk.

Yet all the same from the north she is, although the south does flow in her veins.

What should we do? She will sense the presence of our coven in a moment.

Ah, but she already has.

Silence. Lirith paused, waiting. All around her leaves fluttered, but there was no breeze to stir them. She opened her mind, her thoughts, so that they might see who she was. There were a dozen of them at least, maybe more. It was difficult to be sure amidst the dense life of the grotto.

At last Lirith could stand the silence no more. She opened her mouth, but at that moment a chorus of voices sounded softly in her mind.

Welcome, Daughter of Sia.

44.

The sun had set and the sky was deepening from amethyst to onyx by the time Lirith returned to the hostel. Melia looked up from her chair near the window. The fluffy black kitten yawned and stretched on her lap.

"We've been worried about you, dear."

Melia's voice was gentle, but Lirith winced all the same.

"See, Durge?" Falken said. "I told you she didn't get hopelessly lost, knocked on the head by a robber, or pushed into an abandoned well."

"It is a wonder," the knight replied.

The two men sat at a table, playing a game Lirith did not recognize using small, polished stones. Despite the levity in the bard's voice, his visage was drawn, and Durge seemed even more somber than usual. No doubt they had feared her dead, like the priests of Vathris in the Etherion. After all, there had already been one attempt on her life.

"I'm fine," she said, then realized this was utterly inadequate.

Aryn rushed to her, her blue eyes shining. "Where were you, Lirith?" Then, in Lirith's mind, Aryn's voice continued. *I called for you, but you never answered.*

Lirith noticed Melia's sparkling gaze. She was not so

certain Aryn's words had not been overheard. Aloud she said, "I went to find witches."

Lirith might have spoken to Aryn that night in private, but no matter what Ivalaine said Melia and Falken were her friends. And while the workings of witches made Durge uncomfortable, it was best they all knew what she had learned.

Except what *had* she learned? As the words tumbled out of her, she realized she wasn't entirely certain.

She had gone in search of witches in the city in hopes of learning more about the tangle in the Weirding. After all, it was larger here—far larger than it had ever been in Ar-tolor. Aryn hadn't seen the tangle, but if there were witches in Tarras maybe some of them had. And, Lirith had reasoned, if she could learn more about the knot in the Weirding, she might discover something that would help them find the murderer as well.

At least, that was what she had hoped. The others listened as she described her encounter in the garden. The witches she had found there had been both familiar and strange. They were witches to be sure— daughters of Sia as they had described themselves—for they had known how to weave the Weirding and how to speak across its threads.

However, there were differences as well. These witches were not part of the Pattern that was woven in the Dominions. And while Sia was indeed present in Tarras, it was a muted presence, faded by the bright glare of the New Gods. Many of their spells were weak—like the one with which they had bound the garden gate, and which Lirith had broken so easily. It was also true they had talents that were new and surprising to Lirith.

In particular, they were adept at speaking over the

threads of the Weirding. Lirith imagined followers of such old religions would not be popular in a city dominated by newer deities; no doubt that had driven them to secrecy. As a result, they were able to cast spells in a communal manner Lirith had rarely seen outside the weaving of the Pattern. There had been a coven of thirteen witches in the grotto—she had come upon them during one of their meetings—and Lirith had spoken to them almost as if they were a single entity. Of them all, she had been able to learn the name of only one: the eldest, a brown-skinned witch called Thesta, who was the leader of the coven.

"Had any of them seen it?" Aryn said. "The tangle in the Weirding?"

Lirith nodded. "Some of them. But only those with the gift of Sight, according to Thesta and the others."

Aryn's lips pursed in a frown. "But then why have you seen it, Lirith? You don't—oh!"

Lirith sighed. She still doubted Thesta's words, yet what other answer was there?

Those among us with the Sight have glimpsed the knot you speak of, the witches had said, sometimes speaking with Thesta's voice alone, sometimes speaking in shimmering chorus. *It first appeared two moons ago, and it has been growing larger ever since. We know not its source, but we fear what it portends. Some of the others have had dreams such as yours, the dreams of the golden spiders, and the one in the shadows that seeks to devour everything caught in its web.*

Lirith had gasped at this, for she had not told the witches of her dreams. Now she forced herself to meet Aryn's gaze.

"I don't know, Aryn. I suppose maybe I do have some small shard of the Sight. I suppose I've always known it, although I never could bring myself to admit it."

"But why in Sia's name not?" Aryn said, gripping Lirith's hand. "It's wonderful!"

Lirith stiffened. Could she tell Aryn the other words Thesta had spoken to her?

Yes, I see it. You have kept it hidden, like a curtain drawn over a window. But now the curtain is unraveling. The Sight runs strong in you. Those who suffer sometimes gain such power, and your past is marked with sorrow.

As is my future, Lirith had said, thinking of the old Mournish woman's card, and then she had left the strange witches in their secret grotto.

"There's something I don't understand, dear," Melia said, and Lirith was glad for the lady's question. She didn't know how to answer Aryn, and Durge looked positively queasy at the direction the conversation had taken. "Are there not witches in the Dominions who possess the Sight? Why have none of them seen the unraveling of the Weirding?"

"I'm not sure," Lirith said. "But Thesta made some mention that the knot in the Weirding was a thing of the south, and that perhaps the south ran in my blood. But I'm not sure what she meant by that."

"Really, she said that? Of the south?" Melia's eyes grew distant. "Perhaps it is so. . . ."

Did Melia understand Thesta's words? If so, she offered no further explanation.

"You weren't the only one who did a little investigating today," Falken said. "Durge, why don't you show Lirith what you found?"

She drew close as Durge unwrapped something contained in a bit of cloth. It shone dully on his palm: a flattened piece of gray metal. Something dark and sticky stained the thing; Lirith's gorge rose as she realized it was blood.

"What is it?" she managed.

Durge set the piece of metal on the table next to the unfinished game. "I returned to the Etherion today, to the place where the priests of Vathris fell. I hoped to find something that might help us understand how they died. What I found was this, embedded in one of the walls of the corridor. I believe this was one of the objects that pierced the bodies of the priests."

Lirith remembered the fallen men, the pools of blood. "I don't understand. Surely such a small piece of metal could not be driven through a man's body and into a wall of stone."

"It might, if it was somehow propelled fast enough."

"But what could do that?"

However, even Durge's scientific mind had produced no answer to that question. Despite what he and Lirith had learned that day, their investigation had been stopped as surely as the bit of metal in the marble wall of the Etherion. What was more, according to Melia, the Etherion was in chaos; after the deaths of the priests of Vathris, it was doubtful when—or if— another discourse would be called. And the Minister of Gates still refused to bear Melia's messages to the emperor. Lirith feared the Weirding would unravel long before this mystery did.

"Worry makes me hungry," Falken said. "I think it's time we asked Madam Vil for our supper."

45.

They ate cheerlessly as stars appeared outside the window. Lirith knew the food was delicious, but it tasted like ashes on her tongue. None of them had any idea what to do to stop the murderer. And whether it was the Sight or not, somehow Lirith knew there would be more deaths before this was over. Would her own be one of them?

"Falken," Melia said, as servants cleared away the remains of the supper and left the room, "perhaps a song or tale is in order this evening, something to take our minds off a long and wearying day."

Falken retrieved his lute from its case. He seemed to think a minute, his wolfish face motionless, then he nodded. "I believe I'll tell you about the New Gods, and how they came to Falengarth. That seems an appropriate subject given the history of this city."

Melia gave the bard a sharp look. "And I'm certain you'll do justice to the tale, with no favor toward one side or another." On her lap, the kitten hissed and spat.

Falken laughed. "Don't worry, Melia. The Old Gods won't come off looking better in this tale. I promise you that."

Melia said nothing more, and the others drew their chairs close to the bard. He strummed a soft, melancholy song. It made Lirith think of beautiful things lost, things that had faded long ago yet were not entirely forgotten.

"Do you remember the drawing we saw in the wilds between Toloria and Perridon?" Falken said in his resonant voice. "The giant on the side of the hill?"

Aryn nodded. "It was one of the Old Gods. Mohg, I believe you called him."

Durge cleared his throat. "I mean you and your Old Gods no offense, Falken, but from that drawing Mohg did not appear to be a terribly kind fellow."

Lirith remembered the god's single, staring eye, his long fangs, and the people writhing in his hand.

"That's because he wasn't," the bard said. "Mohg was a god consumed by poison and shadow; he wanted nothing less than to shatter the world. But he wasn't always that way. And that's part of this story as well."

The stars spun outside the windows as Falken told a story that alternately stirred Lirith's blood and froze it.

"Long ago," Falken began, "the Old Gods dwelled deep in the forests of Falengarth in the north of Eldh. With them dwelled their children, the Little People, who were of myriad forms and manners: mischievous greenmen, clever dark elfs or dwarfs, and the light-elfs—or fairies—who of them all were closest to the hearts of the Old Gods.

"There were no men in Falengarth then, save the Maugrim, who were not like the men of today. The Maugrim lived in the forests, wearing the skins of animals, making their homes in caves, and hunting with knives of stone, for, like the Little People, the Maugrim could not bear the touch of iron.

"For eons, the Old Gods were the mightiest beings in all of Falengarth: Olrig One-Eye, Ysani of the Meeting of Ways, Durnach the Smith. And Mohg, Lord of Nightfall, who was stronger than all but Olrig when the sun slipped beneath the edge of the world and the day died."

"So even then he was wicked," Aryn said.

"No," Melia countered. "There is no evil inherent in the night. Only what men and gods would bring there."

Falken nodded. "Melia's right. But then, more than a thousand years ago, things began to change. While only the Maugrim dwelled in Falengarth, for eons men had dwelled in Moringarth, the great, hot land south of the Summer Sea. The Old Gods never ventured to Moringarth, preferring the cool, moist forests of the north, and so the shining cities of men did not trouble them.

"But there came a great conflagration in the south, and many men fled north across the sea to Falengarth. There they founded many cities, including one that, in time, would become the greatest city in the world."

"Tarras," Lirith murmured.

"That's right," Falken said. "Now, the founding of Tarras and the other cities along the south of Falengarth sent a tremor through the Old Gods and the Little People like a wind through a forest. They did not understand these people who came across the sea in red-sailed ships, who piled stone into high towers and worked bright metal into sharp swords. But it was not just iron that men brought across the sea. For they brought their gods as well—strange, new gods."

Melia folded her arms. "I resent that, Falken. We are *not* strange. Nor are we particularly new."

"And yet the Old Gods are more ancient still," Falken said. "They were deities of forest, stone, water, and sky, called into being by the runes spoken by the Worldsmith as were all the things on Eldh. However, the New Gods of Tarras were different. The Nindari were gods of men, granted their godhood by the belief of their worshipers, and their birth was a mystery. League by league, the men of Tarras pushed farther north, bringing their gods with them, and the Old Gods sensed that their days upon Falengarth were waning. One by one, along with the Little People, they began to fade into the Twilight Realm, the land that is no land, which is everywhere and nowhere at once.

"However, there was one among the Old Gods who refused to fade into the Twilight Realm. The sight of men marching into Falengarth filled him with a burning rage, and he accused Olrig, leader of the Old Gods, of treachery and cowardice for his unwillingness to fight."

"And this god," Durge said, "it was Mohg?"

Falken nodded. "And in his words, the other Old Gods sensed at last the ancient jealousy Mohg harbored for Olrig. Mohg felt that he should be leader of the Old Gods, but they turned their back on him. Yet that only fueled Mohg's hatred, like wind on a flame. He went in search of one who might yet help him—a dragon. Now from the beginning of the world, the dragons were ever the foes of the Old Gods, seeking to bring down and destroy everything brought into being by the Worldsmith."

"Or Sia," Lirith murmured. She met the bard's eyes. "In some stories, at least."

Falken gave her a sharp look. "Or Sia, if you will. Mohg went to the Barrens and climbed a mountain so high it pierced the sky, a mountain which has since been cast down into rubble. The sharp stone sliced his hands and feet to ribbons, but at last, bloodied and battered, Mohg reached the top, and there he found the dragon Hriss.

"Now Hriss was a great and ancient dragon, for she

was one of the brood of Agamar, who was the first of
the dragons, and she was terribly wise. Like all the
Gordrim, she coveted knowledge and hoarded it, and
in Mohg's coming she saw an opportunity to gain
knowledge she had always craved.

" 'I will grant you the knowledge you require,' Hriss
told Mohg. And with her own talon she cut a deep
gash in her belly, and blood flowed, and she bid Mohg
drink it, which he did greedily. Her blood was hot and
thick with wisdom, but even as he drank, Hriss
stretched her neck so that she might reach Mohg's
body, and while he was drunk with the taste of her
blood, she ate his living heart from his breast, for she
had always wondered what the taste of a god's heart
would be, and at last she had that knowledge. Satisfied,
she flew from the mountaintop, leaving Mohg to be
picked at by vultures.

"God though he was, Mohg would have died there
on the mountain but for the pity of a witch named
Cirsa, who saw Mohg in a vision. Cirsa climbed the
great mountain with a lump of Tarrasian iron, and this
she placed in his breast, enchanting it with spells, so
Mohg lived."

Falken's visage was grim. "To drink the blood of a
dragon grants the drinker great wisdom. But the price
of that wisdom is that it darkens the vision, so that
never again can one see good in something, or beauty,
or kindness. Rather, all the world becomes cold, hard,
ugly, and cruel—a thing ceaselessly in decay. Seeing
that in Mohg's eyes, Cirsa realized what a terrible
mistake she had made, but before she could undo her
spell, Mohg cast her off the side of the mountain. Such
was her reward for helping him."

Aryn clenched her left hand into a fist. "She should
have cursed him."

"And she did," Falken said. " 'Love shall yet defy you!' she cried as she fell, then she perished on sharp rocks far below. Of course, Mohg cared nothing for love now that he had a heart of iron, and so he forgot her words. And the blood-wisdom had given him what he had desired—a way to defeat the southmen and their gods.

"You see, centuries before this, the three Great Stones—the Imsari—fell to Eldh, where they were found by the dark elf Alcendifar. With his craft, the dwarf bound the powers of ice, fire, and twilight into the Stones, and then he hid them away, for he was jealous of their beauty, and he did not want the eyes of others to steal it away.

"With his new wisdom, Mohg knew that if he could gain the Imsari, he would have the power to break the First Rune, which was named Eldh, and which the Worldsmith had bound into the Dawning Stone at the beginning, so that the world would know permanence and never fade. Once he broke the First Rune, Mohg would be able to reforge Eldh in his own image, an Eldh where he was master and all others—men and gods alike—were his slaves.

"But first Mohg required servants. He knew that to fight men he needed a man of his own. Now, somewhere in the mists of time, men had come into Eldh, into the far north of the world in Toringarth. They were like the men of Moringarth, but taller, paler, and barbaric in manner.

"In the guise of an old, blind seer, Mohg went to one of the chiefs of these barbarian tribes, a man named Berash, who was as bold, arrogant, and foolish as a man could be. With sweet words and promises of power, Mohg convinced Berash to trade his living heart for one of iron, and in so doing Berash became dread and powerful indeed—a being known ever after as the Pale King—but also Mohg's eternal servant."

Falken paused in strumming his lute. "I think you all know the rest of this story. Mohg seduced thirteen of the New Gods and bound them in undying flesh, and they became the Necromancers. The Necromancers went forth into Eldh and discovered Alcendifar's hiding place. They wrested the Imsari from the dwarf, slew him, and returned to Imbrifale, to give the Great Stones to Berash that he might present them to Mohg himself. But when the Pale King rode forth from Imbrifale—"

"He found an army waiting for them," Aryn said, her eyes shining. "Ulther of Toringarth and Elsara of Tarras had forged an alliance, and together they drove the Pale King back into Imbrifale and took the Imsari from him."

"That's right," Falken said. "In a desperate gamble, Ulther and Elsara both sent armies to Shadowsdeep. Ulther arrived first, and he smote the Pale King with his sword Fellring, which had been enchanted by the blood sacrifice of three fairies. Both Fellring and the Pale King's heart shattered. Ulther would have died himself then, for all his army had perished, but at that moment Elsara rode into the vale with the army of Tarras, and the tide of the battle was turned. The Necromancers fled back into Imbrifale with their fallen master. Elsara had saved Ulther."

"She loved him, you know."

All looked at Melia. The lady petted the kitten, a secret smile on her lips. "Ulther journeyed from Toringarth all the way to Tarras to warn the empress of the Pale King's coming. At first she denied his request for an alliance, saying she cared nothing for wars in the frozen north. However, Ulther persisted, and at last

Elsara agreed. But it was not only because she had come to believe in the peril he described. It was because she had come to love him, even as he loved her."

Falken set down his lute. "If that's true, then their love was never requited. Their peoples would never have accepted a marriage between a barbarian king and an empress of the south. But when they created the kingdom of Malachor, to keep watch over the gates of Imbrifale, each gave a child to the new kingdom: Ulther's daughter and Elsara's son were married, and their heirs ruled over Malachor until . . ."

Falken's voice faltered, but Lirith knew what he had been about to say. *Until that kingdom fell.*

"Wait a moment," Durge said in his rumbling voice. "We know the Pale King was defeated in the War of the Stones. However, you have yet to tell us of his master. What became of Mohg?"

Falken picked his lute back up. "It's a story few know, for while the War of the Stones was fought here on Falengarth where all could see, the war against Mohg took place on the shadowy borders of the Twilight Realm, where no man may tread, save perhaps the Maugrim in their time. However, just as the armies of north and south allied themselves against a common foe, so did the Eldhari and the Nindari."

Lirith sat up straight. "You mean the Old Gods and the New Gods worked together?"

Melia nodded. "It's true, dear. We did. I can't say we understood one another very well, but we all knew it was the only way to save Eldh from Mohg."

"Together, all the gods created a trap," Falken said. "They wove a shining illusion of the three Imsari and the Dawning Stone. In his lust, Mohg raced toward what he perceived as the keys to his victory. But even as he grasped for them, they dissolved into shadows, and he knew he had been tricked. However, it was too late. In following the illusion, Mohg had stepped outside the circle of the world. With powerful runes, the Old Gods bound the circle, imprisoning Mohg beyond the borders of Eldh. Forever.

"The trick was not made without sacrifice, however, for it was said that a few of the Old Gods wove the spells of illusion to the last moment, and they were shut outside the circle of the world with Mohg."

A sharp pain pierced Lirith's heart. Could one really love something so much one would abandon it? The thought was beautiful, but so terribly sad.

"What happened to the rest of the Old Gods, Falken?" she asked.

"Their time was over. The world of men held no place for them. They faded into the Twilight Realm, and the Little People with them." He cast a sidelong glance at Melia. "But then, as we learned last Midwinter's Eve, while they are mostly forgotten, the Little People are not entirely gone."

Lirith had not been there, but Aryn had told her the tale, how tall, radiant fairies had carried Beltan's wounded body into the great hall of Calavere, and how queer figures had gathered the dead *feydrim* in twisted arms and carried them away. But then, the *feydrim* had been Little People once, before they were corrupted by the magic of the Necromancers.

"So the fate spoken by the witch Cirsa came true," Aryn said.

Falken cocked his head. "How so?"

"It was because of Ulther and Elsara's love that the Pale King was defeated and that he did not give the Great Stones to Mohg." The young woman smiled, pressing her left hand to her breast. " 'Love shall yet defy you.' "

Falken cast a startled glance at Melia, then looked back to Aryn. "Perhaps you're right at that," he said gruffly.

Lirith sighed. She might have thought the bard would tell a lighter tale as an antidote to their somber mood. Yet this one had been appropriate in its way. Once again she found herself wondering who could possibly murder not one god, but two. A dragon had nearly slain Mohg, but then only by his own willing participation. Whoever had murdered Ondo and Geb must have incredible power—enough to threaten all the world even as Mohg had once done.

But the Old Gods had banded together with the New Gods to save the world. Was there even the slightest chance they might be able to help again? After all, if the Little People could return from the Twilight Realm, why not them? She opened her mouth to ask Falken—

—and a scream came forth.

A dark thing fell onto her lap with a *plop*, then wriggled across the gauzy fabric. It was a spider: black, shiny, and large as a coin. She leaped to her feet, and the spider fell to the floor.

The spider started to scramble away, but Durge stood and placed his boot over it. There was a wet sound. However, terror still surged in Lirith's veins.

"It is only a spider, my lady," the knight said, his brown eyes grave. "There is nothing to fear."

The others gazed at her in confusion. Lirith knew she was going to have to explain. She reached into her gown and pulled out the Mournish spider charm. Then she told them of the dreams she had been having, of the golden spiders, and the hungry thing lurking in the shadows. However, she did not tell them of Sareth. He was not important, she told herself, although that was a lie. But he was secret, and so she said nothing of his place in her dreams.

Melia touched her arm when she finished. "I can see to it you sleep tonight without dreams, dear. If you'd like that."

Lirith gave a stiff nod. She started to slip the Mournish charm back beneath her gown, then with a jolt memory came to her. "Melia," she said, "this reminds me of something I wanted to ask you after I visited the goldsmiths. I completely forgot about it after the attempt on my life." She held out the Mournish charm. "When one of the goldsmiths saw this, she called me a follower of Sif, and she said I would never have the golden amulets I had wanted."

"I can see how she might have thought that, seeing your charm," Melia said. "Sif is the arachnid god. Spiders are sacred to him."

Aryn glanced at Melia. "Was the temple of Sif represented at the Etherion the other day?"

"No, they weren't in attendance."

Falken snorted. "Like half the temples in the city. I suppose they're as afraid as—"

"By the steel of my greatsword!"

As one they gaped at Durge. It was unusual enough for the solemn knight to interrupt another, but for the Embarran to utter an oath was nothing less than astonishing.

"What is it, Durge?" Lirith managed.

The knight's mustaches twitched. "Melia," he said, "tell me, what sort of robes do the priests of Sif wear?"

Melia's expression was puzzled. "They wear robes of dark gray, with pale gray threads woven into them. They're meant to look like spiderwebs, I believe. But why do you ask?"

"Because now I know who the murderer is."

46.

Despite the balmy night air drifting past the curtains, Aryn felt cold. Durge's statement had struck them all like a slap in the face. She cast a glance at Lirith, then spun a quick thread along the web of the Weirding.

What on Eldh is he talking about, sister? Neither Melia nor Falken has managed to discover who killed Ondo and Geb. Durge can't possibly know who the murderer is.

Lirith's reply crackled back across the Weirding like lightning. *If that is what you believe, then you underestimate him. Durge has seen much in his life, has endured much that you cannot even imagine. He is a wise and intelligent man, as well as a philosopher of science, and you do both him and yourself a disservice by so carelessly doubting him. Sister.*

Aryn gasped. The sharpness of these words stung her like cold needles. What had she done to provoke such a rebuke? She never said Durge was stupid. She pulled her gaze from Lirith. Falken stood behind Melia's chair, hands on her small shoulders. Both bard and lady regarded Durge seriously, and Aryn winced. Perhaps Lirith was right, perhaps she was horrible to doubt Durge. It was clear that Melia and Falken did not.

As if by a spell, memories came to Aryn like a bundle of small paintings she could hold in her hand, each one depicting a moment when she had been cruel to

Durge, or had laughed at him. Or, perhaps worst of all, had simply ignored the knight.

No, not like small paintings. Like cards.

You have forgotten about one who bore pain for you.

Was Durge the one the old woman had meant? Aryn recoiled but could not cast down the hand of memories she had drawn. What was wrong with her? No man could be kinder, stronger, truer than the craggy-faced Embarran. Why was it so hard for her to see good in him?

Perhaps it is simply that you do not want to see it, sister. After all, he is more than old enough to be your father. . . .

"Who is it, Durge?" Melia said, her voice tight.

"It was only just now that it all made sense to me," the knight replied in his rumbling voice. He glanced at Lirith. "It was the spider, my lady."

"What does this have to do with spiders?" Falken said.

"Everything," Durge said. "I cannot speak to your dreams, Lady Lirith, or of the visions beheld by the witches of Tarras. However, I do know what I have witnessed with my own eyes. Three days ago, as we departed the Etherion, only moments before the priests of Vathris were slain, I glimpsed several priests who I had not seen participating in the discourse. They were moving quickly, as if they did not wish to be seen. And they wore dark gray robes woven with pale gray threads."

Melia stood up, and the kitten fell with a yowl to the floor, extending its feet only at the last moment to catch itself.

"Priests of Sif." Her amber eyes flashed. "You believe Sif is the murderer."

Durge nodded. "From all we have learned, it can be the only answer. We know from Lirith's visit to the goldsmiths that Ondo had refused to make the amulets of gold the arachnid god desired for his priests. We also know that, recently, the followers of Ondo were robbed of some of their gold. It is my belief that, thwarted in his desire, Sif determined to gain the gold by any means possible. First he murdered Ondo, casting the goldsmiths in disarray. Then he murdered priests of various temples in order to sow chaos and confusion, to make sure the Etherion would not work together to discover him. Finally, he plotted with another god to steal from the guild of goldsmiths."

"Geb," Aryn said, the pieces falling into place in her mind. Lirith was right; she should not have doubted Durge. "That's why you found the gold coin in the sewer."

"So I believe," Durge said. "Only it was not a coin that I found, but a slug. I should have known it immediately, given its smooth faces. I use slugs made of lead in my alchemical work. But gold slugs are used in the making of jewelry. Geb's followers must have stolen the gold and transported it through the sewers beneath the city, dropping the slug in their haste."

Falken ran a hand through his silver-shot hair. "Wait a minute, Durge. If Sif made a deal with Geb to steal Ondo's gold, why did he turn around and murder Geb? It wouldn't make any sense to murder his partner in crime."

"No, it wouldn't," Durge said. "Unless Geb betrayed Sif and kept the gold for himself. After all, Geb is the god not just of beggars, but of thieves as well."

Falken slapped his gloved hand to his forehead. "Of course! That's why Geb's followers are in hiding. They should have been out in force, using the death of their god to gain sympathy and charity, but instead they've hidden themselves deep in the sewers. They don't want the guild of goldsmiths to find out they were in league with Ondo's murderer, and they don't want Sif to take out his revenge on them as he did their god, or to find out where they've hidden the gold."

Melia paced before the window, her small hands clenched into fists. "I should have seen it! Sif ever was a spinner of webs." She moved to Durge. "Thank you," she said simply, and the knight bowed low before her.

"There's still one thing I don't understand," Lirith said. "You told us yourself, Melia, that in all the history of Tarras one god has never slain another. So how did Sif manage to murder both Ondo and Geb?"

"I don't know," Melia said, her eyes glittering like sparks on copper. "But I intend to find out. Let us go to the temple of Sif at once. I'm going to give those priests—"

A sharp knock at the door interrupted Melia. Falken opened it, and a gangly young man rushed through, stumbling as his toe caught the hem of his simple white robe.

"Landus!" Aryn blurted, then winced at her rudeness. But while Landus wasn't the last person she might have expected to come tumbling through their door, he certainly had to be near the bottom of the list.

Durge steadied the acolyte with strong hands. The young man hastily untangled his robe and looked up. As he did, Aryn sucked in a breath. The last time she had seen Landus, his broad face had been full of good cheer. Now his visage was strangely hard, his kind brown eyes glassy and sunken.

"What's going on, Landus?" Falken said.

The young acolyte struggled for words. He must have run from the Fourth Circle all the way here. "It's . . . it's Orsith."

Melia lifted a hand to her throat, the blood draining from her face. "Landus, what is it? Tell me at once that Orsith is well."

"I'm . . . I'm sorry, Your Holiness."

Melia slumped back into her chair, limply, like a piece of cloth cast down.

"I felt a chill come over me a short while ago," she said softly. "I thought it only the night air. But it wasn't the air, was it?"

She looked up at Landus, and the young acolyte's face was a mask of sorrow.

"No, Your Holiness, it was not."

47.

The countless temples of the Second Circle glowed in the pearly light of the moon. To Aryn, they looked like houses of bones shining in the night.

The streets of Tarras were not so busy as during the warm hours of the day, but even in the coolness of midnight they were far from empty. Torches lit the way for drunken revelers to stagger from one feast to another. Music and laughter drifted out of glowing windows, although somehow the sound was more sinister than merry. From time to time cries echoed through the city, but whether they were made in pain or ecstasy was impossible to tell.

Just before they left the Fourth Circle, a man in fine clothes had stumbled before Aryn. He vomited onto the street, laughed, then staggered on. Durge started to move after the man, to rebuke him, but Aryn tugged his arm. Melia had not stopped moving.

The Third Circle had been quiet, for it lay under the watchful eyes of the Tarrasian military. The temple district through which they passed was neither silent nor as raucous as the lower circles of the city. Still, it was clear that many gods favored the shadows of night to the bright sun of day. Incense rose on the air, along with the murmur of chanted prayers.

They passed one temple whose doors stood wide

open. Light spilled down the steps like molten gold. Above the door, a frieze depicted a leering, goat-legged god. In one hand he held a naked maiden, in the other a pretty young man.

Aryn's gaze drifted past the doors. The temple was filled with the smoke of braziers, so that it was hard to be certain what it was she was seeing. But the floor of the temple seemed to writhe as if alive with serpents. Then a night breeze spun the smoke in circles, and she saw not serpents, but arms and legs, tangled together into a living, undulating knot. Moans rose on the air like fractured prayers. They were sounds of pleasure. Or torture.

This time it was Durge who pulled her arm. "No, my lady. Do not look within that temple."

Through great force of will, she managed to wrest her gaze away and let the knight pull her after the others.

Landus led them quickly through the shadowy streets. The young acolyte's face was solemn, and perhaps it was a trick of the moonlight, but even his large, crooked nose seemed far less comical than Aryn remembered. It seemed once again she had under-estimated someone.

By the time they reached the temple of Mandu, the mourning had already begun. The stark interior of the temple was lit by a pale, sourceless radiance, so that the white stone seemed almost translucent. A dozen priests and priestesses stood before the temple's altar, beneath the serene, smiling statue of the Everdying God. Something rested on the stone slab.

Except that wasn't quite right. Whatever the object was, it hovered above the stone surface. At last Aryn realized that it was the form of a man, wrapped head to toe in a shroud of white. Only his face remained uncovered: gaunt and wrinkled, yet in death as peaceful as that of his god.

"Oh, Orsith," Melia whispered.

The priests and priestesses parted as she rushed to the altar, as if they had been expecting this. Melia caressed the old man's face. She bent to whisper to him, but whatever she said was lost as a song rose on the air. Aryn could not understand the strange words the priests and priestesses sang, but there was sorrow in it, and a vast, endless joy that was almost too much to bear.

At last Melia turned from the form floating above the altar and returned to them.

"If it is not too much trouble," she said to Landus, "I would see where he spent his last moments."

The acolyte nodded. "Of course, Your Holiness. It is no trouble. This way."

He led them to a small antechamber that, unlike most of what Aryn had seen of the temple of Mandu, was anything but stark and empty. The walls were lined with wooden shelves and cabinets, stuffed nearly to bursting with tightly rolled vellum scrolls. In the middle of the chamber were a table and a stool, and on the table were baskets of pens and jars of ink, as well as a sheet of vellum. One of the ink bottles had spilled across it, obscuring most of what had been written.

"This was . . . this *is* Orsith's study," Landus said, struggling for words. "He was always so diligent in setting down the records. Orsith loves . . . that is, he always loved histories so."

In the dim candlelight of the study, Landus appeared suddenly frail and thin, old beyond his years. But then, it was plain he had both loved and worshiped Orsith. Aryn hesitated, then moved to the young man and laid her hand on his arm.

"I'm so sorry, Landus," she said.

He looked at her, his eyes containing surprise, then he nodded, a grateful smile touching his lips. "In the end, the circle goes full round for all of us, and Orsith lived a long, prosperous turn. While we all tried to deny it, his health had been failing this last year. It is a shock, but perhaps not quite a surprise."

Falken approached the table. "Was he in here when you found him?"

Landus nodded. "Several of us heard Orsith cry out. I was just down the hallway, so I was the first to arrive. Yet by the time I reached him, he was already gone, slumped here at the table. I fear his heart gave way. But his cry was short; I do not believe that he felt much pain in his passing."

Melia folded her arms over the bodice of her kirtle. "I should have come to Tarras sooner. I could have spent more time before he passed on to the next circle. I wish I had known his heart was so weak."

"That knowledge would have done you no good, my lady."

All of them turned toward Durge. The knight had been kneeling in the corner and now stood.

Melia stared at him. "What are you talking about?"

"It was not Orsith's heart that killed him," the knight said.

Falken scowled at him. "Durge, this is no time for jests."

The Embarran raised an eyebrow at this, and Falken winced, evidently realizing the foolishness of his words.

Aryn moved forward. "You found something, didn't you, Durge? What is it?"

The knight held out a rough hand. On his palm, gleaming in the candlelight, was a spider fashioned of gold.

48.

Falken sat at the table, studying the stained piece of vellum. Melia stood stiffly, silently behind him, having refused the chair herself. She was as rigid as the statue of Mandu in the main hall of the temple. However, right then there was none of Mandu's serenity in her eyes. Instead, they were hard and haunted.

"Are you certain it was Sif who killed Orsith?" Landus said. The acolyte's eyes were wide, and he was visibly trembling beneath his robe.

"It was Durge who put it all together," Lirith said. "All the evidence points to Sif." She gestured to the gold spider resting on the table. "And this would seem to remove any doubts we might have had."

"I suppose it was some sort of poison," Durge said. "You said you observed no wounds on Orsith's body, Landus. Only poison would explain that."

Landus shook his head, as if dizzy. "I suppose. But why would Sif want to murder Orsith in the first place?"

Falken looked up. "I think for the same reason he murdered those other priests and tried to kill Lirith. And not just to sow chaos in the Etherion. Sif is afraid of anyone getting close to the truth about what he's doing." The bard gestured to the piece of ink-stained vellum on the table, and they all gathered around. "I don't think this was one of the temple records Orsith was writing, Landus. I think this was his personal journal."

Landus nodded. "It could be. Orsith did keep his own history."

Falken picked up the sheet of vellum. "It's hard to read. Most of it was blotted out when the ink spilled over it. But a few fragments stand out. Right here he refers to *the darkness beneath*. Here, lower down, is the word *death*. And then here, at the bottom . . ." Falken pointed to the last smudged lines. "*. . . that the spiders have come again.*"

Melia stepped forward, her eyes bright as flames. "I think it's time we paid Sif a visit."

Minutes later they stood on the steps of the temple of Sif. The temple of the arachnid god was not far from that of Mandu, and Landus had led them there himself. No one had thought to tell the young acolyte he couldn't come with them; his visage was nearly as hard as Melia's.

While most of the temples of the Second Circle were hewn of white marble, the stone of Sif's temple was a gray that shimmered in the moonlight. The doors of the structure were massive and inlaid with glossy onyx. They were also tightly shut.

"Something tells me Sif's priests won't be inclined to answer our polite knock," Falken said.

"Then we'll just have to let ourselves in," Melia said crisply.

The lady breezed past them, then raised her hands over her head. At first Aryn thought it was a trick of the moonlight, then she realized the truth: An azure nimbus surrounded Melia's slender figure.

"Open!" the lady commanded.

Her hands flashed, and there was a clap of thunder.

As if they had been struck by a gigantic fist, the doors of the temple flew off their hinges and fell inward with a *boom*.

Even Falken stared as dust billowed out of the opening.

Melia primly smoothed the white fabric of her kirtle. "This way," she said, and stepped through the opening.

The temple of Sif was vast and dim. Dozens of columns held up the shadowy ceiling, carved of more of the same smooth, gray stone. Tapestries of silver cloth hung down from above like the strands of a monstrous web. In the center of the temple, set into the floor with more onyx, was a circle from which eight radial arms spun outward.

Not arms, Aryn. Legs. It's meant to symbolize a spider— a great, black spider.

There were priests in the temple, but it was hard to get a good look at them, for they were all in the process of fleeing. The priests ducked between columns; doors slammed, locks turned. In moments the temple was empty except for the six visitors.

Falken let out a low whistle. "Something tells me they don't feel like chatting."

"Cowards," Melia said, her lip curling in disgust.

Landus gaped at Melia, his expression one of pure awe. Aryn knew exactly what he was feeling. It wasn't every day one got to see a former goddess in action.

Falken scratched his chin. "Now what?"

"Watch," Melia said.

The lady stepped to the center of the spider symbol. She did not raise her voice, but nevertheless her words rang throughout the empty temple, and somehow her sharp tone was far more ominous than any display of wrath.

"Show yourself, Sif," she called. "I know you can hear me. A spider always knows what's at the center of its web."

Silence.

"Now, Sif, or I'll tear your temple down stone by stone and leave only a stinking black pit where nothing, not even the rudest hovel, will stand!"

Melia raised her arms above her.

"No!" came a shrieking, blubbering voice, echoing from all directions. "You must not, Melindora!"

At the far end of the temple, the air rippled and shimmered. Then, as if a gray veil had been cast aside, the air grew clear, revealing a throne of silvery stone. On the throne slouched a gigantic figure. Aryn drew in a sharp breath and knew she was gazing on a god.

Sif was formed like a man. Mostly. For his arms were four in number, as were his legs, and all of these limbs seemed to be waving at once. He wore a shimmering gray tunic over his round, bloated body, and his head seemed far too small for the rest of him. Two tiny black eyes glittered in the circle of his face.

"Well, I am here, Melindora," Sif said in an oddly clicking voice. "Are you happy?"

"Not really. I think I'm going to tear down your temple anyway for what you've done."

She raised her arms again. Blue lightning streaked forth. One of the columns cracked and tilted.

"Stop!" Sif howled, covering his head with four hands as dust and pebbles rained down on him. "Stop this, Melindora. I do not deserve this!"

"Don't you?" Melia held out the gold spider they had found in Orsith's room. "I think this means you do indeed deserve this. And more."

She reached her other hand toward a statue.

"No, Melia—wait."

This time it was not Sif who spoke, but Falken. The bard laid his hand on Melia's arm, gently pulling it down. She turned to glare at him.

"What are you doing, Falken? Sif murdered Orsith as well as the others, and it's time he paid."

"But you are wrong!" Sif wailed. "It was not me, by my web I do swear it. That spider is not mine, Melindora."

Melia stalked toward the god. "You lie!"

"I do not! Well, at least not *now*. Ask him." Sif pointed with one of his many hands to Falken. "He knows the truth—I can see it in his eyes. You all know as well as I that Ondo never let me have spiders of gold, that pompous fool. And wretched Geb hid away the gold he stole for me."

Melia opened her mouth, but suddenly she seemed at a loss for words. She lowered her arm and stumbled back. Falken held her steady.

"So I was right," Durge said, seemingly unfazed that this was a deity incarnate before him. Instead, it might have been an errant serving boy caught in the act of pilfering bread. "You were angry at Ondo and plotted with Geb to steal his gold."

"Yes, I admit it!" Sif squealed, his voice reverberating throughout the temple. "I despised Ondo for his pride. Ever did he flaunt his gold. Yet I should have known Geb would betray me, and for that I hate him as well." Sif's many arms tangled and untangled. "But I did not murder them. I murdered no one."

"What about the priests of Vathris in the Etherion? Durge saw your own priests sneaking about moments before the others were slain."

"You misunderstand, Melindora. My priests had watched the discourse in secret at my command. They wished only to leave the Etherion without being seen. I know not who slew the men of the bull—only that my priests had nothing to do with it."

Again Melia said, "You lie." But this time it was a faint whisper.

Aryn knew the gods were beyond mortal men, that they were capable of making things seem real when they were not. She was not certain it was really Sif who was before them now. Yet all the same she knew the arachnid god was not lying.

Before she thought about what she was doing, Aryn stepped forward. She didn't know how one was to properly address a god, so she settled for a curtsy. "Pardon me, Lord Sif. But if you did not murder the other gods, then who did?"

"You think I don't want to know the answer to that question, you insignificant nit?" He clenched four hands into fists. "I should crush you like a fly in my web."

Aryn stared, aghast, but before she could say more Durge stepped before her.

"God or no, you will not address a lady in such a manner."

Sif's beady eyes narrowed. "And who are you, speck?"

Melia moved toward the throne. "He's my friend. As was Orsith. And if you know anything, Sif, then you're going to tell me. Now."

Sif drew himself up on his throne, his bulbous belly puffing outward. "You are not a goddess anymore, Melindora. I do not have to listen to you."

"True," she said coolly. "But I think the Etherion will. I'll tell them that you're hiding information about the murders. I suspect the other temples will not be pleased to hear this news. In fact, I imagine they'll likely cast your priests out of the Etherion. Forever."

Sif trembled on his throne, his limbs curling inward. His mouth worked but uttered no sound.

"Think of it, Sif." Melia's words were sharp and precise as daggers. "An eternity with no followers to worship you, no one to send prayers or light candles in your name. An eternity with nothing but your own empty webs to keep you company."

Sif's beady eyes bulged. "You would not dare!"

Melia placed her hands on her hips and raised an eyebrow.

Sif's bulbous form shook as if made of jelly. His body was growing fuzzy around the edges, as if he could barely hold the image of himself together.

"You are hateful as a wasp, Melindora Nightsilver," the arachnid god spat. Then, in a more sullen voice, he added, "But I will tell you whatever you wish to know."

Unfortunately, it turned out Sif knew little. Melia and Falken questioned the god repeatedly, but the only thing he could confirm was that the golden spider did not belong to him or any of his followers, and that he did not know who might have dropped it. At last they gave up.

"I'm tired of you, Sif," Melia said. "We're leaving."

She turned away from the throne, Falken beside her.

"Wait, Melindora," the god called out in a sickly sweet voice. "Since I cooperated with you, I am sure this means you will not tell the Etherion about my little deal with Geb, now will you? Melindora? *Melindora!*"

Spittle sprayed from Sif's lips, but Melia only held her chin high as she walked away from the throne.

"Let us leave this place," she said to the others. "I have never cared for spiders."

Moments later they found themselves outside, at the

foot of the temple's steps. Melia's hard expression softened, and she leaned against Falken.

"So it wasn't Sif after all," Lirith said. She glanced at Durge. "It looks as if you were right about everything. Except who the murderer was."

Durge shrugged. "I suppose it is a wonder I got as much right as I did, my lady."

Aryn sighed. She had thought the mystery solved, but they were no closer to an answer than they had been before. "But who does the golden spider belong to?"

"I don't know," Falken said. "But I think maybe Orsith did. I think that's what he was writing in his journal. And my hunch is that's why—"

A scream pierced the night, high, bubbling—and something other than human.

They turned around. The scream had come through the open doors. Durge and Falken reached the temple first, followed by Melia and Landus. Aryn came last with Lirith. They skidded to a halt, jaws agape at what they saw.

Once again, priests ran back and forth inside the temple, but this time they were not fleeing from Melia's wrath. Instead, they stumbled away from a gaping hole on the far side of the temple: a black void where Sif's throne had been. A half dozen columns had toppled over, their supports removed. Heaps of rubble had fallen from above, and dust choked the air. There was no sign of the arachnid god.

Ignoring the fleeing priests, they wove their way among the wreckage and approached the hole, although as they drew near Falken held up a hand, preventing them from getting too close. The hole was perfectly round, its edges as sharp as if cut with a knife. Inside, the pit was a void of pure darkness. It sucked at

Aryn, dragging her forward. Lirith gripped her shoulders. Durge kicked a stone into the hole. They waited, but they did not hear it strike bottom.

Falken tried to grab one of the running priests, but the man only cried out in fear and twisted away. The bard swore. "What's going on here? And where is Sif? We need to ask him what just happened."

"You won't find him."

It was Melia. Her voice was strangely soft and weary. She pressed a hand to her forehead, her visage ashen.

"By the gods, what is it?" Falken said.

Melia swayed on her feet. "He's gone. Utterly and completely gone."

Aryn clapped a hand to her mouth to stifle a cry. Sif was dead. The murderer had been there, in that very temple, and they hadn't even known it.

PART FOUR:
THE FAIRY
AND THE GATE

49.

It was the time of owls.

Grace lay on the hard, narrow bed and stared into perfect darkness. She had pushed down the rough sheets with skinny legs, and her faded, too-small nightgown bunched and sweated around her. The dormitory occupied by the older girls was on the second floor of the orphanage, and the air was dead and metallic. It would have been good to open one of the small windows, to let in a whisper of the cool mountain night. But Grace did not bother to get up. All the windows in the Beckett-Strange Home for Children had been nailed shut years ago.

You don't have to do this, Grace. The shadow pulsed around her, thick and hungry. *You don't have to live through this, not again. Just let the flames come. That's the way it ends. You've got to let them burn.*

But there was something important here—something she needed to remember. Grace surrendered to the dark. Somewhere owls wept. She was thirteen again.

Floorboards creaked above her: old pine sagging under a ponderous mass. That would be Mrs. Fulch, going to the bathroom after her bedtime glass of tea and gin. Her room was on the third floor, although Grace never understood why. It took Fulch ten minutes just to get up the stairs.

Then again, all of the faculty had rooms up there—the wardens, the nurse, the housekeeper, the groundsman, Fulch the cook, and Mr. Holiday, the director of the orphanage. Maybe that made it easier to keep the children out. The third floor was strictly against the Rules. Once, when she was eight, Fulch had caught Grace with her shoe on the first step of that staircase and had dragged her to the kitchen to spank her with one of the big wooden spoons she used to stir the soup kettles. Grace had never tried to climb to the third floor again.

Somewhere above her, a door shut. Seconds later came a grunting sound, followed by a labored *whuffling*. It made Grace think of a *National Geographic* special they had let her watch once on the orphanage's flickering black-and-white television. She liked *National Geographic*, even though Mr. Holiday said scientists were all godless sinners. The show had been about animals in Africa. A water buffalo wallowing in a mudhole had made the same exact *whuffling*. It seemed Fulch's own cooking had disagreed with her. Again. That meant three or four more times that night the sound of her waddling to the bathroom would wake Grace up. That was, if Grace had somehow fallen asleep.

"Grace . . ."

The whisper was barely audible, drifting on the air of the dormitory.

"Oh, Gracie . . ."

Giggles.

Grace went stiff. Talking after lights out was against the Rules. So was getting out of bed, no matter how much listening to Fulch made you have to pee.

Bed-wetting itself wasn't against the Rules—and there was lots of it there. Some days the yellow-spotted sheets flew on the clothesline behind the orphanage like flags. All the same, messing your bed was good for a swat or two from Mrs. Murtaugh, the housekeeper, or maybe from her husband, the groundsman, if she was too busy to do it herself—and Mr. Murtaugh's big hands were rough and hard from work. Grace had learned not to drink too much before bed.

"We're coming for you, Gracie." More giggles, quickly stifled. Another whisper, falsely shrill. "It's me, Mrs. Fulch, and here's Mr. Holiday." Slurping, kissing noises. "We want to make you our most special girl, Gracie." Hands reached from the dark, groping for her nightgown.

Grace sat up. "Leave me alone."

She did not whisper the words, even though Mrs. Broud, the second-floor warder, would be sitting in a chair just outside the door.

The hands recoiled.

"You little—" A word Grace didn't understand. "—you'd better shut up."

That was Mattie Winter. She liked to use words she learned by lurking within earshot of Mr. Murtaugh. The groundsman had a habit of uttering a constant stream of curses as he worked; he never seemed to notice it.

"Did she hear us?" came a thin and piteous whisper. Lisbeth Carter. She could only speak in whines; it had something to do with her nose being too narrow inside to breathe right. These days she was Mattie's shadow.

Grace could just make out their outlines in the gloom: one tall and thick, the other a knobby rail. When she came to the orphanage two years ago, Mattie had crowned herself the queen of the girls' second-floor dormitory, and none of the other girls had ever disagreed—at least not without getting Mattie's fist in the stomach as reward. Grace avoided Mattie when she could, but a few months ago the other girl had seemed to tire of Grace's silence. Since then, she had worked nonstop to get a rise out of Grace. She hadn't succeeded yet.

"I said leave me alone." Grace did not lower her voice.

A muffled squeal. Lisbeth again. "Oh God, I *heard* something! Was that the door? What are we going to do, Mattie? Broud hears *everything*."

"Like your sniveling," Mattie hissed. "Shut your trap before I do it for you."

Lisbeth choked on a sob. Her skinny shadow crept away across the room, to a bed on the far side.

Mattie's eyes glittered in the faint light oozing beneath the door. She was listening. Grace listened, too. Broud was a desiccated old woman whose gray hair was pulled back in a tight bun to display long ears like a donkey's. And if she heard a noise in the dormitory, she would barge in, flip on the searing overhead lights, and bray like a donkey as well.

Silence. Not even the dry sound of Broud turning the pages of a yellowed volume of *Reader's Digest Condensed Books*.

And why should I read anything newer? Broud had said once in answer to Grace's question. *Nothing decent has been written in fifty years. Perverts, that's what authors are today. They spew out filth like a sewer and call it* literature. *Well, I don't need* Reader's Digest *for that. I can condense it all to a single word, I can.*

She never said exactly what that word would be, but Grace had a feeling Mr. Murtaugh knew it.

There was no sound from the other side of the door. Mattie leaned close, her breath hot and sour on Grace's face. She groped for Grace's chest, found her nipple, pinched it.

"Nice little tit you're getting, Gracie. Do they twist

it until you scream? Is that when they do it to you?"
She pinched harder.

Grace clenched her jaw, willing herself not to cry
out. Not so Broud wouldn't hear. She didn't care; the
old woman's braying couldn't hurt her. It was nothing
compared to the other things. She just didn't want to
give in to Mattie.

Mattie snorted and let go. Then, in the gloom, Grace
saw the other girl make a furtive movement. Mattie's
hand went to her own breast, squeezed. Again.

Grace couldn't breathe. Didn't Mattie understand?
She reached out a trembling hand and touched the
other girl's arm—

—and in that moment, as if a wire connected them,
she felt it. The hatred, the disgust . . . the yearning. In
the last two years they had come for Grace, and
Lisbeth, and Sarah Feynman and Nela Barnes. But they
had never come for Mattie.

It was as if Grace had stuck her finger into one of the
orphanage's bare electrical sockets. How was she
seeing this? How could she know exactly what Mattie
was thinking?

But sometimes Grace did know things.

Mattie batted Grace's hand aside. The wire was
broken.

"You *bitch*."

Grace knew *that* word. It sounded like Mattie was
crying, but that was impossible.

"You skinny little—" Another word Grace had
never heard before. "What did you do to me?"

"You want it," Grace said, and that time she did
whisper, because sickness strangled her. "You want
them to come for you. But that doesn't make you
special, Mattie. It makes you . . ."

Grace could find no word to explain it. Because

maybe, in the end, it made you into nothing. Maybe that was the only way you could stand it—to be completely and utterly empty. In the dimness, Mattie's eyes shone with rage and hurt. And want. Then, with a sound that could have been a snarl or a sob, she slunk back to her bed.

Grace lay back and stared again into the dark. She forced herself to stop thinking. Once upon a time, at night, she would think about the people who might come someday to save them—people from the government. But then one day a man did come, and his eyes had been red and bored, and his suit rumpled and dirty, and Mr. Holiday had showed him around, smiling broadly, ruffling the hair of kids who passed, and the man had made some notes on a clipboard and left. And life returned to normal.

Of course, Grace had learned early on that life at the Home was anything but normal. Normal kids didn't lie awake at night, waiting for the soft creak of floorboards, and the hands reaching out of the dark.

Except they had come for her less and less of late. Something had begun to change six months ago. She knew it had to do with what Broud called—her long donkey nose wrinkled—*the monthly woe*. But that was only part of it.

It was not that she resisted them. She did not struggle or cry out when they came for her. She simply watched them. And they seemed not to like that. So she watched them harder. Then, one night a few months ago, the one who had come for her stepped back before he began. She couldn't see his face— always they wore the masks—but his hands had been callused and strong. The hands of a workman.

Stop looking at me like that, you little Jezebel, he had snarled.

Like what, Mr. Murtaugh?

She hadn't even said the words aloud, but all the same his eyes had widened behind the slits of the mask. He shook a fist at her, as if to strike her, but did not.

You're not better than me, you little harlot. You think you can harm me with your spells, but you're wrong. You'll pay for this sin!

Only she hadn't paid. She had run back to her bed, and they had not come for her again. Nor had they come for any of the other girls. Sometimes, even without looking, Grace could feel them watching her: Broud as they spoke their prayers at night, or Fulch in the cafetorium. She would look at them and smile. Grace was watching, too, in her way.

Sometimes, as she walked downstairs to the first floor, she would hear voices arguing, quickly stifled when she came into view. And a few times, one of them had stared at her with a funny, squinty look. It was only when she saw the same look on one of the smaller girls that Grace finally understood what it was.

Fear.

Somehow that look made Grace smile. Last week, she had smiled at Fulch in the cafetorium. *Stop it, you horrible girl*, Fulch had said, wheezing for breath. Then she had waddled out as fast as she could, hand pressed to her mouth, and Mr. Holiday came in to tell them Mrs. Fulch was ill, and he served them lunch himself that day.

Silence again. Mattie must have crawled back into her bed, and Lisbeth, too. Sarah snored, and Nela was quietly sobbing in her sleep. She always cried in her sleep, even though the next day she never remembered it.

Creaks from above again. Fulch was lumbering back to her room. Floorboards groaned. A door squeaked as it opened. A long moment of quiet.

Crash!

Grace sat up straight in bed. She saw Sarah and Nela rise up as well, faint ghosts in their white nightgowns.

"*Shit*," Mattie spat. "What was that?"

Lisbeth squealed. "They're coming for us!"

Mattie reached out to hit her. Lisbeth crumpled on her bed, stifling her sobs with a pillow.

Grace cocked her head, listening. There was another sound, duller than the first. Like something soft and terribly heavy falling to the floor.

"Fulch," she whispered.

"What is it, Grace?" Nela said, her small, dark hands clutching the sheet to her chin.

Grace said nothing as she slipped from her bed. She put her hand on the doorknob.

"Grace!" Sarah whispered. "You can't go out there!"

Silence again. No, that wasn't true. There was a faint humming sound, like the vibration of the tuning fork Broud used before she sang carols in her dry voice at Christmas dinner.

"*Grace!*"

She turned the knob, the door swung open, light spilled through.

A battered *Reader's Digest* sat on Broud's chair. The old woman was nowhere in sight. Grace hesitated; leaving the dormitory at night broke so many Rules there weren't enough spoons in Fulch's kitchen. But something was out there. She drew in a breath and stepped into the corridor. There was no need to tell the others to stay. She could hear Lisbeth's blubbering. None of them would follow her.

She walked a few steps down the hallway. There—a scraping sound. It came from above, like rats on wood. She thought she heard a voice speaking soft, foul words.

Grace moved down the corridor. Doors slipped by. None of them opened. A hush had fallen again over the orphanage. Except for the humming. Grace could feel it vibrating along her jaw.

An opening yawned before her. Steps led up into darkness. The staircase to the third floor.

Grace clutched the worn banister knob and stared upward. Her knees turned into rubber bands. She should run back to bed now, before Broud caught her. This was worth a beating. More than a beating. But she couldn't go back. Something was happening. She felt it, like she had felt Mattie's hurt.

As if of its own volition, her right foot rose and brushed the first step. Above her, livid silver light welled forth. It rolled down the steps like glowing mist.

Do it, Grace.

The humming rose to a high-pitched whine. Grace opened her mouth, but no sound came forth. The hum was the only sound. The light spilled down the steps, pooling around her ankles; it was cool against her skin.

You've got to go up the stairs. You did it once, when you were thirteen. You can do it again.

Gripping the banister, Grace set her foot down on the step—

—and the world turned into fire.

No, this wasn't right. The flames hadn't come yet, not until later. Not until she had seen. She had to go up the stairs.

But the fire roared all around now. Grace curled into a tiny ball on the steps and wept the tears, not of a thirteen-year-old girl, but of a grown woman. Then the shadow swelled all around her and pressed out the fire.

50.

Travis pushed back heavy curtains, letting bright October light pour into the room. He moved back to the bed and sat on the corner.

"Grace," he murmured.

A soft moan escaped her lips, and her head rolled against the pillow, but her eyes were clasped shut. She was dreaming.

No, not dreaming, Travis. It's more than that. She's there again, living it. The shadow of the past.

He laid his right hand on her forehead and felt a tingling beneath his palm. "Grace, it's time to wake up. You're in downtown Denver, in a room in the Brown Palace. Yes, I know it's a little fancy compared to the Blue Sky Motel, but don't worry. It's on the Seekers."

The corners of her mouth pulled downward. Her hands curled into fists, twisting the covers.

The previous night, after the attack at the motel, Vani had driven them there. Neither he nor Grace had known where the Seekers were staying, but somehow Vani had. She had led them to a room on the third floor, knocked. But when the door opened and Deirdre gazed out with surprised eyes, there had been no one in the hall besides him and Grace.

As best they could, they had told Deirdre and Farr what had happened, then they had watched the report on the Channel 4 ten o'clock news. Travis had been only mildly shocked when photos of him and Grace were flashed on the screen.

Police are looking for these two individuals, who they believe are connected to the violence at the Blue Sky Motel, the robotic news anchorman had said. *They are considered dangerous, so if you see them do not approach. Instead, contact the police immediately.*

Apparently their good friends at Duratek had been busy. Travis was amazed they had the energy to manage a multinational conglomerate what with all the time they spent manipulating his and Grace's lives. Then again, it seemed they had had help in the matter. Again he thought of the figure in the gold mask, the one Vani had said was the master of the *gorleths.* Somehow, with a motion of his hand, the other had made Travis's heart stop beating. Had it not been for his dagger enchanted by the Runelords long ago, Travis knew he would be dead now.

Thank you, Jack, he said silently.

After the news, Grace had not been able to stop yawning and had crawled into bed without even taking her clothes off. But there had been no sleep for Travis. He had stayed up well into the night, sitting in the suite's main room, talking with Deirdre and Farr, telling them every detail he could remember about the attack. Finally, Farr had gone into his room to contact the Seekers. Deirdre had brewed Travis a cup of what he thought was herbal tea, but which must have contained a few other active ingredients, because the next thing he knew he was lying on the sofa, the red light of dawn creeping between the tall buildings of downtown to set the room's window afire.

Grace's eyelids were still shut, but he could see rapid

movement beneath them. He bent down and kissed the damp surface of her brow.

"I love you, Grace."

Her eyelids opened.

Grace pushed herself up and pawed at tangled hair. "Travis. Did you . . . say something?"

He smiled and placed his hand on hers. "I just said it's time to wake up."

"I'm sorry. I was at . . . I mean, I was only . . ."

"It's all right, Grace. I know." He tightened his grip on her hand. "I was there, in Spardis. I saw the shadow."

She went stiff and started to pull her hand away, but he didn't let go.

"You should have told me," he said softly. "About the regressions. You've been having them ever since we got back to Denver, haven't you?"

Now she did pull back. "You have enough to worry about, Travis. I didn't want to bother you with a bunch of old memories."

He didn't know whether to laugh or cry. It was completely maddening. Why did she always think she had to do everything by herself?

"Bother me, Grace. Please. I mean it."

She stared at him. Then a thin, fragile smile touched her lips. Slowly, as if she wasn't certain exactly how to do it, she lifted a hand and pressed it to his cheek. "So when exactly in the course of this complete disaster did you turn into the strong one?"

Now it was his turn to blink, astonished at her words. He leaned back, then finally he shrugged. "I don't know, Grace. I really don't know."

She looked away. "I can't stop them, Travis. The memories. Sometimes I think the past is going to drown me."

"What's gone is gone, Grace. The past can't hurt you."

"Can't it?"

He stood. "Come on. Deirdre called for room service. Let's see if this hotel knows how to brew a decent cup of *maddok*."

51.

Deirdre was already pouring from a silver pot when they stepped into the suite's main room. She handed them steaming cups before speaking a word, and Travis wondered how he had ever doubted she was anything but a friend.

"Thanks," he said, lowering his cup. It wasn't *maddok*. It was the real stuff: rich, dark, perfectly brewed coffee.

"You owe me one," she said.

Grace curled into a chair and took small sips. Before Travis could say anything, the door to the second bedroom opened, and Farr stepped out. He wore the same rumpled clothes as last night, as well as a frown.

"What did the Philosophers say?" Deirdre asked.

Farr ran a hand through his dark, curling hair. "Nothing. They said absolutely nothing."

Deirdre frowned. "But that's not possible. Stewart and Erics are dead, and we've broken Desiderata left and right. They have to say *something*."

"Evidently they don't."

Farr and Deirdre locked eyes, and Travis sighed.

"Excuse me, but in case you'd forgotten, not everyone in this room is fluent in Seeker-speak. Could you translate, please?"

"I'm not certain I can," Farr said, tucking in a wayward shirttail.

Travis squinted over his cup. "What do you mean? You're the ones who always speak in mysterious riddles and drive up in black cars at all the right moments. I thought you Seekers had the answers to everything."

Farr's gaze was distant. "So did I," he murmured.

It was Grace who broke the silence. "All right, now what do we do?"

Travis hadn't really thought beyond coffee. Duratek still had Beltan, only now they had mutant-controlling sorcerers in gold masks as well. What could they do? He didn't have the slightest clue.

Fortunately, another voice answered in cool, carefully inflected words. "We must find your friend, the knight Beltan. And quickly. We do not have much time."

It took Travis's eyes a moment to focus, as if the air unfolded around her. There was a *click* as the suite's door swung shut. He didn't remember hearing it open.

"Vani," he breathed. "You came back."

She smiled, the expression sharp as a knife yet not without mirth. "Incorrect, Wilder. I never left. I have been keeping watch over this hotel. It is safe—for the moment." She cocked her head; her short, tousled hair glittered in the morning sun. "Is that coffee?"

"Let me," Deirdre said, clearly too stunned to say anything else. She poured.

"Thank you, Seeker." Vani took the proffered cup.

"It's not *maddok*, you know," Grace said with a grimace.

Vani breathed in the rising steam from the cup. "It will do, Grace Beckett. It's been . . . a long night."

Vani sat on the sofa, and for the first time Travis noticed the shadows beneath her golden eyes. She still wore sleek black-leather pants and boots, but her jacket was gone, and she wore only a black tank top. As she lifted her coffee cup, Travis saw the tattooed symbols that snaked up her arms. More symbols coiled around her neck. He did not know what they were, except that they weren't runes.

"So you know us," Farr said. Awe shone on his face, but then Farr had made a career of searching for evidence of other worlds. Now a woman born on another planet was sitting in his hotel room, drinking coffee.

"You're Seekers," Vani said.

Farr nodded. "And why have you come here to Earth? Can you tell us?"

Vani set down her cup. "Have not Travis Wilder and Grace Beckett already told you? I have come to bring them back to Eldh."

Deirdre opened her mouth to speak, but Farr made a small motion with his hand, silencing her. She shot him a questioning look, but Travis thought maybe he understood. Wasn't that one of their rules? To watch, and to see what those with otherworldly connections did of their own free will?

Grace sat up, her cheeks flushed from caffeine. "How did you get here, Vani? How did you come to Earth? I need . . . *we* need to know."

Vani seemed to think about these words. At last she nodded. "Let me begin my story this way. Long ago, my ancestors dwelled in the far south of Eldh, in the hot lands of Moringarth, in the city of Morindu the Dark. Of all the cities of Amún gathered along the banks of the great River Emyr, only Kor was older. And while Kor was largest of the city-states, none was home to so many sorcerers as Morindu the Dark."

"Sorcerers," Travis said. "Last night, didn't you call the one in the gold mask a sorcerer?"

"Yes," Vani said, her eyes narrowing.

"So what are sorcerers? Are they like the Runelords?"

"No, sorcerers have nothing to do with the wizards of the north. At least as far as I know. For all that my people remember, much has been lost since our exile from Morindu and the lands of Amún. But simply put, sorcerers are those who can beckon and command the *Morndari*."

"The *Morndari*?" Deirdre said.

Evidently she had forgotten Farr's instruction as she shifted to the edge of her chair.

Vani nodded. "In the ancient tongue of my people, it means *Those Who Thirst*. Ever were the *Morndari* thirsty, from the time the first men of Amún discovered them. They are . . ." She gazed at the ceiling, as if searching there for words, then lowered her gaze. "They would be called spirits, I think, in your tongue. Although not the spirits of dead men. They are ancient—as old as the world. Or, perhaps, older still. They are aware in their way, but they have no bodies, no form, and they are not truly alive. Yet they have power. And as the first sorcerers found, they could be enticed with blood. And that is how they came to be named."

"Blood," Grace said. She shuddered. "You mean the blood of animals?"

Vani shook her head. "If a sorcerer would hope to command them, it was his own blood that had to be offered. Once they had drunk, they grew dull and sated, and the sorcerer could bid them to do things."

What things? Travis wanted to ask, but his tongue seemed welded to the roof of his mouth.

"The shining cities of Amún fell over two thousand years ago," Vani said. "The sorcerers rose up against the god-kings, but they were thrown back down and destroyed, and the course of the River Emyr was changed in the last conflict so that Amún became what it is today: the Morgolthi, a desert of dust and bones."

Grace hugged her knees to her chest. "I like history, Vani, and your story is interesting. But what does it have to do with how you came to Earth?"

Vani smiled. "The present has deep roots, Grace Beckett, and moments are like leaves on a tree. Even a simple happening comes to pass only because a thousand other things came first. My people call this fate."

"I'd call it chaos theory," Grace said.

Vani shrugged. "Whatever the words, the result is the same. You see, there were sorcerers who, in the midst of the war against the god-kings, sought to wrest secrets away from Morindu the Dark—secrets of great power. Rather than allow this to come to pass, the sorcerers of Morindu sealed the gates and destroyed their own city from within. Thus was Morindu buried forever beneath the sands of Amún, and its secrets with it."

Travis clutched his empty cup. "Vani, these sorcerers who wanted to steal the secrets of power from Morindu. Did some of them wear gold masks?"

Vani gave a stiff nod. "There was a city in Amún called Scirath, which from the dawn of the age of the god-kings was a rival to Morindu. It was the men of Scirath who first named the city of my ancestors *the Dark*, for they sought to poison the minds of others—to make them fear the Morindai and hate them. Ever did the Scirathi covet the knowledge of Morindu and seek to gain it for themselves. But the Morindai took the name given them in scorn and wore it proudly. And yes." She met Travis's eyes. "The sorcerers of Scirath wore masks of gold."

Grace rose. "Vani, I thought you said all the sorcerers were destroyed in this war."

"Most. Not all."

"But it still doesn't add up. Why would a bunch of two-thousand-year-old sorcerers be interested in me and Travis?"

"For the same reason my people are," Vani said.

Grace stared, then plopped back down in the chair.

Vani gazed at her wrists; her eyes traced the intricate tattoos. "Even as some of the people of Morindu survived, so did some of the men of Scirath. They have never ceased in their effort to uncover the lost secrets of Morindu. And we have never ceased in our efforts to prevent them from doing so. It was one of the Scirathi who attacked you last night. Even had you not seen him, Wilder, I would have known it. Only they ever used *gorleths* as their slaves."

Grace shivered. "What are they, Vani? *Gorleths.*"

"I know not what shadowed sorcery the Scirathi use to create them. They are made by combining the blood and flesh of different creatures, that I know. But I have never seen *gorleths* such as these. They were stronger than any I have ever heard of. Faster."

"And smarter," Grace said. She looked up. "Aren't they?"

Vani nodded. "In a way, I am glad the Scirathi showed himself. I have suspected these last months that it was one of his order who came through the gate."

Now it was Farr who forgot his own rules. "The gate?" His brown eyes were intent on Vani. "You mean to tell me you know of some kind of portal between Eldh and Earth?"

Vani regarded him. "Long my people kept the artifact of Morindu hidden. However, three years ago we risked its use, and that is how I came here, to Earth, in hopes of finding Wilder and Beckett."

"Three years? But you can't have been on Earth that long. The Seekers would have heard of it."

Vani's lips twisted in a wry expression. "I believe you overestimate the swiftness with which I can learn the language of a new world. And you also underestimate my ability to stay hidden from the eyes of the Seekers."

Farr seemed to have no answer to that.

Travis's nerves buzzed like wires. "If you have a gate, Vani, then you can help us take Beltan back to Eldh."

"No, I cannot."

The flatness of her voice shocked him. He stared, as did Grace.

"The artifact of Morindu is powerful, but even as we used it, we did not fully understand it. You see, the artifact is hollow, and when my people first discovered it, it was filled with dark fluid."

"Blood," Grace said.

"Yes, blood. And after I used the artifact to come to Earth, I learned from my brother that it was empty."

Travis ran a hand over his smooth head. "But I don't understand. Can't your brother just fill the thing up and bring us back?"

"It is not so simple, Wilder. We do not know what sort of blood was in the artifact."

Grace spoke in a quiet voice. "Human blood?"

"No," Vani said, turning toward Grace. "The blood of a man does not open the gate. It was another sort of blood in the artifact, blood of great power. And to open the gate again would take the same kind."

"But doesn't the artifact tell you what it needs?"

Grace picked pieces of fuzz off her baggy sweater. "You know, like the label on cars. 'Unleaded blood only.' Something like that?"

"The artifact does have writing upon it, but although we have been able to translate it from the ancient tongue of Morindu, we do not know what it means. It says that to open the way, we must have blood as powerful as the Blood of Light."

Grace sighed. "And you don't have any more idea than I do what that means."

Vani did not answer.

"So you're stuck here," Travis said. "We're stuck here."

Vani stood and paced before the window, black leather creaking. "We suspected the blood would be consumed in using the artifact. I knew before I came that the journey would be in one direction only. But then, nearly a year ago, my brother sent word to me that the ones we sought had appeared on Eldh—and that their names were Grace Beckett and Travis Wilder."

Deirdre let out a low whistle. "That must have been a blow, having come here with no way back, then finding out the ones you were searching for were back on Eldh."

Vani gazed at Deirdre, mouth twisted in a bitter smile. "You have a great gift for understatement, Seeker. However, two months ago, my brother sent me another message, telling me that Wilder and Beckett had returned to Earth."

Travis fought for understanding. "Wait a minute. If you can't open the gate, how can your brother send messages to you?"

"With this."

Vani reached into her pocket and drew out a triangle

of black stone.

Farr moved closer, peering. "What is it?"

"It is a piece of the artifact of Morindu," Vani said. "It allows my brother to speak to me through the artifact—although at some cost to him. Without this, the artifact is not complete. Which is quite fortunate."

"How so?" Farr said.

Vani tightened her fingers around the triangle. "A month ago, the gateway appeared before me. I thought it another message from my brother. It was not. The gate . . . opened wider."

Grace sat up straight. "The Scirathi."

"I did not know it at the time, not for certain. I was caught off guard and barely managed to keep my life. In the chaos of the moment, I could not see my attacker, but last night confirmed my fears. It was indeed a sorcerer of Scirath who came through the gate. He must have wrested the artifact from my brother. And I believe he brought it with him through the gate."

"Wait a minute," Travis said. "I thought you said you couldn't open the artifact without the right kind of blood."

"Yes," Vani said. "I did."

A thrill coursed through him as he understood the truth. However, Grace was faster. That scientific mind of hers.

"You think the sorcerer has learned the secret. You think he knows what kind of blood you need to enable the artifact."

"He must," Vani said. "Else he could not have come through."

Farr looked at Deirdre, his face grim.

"What?" she said.

He rubbed his stubble-shadowed chin. "This is very

bad. The events of last night can only mean one thing: The being Vani calls the Scirathi is working in coordination with Duratek. The news report about the attack at the motel had Duratek written all over it."

Deirdre sucked in a breath. "Which means there's nothing to stop Duratek from using the Scirathi's gate to gain access to Eldh."

Fear bubbled up inside Travis. If Deirdre was right, it meant the end of everything he had fought for, the end of Eldh as a free and separate world. He looked at Grace, and she returned his gaze with frightened eyes.

"No," Vani said, "do not despair so easily. All hope is not lost."

Farr looked at her. "Forgive me, Vani, but you don't know Duratek. They'll exploit any chance they have to get to Eldh and claim its resources for their own."

"You are wrong, Seeker." Vani's eyes glittered. "I do know this group of sorcerers you call Duratek. I have watched them, even as I have watched you. And while they have the knight, the gate, and the secret of the blood, there is yet one thing they do not have."

Even as she unfolded her fingers, Travis remembered.

"The stone triangle. You said the artifact isn't complete without it."

"Yes," Vani said. "When the prism is separated from the artifact, it acts as a focus for the gate. As long as I have this, all gates opened by the artifact will lead to the prism. To open a gate back to Eldh, both artifact and prism must be brought together."

"Then there's a chance," Travis said. "If we can get Beltan and the artifact, and if we can learn what the Blood of Light is, then we can get to Eldh." However, even as Travis said this, he realized how ridiculous it sounded. Even with the help of Vani and the Seekers, how were they going to do that?

"Vani," Grace said softly, "there's still one thing you haven't told us. Why have you and the Scirathi been looking for me and Travis?"

Vani bowed her head, a black silhouette before the window. Then she looked up, her golden eyes brilliant.

"Because, Grace Beckett," she said, "you and Travis Wilder are fated to raise the lost city of Morindu the Dark from the sands of Moringarth."

52.

Not for the first time, Beltan swam upward through the dark waters of unconsciousness, broke the viscous surface, and found himself naked and motionless upon a hard, cold slab.

He struggled for comprehension. Was this the crypt beneath Calavere where his father slept, the life stolen from him by murder? It was impossible to be certain; a fog lay before his eyes. How had he gotten there? He remembered the fire burning along his veins. Poison. Yes, she had poisoned him and had brought him here in order to turn him into a thing like herself. Kyrene.

Do not take my heart, witch!

But why did it matter if she cut the organ from his chest, if she placed in its stead a lump of cold iron? What need did he have of a heart?

You love him.

No, that was no reason; that was his usual stupidity. What did love matter? He had loved his father, King Beldreas, and what had it meant in the end? Again Beltan saw the image that had once haunted his dreams and now—because of the Necromancer Dakarreth—his waking mind: a knife sinking deep into a man's strong, broad back, and a hand pulling away, covered with blood. Beltan's hand. He had worshiped Beldreas, his father, and he had murdered him—stabbed him when he wasn't looking. Wasn't that what love always led to in the end—pain, betrayal, death?

No, it's not the same. I only want to see Travis Wilder once. That's all. I just want to tell him I'm sorry.

But he wouldn't have the chance. Lady Kyrene was going to cut out his heart. And maybe it was better this way. Maybe it was better to have the thing removed than to destroy yet another who could not possibly return his love.

Except something was wrong. He had seen Kyrene die. And it was too bright here to be the crypt beneath his father's castle. The gray was dissolving into hard, lifeless white.

A metallic *click*, then a voice drifted on the air: a woman's voice, though strangely sharp and guttural.

"Subject E-2, medical log. Seven October, cassette two. Test results and duplicate blood and tissue samples have been forwarded to headquarters for analysis and verification, and we are waiting for a directive on how to proceed.

"Since yesterday, I've had time to review the security videotapes, and I'm convinced now that the aboriginal does not speak English. On the tape's audio track, the subject's speech is unintelligible. The logical explanation is that, startled by his unexpected awakening, I projected words I could understand onto the sounds the subject made. I had been on shift for thirty-six straight, and while meds can keep you going, they can do it only for so long without impairment. But I've had a good seven hours of real sleep since yesterday.

"All the same, on the chance the sounds made by the subject represent indigenous speech, I've forwarded the tape to headquarters for digitization and cross-comparison with the current known lexicon. However, I doubt they'll find any matches. I'm sure now the subject was not speaking in any language, but merely uttering sounds of pain and fear. In the meantime, for security reasons, we are keeping Subject E-2 sedated at maximum safe levels. After such a long incapacitation, even accounting for the effects of the alternate blood serum treatment, the strength he displayed was . . . surprising. We'll wake him up when we receive instructions, hopefully tomorrow. End entry."

The light was growing brighter, resolving into shapes.

But I am awake, witch! he wanted to shout, only his jaw would not work. She had thought her poison would keep him asleep until tomorrow, yet it had not. Once before a witch had underestimated him. Kyrene. That was how he had been able to rise from the stone bier, to throw her down, and to put the torch to her.

Why was it he had twice proved a witch's spell weaker than she had thought? He wasn't sure, but his own mother, Elire, had been a witch after a fashion.

As a young man, before he became king, Beldreas had gone riding into the marches of western Calavan to hunt stag and had come upon Elire in the village of Berent. Her green eyes had drawn him to her bed. However, when he learned the next day that the other villagers held Elire to be the village wisewoman, he had flown into a rage. Never had the followers of Vathris been fond of witches, and Beldreas had been a warrior to the marrow.

He came upon her in the village common, and he would have struck her down in his rage had she not told him that his bastard son was already alive and quickening inside her belly. Young and hot-tempered as he was, even Beldreas would not harm a woman who was with child—his child.

However, she was still a witch, and Beldreas would

have nothing to do with her. He rode back to Calavere, and Beltan had spent his first seven years in Berent with his mother. Often she made him drink bitter teas she brewed, or bade him chew on some foul-tasting piece of root that would make him go green and vomit. He never knew why. She would only tell him, *It will make you strong, my little prince.* But he had loved her and had never disobeyed, and when the potions made him sick, she would take his head in her lap, stroke his hair, and sing until he slept.

Then, the summer he was seven, Elire caught a fever, and while she would have tended to any villager so stricken with some of her simples, there was no one to make simples for her. Despite all she had done for them, no one in the village would lift a hand to bury a witch. So Beltan had placed her favorite green scarf in her stiff hands where she lay on her bed and had kissed her cold cheek. Then with a lamp he had set fire to the little wooden house where they had lived and watched it burn.

Such was the measure of Beldreas's honor—if not his affection—that he would not see his only child, bastard or no, live as a pauper in a provincial village, and so he sent his seneschal, Lord Alerain, to bring Beltan to Calavere. Quickly enough, Beltan grew to adore Beldreas and his new home. But he never forgot his mother, or how in the end her witchwork had betrayed her—and ever after Beltan believed it to be a treacherous art.

Yet Lady Grace Beckett was a witch. And perhaps it was from all the simples his mother had made him drink as a child that he had some resistance to them now. Even as he remembered these things, the room grew clearer. He could see the flat ceiling, and the strange, blue-white lights. He made out a shadow on the other side of the room: slender, sitting at a table, head bowed over something in her hand.

It was good that he had not managed to cry out. This way she did not know that he could hear, that he could somehow understand her words—or at least some of them, for there was much she said that indeed sounded like the words of a witch's spell.

Another *click*. Now she spoke in softer words.

"Personal note. We know that the subject is genetically a fully modern human being. The results of the phylogenetic analysis based on the DNA sequencing came back yesterday, and the most parsimonious tree suggests a divergence from northern European populations five thousand years before the present, with a margin of error of one thousand years.

"My own ancestors came from Norway. In a way, I suppose you could say we're cousins of a sort. All the same—even knowing how close he is to us, to me— there is a brutishness to him I find alien and disturbing. Is this what the Vikings were like, the ones who raped and pillaged their way across Europe?

"Headquarters says the civilization level of the aboriginals is medieval, approximately eleventh century, with some tech-specific variance of plus or minus two centuries. I still find it amazing that development could happen in such parallel with Earth, just lagged a thousand years. But that's what our historians have been telling us all along. Humans are humans. It's population density and probability theory that are the controlling factors, not individual will. Maybe the high-ups are right. Maybe manifest destiny exists after all.

"Whatever the case, it must be a violent period there. The subject can't talk to us, but the scars, the multiple injuries to his bones, tell a story of brutality. I know this hypothesis isn't particularly scientific, but I believe that, were he awake and unrestrained, he would kill me with his bare hands."

Silence.

"This is Dr. Ananda M. Larsen. End recording."

A sigh, shuffling noises, then the scrape of a chair being pushed back. The shadow stood.

Beltan let his eyelids droop shut. That was the first rule of a prisoner of war. Make your captors believe you were helpless. The woman—the *doctor* named Larsen—was not completely wrong about him. Were he free, he would not have killed her, but he would have done anything else it might take to be free of this place and these people who were holding him.

A sound he did not recognize rose on the air—a series of chiming noises. Then came a heavy *thunk* followed by a grinding sound that on any world meant a lock was turning. He was trapped. And alone.

A rattle, followed by a soft *whuffling* of breath.

No, not alone after all.

Beltan opened his eyes and craned his neck. From the steel cage in the corner, the *chin-pasi* gazed at him with intelligent brown eyes.

"Hello," Beltan said, his voice a dry croak. "So you're still here, too."

The creature tilted its head, then ran long, dark fingers over the wire mesh of its cage.

Beltan frowned. "You understand me, don't you? Not my words, maybe, but you're like I am to them. You know more than they think you do."

The *chin-pasi* stretched long, scarred arms toward one of the glowing bone-pictures on the wall: a high, delicate skull with too-large eyes.

Beltan tried to lift his head, found he could a little, and examined his surroundings. He was still naked, but they had cast a thin sheet over him. So perhaps he was not just an object to them, but a man. The myriad wires and tubes of his last awakening were gone, and now there was only one tube that led from a clear bladder above to a needle stuck in his arm. He was still restrained, but the bonds seemed a fraction looser than before, as if carelessly tied. Again, they had not believed he could wake so soon. As far as he could tell, there were three bands beneath the sheet: one that passed over his arms and chest, one that bound his hands beside his hips, and one that held his legs.

Gritting his teeth, Beltan strained against the bonds. Whatever the straps were made of, it was stronger than he. He tried wriggling instead. This was more effective; he was nearly able to pull his right hand free from the strap around his waist. If there was just a little more space. . . .

He strained, but after several minutes—exhausted and right wrist burning—he stopped. There was not enough room inside the strap. The only way he could pull his hand out was if he chopped off a limb.

Think, Beltan. Your muscles are gone, so use your brain for a change, if it hasn't completely withered over the years. Think about saddling your charger. A horse always takes in a breath when you're cinching the girth, so that when it breathes out the girth loosens and the saddle slips down. Breathing out won't do you any good—the strap is around your hipbones. But is there a way you can make yourself smaller?

Then he had it.

He pushed upward against the straps. The looseness left an inch between his back and the steel table, but he needed a little more. He gritted his teeth and felt a cool tingling, like a swarm of pinpricks over his body. The straps creaked as they stretched. Somehow he was stronger after his ordeal than he had thought.

There—it was enough. The fingers of his left hand crept along the metal. He tucked his hand beneath him, into the hollow at the small of his back. Then he pressed his body back down, hard.

He held his breath, and like a horse he forced the air from his lungs. He pulled on his right hand. There was resistance—

—then with a bright jolt of pain it popped free from the encircling strap.

Beltan stared at his right hand. It was bleeding. He'd torn off a good strip of skin. But it was free.

Quit staring, you stoneskull, and move.

The strap around his hips was loose now, and it was simple to pull his left hand free. Loosening the band around his upper arms and chest was a harder feat. However, after much grunting, and a fair amount of popping on the part of his elbow, he was able to work his right hand over to the clasp that held the strap in place. He couldn't see what he was doing, and his fingers were numb; it was going to be impossible to figure out the strange clasp.

Except that it wasn't. Again came the cool tingling, in his fingers this time, which moved with a dexterity he was fairly sure he had never possessed before.

The strap went slack. Beltan sat up.

The sheet fell down, and he stared. The last time he had glimpsed himself, he had been horribly thin, like the people of a village he had passed through one spring, where mold had spoiled the winter store of grain and folk had nearly starved to death.

Not today. He was still thin—far too thin. There was no trace of his old ale belly, and he could easily count his ribs. But his skin glowed with pink warmth, and flat sheets of muscles worked visibly beneath. His wound from last Midwinter's Eve was a rough, white line snaking down his side. He flexed his arms. They were stiff, but he had the feeling he could swing a sword with them if he had to.

But that was impossible. A sickly man could not put on a stone's weight in such a short time.

Whatever the answer to this mystery, it would have to wait. He threw back the sheet. The straps around his ankles were easily removed, but he was less certain about the tube in his arm. He gripped it, clenched his teeth, then jerked it out. There was some pain and blood, but it was not as bad as he had thought. Carefully, he swung his feet around, then pressed them against the cold floor. He pushed himself up from the bed, and for the first time in two months Beltan stood.

It was almost the last time. A rushing noise filled his ears, and the room spun around him. He stumbled and might have fallen, cracking his skull on the hard floor, but at the last moment he grabbed the steel rack beside the bed and hung on it like one of the clear bladders of fluid.

He breathed and spat; gradually the dizziness passed.

Slow this time, he took a few steps. With each one blood and confidence pumped through him. In moments he had reached the door. He was sweating, and breathing ridiculously hard for having walked no more than a dozen steps, but he had made it. Hanging from a hook by the door was a thin, white coat like the doctor had worn. He shrugged it on and held it around him. It was too small, but it was better than nothing.

A soft, hooting sound.

The *chin-pasi* gazed at him through the mesh of its cage. Its brown eyes were soft as it made a low sound. The thing almost seemed concerned for him. But then, maybe it was. Close as he was to it now, he could see it was female.

Beltan grinned. "I'm all right, my lady." He lifted a finger to his lips. "Now, be quiet. We don't want anyone to know what we're up to."

The creature kept watching through the wire.

The door was made of steel. It did not have a bar to hold it shut, like most doors Beltan knew, but there was a steel handle that obviously worked as a lever to open it. Beltan tried to move the handle.

It didn't budge.

He leaned all his weight on it, but it was no use. What kind of lock was this?

Another hoot. The *chin-pasi* had stuck its fingers through the mesh and was waving them at him.

"Not right now, my lady," he muttered. "I've got to find a way to get this door open."

He examined it more closely. On the doorframe was a small box. The box had a glass window in which crimson symbols glowed, eerie as the pale lights behind the bone-pictures. Beneath the window, on the box, were ten raised metal squares. A symbol was engraved upon each of the squares, but he did not know what they were. Whatever power enabled him to understand the speech of this place, evidently it did not allow him to read it. But then, even on Eldh his skill at letters was poor. Reading was for priests, highborn ladies, and kings, not bastards.

Again he ran his hands over the door, but he could see nothing—no opening, no weakness—he might exploit. There were no hinges on this side. Only the box with the squares and the glowing symbols.

He swore. If they found him like this, out of his bed, they would bind him far more tightly. Or cage him, like the *chin-pasi*. He had to get out of here before they came back.

The rattling of wire mesh, followed again by the

hooting sound. It was higher this time, more urgent. Beltan looked at the cage. Inside, the *chin-pasi* moved rapidly up and down, then it squatted, held one hand flat before it, and poked at it with a long finger. What was it doing?

Now the thing rose and once more wiggled its fingers through the mesh, pointing at Beltan.

No, you fool. Not at you. Behind you.

He turned, and his gaze fell on the box with the shining crimson symbols.

"This thing." He moved to the box by the door, then looked back at the creature in the cage. "You want me to do something with this, don't you?"

Once more the *chin-pasi* poked at its hand with a finger. Beltan frowned, then stretched his own finger toward the box. He brushed one of the squares.

A screech startled him. He glanced back. The creature was watching. He touched another of the squares on the box. Again the creature screeched, causing him to flinch. He clenched his jaw and touched a third square.

A soft grunt. Beltan hesitated, then pushed the square.

The window on the box went dark, then a single red symbol appeared as a chime sounded. It was just like the chimes he had heard when the doctor left the room.

Another grunt, urging him on. He froze. Was he mad, letting this half-human beast tell him what to do?

It's smart, Beltan. Too smart, maybe. Who knows what they've done to it? Then again, who knows what they've done to you? You've got to get out of this place. And sure as you're a bastard, this creature has been watching them when they didn't know it.

He moved his finger to another square.

He got this one in two tries. A second red symbol appeared in the window, accompanied by another chime. The next one took several attempts, as well as several clipped screeches, but he got the following one on the first try. The *chin-pasi* let out a low hoot. Beltan licked his lips and pushed the button.

Chime.

A fourth red symbol appeared. Then, for a terrible moment, the small window on the box went black. Beltan started to swear, sure he had done some harm, when the symbols flashed into being again, only not crimson now but emerald green. There was a *chunk* as, somewhere inside the door, metal tumblers turned.

He gave the creature in the cage a look of astonishment. It had watched them, and it had learned their secret. Smart indeed.

"Thank you," Beltan whispered.

The creature sat back on its crooked legs, gazing at him quietly. He turned again to the door, gripped the handle, and pushed. With a *click*, the door swung outward.

53.

"These," Farr said, unrolling several crackling sheets of paper on the suite's mahogany table, "are schematics of Duratek's base of operations in Commerce City, just a few miles north of downtown Denver."

Vani prowled toward the table. "You have maps of their fortress, Seekers? I have learned what I could from watching, but never have I seen what lies within."

Deirdre shot her a crooked grin. "Being part of a mysterious international organization has to be good for something."

"Don't be too thrilled," Farr said. "These blueprints were made for the previous tenant of the building. Duratek has occupied the premises for over two months. They might have rearranged all the interior walls in the meantime."

Vani traced a finger over the map. "No, I don't think so. They have made only a few makeshift alterations to the exterior for security. I do not believe they intend to stay there long. This base was established for a limited purpose, and when that is completed they will abandon it."

Grace glanced at Vani. What *was* the purpose of the Duratek base of operations? To open a gateway to Eldh? If so, then why were they holding Beltan?

Maybe he was just a lucky accident, Grace. A bonus prize,

something to play with while they figure out they can't open the gate without Vani's piece of the artifact.

"All right," Travis said, holding the silver coffeepot, his eyes squinty and his goatee pulled down in a frown. "Is everyone in this room a caffeine addict?"

He tipped the pot over his cup. Nothing came out, earning him four guilty stares.

Grace unfolded her stiff body from the chair. "I'll call room service."

It was something vaguely useful she could do. She doubted she would be much help planning an assault on the secret base of a sinister multinational corporation. Trying to put her friends back together after they failed—that was her job.

She dialed and connected to an earful of tinny music; they had put her on hold. Her thoughts drifted. If the Touch worked here on Earth, maybe she could help after all. . . .

But it doesn't Grace. Not very well, at least. You're not going to be able to sense where in the complex they're holding Beltan until you're a few feet away from him. It's going to be up to Vani and the Seekers to find him.

And then what? How were they going to get the artifact and the secret of its use from the Scirathi?

You've seen her fight, Grace. She does things that don't seem possible given the laws of physics. Vani said she was fated to bring you and Travis back to Eldh. Maybe fate really does exist.

No. She couldn't believe that; she was a scientist. There was no such thing as fate; there was no divine providence shaping their lives. If there was a god, then he was a blind idiot.

But there are gods. You've seen one born, Grace.

All right. So maybe she would take those old spiritual ideas out of the box she had shoved them into years ago, dust them off, and reexamine them. When she had time.

But it wasn't just the idea of gods that troubled her. Because if fate existed, then was it fate she had ended up at the Beckett-Strange Home for Children? No, it was better to believe in a random universe, to know that terrible things happened out of stupid luck and not because one somehow deserved them.

Finally a human voice spoke in her ear. She requested the coffee, hung up, and returned to the others, who still pored over the maps.

"Vani," Farr said, "where in the complex have you noticed the largest concentration of security guards?"

Vani pointed to the topmost drawing. "I believe they are holding him here. But the number of guards is not high. They must be relying on other means to secure the complex."

"Of course," Travis said with a bitter laugh. "Their damned technology. That's what they're counting on to keep us out. They think they can do anything with their little gadgets."

Deirdre shot him a grave look. "Be careful what you speak, Travis. Duratek has developed many things even the Seekers are not aware of."

"But Travis is right on one account," Farr said. "Duratek is arrogant, they always have been. And whatever their strength, their hubris is a weakness we can exploit to our advantage."

Grace opened her mouth but was interrupted by a sharp rapping on the door. All of them jumped—except for Vani. Grace let out a tight breath.

"Room service," she said, moving to the door. "I hope."

It was the coffee. She shut the door, locked it, and carried the tray back to the table.

Deirdre traced a finger over one of the maps. "So you think both Beltan and the artifact are in this wing?"

Vani nodded. "And I believe there is something else there as well."

"Something else?" Farr gave her a dark look. "What do you mean?"

"I do not know," Vani said. "But whatever it is, it is important to them. As important as the knight Beltan and the artifact."

Deirdre turned away, fidgeting with a silver ring on her right hand.

"All right," Grace said, since no one else seemed to be willing to ask the hard question. "So how are we supposed to actually get in there?"

"I have an idea," Farr said.

As it turned out, Farr's idea sounded a whole lot less like a plan than it did an intriguing laboratory experiment with a flock of assumptions attached.

Grace gave Farr her best skeptical look. "So, do you have any certainty at all that any of this is going to work?"

"It's simple enough," Farr said. "Deirdre and I will lead the police to believe you and Travis are located at an address in north Denver. Of course, Duratek will never trust the police to handle the job alone, so they'll send a number of agents as well, leaving the complex more or less unguarded."

"Hopefully less," Deirdre said. "It's going to be up to Vani to get Grace and Travis through the perimeter, find Beltan, and retrieve the artifact."

Grace licked her lips. "You didn't answer my question, Farr."

He met her eyes. "Nothing is ever certain, Grace Beckett."

"What of your Philosophers?" Vani said to Farr. "Is it not part of being a Seeker that you must swear not to directly interfere?"

Travis let out a snort. "If that's the case, I'd say they've broken their promise a time or two."

Farr bristled visibly, something Grace had never thought was actually possible until that moment.

"We have a dispensation in this case," he said.

Something about Farr's words bothered Grace. "So why make you go to all the trouble of swearing you'll do something only to let you break the oath when it's convenient?"

Deirdre and Farr traded glances, but whatever the two thought, they did not voice it.

"I'm going to take a shower," Travis said. "I don't think I can save anyone smelling like this."

He disappeared into one room, and Deirdre and Hadrian started for the other—Deirdre to make a telephone call, and Farr to ready some equipment.

Farr paused at the door. "You'll be all right out here, Grace?"

She glanced at Vani, who stood by the window. "I'll be fine."

Farr gave a stiff nod, then followed Deirdre into the other room.

A rustling. Vani sat on the sofa next to Grace. Grace had hardly seen her move across the room.

"How do you do it?" she said. "Move like that, I mean."

Vani smiled. "I am sorry, Grace Beckett. I did not mean to startle you. I fear I still forget sometimes that I am no longer within the walls of Golgoru. There, everyone is expected to move in this fashion."

Grace leaned closer to the other woman. Vani was dangerous; of that there could be no doubt. Her arms were lean and muscled, and her deep-set eyes and shaggy black hair imparted a fierceness to her aspect. Yet there was a softness to her lips, her visage, that the other things could not quite conceal.

"Golgoru?" Grace said. "What's that?"

"A fortress high in the Mountains of the Shroud. It is where I received my training. Along with these." She gestured to the tattoos on her arms and neck. "And these."

Now Vani brushed her hair from her left ear; the ear was pierced all around the edge. Grace counted thirteen gold earrings.

"I suppose you would say Golgoru is a school of sorts, although its existence is a secret known to few. It is where the T'gol receive their training in the silent arts. Those who endure, that is. There were twenty who began training at the same time I did. In the end, only three of us became T'gol."

Grace considered the evidence, then made her conclusion.

"The T'gol are assassins, aren't they, Vani? Trained to kill people."

Vani did not even blink. "Some would call us assassins, yes. But in our ancient tongue, *T'gol* means *those who preserve*."

"How old were you when you went there?" Grace said, wanting to understand. She liked Vani, was grateful to her. Grace would not believe she was simply a trained killer. To kill; to preserve. Could they really be the same thing?

"I entered Golgoru on my twelfth birthday," Vani said. "It was late. Most enter the Silent Place when they are no more than ten suns old. But I was of the Blood, and so the Masters could not refuse me."

"The Blood?"

"Yes. Royal blood."

"Morindu the Dark," Grace breathed. "You're descended from its rulers, aren't you? You're a princess there."

Vani's smile was beautiful and fragmentary, an ancient vase shattered by the weight of time. "I would be, I suppose, if Morindu were raised again."

Grace went stiff. *And you think I'm going to do it, along with Travis. That's why you came here looking for us. You think we're going to help you dig up a city we've never heard of on a world we can't even get to.*

"Forgive me, Grace Beckett," Vani said. "I can see that I have troubled you." She started to stand.

"Just Grace."

Vani halted. "What?"

"No Beckett." Grace looked up. "Just call me Grace."

The golden-eyed woman hesitated, then it seemed her lips curved in a faint smile, and she sat again. However, once she did, Grace found she had run out of things to say.

"The knight," Vani said, breaking the silence after a minute. "The man Beltan. Are he and Travis . . . that is, are they very close?"

Grace laid her hands in her lap. "Beltan loves him," she said simply.

"And does Travis return that love?"

Vani's eyes were suddenly dull as stones. Something was wrong, but Grace didn't know what.

"Why don't you ask Travis yourself?" she said.

Vani turned away. Grace started to reach for her, but at that moment the door to one of the bedrooms opened, and Travis stepped out. He was wearing the same black jeans and T-shirt, but his head was freshly shaved and his eyes clearer.

"What's going on?" he said.

Vani said nothing, and Grace searched for words, but she was rescued as Farr and Deirdre stepped from the other room. In Farr's hand was a small, black-and-silver device.

"I think we're ready," he said. "I just need Grace to say a few things into this for the benefit of the police and Duratek." He held up the device, along with a yellow notepad. "I hope you don't mind, Grace, but I've taken the liberty of scripting your surrender."

Grace stared at him, and only when he raised an eyebrow did she realize what she was doing—and the reason why.

If this plan succeeds, Grace—if you get through the gate and back to Eldh—you'll never see him again.

That night a year ago, when Farr first helped her escape the ironheart at the Denver police station, there had been so much she had wanted to ask him. In the chaos since the Seekers' arrival, she had never had a quiet moment to talk to him. Now, perhaps, she never would.

Farr drew in a breath, as if to say something. However, Vani stepped forward.

"There are some items we will need to prepare the artifact for use," she said. "Unguents, herbs, candles. Ritual things. I have not had time to gather them."

Travis rubbed his head and grinned at Grace. She nodded. It didn't take the Touch to read his mind.

"I know just the place," he said.

54.

Deirdre stared out the limousine's tinted window, watching through her reflection as dim images flickered by. For a brief moment, a row of redbrick storefronts were superimposed over the ghostly negative of her own face. She twisted the thick silver ring on her right hand and thought of Brixton.

That Duratek was the cause of the deaths at Surrender Dorothy was not the question. A mysterious fire was pretty much standard corporate procedure for them. Then there was the Electria. True, these days Glinda could have gotten the drug almost anywhere; Deirdre knew she hadn't. They had given it to her—to bind her, control her. Only then they had decided to discard her.

Arion told me tonight.

Arion?

The doorman. Everyone's whispering about it. No one knows how, but they've gotten themselves a pureblood. They don't need any of us now. . . .

Again she thought of the forest she had seen when Glinda kissed her, and the solid brick wall the doorman Arion had led her through. Then there was the DNA analysis from Glinda's skin cells. Farr said he had seen similar genetic patterns in those with otherworldly connections. Deirdre didn't need blood samples and a lab to know there were others at Surrender Dorothy who would have displayed those same genetic patterns.

But who were Glinda and Arion and the rest of them? How long had they been gathering at a nightclub in London not three miles from the Charterhouse without the Seekers even knowing about them? And was any of this somehow connected to the present case? Like Glinda's ring, the questions only led in a circle, circumscribing nothing.

She sighed.

"Deirdre?"

She turned from the window and met green-gold eyes that, for a startling moment, reminded her of Glinda's and Arion's in their depth and brilliance. Except that was impossible.

This time Grace's voice was more confused than concerned. "Deirdre, what is it?"

"I'm sorry, Grace. I was just thinking." At least that was no lie, even if it was not the whole truth. But how could she have told Grace what she was thinking about when she had not even voiced the words to herself?

You did not before, Deirdre, and maybe you never would have again. But in that moment, when you kissed her, you loved Glinda with all your spirit.

Grace gave her a wry smile. "Thinking. That's a bad habit. And one I've had a hard time breaking myself."

Despite the weight on her heart, Deirdre let out a soft laugh. She knew Grace Beckett more as a name in a file than as a person. Nor had there been many chances for meaningful talk in the chaos of these last days. All the same, Deirdre had a sudden feeling—one so powerful and certain her shaman grandfather would have told her it was a message from her totem guide— that Grace was someone she could be friends with, if time and the distance between worlds allowed.

Travis and Hadrian sat on the opposite seat, but their heads were bent together, talking in low voices. No doubt Hadrian was questioning Travis about his experiences on the world AU-3. Ever the inquisitor. Vani was riding up front with the driver. *I can see better here*, she had said.

"Sometimes I wish I could stop thinking," Deirdre said. "Just for a minute."

Grace's smile became a grimace. "There's a way. I just don't think you'd like it very much." She lifted a hand, drew her necklace from beneath her sweater, and twirled the jagged pendant absently in her fingers.

"I've never seen it up close before," Deirdre murmured. "Only in pictures."

Grace tightened her hand around the pendant. "What are you talking about?"

"Your necklace."

Like night and day, confusion and understanding passed in alternation across Grace's visage. "That first night I met him, Farr told me they were interested in runes like the ones on this. The ironhearts. I don't know why I've never had Travis look at it. He would probably know what some of the runes mean. Maybe . . . maybe I've never really wanted to know." She let go of the pendant. "But you know, don't you?"

Deirdre shook her head. "Not much—not what the runes symbolize. But we do know one thing. You've heard about Travis's friend, Jack Graystone?"

A stiff nod.

"For centuries, he lived in London under various names, including the name James Sarsin. Then, in the summer of 1883, his bookshop burned and Sarsin disappeared. But we did find an old journal of his that was partially legible. In the journal was a drawing of a sword. A sword covered with runes."

Grace brushed her necklace. "The sword this piece of metal is from." It was not a question.

"There's a copy of the drawing in one of the files in the trunk of the limousine. I'll pull it out and show it to you when we have a chance."

"Thank you. I'd like that."

There was a whir of finely tuned brakes as the limousine slowed. Then, in a soft voice, Grace spoke.

"It's not a blessing, you know. To be drawn to another world."

Deirdre thought about this. "Then what is it?"

Grace said nothing as she tucked the necklace back beneath her sweater.

The limousine came to a stop. Farr asked Travis one more question Deirdre couldn't quite hear. There was so much they hadn't had time to learn about Travis's and Grace's experiences. And now, if their plan worked, they would be losing their two prize subjects. What kind of Seeker was she?

Then again, lately she wondered if she was still a Seeker at all. There had still been no word from the Philosophers. True, Farr had won them a dispensation in this case; they didn't need to ask the Philosophers for approval for their actions. All the same, the silence felt . . . strange. Back at the hotel, when Deirdre had called the Charterhouse in London, Sasha had seemed oddly rushed on the phone, her voice clipped, as she explained there was still no message for Deirdre or Hadrian from the Seekers' governing body.

You're doing the right thing, Deirdre. It's better to let them go than let Duratek capture them.

Only it was more than that. Travis and Grace wanted to return to the world they called Eldh. And who in this world was Deirdre to tell them they couldn't go? Maybe the question wasn't what kind of

Seeker she was, but what kind of human being.

The limo door opened, sunlight flooded in. A lithe, black silhouette stood against the glare.

"We are here," Vani said.

Deirdre climbed out and waited on the sidewalk as the others followed. Farr shut the limousine's door, and together they entered a dim storefront.

Cool chimes sounded as the door shut behind Deirdre. The sound of wind and birdsong floated on fragrant air, and for a second she believed she had once again found herself in an impossible forest. Then she saw small stereo speakers mounted on the walls, and the wire that suspended the gnarled branches from the ceiling.

A waterfall of blue beads clacked, parted.

"Well," a husky voice said, "it's about time you're all here. There's trouble in the cards."

And dark fingers beckoned them deeper with long, red nails.

55.

They gathered in a cozy room behind the shop. Small windows were covered with heavy velvet, and the only light came from candles positioned all around. On a round table, carved with mystic symbols, tarot cards were laid out in an intricate pattern. Deirdre knew it was nearly noon in the outside world, but here, in this room, she had a feeling it was always midnight.

"Marji," Grace said with a tentative smile. "It's good to see you again."

Marji laughed, her teeth brilliant against her ruby lips. "Of course it is, queen. But didn't I tell you we'd meet again? It's fate—there's no denying it. Now sit down, everyone. I know we have lots to chat about."

The drag queen Marji made a sweeping gesture with a lean, dark arm, and as if the motion had the power of a spell, Deirdre found herself sitting along with the others.

Marji stood above the last empty chair. She wore an improbable ensemble consisting of a chartreuse mini-dress, a sequined, short-sleeved evening jacket, and a choker of gigantic faux pearls. Deirdre felt a slight twinge of envy. She had never looked that much like a girl in her life.

"I've gathered you here today," Marji said

ominously, "to read you the last will and testament of your great-grandfather, lately deceased."

Five pairs of eyes stared.

Marji stifled a laugh, then sat, adjusting her jacket demurely. "Sorry. I've always wanted to say that."

Farr glowered at her. "Really, madam, this is no time for jests. We have items we need to purchase, then we need to be on our way."

"Well, I see someone's put on the dark and brooding just a little thick today." Marji coiled a hand beneath her chin, purple eyelids drooping. "It's cute on you, sugar, but I bet Sister Marjoram could turn that frown upside down."

Deirdre clamped her jaw to keep from laughing. Farr muttered something incomprehensible and looked away. A small vein throbbed at his temple.

Vani leaned over the table, studying the cards. "These look like *T'hot* cards. You are an oracle, then."

Marji gave a delicate shrug. "I have a gift. But I've never heard them called *T'hot* cards before. That's an interesting name. Where are you from, sugar?"

Vani did not look up. "Far away."

"I suppose you are that. And let me just say one thing, girl." Marji's voice brightened as she waggled a finger at Vani. "You and black leather. One word: Wow."

Vani looked up, her gold eyes confused. "The leather offers protection while allowing me to move freely. It is practical, if that is what your word *wow* means."

Marji rolled her eyes, then looked at Travis, who sat next to her. "Honey, who are these people you've brought me? And what planet are they from?"

Travis gave her a sheepish grin. "Actually, that's sort of a good question."

Marji lifted a hand to her throat. "You aren't kidding, now are you, honey?"

"No," Travis said, gray eyes serious. "I'm not."

There were points, as Travis spoke in low words, telling their story, when Marji's eyes grew wide and she gripped the edge of the table, but she did not interrupt. Finally, when his voice trailed into silence, she shut her eyes. Then she opened them again, and they were as dark and peaceful as a garden at night.

"So you've been to another world, queen," she said to Grace. "You and the cue ball here." She looked at Vani. "And you're from that world. Well, it makes sense. I've never met anyone on Earth who could pull that look off like you do."

"You believe us?" Grace said.

Now Marji laughed. "Why not, queen? Of course there are other worlds than this. God knows there have to be. I'd go crazy if there weren't."

Deirdre thought she understood. Marji was fabulous and unique. But this world was not always kind to those who were special.

She leaned forward to study the pattern of tarot cards on the table. Deirdre didn't necessarily believe they were magic, but she did believe the cards contained ancient and meaningful symbols, honed over the centuries, that could be illuminating in the hands of someone who was sensitive and thoughtful.

"I've never seen this layout of cards before," she said.

"That's because I invented it myself," Marji said. "But the cards aren't really your bag of tricks, are they shaman girl?"

Deirdre sat up straight. "I'm not a shaman."

"Really?" Marji raised a carefully tweezed eyebrow. "Then why do you wear that?"

Deirdre reached up and clutched the yellowed bear claw that hung around her neck. "You misunderstand. My grandfather was a shaman. He gave this to me before he passed away."

"Okay, sugar. And why do you suppose it was you he gave it to when he knew he was dying?"

Words fled Deirdre, like birds taking wing.

Marji clucked her tongue. "Don't deny your gifts, girl. I just can't understand it, why everyone is so afraid of their own power. Well, Sister Marjoram isn't. Why can't the rest of you take a pointer from her?"

These words caused Travis, Grace, and Farr to look away. Deirdre joined them. Marji was a cheap West Colfax psychic in drag. She couldn't possibly be right.

By the time she looked back, Vani was poring over the cards.

"You said you saw trouble," Vani said. "What sort of trouble?"

"I wish I knew." Marji glanced at Travis and Grace. "I'm afraid I got just a little bit curious after you two showed up on my doorstep the other day, the police hot on your hind ends. So I decided to see if the cards would offer any illumination."

She held up a hand, silencing Travis's question.

"No, don't you worry. I didn't tell them anything when they came in here. But they were looking for you all right. And they came in here again, after your little adventure down at the Blue Sky Motel."

Grace gave a bitter smile. "You really do see all, Marji."

"Actually, it was the morning news that time. Not that I should watch. I still can't believe they give top billing to that hussy Anna Ferraro. And don't you believe those things are any more real than mine are." Marji adjusted her perfectly shaped breasts.

"Marji," Vani said softly. "The cards."

"Sorry, sugar. I digress." Marji ran her fingernails over the cards. "But the fact is, I don't know what they mean. And that doesn't usually happen to Marji. Here, on one side of the triangle, is the Chariot. Someone's been traveling for sure." She glanced at Vani. "But then, I think we've established that fact. And here, next to the Chariot is the Seven of Swords. See the two people in the boat, journeying across the water? The water represents the unconscious. They're both so sad, but they're leaving the past behind them, and look— they're going to a golden city on the sea."

Deirdre frowned. "But all of that sounds hopeful, Marji."

"You'd be right, shaman girl. Except for this."

With a crimson fingernail, Marji tapped the third card of the triangle. A hideous, leering face gazed up. The Devil.

"There's something there," Marji said in a low voice. "Wherever you're going. It's evil. And hungry. And it will destroy anyone who goes near it."

She looked up at Travis, dark eyes shining.

He laid his hand over hers. "We have to go, Marji— if we can open the way. And that's why we need your help."

She smiled: a sweet, sad expression. "I know you have to go, honey. I just had to warn you. That's all."

Farr stood. "Marji, there are some things we need. Herbs, oils, I believe." He looked at Vani.

"I can tell you the things."

Now Marji shot Farr a blinding smile. "Will that be cash, check, or charge?"

It didn't take long. Marji's shelves were well stocked. The main difficulty was that Vani did not know the English names of the herbs she required, but she described them to Grace, who displayed a knowledge of herb lore that surprised and impressed Deirdre; Grace was able to tell Marji what it was Vani needed. It wasn't a great deal: three bags of herbs, a bottle of pure, scented oil, and five black candles.

"I'd use these things for some kind of purification or preparation ceremony," Marji said as she handed the bag to Vani. "What kind of ritual is this you're doing, sugar?"

"One that I hope will take us to a golden city on the sea," Vani said.

Marji nodded.

Farr cleared his throat. "We should probably be going."

However, before they could move, Marji stepped in front of them. "Hold it. No one's going anywhere on an empty stomach. I don't care what world you're from, everyone's got to eat."

It seemed so unimportant—they had so many things to do, things Deirdre could hardly envision. Yet Marji was right. Even in the midst of incredible events, a person had to eat. Neil Armstrong would have fallen flat on his face on the moon despite the low gravity if he hadn't had his Tang and Food Sticks up in the orbiter.

They sat around the séance table in the back room while Marji seemed to produce lunch out of thin air. There were small cheese-and-tomato sandwiches, a bowl of hummus with crackers for dipping, green olives, and macadamia nut cookies.

The repast was good for more than just nourishment. Farr pulled out the map of the Duratek complex, and with Vani they refined some of their earlier ideas.

Marji eyed the blueprints as she cleared dishes from

the table. "That all sounds like some supersecret spy stuff, babies. Now, it goes without saying that Marji knows how to keep a secret. But I sure hope no one else knows what you're up to."

Farr gave Travis a pointed look.

"I haven't talked to anybody." He frowned. "Well, that's not completely true. I did call Davis and Mitchell Burke-Favor, some friends up in Castle City. But I didn't tell them where we were or what we were doing. And that was before . . ."

"Your good friends at Duratek Corporation got wind of where you were hiding," Marji said.

Travis gripped the table. "Wait a minute. You're not saying Mitchell and Davis—"

"I'm not saying anything," Marji said, holding up her hands. "Except that loose lips sink ships."

Farr handed Marji a crisp white business card. "We thank you for your discretion."

She tucked the card into the pocket of her jacket and winked. "If you want, you could be thanking me for other favors, sugar."

Farr hastily moved to the door. "We really should be going now."

"Thank you," Deirdre said.

Marji gave her a solemn nod.

Grace hesitated, then caught Marji in an embrace. "We're so lucky we found you."

Marji clucked her tongue. "Nonsense, queen. Luck had nothing to do with it. It was fate, pure and simple. Now, watch the pearls."

"Oh," Grace said, and stepped back.

"Good-bye, Marji," Travis said.

She moved to him, closed her eyes, and kissed his cheek.

"Marji . . ."

She stepped back, grinning. "Don't worry, honey. There's already plenty of competition for your heart. I know, I've seen it in the cards. Just indulge Sister Marjoram for a moment."

Travis hesitated, then leaned forward and kissed her ruby lips. Marji stepped back, eyes wide, then fanned herself with a hand, at a loss for words for the first time since they had entered her shop. Travis smiled, then turned away.

Vani gazed at Marji, her gold eyes thoughtful. "My people are great seers and oracles, and they have wandered far over the years. Perhaps, somehow, it came to pass that others found their way here, and that their blood runs in your veins."

Marji squeezed her hand. "I like thinking that, sugar."

There was no more delaying Farr. He moved to the door of the shop. The others followed.

Deirdre turned to tell Marji thanks one last time, but all she saw were blue beads, clacking faintly. Then the door opened, and they stepped into white-hot sun and the future.

56.

Marji hung up the telephone, then turned and gazed at the pattern of cards on the séance table.

"I sure hope that was the right thing to do, girl," she said with a sigh.

But they needed help, that much was clear. She moved to the table, sat, and studied the cards again. Marji had never seen so many dark signs come together at once before. Not even the day she lost her bid to become the Queen of Denver's Rainbow Court, and that fat little tart Chi-Chi Buffet won solely because she lured three of the judges into the bathroom for some very personal persuasion.

She tapped one of the cards in the center triangle— the Devil—and a shiver coursed up her back. She felt so cold. But that's what happened when one chose fashion over comfort.

Like you're ever going to change your ways, girl. Being beautiful is your burden.

Although it hadn't always been. Once, years ago, she had been Martin J. Morris, a gangly black teenage boy living in Five Points with an uncle who only ate food that came in cans, only drank things that came in bottles with bulls on the labels, and only spoke in words that would have been bleeped out on the TV reruns Martin liked to watch.

Fame? *What's that crap, Martin? You should be watching* The A-Team. *Mr. T—now that's the man you want to be. 'Cept without all that jewelry. Spin like them dancer boys, and they'll be calling you Fartin' Martin. Are you listening?*

Martin wasn't. He did spin, at night, alone in his attic bedroom.

Things hadn't been so bad when his aunt was alive. She had laughed when Martin had danced for her, holding an egg beater like a microphone as he lip-synced to her old Billie Holiday records. Then, one day Martin had glanced into the mirror in his bedroom, only he hadn't seen his own reflection. Instead, as clear as *That Girl* or Ginger on *Gilligan's Island*, he had seen his aunt walk across a street he knew was two miles from their house. Then he had watched as a garbage truck ran a red light and struck her.

He had always thought people flew through the air when they got hit by cars, tumbled to the pavement, rolled, and got up just like Lindsay Wagner, the Bionic Woman. Instead, his aunt had exploded, as if the frail, heavy fruit of her body had been just barely held together by the force of her life. For a moment the mirror had turned crimson, then he had stared at his own wide eyes.

By the time he got downstairs, the police were there, and his uncle had already popped the top on a bottle.

It was about a year later, one day when his uncle was snoring wetly on the couch, that Martin sneaked into his uncle's room, raided the closet of his dead aunt, and ran back to the attic with an armload of chiffon, velvet, and crisp polyester. And that gray afternoon, at the age of sixteen, color finally found its way into Martin's life in shades of canary, hot pink, and lime green. Sister Marjoram was born.

A year later, when his uncle finally found what had

become of his dead wife's clothes, he threw Martin out on the street. It was the best favor anyone had ever done for Martin in his life.

It's clear you're suffering from depression, low self-worth, and a lack of identity, the slack-eyed counselor at the youth center had told him, staring dully at his tight jeans, tube top, and feather boa. *That's why you're creating a new persona for yourself.*

But the counselor was wrong. Sister Marjoram wasn't the persona. Martin J. Morris was. For sixteen years he hadn't had the slightest clue who he was, had gazed at the skinny boy in the mirror with the uneasy eyes of a stranger. Then, that day, he had finally found what he hadn't even known he was looking for in a pair of high heels and a Chanel handbag. He had found himself.

And she wasn't Martin anymore. She was something different, something marvelous, and—for all the falseness, for all the feathers and sequins, the depilatory cremes, collagen injections, and silicone—something that was utterly true.

She was Sister Marjoram, the Spice of Life.

And, at the moment, she was more than a little confused.

"What is going on here, girl?"

Marji knew she was psychic, just like she knew she looked sensational in lavender chenille while it made Chi-Chi Buffet look like Miss Piggy. A dozen times more in her life she had seen things in the mirror, like the day she saw her aunt die, or the day she saw herself opening Marji's House of Mystery, and each of the visions had come true. But today her talent seemed to have fled her. There were so many clear images, but nothing quite fit together, like a broken mirror she couldn't fix.

She lifted her finger from the card of the Devil. That evil was real and dangerous, but it was distant, surrounded by cards that bespoke traveling, the past, and dreams. She moved her finger to a card in the outer circle. The Knight of Swords, reversed. A powerful man, but his power had been stolen. Only who was it? Next to the card was the Magician. That was him—the delicious bald boy. Travis.

She sighed. "You would have done a few personal favors for him, election or no, wouldn't you, girl?"

A heat rose in her, then cooled to chill dampness. It wasn't just desire. It was darker, stranger, and so much more compelling. She had known it the second she had seen him: that she loved him and could never have him.

"You can't always get what you want, Marji, you know that. That's what wine and credit cards are for."

But if she couldn't have him, who would?

The Knight of Swords. It had to be—the position made it clear. And hadn't they said there was a man they were trying to rescue? But there, on the other side of the Magician, was another court card, the Queen of Swords. So who was it who loved him, then? The Knight or the Queen? Then she knew.

"They both do, girl. Lord above, they both do."

But if the prisoner was the Knight, who was the Queen?

An image flashed through her mind: golden eyes, gazing at another deeply when it seemed no one else had been looking. No one but Marji.

She nodded. Mystery solved. Marji clucked her tongue. "You're going to be one busy boy, Mr. Travis."

She smiled, and the expression was one of sorrow as well as gladness. It hurt to let something so precious slip through her fingers. And it healed to know there were others who needed it more than she did.

"It's your own fault for being so damn together, Marji. But thanks for the kiss, honey. I'll lock it in my heart for always."

Now she was getting weepy. Not a good idea when you wore so much mascara. Marji forced her tears back and picked up the deck of cards. She was due for a reading herself, and maybe it would help take her mind off things. She shuffled until she felt the spark that let her know it was right, then turned the first card.

A grinning skull stared up at her from the black hood of a reaper's robe.

Marji went rigid.

It's just a symbol, girl. Change, the end of a cycle, that's all it means.

That's what the books about tarot said, anyway, maybe just to make people feel better. But sometimes, she knew, the card meant exactly what it read.

Death.

A coldness flowed over her, and this time it wasn't just imagination and skimpy clothes. The velvet curtain covering one of the small windows fluttered, and icy autumn air swirled into the room.

Marji moved to the window. "I thought you were closed. Marji must have breathed in a little too much nail polish remover today." She shut the window and started back toward the table.

Halfway there, she heard it: a low *whuffling*, almost like her uncle used to make after downing a couple of malt liquors and collapsing on the couch.

Marji froze, listening. The *whuffling* ceased. Then she heard the bright sound of glass breaking out in the main shop.

Indignation rose within her. So some creep had let

himself into her store and was now trampling around like a buffalo. She grabbed a stainless-steel nail file from a shelf. Whoever was out there had balls. But not for long.

Marji walked down a hallway, past several doors, then reached the curtain of beads. A stench hit her a second later, so strong she batted her eyelids, but the tears came anyway, and her mascara started to run. Whoever was out there, it smelled like he had rolled in a Dumpster before coming in. Breathing through her mouth, she reached out and parted the beads.

There was a wet grunt, then something dark and sinuous moved from the shadow between two rows of shelves. A small, low-browed head looked up, and pale eyes stared at Marji. With an easy, loping motion, it started for her, letting talons run along the shelves as it came.

More bottles fell to the floor, and Marji's scream was absorbed by the sound of shattering glass.

She stumbled back, letting the beads clack into place, concealing the sight of the thing. But she could still smell it, could still hear it. Whatever that monster was, it was coming for her. Fast.

Groping behind her, she found a doorknob, turned it, and backed into her dressing room. The walls were lined with mirrors, and the top of a large white vanity was cluttered with makeup, hairbrushes, nail polish, and curlers. Beauty like Marji's didn't come naturally; it came in lots and lots of little bottles.

She shoved against the door, but she was too slow. Something struck it, hard and furious, and she stumbled against the vanity. The back of her head smacked the mirror, and jars and vials clattered as they fell.

It came though the door slowly, cautiously.

Whatever it was, it was smart enough to know it had her cornered. She could see it clearly now in the bright light reflecting off the mirrors, and her gorge rose in her throat.

"You are one ugly boy."

The thing reminded her of an ape. Its arms dragged the ground, claws cutting the rug to shreds. Long, matted hair covered its body, and its short snout wrinkled as it bared fangs in a drooling grin. Yet the eyes were the worst: too large, slanted, white as moons. Nothing had eyes like that. Nothing on this planet, anyway.

The creature stalked forward. Marji reached behind her, fumbling with numb hands on the top of the vanity. The stench was enough to induce unconsciousness. Dizziness swept over her. The monster braced short legs and reached for her as it opened its maw.

Marji's hands closed around a pair of hard, familiar objects, and in a motion as smooth as a diva's she whipped them out before her. With one finger she let loose a billowing cloud of hairspray from a can, and with another she flicked the lighter she used to heat eyebrow pencils.

She flashed a wicked grin. "Looks like you're having a bad hair day, sugar."

Fire roared forth, engulfing the creature. It shrieked, lifting impossibly long arms as flames licked up its greasy hair, and fell back.

Marji followed after, can thrust out before her, spraying a gout of flame. Again the thing let out a squealing cry, then it fell backward into the hallway. It jerked, limbs tangling in spasms as the flames ate it.

Marji lowered the can. The thing grew still, curled in on itself like an insect as it burned. It was dead. She reeled backward, eyes burning from smoke, and turned around. Breath fled her. Marji gazed into the dressing room's mirrors and did not see herself.

It was a two-lane highway, leading over the crest of a hill and down into a valley. Beyond, flat slabs of gray stone thrust up like giants leaning against gray-green mountains. Five eighteen-wheelers sped up the hill, past a highway sign. The trucks were painted black except for a single white crescent moon on their sides. Marji gazed at the highway sign, but even as she did the image faded, and she stared at a tall, lean form in a sequined jacket and a beehive hairdo.

It was a faint skittering sound that broke the trance. Marji turned around.

They scuttled through the door, wriggling toward her across the singed carpet, gleaming in the light. Spiders. Gold spiders. She counted ten, twenty. Then she stopped counting as they continued to pour through the door. Again she lifted the can of hairspray and the lighter. Flame burst forth. The first row of spiders melted into motionless lumps.

The can sputtered. The flames wavered, then died out.

Marji threw down the can. She backed up against the vanity.

This is not good, girl. You always looked best in silver. Gold is definitely not your color.

The spiders wriggled closer. She fumbled for the phone on the vanity. There was time for one more call. From her jacket pocket she drew out the card the handsome, grumpy one had given her. She dialed, lifted the phone to her ear.

You have reached a Comlink pager, an electronic voice intoned. *Please enter the telephone number where you can be reached.*

No, there was no time for call-backs. They would just have to be smart enough to understand the message. She didn't know what it was she had seen in the mirror, only that if she saw it then it had to be important. With a hard fingernail, she punched the keys.

Something brushed her ankle. Marji dropped the phone and stamped her foot. A spider fell off. Another stamp, and it was pulverized beneath her stiletto heel.

More spiders followed after it, and more. There was no more room to back up.

"Last dance, Marjoram," she whispered.

More spiders crumpled under the heels of her shoes until she felt the first, sharp pricks of pain.

57

Beltan crouched in the metallic shadows behind a pile of steel crates. He cocked his head, listening: the sound of rapid footsteps, echoing voices, the boom of doors shutting. For over an hour, Beltan had crept through the dim, angular halls of this fortress, encountering little activity. Then, a few minutes ago, the noises had begun. Something was happening.

Perhaps the doctor has gone back into the room and found your bed empty, Beltan.

Except he had heard no alarm, and the distant shouts were not sharp with anger and fear. They sounded more like commands.

It was cold. The thin white coat he had pilfered offered no warmth, and he pulled his knees to his chest. He knew he should get moving again. The guard he had seen a minute ago was gone, off to join his companions in whatever task they had been set to. But he needed to rest, just for another minute. While there was a strength in his bony limbs he had not thought possible, the simple act of moving quietly between hiding places had left him damp, weak, and trembling as a newborn foal.

A low hooting noise.

She was curled up in the corner behind him, long arms coiled around her small head, as if cradling it. She gazed at him impassively, her gentle brown eyes filled with intelligence and pain. The bare patches on her arms glowed in the faint light, scabbed-over cuts marking them like some of Travis Wilder's runes.

"It's all right, my lady," he whispered. "We'll stay here another minute."

She leaned back as if she understood him.

And maybe she does at that, Beltan. She knew the secret of the lock on the door. And she was there, in your dream of the Gray Land. She called to you.

He knew it was risky and perhaps foolish to have brought the *chin-pasi* with him. But he owed his life and his freedom to her—however long each of them would last. He had found a metal instrument in a drawer—its purpose unfathomable, except that it looked as if it could cause great pain if applied correctly—and had used it to lever open the cage's lock. The *chin-pasi* had climbed out on stiff legs and had embraced him, encircling his thin body with gangly, powerful arms.

After that, she had followed just behind him, silently, quickly, seeming to anticipate each of his moves. Twice she had made frantic motions, flapping her long hands as he started down a corridor, and each time as they fell back he had heard voices coming their direction. Beltan wondered what they had done to her. And what they had done to him. The *chin-pasi* was not the only one who seemed to know things.

More than once, as they stole through the fortress, he had felt the tingling creep over his flesh, along with a sensation of danger. Each time he had led the *chin-pasi* to a hiding place. And each time, moments later, a guard came into view, clad in their strange uniform of black boots, tight black trousers, and thin black shirts with short sleeves.

That they were guards there could be no doubt.

Beltan was a disciple of Vathris; he knew a warrior when he saw one. To a one they were large men, arms and necks thick, hair cropped close. Their shirts were marked with a white crescent shape—surely an insignia of some sort. But the clearest signs of all were the objects strapped to their belts. The things were short, stubby, and made of metal. Beltan couldn't say exactly what they were, except that by the way men carried them they were clearly some sort of weapon.

The needle pricks came once again, swarming over his neck and arms as he crouched behind the crate. A heartbeat later the guard came into view. He was not walking on patrol, but rather jogging toward a specific task. He touched a wire coiled around his head.

"This is Clarkson. Alpha and Beta Sections are clear. Moving to Gamma Section now. Trucks one and two are already fully loaded, so start with truck three. Good, then—"

The guard's harsh words were cut off as he rounded a corner. The tingling faded, along with the sense of peril. Beltan turned toward the *chin-pasi*. She gazed at him, eyes quiet in her dark, wrinkled face.

"They've done something to me, my lady," he said, his voice hoarse. "Just like they've done something to you."

The creature pursed her lips and gestured with curving fingers. *Time to go.*

Hunched, he started down the corridor, toward the source of a faint, gray light. The *chin-pasi* loped after him. Beltan wished he could walk like her, leaning on the knuckles of his hands. His sinews felt like wet leather left in the sun to dry; stretching his tall frame upright was painful.

After the noise and commotion, the hallway was now eerily silent. Together, they passed open doors leading to rooms empty save for a few papers crumpled on the floor or a handful of colored wires dangling from the ceiling.

The light grew brighter. A new sound echoed from up ahead, a roaring he could not comprehend. It made him think of the growling of some great beast. However, he did not feel the tingling. Whatever the source of his new instincts, they had gotten him this far. He clenched his teeth, willed his legs to keep pumping, and swung around a corner.

He nearly collided with a man and woman in long white coats.

Beltan's bare feet skidded on the slick floor, then stuck, halting him. With a soft *whuff*, the *chin-pasi* bumped into him from behind. He stared, frozen, waiting for the two doctors to turn around, to see him, and to cry out in alarm.

They did not. The roar was loud now, pouring through the opening in which the two doctors stood. Beyond was bright gray light and chilly air.

The doctors were talking—loudly, to compensate for the grinding noise. They had not heard Beltan and the *chin-pasi*. But why hadn't he felt the tingling? Maybe his new instincts were fallible after all. Or maybe he was not really in danger—not as long as they hadn't heard him.

"—and it's being loaded now," the male doctor shouted above the noise.

The female doctor clutched her coat to keep it from flapping in a stiff breeze. "And the subject?"

"You mean E-1?"

"Yes. The nonhuman."

"He's already on the same truck."

The female doctor turned slightly, and Beltan realized that he recognized the shape of her profile. It was her, the woman in his room, the one he had frightened when he spoke to her. He remembered the words she had spoken as he listened.

This is Dr. Ananda M. Larsen. End recording.

"Do you know why the order came down to evacuate?" Larsen said, her shoulders hunched against the chill.

The man shrugged. "Who can say? We're just the brains, remember. It's the brawn that calls the shots here. But I've heard it's because they discovered our location and are planning a strike."

"Who?"

"You know very well who."

Larsen nodded. She seemed to murmur something, but the word was lost amid the roaring.

Beltan swore under his breath. He wanted to know who it was that planned an assault. Perhaps Beltan could befriend these people and use them to escape.

"Damn, it's cold." Larsen stamped her feet.

"It's not just the wind that makes me cold. There— do you see? Over by the truck."

Dr. Larsen muttered something Beltan did not understand, but which could only be a curse. "I thought he was gone. Wasn't he supposed to be searching for them?"

"That's what I thought. He must have come back for the mobilization."

At last Beltan understood. The activity, the words of the guard, the empty rooms. They had been discovered, they feared an attack, and now they were abandoning their fortress. But where were they going?

It didn't matter. All that mattered was that he got out of there before they discovered he was missing. In the chaos of the mobilization, he just might have a chance.

Larsen grimaced. "He gives me the creeps."

"To say the least. What do you think is behind that mask of his?"

"God, don't even say that. I don't know where they dredged him up, but I wish they'd send him back."

"I agree, but we needed him. He was the one who showed us we could perform gene therapy using the nonhuman's blood serum as a delivery vector. And he was the one who brought us the nonhuman in the first place."

"Fine. I won't argue with you there. But we don't need him anymore. We've advanced our techniques ten centuries beyond his crude methods. Have you seen some of the hybrids he created? Thank God they destroyed them all. They were monsters. Nothing like Ellie."

"You mean your chimp?"

"You wouldn't believe the results I've been getting. Basic manual dexterity skills up seventy-eight percent. Abstract reasoning test scores up one hundred fifty-three percent. It's incredible. I think she's on the verge of achieving language. I don't mean mimicking a few hand signals, but real, complex language."

The male doctor wasn't listening. "You know, I've heard he can't stand it."

"Can't stand what?"

"E-1. I've heard he doesn't like to be near it."

"But he's the one who brought it through."

The man shrugged. "Well, sometimes we have to associate with things we hate in order to get what we want."

Larsen looked away. Again her words were lost in the droning sound. They might have been, *Yes, we do.*

"So, do you think it's going to help us?"

Larsen turned back. "What?"

"The nonhuman. I've heard they think it understands how to activate the artifact. Do you think it will help us?"

"I don't know." Larsen sighed. "I've heard it's in constant agony."

"Well, that's to be expected. We've seen what hybrids go through here. Logic dictates it would be worse for a homogenetic specimen. That's why the lab at headquarters synthesized Electria in the first place, to control their pain." A soft laugh. "The international drug trade is just gravy to help fund interesting little side operations like yours and mine, Ananda."

She took a step back, body curving inward, as if repulsed.

"I've got to go," she said. "I think they're moving on to Gamma Section."

"They won't let you touch anything yourself."

"I know. I just . . . I just want to make sure they treat Ellie and E-2 all right."

The man nodded. "See you at the rendezvous, Ananda."

Larsen said nothing. She took another step back, then turned to move down the corridor.

She stopped, jaw open, and stared. Ten steps away, Beltan and the *chin-pasi* stared back.

For several moments they stood this way, frozen. Then a grin crept across Beltan's face.

Larsen lifted a hand to her chest. "Doyle."

"You still there Ananda?" The male doctor turned around, and his eyes went wide. "Jesus!"

He lunged toward the wall, reaching for a red button. With a screech, the *chin-pasi* sprang toward him. She reached the doctor just as his hand struck the button. A wailing sound pierced the air, and lights flashed. The doctor screamed as he tumbled backward, the *chin-pasi* on top of him.

"Ellie!" Ananda cried. "No!"

Long, black fingers tightened around the man's neck, and the *chin-pasi* let out another screech as she thrust forward. The back of his head contacted the floor with a loud *crack*. The man went limp, and the *chin-pasi* looked up. There was sorrow in her brown eyes, as well as a faint, pale light.

The alarm continued to wail. The guards would be here in moments. Beltan moved to Larsen in stiff, quick steps.

"Please," she whispered. "Please, don't kill me."

Beltan reached out with big hands. "I'm sorry."

He encircled her neck with his fingers, squeezed. Her eyes bulged. She scrabbled at his hands, but she could not break his grip. He began to close his fingers—

—then froze.

What's wrong? Are you a weakling, boy? Finish her.

The sterile corridor was gone. He was in a wintry wood, kneeling in snow stained crimson. Before him lay a young doe, sides heaving for breath. Foam bubbled around the arrow stuck in her side.

I said finish her!

She was so beautiful, so weak. He couldn't do it.

A snort of disgust. A strong hand wrested the knife from him. His father's hand.

I'll do it myself, then, if you're such a coward. Like a girl you are, not a son of my flesh.

Beldreas made one, quick slashing motion, and a river of red steamed as it gushed onto the snow.

The corridor wavered back into focus. Beltan loosened his grip. Larsen choked, drew in a shuddering breath.

He couldn't do it. No matter what she had done to him, she did not deserve to have her blood spilled like this.

He shoved her away. She struck a wall, then sank to the ground, staring up at him. He grinned again, then pressed his finger to his lips. *Quiet now.*

He started forward, stepping over the body of the doctor. The man's eyes gazed upward, dead. Beyond the opening was a flat space bounded by some kind of wire fence. Five long, black, blocky shapes were arranged in parallel, and it was from those the roaring came. Beltan thought he knew what they were. Travis had described things like this to him. These were the *t'ruks* the guard had spoken of. Vehicles, like wagons, for transport. He blinked against a sharp wind, then stepped through the doorway.

Behind him, a scream rose above the wailing of the siren.

"Here—he's down here! Oh, God, help me. I think Doyle is dead."

So Dr. Larsen had not heeded his wish for silence. The sound of booted feet echoed behind him. Beltan turned in time to see two of the guards in black pounding down the corridor. They moved past Larsen, still huddled on the floor, and leaped over the body of the fallen doctor without even glancing at it.

One of the guards was faster than the other. He reached Beltan first. The man coiled a thick arm around Beltan's neck and planted a foot behind Beltan's leg, obviously thinking it would be easy to take down this skinny, mostly naked man.

Beltan let out a roar that was part anger, part delight. He grabbed the man's arm, twisted it back, then stepped across the man's leg and braced his own behind. By Vathris, it was easy. He leaned into the guard. The man cried out—more in surprise than pain—and bent back. There was a wet popping as the man's leg buckled. The jagged end of his thighbone thrust outward through his black pants, along with a gout of dark blood. Now the man's cry became one of agony. He fell to the ground, writhing. Beltan looked up.

"Drop now," the second guardsman said.

He stood five paces away, the metal object that had been at his belt now gripped in two hands thrust before him. There was a click as the man did something to the object. Beltan still did not understand what the thing was, but by the way the man held it, he clearly believed it would protect him.

"I said drop!"

Beltan decided to see if the guardsman was right, if the thing would indeed protect him. After all, what did he have to lose but his own cowardly, murdering life? Beltan tensed, then lunged forward.

There was a high-pitched screech, and something dark and fast sprang from the shadows. Long arms stretched out, and the thing landed on the guardsman. There was a loud boom like thunder that caused Beltan to stop and flinch.

"No!" a shrill voice screamed.

Larsen rushed forward, tears streaming down her face. The guardsman grunted and sat up, shoving his attacker off him. The *chin-pasi* rolled onto her back, arms flopping limply against the ground, empty brown eyes staring upward. In the center of her chest was a deep, bloody hole.

A wave of dizziness crashed through Beltan. He took a staggering step forward. "My lady . . ."

"Ellie!" Dr. Larsen shouted, kneeling beside the crumpled form of the *chin-pasi*.

Still sitting, the guardsman lifted the metal weapon and pointed it at Beltan. "I said drop, you bastard."

"You idiot, don't kill him!" Larsen cried, staggering to her feet in front of the guard, who swore and leaped up.

Beltan only watched, motionless. *Bastard.* So even on this world they knew what he was. The *chin-pasi*'s blood was pooling on the hard, black surface of the ground now. Beltan felt his knees buckle as the strange strength finally fled him. He couldn't seem to get enough air. Before he could fall to the ground, rough hands grabbed him under the armpits, hauling him up.

The guard who had slain the *chin-pasi* stepped forward, face red and puffy. "Let me at that bastard."

Again Dr. Larsen interposed herself between the guard and Beltan. There was fear in her eyes, and her hand trembled visibly as she held it out, but her voice was resolute.

"You will not harm him. Do you know how much we have invested in him? More than you'll earn in your lifetime, you moron. Got that?"

The guard stared at her with a mixture of rage and chagrin.

Larsen turned, addressed the men who held Beltan. "Get him to the truck with the other subject. Now."

Hands started to pull Beltan away. He could not resist.

"Let me go," he croaked.

Larsen took a step toward him, her expression one of wonder. "My God, you really can speak our language."

"I said let me go."

"They won't harm you." Her eyes shone with wetness now. "Don't be afraid."

He bared his teeth, holding her gaze with his own.

"My father was right," he said softly. "I should have killed you."

She stared and lifted a hand to her bruised throat.

A fog seemed to be settling all around now. The guards moved like wraiths in the gloom, and it almost felt like Beltan was floating on a gray ocean.

There was a moment when the fog cleared a little, and he stared at a peculiar sight. A man in a black robe stood near a group of several *chin-pasis*. They scurried, dragging bags behind them and loading them into one of the *t'ruks*. Only something about them wasn't right. The fingers of the *chin-pasis* ended in long, curving claws, and their eyes were not soft and brown, but large and bright as moons.

The man in the black robe touched his face, and as he did several of the *not-chin-pasis* squealed and moved quickly in the direction he pointed. Then the man turned, and Beltan felt his heart wrench in his chest. The man's face was made of gold.

The fog closed back in. It seemed to be seeping into his head now. There was a stinging in his arm. Had they poisoned him again? By the time he was able to blink his vision clear, he saw a set of black doors above him. A hand opened one of the doors. They were loading him onto one of the *t'ruks*. But the others were coming, the enemies of his captors. Only they wouldn't know where he was.

Hands reached down for him. There was no time. Beltan went limp. They weren't prepared for that. Hands scrabbled for him as he slumped forward, against the door that was still shut. It was covered with a layer of grime. Quickly, he pressed a finger to the door. He had to make a mark, a sign others would understand. But he had never been good at letters. He couldn't think. Already rough hands tugged him back.

Then he saw it—a symbol he remembered.

His finger was shaking, and they were pulling him. He couldn't be sure he had made the mark right. Then the hands lifted him into a dim, long space. It was crowded. They shoved him past stacks of steel crates. One of them was empty, its hatch open. The hands forced him inside.

No, don't do this! he tried to scream, but instead different words came out of his mouth.

"Fa! Oel im ethala inhar!"

The hands pressed harder. He curled up inside the steel box, like a babe in a cold, lifeless womb. There was a *clang* as the hatch was shut, and another as its latch was driven home. Outside the box, shadows receded. There was a loud noise as the door of the *t'ruk* was shut.

"I'm sorry, my lady," he whispered.

But she couldn't hear him. He was a coward and a weakling, just like his father had said. She had died for him, and now he was alone.

A faint, chiming sound.

He listened. The sound came again, and it made him think of ice on a starry night. The tingling returned, all over now, and the fog seemed to recede a fraction. Beltan shifted in the box and peered out a small vent.

He felt it should have been dark inside the *t'ruk*, but it was not. A soft, silvery glow illuminated the boxes and crates all around. Most were steel like his own, although one was different. It was smaller and looked as if it was fashioned of stone, its surface covered by odd, angular symbols.

The light grew brighter. Beltan saw now that it emanated from one of the steel boxes near his own. Something moved within, folding long, slender limbs behind the wire mesh. The tingling grew stronger now, a sensation like lightning about to strike. He forgot weariness, forgot fear, even as he felt the *t'ruk* rumble into motion.

Beltan pressed his face against the grate. "Who are you?"

Inside its cage, the thing lifted a large, round head and gazed at him with tilted eyes like white, depthless jewels.

58.

"How much longer?" Grace said, squatting next to a puddle in the dimness beneath the viaduct.

Travis scowled at her. "You mean since the last time you asked that question exactly seventeen seconds ago?"

Grace opened her mouth for a hot reply, but her words were lost as a particularly heavy truck hurtled over the viaduct above them. Small flakes of cement fell down like hard snow. Travis knew the real question was not how much longer they had to wait for the call from the Seekers, but how much longer they had until the entire overpass came crashing down on top of them.

"It is nearly time," Vani said. She crouched on the base of a cement column, gazing into the grayness of the day, her visage intent.

"Thank you," Grace said. She shot Travis a sour look.

He scowled. "Fine. Trust the enigmatic woman from a medieval world who doesn't even have a watch."

Then again, he had a feeling Vani was one of those people who could tell time without the convenience of a digital clock. She probably kept a running count of the seconds in the back of her mind. He supposed

she could also start a fire with two Q-Tips in the rain
and hot-wire a car with a gum wrapper and some
twine. She was one of those terminally *capable* people.
Unlike Travis, who had always found it cause for
minor celebration when he actually remembered how
to use a can opener.

He was glad she was with them.

The Seekers had dropped them as close as they dared
to the location of the Duratek complex. This was
Commerce City—a shiny, optimistic name that could
not change the fact it was a grim, dirty industrial area
north of downtown, home to oil refineries, storage
facilities, and dog-food factories.

A hundred years ago, all of this had been tall-grass
prairie sprinkled with wetlands. Now smokestacks rose
above the viaducts, spewing billowing clouds of vapor
that merged with brown-tinged clouds. But that was
the price of *Commerce*. No doubt Duratek was right at
home here. After all, if they had their way, in just a few
years this could be Calavan or Toloria.

They had parted from Farr and Deirdre with few
words. But then, they had already picked over the
scant bones of their plan a dozen times. And what did
you really tell someone who, if all worked as intended,
would soon be a world away? *See you around? Let's keep
in touch?* He had settled for shaking Farr's hand, and for
kissing Deirdre's cheek as he whispered, *Thank you.*

Be safe, my gentle warrior, she had told him.

It was only as he and Grace made their way through
a maze of parking lots, junk heaps, and storage tanks,
following behind Vani in a poor imitation of her sleek
stealth, that the absurdness of what they were trying to
do really struck him.

*This is impossible, Travis. Even if by some miracle we get
Beltan away from Duratek, how are we going to use the*

artifact to open the gateway? This is one case where even Vani doesn't have all the answers.

Another truck. More cement snow.

Grace shook the stuff from her hair. "If he's not conscious, how are we going to transport him?"

Travis huddled inside his black trench coat. "What?"

"We didn't think of that. We can't carry him and fight at the same time. And even if he's conscious, he's experienced severe muscle atrophy. He's not going to be able to walk. Maybe we should let them keep him, at least until he's stronger." She leaned back against a clump of rusted rebar. "But what will they do to him in the meantime? No, it has to be now."

Travis shuffled toward her, avoiding one oily puddle only to step in another. He stared at his wet, rapidly cooling foot. Maybe it didn't matter what you did; maybe the result was bound to be the same no matter what action you took. Maybe, like Vani had said, all this was just fate.

"You're babbling, Grace."

She reached out, gripped his hand. He squeezed.

Gravel crunched, then Vani was there.

"I believe I can glimpse their fortress. Do you see? Past that empty space, beyond the wall."

Travis did not follow her gesture. He gazed at her instead. "What was it like?" he said. "Coming through the gate, knowing you might never get back to your home?"

She fixed her gold eyes on him. "I will return home. The cards have told me."

Her words were confident, but he caught the slight wavering in them, and she looked away. So, even Vani didn't believe completely in fate. Maybe it wasn't too late, maybe he could stop this before—

A piercing trill emanated from the cellular phone

Farr had handed to Grace as she stepped from the limousine.

Grace pushed a button. "Hello?"

She listened a few moments, then lowered the phone. "It's time."

Vani moved from the cover of the junk beneath the viaduct, down a gap between two fences choked with dead weeds. Travis and Grace exchanged looks. He stuck the phone in a small backpack, shouldered it, and they followed Vani.

There was no need for Grace to discuss the call. It meant that Farr and Deirdre were in position, at an address somewhere north of here. It meant that, by means of Farr's digital recording device, Grace had just had a conversation with the police. The nature of the device had allowed Farr to record twenty separate snippets of her voice, some complex and rambling, others as simple as *Yes* or *Could you repeat that?*

Any of the snippets could be accessed at the touch of a button. That meant Farr could hold the recorder to the phone while he listened and choose the sampled bit of Grace's voice that worked best as a reply to whatever was said.

And it had worked. That's what Farr's call had meant. He had stayed on the phone long enough for the call to the police to be traced, then had called Grace. At that moment, he and Deirdre were speeding away from the location before the police arrived. Along with Duratek.

It took another fifteen minutes for them to reach the fence surrounding the complex. That had been by design. They had wanted to give Duratek enough time to intercept the messages on the police radio bands, to gather a force together, and to leave the building in hopes of capturing Travis and Grace.

Incredibly, it seemed to have gone as planned. The three paused behind a broken chunk of a cement culvert just outside a chain-link fence. A hundred yards beyond was a low, long, industrial building. In between was a parking lot, empty except for a few faded, peeling cars.

"It looks like they've left," Grace said.

"Stay low," Vani whispered. "They will not all have gone, not with what they are holding within."

Travis slipped his sunglasses over his eyes. Even the gray light of the dreary afternoon was too much for them. "I don't see anybody."

"There is no way to approach the building by vehicle from this side," Vani said. "I do not imagine they will be expecting three people on foot."

Travis nodded. "Yeah, whoever tried something like that would have to be idiots."

Vani crept to the fence and drew a small object from a pocket of her jacket. She unfolded it and, in a series of neat motions, clipped through a dozen links. With a tug she opened a gap in the fence.

"You go, Wilder."

He gazed at the ragged hole. "So, what happened to ladies first?"

"That's the other planet," Grace said.

They climbed through the fence, Vani last, then crouched behind the cover of one of the abandoned cars.

"Anything?" Travis whispered.

"No," Vani said. "Their forces here must be smaller than I guessed. They must be concentrating what security remains on the front of the building."

Grace leaned against the car's dented door. "Arrogance and caution don't exactly mix. They probably think nobody knows about this place. And right now most of them are likely on their way north, thinking they're going to pick up me and Travis."

"This way," Vani said.

They crept from car to car until they were thirty feet from the side of the building. There was no more cover.

"I want you both to make for that door," Vani said, pointing. "Run as quickly as you can, but stay low. Do not stop until you get there."

"What about you?" Grace said, her visage tightly drawn.

"I will watch in case someone sees you. Now go."

Travis swallowed hard as Grace gripped his hand. He drew a deep breath, then they were running.

He felt like a complete idiot, as if everyone in the city could see him at that moment, hunched over, galloping clumsily with Grace. He kept expecting the sound of an alarm to pierce his skull. But there was only the thrum of distant traffic. He pressed himself against the wall next to the door, Grace beside him. There was no sign of Vani. He started to say something to Grace. . . .

The air folded and blurred in front of the door, then grew smooth again.

Quiet, Vani mouthed.

Travis swallowed his words. Vani tried the doorknob, but it didn't move. This did not seem to faze her. She cupped the knob with both hands, shut her eyes, and pressed her body against the door.

He never saw exactly what she did. A single ripple seemed to pass over the red-painted surface, as if it were a pond into which a pebble had been tossed. Without a sound, the door swung open. Vani's hands went up, ready.

Nothing came through the door.

Her hands went down. "This way."

They stood at the end of a long, featureless corridor. A line of fluorescent lights buzzed overhead, stretching toward the vanishing point. Half of them were dark, casting the hallway into alternating brilliance and shadow. Travis thought of a ball bouncing along the tracks of a roulette wheel. Where would it land? White or black, life or death. Everyone place your bets.

Vani moved down the corridor with barely a whisper of sound. Grace and Travis followed after, trying not to sound like a herd of wild pigs in tap shoes. They passed several doors, all of them open and leading into empty rooms. Dread crept down Travis's spine. He almost wished they would just show themselves, burst out a door, laugh, and throw nets on them. Actually getting caught couldn't possibly be as bad as fearing it.

More doors, more empty rooms.

"Where are they?" Grace whispered, then bit her lip at a harsh glance from Vani.

Travis pressed his shoulder against hers. *I was about to say the same thing,* he verbalized in his mind, just in case she could use the Weirding to tune in to his brain. He didn't know if it worked, but she pressed back.

They reached another door. This one was shut, and it was larger than the others. Travis heard a faint humming noise. He touched the surface of the door. It was vibrating slightly.

Vani gave them sharp looks. The message was clear: This was it. Grace and Travis stepped back as Vani gripped the handle of the door. Once she turned it, the time for subtlety was over. It was up to Grace and Travis to stay close but to stay out of Vani's way while she worked. And they had to get to Beltan the moment they saw him.

"Now," Vani whispered.

In one fluid motion she turned the handle, threw open the door, and dived through in a black blur.

Travis and Grace rushed after. He tensed, expecting to see Vani's limbs moving at impossible speeds, throwing Duratek agents around like rag dolls, clearing the way.

"Oh," Grace said next to him, her voice echoing.

Vani stood motionless, hands on her hips. Travis took a staggering step forward and tore off his sunglasses.

"Empty," he said. "It's empty."

The room was large, a hundred feet across, and there was nothing in it. A few empty boxes, some crumpled papers; that was all. High walls stretched toward bare beams and shadows overhead. There were only a few murky lights, and on one wall was a large exhaust fan, spinning slowly—the source of the hum.

"Maybe they're somewhere else," Grace said, hugging herself. "There are more doors."

"No," Vani said, her words like knives. "They are gone. All of them."

But it didn't make sense. They wouldn't all have gone after him and Grace. "How can this be?" Travis croaked.

Vani turned toward them. "They knew we were coming."

It struck him like a blow. Somehow they had known and had cleared everything out. The artifact. Beltan. Everything. He felt Grace's weight as she sagged against him.

"Now what?" he said, holding on to Grace, wondering what was going to prop him up when his own legs gave way.

Vani started to move. "Now we must—" Her

words ceased, and she halted.

"Vani," Grace whispered. "What is it?"

Even as Grace said this, Travis saw them. Lean, gangly, hunched shadows scuttled from behind fallen boxes, crept from dim corners, and dropped down from the steel beams above.

"It is a trap," Vani said.

59.

Deirdre sank back against the leather seat as the limousine accelerated, leaving behind the dilapidated rental house where they had made their phone call to the police.

"You know," she said, arms crossed over her black-leather jacket, "that was completely illegal."

"Only on this world," Farr quipped.

He didn't look well. He hadn't shaved that day, and the stubble of his beard cast a shadow over his face. His dark eyes were sunken, and his lips—usually so full and sensual—were drawn in thin lines. He fiddled with the controls on a small radio. Voices crackled out of the speaker. He was scanning the police bands.

Deirdre sighed and supposed she didn't look so marvelous herself. "So, do you think the police will really come?"

He bent his ear to the radio. More voices hissed and popped. Farr looked up, eyes glinting. "It seems they're already on their way."

If the police were coming, Duratek couldn't be far behind. Which meant the plan had actually worked—at least their part of it. Deirdre could only hope the others were having similar luck.

Not that luck would have much to do with it. Travis and Grace had described the things Vani was capable of. Duratek would leave the complex sparsely guarded in order to follow the police, and Vani would get them inside, get the artifact, and free Beltan. Even if they couldn't find a way to activate the artifact and return to AU-3, at least they would be able to escape with it, which would keep Duratek from discovering the secret of the artifact themselves. It wouldn't be a total loss.

And may the spirits cast woe upon you, Deirdre Falling Hawk, for that is an untruth. You don't want them to find out how to activate the artifact. You don't want them to leave.

Perhaps that was just the Seeker in her, the part that wanted to be able to continue studying her fascinating subjects. And yet that was a lie as well. The reason she didn't want Travis and Grace to go was simple: She was going to miss them.

"How long until the police arrive?" she said.

"Their ETA is three minutes. We'll be well away by then."

Farr had set down the radio. He was flipping through a folder of papers now—documents related to the cases that had all become inextricably linked: Sarsin, Beckett, Wilder. And what other cases were connected to these without their knowing it? When she joined the Seekers, she had always hoped one day she would find those who had otherworldly connections. She never thought she would be the one with such ties herself.

More chatter on the police radio. Farr seemed not to notice. He stared at something in the folder on his lap, brushed it with a finger. It was a strangely tender motion for the usually brusque Farr. Deirdre craned her neck, then saw what he was looking at. It was a photo. A tall, elegant woman with pale hair ran down a set of steps before a concrete building. She was looking to one side, gazing into the darkness, her expression desperate and regal.

In the space of a heartbeat it struck Deirdre. Her grandfather would have said it was a message from the spirit world, for such messages come suddenly, and often with pain, and they were always true.

"Damn you," she murmured.

Farr looked up, brown eyes startled. "Deirdre?"

She sat up straight on the seat, heat rising. "Damn you, you really think you are him, don't you? Marius Lucius Albrecht. The greatest Seeker in history. You're not just trying to follow his career. You're trying to *be* him."

Farr splayed his hand on the photograph. "What on Earth are you talking about?"

"No, this has nothing to do with Earth." The words exploded out of her: angry and true. "Albrecht fell in love with her—Lady Alis Faraday, the woman the Philosophers sent him to study. And now you think you love *her*. Grace Beckett."

He opened his mouth to speak, but she didn't let him.

"By the Book, are you insane, Farr? Do you have a list of all the accomplishments of Albrecht's life so you can check something off once you've matched it? All of this—everything we've done here in Denver—it was all so you could have her, wasn't it? Well did you? Did you get your moment alone with her? Did you check that off your list as well?"

She was shaking now, fists pounding against the knees of her black jeans. "The others were right; I didn't want to believe them when I first started working with you, but now I do. You are one cold, arrogant son of a bitch, Hadrian Farr. And if you really are the next Marius Albrecht, then he was a bastard just like you are."

Deirdre flung herself back against the seat, glaring. He did not move, did not counter her words with smooth, eloquent arguments as she would have expected. Instead he gazed at the photograph through his fingers. Then, slowly, he closed the folder and looked up at her with haunted eyes.

She gasped, and the anger drained from her in a cold flood, leaving her hollow.

"No," she whispered. "God, no, don't say it."

It was too late.

"I do love her," he said.

The words were small and broken. There was no room for irony in them, nor carefully calculated effect. She had never heard Farr speak like this—this plainly and without guile. The cost to him must have been more than she could imagine.

"You can't have her," she said. "Everything in the Book forbids it. In the end, even Albrecht gave up Lady Faraday."

He leaned forward, elbows on knees, head bowed. "I know."

The whir of traffic seeped through the windows. They were heading toward her even at that moment— Grace Beckett. But now Deirdre found herself hoping that she and Travis and Vani did manage to use the artifact, that they did step through an impossible gate into another world. Farr had always been the very paragon of a Seeker, sometimes admirable, sometimes despicable, always mysterious, powerful, and alluring. To see him like this—undone by his own fallibility— it was almost more than Deirdre could bear. She reached a hand toward him, although whether to comfort or strike him she did not know.

An electronic chime pierced the air. Deirdre and Farr stared at the pager that rested on the seat next to him.

He grabbed it.

"Is it them?" Deirdre said.

"It can't be. It's too soon. And I told them to call, not page." He pressed a button, frowned. "I don't recognize this telephone number."

"What is it?"

"It's 268-533-7128."

"I don't know it. Maybe whoever called entered it incorrectly by mistake. Can you see what phone number the call originated from?"

Farr pressed another button. "Yes."

Deirdre fired up a small notebook computer. It was good to have something mundane to focus on. He read off both numbers, and she punched them in. Before coming to Denver, she had loaded a database of all Colorado phone numbers on the computer. Standard procedure. She started the search, then in a moment she had it.

"The number where the call originated belongs to an address in Denver. On West Colfax. It's a business. Name is . . ." Her fingers froze on the keys. "Marji's House of Mystery."

Deirdre pushed aside the computer and grabbed a cell phone. "I'm calling her." She punched the number, waited as it rang. And rang. She pressed a button and lowered the phone. "Marji's not answering."

"Nor will she," he said softly. He had been bending close to the police radio. Now he turned up the volume.

"—that's on West Colfax," a sharp, disembodied voice spoke over static. "Denver Fire and Rescue just arrived. Right now we think one person is trapped in—"

More static. Farr turned down the volume, his

brown eyes wide. Deirdre realized this was the first time she had ever seen him frightened.

"It's her, isn't it? Marji. She's the one trapped inside. But maybe they'll . . ."

Deirdre didn't bother finishing. It didn't take a message from the spirits to know that, just like in Brixton, no one would be coming out of that fire. Duratek didn't work that way.

"They know." Anger transmuted Farr's dull expression. He slammed the seat with a fist. "Damn them, they know everything!"

"They must have heard us. At Marji's. They must have followed us from the hotel and heard us talking there. Or maybe they had the place bugged. The police had been there, looking for—" A cold hand clamped around Deirdre's heart. "Travis and Grace."

Farr had already grabbed the cell phone. He dialed, then a moment later set the phone down. "It's not turned on." He laughed—a forlorn sound. "I told Grace to keep the phone turned off until it was time to call us. I didn't want a wrong number ringing it while they were sneaking around the complex. I guess it's a little late for worrying about that."

"Now what?" Deirdre said.

Farr raised the phone. "I'm calling the Seekers. This is beyond us now. We may have to get law enforcement involved. Get the police there, on scene, just to keep anything from happening. Even Duratek can't kidnap someone with the police standing watch—that's just the kind of attention they can't afford. We can sort out the mess later, even if it means having to pay a bond to get Travis and Grace out of jail. It's not like the Seekers don't have money and lawyers enough."

Farr dialed. Deirdre hoped he was right. It was true

that the Seekers had good lawyers. And if the police were involved, even Duratek would have to play by certain rules.

Farr spoke into the phone. "Yes, hello, it's Farr. This is a crisis. You must get a message to the Philosophers immediately. We have lost control of—"

He stopped speaking. Then, slowly, he lowered the phone and switched it off.

Deirdre nearly screamed the words at him. "What the hell are you doing?"

"They hung up."

She dug her fingers into the seat. "Hung up?"

He looked up, visage weary. "Yes, hung up. It was Sasha. Once I spoke my name, she said she was sorry, that she couldn't talk to me, that no one was allowed to talk to me or to you, that they could not interfere. Then she disconnected."

Deirdre lunged for the phone. "We have to call them back. We have to let them know what's—"

Gently, Farr pried the phone from her rigid fingers.

"No, Deirdre. I don't know why I didn't see it sooner. I guess I've always been blind to what it's like for those on the other side of the investigation. They won't talk to us. We're on our own now."

This was impossible. The Seekers didn't abandon their agents. Not like this.

"I don't understand. . . ." But even as she spoke, she *did* understand.

Farr nodded. "Desiderata One. A Seeker shall not interfere with the actions of those of otherworldly nature."

Images flickered outside the tinted windows, as dim as ghosts. Everything Deirdre had known had melted to a sea of shadow, and she and Farr were adrift alone.

"We're not the Seekers anymore," she said. "We're

the subjects of the investigation."

Farr gave a grim nod. "The watchers have become the watched."

"Do you think they're watching us now?"

"Most likely they've got some form of surveillance on us." His lips twisted in a bitter smile. "It's what I'd do."

Still Deirdre couldn't completely understand. "But why?"

"They want to see what we'll do, of course. Evidently the Philosophers have decided we have become too closely involved in this case, that we are no longer observers but rather players." He brushed the file folder. "It seems we are less useful as investigators and more so as subjects with otherworldly connections. They want to see what we do of our—"

Deirdre sucked in a breath. "Of our own free wills."

She and Farr locked eyes. Yes, he was thinking the same thing she was. If the Seekers had cut them loose, that meant nothing was binding them anymore. Not the Desiderata. Not the Vow. Which meant . . .

"We can do anything," she said. "Anything we want."

Farr grinned, like a wolf invited in among the sheep. He opened a small cabinet in the door, then pulled out two objects. They were guns—nine-millimeter semiautomatic pistols. He held one out toward her. Forcing her hand not to tremble, she closed her fingers around the gun. It felt smooth against her hand, and she had to grip it tightly, like it was a living thing.

Farr leaned forward, punched a button on the seat's armrest. "Driver, get us to the location in Commerce City as fast as you can. I don't care what you have to do."

Deirdre felt resistance as the limousine sped up. But

she knew it was still at least fifteen minutes to the complex. They were going to be too late.

And maybe it didn't matter. There was something here, something they were missing. Why, in her final moments, had Marji called them? She picked up the laptop and stared again at the first number on the screen: 268-533-7128.

"Hand me the phone," she said, and Farr gave it to her.

She dialed the number. A series of sharp tones, then a computer-generated voice told her the number did not exist. Somehow that didn't surprise her. Marji had called them just before her shop had burned. She must have been trying to tell them something. But what? Farr's pager only accepted phone numbers.

And what if it wasn't a phone number she had wanted to give you? There aren't any limits on you anymore, Deirdre. So think. Marji was a psychic. Tarot cards. Tea leaves. Palms. Numerology . . .

She picked up the phone, stared at the keypad. There were no letters on the one. Forget the last three digits for the moment then. She looked at the others. Two. That was a "B" on the keypad. Six was an "O." She typed them on the laptop as she transcribed them. Then she leaned back.

Farr studied her. "What is it, Deirdre?"

She could not take her eyes from the word she had typed on the glowing screen:

BOULDER128

"Boulder," she murmured.

"What?"

She slammed shut the lid of the computer. "They're taking Highway 128 to Boulder. Duratek. After they heard us talking, they must have been afraid of a full-on assault from the Seekers, and they bolted. Maybe they have another base of operations in Boulder. It's only thirty miles north of here."

"Are you certain, Deirdre?"

She gripped the yellowed bear claw hanging at her throat. "I'm certain."

Farr pressed the button again. "Cancel that last order, Driver. Get us onto Highway 128 to Boulder. Now. And don't stop for anything."

Deirdre lurched in the seat as the vehicle made a hard turn. By the time she righted herself, she saw that Farr wore a fierce grin. He looked quite mad.

But maybe he wasn't. The Desiderata were rules set down in a musty, five-century-old book. What could they possibly have to do with the human heart? She set the gun on the seat beside her and touched the silver ring on her finger.

"So what about Travis and Grace?" she said.

"If you're right, they should be calling us any minute to tell us Duratek has evacuated the complex. They're perfectly safe at the moment."

Deirdre nodded. Duratek was headed north, and she and Farr would intercept them, stop them somehow. That was their choice. Besides, even if Duratek had left a few stragglers behind at the complex, she had little doubt Vani would be able to handle them.

She shot a grin back at Farr, one she knew was every bit as mad as his own.

"Here's to free will," Deirdre said.

60.

"You can handle them, right, Vani?" Travis rasped, as they backed toward the open doorway.

Shadows undulated toward them slowly. Wet grunting noises echoed off bare walls. Grace shuddered. What could they possibly be waiting for?

Vani held her hands before her, ready. "As I said once, these *gorleths* are different than any I have heard of. They are strong. And clever."

"That didn't exactly answer my question," Travis said through clenched teeth.

"Three of them. Perhaps four, if I am fortunate."

Travis made a strangled sound. "In case you hadn't noticed, there are something more than four of them."

Vani kept her gold eyes on the sinuous shadows. "I had noticed, Travis. Surprising as it may seem to you, people from other worlds are indeed able to count."

Grace pushed clinging bangs from her damp brow. It was hard to keep hold of them with her eyes. The *gorleths* wove back and forth, vanishing and reappearing, sometimes closer, sometimes farther away.

"Why aren't they attacking?" she said, because if she didn't say something she was going to scream instead.

Travis ran a hand over his bald cranium, wiping away fine beads of sweat. "I think they're playing with us."

"No," Vani said. "*Gorleths* do not play games. I am not certain, but I do not believe their master is here. He must have commanded these *gorleths* to guard this space. If we leave, I do not believe they will be able to follow us, for that would violate what the sorcerer has ordered them to do."

Travis groaned. "That's great. You're telling me our lives are riding on the fact that these are *anal-retentive* monsters?"

"I wouldn't listen to him," Grace whispered to Vani.

"Do not fear, Grace. I am not."

They kept backing up. Grace felt a puff of air behind her. They had reached the doorway.

Vani spoke in low, even tones. "You must retreat through the door. But do it slowly, so that they are not aroused."

"I thought you said they couldn't leave the room," Travis whispered.

"That is my hope. But then, in addition to guarding this space, the Scirathi may also have ordered them to attack anything that runs from them. Do you wish to find out?"

Grace gripped his elbow. "Come on."

Together, Grace and Travis moved back through the doorway into the empty corridor beyond. They waited several heartbeats.

"Vani—" Grace started to call out softly.

At that moment the air melted, then resolidified, and Vani was there. Grace never saw her hand move, but all the same the steel door swung shut behind her, closing with a solid *thunk*.

Travis pushed his sunglasses up. "So, when are you going to teach us how to do tricks like that?"

Vani snapped her black-leather jacket into place. "I could teach you, Travis, but—"

"Then she'd have to kill you," Grace finished with a smirk.

Vani cocked her head. "How do you know so much about the ways of the T'gol?"

"Lucky guess," Grace said, trying not to choke. "Can we get out of here now?"

"Yes. I do not believe they are following."

Grace shut her eyes and reached out with the Touch. The shadow reared all around her, but she let it slide over her, past her. Right now there were more pressing fears than those of the past.

There. Eight—no, nine—twisted blots moved through the fabric of the Weirding. Grace felt her gorge rise in her throat. They were abominations: life that had been twisted, misused, made a mockery of what it once had been. With a gasp she let go of the thread and opened her eyes.

Travis was watching her, his expression solemn. "Are you all right, Grace?"

She hesitated, then shook her head. "Come on. Vani is right—they aren't following. Let's get out of here and find out where they've taken Beltan."

Grace started jogging down the corridor, back the way they had come.

A high, electronic wail pierced the air.

She turned around and pressed her hands to her ears, but the sound cut through flesh and bone like tissue paper.

"What is it?" she shouted.

"Some sort of alarm," Vani called, her voice barely audible above the siren.

"That doesn't make sense!" Travis shouted. "Why didn't it go off on our way into this place?"

"Because they wished for us to get into the building. Not out."

It came a second later: a boom as something struck the other side of the heavy metal door.

Again Grace reached out with the Touch, then her eyes flew open. She had seen it against the brightness of the Weirding: a black, seething knot just on the other side of the door.

"They're trying to get out!"

Vani backed away from the door as it shook under another blow. "It seems the alarm has invoked a second command given by their master. A command to hunt us."

For one more heartbeat the wail of the alarm paralyzed them, making it impossible to think. Then they were running.

Another boom behind them. Grace glanced back over her shoulder in time to see the surface of the metal door bulge outward. She turned back, running on Travis's and Vani's heels. Openings flashed by to either side. The door they had entered the building through grew in her field of vision: a rectangle of gray light.

The light turned black.

Thirty feet ahead of them, dark shapes slipped through the door. Pale eyes locked on the runners. Two hunched forms began loping down the corridor toward them.

Gorleths. Even as she watched them come, more shadows appeared.

Grace nearly ran into Vani and Travis.

"Turn," Vani said, her words as piercing as the siren. "Run the other direction. Now!"

Thought connected with nerves and muscles. Grace spun around, and she and Travis lurched down the corridor together. Her feet felt like they were made of lead. Ahead of them, to the left, the door that held back the other *gorleths* deformed further with another *boom*. Behind Grace, masked by the sound of the alarm, came wet, popping noises, then a piteous cry that was not human in origin. A black comet seemed to streak past her, then Vani was there, running just ahead of them.

"I have removed the two *gorleths*," she called over her shoulder. "But more come that way."

Grace had no breath to respond. They had reached the door that led into the empty warehouse space. Even as Grace dashed past it, metal shrieked, parted, and a long arm punched through a gap, scrabbling for her with gleaming claws.

It would have sliced her jugular if Travis hadn't grabbed her sweater and jerked her toward him. Her limbs tangled around his. They both nearly went down. Then Vani was there, steadying them with strong arms.

The sound of rending metal echoed behind them, merging with shrieks of hate and hunger. Grace didn't need to look back to know that dark forms slunk through the mangled door, joined with others that loped down the corridor, and turned to pursue their fleeing prey.

The corridor ended in a door. Travis got there first. He threw himself against it, pressing the latch bar.

He stumbled back. The door was locked.

"Stand away," Vani said.

She leaned her body against the door, hands splayed out on steel, and shut her eyes. The alarm still sounded, but along with it came a new, shrill, scraping sound that shredded Grace's nerves. It reminded her of fingernails on a chalkboard. Only louder. Much louder.

"You might want to hurry it up, Vani," Travis said, his face ashen.

Vani did not answer. Her jaw was clenched.

Beneath her hands, the surface of the door began to warp, ripple, like paint on fire.

Dread pulled at Grace, and she looked behind them. The creatures moved swiftly down the corridor. A knot of five coursed some distance ahead of the others. Their long arms dragged as they ran, their talons digging deep furrows in the floor. That was the source of the horrible sound.

"Vani . . ." Travis said, voice rising.

Grace snapped her head around. The door looked as if it were fading in and out of being. Here and there she caught glimpses of things beyond: a patch of gray sky, part of a parked car.

"Now!" Vani cried.

The door burst open.

They dashed out into the gray afternoon, feet pounding against asphalt. It was a parking lot on the opposite side of the building from where they had entered. Beyond a high, wood fence, Grace could hear the sounds of traffic. She looked back at the open door. Vani had shut it, but already it shuddered under a blow. She backed away. They had seconds at most.

"Run," Vani said, still backing up, hands before her, ready to strike. "Climb over the fence, get to the road, and flag down a vehicle."

Grace reached out a hand. "What about you?"

"I will delay them."

"No," Travis said. His face was hard. "There are too many. We won't leave you, Vani."

Vani turned around, a strange, soft light in her gold eyes. However, before Grace could decide what it really meant, the light was replaced by sparks of anger.

"Do not become a fool, Travis. I will be slowed if I am forced to protect you and Grace. The only way you can help me is to go."

She was right. Grace grabbed his arm. "Listen to her, Travis. We have to—"

Her words were cut short as something dark and heavy struck her from the side.

Grace rolled to the pavement, stones and bits of broken glass gouging into her hands and cheeks. A sunburst of agony exploded in her stomach, radiating outward from her solar plexus. She managed to raise her head, grimacing in pain, unable to breathe.

It crouched over her, maw open. Ichor drooled from tusklike fangs. It ran a talon over her chest almost gently, as if deciding exactly where to make the incision. Then it pulled its spindly arm back, talons extended, ready to tear her guts out.

The air shimmered behind the *gorleth*. Before it could strike, its arm bent at a queer angle, eliciting a sharp *crack*. The thing threw its head back to scream, but there was another blur, and its head twisted on its neck. The *gorleth* slumped to the asphalt next to Grace. The air grew smooth, and Vani was there.

"Travis!" she called out. "Drop. Now!"

Twenty feet away, Grace saw Travis fling himself to the ground. A snarling shape lunged for him. Vani extended her arm in a precise motion, and a trio of small objects flew out from her coiled hand. Only when they struck their target did Grace see what they were: three sharp triangles of steel.

The *gorleth* staggered back from Travis, the steel triangles protruding from its chest. It scrabbled at them with its talons, ripping its own flesh, then toppled backward onto the asphalt. The creature convulsed a moment, then grew still, foam bubbling from its gaping mouth. The triangles had not bitten deep. Grace didn't need to ask to know they had been poisoned.

At last she drew in a ragged breath. The two *gorleths*

that had attacked them were dead, but where had they come from? Then her eyes moved to the roof of the building.

"Yes," Vani said. "They came at us from above. You must go before more follow."

She helped Grace up. Travis had climbed to his feet. He started to speak, but at that moment the door of the building flew outward with a sound like thunder. Huddled in a black ball, five *gorleths* loped toward them across the parking lot.

In an instant, Grace judged the distances and made the calculations. Even Vani would not be able to move swiftly enough. The *gorleths* would reach Travis first. She steeled herself, preparing to watch her friend get torn to bits.

A sound rose on the air like a scream. The sound grew louder, and something swung into view around the corner of the building. There was a deep roar, followed by another squeal. In a green flash the thing hurtled forward. The *gorleths* turned their heads, their lidless eyes staring, just in time to see it strike them.

Five hairy bodies flew through the air, gangly limbs flung wide. Blood sprayed out in a glittering arc, misting Travis with crimson as he turned his head away. The *gorleths* seemed to hover in midair, so long that for a terrible moment Grace thought the things could fly. Then they came crashing to the pavement in five tangled, oozing heaps. They did not get up.

The thing raced back around in a tight circle. Only as it squealed to a halt between her and the others did realization cut through Grace's dullness. It was a truck—a big, green, double-cab pickup truck, blood smearing its now-dented front hood. Two rifles were nestled in a gun rack mounted on the back window, and a rainbow air freshener swung wildly beneath the rearview mirror. On the truck's front bench sat two men.

No, not men, Grace. Look at the hats. They're cowboys.

The lean man on the passenger side let out a whoop as he squinted through the windshield with crinkly blue eyes. "Now that's what I call roadkill, Mitchell."

The driver didn't answer him. Instead, he turned to gaze at Grace through the window, his eyes serious behind wire-rimmed glasses.

"Need a lift, ma'am?" he said in a deep, melodious drawl.

61.

Travis glanced out the rear window of the pickup, but all he saw were cars and pavement. The industrial building was at least a mile behind them now. Even if the Scirathi had ordered the *gorleths* to pursue, they could not run so far so fast. He felt another hand squeeze his. Grace. He forced himself to turn around.

"So, Travis," Davis Burke-Favor said, leaning over the back of the front seat, "are you going to introduce us to your friends or not?"

They had all tumbled into the back bench of the pickup in a frenetic dash to escape before more of the creatures burst out the door of the building, and Mitchell had peeled out of the parking lot before they were completely inside.

"This is Grace Beckett," Travis said. "She's a doctor. And this is Vani. She's . . ."

His words faltered. What exactly *was* Vani. A spy? A protector?

"I am their friend," Vani said.

Travis gazed at her. She raised a single eyebrow, and he smiled.

"That she is," he said.

Davis tipped his gray Stetson, his lean, tanned face crinkling again in a grin. "Pleased to meet you both."

"All right, Travis," Grace said. "Now it's our turn."

She leaned back on the seat, her face pale, her ash-blond hair a snarled mess, but her eyes strangely brilliant. Her face was scraped in several places, and Davis's handkerchief was wrapped around one of her hands, which had been bleeding after her fall.

Travis finished the introductions. "Grace, Vani, these are friends of mine from Castle City, Davis and Mitchell Burke-Favor. The funny one who laughs at everything is Davis. The good-looking one with the radio voice is Mitchell."

"See, Davis?" Mitchell drawled, not taking his eyes off the road as he drove. "I told you I was the handsome one."

"No, you're the old one."

"I'm just getting better with age."

"That's not fair. I'm handsome, too."

"No, you heard the man. You're the funny one."

"That's funny as in comedic—you know, the life of the party. Not funny-looking." Davis looked back over the seat. "Isn't that right, Travis?"

Travis glanced at Vani and Grace. "In case you couldn't tell, they're sort of together."

"I believe we had gathered that fact," Vani said, a faint smile on her dark red lips.

"That obvious?" Davis said.

Grace nodded. "The his-and-his rifles are dead giveaways."

Davis let out a hoot of mirth, slapping the seat, and even Travis laughed, though it hurt; his lungs still ached from their mad sprint. Then, gradually, his laughter dwindled.

"So how did you know? How did you know where we were, and that we needed help?"

Mitchell's eyes were puzzled in the rearview mirror. "You mean you didn't know she called us?"

"Who called you?"

"It was your Denver friend, Marji."

Travis felt Grace's hand tighten around his.

"Marji called you?" she said. "When?"

Davis checked his watch. "Must have been a bit over two hours ago. As soon as Mitchell hung up, we hopped in the truck, and Mitchell drove like a shot down the canyons."

Travis looked at Grace, but she shrugged. She didn't know either why Marji would have called. Travis didn't even know how she had known about Davis and Mitchell—

—and then he remembered her question, wondering who might know about them, and Travis had mentioned his friends up in Castle City. She must have remembered, then gotten the number from information. But that still didn't explain why.

Travis folded his arms on the back of the seat. "What did she tell you?"

"Not a lot," Mitchell said. "Just that you were in trouble, and where we could find you. She said you've been . . . that you've been somewhere far away, and that you need to get back. Only that pack of wolves from Duratek have something you need. And a friend of yours, too. Is that right?"

Travis gripped cracked vinyl. "That's pretty much it."

"You have put yourselves in great danger by coming here," Vani said.

Davis made a dismissive wave. "It was nothing, ma'am. Mitchell will bang those dents right out of the hood. Won't be the first time."

"Thanks to your driving," Mitchell said.

"Hey, it's not my fault half the bucks in the valley are suicidal." He glanced back at Grace. "You're a doctor, ma'am. Is there such a thing as Prozac for deer?"

"I'd suggest counseling," she said. "They might have elk envy. You know, bigger antlers."

That elicited another whoop.

"Travis," Mitchell said, his deep voice solemn, "there's something else you need to know."

At once Davis's laughter ceased. Mitchell kept talking.

"On the way out of Castle City we saw something, on Summit Road. I think you know it, Travis. Dirt road, runs just east of our ranch. Just about no one uses it these days except for us, and only when we want a shortcut to the highway. But today we saw a car, and a couple of those black-suited men."

Travis said the word through clenched teeth. "Duratek."

"That's right. We know the two. They came by our ranch looking for you a couple of days after you called us. We didn't tell them anything. But then we saw you on TV, just for a second, in a news story about that new cathedral they're building in downtown Denver, so we called Deputy Windom. And . . ."

Mitchell's melodious voice faltered.

"What is it?" Travis said, his mouth dry and metallic.

Davis answered. "There was a sheriff's vehicle next to the black-suits' car. We saw her, leaning out the window, talking to them. It was—"

Connections sizzled in Travis's brain. "It was Jace— Deputy Windom. She's been talking to Duratek. That's how they found out Grace and I were in Denver."

"I don't know why she'd do it, Travis," Mitchell said, eyes sad. "I don't know why she'd deal with those wolves."

But Travis did. She had loved Max, and Max had burned. Because of Travis.

He leaned back, rubbing his right hand. How many more people would be drawn into the web around him? How many more people would be harmed because of what Jack had done to him?

You should never have come, he wanted to tell Davis and Mitchell. *You should keep away from me*. But his tongue was so dry he couldn't form the words.

Davis scratched his neck. "So, do you mind if I ask what those animals were back there? Whatever zoo they escaped from, I think they've been feeding on toxic waste in the meantime."

Grace sat up straight. "That's it. That's why they looked so familiar. They've taken Earth animals and altered them." She curled a hand beneath her chin. "But how? Cloning? There's no time to have grown adult animals from embryos. Gene therapy—that has to be it. Encase the genetic material in a virus, infect them, or use some other vector to introduce it. But what genome have they been using? It can't . . . it can't be local."

Davis's forehead wrinkled, pushing up his hat. "So does she always talk like a mad scientist?"

"Pretty much," Travis said.

"Sorry," Grace said with a chagrined look. "It's just that you made me realize something, Davis. They did look like chimpanzees, didn't they?"

Travis understood what she was getting at. The *gorleths* had been chimpanzees . . . at least they had been once. But they had been changed, just like the Necromancers changed the Little People into *feydrim*. Only what had been used to alter them? He thought of their pale, slanted, too-large eyes. But there was only one thing he had ever seen that had eyes like that. And they were gone, they had to be. He had healed them with Sinfathisar.

He opened his mouth, not sure what he was going to say, but Vani spoke instead.

"The Seekers." She gazed past Travis, at Grace. "They do not know what has happened."

Grace smacked her forehead. "We were supposed to call them." She fumbled in the backpack Travis had been carrying, and which held his few precious objects: Jack's dagger, and his mistcloak. Grace pulled out the cellular phone Farr had given them. She punched a button, held it to her ear.

"It's me," she said.

Travis watched her as she listened. He could hear the faint buzz of a man's voice emanating from the phone. Farr—although Travis could not hear what he was saying.

It happened suddenly. Grace's fingers went white around the phone, and her eyes grew dull. She listened another minute, then nodded.

"We're coming," she said, then lowered the phone.

Travis took the phone from her, switched it off. Something was terribly wrong. "What is it, Grace?"

She gazed out the window. "Marji is dead. There was a fire at her shop about two hours ago." She turned her gaze on Mitchell and Davis. "It must have been just after she called you."

Travis fought for understanding. Marji—tall, outrageous, gorgeous Marji. . . . Dead? Rage rose in him, only to be crushed down by a ponderous sorrow. Once again someone who had dared to help him had paid for the deed with her life.

"How?" was all he could say. But he already knew.

"Duratek," Grace said. "Farr thinks one of their agents followed us to Marji's and heard us talking. He thinks that's how they knew about our plan, and why they evacuated the complex."

Vani peered at the blur of grimy buildings outside the window. "But where have they gone?"

"Boulder. On Highway 128." Grace leaned forward, her head next to Mitchell's. "We've got to go there."

Travis struggled to keep up with her words. "How do you know that's where they are?"

"I don't. It's what Farr said. He and Deirdre are on their way. We've got to follow them. Now."

"Boulder it is, ma'am," Mitchell drawled.

All of them were flung to one side of the cab as he turned hard on the wheel, swinging the truck onto the dirt median. Dust and gravel flew as the vehicle spun in a half circle. Then Mitchell double-shifted and punched the accelerator, and they were flung back against the seat as the pickup lunged forward. It sped in the opposite direction now, gray mountains looming in the windshield.

This time it was Mitchell who was grinning, his brown eyes sparkling behind his wire glasses in the rearview mirror. "That was a little trick I learned herding cattle on my grandfather's ranch in Montana."

"Nice," Travis said, holding on to the seat with a death grip. "Now tell me where in this thing you keep the barf bags."

62.

Grace was beginning to think Travis's request hadn't been out of line. It was clear the pickup had lost its suspension somewhere on the rugged landscape of Davis and Mitchell's high plains ranch, and the two men hadn't bothered to go look for it. She bounced on the seat, periodically whacking her shoulder against Travis or her head against the ceiling.

They had called Farr again. Travis had spoken to the Seeker, explaining that they had a vehicle and were driving fast. Then, in mid-sentence, Travis frowned and lowered the phone.

"I think the battery just died."

Grace hoped that wasn't an omen.

Now a glittering complex of office buildings slid out of view behind them, and the pickup crested a rise. Colorado Highway 128 stretched ahead—two asphalt lanes winding up and down a series of rolling hills. Urban sprawl hadn't reached this place yet, and the land was empty and brown: beautiful with the forlornness that comes only to lonely spaces. Ahead, to the west, rose the tumbled granite slopes of the Flatirons, which Grace knew dominated the skyline above Boulder.

"Any sign of them?" she called over the whining of the engine. She didn't know how many gears this truck had, but whatever it was it didn't seem to be enough.

Davis squinted blue eyes. "I don't see anything. No, wait—there's something going on up there."

It was a construction zone. There were a couple of backhoes parked at odd angles, and a dump truck took up most of the road. Orange cones were scattered all around, and a man in a matching orange vest held a stop sign. Mitchell slowed the truck.

"We don't have time for this," Travis said.

The dump truck rolled a few feet, closing the small gap that remained, then came to a halt.

Grace clenched her jaw. They didn't know how much of a lead Duratek had—they could already be to Boulder by now. And there were a dozen major roads into and out of the city.

The construction worker was waving the stop sign now.

"You'd better slow down, Mitchell," Davis said.

A few other cars were stopped. Mitchell started to bring the pickup to a halt behind them. None of the pieces of construction equipment seemed to be moving now. How long was this going to take?

"Travis, Grace," Vani said quietly, "I am not yet familiar with all the customs of this world. But if these are workmen, tell me why are they dressed in such fine clothes?"

Grace leaned forward, peering through the windshield. The pickup was nearly stopped. Two of the workmen in orange vests were approaching. One of them reached into the pocket of his black dress pants. Beneath the orange vest, he wore a white button-down shirt and a tie. Then she saw it, lurking near one of the backhoes: a shiny black sedan.

Of course, you should have known. The dump truck is empty, and the road hasn't been torn up.

The men were a dozen feet away. The one started to draw his hand from his pocket. There was something in it.

"Mitchell!" Grace shouted. "Get us out of here—now!"

He must have realized the truth at the same time she did, because even as she screamed the words he punched the accelerator and the pickup sprang forward. Mitchell cranked hard on the wheel, clipped the bumper of the minivan ahead of them, then maneuvered the truck onto the right shoulder. The approaching men scrambled to avoid being struck.

Davis grabbed the dashboard. "Might I ask where you're going, honey?"

"I haven't exactly figured that out yet."

The shoulder was too narrow. On one side was a steep embankment, on the other one of the backhoes. It wasn't going to work. Mitchell hit the brakes, leaned into a hard turn. The pickup spun in a half circle, then charged straight across the road.

A sound like a backfire set Grace's ears ringing, then the back window of the truck disintegrated into a glittering cascade of crumbled glass. She shook glass from her hair, then glanced back through the empty space. The two men in dark suits and orange vests held guns out before them.

"Get down!" Travis yelled.

Grace huddled against the seat with Travis, but not Vani. There was another report, and a hot whistling sound.

The sound ceased abruptly, and Grace glanced up. Davis stared with wide blue eyes at Vani's closed fist two inches from his face. Vani opened her fingers. In her hand was a small, bright bullet.

The truck lurched again.

"Hold on, everyone!" Mitchell called out.

Grace couldn't see from her vantage. The arm of a backhoe flashed by the window, then suddenly the world outside the pickup tilted wildly. She saw sky, then the flat line of the horizon leaning at a peculiar angle. A curious feeling of weightlessness came over her. The truck was going to roll.

"Now, Mitchell!" came Davis's shout.

Again the pickup lurched, then with a jolt that caused Grace to clamp her teeth down on her tongue, sky and earth righted themselves outside the windows. The engine roared as the truck gathered speed.

Trying not to cut herself on broken glass, she pulled herself upright alongside Travis. The construction equipment was rapidly shrinking outside the back window. She could see the tire gouges in the embankment on the south side of the road—which was barely less steep than the other, and which Mitchell must have used to gain their freedom. She saw the men in black suits throw off their orange vests and run to the sedan. But it was on the other side of the dump truck. They waved their hands frantically, but the shadow inside the dump truck seemed to be having trouble operating it, and it struck one of the backhoes.

The pickup descended over a hill, and the scene was lost to view. Grace turned around. Travis was watching Davis and Vani. She handed Davis the bullet.

"Keep this for luck," she said.

Davis still stared at the bullet. "That I will, ma'am. That I will."

Travis studied Vani, his gray eyes intent. As if aware of his attention, she lowered her head, gazing at her hands in her lap.

The land rose and fell beneath the truck. The mountains loomed closer.

"How much farther to Boulder?" Grace said.

Davis answered. "I don't think it's far. If I remember right, this road hits Highway 93 just east of the foothills. It's 93 that heads on up to Boulder."

"And it also heads south to Golden," Mitchell said.

"Faster," Grace breathed in Mitchell's ear.

She watched the speedometer climb to the right: 70, 80, 90. The truck rattled as if it were going to fly apart.

A green sign flashed by outside the window, too quickly for Grace to read. They reached the top of a large hill, and the land fell away into a deep, dun-colored bowl. Where the highway flattened out at the bottom was a black tangle.

Five eighteen-wheeled trucks were stopped on the road. The first one had jackknifed and fallen on its side, blocking the road. A column of black smoke billowed into the air. The second truck had smashed into the first. The others had managed to avoid a collision, but the drivers had steered them in various directions to keep from striking the trucks ahead.

"There!" Travis said, pointing through the windshield. "Do you see it? Just past the first truck."

His new eyes were too good, and there was too much smoke. Then the smoke coiled, breaking apart for a moment, and Grace did see. Lying across the road was a black limousine. Its side was smashed in by the impact with the first truck. It must have pulled out onto the highway just as the caravan reached it. There had been no time for the trucks to stop—or for the limousine to roll out of the way.

"Deirdre," Travis whispered, voice hoarse.

In her mind, Grace spoke another word. *Farr.*

On the sides of the black trailers, crescent moons gleamed in the waning daylight. Dark figures were climbing out of the cabs, stumbling among the wreckage. The accident must have just happened.

"All right," Mitchell said. "We found them. Now what?"

It was Vani who spoke. "There is room to the right side of the road. You must use it to get us to the head of the caravan. If they are yet alive, the Seekers will be there. Perhaps they will have discovered in which vehicle the knight is being held."

Mitchell shifted gears. "Yes ma'am."

The pickup roared down the hill.

Be all right, Farr, Grace said to herself, not even sure why she did, only that it was all she could think of right then. *Damn it, you had better be all right.*

The black length of the rearmost truck sped by. Two big men in black jeans and T-shirts looked up, faces dazed. Guns were holstered to their sides. One of them clasped a hand to his head while blood seeped through his fingers. Before they could react, the pickup blazed by.

Mitchell wove around the next trailer. Another of the guards dived and rolled on the asphalt to avoid being run over. Mitchell gunned the engine, swerving back across the road.

"Stop!"

It was Travis.

Mitchell slammed on the brakes, and Grace nearly flew into the front seat. Only Mitchell's thick shoulders stopped her.

Davis eyed the truck's mirror. "We're going to have company soon. This is not necessarily a good place to stop."

"Look, Grace. Do you see it?" Travis pointed to the back of the eighteen-wheeler they had just been about to pass. "Low on the left door."

She saw them: three horizontal lines had been drawn with a finger in the dirt on the door.

"It's just graffiti."

"No." His voice was soft. "No, you're wrong."

He reached into his shirt, drew something out. It was a piece of bone on a leather string. Etched into the bone were three parallel lines:

$$\equiv$$

With a jolt of energy, Grace understood. "It's a rune."

He nodded. "The rune of hope."

"What's it mean?" Davis said, frowning.

Vani opened the door of the pickup. "It means their friend is in this vehicle."

"We'll be needing those rifles," Mitchell said.

Grace brushed broken glass from one of the rifles, then wrested it from the gun rack. Travis grabbed the other, and together they piled out of the pickup.

"Stop now and drop those guns," a deep voice said.

Grace froze next to Travis, Mitchell, and Davis.

The man stood twenty feet away, the bulging muscles of his arms hard as he thrust the sleek pistol out before him. A trickle of blood ran from a cut on his cheek. With his small eyes fixed on them, the guard released the pistol with one of his hands and adjusted the skewed audio headset he wore, bringing the microphone close to his mouth.

"I've got them contained," he said. "We're behind transport three. I need a—"

His words ended in wet gurgle as his head twisted to one side. There was a *crack*, and the guard went limp, his heavy body crumpling to the ground. Both Davis and Mitchell stared at the dead man, their faces pale. Even before the air rippled, smoothed, and her eyes caught up with the too-swift motions of the other, Grace knew what—no, *who*—she would see.

Vani wiped her hands on her leather pants. "There are more guards in the frontmost part of this vehicle."

A bullet whizzed not far above Grace's head. Together, the five pressed themselves against the back of the truck, out of view of the front cab. Slowly, Davis peered around one side, Mitchell around the other.

In stereo, rifle blasts thundered on the air. A second later came the sounds of two doors shutting.

"I think our friends decided they'd rather stay in the cab for a while," Davis said, his grin back at full strength.

"Keep watching that direction," Vani said. "I will guard the rear of the vehicle."

The air shimmered, and she was gone.

Davis let out a whistle. "How the hell does she do that?"

"Keep your eyes on your man, Davis," Mitchell said.

"I thought you were my man."

"You know what I mean."

The two cowboys held their rifles ready, keeping watch on the front of the truck. Grace could hear booted feet against asphalt. Somewhere came a faint, gurgling cry of pain, quickly cut short. Vani was out there somewhere.

"We've got to open these doors," Grace said.

Travis tried the handle. It didn't move; the truck was locked. Panic flooded Grace. What were they going to do?

Before she could speak, Travis pressed both his

hands against the doors. He bowed his head, eyes shut, jaw clenched.

"*Urath,*" he murmured.

Grace waited, but nothing happened. It was no use. Just like the Weirding, his rune magic was too thin, too weak here on Earth. Travis staggered away from the truck.

The doors swung open.

She stared. "But I thought . . ."

He held up his right hand, wonder on his face. On the palm, a symbol glowed as if it had been drawn on his skin with molten silver: three crossed lines.

"Something's different," he said. "My power—it's stronger here."

"What's going on back there, Travis?" Mitchell said, eyes still fixed forward.

He glanced at Grace; she nodded.

"We're going in," he said.

Travis put a boot on the rear bumper, then climbed into the back of the truck. A hand reached down for Grace. She took it and climbed in after him.

She had thought it would be dark inside. It was not. A soft, metallic radiance hung on the air, although where it came from she could not say. The trailer was a jumble of large steel crates. Many of them had shifted and tumbled over in the truck's rapid stop.

A low moan rose on the air. Grace turned, then she saw it. Something stretched forth from a hole in one of the crates. It was a hand.

The word erupted from Travis in a roar. "Beltan!"

He and Grace reached the box at the same time.

Grace gripped the knight's big, bony hand. "Beltan, we're here. We'll find a way—"

—*to open the crate*, she was going to say, but there was no need. This time Travis shouted the rune.

"Urath!"

The door of the crate flew open. Whatever was affecting his rune magic, it was even stronger now.

Grace let go of the hand. It disappeared back through the hole. Then, slowly, shakily, something unfolded itself from the crate and stretched upward: a tall, pale, gaunt but blessedly familiar figure.

He grinned in the dim light, and despite the sunkeness of cheeks, despite his scraggly beard and the bruises beneath his eyes, in that moment his homely visage became so brilliant and beautiful it took Grace's breath away.

"Beltan," Travis said, his voice a whisper now.

The knight's grin shifted into a faint frown. "By Vathris, what's happened to you, Travis Wilder?"

And tears streamed down Grace's cheeks as Travis caught the big man in a fierce embrace.

63.

Travis tightened his arms around Beltan. Always before, the blond knight had seemed so strong, so invincible. Now, beneath the white lab coat, Beltan felt thin and terribly brittle. Travis knew he could easily pick the knight up in his arms and carry him if need be. But maybe that was all right. Maybe he was the protector now.

"Travis," Beltan said, his voice hoarse. "Travis, there's something I have to tell you."

Grace cast them a nervous look from her position by the open door of the trailer. "We should get going."

"She's right," Travis said, starting to pull away. "It isn't safe here. We can talk later."

Somewhere outside gunfire sounded.

"No, it can't wait."

Beltan gripped his shoulders. Despite their thinness, there was a hot strength in the knight's hands, holding Travis in place. Beltan struggled for words, his green eyes bright.

"In the baths, at Spardis, I . . . I told you I wasn't sorry. But I only did that because I thought I was going to . . . I know you haven't heard the call and . . . and I'm sorry, Travis. I'm sorry that I—"

"No." Travis spoke the word firmly, a command. "No, don't you dare be sorry, Beltan. No one should ever be sorry for loving someone."

Beltan stared, his gaunt visage stricken.

"Yes, you surprised me a little." A small laugh escaped Travis. "Okay, truth be told, more than a little. But it's all right. I've had time to think about it. And while I'm still not sure I understand how I managed to deserve it, it doesn't matter. I know that now." The words burned in Travis's mind, as clear as runes. Yes, this was how it was meant to be. "You see, Beltan, I—"

The light streaming from the rear of the truck dimmed, and a lithe silhouette appeared against the gray opening. Travis turned. Gold eyes locked on his. Startled, he stepped away from Beltan.

"The guards are pressing toward us," Vani said, moving into the trailer. "There are not many—I do not believe they expected pursuit. I imagine they thought the *gorleths* at their fortress would destroy us. All the same, the weapons of Davis and Mitchell cannot hold them off for long. We must hurry."

The knight's green eyes narrowed as he gazed at Vani. "Who is *she*?"

"She's . . ." Travis licked his lips.

Vani rested her hands on her half-cocked hips, her gaze a mystery.

"This is Vani," Grace said. "She's a . . . a warrior from Eldh, and we owe our lives to her."

Beltan seemed to study her, then he nodded. "Then I owe my life to you as well. Vani."

Her gaze moved to Travis, then back to Beltan. "Your thanks may be premature, knight of Calavan. Come, we must go."

"Wait," Beltan said. "We can't leave yet. There's someone else who needs our help."

He turned around, started to move one of the fallen boxes, then staggered.

Travis steadied him. "Beltan . . ."

The knight pulled away. "You don't understand, Travis. We have to free him. We—"

Silvery light welled forth. It was faint and flickering, and it quickly dimmed again, but there was no mistaking where it had come from. Travis felt a tingling in his right hand. He stared at Beltan. Then he was moving.

Vani reached the crate the same time he did. Together, they pushed it over, righting it. There was a small door on the crate made of wire mesh. Something moved inside. Again pale illumination flickered within, like the light of a dying, silvery firefly.

"Hurry," Beltan said. "I'm not sure, but I think . . . I think it's ill somehow."

Travis knelt beside the crate and peered inside. Large, tilted eyes gazed back at him. An ancient sorrow filled them, and deep pain, and something else as well. It might have been . . . joy. Like a wind, recognition passed through him. Yes, he understood.

"Iron," he said. "It can't bear the touch of iron. Or steel, I suppose. None of them can. That's why it can't escape."

"What can't stand iron?" Grace said. "What are you talking about, Travis?"

He didn't answer her. Instead, for the third time that day, he spoke the rune of opening.

"*Urath.*"

Yes, this was the source of his suddenly renewed power. The lock fell off, the wire door swung open.

With a sound like distant chimes, the fairy floated out of the crate. The four humans watched, breath suspended.

Last Midwinter, in Calavere, Travis had used the power of Sinfathisar, the Stone of Twilight, to heal a band of wraithlings, to make them again the fairies they had been. They had followed him to Shadowsdeep, and there they had saved Beltan's life.

Those fairies had been tall, luminous beings, so radiant he had hardly been able to gaze upon them. But the fairy before them was a shadow of those beings. It was so thin—far thinner than Beltan, as if it were made of twigs—and its skin was a dull gray. Its head seemed far too large for its spindly neck, and it was naked, so that he could see it was neither male nor female.

All the same, it was beautiful. He started to sink to his knees before it.

The fairy reached out spidery arms, brushed him with cool fingers, and he found himself standing once again. But the fear was gone. Instead, a cool peace filled him.

"How—?" Grace pressed her hands to her heart. "How can it be here?"

"They were holding it captive," Beltan said. "Like me. They were doing experiments on it."

Even as the knight said this, Travis saw the thin, white scars on the fairy's delicate arms.

Vani's golden eyes were thoughtful. "It must have come through the gate with the Scirathi."

At her words, the fairy nodded. Then a tremor shook its form, like a gale shaking the bough of a tree. It was so dim here, its radiance quelled. Being on Earth caused it pain—terrible pain.

The fairy reached a trembling hand toward the crate, then snatched it back when it brushed the metal edge. There was a high, soundless cry of pain. It wanted something—something in the crate.

Grace knelt, reached inside, then leaned back. In her hand was a plastic bottle. In the bottle were purple pills, each one marked with a white lightning bolt.

Grace looked up at the fairy, then she gave a stiff nod, twisted off the lid, and held the bottle out. With long, trembling fingers, the fairy took three of the pills. It seemed to hesitate, then it brought them to the thin, lipless line of its mouth and swallowed them. It passed its hand over its jewel-like eyes. When it lowered its hand again, the pain was gone from its gaze.

Grace looked down at the pills. "Those bastards— that's why they developed it. It's for them, to keep them alive here on Earth." She looked up at Travis, her green-gold eyes stricken. "Electria is for fairies."

The light elf reached out and cupped her cheek with a willowy hand. Grace gasped, eyes going wide. Slowly, she lifted her own hand and touched it to the fairy's dull gray cheek.

A call came from the rear of the truck: a deep, twanging voice. Mitchell.

"You all might want to hurry it up in there. They've been lying low for the last few minutes, but now it looks like we've got some strange company coming."

The sound of a rifle being cocked followed Mitchell's voice.

Travis turned, met Vani's gaze. She nodded.

"Vani and I will go," he said. "Grace, stay with the fairy and Beltan."

The blond knight took a stumbling step forward. "I'm coming with you, Travis. I'm your protector."

Travis paused, then reached out and laid his hand on Beltan's chest. "No, Beltan," he said gently. "Not now."

The knight gaped, then staggered back and leaned against a crate. Sorrow etched Travis's heart. He wanted to move to the knight, to hold him, but there wasn't time.

"Travis!"

That was Davis's voice. Together, Travis and Vani

moved to the end of the truck and leaped out the doors.

It didn't take long to spot the problem. Davis and Mitchell stood, rifles ready. A moment later the things appeared around the cab of the closest truck, long arms dragging the asphalt as they loped nearer. Travis counted three. Five. Then he stopped counting.

Thunder sounded as Mitchell squeezed the trigger of his rifle. A second report came as Davis followed suit. Two of the *gorleths* squealed and fell to the ground.

More continued to appear from around the truck. Davis and Mitchell cocked their rifles, fired again. Two more fell. It wasn't enough; they were coming faster than the two men could drop them. Travis felt Vani tense beside him. Then his heart froze in his chest as another figure came into view.

He walked slowly, black robes billowing behind him. The light of the westering sun had broken through the clouds, and it gleamed off his mask of gold. Travis saw now that the expression on the mask was wrought into a lifeless smile, the eye slits thin and leering. The Scirathi raised a hand, and Travis's heart shuddered in his chest.

Vani clutched him. "Travis!"

He tried to speak but could not.

Gunshots split the air. Only it didn't come from Davis and Mitchell's rifles. Another of the *gorleths* fell, screeching. But the second bullet missed its mark. Instead, there was a bright *ping* as it struck something metal.

The sorcerer halted, head bowed, as something sparked and skittered away across the pavement. The *gorleths* faltered, then ceased their advance. Travis drew in a ragged breath, his heart beating once more. What was happening?

The Scirathi lifted its head, and the black cowl

slipped back. The gold mask was gone. The bullet must have struck it, knocking it off, exposing the sorcerer's face.

Or what was left of his face. Two black eyes peered from a tangled mass of livid pink scars. The sorcerer's mouth was a crooked gash, and his nose two pits amid the ruin of his face. Travis fought for understanding—

—then gained it. Vani had said the sorcerers used blood to work their magic. How many times had the Scirathi been forced to cut himself? How many times before his arms, his legs, his torso became too damaged to heal, too damaged to bear more wounds? How long until there was nowhere left to cut. . . .

A flash of gold. Light glinted off the sorcerer's mask. He saw it at the same time as Travis, stopped against the tire of one of the trucks. The sorcerer lunged for it.

He was too slow. In a black, howling knot of fury, the *gorleths* sprang at the Scirathi. Davis and Mitchell lowered their rifles, horror on their faces. Travis took a step forward, but Vani's strong hand held him back.

"So the old stories are true," she said. "The masks truly are the focus for their power. Without it, the sorcerer cannot control the *gorleths*."

Free from his will, they turned on him—their maker and their torturer. Travis felt his gorge rise in his throat, but he could not look away.

The monsters made quick work of their master. His screams ended as they tore his arms from their sockets. In moments all that remained were shards of bone, and shreds of meat and black cloth. Travis thought the *gorleths* would turn when they were finished and resume the attack, but they did not. Instead, they hissed and tore at each other, ripping their own bodies with long talons. Free of the command to kill others, they turned on themselves and their own suffering.

At last Travis forced himself to turn away from the grisly spectacle. Davis was vomiting on the pavement, and Mitchell was holding his shoulders with strong, gentle hands.

Footsteps on asphalt. Travis jerked his head up, fearing that he would see gun-wielding guards. Instead, the pistols were gripped in familiar hands.

"Deirdre." He said the word like a prayer, then caught her in a tight embrace.

Farr lowered his gun, gazing at the now-still heap of fur and flesh that had been the sorcerer and the *gorleths*. "That was a lucky shot, Deirdre."

She stepped back, her dark eyes serious. "No." She gripped the yellowed bear claw that hung around her neck. "I think maybe it was fate."

Davis was standing upright, although his face was pale. Mitchell kept an arm around him.

"I don't see any more of the guards," Mitchell said. "I think they've run off. Can't really say I blame them."

Farr shook his head. "No, they've retreated, that's all. They're waiting for backup from Duratek. And it will be here in minutes. We've got to—"

A crystalline chiming drifted on the air, along with silvery light. They gazed up at the open back of the truck. Grace stood beside a slender gray being, not quite touching it, as it raised a hand to shield its eyes from the last remains of the daylight.

"Good Lord," Davis said softly. "What is that?"

The awed stares of Mitchell, Deirdre, and Farr echoed the question.

"It's a fairy," Travis said simply.

Beltan appeared behind the fairy. With a groan, he set something down on the edge of the trailer. It was a small box made of dark stone, its sides etched with symbols.

Vani drew in a sharp breath. "The artifact of

Morindu."

"The fairy showed it to us," Grace said. "We never would have seen it in the mess."

Grace climbed down from the truck, and Travis and Farr helped Beltan to follow. The fairy stretched forth slender arms. Davis and Mitchell gazed at each other, then they reached up strong, rough hands and lowered the creature to the ground. It tilted its head, then touched Davis's face. He laughed, then hugged Mitchell as the fairy drifted away.

It drew close to the stone box.

"Is that it?" Farr said, his eyes solemn. "Is that the gate artifact?"

Vani knelt beside the box. "No, this is new—it is merely a container. I would guess it was made by the Scirathi to protect the artifact." She ran her hands over the smooth surface of the top, the sides, then shook her head. "It is bound with spells of blood sorcery. I do not know if I will be able to—"

The fairy bent, like a sapling before a wind, and touched the box. The lid fell aside. Vani hesitated, then reached into the box and drew something out. It was a small piece of perfectly black stone.

From his vantage, Travis saw there was a kind of angular writing on the artifact. It was pyramid-shaped, with a total of four sides. However, the shape of the artifact was not perfect. The top of the pyramid was flat, as if it had been lopped off, and Travis could see there was a small reservoir in the interior. With the flat top, it seemed incomplete. Where was the rest of it?

Even as he thought this, Vani reached into her pocket and drew out the small, triangular piece of stone she had showed them before. The prism. She started to bring it close to the artifact, to complete it.

The fairy touched her hand, staying it. Vani

frowned, her expression one of confusion. Travis was confused as well. What was the fairy doing? It lifted a finger to its breast, pressed the tip against its gray skin——

——and into its body.

The fairy's mouth opened in a silent circle of pain. It dug another finger into its body, and another, pushing them deeper. Blue-white light seeped from the wound. Then, with another cry, the fairy pulled something out of the wound in its chest. The creature held it forth, wet and glistening.

It was a stone.

No, not just a stone. Travis approached the fairy.

"Travis," Grace murmured. "What is it?"

The fairy nodded. He didn't know how he knew, only that he did, that it was for this reason the fairy had let itself be captured by the Scirathi and had come to this world—to give him this, this Stone that it had concealed in the only place it would be safe.

"It's Sinfathisar," he said.

He reached out with his left hand and took the Stone of Twilight, still wet with the fairy's blood. More blood oozed from the hole in the fairy's chest, at once dark and glittering. The being turned toward Vani and spread its arms.

Vani stared—then leaped into action. She raised the artifact, catching the dark trickle of blood. In moments the small reservoir was filled. The fairy pressed its hand to its breast, stopping the flow of blood, and a pale radiance welled between its fingers.

"The blood of light," Vani breathed.

"What does it mean?" Beltan croaked.

Travis gripped his hand. "It means we're going home."

64

Minutes later they were ready.

Grace had retrieved the small backpack from the pickup and pulled out the things they bought at Marji's shop. Marji, who was gone now because of them. But Travis would have to think that through later, when there was time. He wouldn't let Marji's death be for nothing.

They worked in the shelter by the rear of the truck. Vani had set the artifact on top of the box, and had placed four of the candles around them. They guttered in the wind but did not go out. She had mixed the herbs and oil together, making an incense, and she lit this with the fifth candle. A heavy, fragrant smoke coiled upward on the air. Travis breathed in the fragrance, his mind clearing.

He looked at Deirdre and Farr, then Mitchell and Davis. "So, how are you all getting out of here?"

Davis's face crinkled in a grin; the greenness had left his face as he breathed in the incense. "Now, don't you worry about us. Your friends' limo may be so much tinfoil, but there's still plenty of gas in the pickup."

"We can still get out of here," Mitchell said. He glanced at Farr. "If there's time."

Farr nodded. "I believe we'll make it. We'll need to pick up our driver. Crashing into a convoy of trucks wasn't in his job description, so we dropped him off by the road a mile back."

"Wait, there's something you should know," Grace said, moving to the Seeker.

Farr stared at her, his handsome face stunned.

"Electria," Grace said. "I know why Duratek invented it. It's for fairies, to keep them alive on Earth."

Farr blinked. Whatever he had thought she was going to say, clearly this hadn't been it. He started to lift a hand, then—slowly, as if by great force of will— he lowered it again. His expression was haggard, broken.

"Thank you, Dr. Beckett," he said.

Deirdre looked down at her hand. "Fairies?"

The gray being moved close to her, lifted her hand, and touched what Deirdre had been gazing at: a silver ring. Gently, the fairy closed its fingers around her hand, then moved away. As it did, Travis saw there were tears in Deirdre's eyes.

"The artifact is ready," Vani said.

"Wait," Deirdre said, fumbling in a pocket. "Grace, I almost forgot. Here—it's the drawing I told you about. The one that shows the sword from Sarsin's journal."

Grace accepted the folded piece of paper. "Thank you."

Deirdre smiled, nodded, then stepped back.

Vani knelt close to the artifact. Travis and Grace stood above her, Beltan gripped between them. The fairy drifted close. Vani hesitated, then placed the prism atop the artifact.

At once the air shimmered, and the gate sprang into being, its shining edges dancing and rippling like the Aurora Borealis. Beyond was swirling gray.

"You must help me envision our destination," Vani said. "Hold the image in your mind. We must go find my brother, in Tarras. A city—"

"A city of gold by the sea," Grace said.

Vani nodded, then stood. The gate shone before them. Through it, Travis could still see the two Seekers, and Mitchell and Davis, but they were dim, as if already fading.

"You all . . . you all take care of yourselves," Mitchell said, and Davis nodded, still grinning.

Deirdre was weeping now, gripping her bear claw necklace. "May we meet again, if not on this world, then in another."

However, Hadrian said nothing. He merely watched them with haunted brown eyes.

Travis raised his hand, to tell them all thank you and good-bye. But before he could speak, the fairy spread its arms. The gate expanded, growing outward, encapsulating them in shimmering light.

Colorado dimmed to a shadow, and was gone.

PART FIVE:
THE SHADOW
OF THE PAST

65.

Nothing. All around Travis there was nothing. A vast, aching void without end.

He tried to scream that something had gone horribly wrong with the gate, but he had no mouth, no lungs—no body at all. He had been reduced to a single point: a buzzing spark of energy, like a gnat so minuscule it was all but invisible.

He tried to search around him for the others—for Grace and Beltan and Vani—but there was no sign of them. Only the empty grayness. Yet even calling it gray was granting it too much substance. Gray was a blending of light and dark. This place was the absence of both things, of all things. And as far as he could sense, it went on forever.

Even as he tried again to scream, he became aware of something coming toward him. No, *somethings*. He could not see them; they were bodiless, just as he was. Instead, a distortion spread through the colorless fog in their wake, like the wrinkles made by insects as they skim over the surface of a puddle.

Then it hit him, surging before them like a wave. Hunger. Vast, ceaseless hunger. A primal desire to consume. The empty fog warped and flowed around him as they closed in.

This way.

Travis didn't hear the voice. All the same, he felt the words resonate through him like the music of bells. He tore his awareness away from the approaching things and saw it: a shining circle in the middle of the nothingness. And on the other side of the circle was . . . light. Real, golden light.

The grayness roiled around him. The ravenous specks buzzed and darted like stinging insects, ready to suck away his very being. Travis willed himself away from them, stretched toward the glowing circle—

—and tumbled onto hard stones.

"Oof," he said, and both sound and pain let him know that he was alive.

Three more *oofs*, and three more bodies tumbled to the stone next to him. And a whisper, like a gentle wind passing through a snow-mantled forest.

Travis sat up and stretched out cold, trembling hands. His clothes and skin were covered with a layer of fine frost. He lifted his left hand, moving it from shadow into a slanting beam of honey-colored light. For a moment the frost crystals shone like gems. Then they melted and were gone.

There was something in his hand. Travis willed opened stiff fingers. On his palm was a round, mottled, gray-green stone. Sinfathisar. He closed his fingers around it again.

They were in some sort of alley: a dim, narrow space between two white buildings. Here and there, wayward rays of sunlight fell down from a blue shard of sky above. Vani was already on her feet, her black leathers gray with frost. Grace and Beltan huddled against one wall, skin faintly blue, hair and eyebrows prematurely white with ice. Grace opened her eyes, and snow fell from her eyelashes. There was no sign anywhere of the gate.

It took Travis a moment to find his voice. "What was that place?"

Vani slipped the obsidian artifact inside her jacket. "It was the void between the worlds."

"And you . . . you passed through it before, when you journeyed to Earth?"

"Yes."

How could she have stepped through the gate knowing what was on the other side? Or rather, what *wasn't*. Travis didn't think he could bear that again, not without going mad.

"What . . . ?" It was Grace, although the word was barely a croak. She swallowed, and this time her voice was clearer. "What were those things in the void, Vani?"

"They were *morndari*."

Beltan frowned, cracking the ice that clung to his scruffy gold beard. *"Morndari?"*

"Those Who Thirst," Grace breathed.

The knight's green eyes were still confused; Travis would explain it to him later. When speaking was not such an ordeal.

Vani stalked to the mouth of the alley, peered out. "Come, all of you—move nearer the sun. It will help to warm you. I do not believe our arrival was noticed, which is well." She gazed back at the rest of them. "My people are always in Tarras at this time of year, so we must believe the Scirathi are here in the city as well."

These words sent another shiver through Travis. So there were sorcerers here.

"Do not fear, Travis, the effects of the gate will wear off soon enough."

Vani must have mistaken the source of his shaking. She reached down with a strong hand and helped him up. Then, with a gentle motion, she brushed the frost from his cheek.

A low grunt came from behind Travis. Grace had helped Beltan to his feet. The knight stood, broad shoulders hunched, grasping the wall with a bony hand for support. His green eyes were fixed on Travis and Vani, his gaunt face a grimace of pain. Travis stepped away from her, suddenly warm, although he had not moved into the sun. He searched for something to say.

Light welled forth—not from the street outside the alley, but from deeper in. The light brightened, and a crystalline sound floated on the air. All at once the light coalesced into a tall, slender, shimmering form.

Travis forgot the aching and stiffness in his joints, forgot the fear inside him. He gazed into ancient, depthless eyes and found, for a moment, peace.

The thin, gray being they had freed from the steel crate was still there—Travis could see it amid the radiance—but it stood tall and straight now, taller than Travis or Beltan, like a willowy tree. It was no longer naked, but rather clad in light, so that it seemed it wore a coruscating robe and a crown of white fire.

"You," Travis whispered. "It was you who showed me where the gate was in the void."

The fairy nodded, although the gesture bespoke not a mere *yes*, but a thousand words that could not be uttered in any language. Again Travis gazed down at the Stone of Twilight in his hand. It seemed to catch the fairyglow, spinning it into a gray-green gauze.

Beltan took a staggering step toward the fairy. "You are well now. I am glad to see it."

The fairy drifted toward Beltan. With a slender finger it touched a small, round wound on the knight's arm, then it turned its own arm over. They were faint and almost lost amid the radiance, but Travis could still see them: long, white scars.

A choking sound escaped Beltan. "By Vathris, that's what they did. They put your blood in me, didn't they?"

Again the fairy nodded. Beltan swayed, started to fall. The knight was still so terribly thin. Both Grace and Travis reached for him, but they were too slow.

With slender arms, the fairy caught Beltan, holding him in a gentle embrace. The knight looked up, eyes wide. Then tendrils of white light spun outward from the fairy, coiling around him.

Now Beltan did stagger back, but he did not fall. He stood stiff, arms thrust at his sides, as the light spun faster and faster around him. The light grew more brilliant. It seemed Beltan's skin was translucent as glass. Travis could see muscles undulating beneath, then the knight's beating heart. Then even flesh was transparent, and his bones were silhouetted against the glare. The light flared, turning everything to white—

—then dimmed.

Shadows closed back in on the alley, and a breath of wonder escaped Travis.

Beltan held his hands out before him, mouth open. The lab coat had evaporated like the frost under the force of the light, and Beltan was naked. Travis knew he should not stare, but he could not turn away. The knight was no longer emaciated, but rather lean and rangy like a tawny lion. Sheets of muscles flexed beneath his pale skin. His thinning, white-blond hair tumbled over broad shoulders, and his scruffy beard was as gold as the sunlight outside the alley. On his left side, where the Necromancer Dakarreth had reopened his wound, there was only a pale line.

Beltan gazed at the fairy, astonishment on his face. It

was hard to see for the radiance, but it seemed to Travis that the fairy smiled.

The last tendrils of light vanished from around Beltan. Smiling, Grace looked away, and Vani studiously averted her eyes.

Beltan glanced down, then his head snapped up. "By the Blood of Vathris! Sorry, my ladies. Er, Travis . . ."

Travis pulled his mistcloak from the backpack he still had slung over a shoulder and threw it around the knight. His hands lingered on Beltan's chest; it was warm and firm. "How do you feel?"

The knight gave him a wry grin, holding the cloak around him. "A bit embarrassed. But otherwise fine." Then wonder crept into his eyes. "More than fine. Not even an ache or pain from any of my old battle scars."

A chiming sound. The fairy drifted past them, toward Vani. It made a graceful gesture. Vani seemed to understand. She drew the gate artifact from her jacket and removed the prism. Travis could see the artifact was empty now.

The fairy took the artifact in long fingers and drew it close to its body. There was a flash, and a sharp, crystalline sound, almost like a cry, then the light dimmed, and Vani was holding the artifact again. It was no longer empty, but filled once more with dark fluid.

Vani replaced the prism, sealing the fairy's blood inside. However, Travis noticed she made certain the prism was turned at an angle, so that its sides were not aligned with the sides of the artifact. He supposed she did this so that gate would not be activated.

"Thank you," Vani said simply.

Travis moved to the fairy, gripping the Stone of Twilight, the Great Stone he had entrusted to the

Little People of Gloaming Wood not long after last Midwinter's Day. "You let the sorcerer capture you and take you through the gate, didn't you? You did it so you could come to Earth and bring me Sinfathisar. But why?"

The fairy tilted its head, then words chimed around Travis, and inside him.

To choose what it shall be.

He didn't understand. What was he supposed to choose? However, before he could ask, the fairy drifted away. The radiant being paused before Grace. Then, slowly, it bowed to her.

Grace lifted a hand to her throat, the light of the fairy shining in her vivid eyes. For a moment its light wavered, and the being seemed to reach a hand toward her. However, Travis must have imagined it, for the silvery corona that surrounded the fairy suddenly brightened, expanding like a star, then collapsed, leaving only a white-hot spark of light. The spark circled around them once, then sped away down the alley and was gone.

Travis gave Grace a questioning look, but she only shook her head, then moved to Beltan. First she lifted one of his hands, then the other, then studied his face.

"This is impossible. You were in a coma for two months, Beltan. Your muscles had experienced severe atrophy, and you were osteoporotic. And now"—Grace stepped back—"now you're perfect."

Beltan's eyes sparkled, and he gave a bow. "Why thank you, my lady. So I've always liked to believe."

"No, that's not what I meant—"

He sighed, the mirth dimming in his eyes. "I know what you meant, my lady. My body is hale, that's all." The knight gazed down at his hands. "And I am anything but perfect."

A note of alarm cut through the relief in Travis's chest. What was Beltan saying?

Grace spoke again. "You said something about the fairy's blood, Beltan, about them infusing you with it."

"I believe so, my lady. There were tubes going into my veins when I woke in their fortress. They must have used them to put the fairy blood in me. I think . . . I think that was how I knew things I had no way to know, like how to speak their language."

This struck Travis like a slap. Grace and he still had the silver half-coins Brother Cy had given them, and he had thought it simply the magic of the coins that had allowed him and Grace to understand Beltan. But Deirdre and Farr had been able to speak to Beltan as well, and Davis and Mitchell. So there had been another sort of magic at work.

"The *chin-pasi* at the fortress," Beltan went on, "I think they put the fairy's blood in it as well."

"The chimpanzee?" Grace crossed her arms. "Yes, that has to be how they did it—that's the delivery vector they were using for the gene therapy, and that's how they made the *gorleths*. Which would mean—" She gazed at the knight. "Oh, Beltan . . ."

Travis moved closer. "What did they do to him, Grace?"

Beltan's visage was solemn. "They were trying to make me into a killer." He turned away, hands clamped together. "I guess they didn't know I already was one."

What was Beltan talking about? Travis looked at Grace.

"I don't think we need to worry. I don't see any outward morphological changes. And the fairy . . . I think all it did was heal him. He's still our Beltan." She smiled. "Just a little better than before."

But that wasn't entirely true. Beltan *looked* well enough. More than well. Before, Beltan's face had always been rough and homely in a good-natured way, his handsomeness a secret that shone forth only when he smiled. But now it was as if Travis could see that part of him whether Beltan was smiling or not. Only there was something else, something that dimmed that light. . . .

A shadow blocked the sun. Vani stepped into the mouth of the alley. When had she gone?

"Here." She held out a bundle of clothes. "Put these on. Then we must go."

Travis eyed the garments. "You didn't steal these, did you?" It seemed like people were always stealing his clothes for him on Eldh.

Vani's gold eyes flashed. "You cannot wear your Earth garb here. It will attract undue attention."

Travis sighed. Stolen all right.

Moments later they were dressed. Grace wore a simple shift of pale green, but she looked regal all the same. Vani wrapped a yellow cloth around herself. It hid her black leathers, but it could not disguise the sleek power of her movements. Travis and Beltan both wore long white shirts that came to their ankles.

Vani handed Travis a cloth sack. "Use this for your things."

He stuffed his mistcloak into the sack, then transferred the few other items from his backpack: his gunfighter's spectacles and Malachorian dagger, and the drawing of the sword Deirdre had given Grace. He cinched the sack's rope and slung it over his shoulder.

"Can you walk?" Grace said to Beltan.

The knight nodded. "It's odd, but I think I can. Although a pot of ale would give me strength."

"We have no time for ale."

"Nonsense," Beltan said. "There's always time for ale."

Vani moved to the mouth of the alley. "We must find my brother at once."

"But how do you know he's here in Tarras?" Travis said. "You haven't talked to him in months."

"I saw the markings on a wall near where I took— that is, where I found the clothes."

Travis frowned. "You mean you know your brother is here because he's a vandal and likes to write on walls?"

"They are arcane signs, Travis, used by my people to signal one another of our presence. To the dwellers of this city, they would look like scratches, nothing more. Now come."

66

Melia was dancing again.

Lirith stood in the doorway of the lady's room, hand to her mouth. The coppery light of afternoon shone through the window's sheer curtains. They had all been trying to rest, for none of them had slept after their visit to Sif's temple last night, not after witnessing the murder of the arachnid god. Aryn had finally fallen asleep, but rest eluded Lirith, so she had gone to Melia's room. There were some things she wanted to ask the lady. Things about spiders.

Falken stood just inside the door, watching Melia. The small woman danced on a red carpet in the center of the room, placing her feet in precise positions, the rings on her toes gleaming. She murmured a soft, mournful song that once again reminded Lirith of the music of the Mournish.

Lirith glanced at Falken. "How long has she been like this?"

"I'm not certain," he said softly. "She retired to her room about an hour ago. I've only been here a few minutes."

Melia spun in a circle, bowed, then began the circle again. It was the same dance Lirith had witnessed before, in the shrine of Mandu in Ar-tolor. However, there was an urgency to it that had not been there the last time.

Lirith clutched the spider amulet at her throat. "What is she doing, Falken?"

"I think she's reenacting her mystery."

"Her mystery?"

"Yes, the story of how she became a goddess." The bard tore his gaze from Melia. "Each of the New Gods has a mystery—a story around which their cult is centered. Like Vathris, who slew the white bull, and a red river of blood poured forth, quenching his parched kingdom. Or Jorus Stormrunner, who was thrown into the sea to die, only he was transformed into a horse and rode the waves back to crush his enemies."

"Or like Tira," Lirith said.

Falken lifted a hand to his chin. "Yes, I suppose you're right at that. Like Tira, who was burned in fire, and who ascended with a star into the sky."

"But what's Melia's mystery? I don't know it."

"Listen," the bard said.

Only as he said this did Lirith realize that Melia was no longer singing. Instead she spoke, her voice a singsong chant that rose and fell in time with the motions of her feet, her hands.

". . . that I shall marry him not, my sister. For last night I heard him, drunk on wine and boasting with his men at table. It was he! It was he who slew our people, who spilled their blood upon the ground. It was he who took our mother and father from us. It was he who tore our brothers limb from limb and scattered their bodies for the vultures."

Melia's movements changed, reversing the circle, and her voice changed at the same time, growing higher, softer, as if it were another who spoke. And perhaps it was.

"But his word is law, Melindora. You dare not refuse him, or he will murder us both and what few of our people remain. He has chosen you, and nothing you might do would make him change his will—save only if you were made a woman by another man. But no man will touch the one he has chosen. To do so would be death."

Again Melia's voice and direction changed.

"No man will touch me? Very well, my sister. Then no man will I lie with, and no man will I marry, and no man will save me from this murderer's bed. There, do you see him, so beautiful and brilliant? Ever has he been my companion. I shall marry the moon, my sister. I shall dance a dance of joining in his pale light, and by it I will be his wife."

Lirith gazed at Melia in wonder. How could a young woman, grief-struck at being forced to marry the warlord who had slain her family, wed the moon instead? Yet that was why they were called mysteries. If desire was great enough, sometimes the impossible happened, and a god or goddess was born.

"Lirith?" a cool voice said. "Falken? What are you doing here? Last I recalled, this was my chamber."

Melia stood hands on hips, wearing a frown.

Falken sighed. "Dear one . . ."

Those words were enough. Melia looked down at herself, then glanced back up, her amber eyes startled.

"I was . . . I was gone again, wasn't I?"

Lirith did not hesitate. She rushed forward and caught the woman in a fierce embrace. "You were so brave to refuse to marry him."

Melia stiffened, then melted into the embrace. "Or foolish, dear. And yet the gods do have a way of preserving fools. But all that is so long ago. And whatever the source of my memories, they are gone now, in the past where they belong." Gently, she pushed Lirith away.

Falken's mien was thoughtful. "Yes, Melia, all that was indeed a long time ago. And yet it seems it is as real for you as what is happening now."

Melia turned away. "And at times even more real." She turned back, her eyes clear now. "I do not know the source of my spells, Falken. They come without warning and are gone as quickly. But I know now I am not alone in them."

"What?"

"Last night, I held counsel with my brothers and sisters. Those who would talk to me, at least. I suppose we are like a great, tangled family, and as in any family not all of us are on speaking terms. Especially now."

Lirith wondered how Melia could speak with the other gods without even leaving the hostel. But then, couldn't anyone speak to the gods in secret silence? It was called prayer. And Lirith had a feeling Melia's prayers were paid a bit more attention than those of the average worshiper.

"What do you mean, Melia?" Falken said.

She moved to the window. Outside, brilliant light gleamed off gold domes. "It's not just me. Many of the gods have been reliving their mysteries. And the experience is even more profound for them, for I am no longer a goddess. It is not just fear that is causing silence on the part of the gods. It is confusion. Many of the gods are so lost in dreams of ancient days that they no longer answer the prayers of even their highest priests."

"That would help to explain the chaos in the Etherion," Lirith said, thinking over Melia's words. "It sounds as if the priests aren't receiving any guidance from their gods. That makes them frightened. And fear tends to make people angry and defensive."

Melia smoothed the folds of her white shift. "I believe you're right, dear."

Falken let out a sound like a low growl. "So, not only is someone murdering gods, they're also making sure none of the other gods do anything about it by casting them under some sort of spell that entangles them in dreams of the past. But who could do such things?"

Melia moved toward the bard. "I don't know, but this has gone on quite long enough without any comment from the emperor. I don't care whom I have to tamper with, I am getting into the First Circle to see him today."

They found Aryn and Durge in the main room. Madam Vil had sent up a pitcher of chilled *margra* juice, and by his pink lips Durge had drunk most of it himself.

"What's going on?" Aryn said, blue eyes startled.

Falken shot the young baroness a wolfish grin. "I believe we're going to see the emperor."

Minutes later they walked through the crowded streets of the Fourth Circle, making their way to the city's main avenue. Melia moved with swift purpose, and people scrambled to get out of her way. Lirith couldn't blame them. Better to stand in the path of a herd of wild horses, she reasoned.

"How peculiar," Aryn said next to her.

Lirith gave the young baroness a questioning glance.

"Over there, in the fountain."

Lirith followed Aryn's gaze. Across the plaza, in the bubbling waters of a large, tiled fountain, an elderly man and woman splashed about, robes hiked up above their knobby knees, laughing with glee. Two small children stood outside the fountain, arms crossed, frowns of displeasure on their round faces.

Lirith stopped to stare. "But that doesn't make sense."

"I know," Aryn said with a laugh. "Shouldn't it be the other way around? I think they've gotten things mixed up."

For some reason, Aryn's words troubled her. Where had she heard them before? Then she remembered the wine vendor, his eyes confused as he looked at the wine he had poured on the street.

I keep mixing everything up, I do. . . .

Energy buzzed through Lirith. Something was going on here, something important.

A shadow touched Aryn's brow. "Sister—what is it?"

Lirith started to answer, then movement caught her eye. Two men stood in the dim mouth of an alley. There was a flash as coins were exchanged, then one of the men stepped onto the street, a wooden cup in his hand. The man downed the contents of the cup, then let it fall from his fingers as he moved across the plaza. He leaned against a wall and slid to the ground to sit, joining a score of men and women who had done the same.

Lirith bent and snatched up the cup the man had discarded—the cup she was certain had contained a draught of the Elixir of the Past. She sniffed the residue, then coughed and tossed the cup back down. Her nose had detected cheap wine and a handful of common, bitter herbs—nothing else. There was no magic in this potion, nothing that could cause people to see visions of things that were no more.

But if that's true, sister, then what is causing them to drift in the past?

Her eyes moved again to the wall. Like the others, the man now stared at the sun with empty eyes, flies crawling on his face, a smile on his purple-stained lips.

A touch on her arm drew Lirith's gaze around. Aryn wore a confused expression. However, before she could speak, Durge drew close to them.

"My ladies, Melia and Falken continue on. We should not fall behind."

"Aryn, Durge," Lirith said, her words urgent, "have you noticed anything odd since we arrived in Tarras?"

The knight stroked his mustaches. "You mean besides indoor plumbing and gods being slain?"

Lirith forced herself not to groan. "Yes, Durge, besides those things."

Aryn shrugged, but after a moment Durge nodded.

"Now that you mention it, my lady, there was a boy I saw. It was in the Fourth Circle. He was crying in the street."

"That's not strange, Durge," Aryn said. "Children often cry."

The knight sighed. "Especially, I find, when I am near. But there was something odd about this child. He was wearing the robe of a priest. A robe clearly intended for a grown man."

A chill crept up Lirith's spine despite the balmy air. What did Durge's story mean? She wasn't certain, not yet, but there was one thing she did know. It wasn't only the gods in this city who were getting tangled in the threads of time. It was their followers—the people of Tarras—as well.

And you yourself, sister.

Again she thought of Corantha, and memories welled up, thick and dark. Lirith pushed them aside. She would not become a slave to the past, not like the people who leaned against the wall.

"Come on," she said. "We'd better not make Melia wait for us."

They had just reached the bard and the amber-eyed lady when Aryn spoke—in Lirith's mind rather than with words.

We are being followed, sister.

Lirith spun a quick thread out to the Weirding. Yes, there it was . . . like a shadow trailing after them.

Aryn's voice came again. *Do you think it's the one who tried to harm you?*

Lirith probed. The presence of the man in the black robe had filled her with foreboding, but this shadow was like that other she had glimpsed from time to time on their journey south to Tarras. Its presence did not fill her with fear but rather curiosity.

She thought about it a moment. Then she brushed her hand against Durge's and used the connection to bring her thread close to his.

Durge.

She felt surprise and dread. Of course, the last time she had touched him like this she had stolen his memories away from him. But all she wanted to do was give him a message, and to do it without speech that could be observed or overheard. She pressed her hand harder to his.

Please, Durge. Don't pull away. We're being followed. Behind us and to the left. There, in the shadow behind that stack of clay jugs. Do you see it?

Lirith used the Weirding to form the image for him, then felt understanding. She released the thread and heard a sigh beside her. However, when she glanced at Durge, his face was already resolute. He had strapped his greatsword to his back today, and his fingers twitched as if eager to draw it.

Ahead, Melia and Falken turned down another street. Lirith, Aryn, and Durge followed. As soon as they rounded the corner, the Embarran moved into action. He drew his massive blade and pressed himself to the wall.

Help me, sister, came Aryn's voice.

At once Lirith understood what the young woman was trying to do. Aryn had the power but not the skill. Lirith reached out invisible hands, guiding the young woman's. Together, they wove the threads of the Weirding into a shimmering curtain before them. In a heartbeat it was done. Anyone gazing at them would see only a blank wall.

They waited. Then a figure clad in a black robe came into view, moving with stealth. When the figure was even with them, Durge stepped through the spell of illusion.

Their shadow tried to move, but the knight was too fast. His greatsword flashed, and the point came to a rest an inch from the other's heart. Their stalker froze. Aryn and Lirith stepped forward as the last of the illusion unraveled.

"Show yourself," Durge rumbled.

The figure hesitated, then lifted two brown hands and pushed back the hood of the robe. Lirith gazed into eyes the color of old copper coins, and her heart ceased beating.

"Greetings, *beshala*," the man said in his deep, chiming voice, a bemused expression on his sharply handsome face.

Aryn gasped, and Durge let out a grunt.

"I recognize you," he said, lowering his greatsword. "You're that Mournish fellow, the one who took us to his grandmother's wagon at Ar-tolor."

Sareth opened his mouth to answer, but before he could Melia and Falken approached.

"There you are," Melia said. "We haven't time for dawdling if we're—" Her amber eyes alighted on

Sareth. "Oh, I see you were distracted."

Falken studied Sareth's visage. "So, who's your Mournish friend?"

Lirith tried to speak, but now her heart seemed to have fluttered up into her throat. Beneath her gown, her skin broke out in a sweat.

"Sareth!" a woman's voice called.

They turned, searching for the source of the voice.

"Sareth!"

The call was closer this time. Sareth turned around, then his eyes went wide, and he threw back the robe.

"Vani!" he called.

Finally Lirith saw her—a woman wrapped in yellow, her skin and eyes as coppery as Sareth's, moving toward them with swift, sinuous grace. Now the sweat made Lirith's skin clammy. The woman was absolutely beautiful. To Lirith's dismay, the woman threw herself into Sareth's arms, and the Mournish man caught her in a tight embrace, his eyes glowing.

"Vani," he murmured, and the love was plain in his voice. "How can this be? How is it you are here?"

Lirith wondered the same thing. Sareth had been following them ever since Ar-tolor. Had been following *her*, she might have let herself believe. But what a foolish thought that was, for this strange woman had thrown herself at him, and he seemed not to mind it in the least.

She started to turn away, so as to not have to witness the terrible spectacle any further, when Aryn gasped and Durge let out a soft oath. Lirith followed their gazes, then amazement stunned her as well.

Following the strange woman, three figures walked toward them: a tall, blond man, another man with a bald head, and a regal woman with eyes like sun on leaves. Lirith staggered, and had the wall not been behind her, she would have fallen.

"Sister," she said softly, but by the time she spoke the word Grace was already there, along with Travis and Beltan, all of them grinning, their expressions every bit as astonished and joyful as Lirith's own.

"My dear ones," Melia said, eyes shining. "You have such wonderful timing."

67.

It was strange, but in all their urgency to return to Eldh, Grace had never stopped to think about what it would be like when they finally did. Not that it mattered; she would never have been able to imagine feeling like this. She could not remember a time in her life when she had laughed so effortlessly, had embraced others with such abandon, or when she had felt so light and full at the same time.

The symptoms are clear, Doctor. You're experiencing joy. Not something you're used to, granted, but I hear it's far from life-threatening. You might actually get used to it someday.

She hoped not.

There was much hugging and talking. So much, in fact, that they began to win stares from passersby, and the man whom Vani had called Sareth—and who, given his sharp, dark features, was clearly the brother she had been looking for—herded them all into a shaded grotto where they could speak out of the glare of the sun and public attention.

As glad as she was to see her friends, there was something else Grace ached to embrace, something she had craved all those months on Earth. As they stepped into the green, moist air of the grotto, she let herself shut her eyes, reach out, and Touch the Weirding.

A thrill coursed through her. On Earth, it had been

so worn and dirty that she had forgotten just how wondrous it was. The threads of life wove all around her in an elaborate web, shimmering and perfect. . . .

No, Grace. Not perfect.

She hesitated, then began to probe. Something was wrong—all her instincts as a doctor told her so. But what? Every thread she touched was bright, flawless. Then she understood. At the hospital, she had learned that sometimes it wasn't what you observed, but rather what you *didn't*. She glimpsed them—small, dark areas in the web, places where strands should have shone but which were empty instead.

Grace, are you all right?

It was Aryn's voice, speaking in her mind. Eyes still shut, Grace could see Aryn clearly; the young woman's outlines glowed in the pale blue light of her life thread.

I'm . . . I'm not sure, Grace managed to answer.

Now Lirith was there, her outlines dimmer than Aryn's, but warmer in color and more clearly focused.

You see it, don't you, sister? The flaw in the Weirding.

Grace struggled to explain. *Not exactly. Everything I sense is perfect. But it's as if I'm not sensing everything I should be. It's as if some of the threads of the Weirding are missing.*

She felt sadness spin outward from Lirith. And fear.

I know where they have gone, sister. . . .

Lirith's thread reached for Grace's, connected. Images flashed through Grace's mind, and in an instant she saw everything: the tangle in the Weirding.

Her eyes fluttered open. Now she stared at Aryn and Lirith with mundane sight. "What is it?"

Lirith sighed. "I am not certain. But I have spoken to Melia, and she believes it has to do with what is happening here in Tarras."

Grace struggled for understanding. "But what are

you talking about? What's happening in Tarras?"

Shaken as she was, she had spoken the words loudly, and it was Falken who turned around to answer her.

"That's a good question, Grace. You've returned at a dark time. I don't know how to explain it quickly other than to say that gods have been murdered—three of them—and we're on our way to see the emperor to do something about it."

"No," a deep voice said.

As one, they turned toward Sareth.

"You must not go to the palace. The peril is too great for you here. You must leave the city at once."

Durge glowered at the dark-haired man. "Why were you following us? Are you not the cause of our peril?"

Vani moved to Sareth, her golden eyes filled with concern. "Sareth, what is happening? And what has happened to you?"

Her gaze flickered downward. Grace looked down as well. His billowing pants partly concealed it, but by the way he moved Grace guessed the amputation to be just below the knee. And this world offered no custom-fitted, flesh-colored prostheses. Instead, his left leg ended in a carved wooden peg.

Sareth took Vani's hand, squeezed it. As he did, Lirith turned away, but there was no time to ask the slender witch what was wrong.

"There is much I have to tell you," Sareth said, his gaze intent on Vani. Then he looked at the others. "I would guess we all have much to say to one another. But it is not safe for you in Tarras. It would be best if you would come with me now. Our caravan is not far from the city. We can talk more safely there."

Grace saw the suspicion in Durge's face. Falken and Melia exchanged glances and unspoken messages.

Grace didn't know why they were in Tarras, or why Sareth had been following them. But Sareth was Vani's brother, and Vani had done more than just save their lives. She had proven herself a friend.

"You should trust him," Grace said. She glanced at Vani. "You should trust them both."

As if Grace's words were a command, Durge sheathed his sword and bowed to Sareth and Vani.

"You are friends of my mistress, and I have insulted you. I am certain my mistress will reprimand me severely." The knight sounded almost hopeful.

"No, my good cloud," Sareth said. "You were right to be suspicious. Especially in this city. But we can talk more later. We must leave at once."

Melia glided forward. "We must at least stop by the hostel to settle our account with Madam Vil."

"You cannot," Sareth said.

Falken frowned. "What do you mean?"

"The House of Nine Fountains is no more."

"What do you mean, it's no more?" Aryn said with a gasp.

Sareth made a sharp motion with his hand. "I mean it is gone, just like the nave of the temple of Sif. There is only an empty pit where the hostel stood this morning."

Grace didn't know how a building could vanish, but by the expressions on the faces of the others they had an inkling.

Melia lifted a hand to her breast. "How many? How many were inside the hostel?"

"No one I overheard was certain," Sareth said. "Perhaps a dozen guests and servants. And the proprietress of the hostel."

Tears shone on Aryn's cheeks now. "Madam Vil. But why? Why would they do such a thing?"

It was Lirith who answered, voice hard. "They found out where we were staying, and they wanted to eliminate us."

Sareth hesitated, then nodded.

"You know how they're doing it, don't you?" Falken said. "You know how they can make buildings vanish just like gods."

"I will tell you, ancient one. But not here." Sareth glanced around, as if he feared an attack.

"All right, everyone," Falken said. "I'd say try to look as discreet as possible as we move through the city, but that's probably a little hard for this group. So let's at least move as quickly as we can."

Travis laid a hand on Beltan's arm. "Can you walk?"

The blond knight nodded. "I can." He seemed to hesitate, then he laid his hand on top of Travis's.

Vani turned away from the two men and moved to Sareth.

"Let us go," she said, her voice as flat as her gaze.

68.

It was late afternoon by the time Grace and Lirith followed Vani along a track that led up the side of a rocky hill a half league to the north of Tarras. They had left the grotto in small groups, spacing their departures by a quarter of an hour, in order to be less conspicuous as they moved through the city. However, Durge had not been happy that Vani, Lirith, and Grace were to bring up the rear.

"Three ladies should not go unattended when there is danger about," the knight had rumbled.

Grace had glanced at Vani, then had smiled. "I don't think you need to worry about us ladies."

Now Grace and Lirith panted as they tried to match Vani's swift pace up the slope. Just when Grace was beginning to think her knees were going to give out, the track did instead.

They stepped onto the summit of the hill: a flat space crowned by a circle of *ithaya* trees that rose like columns toward the sky. *Ithaya* were also called sunleaf trees, and at that moment Grace understood why. For the slender, yellow-green leaves caught the heavy light of the sun and spun it into a gauze of gold that mantled the grove.

On the far side of the grove, the hill fell away abruptly, and Grace realized they must have ascended to the top of one of the white cliffs that rose above the city. Far below, Tarras rose in five concentric rings of white stone, the sun setting fire to its domes. Grace turned around to tell Lirith how beautiful it was.

Instead, a gasp escaped her. She must have somehow missed it as they entered the grove. Now she saw it, lurking there among the tall trees. Its wings were folded tight against its body, its neck coiled, but there was no mistaking the scaly body, the saurian head.

"Lirith, a dragon!" she murmured, fear and wonder melding as one in her chest.

Lirith let out a warm laugh, and Grace managed to wrest her gaze away from the creature long enough to stare at the dark-eyed witch. How could Lirith laugh at a dragon?

"Look closer," Lirith said.

Grace turned back. Again a thrill of terror shimmered through her—

—then faded as she saw the peeling paint, the spoked wheels, the small green door where the dragon's tail should have been.

It was a wagon. And now Grace saw there were other wagons among the trees, all shaped like animals both fantastical and mundane. There were a toad, a rabbit, and a snail, as well as a unicorn and a lion with wings like an eagle's. Flags hung between the wagons and the trees, filling the grove with sparks of color. People in bright clothes moved in and around the circle. A group of them started toward the new arrivals. Grace saw Travis, Beltan, Melia, and Sareth. Durge, Aryn, and Falken came close behind.

Vani started toward the others, and Grace and Lirith followed.

"Don't worry, sister," Lirith said. "I thought it was a dragon as well the first time I saw it."

This startled Grace. "You mean you've met Vani and Sareth's people before?"

"Not exactly, sister. They came to Ar-tolor at the end of summer, and Aryn, Durge, and I went to visit their caravan. But I've heard it said that no one can really know the Mournish."

"You mean the Morindai," Grace said.

The dark-haired witch shook her head. Clearly she had never heard the word before. The two groups had come together now in the center of the grove.

"Vani," Grace said, "didn't you tell us your people are called the Morindai?"

"That is what we call ourselves. But in Falengarth we are called the Mournish. Or the Vagabond Folk. Or, often, less complimentary names."

Falken scratched his chin. "Morindai. Now why is that name familiar?"

Vani cast a glance at Sareth, and he gave a small shrug.

"It means *People of Morindu*," Vani said.

The bard's faded eyes went wide. "Morindu? You mean Morindu the Dark, the lost city of sorcerers?" He gave Melia a stunned look.

The lady's amber eyes gleamed. "I confess, I had often wondered if it might be so. But I was never certain."

Before the bard and lady could speak more, a shrill voice drifted from the open door of the dragon-shaped wagon.

"Sareth, where are they? Bring them to me at once. I could perish at any moment."

Sareth grinned. "Nonsense, al-Mama," he called back. "You know exactly when you're going to begin the Great Journey. You told me yourself you saw it in the cards."

"Vile young man!" the shrill voice came back. "I'll put a *va'ksha* on you as my dying act, do you hear me? Now come!"

"What's a *va'ksha*?" Grace asked.

"A curse," Vani said with a sharp smile.

Beltan clutched a small clay cup. "I would go if I were you." He took a sip from the cup, grimaced, then managed to swallow.

Aryn's nose wrinkled. "Beltan, that healing tea she made you smells dreadful. How can you possibly drink it?"

"She said I had to finish it all or she'd put a *va'ksha* on me that would make my—" His cheeks turned pink, and he hastily lifted the cup for another sip.

Vani started toward the wagon.

"My al-Mama will see your fate now," Sareth said to Grace. "She has already seen the others."

"But what about Lirith?" Grace said.

Lirith turned away, her arms crossed over her gown. "I will stay. I already know my fate."

Sareth gazed at Lirith's back, but Grace could not fathom the expression in his eyes.

"This way," he said to Grace, and she followed him and Vani toward the wagon.

It took Grace's vision a long moment to adjust to the dimness of the cramped interior. Then motion caught her eye, and she made out a thin, birdlike figure swaddled in blankets.

The woman lying on the bench was ancient. An accurate estimate of age would take closer examination, but Grace was certain she was over a hundred. Her arms were withered sticks, and her nose a vulture's beak, but her eyes were bright and clear as harvest moons.

"Leave us, Sareth," the old woman rasped.

Grace heard his wooden leg beat hollowly against the steps outside, then he was gone. She opened her mouth, not sure what she should say, yet certain she should say something.

"Shut your mouth, girl, and let me look at you," the old woman said in her harsh voice.

Grace snapped her mouth closed.

"Humph." The old woman bit a finger with what seemed to be her sole remaining tooth. "Well, you are skinnier than I would have thought, for one who has so much to do. Yet looks can deceive, can they not?" She cackled, touching her all-but-hairless skull. "Now, give me your hand."

Grace hesitated, but a bony arm shot out and thin fingers grasped her wrist with a surprising strength, pulling her forward. The old woman turned Grace's hand over, palm up, and pored over it. She cackled again.

"Yes, yes, I can see it in you. You are strong, girl—perhaps, in the end, the strongest of all. So many of them will break before all is done, but not you, girl. In the end, it is you who will break others. That is your fate."

Grace fought for breath. No, the old woman was wrong. She was not strong. She was broken, a thing used, damaged, and thrown aside. Even now she could see it: the shadow pulsing on the edge of vision, as hungry as the bodiless beings she had glimpsed in the void between worlds. She snatched her hand back.

The old woman grunted. "Do not think I do not see it, girl. A darkness lies upon you, heavier than upon any of the others, memories of what once was. Those who say the past cannot harm you are liars. It can consume everything you are and leave only an empty husk. But"—the old woman leaned forward, pointing a finger toward Grace's chest—"only if you let it, girl!"

Grace fought for words. "But you said you believe in fate. What if I don't have a choice?"

"Bah!" The old woman waved a hand in disgust. "Fate is only what you make of it, girl. Every day we make a thousand choices. Do I turn left or do I turn right? Do I drink water or do I drink wine? Fate is where, in the end, all these choices lead us. It is nothing less, nothing more. Just because you cannot escape fate does not mean you cannot shape it."

Grace started to shake her head again, then hesitated. Maybe the old woman's words weren't so mad after all. After all, it sounded less like magic than it did chaos theory.

But chaotic systems are hopelessly complex, Grace, you know that. Countless factors work together in unpredictable ways to determine the outcome. You can't control it, so it might as well be fate.

Still, despite the dread in her throat, the old woman's words filled her with a fraction of hope.

Vani knelt beside the old woman's bench. "What did you see for him, al-Mama?"

"Who do you mean, girl?"

"You know very well who I mean, al-Mama. Travis Wilder."

The old woman shrugged shoulders as sharp as knives. "What do you think I saw, child? He is the one, you know it as well as I do. But he is not what I expected. His hands are without mark. Even a newborn has lines upon its hands, Vani, but not him!" She clucked her tongue. "He is a man with no past and no future."

Vani shrank back, as if the old woman had struck her a blow. "He has no fate, then?"

"So, you think he is *A'narai*?" The old woman

folded her arms, bracelets gleaming around her skeletal wrists. "Perhaps, girl. I had not thought of that. Or had not dared to. These bones are too old to bear such wonders. But perhaps you are right, perhaps he is one of the Fateless after all. It was said, long ago, they were the only ones who might enter the chamber where Orú dreamed without their minds being stolen by madness. And if he is indeed the one . . ."

Vani and the old woman locked eyes.

Grace worked her parched tongue. "What are you talking about?"

"Come," Vani said, standing. "We must leave my al-Mama to her rest."

Grace started to protest, but Vani was already steering her toward the door of the wagon.

"Take great care with her, Vani," the old woman called. "Never will he reach the City of Secrets without her. That fate is clear above all others."

The curtain parted. Grace stumbled down the steps, then found herself among swaying *ithaya* trees. The sun had set, and the sky had turned from sapphire to jade. Over the sea, a great, round moon was rising, a dozen times larger than any moon ever glimpsed on Earth.

Sareth was waiting for them.

"Tell me everything she said."

Vani nodded, took Sareth's arm, and together the two moved across the grove, heads bent together in talk.

A sigh sounded beside Grace. She turned to see Lirith standing behind her.

"Where are the others?" Grace said.

Lirith's brown eyes gazed into the deepening gloom. "He loves her, doesn't he?"

"Loves her? I'm sure of it."

Lirith gave a stiff nod. "Well, then. Good for him. I

hope . . . I hope they are happy when they are married."

"Married? What are you talking about, Lirith?"

The slender witch blinked. "Vani and Sareth. If they love one another, are they not to be wed?"

Finally Grace understood. How could she have been such an idiot? But then, while she could listen to the heart of another with a stethoscope, there was no instrument that would let her glimpse what lay within it.

She laid her hand on Lirith's arm. "Vani and Sareth love each other because they're brother and sister."

"Brother and sister?" Lirith's jaw worked as she fought for words. "Then you mean . . . ?"

The slender witch turned away, arms folded over her chest. A tremor passed through her. Grace couldn't be certain, but it seemed to her it was a sob. She hesitated, then reached a hand toward Lirith.

"Grace, there you are!"

She turned around, as did Lirith. It was Travis.

He glanced at Lirith, then cocked his head. "Are you—?"

"We're fine," Grace said, finding Lirith's hand and squeezing it.

He nodded. "Come on. Falken is practically rabid to talk to Sareth, but it seems they're going to throw us a feast first. I gather it's not often the Mournish—the Morindai—accept guests into their circle, so when they do they have to make a big deal of it."

Grace glanced at Lirith. The witch's eyes glittered in the darkness.

I am well, sister.

Grace tightened her grip on Lirith's hand. "Lead the way," she said to Travis.

69.

The Mournish might have forgotten many things in their millennia of wandering, but how to throw a party was clearly not one of them.

Travis watched as sparks soared upward from a bonfire toward the strange stars above, along with wild strains of music. His belly seemed to contain more spiced meat, flatbread, and olives than should be physically possible, and he held a cup of some sort of red, fiery wine in his hand—the reason the pleasant warmth he felt came not only from the fire.

He stood on the edge of the circle of light, near Aryn, Lirith, and Durge, while the others were gathered across the fire. Melia and Falken sat on piles of cushions as if they were royal guests. Some of the Mournish sat on the ground, making their music with drums, wooden flutes, things that looked like fiddles, and instruments of bone Travis did not recognize.

Those Mournish not making music were dancing to it, swirling in patterns that seemed utterly chaotic, yet which suddenly formed into precise circles or interlocking squares, then just as quickly dissolved into whirls of color again. Even the children made music and danced, the girls wearing bright dresses and scarves, the boys in loose pants and colorful vests.

All the Mournish—whether infant or ancient—

wore jewelry: bracelets, necklaces, and rings on their fingers, their toes, and in their noses and ears. However, Travis noticed that only Vani bore tattoos: the strange symbols that coiled up her arms and neck. Grace said they were symbols of her training. Of her skill as a T'gol.

She's an assassin, Travis. That's what the T'gol are. Vani has been trained since she was a girl in the art of killing people in the swiftest and most efficient ways possible.

Travis gazed across the fire. For a moment golden eyes gazed back at him, then turned away.

Earlier, he and Grace had stepped away from the fire for a moment to talk.

They think you're A'narai, Travis.

A'narai?

It means fateless. Vani and Sareth's grandmother said you have no past and no future because your hand doesn't have any lines anymore.

So that's what they meant. The old woman—she said it was not my fate to uncover Morindu, but that it was the fate of the Mournish that they would regain Morindu through me. That didn't really make sense.

Agreed. And what makes less sense is that they think I'm going to be the one who gets you to the lost city of Morindu so you can raise it from the desert for them. According to her, that's my fate.

What do you think your fate is, Grace?

But she had only looked away, and Travis couldn't decide which was worse. Knowing your fate—or not having one at all.

Colors whirled before Travis, and when they stopped he saw a Mournish woman clad in jewel-colored scarves.

"Dance with me," she said in a lilting voice.

Travis started to stutter his decline when he realized

her rich brown eyes were not gazing at him, but at Durge—or rather, at Durge's hard chest visible through his open vest. The Embarran hastily crossed his arms, but this only caused his biceps to bulge. The Mournish woman draped a scarf around his neck, pulling him toward the music and the light.

"This is not proper, my lady," Durge sputtered.

"It is quite proper among my people, *sayeh*. And it is among my people that you are at present."

Durge cast a desperate look at Travis, but Travis only grinned and waved, knowing there was nothing he could do to save the hapless knight. Towing him by a scarf, the Mournish woman led him into the throng.

"Poor Durge," Aryn said with a sigh. "He must be dreadfully embarrassed."

"Actually, sister," Lirith said with a laugh, "he seems to be doing rather well."

Lirith was right. The Mournish woman used her scarves to guide Durge in the dance, but in moments the knight seemed to have figured out the complex steps and moved in perfect unison with the woman. She lowered her scarf until it encircled his hips and used it to draw him closer.

Aryn's blue eyes grew squinty, and her left hand clenched into a fist. "That . . . that harlot. She doesn't actually think she can have Durge, does she?"

"No, sister. They cannot . . ." Lirith's voice wavered, her visage suddenly stricken. "That is, I've heard that the Mournish can never marry outside their clan."

Aryn seemed puzzled by this, but Lirith turned away from the fire, her face lost in shadow. Had Lirith drunk too much of the heady wine? Travis started to move toward her, then paused. He saw another figure standing apart from the light and music. Despite the gloom, Travis's new eyes made the other out clearly.

He hesitated, then left Lirith and Aryn and moved toward the shadow beneath the trees.

"Beltan, what are you doing way out here?"

The knight stared into his cup; it was still full of wine. "I'm afraid I'm not much in the mood for merriment."

"Then I don't think the fairy did heal you, at least not completely."

"It's not that. The fairy patched me together well enough. I suppose I owe it my thanks for that."

Travis stepped closer. It was surprisingly cool away from the fire. He could feel heat radiating from the other man.

"Then what is it?"

Beltan was silent, his eyes glittering in the cast-off light of the fire. "I learned something about myself, Travis. In Spardis, in the baths. Dakarreth told me. It's . . . it's something I did. A terrible crime."

The big knight was trembling. What was wrong? Travis didn't know, but he did know one thing: not to trust the words of a Necromancer. He reached out, took one of the knight's hands, and held it between his own.

"Beltan, I don't know what Dakarreth told you, but he was evil—he wanted to hurt you. It can't be true."

"No, it is true," Beltan said, his voice hoarse. "I know it is. Five years ago, in Calavere . . . I was the one . . ."

Beltan's words trailed off. In the hospital, in Denver, Travis had dared to bend down, to press his lips to the knight's. But that had been a cowardly act, one the recipient could never possibly respond to—or pull away from. Travis let out a breath, then leaned forward, bringing his lips nearer the other man's.

"Travis? Are you there?"

He sucked his breath in again and stepped back. Beltan stared, expression confused, his hands frozen halfway before him, although whether in the act of reaching out or drawing back Travis couldn't say. The darkness stirred, and a lithe figure stepped into the moonlight.

"You should come back to the fire," Vani said. "Both of you."

Beltan's eyes narrowed. "We were doing fine out here."

Travis worked his jaw, suddenly anxious for something to say. "What's wrong, Vani? Do we need to be watching for the Scirathi? You said they could be here in Tarras."

She broke her gaze from Beltan and spoke in a crisp tone. "They are indeed here in Tarras. Sareth told me he has seen their signs. But I do not think they will attack us openly, not here in the caravan. They yet have some fear of the Mournish. As well they should."

Travis thought about this. "Your people are sorcerers as well, aren't they, Vani?"

"No, it is forbidden for us to work blood sorcery until we return to Morindu the Dark. But we have . . . other means of keeping the Scirathi away."

Travis studied her lean form, her easy stance. He supposed they did at that. Things like the T'gol.

Beltan seemed to notice Travis's gaze, and the knight scowled.

"Come on," Travis said, suddenly wanting to be near light again. "Let's go back to the fire."

The Mournish had just called for a song from Falken, and they were laying down their drums and flutes to watch the bard. Travis saw Grace, Melia, and the others and moved toward them, Beltan and Vani following. Grace looked up, smiled at him, and he smiled back. However his smile faltered after a moment. Something had happened there in the shadows beyond the fire. He had been about to kiss Beltan. Why had he pulled back?

Falken stood and strummed a chord on his lute. "I think this song is appropriate for this place and this night. It's called 'The Lay of Ulther.' It's a song about the south and the north, and how they came together long ago."

> *"With Fellring sword of Elfin art,*
> *Ulther smote the Pale King's heart—*
> *The magic blade was riven twain,*
> *But Berash did not stand again.*
>
> *"Then came the Runelords to the vale,*
> *To bind the gates of Imbrifale—*
> *And witches too with their fey art,*
> *Wove passes high with perils dark.*
>
> *"Lord Ulther knelt before the Queen,*
> *And a pact they forged between—*
> *They set the guard of Malachor,*
> *That shadows gather nevermore."*

The last strains of the bard's music faded, and the night was silent. The Mournish still watched the bard, their faces strangely solemn. Then, in twos and threes, they stood, bowed to Falken and Melia, and departed the circle of the fire. In moments, the eight companions stood alone in the firelight, along with Vani and Sareth.

"I guess the party's over," Travis said to Grace.

She gazed into the fire, gripping the steel pendant that hung at her neck.

"Grace, what is it?"

"That song. I . . . I know it."

"Maybe you heard Falken sing it before."

"No, that's not it."

Grace moved to the bard, who was putting his lute back into its case.

"Falken, could you play the music for the first verse again?"

Melia smoothed her white shift on the pillows where she sat. "Whatever for, dear?"

"I'm not sure. Falken?"

The bard nodded. "Very well."

He took his lute back out, then strummed the now-familiar chords of "The Lay of Ulther." Then, to Travis's surprise, in a husky voice, Grace began to sing:

> *"And farewell words too often part*
> *All their small and paling hearts.*
> *The fragile glade and river lain,*
> *Beneath the hush of silent rain."*

Falken's hand fell still on his lute. He looked at Grace with piercing eyes. "I've never heard those words sung to this tune."

Melia rose to her feet. "But they sound similar, don't they?"

Falken nodded. "With Fellring sword of Elfin art . . ."

"And farewell words too often part. . . ." Grace looked up, her own eyes startled now. "But I used to sing that song as a child. I don't understand."

Sareth stepped forward, his sharp features cast in stark relief by the firelight. "Perhaps you can consider this mystery later. I think now it is time for us to talk."

70.

The fire burned down to a circle of glowing coals as Vani spoke of the three years she had spent on Earth: how she had searched for the ones fated to raise Morindu the Dark from the blasted sands of the Morgolthi, how she had learned in a message from Sareth that Travis and Grace were the ones she sought, and how together they had fled Duratek, the *gorleths*, and Denver on that last terrifying day.

It was only when Aryn spoke that Travis realized Vani had finished her tale. The young baroness's eyes were large as she looked at Grace and Travis.

"So you're supposed to help the Mournish find the lost city of their ancestors?"

"The fabled city of Morindu," Falken said. "But how can that be? What do Travis and Grace have to do with the City of the Dark?" He looked at Melia.

The amber-eyed lady shrugged, shifting on her cushion. "Well, don't ask me. I wasn't even born when the cities of Amún were destroyed in the War of the Sorcerers. Nor were any of my brothers and sisters."

"No," Falken said, rubbing his chin. "No, they weren't."

"How, Vani?" Grace said simply. "I would like to help you, to thank you for what you did for us, but how are we supposed to find a city that's been lost for millennia?"

It was Sareth who answered. "I believe we were hoping the two of you would have some ideas about that. All the *T'hot* readings tell us is that it is your fate to raise Morindu the Dark."

Travis let out a groan. "You mean you have no idea how we're supposed to find this place?"

"If we did," Vani said, "would we not have journeyed there and dug it up already?"

Great. He and Grace were fated to do something no one had any idea how to do—least of all themselves.

Sareth held his hands toward the fire. "The cards only tell us what will happen, not how. Or when. For all we know, it could be years from now that you journey to Morindu. And right now there are other secrets to concern us. Ones that, unlike those of Morindu, have already been exhumed."

Durge grunted. "How about telling us the secret of why you have been following us ever since Ar-tolor."

The Mournish man sighed. "I suppose that is as good a place as any to begin. I am sorry for any mistrust I have caused with my silence. However, it is not usually our way to speak with outsiders. Only the urgency of events causes me to do so now. As does the nature of those to whom I am speaking. But to answer your question, my good cloud, we followed you from Ar-tolor for the same reason we journeyed there in the first place: to keep watch."

Lirith drew her knees to her chest. "But why?"

Sareth opened his mouth, but Grace was faster. That analytical mind of hers, Travis knew.

"Because we're your friends, Lirith. They think Travis and I are going to help find their lost city, but then we went back to Earth, so they decided to keep an eye on all of you in case we showed up, figuring you'd be the first people we'd contact here on Eldh."

Sareth laughed softly. "It seems we Mournish are not so mysterious as we would like to believe. What you speak is true. Our seers told us the one we sought would be a wizard of northern magic, yet that he would not come from the north but rather another world. That was why Vani dared to use the artifact to journey to your Earth." He looked at Travis. "Then, when we heard the tales about what you did at Calavere last Midwinter's Eve, we knew you had to be the one. However, before we could reach Calavere, you had returned to your world."

Sareth stirred the coals, sending sparks snapping upward. "A few months ago, we learned that you had returned to Eldh, but the ravages of the Burning Plague made travel difficult, and by the time we reached Castle Spardis in Perridon, you were both already gone. But we kept watch on your companions. And I sent word to Vani that you had returned to your world once again."

A thought occurred to Travis. "Sareth, Vani never explained something to us. How were you able to use the artifact to send messages to her?"

The Mournish man's eyes glittered, and he pulled down the sleeves of his shirt. But not before Travis caught the pale gleam of scars in the firelight.

"I thought you said the Mournish were forbidden to work blood sorcery."

"Sometimes that which is forbidden must be done in order to prevent a far greater danger."

Travis thought maybe he understood. In a way, it was like Farr's dispensation from the Seekers. Rules were made to protect people, but sometimes the rules had to be broken in order to save them. While it took a fairy's blood to send a person through the gate, it seemed human blood was enough to send words.

Aryn edged closer to the fire. "So when we left Artolor, Sareth, you followed us here to Tarras."

"That is partly true. But there is another reason we had to journey to Tarras."

Falken looked up. "The murdered gods. You know what's happening, don't you? You know how and why they're being slain."

"And we spent all this time trying to find the murderer," Aryn said. "Why didn't you just tell us, Sareth?"

The Mournish man gave a bitter smile. "Wagons are not so swift as ships, fair lady. You arrived in Tarras several days before us. I did not reach the city until the day the Scirathi attempted to harm you, *beshala*." He said these last words to Lirith, his eyes intent.

Lirith did not meet his eyes. "The Scirathi. You mean one like the sorcerer who attacked Grace and Travis on their world."

Sareth nodded. "Although there was something strange about the sorcerer of Scirath who attacked you, *beshala*. What, I cannot say—but that he was Scirathi there can be no doubt. Only they wear masks of gold."

"Masks," Grace murmured. She met the questioning gazes of the others. "The masks are the focus for their magic. We saw that firsthand."

Beltan cleared his throat. It was the first sound the blond knight had made since they had gathered around the fire. "All right, let me see if I'm following this. These sorcerers—the Scirathi—they're the ones behind the murders of the gods?"

Sareth hesitated, then nodded.

Melia clenched small hands into fists. "They will pay for this!"

"But how?" Falken said. "Even a sorcerer should not have the ability to slay a god."

The Mournish man looked down, silent for a long moment. Travis realized he was gazing at his wooden leg. At last he looked up.

"It is a demon," he said.

Vani clamped a hand to her mouth in an expression of open horror. Clearly she knew what Sareth's words meant, and by their grim expressions Melia and Falken did as well. But Travis had no idea.

"A demon?" he said.

"Yes," Sareth answered. "A relic of the War of the Sorcerers long ago. When the sorcerers rose up against the god-kings of Amún, they created the demons as their greatest weapons. A demon could lay waste to an entire city, destroying every last grain of its walls, leaving only bare sand."

Aryn shuddered. "Just like Madam Vil's hostel."

"But the demons, what were they?" Travis said.

"They were *morndari* made incarnate. The *morndari* were ever bodiless and hungry spirits—that is how blood could be used to draw and control them. But a few of the sorcerers found a way to bind the *morndari*, encasing them in bodies of stone. These were the demons. Incarnate, they could walk across the land, but their hunger was not lessened in their physical form. They consumed everything in their path, and they were never sated."

These words sickened Travis. He could almost see them—vague, shadowy creatures opening vast maws to eat entire cities as people tried in vain to flee.

"If they were never sated," Grace said, "then how were they stopped? Why didn't they consume everything in Amún?"

"They very nearly did. It is because of the demons

that the lands of Amún are now the Morgolthi—a wasteland of bones, dust, and death. However, in the end, the sorcerers who created them realized their folly and managed to undo their magic, destroying all the demons."

"But not all of them," Falken said. "Not if you're right."

Sareth turned toward the bard. "We can only guess that one of the demons crossed the Summer Sea, to the shores of Falengarth."

"But why didn't it destroy things here?" Lirith said.

"It was bound somehow, imprisoned in a chamber beneath the very hill upon which Tarras was later built. Although who bound it there we do not know. It must have been a sorcerer of vast power."

Travis forced himself to stop biting his lip. "But if it took such a powerful sorcerer to bind the demon the first time, how can it be locked up again?"

"The demon is not free," Sareth said. "Not completely, for were that so there would be only a void where Tarras stands. Its prison has grown weaker, yes, due to the actions of the Scirathi. But I believe the sorcerers have found a way to use the demon for their own ends without releasing it."

"Their own ends," Melia said, her voice rising with fury. "You mean to murder the gods!"

Sareth regarded Melia with solemn eyes. "No, great lady, that is not so. To murder the gods is not the reason the Scirathi are using the demon. Instead, the deaths of the gods are merely meant to appease the thing—an attempt to sate it—so that they might safely pass by it."

"You mean," Falken exclaimed, "the Scirathi are sacrificing gods to the demon just so they can get past it?"

Melia was shaking with rage. "That's . . . that's utterly perverse!"

Travis's heart rattled in his chest. Something was wrong—and not just the existence of an ancient monster or the pointless deaths of three gods. Then, with a chill, he understood.

"Sareth," he said, "you told us that the Scirathi are sacrificing gods to the demon in order to sate it."

"That is so."

"But you also said demons can never be sated, no matter how much they consume."

"No, they cannot."

"Then what's to keep it from getting stronger as it feeds, strong enough to escape completely?"

Sareth gazed at his wooden leg and said nothing.

71.

It was Vani who broke the silence.

"Brother, you have yet to tell us how you learned of the demon beneath Tarras."

Sareth bowed his head, and he seemed to be murmuring something. Was he gathering his thoughts? Or was it a prayer? Before Travis could decide, the Mournish man looked up, his dark eyes haunted.

"It was two years ago that I learned of the demon— not long after you left us, Vani. A dervish came to our caravan where we were camped, at the foot of the Mountains of the Shroud."

"A dervish?" Falken said, and this question surprised Travis. He had always thought Falken knew everything about the people and history of Eldh. Evidently there were limitations even to the ancient bard's knowledge.

Sareth glanced at the bard. "The free working of blood magic is forbidden among the Mournish until the time we regain Morindu the Dark, lest we become like the Scirathi—covetous of power. However, there are those who have chosen to forsake this law, and who strike off alone to master what secrets of sorcery they can. These are the dervishes. Most of them are mad—that is the price they pay for their solitude and the secrets they learn—and this one was no exception.

"He was dying when he stumbled into the caravan. I think that was the only reason he spoke to me, to boast of the mysteries he had learned before death took him. He was dry and thin as bones left in a desert, and his face was a mask of scabs and flies. He said he had come from the Morgolthi, the Hungering Land, and I did not doubt him. He said he had dug there, in the burning sands, and he had found . . . this."

Sareth drew something from a pocket. It looked to Travis like a thick, wedge-shaped piece of pottery, covered with angular markings.

"All that night, as I watched over him, the dervish babbled in his sleep. He was burning with fever, and little of what he said made sense. But a few words I heard over and over. *The Dark shall rise again*, he said. And, *His blood is the key*. At dawn I watched the life leave him, and we buried him there."

Vani reached out, took the shard of pottery from Sareth. "What is it? What did the dervish give his life to dig from the sands of the Morgolthi?"

"It's a piece of a tablet," Sareth said. "That I knew at once, although I could not read it. However, Mirgeth could when I took it to him. It is written in the ancient tongue of Amún."

"What does it say?" Falken asked.

"Very little. A few fragments of words, enough to let us know it was written during the War of the Sorcerers, that was all. I was prepared to forget the dervish and his ravings when, accepting the shard back from Mirgeth, I dropped it. It struck the ground and . . ."

Sareth took the shard back from Vani. Carefully, he pulled the shard into two halves and drew something out. It was a thin circle of gold.

Vani sat up straight. "A *fa'deth*."

"Yes." Sareth glanced at the others. "It is a *fa'deth*, a

message-disk, used by the high sorcerers of Morindu to send missives to one another."

In the crimson glow of the coals, Travis could make out fine engravings on the disk. "What does it say?"

"Make it speak for us, Sareth," Vani said, her eyes as bright as the golden disk.

He shook his head. "To do so requires blood. Once the elders let me use the *fa'deth*, but once was enough, and I must not shed more blood for it carelessly."

"You mean that it can speak to you?" Grace said.

"As I said, it is how the highest sorcerers sent messages to one another. Even if the disk were intercepted, the thief would not be able to hear the missive."

"Unless the thief was a sorcerer as well," Travis murmured, not realizing he had spoken until he saw Sareth gazing at him.

"What did it tell you?" Vani said.

Sareth drew in a breath. "That a demon had been imprisoned in a mound of white stone north across the sea—a mound, from its description, I knew to be the very hill upon which Tarras now stands. And it also told how something else was entombed with the demon. A relic of Morindu the Dark."

"What relic?" Vani whispered, leaning closer.

"A scarab," Sareth said. "A scarab of Orú."

Vani gasped, but by the puzzled looks on the faces of those around him, Travis wasn't the only one who was confused.

"Isn't a scarab just a piece of jewelry?" he said.

Sareth laughed, a deep and chiming but somehow mirthless sound. "You might as well say the sun is just another flame like a candle. Of all the secret magics of Morindu the Dark, there was none so powerful as the scarabs of Orú."

"Wait a minute," Grace said. "I heard your grand-mother say that name. Orú. Who was he?"

Vani rested her hands upon her knees. "For three hundred years, he was the god-king of Morindu the Dark."

"Nonsense," Durge rumbled. "No man can be king for three centuries."

Again Sareth laughed. "Yes, that is true, my good cloud. No man. But a god?"

"Orú was not truly a deity," Melia said, her expression outraged. "The god-kings of Amún were just tyrants who posed as deities so they could claim a divine right to rule their cities. It was despicable!"

"And yet," Falken said, "some believe that, without such harsh rule, the first cities could never have been carved out of the deserts of Amún. And certainly it was those fleeing the destruction of Amún who brought civilization to Falengarth. Without the god-kings of Moringarth, Tarras would never have existed."

Sareth weighed the gold *fa'deth* in his hand. "It is true that Orú began life as any ordinary man—in fact, he was the son of a beggar. You see, in Morindu, a king or queen did not rule by right of birth but rather right of magic. The greatest sorcerer of each generation was crowned king or queen. And in the thousand years of its history, no sorcerer was greater than Orú. While the other rulers of Amún dared to call themselves gods, only Orú was truly as powerful as a god."

"But if he was born to such rude beginnings," Lirith said, her eyes focused on the fire, "how did he become so powerful?"

"I fear the answer to that question is buried with Morindu beneath the sands of the Morgolthi," Sareth said. "And even when Morindu stood, I do not think many knew the secret of how Orú became as a god.

Perhaps his wife and his seven high priests—certainly no one else. But I do know this. If a river of human blood was required to work a magic, then the same magic might be done with but three drops from Orú's veins.

"Once, the legends say, a hundred sorcerers of Scirath sacrificed themselves at the same moment, driving black knives into their hearts and filling a great pool with their blood—all to work a magic that extended the life of the king of Scirath by ten years." Sareth's eyes gleamed in the firelight. "Ten years—that was what the blood of a hundred sorcerers bought Scirath's king. And by the time Morindu fell during the War of the Sorcerers, Orú had been alive for over three centuries."

Beltan crossed his arms. "So if this Orú was such a great king, why didn't he save his city?"

"He could not," Sareth said. "For you see, he was asleep."

Grace hugged her knees to her chest. "Asleep?"

"Yes, asleep. Even as the centuries passed and his power grew, Orú became harder and harder to rouse. Sometimes he would sleep for days at a time, and he would moan and thrash with great violence, as if caught in the throes of dread nightmares, so that his priests were forced to shackle him to his throne. Then the days became weeks, and the weeks months, until . . ."

"He never woke again," Aryn finished with a shudder.

Sareth nodded. "Ever after, Orú was called the Shackled God, for he dreamed, chained to his throne, while his seven sorcerer-priests ruled in his name. And in time, the seven discovered a terrible and powerful secret. For they pricked Orú's finger and drank his blood, becoming great sorcerers themselves. However, they did not consume all the blood they took from him. Some of it they sealed in jewels of gold."

Understanding crackled through Travis. "Scarabs. That's what scarabs are. Jewels that contain the blood of the god-king Orú."

"Yes," Sareth said. "How a scarab came to be sealed in the tomb of the demon I do not know—only that the *fa'deth* told of it being there. However, there is no relic of Morindu the Dark that is more powerful. Or more dangerous."

A piece of dark wood hissed and fell apart, consumed by fire. At last Vani spoke.

"Sareth, there is a part of this story you have not told us. You were . . . whole when I saw you last." She gazed, not at his face, but at his wooden leg.

He looked down at his hands. "There is no blood more powerful than that of the god-king Orú. The blood of five hundred sorcerers could not equal that contained in one scarab. With a single drop, wonders could be worked. Or . . ."

"The artifact," Grace said. "You wanted to find the scarab so you could use the blood of Orú in the gate artifact and get Vani back from Earth."

Sareth gave a stiff nod. "It was earlier this year, after we had learned that Travis Wilder was here on Eldh, but before he returned to his Earth. I could not . . . I could not bear the thought of you stranded there, Vani, with no hope of . . ."

Tears shone in Sareth's eyes. Vani reached for his hand, held it tight. "I am here now, brother. But you must tell me. What happened to you?"

Roughly, he wiped away his tears. "The elders forbade it, of course, but I defied them and went anyway. Only I did not go alone. Xemeth came with me." Sareth glanced at the others. "As children,

Xemeth and Vani and I were impossible to separate. We did everything together. He was like my brother. Only, when we were older, the cards—"

Vani looked away. Whatever Sareth had been about to say, he swallowed the words.

"So Xemeth went with me to Tarras. From the followers of the Rat God we learned of a crack that ran from one of the sewers deep into the rock beneath the city, one which even they had never dared follow to its end. We descended the crevice, until at last we came to a great cavern. And there . . ."

Sareth's hands began to tremble. He clenched them together but could not stop the shaking. "I cannot tell you exactly what happened in that cavern. Like a nightmare, it is both dim and horribly clear. I saw the scarab, shining like a golden star, resting on an altar. Xemeth started to move toward it. And then . . . a shadow fell over us. A shadow whose center we could not see.

"I think . . . I think the demon was still bound by the old magic. Otherwise I would never have escaped. I felt only a great coldness in my leg, and then I could not walk. But Xemeth . . . he was closer. One moment I saw him, then the shadow grew. There was a great noise, and the ground shook. Then he was . . . gone."

Lirith clamped a hand to her mouth.

"I fled then, like a coward," Sareth rasped. "I dragged myself up the crevice by my hands. How I returned to the sewers beneath Tarras, I do not know. It was only when the people of Geb found me and lifted me up that I realized what I had lost." He brushed his wooden leg. "Our people came for me then, and returned with me to the caravan. I thought they would punish me for my foolishness, but they did not."

"They believed you had been punished enough," Falken said, flexing his black-gloved hand.

Vani folded her arms. "Poor Xemeth. I never got to . . ."

Her words trailed into silence, and Travis thought maybe he understood. As the childhood friends had grown older, he guessed Xemeth had fallen in love with Vani. But it was a love she had not been able to return. Something had prevented her . . . something she had seen in the cards.

"So you think the Scirathi want the scarab," Grace said.

Sareth looked up, the line of his jaw hard. "I know that they do. Even as we have always worked against them, so they have always sought relics of Morindu— and there is none so powerful as a scarab. With it, there is no telling what sort of foul sorceries they might work."

"Like raising Morindu the Dark?" Travis said.

Sareth gave a stiff nod. "Somehow, the Scirathi learned of the demon and the scarab beneath Tarras. Two months ago, one of them attacked me and wrested the gate artifact from me."

"We know," Vani said.

He gazed into the glowing coals. "I had believed that's how they were doing it—how they were feeding the demon. I thought that somehow they must be using the artifact to open gates between the cavern beneath Tarras and the temples of the gods. To pass between worlds takes blood of great power—blood such as that of the being of light Vani told me of, the being who came through the gate with you. But the blood of a sorcerer might be enough to open portals within the city."

Grace frowned. "But wouldn't that be impossible

without the artifact's prism? And Vani had that on Earth."

"Yes, I know that now," Sareth said. "And as it turned out the artifact was taken to Earth anyway. Which leaves only one answer."

This time it was Travis who got it first. "The Scirathi have another gate artifact."

"Yes," Sareth said.

Falken sighed. "So the sorcerers of Scirath are behind all the murders in the city. They've sacrificed gods to the demon in hopes of sating it so they can get past it and gain this scarab. And they've been killing anyone who gets close to discovering what they're doing."

For a moment sorrow flickered across Melia's visage, then her expression grew hard. "They will not succeed. We will not let them."

"But how?" Grace said. "How are we going to stop them if they have a demon on their side?"

A cool tingling passed through Travis. Once again words whispered in his mind.

To choose what it shall be. . . .

He didn't know how, only that it had to be so, that this was the reason it had let itself be captured and carried across worlds to him. Carefully, he drew the Stone out of his pocket. It shone dully on his hand, seeming to absorb the firelight. Sinfathisar. The Stone of Twilight.

"We're going to do it with this," he said.

72

Lirith stepped from the back of the wagon in which she had slept and breathed in the moist scent of dawn. White-gold light stole among the circle of *ithaya*, and the tall trees swayed in a wind that swept off the sea. Gulls circled in the sky, their calls drifting down like the faint voices of ghosts.

Last night, when she had stumbled into the wagon to sleep, she had been too weary to really look at the craft. Now she saw that the wagon was shaped like a toad. She was grateful it was not a spider.

She left the wagon's steps, and her bare feet sank into the dewy grass. A sharp, clean scent rose from it. She moved among the trees until she could see it far below: the white towers and gold domes of Tarras. They gleamed brilliant and perfect in the dawnlight.

No, not perfect. From the city, several thin, dark lines rose into the sky. Tarras was burning. Only in a few places, yet to Lirith it meant one thing: the darkness and confusion they had glimpsed in the city was growing. How many people had abandoned their hearths, their businesses, their loved ones to drink the Elixir of the Past and stare at the sun with blind eyes? But maybe it didn't matter; maybe soon there would be no city and no people left to worry about. Lirith hugged herself against the wind. To her eyes, the lines of smoke looked like black threads reaching toward the sky.

She hesitated, then shut her eyes and reached out with the Touch. Yes, she could see it: the tangle in the fabric of the Weirding. It seethed and grew as she watched, and sickness welled up in her. All the same, she forced herself to look closer, to peer into the heart of the tangle.

There, she could see it, or rather sense it: the black void at the center. Even as she watched, a thread was drawn close to the tangle—then flashed and was gone. So it was doing more than merely entangling the threads of the Weirding. It was eating them.

But, after what she had learned last night, that only made sense. That the demon was the source of the tangle in the Weirding as well as the change in the garden of the gods there could be no doubt. Yet why had Lirith first seen the knot all the way back in Artolor?

Think, sister. What happened that day you first glimpsed the tangle? The guard came to your door, waking you. It was . . .

It was the day Melia had arrived at Ar-tolor.

Yes, it all makes sense. Melia has been getting lost in thoughts of the past, and the moment she arrived at Ar-tolor, the same thing began happening to you, sister. And now it is happening to the people of Tarras, even as the other gods become caught in the web of the past.

Lirith supposed the tangle she saw in the Weirding was simply a vision—a construct of her ability with the Sight, one which strove to give form and shape to the peril she had been sensing. But why was the demon causing Melia and the other gods—as well as people near to them—to mix past, present, and future? It was as if the demon was unraveling not just the threads of the Weirding, but the very fabric of time itself.

Lirith sighed. These were questions she could not answer, but she resolved to ask the others. That was, if there was time. For last night, by the dying light of the fire, they had forged what seemed to Lirith a desperate plan.

I think I'm supposed to go beneath the city, Travis had said. *I think that's why the fairy used its blood to fill the gate artifact again. It wants me to go through, take Sinfathisar, and stop the demon before it gets loose.*

We'll need to distract the Scirathi, Sareth had said. *They will be keeping watch on the cavern where the demon is imprisoned. Your magic Stone will do you no good if you never manage to get near the demon. We need to keep the sorcerers as far away from you as possible.*

I believe Emperor Ephesian will help us in that regard, Melia had said, her eyes gleaming. *Whether he wishes to or not.*

It was Grace who had finally spoken the question on all their minds. *How, Travis? How can you use Sinfathisar to stop the demon?*

I don't have that one entirely figured out, Grace, he had said with a wry smile. *But the fairy seems to think the Stone can do it. And I did use Sinfathisar to seal the Rune Gate. I'll have to believe it can do this as well.*

They had gone to bed then, Sareth and Vani showing them to different wagons where they could sleep. However, Lirith had had one more conversation before she let sleep come, speaking in the dark with Aryn as they lay in the wagon. They had spoken without words—nor had they included Grace in their conversation, for she had fallen at once into the profound sleep of exhaustion. Besides, Lirith did not know how they were going to tell Grace that the Pattern required her to betray her friend.

Except Grace wasn't at the High Coven, sister, Aryn had spoken in her mind. *She isn't part of the Pattern.*

That was true, only Lirith didn't understand what it meant, not fully. She would have to consider it later. Right now there other matters at hand.

We must send word of Travis Wilder's arrival to Ivalaine at the first opportunity. That much the Pattern requires.

Lirith had sensed the hesitation on the other end of the thread. She felt it herself.

I know, sister. You are not the only one who was joyous to see Travis—then despaired at the sight of him. I still find it hard to believe he would seek to harm Eldh. In everything I have seen him do, he is a kind and gentle man. But he has power, great power. That much neither of us can deny.

But what do we do, Lirith?

Just what I have said. The Pattern requires only that we send word back to Ivalaine and that we watch him. No matter how he might threaten Eldh in the future, right now Travis is the only one who has a chance of preventing the demon's escape, and we must not hinder him in this.

But what if he makes a mistake, sister? What if he accidentally allows the demon to escape, and that's how Eldh is destroyed?

Lirith had not considered that. However, she knew the perils of interpreting prophecy. Sometimes, in trying to avoid what was foretold, one could cause it to happen.

No, Aryn, we will take no action other than what we were commanded. We will send a missive to Ivalaine as soon as we can, and we will watch Travis. That is all.

And how will we tell Grace?

Good night, sister, Lirith had said. *You will need your sleep.*

But she had slept little, and when she did she dreamed of pushing Travis Wilder into the tangle in the Weirding while a man and a woman cried out in dismay. The man was Beltan, of course; he loved Travis. At first she thought the woman to be Grace, but then she saw that the other had eyes of gold. Before she could look closer, the threads tangled around Travis, drawing him into the dark center of the tangle, and in an instant he was gone. Except the tangle kept growing until it devoured everything, including Lirith herself.

Now, somewhere behind her, she heard the sounds of voices. The Mournish were beginning to stir. The others would be up soon. Lirith turned.

"Hello, *beshala*," Sareth said, his brown-gold eyes soft in the morning light.

Lirith lifted a hand to clutch the spider charm at her throat, but any words she might have spoken were stolen away by the wind. Above, gulls cried.

She must have walked right past him. He leaned against the trunk of an *ithaya* tree, wearing his billowing pants and open vest. The morning light shone off the bronzed skin of his chest, and the wind tousled his black hair. In his hand he held a card. A *T'hot* card. She could not see its face.

Last night, in the darkness, she had been able to forget how handsome he was. Not now. She felt weak at the sight of him. Then her eyes drifted down to the leg that ended not in flesh but wood. His lips twisted in a grimace. He dragged his wooden leg back.

Lirith looked up in horror. She didn't mean to make him hide his leg. It was part of him, like his fine hands, or the sparse, pointed beard on his chin. She would change none of it. Again she tried to speak but could not.

This is foolishness, sister. Tell him. Tell him what you are feeling!

"It brings good luck, the old women say," he said in his deep, thrumming voice.

She tilted her head, confused. He pointed to the spider charm, which she still gripped.

Lirith let her hand fall from the charm. "Do they? I'm not sure that it has."

Last night, Vani had told how the Scirathi used magical spiders of gold to poison those they wished to kill. That was how they had murdered Orsith. And she had seen them in her dreams. . . .

It seemed he sensed her thoughts. "No, do not let the work of the Scirathi decide what you believe. It is as a mockery that the sorcerers of Scirath use spiders to work their evil. For in Morindu, spiders were held to be sacred. And so my people still consider them. In our legends, they are the weavers that bind the world together."

Lirith sighed. "We had thought it was Sif who was behind the murders, because we found one of the spiders where the priest Orsith was slain. But that was just coincidence, wasn't it?"

"Maybe not entirely. I imagine the Scirathi saw in the arachnid god an opportunity to mislead and confuse any who sought to discover the source of the murders."

Lirith nodded, but it was not of spiders that she wished to speak.

"I have heard . . ." Her voice faltered, and she moistened her lips. "I have heard it said that outsiders are never allowed to marry into the clans of the Mournish."

Sareth stared past her, motionless. "What you have heard is true."

The words were a dagger, but one she had known was coming. She turned away to hide the wound that surely had appeared in her breast. "I see."

But maybe it didn't matter. Who was she to think a man would marry her? She recalled the dream, how Sareth had turned to stone in her arms. For her, was not the dream already true? A man would find no warmth within her, no life. No children.

A rustling behind her. She smelled clean sweat and spices, and her throat went dry. A warmth touched the back of her neck: the breath of a man.

"*Beshala . . .*" he whispered.

She closed her eyes. "You keep saying that word, but I don't know it. What does it mean?"

"In the tongue of my people, it means *beloved.*"

A gasp escaped Lirith; it was a sound of pain. She turned, searching his face for answers. "No, it can't be. *Beshala.* I remember—that was what you called me in Ar-tolor, the first moment you saw me."

His eyes were solemn. "So I did."

"But . . ."

"What man of the Mournish does not know his fate when he sees it? *Beshala.*"

They stood like the trees, swaying in the wind as the gulls called out above them. Then slowly, against the wind, they bent toward one another.

"Lirith, there you are!"

She stumbled back, looked up. Grace walked between the sunleaf trees toward them, Travis at her side. Lirith felt her cheeks glowing hotly, and Sareth moved hastily away. However, if either Travis or Grace had noticed anything, they did not say.

And nor was there anything to notice, sister. You heard his words. Whatever his fate, he can never marry an outsider. And you know what fate holds for you. The Raven . . .

"Melia is up," Travis said. "She wants everyone to get together. Now."

Grace gave an apologetic shrug. "I tried to tell her that no one is saving any world before *maddok*, but you know how she gets."

"Indeed," Lirith said in a voice she hoped sounded light and casual. Again she wondered how she was going to tell Grace what the Witches had decided about Travis Wilder.

"Lirith?" Travis cocked his head, gazing at her.

"Yes?"

"You were staring at me. What? Is my hair a mess? Oh, wait." He rubbed his bald head and grinned.

"Forgive me," she said. "I'm not . . . I'm not quite awake yet."

Travis only nodded in agreement, but Grace studied her with questioning eyes. Fortunately, before Lirith felt compelled to start babbling about everything the Witches had decided, Travis spoke again.

"Good morning, Sareth. What have you got there?" Travis gestured to the card in Sareth's hand.

"Perhaps you can tell me. When I rose this morning, I drew a card from my al-Mama's deck to see what the day holds."

He turned the card over. Lirith clapped a hand to her mouth. The card showed a man pierced in the back with three swords.

Travis winced. "I have to say, that doesn't seem like a very good sign."

"No," Sareth said. "It does not. This card signifies treachery. I would say there is betrayal ahead of us this day."

"But by whom?" Grace said.

Lirith crossed her arms and turned away. "We had better not keep Lady Melia waiting."

73.

It was midmorning, and the white sun was bright on white walls as they moved along the main avenue that led up through the five circles of Tarras.

"All right," Travis muttered, "am I the only one who feels just a little bit less than inconspicuous?"

He adjusted his new garb: knee-length trousers, loose white shirt, and a red vest embroidered with yellow thread. A scarf covered his bald head, and his silver earrings only added to the effect. Were it not for his pale, still-new skin, he would have passed perfectly as a Mournish man.

Back at the caravan, Sareth and Vani had given all of them new clothes to wear.

It is simply a precaution, Sareth had said. *We are less likely to draw undue attention from the Scirathi if we appear to be only a simple band of Mournish come to the city to tell fates and sell trinkets.*

Grace's attire was not so different from Travis's. She was taller than everyone in their group save Beltan and Travis, and none of the clothes of the Mournish women had fit her. Her ash-blond hair was drawn up beneath a floppy, brimless hat. Vani had even given her a short sword to wear at her hip. The others all wore brilliant colors and gleaming jewelry. Even Durge, who had submitted to trimming his mustaches short and keeping the whiskers on his chin in the Mournish style—albeit not without some grumbling. However, when Aryn mentioned that he looked ten winters younger, his grumbling had ceased.

"At least it's working," Grace said in answer to Travis's complaint. "Look. Nobody is even coming near us."

"Well, can you blame them? Marji would have arrested us in a second for high crimes against fashion."

Grace sighed, then touched her embroidered vest. "No, I think she might have liked it."

The more she thought about it, the more Grace realized how good Sareth's decision to disguise them was. The Scirathi hated the Mournish, but they also held the Vagabond Folk in contempt. They would care little about a ragtag band who came to the city to scrounge a few coins. Instead, the sorcerers would be watching for Melia and Falken as well as Lirith, Durge, and Aryn. And there was no way the sorcerers could know Travis, Grace, and Vani were in the city.

Except, as they went, Grace began to think it wasn't simply their disguise that let them pass without notice. Lirith was right. The people of Tarras seemed dazed and distracted. Many of them wore looks of open confusion, standing in the middle of the street, holding a bucket or a child or a basket of goods, as if they had absolutely no idea what they were supposed to be doing next. Then there were the people slumped against walls, flies crawling over their purple-stained lips, empty cups in their hands. Yet it didn't make sense—Lirith had said there was nothing magic in this so-called Elixir of the Past.

It's the demon, Grace. That thing is the source of everything that's changing in this city. But how is it entangling Melia and the gods in the past, along with the people close to them?

Grace didn't know. And while she had been a world away from Melia and the other gods, every day the remains of the past seemed more real to her, and the present more like a parade of ghosts.

They reached the Second Circle of the city. From what Grace had gleaned, this was the holy district. She had never believed in gods on Earth, and even here on Eldh, where the gods were real and present, she was still not certain what she thought of them. They were at once weaker and more dangerous than she would have imagined. All the same, there was a grandeur to the temples of white stone she could not deny. Above them rose a great blue dome. That must be the Etherion that Melia had mentioned.

When they reached the gate to the First Circle, they found its gilded doors tightly shut. It seemed the emperor had not had a change of heart.

Melia adjusted the veil that concealed her face, then glided toward a smaller red door set into the wall near the gate. She knocked on the red door once, twice, then a third time. She started to thrust both hands before her, and Grace had the feeling she was about to blast the door to pieces when the top half of it swung open to reveal a thick-necked soldier in a bronze breastplate.

"Please inform the Minister of Gates that I require his presence," Melia said pleasantly.

"The Minister is seeing no one without an appointment today."

"Forgive me." Melia laid her hand on the soldier's arm. "I can see you're quite stupid, so let me put it in simple words. I *will* speak with the Minister."

The soldier blinked. "Of course, Your Holiness. As I said, I will fetch the Minister at once."

The door shut. Grace was about to ask Melia exactly

what she had done—was it something that might be reproduced with the Touch?—when the door flew open again. The Minister of Gates was a strikingly handsome and opulently attired man of an age with Grace or Travis. His beard shone with oil, and gems glittered on his fingers. He took one look at Melia and the rest of them, then frowned, the expression stealing all the beauty from his face.

"I know not why thieves and vagabonds are tolerated in this city," he said in a voice rich with disdain. "But I know they are certainly not welcome in the shadow of the emperor's palace."

Melia folded back the veil, revealing her face. "It is true I am something of a wanderer, Minister. However, this city has been my home for nearly two thousand years. I do not think it is your place to tell me I am not welcome here."

The Minister's eyes went wide—then quickly narrowed again. "Lady Melindora. Forgive my rudeness. I did not recognize you in such . . . rustic attire. However, I must inform you that the emperor has not changed his mind regarding your petition. If you would let me know where I might send a message, then I will inform you the moment the emperor ends his mourning period."

"No, Minister," Melia said, voice cool, "you will open these gates at once and see us to the emperor." She made a subtle motion with her hand.

The blood drained from the Minister's face. "Do not dare play your tricks on me. If you try, I will call on Misar, my god, and you will be taken before the Etherion for your action. Even you are not above the gods, Melindora."

"Go right ahead. I'll be very curious to hear what Misar has to say about this."

The man gripped an amulet shaped like a gold feather that hung by a chain around his check. "I swear by Misar, I'll do it!"

Melia folded her arms. "I'm waiting."

The Minister squeezed the amulet, fingers going white, then shut his eyes as if to pray.

He screamed, then let go of the amulet and staggered back. The red imprint of the amulet was clear on his palm. It was already blistering.

"Misar has forsaken you!" Melia exclaimed. "What evil have you done to deserve this? No, I do not care to know. Let us in, or I'll see to it that all the gods spurn you as Misar has done. None will heed your prayers, and when you die your bones will be left for the vultures to pick. There will be no salvation for you after death, Minister, only eternal loneliness and pain!"

Such was the force of Melia's words that even Grace shuddered. The Minister babbled gibberish, then turned and shrieked something down a corridor. The red door slammed shut, and a moment later, with a grinding sound, one of the huge gilded doors swung open.

"This way everyone," Melia said with a pleasant smile.

The Minister was nowhere to be seen on the other side of the gate, but there was a quartet of soldiers waiting to lead them to the emperor. They followed the soldiers across tiled plazas and past pools in which swam jewel-colored fish.

"What happened back there, Melia?" Falken said in a low voice. "Did Misar really forsake the Minister of Gates?"

"More than that," Melia answered. "Did you see the way the holy symbol burned him? Misar has placed a malediction on the man."

"A malediction?" Grace asked.

"It's a sort of curse, dear," Melia said. "The gods use it rarely—and only for those who have committed a horrible crime, something that goes against everything the god in question stands for."

What crime had the Minister done? Before Grace could ask more, the soldiers halted at a set of ornate doors almost as large as the gate of the First Circle. A huge white edifice rose above them, crowned by a dome that gleamed gold in the sunlight. To either side of the door hung white banners embroidered with the symbols of three trees and five stars.

One of the soldiers turned toward Melia. "I will inform the emperor you are here, Your Holiness."

"Thank you, dear, but that won't be necessary."

The small lady raised her arms. For a moment a blue nimbus shimmered around her hands, then the doors swung inward. Before the soldiers could react, Melia swept through, and the others hastily followed. They found themselves in a space so vast it took Grace several moments just to arrive at any sense of scale. Those specks on the far side were actually people.

Melia was already gliding across the white floor. Grace hurried to catch up. Cream-colored cats darted to and fro across their path. The felines looked so soft Grace had the desire to pick one up and stroke it. She resisted. For all she knew, petting the emperor's cats was a crime punishable by removal of the offending hand, if not more. Grace noticed that many of the cats seemed to be following after Melia in a soft, undulating throng.

After a full minute of walking, the specks on the far side of the hall finally resolved into recognizable figures, and Grace was dumbstruck for a second time.

On a throne of white marble veined with gold sat a

man who could only be the emperor, for he was nearly as large as an empire himself. His loose white tunic draped but did not conceal the great, rolling mounds of flesh that made up his body. Arms as big around as Grace's waist rested on the sides of the throne, and legs like tree trunks ended in surprisingly dainty, sandaled feet. The emperor's head—which seemed far too small given the size of the rest of him—perched upon several folds of flesh that might once have formed a neck. His face was round but surprisingly well shaped, and his eyes were intelligent—although there was a dullness to them as well. On his head sat a lopsided crown of gold *ithaya* leaves.

Surrounding the emperor on the dais were—what? His servants? His slaves? The palace prostitutes? The only thing Grace could be certain of was that, to a one they were young, beautiful, and—if one didn't count jewelry—quite naked. A pair of unclothed young men fanned the emperor, their oiled flesh gleaming, while several maidens tried to entice Ephesian with fruits that were only slightly less ripe than their bare breasts. More of the young things plucked out music on harps, or danced for the emperor's pleasure.

And when they move together like that, I don't think you can call it just dancing, Grace.

Cheeks warm, she turned away, only to see that all the men in their party were staring. It looked as if she was going to have to use a scarf to tie Durge's jaw back into proper position.

Unlike Grace's male companions, the emperor hardly seemed to see the firm, oiled flesh writhing around him. He held a cup of wine loosely, as if forgotten, in one of his hands. Grace began to think she understood the dullness in his half-shut eyes. It was boredom.

"Your Magnificence," Melia said, "it is so good to see you."

The emperor sat up a bit. For a moment he frowned in confusion, squinting as he peered forward. Then all at once the dullness left his eyes, replaced by a bright light.

"By all the gods, Melindora Nightsilver!"

The emperor's voice was not what Grace had expected: It was a clear, lovely tenor.

"At your service, Your Magnificence," Melia said with an elegant curtsy Grace could never have matched in a thousand years. All the same, she found herself following suit as she and the others paid obeisance.

Ephesian gestured for them to rise. "This is the first interesting thing to happen all day. And here is Falken Blackhand with you. Up to your usual mischief, are you, my melancholy bard? Ruined any more kingdoms lately? And these are some friends of yours? They're not really Mournish, are they, Melindora? They don't look it, save for those two there. Brother and sister, are they? And maybe that dark one. And have you all just arrived in Tarras?"

Grace got the impression Ephesian didn't really expect anyone to answer his questions. All the same, Melia managed to interject an answer.

"No, Your Magnificence. We've been in the city some time."

"What?" Ephesian slammed a meaty hand against the arm of his throne. A few of the naked young things jumped. "And you've only just now come to me? What have you been doing all this time, Melindora? Can something else possibly be more pressing than paying a visit to me, your beloved emperor?"

Again Melia deftly interposed an answer between his

questions. "I did try, Your Magnificence. However, the Minister of Gates said you had rejected my petition to see you."

"Nonsense! The Minister told me of no such petition."

"After my encounter with him a short while ago, that does not surprise me, Your Magnificence."

Ephesian glowered. "Well, I thank you for giving me something intriguing to do, Melindora. I shall get to the bottom of this."

He snapped chubby fingers, and a soldier stepped forward. Grace had not noticed him before, but now that she looked she saw that a score of soldiers ringed the throne room. She supposed this was necessary for the emperor's protection. All the same, it made this feel less like a palace than it did a prison.

"Go fetch the Minister of Gates," the emperor said to the soldier, who bowed and ran from the throne room.

"You will partake of refreshments while we wait," Ephesian said.

Several of the nubile maidens descended the dais. Durge's eyes bulged, and Grace wondered if the stalwart knight was on the verge of a coronary.

Lirith touched his arm. "He means wine, Durge."

The knight sagged in visible relief, and accepted a cup from one of the maidens. Aryn clapped a hand to her mouth to stifle a laugh.

A well-shaped young man gave Beltan a cup of wine. The blond knight grinned. "A fellow could get used to this."

"I think that's the problem, Beltan," Grace said quietly. "He *has* gotten used to it."

On the throne, the emperor let out a groan as several of the maidens tangled their fingers through his hair.

He batted them away.

"Begone with you! All of you! Starting tomorrow, I'm going back to eunuchs. They're dull as stones, but at least they don't giggle all the time."

Lirith hesitated, then approached the dais, where she curtsied nearly as elegantly as Melia.

"Forgive me, Your Magnificence."

The emperor glared at her. "Why should I forgive you, girl? Have you insulted me?"

"Just a precautionary apology, Your Magnificence."

Ephesian laughed. "I like this one, Melia. She's clever. Can I have her?"

"I fear she's not mine to grant."

"Too bad. Well, go on, girl, you've made your apologies. I'm in a good mood at the sight of Melindora, so I'm quite likely not to have you flogged for your insolence."

Lirith swallowed. "I just thought I might make a suggestion, Your Magnificence. If all of this"—she gestured to the bodies clustered around the throne—"this decadence and indulgence has grown tedious to you, you might consider an alternative."

The emperor rested his hands on the shelf of his stomach. "An alternative? Such as what?"

"Well, such as virtue and morality."

Ephesian mouthed these words as if they had been spoken in a foreign tongue. "Virtue and morality? Let me be certain that I understand you, girl. You mean, give up indulging in wine and food and sex?"

"You don't have to give them up, Your Magnificence. Not entirely. Just partake of them in moderation."

"Moderation?" The emperor clapped his hands together, eyes shining. "Yes, moderation. How positively perverse! People will be absolutely disgusted—I adore it. Please, you must tell me more about this *virtue*, as you call it. It's a northern concept, no? All wind and stone and icy water up there, I hear. It twists men into deviants, right?"

Lirith opened her mouth to answer, but at that moment the soldier the emperor had dispatched earlier sprinted across the throne room to kneel before the dais.

Ephesian scowled. "I thought I told you to fetch me the Minister. Yet I do not see him."

"Forgive me, Your Magnificence," the soldier said. "I could not bring the Minister to you."

"And why not?"

"Because the Minister is dead, Your Magnificence."

Grace felt her heart skip in her chest.

"Dead?" Ephesian said with a frown. "But how? I don't recall ordering his execution today."

"It was poison by the look of it, Your Magnificence. And we found something with him. Something strange."

These words sent a jolt through Grace. No, it couldn't be.

"Well, what is it?" Ephesian demanded.

The soldier held out a hand. On it, crumpled but still recognizable, was a spider made out of gold.

74.

Ephesian peered forward, squinting as Melia and Falken described what they had learned about the murdered gods. The nubile maidens and pretty young men had all been sent away—in search of some clothes, Grace hoped.

"Is this all true, Melindora?" Ephesian said, scowling. "You knew what faction was behind the deaths of Ondo, Geb, and Sif, as well as the vile attacks on my city's temples, and yet you did not tell me?"

"Please recall, Your Magnificence," Melia said as one might speak to a dear but somewhat trying child, "prior to today, the Minister of Gates refused me entry to the First Circle, nor did he bring you my petitions."

"And I think now we know the reason why," Falken said. "The Minister must have allied himself with the Scirathi. These sorcerers didn't want you to know the truth about the murdered gods, Your Magnificence, and they were keeping anyone who might be able to warn you from entering your palace. But the god Misar must have discovered the Minister's treachery. And when the Minister finally did let us inside, the Scirathi rewarded him at once. With death."

Ephesian gripped a jewel-encrusted goblet. "This is unacceptable. I do not tolerate deception and treachery in this city—unless I am the source of it. I wish the Minister wasn't already dead so I could have him executed myself in some suitably horrible manner." He started to lift his cup to his lips, then wrinkled his nose, lowered the cup, and sighed.

Melia drifted up the first step of the dais. "Is something amiss, Your Magnificence?"

"Nothing, Melindora." His expression one of disgust, the emperor tossed the cup to the floor. Crimson wine spilled across the white stone like blood. "Except that it seems others have to tell me what is going on in my own empire."

"But it's a large and great empire, Your Magnificence."

Ephesian grimaced. "Yes, so my advisors tell me over and over. Yet I am not quite so soft and dull as they believe they have made me. I know that my empire has receded over the years even as my girth has expanded." He adjusted his crown with a pudgy hand. "Well, perhaps it's time I paid less attention to my vices and more to the concerns of my empire."

Lirith gave an approving nod. "You'll find that's one of the happy side effects of virtue, Your Magnificence. It leaves your mind and your schedule clear for so many other things."

"Is that so?" Ephesian said, rubbing his chin. "Absolutely fascinating. I command you to tell me more about this *virtue* of yours."

Melia ascended another step. "Your Magnificence . . ."

Another massive, imperial sigh. "Yes, yes, Melindora. I can see quite well this is not a social visit. The gods forbid you ever come to Tarras simply to pay your beloved emperor a simple, polite obeisance. Out with it then. What do you need?"

"The Dome of the Etherion," Melia said. "Just for the day. Oh, and soldiers. Lots of them."

The emperor cocked his head, then his rubbery lips curved in a smile. "Well, this is turning out to be an interesting day after all."

A short while later they gathered in what Ephesian had referred to as, "a modest side chamber where you can wait while Melindora's requests are prepared." Evidently, on an imperial scale, *modest* meant something the size of a warehouse. They rattled around the vast, marble-columned hall, frequently losing sight of one another along with all sense of direction.

There was no sign of Lirith yet. She had remained in the throne room so Ephesian could question her on the foreign but intriguing concepts of *morality* and *decency*. Grace's last glimpse of the two had revealed Lirith sitting on the top step of the dais, speaking cheerfully, while the emperor gazed forward with shining eyes, rubbing his jowls and chuckling.

Then again, perhaps it was not such a wonder the emperor was ready for a change.

He's myopic, Grace. You saw the way he squinted at whoever was speaking. And that's why all those naked young things were so uninteresting to him. He couldn't really see them.

There was no way she could make a pair of glasses for the emperor on this world. All the same, she had a feeling Lirith was helping Ephesian see in other ways.

Grace strolled through slanting beams of light, some distance from the others. These last days had been so jarring. It felt good to be quiet, if just for a moment. She glanced down at the wine cup in her hand; it was empty. Grace walked toward a servant who stood on the far side of the hall.

Then jogged. Then ran.

By the time she reached the other side of the hall her heart was pounding, her lungs were heaving, and there was absolutely no sign of either servant or wine. The others were small shadows in the distance. There was nothing to do but head toward them and hope she made it back before she expired.

Just take it slow, Grace. You'd think with all this dashing between worlds you'd be in better shape.

She was halfway across the hall when she noticed a statue she must have passed in her vain attempt to get more wine. It was the statue of a man, half again larger than life. Grace wasn't exactly certain what made her stop and gaze at it. The statue seemed out of place here. But perhaps that was what made it so compelling.

Unlike the smooth, white marble all around, this was hewn of rough, gray stone. All the same, there was a vividness to it that brought life to the subject. The man was clearly a warrior of some sort, dressed for battle, holding a massive sword in his hand. There was a crudeness to his garb—the stone cleverly carved to suggest leather, fur, bone, and beaten plates of steel— as well as a wildness to his sharp features and shaggy hair that lent him a rough, wolfish look. All the same, he was handsome. More than handsome—imposing. This was a man others would kneel before. Then Grace noticed the circlet resting on his brow, and she knew this man had been a king.

Except that didn't make sense. Tarras had emperors, not kings, and Grace had a feeling none of them had ever looked this barbaric. The statue was chipped and worn; it was clearly very old.

"What have you found here, Grace?" a musical voice said behind her. "Well, look at that."

Only as Falken spoke did Grace realize she had been staring at the statue. How long had she been standing there? She turned toward Falken. The others were drifting in her direction as well.

"What a king he must have been," the bard said softly.

So Grace had been right. "Who was he, Falken?"

"It's Lord Ulther, the king of Toringarth a thousand years ago. I think you know his story, Grace—how he and Elsara, Empress of Tarras, worked together to defeat the Pale King in the War of the Stones." Falken stepped closer to the statue. "So that's what Fellring looks like. I've always wondered. I had always believed its likeness was never recorded before it was shattered. But Elsara must have commissioned this statue of him when he came to Tarras to beg her aid."

Grace felt strange, light. The warm, spicy air was suddenly stuffy and cloying. "Fellring?"

"Yes, that's the name of Ulther's sword. Do you see?" Falken pointed to the blade gripped in the statue's hand. "It's writ with runes of power."

Grace's attention had been on the statue's face; she had hardly glanced at the sword. Now she did—

—and the floor fell away from her feet as the world went white.

When her vision finally cleared, she saw faces hovering above her. Falken, Melia, Travis, and the others as well. At last the ringing in her ears receded, and she could hear voices.

"—you all right, Grace?" Travis was saying.

"Please, dear," Melia said, her amber eyes concerned. "Can you speak to us?"

Two more voices sounded in Grace's mind, weaving together as one. *Sister, what is wrong?*

All this attention made Grace acutely uncomfortable. She managed to disentangle herself and stand.

"I'm all right." Except that wasn't true. At the

moment, she was anything but all right. She was . . . But she didn't know anymore. Perhaps she never had.

"You're the doctor, Grace," Travis said, his gray eyes intent, "but even I know people don't keel over when nothing's wrong with them. What's going on?"

There was no point in hiding. Besides, she wanted to see—had to see—if she was right. With shaking fingers, she drew a piece of paper from her pocket and unfolded it. It was the drawing Deirdre had given her before they stepped through the gate.

The drawing of a sword.

There could be no doubt about it—even she could see that the runes were identical—and by Falken's oath he saw it as well.

The bard looked at Grace, blue eyes stunned. "I don't understand, Grace. How can you have a drawing of Fellring?"

"Not . . . just a drawing, Falken." Shaking now, she reached beneath the loose-fitting Mournish shirt and drew out her necklace.

Usually she kept it hidden, a secret relic of the childhood she had never known. She supposed, for all their time together, Melia and Falken had never seen her necklace before.

Falken actually staggered, his hand to his chest. "It can't be. By the Seven, it can't."

Beltan groaned. "Enough mysteriousness, Falken. Would you please be kind enough to explain to the rest of us exactly what it *isn't* supposed to be? I think we'd all like to be shocked, too."

Vani's gaze was half-lidded, curious. "It is a shard of the sword, is it not? The blade the statue holds."

"The shard of Fellring," Falken murmured. "But how can it be?"

Grace was struggling for understanding herself. The

air seemed to throb around her, and her mind was buzzing.

"I've always had this," she said, gripping the pendant. "I was wearing the necklace when the people from the orphanage found me. I don't remember it, but I couldn't have been more than three years old at the time."

"But that's impossible. I know it is. The only person who could possess that necklace as a child would be—"

"Would be Ulther's last descendant and heir," Melia said.

Falken and the others stared at Grace as if she had suddenly sprouted wings. Grace struggled for words but found she had none, so she struggled for understanding instead. According to Melia, the man in the statue— King Ulther of Toringarth—was her great-thirty-something-times-over-grandfather. Which meant, all this time, she was not from Earth at all. She was from . . .

Travis's voice was soft with wonder. "You're from Eldh, Grace."

No, it couldn't be true.

Except it was, and she knew it. Three years old, alone on the side of a mountain, and all she had was a piece of his sword. That and a fragment of a song she had heard as an infant. A song from another world. Her world.

And farewell words too often part . . .

"With Fellring sword of Elfin art," Grace murmured aloud.

Melia caught Grace's hands in her own, beaming with joy.

"Welcome home, Ralena."

75.

Grace listened, utterly numb, as Falken and Melia told a tale—*her* tale—describing how for centuries they had, in secret, kept watch over the heirs of the lost kingdom of Malachor. At some point Lirith must have come from the throne room, although Grace didn't see when. All at once she was simply aware that Lirith was there, eyes shining as she gazed at Grace.

"I don't understand, Falken," Beltan said when at last the bard paused in his telling. "All the old stories I've ever heard say that the royal line of Malachor was completely wiped out when Malachor fell, that no heirs survived."

"You're right, Beltan," Falken said, gazing at his black-gloved hand. "That *is* what the stories say. That's what I wanted the stories to say when I wrote them down seven centuries ago."

His words seemed important, but Grace's brain was too dull to comprehend what the bard was saying.

"I think maybe I understand," Travis said. "One member of the royal line of Malachor *did* survive, only you and Melia didn't want anyone to know about it."

Falken's wolfish visage was haggard, as if the centuries suddenly weighed heavy upon him. "It was the king and queen's only child, their infant son. With a knife I cut him crying from her womb where she lay dead—only a day after the king himself was slain."

Lirith moved closer. "You were afraid those who had murdered the king and queen would kill their child as well."

"But how did it all happen?" Aryn said, blue eyes questioning. "The stories say that Malachor fell, but they never really say how. Only that you—"

Melia cast a sharp glance at the young baroness, and Aryn hastily bit her tongue. However, Grace knew what she had been about to say.

That you were the reason the kingdom fell.

"No, my lady, that is not a tale I will tell today." The bard looked up, and his wolfish visage brightened. "Nor does it matter, not now. Not when you've come back to us, Ralena."

At last Grace managed to find her voice. "Why do you keep calling me Ralena?"

Melia smiled. "Because it's your name, dear. At least, it's the name your parents gave you."

These words were like a blow to the center of Grace's chest. "My parents? You knew them?"

"Yes, dear, quite well in fact." Melia sighed. "They were so young, so bright—sometimes around them I felt as if I were still only a thousand years old."

Durge's eyes bulged, and even Grace felt a mad impulse to laugh. But the feeling passed as sorrow filled Melia's gaze.

"What happened?" she whispered.

It was Falken who answered. "Raiff and Anilena— your parents, Grace—were married young. Too young, Melia and I both thought at the time, but I believe they felt some urgency in the matter. You see, Anilena was at the time the sole living heir to Malachor—the direct descendant of the last king and queen. Her parents had died young, her mother while giving birth to her, and her father while out boar hunting only a year after."

Melia touched Falken's arm. "He let the beast take him, Falken. You know it's true. He could not bear to live without his beloved."

The bard laid his hand over hers. "It fell to Melia and me to raise Anilena as best we could. It was not the first time, over the centuries, we had seen a child of the line of Malachor to adulthood, but never had we raised one from such a tender age, and so Anilena was special to us.

"Of course, we did have help. Gevriel Warden dwelled with us, along with his two sons. Gevriel was of the family of wardens who had served the kings of Malachor, for the line endured after the kingdom fell. Always there was at least one warden to keep watch over the current heir. At the time when Anilena was a child, we were all living in southern Calavan, in a small manor near the banks of the River Goldwine."

"It was so beautiful there," Melia said quietly. "I shall never forget the light on the river at sunset."

Grace forced herself to breathe. "Did she . . . did Anilena know who she was?"

"Not at first, dear," Melia said. "We wanted her to grow up as any child might. She did know her parents had died, and she thought of us as her aunt and uncle. Then, on her eighteenth birthday, we gave her the necklace you wear now, and we told her the truth. At first she was angry, but in a short time she was able to accept the burden that had been placed upon her." Melia reached out and touched Grace's hand. "Ever were the women of your line strong, dear."

Grace had to resist the urge to pull back.

"And don't forget willful," Falken added. "Not a month after we told her of her heritage, Anilena ran off and married Raiff, the elder of Gevriel Warden's two sons. In truth, I'm surprised it took that long before the two lines were united. Regardless, Anilena loved him, and it seemed she was determined to produce an heir as soon as possible. In case something dire happened."

"And it did," Durge said in a grim voice.

Now it was Falken who seemed to lose his tongue.

"Black knights," Melia said. "It was four years later. Anilena and Raiff were so happy together, and happy with their daughter Ralena—with you, Grace. Then one day, Falken and I took a short journey to Gendarra, to pay a visit to our old friend Tome, who was there at the time. We took you with us, for Tome had never seen you, and Raiff and Anilena had promised him they would let you visit him. You were just three winters old. To be certain we were safe, Anilena and Raiff sent Merric Warden with us—he was Gevriel's other son, and Raiff's young brother."

"As it turned out," Falken said, "we weren't the ones who needed protection. After visiting Tome, we returned to the manor and found it burned. There were few left alive, but we discovered Gevriel in the wreckage, although he was gravely wounded. He told us what had happened, how a band of knights in black armor had ridden up to the manor on black horses. Without even stopping to speak, the knights had attacked and set the manor afire. They slew Raiff while he tried to protect Anilena. She took up his sword, but they . . ."

Falken squeezed his eyes shut, then opened them again. "They murdered Anilena where she stood. Then, without another word, the knights turned and rode away as quickly as they had come. Gevriel told us these things, then he died as well in Merric's arms."

Grace listened to these words in horror. In the space

of a few minutes Falken and Melia had given her the parents she had never known, then as quickly had taken them away again.

"Who?" she finally managed to say. "Who were they? The black knights who killed my parents?"

"I'm afraid we were never sure," Melia said.

Falken gazed at her, eyes fierce. "I am. It was the Pale King who sent them. Only Fellring ever had the power to harm Berash, and only one of Ulther's heirs could wield the sword were it ever reforged. He wanted to make certain that never happened. And we know now he was stirring again at the time, preparing to break the Rune Gate as he nearly did last Midwinter."

Melia looked at the bard but said nothing.

"That's a dark tale, Falken," Beltan said. He looked at Grace, his usually jovial face somber. "And I'm sorry you lost your parents. I know what that's like. But this still doesn't explain how Grace ended up on Travis's world."

"That was my doing," Melia said.

Travis gaped. "You mean you have the power to send people between worlds?"

The amber-eyed lady smoothed her robe. "Not precisely. I had a little help in the matter."

Falken folded his arms and raised an eyebrow.

"Oh, very well, so I had a great deal of help. But the New Gods owed me—I had saved up quite a few favors over the millennia."

"So you and the other New Gods sent Grace to Earth," Travis said.

Now it was Grace's turn to stare. "Why?"

"To keep you safe, dear. Wherever they came from, the black knights had one goal in mind: to slay the heirs of Malachor. You were all that was left, and we knew it was only a matter of time before the knights discovered you were alive. Desperate measures were called for."

Vani moved closer, leather creaking. "So you knew of this other world, this Earth, even as the Mournish did. I thought only the sorcerers of Morindu knew of the place that could be reached across the void—the *morndari* told them of it long ago, and that was why they built the gate artifacts."

Melia patted Vani's cheek—a gesture which seemed to shock the assassin.

"Don't completely underestimate us, dear. Foolish and petty as we can be, we immortals do know a thing or two. We first became aware of the other world more than a millennium ago, when we aided the Old Gods in binding Mohg beyond the circle of Eldh. We glimpsed—if only for a moment—a world beyond what we knew."

Travis gazed at Melia, his gray eyes thoughtful. "So the New Gods were able to open a gate to Earth."

"It was not quite so easy as you make it sound. It took nearly all of us working in concert to do it—an alliance which I fear will never occur again. And even so, I do not think we would have succeeded if there had not been something working to open the way from the other side."

Now Grace was completely lost. "What do you mean? What could have been working from the other side?"

However, before bard or lady could speak, Travis did. "It was this, wasn't it?" He drew something out of his pocket: a gray-green Stone. Sinfathisar.

Falken nodded. "We believe so. Now, at least—for at the time we didn't know the Stone of Twilight was on Earth. But its magic acted like a beacon for the power of the New Gods, drawing it to your Earth and opening a gate."

"That's why you came to Castle City, Grace," Travis said. "And that's why the people from the orphanage found you there. It was because Jack Graystone had Sinfathisar. And I suppose that's how the ironhearts and wraithlings ended up in Castle City last autumn. They were drawn there by the very thing they were seeking." He tightened his fingers around the Stone.

"We can't be sure," Falken said. "But it makes sense. We know the Pale King had the Great Stone Gelthisar. It must be that its power was great enough for him to send some of his servants to your world. And just like Grace, they all ended up near the place where Sinfathisar was being kept."

Grace's eyes were hot, and she felt tears filling them. At last she knew she had not been abandoned as a child. They had loved her, and they had been trying to protect her. So why did she feel so lonely she couldn't bear it?

"Why?" she whispered. "Why did you let me go there alone? Why did you send me . . . ?"

Why did you send me there, to the orphanage, to the shadow? she wanted to ask, but the words stuck in her throat.

Melia hesitated, then she took both of Grace's hands in her own. "We didn't send you alone, Grace. At least, we didn't want to. Merric Warden held you as we opened the gateway. He was to go with you, to watch over you. But . . . something went wrong."

Grace shook her head, beyond words now. Melia tightened her grip.

"You were so small, so fragile. You were wearing a dress Anilena had made for you, and Falken had placed the necklace around your neck, for he had found it on Anilena. Then, even as Merric went through the gate, we all sensed it: a presence on the other side. What it was—or who—we still do not know. But it was great, and powerful. And it was evil. I watched as Merric cried out in agony. I could see the other side of the gate—the mountain where they must have found you. With his last effort, Merric heaved your tiny body forward. I saw you fall, tumbling to the grass, crying. Then Merric screamed again, and he was torn apart by something none of us could see. After that the gate closed, and we could not open it again."

Now Melia released her hands. "I'm so sorry, Ralena. I'm so sorry we left you alone. We wanted to protect you, and I fear it was the opposite that happened. Please . . . can you ever find a way to forgive us?"

Grace tried to speak but could not. Instead a low moan escaped her as she shook her head. Pain hazed Melia's visage, and the lady stepped back. No, she misunderstood. Desperate, Grace reached for words, found them, put them together.

"There's nothing to forgive. You did everything you could for me. And I'm alive."

And broken. But she did not speak those words aloud. That was not Melia's fault, nor Falken's. They had devoted their lives to protecting her family. If it were not for them, Grace never would have been born in the first place.

Falken was grinning now. "It doesn't matter what happened, Grace. You're well, and you're here. That's all that counts. And one day Malachor will shine again under your rule."

These words were like a slap. However, before Grace could speak, Melia clapped her hands.

"Oh, Ralena! I had thought I would never see you again. Then, that day we came to Calavere last winter, and I saw you standing there—I thought my heart would shatter with joy."

Falken's eyes nearly popped out of his head. "*What?* You mean, all this time, you knew Grace was Ralena?"

Melia smiled sweetly. "Of course, dear."

The bard's face turned a fascinating and completely unnatural shade of purple. "And you never thought it important to share this little fact with me?"

Melia rolled her eyes. "Well, I didn't think it would take you so long to figure it out. I recognized her at once—even if she did see fit to keep her necklace hidden. Only a child as lovely as Ralena could grow into a woman as beautiful as Grace. Besides, I imagine no one on any world has eyes quite like hers. They haven't changed a bit, dear."

Falken looked ready to explode, but before the bard could speak Durge stepped forward. His lined face was sober as always, but there was a light in his brown eyes Grace had never glimpsed before. It was certainly pride. It might also have been joy.

"I knew it," he said softly. "You are indeed a queen. Of men, if not of fairies." Then, to her astonishment, Durge knelt on the floor before her and bowed his head.

As if that were not enough, a moment later Falken followed suit, then Beltan, then all of the others. Travis knelt, grinning, and Lirith and Aryn with eyes sparkling. Even Melia, and Sareth and Vani. They all knelt on the floor before Grace.

This was horrible. Didn't they understand? She couldn't possibly be royalty, let alone a queen.

But you are a queen, Grace. Much as you'd like to deny

*it, you can't, so you'd better get used to it. Besides, you're
the ruler of a kingdom that hasn't existed for centuries. It's
not as if there's anything to be queen of. So what is there to
worry about?*

Plenty. Falken's blue eyes were brighter than she had
ever seen them. It was clear the bard thought she was
going to restore Malachor—the very kingdom all the
legends said he had helped to bring down. She looked
at Vani and Sareth. Why did everyone around here
think she had a natural talent for resurrecting dead
civilizations?

She wiped her tears from her cheeks, then reached
down and gripped Durge's thick shoulders, pulling
him upward.

"Rise, Durge, please. All of you. Do you know how
stupid you all look?"

Travis was still grinning as he stood. "As you wish,
Your Majesty."

She glared at him. He was going to pay for that one,
and by the way his grin turned into a grimace he knew
it.

Sareth moved forward. "This is an amazing story
you have told us Falken, Melindora. But may I remind
you . . ."

Melia waved his words aside. "Yes, Sareth. We have
hardly forgotten. Come, everyone. I imagine my
requests to the emperor have been seen to. It is time
we paid Ephesian our respects and said farewell."

Grace followed the others from the hall, forcing her
legs to function. She could feel the others gazing at her
with a mixture of awe and respect. Even Travis. It was
utterly dreadful. Then, thankfully, Aryn was there.
The young woman gripped Grace's hand in her own
good one.

"So King Boreas was right all along, Grace. You

really are royalty. Only you're not a duchess, but a queen."

Queen. That was what Marji had called her. Why was Grace always the last to know?

"In fact," Aryn went on, "as Queen of Lost Malachor, I imagine you'd even outrank Boreas."

To her surprise, Grace found herself laughing, and the act was steadying, healing. "I don't think I'm going to be the one who tells Boreas *that.*"

Aryn joined in her laughter. "Well, don't look at me!"

They were still laughing when they reached the dais and Ephesian's throne. The emperor's myopic eyes lit up when Melia told him of their discovery and of Grace's royal nature.

"We shall have a celebration!" Ephesian said after roaring with mirth. He turned his attention to Grace. "We're cousins of a sort, Your Majesty. I am descended from Elsara's eldest son, and you from her second. Thus I decree that all of Tarras will honor you. We'll have nine days of feasting and music and dancing. What's more, you and I can ride together in a parade on a golden barge, and while the people watch I'll give you some advice on how to run an empire."

Grace had absolutely no idea what to say to that, so she simply murmured, *Thank you, Your Magnificence.*

Now Ephesian regarded Melia. "I must thank you, Melindora. This is quite possibly the most interesting day I've ever had."

"And nor is it quite over yet, Your Magnificence," Melia said. "So let's not celebrate prematurely."

Ephesian called forth one of his soldiers, who reported that the Etherion had been made ready as Melia commanded. After this, the companions bade their farewells to the emperor—with both Lirith and

Grace promising to visit soon—then departed, marching across the vast throne room and leaving the emperor alone. The gilded doors of the palace swung shut behind them with a *boom* that reverberated through Grace's body.

The vibration grew in force. A roaring filled the air, and the tiled surface of the courtyard rose and fell violently under Grace's feet. She cried out as she and the others tumbled against one another. It wasn't the vibration of the doors closing, Grace finally realized. The ground was shaking.

"What's happening?" Falken shouted above the roar.

However, even as the bard spoke, the trembling of the ground ceased, and an eerie silence fell over the palace, punctuated by the distant barking of dogs.

Grace struggled to regain her feet, letting go of Sareth, whom she had clutched to keep from falling. A webwork of fine cracks covered the tiled courtyard. She was certain the cracks had not been there moments before.

"That felt like an earthquake," Travis said.

"I do not like this," Sareth said, gazing at Vani. "The cavern of the demon lies beneath the city. This trembling cannot bode well."

Vani opened her mouth to answer, but a moan of pain interrupted her. Nearby, Melia staggered, her face ashen.

Falken rushed to her. "Melia, are you hurt?"

She shook her head.

"What is it?"

At last Melia managed to croak a single word. "Misar . . ."

Grace knew enough of what had been happening in Tarras to understand. Another god was dead, consumed by the demon.

76.

Travis craned his neck, gazing up at the blue dome high above. It was hard to believe it *wasn't* the sky he was looking at. Birds dived and darted, then soared toward white clouds. It was only after staring for a minute that the illusion finally became apparent. The clouds never moved, painted in place. Melia had led them to a large balcony at the level of the sixth tier. Except for the birds, they had the place to themselves.

Grace stood a little apart from the rest of them, gazing at the white floor of the Etherion far below. Travis couldn't help but grin. The first time he had met her, in the great hall of Calavere, he had assumed she was from Eldh. And even later, when he knew she had come from Denver, he had always felt like she belonged here in a way he never would.

It turns out you were right, Travis. She does belong on Eldh. And if Falken's right, then I suppose a good chunk of Eldh belongs to her.

Only why was there such a look of sadness on her face? Shouldn't she have been happy to know the truth about her parents? But maybe he knew the reason. Melia and Falken had sent her to Earth to protect her, only she had ended up at the Beckett-Strange Home for Children. And there she had found anything but safety. Travis knew; he had seen the shadow, her shadow.

Yet now she was back on Eldh, back where she belonged. Brother Cy had seen to that.

Travis reached into the pocket of his loose-fitting Mournish pants and pulled out the half-coin the strange preacher had given him, and which had twice transported him back to Earth. Grace had the other half of the silver coin, but not long after their return to Denver, Travis had placed the halves together to study the symbols on both sides.

With the coin complete, he had finally recognized one of the two symbols: a circle with a dot inside. It was the rune Eldh, the symbol of this world. Travis hadn't recognized the rune on the other side of the coin—a triangle with a line above it. In a way it had reminded him of the rune of ice, but he guessed it had another meaning.

They're just like two sides of the same coin, aren't they, Travis? Sister Mirrim told you that—when one world burned, so did the other.

The rune on the opposite side of the coin could only be the rune for Earth.

All right, that was one mystery solved, but it begged another—who was Brother Cy? And how could the preacher send Travis and Grace back and forth between the worlds with what amounted to a wave of his hand when other people, Duratek and the Scirathi included, were scrambling for magic blood and ancient artifacts to do the same thing?

Travis wasn't sure. But the magic of the *morndari* seemed to allow passage across the void between the worlds. And clearly the Imsari did as well—that was how Jack Graystone had come to Earth. And once Jack was there, Sinfathisar had functioned like a beacon, drawing Grace to Castle City. Along with the Pale King's servants and the runelord Mindroth.

So was Brother Cy related to one of these powers? Travis wasn't certain. But in a way the half-coins were similar to the gate artifact. Although they required no blood.

Travis sighed. There was no way to answer his questions now. But if he ever had the chance to talk to Brother Cy again, he was determined to get some answers. He slipped the coin carefully back into his pocket.

"All right, Melia," Falken said, hands on hips. "We're here. And there must be three entire companies of Tarrasian soldiers surrounding the Etherion. Now what?"

Melia's visage was still pale. However, her expression was resolute, and ire sparked in her eyes. "Sareth has told us that if Travis is to go beneath the city, we must provide a distraction for the Scirathi so they do not accost him. And distracting the sorcerers is exactly what I plan to do."

"And how exactly are you going to accomplish that?"

"You shall see."

Before the bard could ask more questions, the lady spread her arms, shut her eyes, and tilted her head back. "Mandu, my dearest brother, are you here?"

Melia's words dissipated on the hazy air, and silence filled the Etherion. He began to think Melia's question had been uttered in vain—

—when a voice spoke. The voice came from all directions and nowhere at once: deep and thrumming with power, yet strangely hesitant, as if the one who spoke was rusty at the craft of using words.

"I am . . . here . . . dear sister."

A queer calm came over Travis. He knew he had to go beneath the city, had to find a way to bind the demon with Sinfathisar so that it could not complete its escape. All the same, peace filled him.

Aryn sighed, her blue eyes glowing. "Mandu."

"Who is Mandu?" Travis quietly asked the baroness.

"The Everdying God." It seemed Aryn wished to say more, but then she simply sighed again.

Melia stepped forward. "Oh, Mandu, it is so good to see you once more. It has been so terribly long."

"And you . . . dear sister."

The air rippled like water, and before Melia stood an old man clad in a shining white robe.

"I am . . . keeping watch over them. As you have asked . . . dear sister."

Travis let out a soft breath. The old man was beautiful. His wrinkled skin was as thin as tissue, yet luminous, as if light shone beneath it. Wispy white hair floated around his head, and his gold eyes were filled with gentle wisdom. The old god's form flickered, growing alternately translucent and opaque.

"I am glad, Mandu," Melia said. "They have need of a shepherd since they have lost theirs. And I fear there are now more lost lambs to join them."

"Yes . . . dear Misar has completed his circle. But do not fear . . . dear Melindora. I will watch Misar's flock as well. I am nearly ready . . . to complete another circle myself. Yet I will stay . . . for a while at least. I have grown perhaps . . . too distant in my progression. To stay for a time will be good for me."

Melia was beaming now. "Oh, Mandu, I am glad to hear it. We shall all be better for your presence, especially in these dark times. Were you able to do what I described?"

"I have. Even now does the flock of Geb . . . speak the rumors as you directed."

"Wonderful."

"I will go now . . . and rest. I fear I am not used to being so . . . *present*."

"Of course, dear brother," Melia said softly. "When all is done, I shall speak to you again."

The brilliant aura around the old man flared, so bright Travis was forced to turn away. When he turned back, the old man was gone, and Melia was already walking toward them.

Lirith regarded her. "I thought you said Mandu tended to remain apart from the affairs of the other gods."

"Usually he does, dear. But recent events have made Mandu feel that perhaps he has become a bit *too* distant. He has agreed to help those who have lost their gods. At least until new gods arise to take the place of Ondo and Geb, and Sif and Misar."

Beltan scratched his thinning blond hair. "Excuse me, Melia, but that doesn't make sense. The gods have been around for ages. How can new ones suddenly appear to take the place of the ones who have been murdered?"

"Even I don't know, dear," Melia said. "That's why the cults are called mysteries."

"Tira," Grace said softly. "She became a goddess. We watched her rise into the sky. Will some of those who lost their god follow her?"

Melia seemed to think of this. "In time, perhaps. Even though she is a goddess now, it seems to me Tira is yet a child. It might be a long while before we really begin to understand what her purposes are."

"What was Mandu talking about?" Falken said. "He mentioned something about the flock of Geb speaking rumors."

Melia smoothed her blue-black hair. "Yes, Mandu has spoken to the beggars and thieves of Tarras. Even now they are spreading rumors throughout the city."

"Rumors of what, my lady?" Durge asked.

"Rumors that tell of a relic of the ancient south. A relic that is even now being held by the emperor in the Etherion."

Sareth's eyes went wide. "The scarab! You're trying to convince the Scirathi that the emperor has somehow gained the scarab and is guarding it in the Etherion. That's why you asked for all the soldiers."

Melia smiled. "And do you think it will work, Sareth?"

The Mournish man rubbed his bearded chin, then a grin cut across his face. "The lust the Scirathi hold for the scarab knows no bounds. They will not be able to resist discovering for themselves if the rumors are true. They will come."

Travis gathered his will. "And that will give me the time I need to go beneath the city and . . ."

And what? He didn't really know, so he said nothing more.

It was time. If Melia's plan worked, the Scirathi could begin showing up at the Etherion any moment. Vani took the obsidian artifact from a pouch and set it down in the center of the large balcony. The prism was still askew.

Sareth handed candles and a small sack of herbs to Vani. They were going to work the purification spell. Two minutes, maybe three—that was all Travis had before he went below the city. When Sareth faced the demon, he had lost his best friend as well as his leg. What would Travis lose? Everything, perhaps.

His gaze wandered across the balcony, to a tall, rangy figure. Beltan. The blond knight gazed out over the vastness of the Etherion, big hands gripping the stone railing. The knight looked whole and strong. All the same, something seemed to hang over him, dimming his light, and once again Travis wondered what Duratek had done to him.

They were trying to make me into a killer, Beltan had said. *I guess they didn't know I already was one.*

Did those words have something to do with the crime Beltan had talked about last night? But whatever the Necromancer said he had done, it had to be a lie. Beltan was good, kind, and brave, not someone who had the power to destroy. Not like Travis.

I'm the monster, Beltan. Not you. I'm the one who's supposed to destroy Eldh. That's what the dragon Sfithrisir said. And Grace said the Witches believe it, too.

Travis started to move toward Beltan—

—then hesitated as a soft voice spoke behind him.

"You can see it, can't you? His shadow."

Travis turned to stare at Grace. "What?"

She wasn't looking at him; her eyes were on the big knight. "I first saw it on the journey to Spardis, and then again when I bound our threads together. He has a shadow just like I do. Just like we all do."

He gave her a questioning look, and she met his gaze.

"This morning, on our way into the city, I used the Touch to look at your thread, Travis. Yours and the threads of the others. Even Melia and Falken. It's not just me and Beltan. Some are greater, some lesser. But we all carry shadows with us."

Travis understood. They all had their ghosts that haunted them. He sighed. *I love you, Alice.*

For a moment he was almost there again, in the silent farmhouse in Illinois where his sister had died. Then his vision cleared, and he saw Grace gazing at him.

"Do you love him?" Grace said.

The question was flat, a doctor asking him if he had noticed any discomfort in his chest while she took his pulse.

"Yes," Travis said, surprised at the certainty in his voice. "I've never really known anything in my life, Grace. Half of the time I can't even tell left from right. But I love Beltan. That's the one thing I do know."

Grace's eyes pierced him. "Then why aren't you with him now?"

Travis opened his mouth, but no words came out. Now, just as on the previous night, something was holding him back. But what?

"Vani," Grace said.

Only as she spoke the word did he realize he was no longer gazing at Beltan, but at the assassin. As if she sensed his attention, she looked up with gold eyes. Then she turned her gaze back to the artifact.

"What's going on, Grace?" he managed to croak.

"I don't know. I think maybe . . ." Grace drew in a breath. "Back in the hotel room, in Denver, Vani asked me about you and Beltan. She asked me if you loved him. When I said yes, she seemed . . . broken."

Understanding washed over Travis, along with a sick feeling. "Last night, when Sareth was talking about their friend, Xemeth—the one who died—it was clear that Xemeth loved her. But Vani mentioned something about the cards, something they had said to her."

Grace seemed to think about this. "The Morindai believe in fate, Travis. Maybe the cards told her who she was fated to fall in love with, and maybe it wasn't Xemeth. Maybe—"

No, he didn't want to hear it. Beltan loved him, and he loved the knight. That was the one thing he had finally managed to figure out in this mess of a life, and nothing was going to take that from him.

Except Grace spoke, and she did.

"Maybe it's you she loves, Travis."

In the center of the balcony, Vani stood up. The blue smoke of incense coiled around her like ghostly fingers. "Are you ready, Travis?"

He looked at Grace, but there was no more time for words. And maybe it was better this way, going beneath the city to face the demon—one monster to another. Better that than choosing between two people, both of whom deserved so much better than he.

Travis moved to the artifact. He reached into his pocket, felt the smooth surface of Sinfathisar. Despite the dread in his chest, he found himself grinning. Whether he lived or died, at least he was trying to do something good. Whatever fate would make of him in the end, that had to count for something.

"Ready as I'll ever be."

Melia stood on her tiptoes to kiss his cheek. "Do be careful, dear."

Aryn clutched the bright blue fabric of her dress. "But he can't go alone. We have to watch . . . that is, someone has to go with him."

Lirith shot the young baroness a sharp look.

"I will be going with him," Sareth said. "I am the only one of us who has been to the demon's cavern before. Which means I must open the gate."

Grace stepped toward the gate. "Well, we've been through this much together, Travis. Don't think you're going to get rid of me now."

Her words pierced his heart like knives. This was ridiculous. It was too dangerous; they might never come back. And she was the queen of a lost kingdom. There was absolutely no way she could go.

Then again, if she was a queen, who was he to question her?

"Oh, Grace . . ." he said, and it was enough.

"Things are going to be bleak and perilous below," Durge rumbled. "I imagine there's no hope of any of you coming back. But never let it be said it was not because you didn't have a sword with you."

The knight moved to the artifact.

"Well, Grace," Lirith said crisply, "it is unseemly for you to be the only lady amid this brutish gaggle of men. I shall accompany you, for propriety's sake."

The witch cast a glance at Aryn, then moved to stand next to Durge.

Falken crossed his arms and glared. "Is *everybody* going beneath the city?"

"No," Melia said. "Just those who need to, I think. If they will be so kind as to remain with us, Beltan and Vani will help me with any sorcerers who might somehow get past Ephesian's soldiers. And you, Falken, can keep watch over Lady Aryn in such an event."

Beltan's face was hard. He gripped the curved Mournish sword strapped at his hip. "No sorcerers will get past me, Melia."

"They will not get past either of us," Vani said, folding her arms across her black-leather jacket.

The assassin gazed at Beltan. The knight returned her gaze, then after a moment he nodded.

Travis looked at Grace, Lirith, and Durge. None of them had to come with him. They should stay up here. All the same, he was glad for them.

"Thanks," he said. It was utterly inadequate, but it was all he could manage.

Aryn let out a gasp. "Something is coming. No, *somethings*—I can feel them."

"Scirathi," Vani said.

Beltan drew his sword, and Falken moved closer to the baroness.

"The sorcerers have heeded the rumors," Melia said. "You had best hurry."

Sareth knelt, touched the small stone prism, and turned it so its sides aligned with those of the artifact. There was a crackling sound, like distant lightning. The air parted, and it was there: a jagged oval of darkness, edged by blue fire.

Travis felt a hand grip his. Grace. He squeezed back. Durge and Lirith moved close.

"Think of nothing as we pass through," Sareth said. "You must let me envision the cavern. And we must keep close together no matter what. Do you understand?"

They nodded.

"May the gods go with you, dears," Melia said.

Travis cast one last glance at Vani and Beltan, but neither of them was looking at him.

"Now!" Sareth said.

And in a tight knot, Travis, Grace, Lirith, and Durge followed after the Mournish man, into the crackling circle of the gate.

77.

It was hot beneath Tarras.

The stifling air of the tunnel wrapped itself around Travis like black blankets, rendering breathing an exhausting labor. Sareth held a small lantern, although he had positioned the tin shield so that only the scantest fragments of light escaped. It was not difficult for Travis to make his way along the undulating passage; despite the darkness, his new eyes easily discerned the smooth, rippling walls and floor. However, Grace, Durge, and Lirith stumbled constantly, groping blindly as they went. He could see the desperation on their faces.

"How much further?" Travis whispered to Sareth.

The Mournish man had said nothing since the shimmering gate vanished. A few times he had hesitated as a side tunnel branched off from the passage they trod, muttering under his breath, but after a moment he always continued onward. As far as Travis could tell, they had moved consistently downward.

"I directed the gate to deliver us to a place just outside the cavern," Sareth said in a barely audible voice. "However, it seems we arrived somewhat farther away than I intended. Still, we are nearly there. I think."

The grinding of Durge's teeth was considerably louder than Sareth's words, as was Lirith's sigh. The sound of it seemed to hiss around them like invisible snakes. Lirith quickly clamped a hand to her mouth.

"It feels like the whole world is weighing on this place," Travis murmured to Grace.

"No, just a city."

Sareth came to a halt. Once again the passage forked. The Mournish man rubbed his chin, staring first at one opening, then the other. He was muttering, louder than before.

Panic rose in Travis's throat. The only way they could get back to the surface was to reach the cavern and find the passage Sareth had once taken from the sewers. Sareth still had the gate artifact, but it was empty now, the fairy's blood consumed by its magic. If they didn't find the passage, they would be trapped down here forever.

But that wasn't true, either. The Scirathi would find them sooner or later. If the demon didn't consume them and the entire city first.

"This way," Sareth said, moving toward the left-hand passage.

They pressed on down the sinuous tunnel. Travis found himself wondering how these passages had been formed. Not by water. Although they were smooth, here and there sharp edges protruded from the walls. Nor had these tunnels been hewn by men; they were too . . . organic. All in all, they reminded Travis of the branching pattern of arteries and veins in a body.

Sareth held up a hand. "I recognize this place," the Mournish man whispered. "We are near."

"But I sense only emptiness ahead of us," Lirith said, fingers pressed lightly to her temples.

"Truly, my lady?" Durge rumbled. "For I was thinking I had never in my life breathed air so thick with danger."

"Emptiness is all there is to the demon, *beshala*," Sareth murmured. "Perhaps that is what you sense."

"No, there *is* something ahead," Grace said quietly. "But it's hard to make out—like a shadow on black." She let out a breath. "It's gone now."

Travis reached into his pocket and gripped the hard orb of Sinfathisar. "I suppose I had better lead from this point on. The rest of you stay back."

Lirith started to protest. "But the light—"

"I don't need light," Travis said, and started down the tunnel.

Fear rose in him with each step.

This is stupid, Travis. Beyond stupid. Sareth said the demons were capable of eating entire cities. They turned most of the southern continent into some sort of wasteland. What makes you think you can stop it?

He couldn't—but Sinfathisar could. And because of what Jack Graystone had done to him, making him a runelord, Travis was the only one who could touch one of the Imsari and live. That was why the fairy had brought the Stone to him.

The Stone of Twilight is going to do all the work, Travis. You're just the deliveryman. It's not a great job, and not one you asked for, but you can manage it.

They had not gone far when Travis noticed a faint light on the air, like the splotchy purple afterglow one saw after staring at a bright light. Behind him, Sareth blew out the lantern flame, and Travis guessed it wasn't only he who saw the light. With each step the purple glow brightened, rippling on the heavy air.

Travis felt it before he saw it. A puff of slightly cooler air moved against his face, and the faint echoes of his footfalls no longer returned to him so quickly. There was a space ahead. A big space. The purple light mottled the darkness now like a livid disease. An acrid reek permeated the air. The walls fell away to either side.

Had it not been for his preternatural eyes, he never would have seen the edge. As it was, Travis's right boot skittered over the precipice. The rest of his body nearly followed, then strong hands caught his shoulders. Durge.

"I thought you were supposed to be keeping back," Travis whispered.

"As you wish, Goodman Travis. I will heave you over the edge and return to my place."

Travis winced. "That won't be necessary. And thanks."

The others drew nearer, and Durge's outstretched hands kept them from drawing too close to the edge. They stood on a flat slab of stone that jutted out into the void. In the center of the slab stood a cylinder of dark stone, about four feet high and as big around as Travis might encircle with his arms. It looked like some kind of pedestal.

The purplish light flickered in all directions like heat lightning, making it impossible to gauge the size of the cavern. It was huge, that was all Travis could tell—so huge he wondered why the entire city hadn't already collapsed into it.

Sareth let out a hiss. "It has grown. The cavern was not half this size when I was last here."

"The demon," Lirith said quietly, although her words still echoed. "Where is it, Sareth?"

"Should it not be upon us in its hunger?" Durge said. He was holding his greatsword now, as if the massive blade could damage a being that didn't truly have a body.

"I do not know," Sareth breathed. "The demon is . . ."

"It's gone," Grace said simply.

The others turned around.

"What do you mean *gone*?" Travis said.

She spread her arms. "Gone. The threads of the Weirding are all tangled, just like you said, Lirith. And some of them are half . . . eaten. But the thing that did it isn't here anymore. I'm sure of it."

"The ground tremble we felt," Durge said. "Could that have been caused by the demon's escape?"

Sareth clenched his hands into fists. "No, that is impossible. Had the demon escaped at that moment, there is no doubt we would have known it."

"Then maybe it just broke free," Travis said. "Just minutes ago, after we passed through the gate."

Durge scowled at this. "Surely we would have felt more tremors in the tunnels if it had done so. Logic says that the demon could not have escaped this place so recently. Which means it must still be here."

"Except it's not," Grace said.

Lirith crossed her arms. "One of you has to be wrong. The demon can't possibly be here and not here at the same time."

Travis's mind buzzed. *Time*. Then, in a flash, he had it.

"Time!" he said aloud, and the word ricocheted all around the chamber. "That's it, Lirith."

Sareth glared at him. "What are you talking about?"

Understanding fluttered in Travis's brain, moving so quickly it was hard to pin down. "You were talking about it last night, Lirith. And we saw it when we walked through the city this morning. Gods and people are getting lost in dreams of the past. It's the demon—it's been distorting the flow of time here in Tarras, first for the gods of the city, and now for its citizens."

Lirith nodded. "The demon is not just consuming the Weirding. It's tangling the very threads of the tapestry of time."

Grace's eyes lit up. She turned toward Sareth. "Vani told us the *morndari* don't have physical bodies. Is that right?"

"It is."

"Travis," she said, "do you know anything about the theory of relativity?"

"You're the doctor, Grace."

"Yes, but unfortunately not a doctor of physics. Yet from what little I know, relativity says that time, matter, and space are all linked. If something had no body—no mass—it could move at the speed of light. And doing that would have relativistic effects on time."

Sareth's angular visage was grim. "I do not pretend to understand what you say, Grace. But while the *morndari* do not have bodies, the demons do. They were *morndari* given form by the sorcerers of Amún."

"That's right," Grace said, chewing her lip. "But what does it mean?"

Travis laid a hand on her arm. "We'll chat about Einstein later, Grace. However the thing managed it, the demon isn't here anymore. We have to find Sareth's passage and get out."

"Give me a moment," Sareth said, stepping to the edge of the precipice. "Things have changed since last I was here. I have to think about where the passage to the sewers would be."

Durge tightened his grip on his sword. "I would urge you to make haste in your determinations. We cannot expect the Scirathi to be tricked indefinitely by Lady Melia's ruse. And do not the sorcerers have a relic by which they might transport themselves here?"

Sareth said nothing as he scanned the darkness.

"You need light," Lirith said. She made a weaving motion with her fingers, then held aloft a softly glowing orb of greenish light. The darkness receded a fraction. Grace's forehead creased in a frown, then she repeated Lirith's actions. A second globe of greenish light appeared, this time in Grace's hands.

Still the darkness pressed close.

"*Lir,*" Travis whispered, and the silvery radiance of his runelight joined that of the witchlights. The darkness retreated another fraction. It would have to be enough.

Sareth turned to continue searching. Grace, Lirith, and Durge moved after him. Travis started to follow, then something caught his eye: spidery outlines flickering in the green-and-silver light. He moved toward the circular pedestal he had glimpsed earlier.

No, not pedestal, Travis. Altar.

A thrill coursed through him as he knelt beside it. He reached out a hand, hesitated, then touched the symbols carved into the smooth, black stone of its sides, symbols that gleamed in the magical light.

"Everyone," he said softly, although the word echoed all around, "I think you should come look at this."

In moments the others were there. By then, Travis had already realized the purpose of the symbols. They weren't runes or another kind of writing, but rather sharp, angular pictographs: drawings meant to be read without language.

"It's a story," he said.

Lirith knelt beside him. "A story about what?"

"A sorcerer," Sareth murmured, dark eyes gleaming in the witchlight. "Look, there he is."

Sareth pointed to a stick figure. The figure gripped

a curved shape in one hand, and from its other trailed a line of small dots.

"But what is he doing?" Durge said, the pale illumination deepening the creases in his face.

Grace touched the altar. "He's binding the demon."

Together, glyph by glyph, they deciphered the story. The sorcerer shed his own blood, enticing a being that was represented only as a dot surrounded by concentric lines of power. The demon. Jagged outlines suggested a crag that could only be the hill of Tarras. The sorcerer created a hollow in the hill and with more of his own blood lured the demon inside.

"But it wasn't just his own blood," Lirith said, pointing to a glyph. In the stick-sorcerer's hand was a dot with eight small lines radiating from it.

Quickly, they read the rest of the story. With the scarab, the sorcerer enticed the demon into the prison in the rock, then worked a great magic. The very last glyph showed a rain of dots pouring from the sorcerer's body as the circle of the demon shrank in on itself.

"That's all?" Durge said, frowning. "But the story does not seem complete."

"I don't think we're seeing everything," Travis said. "Look, here's the edge of another glyph. But the rest has been erased somehow."

Then he understood. On one side, the stone of the altar was warped and rippled like the walls of this place. Whatever power had carved the tunnels had deformed the stone of the altar, wiping out the last part of the story. However, Travis thought he could guess the final symbols: the sorcerer, with his remaining power, carving his story here.

They rose, standing around the altar.

"So it was the scarab of Orú," Sareth said, wonder

on his face. "That was how the sorcerer bound the demon in this place. He used the jewel as the focus of the binding and sacrificed his own blood to forge the magic. I suppose we will never know his name, but he must have been one of the greatest of his kind—perhaps one of the sorcerers who first created the demons before they realized their folly."

Travis felt a pang in his chest. The sorcerer had sacrificed himself to undo his own magic and save the world. He clenched his right hand into a fist.

"Sareth," Durge rumbled, "you say the scarab was not consumed by the sorcerer's magic, but was rather the focus of it."

"That's right."

"Then I think you should look at this."

The knight brushed dust from the top of the altar. On one side the stone was melted and deformed, but on the other it was unmarred. On this side, set into the surface of the stone, was a shallow round depression.

"It looks like something is supposed to fit in there," Grace said.

Travis swallowed hard. He brushed away more dust, revealing eight grooves radiating from the circular depression. "Something with eight legs. . . ."

They gazed at each other, eyes wide in the flickering green-and-silver light. A faint sound echoed on the air, like a small stone skittering before falling into endless dark.

Dread solidified Travis's heart. "Lirith, Grace, can you sense any sign of the Scirathi nearby?"

Lirith's eyes were shut; she was already working. "No, there's no one else here but us. I—" She drew in a hissing breath.

"Something's coming toward us," Grace said, her eyes flying open. "Something—"

Part of the darkness swirled, separated, and drifted toward them: a figure clad in a billowing black robe. Silver runelight and green witchlight glinted off a motionless, serenely smiling face made out of gold.

"Scirathi!" Sareth spat, drawing his sword.

Durge stepped forward, his greatsword raised.

"The mask!" Grace said. "It's the source of his power."

Lirith pressed close against her, already weaving her fingers in a spell. Travis swallowed, waiting for the attack of the *gorleths*. Surely the sorcerer had his slaves with him.

The Scirathi came to a halt a dozen feet away.

"Come on, you *va'keth*!" Sareth hissed. "Come on so we can kill you."

Low at first, then rising eerily, a sound emanated from behind the gold mask. It was the sound of laughter.

"Really, Sareth." The sorcerer spoke in a strangely lisping voice. "Is that the only greeting you have for your oldest and dearest friend?"

The Scirathi lifted black-gloved hands to the gold mask. There was a faint *click*. Then the sorcerer lowered the mask, revealing the face beneath.

Or what was left of his face.

Travis's gorge rose in his throat. On the left, the man's visage was normal, the skin coppery, the eye dark brown. In a way he looked not unlike Sareth, although dull and plain where Sareth was sharply handsome. But it was to the right side of the man's face that Travis's gaze was drawn—or rather, where the right side of his face should have been. Travis could see bone, and teeth, and leathery skin that had been stretched tight in an effort to conceal the deep concavity. However, without the mask, there was no hiding it: the right side of the man's face was eaten away.

"By the Blood of Orú!" Sareth swore. "It cannot be you. You are dead!"

The Scirathi's words were slurred yet cutting. "And it's so good to see you as well, old friend."

Sareth sputtered. "I only meant . . . the demon . . . I saw it take you!"

"Did you, Sareth?" the other said, moving closer. "Perhaps that was only what you wished to see. For here I am before you—alive if not exactly whole." The left side of the man's mouth curled up in a sneer, and he nodded toward Sareth's wooden leg. "But then, neither are you. Yet I would say you are still the lucky one." His fingers fluttered across the ruined side of his face, and a shudder coursed through him. Pain.

Sareth licked his lips. "Xemeth."

"Yes, it is I—the friend you brought with you to the demon's lair, the one you left to die while you fled."

"But you didn't die."

"Obviously. You always were an idiot, Sareth. Evidently your parents had but one brain to give, and Vani got it. But do not fear. I am not angry anymore. In fact, I am grateful for what you did to me. Were it not for you, dear Sareth, I never would have gained what I have now—the key to everything I have ever desired."

Sareth hesitated, then took a step closer. "What are you talking about, Xemeth? What have you gained?"

"This." Xemeth reached into his robe and drew something out. Soft gold light welled between his fingers. Then he held out his hand.

It rested on his palm, its legs moving slowly against his flesh: a spider made of gold.

At once Travis knew it was not one of the spiders

the Scirathi made to carry their poison. It was larger, and vastly more beautiful. Its eyes were like many-faceted opals, and a sparkling red gem was set into its back. Power radiated from the gold spider along with the light. It seemed a living jewel.

"The Scarab of Orú," Sareth whispered.

78.

The demon might have been gone, but Grace didn't need Durge to tell her that they were still in grave peril. Sareth had drawn as close to his old friend as he could, but Xemeth would not let the Mournish man come too near, and he would move away if Sareth drew within five paces of him.

He's not really a Scirathi—he can't be. If he was a sorcerer, we'd all be dead by now. He's just dressed like one of them. But why?

Travis and Lirith stood next to Grace, eyes on Sareth. Durge had stepped a little farther away. He still held his greatsword, but he did not move. Xemeth might not have been a sorcerer, but he did have the scarab, and from what Sareth had said there was no telling what Xemeth might be capable of doing with the relic in hand.

Sareth moistened his lips. No doubt the Mournish man was carefully calculating what to speak.

"This is a wonder, Xemeth. You have done what we came here to do that day—you have saved the scarab from the hands of the Scirathi. And I am beyond joy to know you are well. Only why did you not come to us sooner and let us know you were alive? All the Mournish would have been glad." He paused. "Vani would have been glad."

A tremor passed through Xemeth. For a moment the left side of his face seemed to go slack. Then the intact half of his expression hardened again.

"Clever, Sareth. However, false platitudes will not make me forget how you left me to die. Nor will your pretty words give me back my face."

"I am so sorry for what happened to you, my friend. I truly am."

"And now you offer me false pity," Xemeth snapped, "an even less potent remedy for what has happened. And while it is satisfying to know that you lost part of yourself as I did, do not think it makes us equals. For what is a missing leg to what I have suffered?"

Again his fingers fluttered over the pit where the right side of his face should have been. Grace knew Xemeth had beaten the odds surviving that injury—especially on this world, where even a small wound could lead to a fatal infection.

But it was sterile excision, wasn't it, Doctor? Just like Xemeth's leg. The demon doesn't really eat things—not with a mouth and teeth. Whatever it touches simply . . . vanishes. Like the stone in these tunnels.

Or like flesh.

"How, Xemeth?" Sareth said. "How did you survive? And why are you dressed as one of the Scirathi?"

"What, old friend, do you and your companions wish to hear a tale?"

Sareth's gaze was pleading. "No one should have been able to survive the demon, yet you did."

Xemeth's remaining eye shone. Grace understood; Sareth was appealing to Xemeth's vanity and self-importance, trying to buy them time. But time for what?

"Very well, Sareth. I confess, now that you have

come here, I would be disappointed for you to perish without first hearing my story. And I believe there is time enough to tell it." Xemeth laughed, a bubbling sound. "Time certainly means little to *it*. And I imagine, soon enough, I will have all the time in the world." He tightened his grip around the radiant scarab.

Grace saw Travis slip his hand in his pocket. Would the Stone be able to stop Xemeth if he tried to harm them? Grace didn't know enough about its powers. Durge still gripped his sword, and Lirith's fingers were moving behind her back, weaving.

Grace spun a thread toward the slender witch. *A spell?*

Yes, sister, a spell of binding. Although I do not know if it can hold him. Do you feel it? The scarab pulls apart the threads even as I try to weave them together.

Let me help.

It was hard to work with her eyes open, but they couldn't let Xemeth know what they were doing.

". . . and the demon came upon us," Sareth was saying. "I made it to the passage, then turned around and reached for you. Only then I felt a coldness in my leg. The shadow seemed to swallow you, and you were gone."

Xemeth stroked the scarab with a finger. "What you saw was not quite what happened, *friend*. The demon did come upon me. I felt it surround me, and as you described with your leg, I felt my face go cold. Then the ground shook, and a crack opened beneath me. I fell."

"So that's why it seemed to me the demon had consumed you. I could not know you were still alive."

Xemeth made a strangled, snarling sound. "Do you think that absolves you of your crime? If you had remained, then you would have heard my cries of agony. For a full five fathoms I fell. When I hit the bottom I know not how many bones were shattered. And as I lay there, the numbness in my face faded, and the pain came."

Grace could not even imagine the horror and the agony. In a way, she could not blame Xemeth for his rage.

"Then what?" Sareth said.

"How long I lay there, broken upon the rocks, I do not know. A day, perhaps more. There was no light, nothing with which to measure the passage of time. I was dying, slowly but steadily. I tried to crawl, but to move inches took me hours. Finally I felt myself weakening, and I knew the end was close. One more time I heaved my body forward over sharp stones— and that was when I found it."

Another laugh escaped him. "Ironic, I know, but had I not been injured I never would have found the means of my escape. In the dark it looked just like all the other stones. But I had cut my hands, and when my blood fell upon the thing, it . . . awakened at the taste."

Xemeth slipped the scarab into his robes, then drew forth something else: a triangular object of black stone.

"The second artifact!" Sareth said.

Xemeth's ruined lips twitched upward in a smirk. "So, you know that was how we were doing it, how we were sacrificing the gods to the demon. But I am not displeased. Indeed, I had hoped the Mournish would surmise what was happening, and that they would interfere with the Scirathi. I was counting on it, really. That was all part of my plan for getting both the demon and the sorcerers out of my way."

"You mean you haven't joined them?"

"Join those *va'keths*? I may have been homely, I may

have been clumsy, but I have never been stupid." Xemeth touched the gold mask, which now hung from a cord around his neck. "True, their costume has suited me. It has allowed me to keep my face and form concealed as I move about the city."

"You!" Lirith gasped, and Grace felt the witch's attention slip away from the spell they were weaving. "You were the one who tried to murder me!"

Xemeth let go of the mask. "Once I saw her arrive in the city, I knew that meddling bitch Melindora Nightsilver wouldn't be able to keep her nose out of things. I tried to kill you while wearing this garb because I wanted her to believe that the Scirathi were behind the deaths of the gods. I knew that, once she suspected the Scirathi, she would do everything she could to impede them. Just as she is doing now. And I would indeed have killed you had not my dear old friend arrived to save you."

Lirith lifted a hand to her heart and gazed at Sareth. "It was you who saved me?"

His eyes were solemn. "It was I, *beshala*."

"Beshala?" Xemeth repeated in a mocking voice. "Oh, Sareth, this is too marvelous. It makes it only sweeter that you have brought her with you, and your other friends as well. Although I must say, the garb of our people does not suit them as it suits her."

Sareth ran a hand through his hair, his eyes wild. "What are you going to do, Xemeth?"

"Please, Sareth, you know perfectly well I'm going to kill you. Just as the demon will slay all of the Scirathi."

"You mean you're betraying them?"

Xemeth sighed. "Now you're just being dull. Of course I'm betraying them. Just as you betrayed me."

Grace sucked in a breath. The *T'hot* card Sareth had

drawn that morning—the Three of Blades. Didn't he say it had foretold betrayal that day?

Sareth struggled for words. "I don't understand."

"Must I spell it out for you? Very well, but only briefly. Time is running out now, for you and the sorcerers of Scirath." Xemeth held up the gate artifact. "When I found this in the hole where I lay dying, I knew I had found my salvation. Why it had been put in this place so long ago, I am not certain. Perhaps the sorcerer who bound the demon thought he might use it to escape after working his magic. If so, he perished before he had the chance.

"Regardless, my blood awakened the artifact, and when I opened it I saw there was yet blood of power within it. I used it to create a gate to the surface and crawled through. I was dying, and I had given the gate only a vague idea of where it should take me, but it seemed fate was on my side, for I came through in the countryside west of Tarras, and I was found by a shepherd. He was a kind and lonely man, and he nursed me back to health. Too bad. Once I was strong again, I was forced to repay his kindness by killing him. But he had seen the artifact, and I could not let word of it get back to the Mournish. Not then, before I had my allies."

"The Scirathi," Sareth said through clenched teeth.

"Now you're catching on." Xemeth set the artifact down on the altar. "I was determined to come back here and gain the scarab for myself, only I knew I had to find a way to get the demon out of the way. That was where the Scirathi became of use. I approached them, revealed the artifact to them, and told them of the scarab.

"As you can imagine, the sorcerers of Scirath were quite interested. Long have they searched for artifacts such as this. It is because they seek something in the other place beyond the void, the place which only the artifacts can reach. They have allies of some sort there."

Grace glanced at Travis. He mouthed the word that burned across her brain. *Duratek.*

"I confess," Xemeth went on, "I didn't pay much attention to these distant friends of the Scirathi. I'm not even sure how the sorcerers came in contact with these people of the other world without the benefit of an artifact. I believe there is someone here in Falengarth who the sorcerers are in league with, someone who approached them and told them what the Morindai learned long ago, that there is another world across the void. All I know is that these people across the void seek a way to Eldh, and that the Scirathi have agreed to help them get here in return for some unknown favor or payment.

"Not that any of this really matters to me. All I care is that, to indebt them to me, I let the sorcerers use the artifact to communicate with their allies in the other world. Such is their skill at blood sorcery that they were able to send messages back and forth across the void. They even managed to draw forth a few objects from the other world, including some kind of weapon made by their allies across the void—metal sticks that can slay at a distance." Xemeth chuckled. "Of course, the sorcerers who attempted to pass through were consumed by the *morndari* in the void. To open a gate through which living men could pass, they needed blood far more powerful than that of a mere sorcerer of Scirath."

"You mean like the blood of Orú," Sareth said.

Xemeth drew the scarab forth again. "Exactly. I told the Scirathi about it, and I helped them forge a plan—the plan you are now aware of. Using the artifact and the blood of many sorcerers, we opened gates to the temples of the gods and fed them to the demon in order to sate it, so that we could get past it and gain the scarab."

Sareth raised a fist. "But you cannot sate a demon! Once free, it will never stop consuming."

Xemeth appeared bored now. "You think I don't know this, Sareth? Believe me, I understand far more of demons than you do. I cared only to distract both demon and Scirathi so I could get the scarab. Oh, and one more thing. You might like to know it was I who told the Scirathi about the gate artifact the Mournish possessed."

Sareth was shaking now, beyond words.

"Why, Xemeth?" Grace said, surprised at her own words. "Why do you want the scarab?"

He turned his disconcerting gaze on her. "Tell me, northwoman, is it not the least I deserve after what I have suffered—what I have suffered all my life? Always I was second to Sareth's first, and when I wanted the one thing he couldn't possibly have, I was denied that as well." He stroked the scarab. It probed his finger gently with slender gold legs. "Once I drink the blood of Orú, I will become the greatest sorcerer alive. Even the demon will not stand before me, and I will imprison it again."

At last Sareth found words. "Vani would be ashamed of you."

Of all the words Sareth had spoken, none of them had seemed to penetrate Xemeth but these.

Xemeth cringed. "Is she here in Tarras?"

Sareth nodded, and once again Xemeth touched his face. If he had been plain to look at before, what would Vani think of him now? But Grace knew it wasn't his looks that had made Vani turn him away. She believed she was fated for Travis. However, something told Grace that was knowledge Xemeth didn't have.

Xemeth stumbled back from the pedestal. He seemed suddenly lost, shaking his head, muttering. Sareth cast a glance back at the others; this was their one chance, while Xemeth was distracted by thoughts of Vani. Durge raised his sword. Travis reached into his pocket.

Ready, sister? Lirith's voice said in her mind.

Grace tightened her hold on the Weirding. *Ready.*

As one, they moved forward.

"Stop!" Xemeth cried, holding up the scarab.

The golden radiance was like a wall. Sareth, Travis, and Durge stumbled back. Lirith cried out, and Grace felt a sharp jab of pain as the threads of the Weirding were ripped from her mind. She reeled away from the others.

"What are you thinking?" Xemeth shrieked. "That you can stop me now? Do you know what this is? What I hold is a scarab, the greatest relic of power that remains from Morindu the Dark. With a drop of Orú's blood, sorcerers have thrown down mountains, boiled seas, and blackened the light of the sun with plagues of locusts. You cannot possibly stop me."

Sareth lifted a hand to shield his eyes from the golden radiance. "The demon, Xemeth. Where is it?"

"It is free," Xemeth said in triumph. "My spies in the palace overheard Melindora's little plan this morning, so I opened a gate to the Etherion above. And this time the demon was strong enough not merely to reach through the gate, but to pass through entirely. It is weak and slow after millennia of starving here in its prison, and it will have to consume much before it remembers its true power. All the same, it is a demon. Even now, I imagine it is disposing of the

Scirathi as well as Melindora Nightsilver and her companions. Then, once it is finished but before it grows too strong, I will bind it again—with the power of the god-king Orú!"

Xemeth lifted the scarab high, tilted his head back, and opened his mouth. His fingers tightened around the glistening scarab, crushing it. Three dark red drops dripped from the jewel into Xemeth's mouth.

The transformation was sudden and shocking. Flecks of gold light—faint at first, like dim fireflies—fluttered beneath his skin. They grew brighter, swarming all over his face, his neck, shining through the fabric of his robe, until Xemeth's entire form shone as brilliantly as the scarab.

He threw the crushed jewel aside and thrust his arms out.

"Yes," he cried, his voice thundering in the cavern. "Yes!"

The gold specks danced over the right side of his face. First bone and teeth appeared, then muscle and skin. The sparks dimmed to a soft, gold corona that encapsulated him. He smiled—and the expression touched both sides of his face. Slowly, he reached up, probing his renewed flesh.

"Whole," he murmured, two eyes shining with wonder. "I am whole. And I can feel it flowing in my veins. His blood. Surely I am the most powerful sorcerer since Orú himself!"

Sareth's face was a mask of anguish. "You are a fool, Xemeth. Vani . . ."

Xemeth's glowing features shifted into a frown. "What of Vani?"

Sareth met Xemeth's glowing eyes. "Vani is in the Etherion."

Xemeth stared, frozen, then looked up at the stone

ceiling far above. "The demon . . ."

With a roar of fury, Sareth launched himself forward. He was nearly quick enough. Then, in an easy gesture, Xemeth moved his hand, and crackling gold sparks burst from his fingers, striking Sareth in the chest. He flew back, landing near the edge of the precipice with a grunt of pain. Lirith let out a cry and rushed to him, holding him back from the edge.

Durge and Travis started toward Xemeth, but they were too far away. Only Grace was close, but the threads of the Weirding slipped through her fingers as she tried to weave a spell.

Xemeth picked up the gate artifact from the pedestal, then thrust his hand onto one of its points. Blood oozed forth, covering the artifact.

"I am coming, Vani!" he cried, and the gate appeared: an oval of darkness ringed by blue fire.

Xemeth threw himself into the gate. As he did, the ring of blue magic flashed and expanded. Grace tried to twist away from it, but her foot slipped on a stone, and bright pain flared in her ankle. With a cry, she stumbled the opposite direction.

"Grace, no!" she heard Travis cry.

Then the cavern vanished as Grace fell into the gate.

79.

Magic crackled. Like a seed being spat from an angry mouth, Grace flew from the orifice of the gate and landed with a grunt of pain on hard stone.

Sizzling, the gate snapped shut above her. She pushed herself onto her hands, gasping for breath. This time, passing through the gate had been like swimming through thick, black water. And it had been cold, so horribly cold. Her muscles were clay, her brain a lump of ice.

There's something you have to remember, Grace, something you're supposed to look out for. . . .

With a shudder it came to her. Xemeth. Where was Xemeth?

She forced her muscles to function. Frost clotted her vision; it was hard to see. All she could tell was that she was in a large space and that a storm raged around her. Wind shrieked and groaned, ripping at her hair and clothing. Blotchy shapes flew through the air, but she couldn't be certain if they were really there or if they were artifacts of her impaired vision.

"Grace!" a man's voice shouted over the roar of the storm.

No, not a storm. Her vision cleared enough for her to see marble columns and a high blue dome. So this was the Etherion. But there couldn't be a storm inside a building, even a building as big as this.

Something tugged at her hard—once, then again. No hands touched her. All the same, she felt her body slide several feet over polished stone.

"Grace, you've got to hold on!"

At last the heat of her body melted the frost, and she blinked the water from her eyes. A familiar form crouched several feet away. He held on to a column near a wall, his blond hair whipping in the wind. Grace slid another few feet along the floor. She was almost within arm's reach of him.

"Beltan!" The wind seemed to snatch the words from her lips. "Beltan, what's happening?"

The knight's eyes gazed past her. She started to turn, to see what he was looking at.

"No, Grace. Look at me, do you understand? Don't look at anything but me."

Grace nodded. Again invisible hands tugged at her. She tried to resist, but it was no use. She slid another foot.

"Get her, Beltan!" Vani shouted.

The assassin gripped another column near Beltan. Melia clung to the same column, blue-black hair swirling wildly. Just beyond, Falken and Aryn held on to a stone bench that must have been bolted to the floor. Clinging to another bench not far from the bard and the baroness was a figure in a black robe.

Grace's heart lurched. Xemeth?

No. The sorcerer turned his head away from the wind, toward Grace. His gold mask was dented and cracked, and it had slipped aside, revealing a face twisted in terror. It was not Xemeth.

Grace skidded a few more inches away from the knight.

"You had best hurry, dear," Melia called to Beltan, her words calm yet commanding.

Beltan hooked one of his legs around the column, then inched forward on his belly. Bits of paper and shredded cloth streaked past him. A chair sailed out of a nearby alcove, striking Beltan's head and shoulders, and he grunted in pain.

The chair tumbled over the knight, then scuttled across the floor past Grace, like a thing alive. She started to follow it with her gaze.

"No, Grace! Look at me and nothing else."

She kept her eyes on Beltan. Blood streamed from a cut on his forehead.

"Take my hands, Grace."

He stretched out his arms. She reached for him, but it was no use; a gap a foot wide remained. Carefully, Grace lowered herself onto her belly and extended her arms toward Beltan.

It was a mistake. She had no friction in that position. At once she felt herself start to slide across the stone.

"No!" Aryn screamed.

Grace tried to lift her head, to get one last look at her friends before she careened away.

"Got you!" Beltan said, grinning fiercely as he clamped his hands around her wrists.

His grip was so strong it hurt; Grace didn't give a damn. Beltan pulled her back. Vani was holding his legs, anchoring them to the column. The blond knight gave one last heave, Vani pulled, Grace kicked, and then all three of them were huddled together, pressed against the column.

Melia sighed. "Thank the gods."

"That was close," Falken said, his voice all but lost in the wind.

Grace turned her head. Her hair tangled in front of

her eyes, then blew back, and a coldness filled her stomach as she saw what Beltan had told her not to look at.

They were on the same broad balcony where they had gathered before, overlooking the floor of the Etherion fifty feet below. Half of the balcony's balustrade had been broken away, leaving only a sheer edge. Grace had been no more than three feet from the precipice. Had Beltan not grabbed her when he did . . .

Another chair hurtled past them and flew over the edge of the balcony. However, it did not fall to the floor. Instead, it sped through the air, into the vastness of the Etherion—

—then abruptly slowed and changed direction. Grace watched, breath suspended, as the chair began to describe a circuit around the edge of the Etherion, drifting in midair.

The chair was not alone. Hundreds—no, thousands—of other objects cluttered the air. There were more chairs, and tables, benches, statues, vases, metal bowls, cups, and chunks of broken stone large and small. As she watched, a piece of the balcony's balustrade drifted past. Several parchment scrolls followed, then an entire marble altar. All of the objects floated in a circle around the center of the Etherion.

No, not a circle, Grace. A spiral. . . .

She could see the pattern now. It looked like something straight out of her college astronomy class, like a miniature model of a galaxy: flattened at the edges, thicker at the middle, all the matter orbiting around a central point, growing closer and closer with each revolution.

A brilliant spark of light ignited in the center of the spiral and just as quickly faded. What was happening?

The objects were so thick in the middle of the spiral Grace couldn't see.

She cast a wide-eyed look at the others. "What happened here?"

"A band of sorcerers broke through the emperor's soldiers," Vani said through clenched teeth. "That was one of them."

She nodded toward the sorcerer who still clung to the bench beyond Falken and Aryn. He gazed back with frightened eyes; with his mask damaged, he was powerless.

"Together, Melia, Beltan, and I were holding them off," Vani went on. "And then—"

"A shadow came," Beltan said. "A shadow like none I've ever seen before."

Grace followed his gaze back out into the Etherion. With a jolt of sickness, she saw them drifting among the other objects: forms in black robes, their gold masks gleaming. She counted at least five. They were motionless as they drifted. Were they asleep, paralyzed? Dead?

She saw other motionless forms floating amid the flotsam: dark, furred, twisted. *Gorleths*. And there were men scattered throughout the wreckage as well, Tarrasian soldiers. They drifted on their backs, eyes shut, as if asleep on the sea. Inexorably, they spiraled with the other objects toward the center of the Etherion.

At last, with dull horror, Grace understood. With each orbit the floating objects drew closer to the shadow in the center. And when they reached it, they were . . .

. . . consumed.

"The demon," she breathed.

"Grace, dear," Melia said, amber eyes serious, "how is it that you are here?"

"We were—"

"Travis," Beltan said, his voice hoarse. "Is he all right? And the others?"

Grace struggled to speak over the wind. "They're all right. At least I think so. I came through . . ."

A new fear flooded her. In the chaos of her arrival she had forgotten. Xemeth had to be here somewhere. She craned her neck, searching.

The sorcerer clinging to the bench screamed. With a groan, the bench lurched from its moorings. The sorcerer screamed again. His gold mask flew spinning through the air—then its trajectory abruptly slowed as it became part of the procession to the center and oblivion.

With another groan the bench pulled free. The sorcerer's arms flailed—then his hands wrapped around Aryn's ankle.

The young baroness cried out; her grip on the bench was broken.

"No!" Grace shouted.

Falken was faster. He snaked out his black-gloved hand and caught Aryn's left wrist. The young woman jerked to a halt, as did the sorcerer still holding her ankle. The sorcerer clutched Aryn, scrabbling at her leg, while Falken held on to her with one hand, the elbow of his other arm hooked around the bench, his face lined with effort.

"I can't hold them!" the bard shouted.

Beltan and Vani both started to reach toward the next column in an effort to reach Aryn and Falken, but Grace knew they would never make it in time. There was only one chance.

Grace pressed her eyes shut. *Aryn.*

A pause, then a wavering voice sounded in her mind. *Grace?*

Aryn, listen to me. It was hard to use the Touch; the

force of the demon pulled at the threads of the Weirding.

Grace, I don't want to fall!

You're not going to fall. Weave a spell around him. Weave it now—a spell of pain.

I can't . . . I can't hold the threads. . . .

I'll help you.

But—

Do it, Aryn.

In her mind, Grace reached out invisible hands, clutched the undulating threads, held them in place for the young woman.

Now!

Grace sensed hesitation—then a hardness of will so strong and deep it shocked her. The threads came together in a shining cloth.

"My eyes!" the sorcerer shrieked. "*Deh'ru*, my eyes!"

He let go of Aryn's leg and clutched his face, blood gushing through his fingers. He tumbled through the air, then reached the edge of the spiral. At once he began to drift along with the other matter, body motionless, staring upward with crimson sockets.

Falken reeled Aryn in. Grace felt the shadow—*her* shadow—pulsing on the edge of her vision. It had loomed when she helped Aryn with the spell, and it had not retreated. She felt the past weigh dark and heavy upon her.

She gazed into the shadow at the center of the Etherion, and in that instant came understanding. She thought of the pictographs on the altar, of the dot surrounded by circles of power. Yes, it all fit. It was a thing with endless gravity contained in a stone no larger than her hand—a thing that bent and twisted both time and perception, that drew matter into it with insatiable voracity.

It's like a black hole, Grace. The demon. Everything is spiraling toward it, falling into its gravity well, with no way to escape. Even time itself. That's why past and present have been getting so muddled here in Tarras.

She opened her mouth to explain to the others what she now knew, but she had no idea how to explain theoretical physics to a group of medieval people; she wasn't sure she really understood herself. Nor, she supposed, did it matter. The shadow of her past bubbled upward, reaching for her. Soon it would consume her—if the demon didn't first. Or maybe they were the same thing.

"We cannot let it escape," Melia said. "I have to try to stop it."

The amber-eyed lady pulled herself to her feet beside the column, her face hard, her kirtle streaming in the gale.

Falken reached for her. "No, Melia, you can't. It will take you!"

"I must try, dear."

Melia started to let go of the column—

—then halted as a figure drifted down from the heights of the Etherion. The figure's black robe fluttered on the wild air. Instead of a face, a gold mask gazed from the cowl of the robe with serene, dead eyes. Without sound, the figure's feet touched upon the stone of the balcony.

"A sorcerer!" Beltan cried.

The figure in black stepped toward them easily, unaffected by the pull of the demon. A gloved hand rose to the mask, then drew it aside. Although made of flesh, the face beneath seemed every bit as golden as the mask.

"Xemeth!" Vani said in wonder.

80.

Xemeth smiled, his face whole and perfect. Vani shook her head, her expression one of disbelief. "Xemeth, can it really be you?"

"Indeed, Vani. It is I."

Tears rolled down Vani's cheeks before the wind snatched them away. "But Sareth said . . . he said you were dead."

"Sareth lied to you. As you can see, I am quite well. Better than well." He moved closer.

"You're glowing, Xemeth. What has happened to you?"

"Let us leave this place, and I will explain everything." He held out a shining hand. "Come with me, *beshala* . . ."

Vani's sharp eyes seemed suddenly dull, her expression slack. She started to reach a hand toward Xemeth's.

"Vani, no," Grace said, making her voice into a scalpel. "Xemeth is the one who freed the demon. He's drunk the blood of the scarab."

Vani blinked, then snatched her hand back. Xemeth's smile turned into a leer.

"Oh, dear," he said in a mocking voice. "My deeds have been found out. Whatever am I going to do?" Shrill laughter fell from his lips. "Wait, that's right—

I'm the greatest sorcerer in the world. I'll do whatever I want."

Xemeth thrust his hands above his head. Gold sparks shot upward, striking the dome of the Etherion. There was a clap of thunder, and dark lines snaked across the dome. There was a deep, roaring sound, and chunks of stone rained down from above.

Grace ducked her head, but she should have known what would happen. The stones plunged downward—then were caught by the demon's pull, joining the spiral of matter around it.

She looked up. Now she could see real sky through a jagged hole in the dome of the Etherion. Cracks still spread outward from it. She wondered if the whole building was going to collapse. But it wouldn't matter to the demon; the thing would eat the rubble. Xemeth had said it was still weak after its imprisonment, but with every object it consumed it would only grow stronger. And faster.

Xemeth lowered his hands, gazing at them with an expression of amazement. Then he laughed again. "This is most amusing." He turned his molten eyes on Grace. "But what do we have here? It looks like a little mouse sneaked through the gate with me. I shall have to squash it."

There was no time to react. Xemeth flicked a finger, and gold sparks blazed forth. Grace braced herself, waiting to be annihilated.

It was the column next to her that exploded instead. It burst apart into a spray of dust and stone shards—all of which flew toward the spinning disk of debris. Xemeth stumbled, then let out another burst of shrill laughter.

He's intoxicated, Grace. All the signs are there—the dizziness, the poor coordination. The blood of the scarab has made him drunk, and he can't control his new power.

"It seems I missed. But don't worry, little mouse. I won't miss this time." He pointed a finger directly at her chest.

"Xemeth!" Vani said, struggling to her feet, still holding on to a column. "Why have you come for me?"

Xemeth lurched around, then took several wavering steps toward Vani. "But surely you must know, *beshala.* I have come to make you mine at last. As you should have been long ago."

Vani pressed her cheek to the marble column. "So you . . . love me, then?"

"Love you? I worship you, Vani. Ever since we were children, I knew there was nothing in the world I wanted so much as you. And then . . ." A grimace twisted his face.

"I'm sorry, Xemeth," she said.

He drew closer. "No, do not be sorry, *beshala.* You will never have to abase yourself before me, not like these dogs. I was not worthy of you before, I know that now. But that is not true anymore. I can be anything you want me to be, *beshala.*"

Xemeth passed his hands before himself, and suddenly his robe was gone. Now he was clad in loose black trousers and a crimson vest. His bare arms and chest were gleaming and muscled, and his face chiseled and handsome. A short black beard adorned his chin.

Vani winced, and Grace understood.

He's made himself look like Sareth. Sareth, who he always felt was better at everything when they were children.

Xemeth must have noticed Vani's reaction, for his lips turned down, casting a shadow on the beautiful visage that was a mask as surely as the face of gold he had worn before.

"What is wrong, *beshala*? Does my new countenance not please you?"

Vani's eyes were solemn. "I am fated for another, Xemeth."

He brushed these words aside with a sloppy gesture. "What is fate to one such as I? I am the greatest sorcerer since the god-king Orú. I can make fate as I will—or I can break it. Tell me what I must do to win you, and it shall be done."

Again Xemeth stumbled and caught himself. Grace traded a look with Beltan, and the knight nodded. He had reached the same conclusion Grace had.

"Very well," Vani said, her voice rising above the sound of the wind. "There is one way you can win me, Xemeth."

Grace saw the hard light in the assassin's eyes. Vani was buying them time.

"What is it, *beshala*? Tell me what I must do to make your heart mine."

"Bind the demon, Xemeth. You have the power— I can see it in you." Vani reached out a hand and brushed his radiant cheek. "I know you can do it . . . *beshala*."

Xemeth's eyes went wide. For a moment Grace could see him—the small, sad boy who could never get what he wanted. Pity started to blossom in her heart. With a thought as cold as a knife, she excised it.

"Very well, *beshala*. I need the demon no longer. The Scirathi have been disposed of, and no one else can possibly stop me now. It will be done as you wish, and then we will be away from here. Together."

"Yes, Xemeth. Together."

He turned from her and approached the edge of the balcony. The wind tugged at his clothes, but that was all; the demon had no effect upon him.

The air of the Etherion was clearing. The spiraling flotsam was nearly gone. Grace could see it hovering there in the center of the Etherion: a spot of perfect blackness. Her eyes could not seem to hold on to it, and a sickness welled up in her stomach. Every few seconds there was another burst of light as something reached the center of the spiral. Grace thought she saw a figure in a black robe draw close.

Flash. It was gone.

She forced her gaze to Xemeth. He tottered on the edge of the balcony, then steadied himself.

"Behold the power of Orú!" Xemeth called out.

He stretched his arms toward the demon, and a corona sprang into being around his body, like that around the sun. Golden rays shot from his hands, speeding toward the center of the spiral, striking the demon.

Grace did not hear it cry out so much as felt it. Like a shock wave it spread outward, rippling through air, stone, and flesh.

What is he doing to it? Aryn said in her mind.

Grace tried to answer her, but the threads of the Weirding twisted and snapped, and she could not grab hold of them. The walls of the Etherion seemed to pulse. The very fabric of being was unraveling.

Xemeth threw back his head, exultant.

"This is for you, Vani!"

The gold rays extending from his hands grew brighter yet, striking the dark blot of the demon. Grace watched, her fear forgotten in awe. Xemeth was going to do it. He was going to bind the—

Xemeth shuddered and skittered an inch closer to the edge. He shook his head, gazing down at his hands. Gold light still streamed from them toward the demon.

Again a spasm passed through his body. His flesh

seemed to ripple like the stone walls of the Etherion.

"I don't—" he said, but the rest of his words were pulled away from his lips.

Grace blinked. Xemeth's arms seemed to be growing longer, stretching away from his body and toward the demon. He tried to pull them back.

He did not succeed. The gold rays still reached from his hands to the demon. His fingers elongated to impossible proportions, stretching thinner as they did.

Xemeth screamed. "I cannot let go!"

His words were weirdly distorted, the tones shifted downward like the whistle of a receding train. Xemeth's arms were a dozen feet long by then, and his fingers were so thin they merged with the rays of light plunging into the demon.

"What's happening to him?" Vani said, her expression one of horror.

Even as she spoke, Grace understood. The cry of the demon—it hadn't been agony. It had been delight. Sareth had said the *morndari* craved blood. The demon had starved in its prison for more than two thousand years. And now it had tasted blood of unfathomable power.

"It's pulling him in," Grace said. "And Xemeth doesn't have enough control over his power to stop it."

Xemeth's arms stretched to spindly strands twenty feet long, as if the gold rays were lines the demon was using to reel them in. His screams wavered strangely. Now his head was being drawn toward the demon with the rest of him, his neck and shoulders elongating like his arms to grotesque lengths. Twenty feet. Thirty. Fifty. His scream still rang out, but he couldn't possibly be alive anymore. Such distortion would kill a man in a second.

And what does a second mean when you're been pulled into a black hole, Grace? Time stops, and a second is forever.

Gagging, Aryn averted her gaze. Falken pressed her head to his chest. Melia's visage was solemn, and both Beltan and Vani stared with a mixture of revulsion and fascination.

The liquid sound of Xemeth's scream seemed to freeze as the moment of his agony extended into infinity. Only his legs remained on the balcony. His body above the waist had become a slender rope, snaking its way along with the golden rays of magic toward the demon.

In the blink of an eye it happened. Like a taut wire suddenly freed at one end, Xemeth's form snapped away from the balcony, whipped through the Etherion, and was reeled into the shapeless shadow.

Flash.

He was gone.

"Xemeth . . ." Vani murmured, her face hard, yet touched by sorrow all the same.

"Did you . . . ?" Beltan licked his lips. "Did you know that was going to happen?"

Vani shook her head. The assassin had only been trying to gain them some time; she couldn't have known that Xemeth's newfound magic—the power he had always craved—would be his undoing.

There wasn't much debris left in the Etherion. Only a few pebbles, and in bright flashes even those were consumed. All at once the far wall of the Etherion bulged and burst outward in a spray of white stone that swept quickly into a spiraling course toward the demon. The blood of Orú had strengthened it; the demon was going to rip the Etherion apart.

We have to get out of here, Grace started to say.

Another voice spoke first.

"I am so weary, my sister. So terribly weary. I can dance no more."

"Melia!" Falken cried out. "No!"

Grace jerked her head up in time to see Melia let go of the column to which she had been clinging. Eyes shut, the lady rose into the air. Her small body rolled, until she lay upon her back. Then she drifted away from the balcony, circling with the other debris toward the center of the Etherion.

"Falken!" Beltan shouted. "Hold on to Aryn!"

It was too late. Like Melia, Aryn rose into the air, her eyes shut.

Aryn! Grace tried to shout across the Weirding. *Aryn, can you hear me?*

But the only answer was from the shadow attached to Grace's life thread. It pressed around her, close, smothering. Grace was too tired to resist anymore. Her eyes drooped shut.

No, that's what it wants you to do. It wants you to give in to the shadow of the past so it can consume you.

Grace forced her eyes open. Before her, Beltan's head lolled on his shoulders.

"Beltan! You've got to stay awake."

She started to shake him, but his arm was ripped from her grasp as he rose into the air to float in the wake of Melia and Aryn. Vani rose up after him. The assassin's limbs were still, her eyes shut.

The shadow pulsed all around Grace. Everything seemed to grow dim. The call of owls sounded in her mind.

Falken, she tried to shout, but she couldn't form words. Nor was there any use. Through the fog she could just make out the shape of the bard drifting up to meet the others. She clutched the stone column.

Don't close your eyes, Grace. Don't give in to it. The past can't harm you. It can't—

But even words were too much effort. The column seemed to melt under her fingers. She felt her body grow unbearably heavy, and she could not resist the gravity of the shadow. Grace shut her eyes, and the past swallowed her whole.

81.

"It is no use," Sareth said, turning from the edge of the precipice and holding a hand to his eyes.

The Mournish man's words echoed throughout the vastness of the cavern. Lirith gazed at him with worried eyes.

"So there is no sign of the passage," Durge said.

Sareth shook his head. "Nothing here is as it was. If the passage to the city yet remains, then I can see no trace of it. In truth, I fear the passage is no more."

"So we're trapped here," Travis said.

It wasn't accusation, merely realization. All the same, Sareth flinched.

"I am sorry."

Lirith moved to the Mournish man. "This is not your fault."

"No, you are wrong. It is entirely my fault." He turned away from her.

The four of them were still gathered on the finger of stone that thrust into the void, near the altar where Xemeth had found the scarab. For minutes that seemed like hours, Sareth had searched the darkness for signs of the passage he had once used to escape the demon. The green glow of Lirith's witchlight was comforting, but it pushed back the shadows only for a dozen paces all around them, so Travis had sent his silver ball of runelight darting through the emptiness, moving it into cracks and crevices to illuminate them.

As Sareth had said, it was no use. One hole in the stone looked like another, and there was no telling where any of them might lead—if anywhere at all.

Lirith gazed at Sareth, her eyes filled with sorrow. Then the witch folded her arms across her chest and moved away, toward the altar.

Travis sighed. Sareth shouldn't blame himself. It had been Travis's idea to stop the demon; he should have come down here alone. But it didn't matter now— blame was not going to help them find a way out. And it wasn't going to help Grace and the others.

If it's not already too late.

He peered into the darkness above, and a clammy sweat broke out on his skin. Was the demon still up there? Or the Etherion for that matter? And what of Melia, Falken, and Aryn?

But it was not on the lady, the bard, or the young baroness that Travis's thoughts dwelled. Instead he found himself thinking of Beltan . . . and Vani.

And if you could save only one of them, Travis, which one would it be?

He didn't know where the question came from, only that it was as cold and cruel as a needle in his heart. Nor was there any point in answering it. Right now he couldn't help either of them.

"Can we not use the gate artifact to reach the Etherion?" Durge said.

Sareth hefted the black stone pyramid. "We cannot, good cloud. The magic of the artifact requires blood of power, and all of the fairy's blood was consumed when we opened the gate to this place. Xemeth had drunk from the scarab, and the blood of Orú had mingled with his own blood—that was how he was able to open a gate."

"But were not the Scirathi also able to open gates within the city using the second artifact?"

"They are workers of blood magic," Sareth said. "The blood of a sorcerer is enough to open a gate within the city, although not across worlds."

Durge seemed to think a long moment, then suddenly he looked up. "Goodman Travis is a wizard. Are not wizards similar to sorcerers?"

Travis swallowed mad laughter. "It wouldn't be the first time I've donated blood."

"No, Travis," Sareth said. "Your rune magic is strong, but it is of the north. It has nothing to do with the sorceries of Morindu the Dark."

A frown crossed Durge's craggy face. "Is there not something else you can do, Travis?"

"I wish there was, Durge. But I don't know any runes that can get us out of here."

"And what of the Great Stone?"

Travis drew out the Stone of Twilight. It glittered in the green glow of the witchlight: quiescent, a mystery. Travis barely understood its powers. It could make things whole, that was all he knew. He had used it to heal wraithlings in Calavere, and to bind the Rune Gate. And the fairy seemed to believe he could use it to bind the demon. But as for how the Stone could get them out of this cavern . . .

He held Sinfathisar out toward the knight. "Have you got any ideas how to use it?"

Durge took a step back. So much for Embarran logic. Travis slipped the Stone into his pocket. "We're not going to be able to help them, are we?"

Sareth's visage was grim. "There is no way out of this place."

"Actually," Lirith said in a rising voice, "I believe that there is."

The three men turned to look at the witch. She stood beside the altar, leaning over it.

"What is it, Lirith?" Travis said.

"I think you had better come see."

"What is it, my lady?" Durge said as they drew near.

"Look here." Lirith touched the shallow depression on one side of the top of the altar.

"That's where the scarab was resting before Xemeth took it," Travis said. "But I don't see how that helps us."

"It doesn't," Lirith murmured. "But I think perhaps this does." With her fingers she brushed dust from the section of the altar top that had rippled and warped.

If it hadn't been for the witchlight hovering above them, Travis would never have seen it. As it was, it was no more than a tiny spark of gold embedded in the half-melted surface of the pedestal.

Sareth looked up. "We have to break away the stone!"

"Why?" Durge said, glowering.

"Because," Lirith said, "it might be—"

Travis was already working. He laid a hand on the altar and spoke a word.

"Reth!"

There was a bright sound as rock cracked, then the surface of the altar shattered into small fragments. Travis drew his hand back.

"Look," Lirith murmured.

The four of them held their breath as a few of the fragments shifted. Filaments like slender wires reached up, searching for a hold. Then they pushed a flake of stone aside, and it crawled up onto the scattering of shards: gold, shining, and utterly perfect.

A scarab.

"How—?" Travis said, but he could get no further.

Soft gold light played across Sareth's face as he knelt beside the altar. He swore softly. "We are fools. Here it was right before us."

Travis and the others bent down beside him. Sareth passed his finger over one of the pictographs, brushing away millennia of grime. In one of the sorcerer's hands was a circle with eight lines. And in the other hand was . . . the same.

Sareth rose. "There must have been two scarabs set into the altar as part of the binding, not one. But as the demon grew stronger from consuming the gods, it began to reshape the stone in this place. The altar began to melt, and one of the jewels was all but covered."

"So Xemeth missed it," Durge said.

"As we would have," Sareth said, "were it not for your sharp eyes, *beshala*."

He was grinning now; she smiled back at him.

Travis held out a hand. With slow, delicate motions, the scarab crawled onto his fingers, then curled up in his palm. It was warm to the touch.

"So how do we use it?"

"According to the tales," Sareth said, "each of the scarabs was made to contain three drops of the blood of Orú."

Lirith touched the jewel with a gentle finger. "Blood of power. . . ."

In a minute they were ready. Sareth had set the gate artifact on the altar and had removed the prism, exposing the empty reservoir within.

"What of the purification spell?" Lirith said.

"There is no time," Sareth said. "And its purpose is only to calm the mind of the traveler, that he might better concentrate upon the destination."

Durge cleared his throat. "Then let us all work to envision the Etherion and be sure we are not distracted with idle thoughts of our childhood homes or some such fancy. I would rather our bodies not be divided between multiple locations."

"How do I make it work?" Travis said. The spider-shaped scarab moved gently back and forth on his palm.

"Hold it over the artifact and squeeze it," Sareth said. "But gently. Let only a single drop flow forth."

"Will one be enough?" Lirith said.

Sareth met her eyes. "A sea of Scirathi blood would not equal one drop from the veins of the god-king Orú. Even the blood of the fairy would be like water compared to it."

Travis drew in a breath. "You know, this is something I really never imagined having to do in my life."

"Now, Travis."

He squeezed the scarab, firmly but not roughly. Dark red fluid welled forth, forming a single glistening drop. For a moment the drop hung there, suspended, then Travis tapped the scarab, and the drop fell into the stone vessel below. Gently, he slipped the scarab into his pocket.

"You stay there," he said to the living jewel.

Sareth gazed at each of them in turn. "Ready?"

They nodded. The Mournish man lifted the triangular prism and set it atop the artifact. Instantly the gate sprang into being, blue fire mingling with gold around its edges.

"Remember," Durge rumbled, "the Etherion."

"The Etherion," the others repeated.

Together they stepped through the gate.

82.

Grace stood in her nightgown at the foot of the stairs, thirteen again.

All around her the orphanage was quiet. Too quiet. There was no trace of Mrs. Broud, the donkey-faced warder of the second floor, and Lisbeth Carter must have been stifling her sobs with a pillow because Grace could no longer hear them behind her. Even the owls had fallen silent.

But a few minutes ago Grace *had* heard something. She had listened to Mrs. Fulch's grunts and groans drifting down into the girls' dormitory as the red-faced cook made her way back from the bathroom. Then had come a crash, followed by a dragging sound. Something had happened up there. But what?

You've got to find out, Grace. That's why you're here again. It has to be.

Grace gazed up the dark shaft of the staircase to the third floor and shivered; she had long ago outgrown the thin nightgown, and her bony legs stuck out from it like white sticks. The night pressed against her. Only it wasn't just darkness that filled the hallway.

It's the shadow, Grace. Your shadow—the blot attached to your life thread. This is it, this is its very heart. It's inside you. And you're inside it.

She wanted to turn, to dash down the stairs, to run

outside beneath the cold mountain stars. Instead, gripping the banister, she placed her foot on the first step.

Silver light burst into being, pouring down the staircase like livid mist. Now she could hear it, vibrating on the air and in the wood beneath her feet. A heat rose within her.

No, it's too soon for the flames. That was after you came down, after you saw something upstairs. You've got to go up there, you've got to remember. . . .

The heat receded. Her hand slid up the smooth wood of the banister, and her feet ascended another step, and another. The silver light coiled around her bare ankles, its touch cool.

Her eyes drew level with the floor above, and the light grew brighter. She hesitated, but there was no alarm, no sound of Mrs. Broud's braying at catching her in the act of violating the Rules. Grace drew in a breath, then in five quick steps vaulted the rest of the way up the stairs.

She stood at one end of a long corridor that ran the length of the orphanage's third floor. Pale light flowed without a whisper over the worn floorboards. It poured from beneath a door at the far end of the hallway.

That was where she had to go.

The humming was louder; her jaw ached with it. Her bare feet making no noise, she moved past shut doors, toward the one with the white-hot line beneath. When she was halfway down the corridor she heard it: a low sound, rising and falling in alternation. It made her think of voices singing. Only it wasn't singing. There was no music in that sound.

Grace halted before the door. The humming filled her now, trying to shatter her body like glass. She almost thought she could make out words in the chanting—words that danced just on the edge of understanding, as if she had heard them long ago. In a story, perhaps. Or a song.

Grace cocked her head, listening. Then the sound of the voices ceased, and a new sound came from behind the door: a wet moan of pain, swiftly muffled. A moment later came a cracking sound, as of something hard being broken.

Open the door, Grace.

She hesitated, then reached out a hand and clutched the knob.

Do it now!

The door was locked, but somehow that seemed not to matter. Metal flowed and rearranged itself beneath her fingers. The door flew open. Silver light gushed out, and in an instant Grace saw everything.

They stood in a semicircle in the cluttered room, seven grown-ups—the whole staff of the orphanage, except for one. They wore black masks like they did when they came to take one of the children away, but it was as if their faces were outlined with shining green threads. If Grace squinted, she could see right through the disguises.

There was Mr. Murtaugh the groundsman, staring at her in fury, and Mrs. Murtaugh next to him, the look of lust on her face twisting into an expression of dread. Broud and all the wardens were there, and in the midst of them all stood Mr. Holiday, his face handsome even in astonishment.

Hanging on the wall behind the grown-ups was a black cloth covered with silver drawings. The drawings seemed almost familiar, although she didn't know when she had seen them before. Most prominent among them was a single, staring eye. The eye was set in the middle of a vaguely human face that bared sharp teeth in a terrible smile. Whoever the being in the drawing was, it was a thing of hate and hunger.

Her gaze returned to the adults. In front of them, sprawled on a battered chaise longue, was Mrs. Fulch.

The cook was motionless, her eyes staring upward without seeing. They had torn open her dowdy gray blouse, and her huge, pendulous breasts sagged to either side, away from the ragged hole in the middle of her chest. Blood smeared her skin, her clothes. Even as Grace wondered what they had done to her she saw the fist-sized lump of flesh in Mr. Murtaugh's hand, still dripping red liquid, and she knew it was Mrs. Fulch's heart. Mr. Holiday held another lump of similar size, but this one was a dark, metallic gray.

Mr. Murtaugh was the first to speak, shouting a string of expletives, none of which Grace recognized.

"What do we do?" Mrs. Murtaugh shrieked. "She's seen us. What do we do?"

Broud glared at the frantic woman. "By His Perfect Dark, shut up or it's your heart next." Now she turned her urgent gaze to Mr. Holiday. "Hurry, Damon—finish the act of creation before it is too late."

Mr. Holiday gripped the dark lump—

It's iron, Grace. A lump of iron.

—then roughly shoved it into the gaping hole in Fulch's chest.

Mrs. Fulch sat up.

Her flabby limbs flopped about as she drew in a wet, shuddering breath. Then she looked up and smiled—a hungry, hateful expression. She spread her sagging arms.

"I am ready, master!" she cried in a shrill, bubbling voice, her eyes mad, her lips flecked with blood. "By

our hands shall you return to your rightful world, and
the Lord of Nightfall shall rule all!"

Grace took a step back. Despite Mrs. Fulch's
movements and speech, Grace was quite certain the
cook was not alive. She looked at the others, looked
deep, down to the shimmering green threads beneath
their skin. Not Mr. and Mrs. Murtaugh, nor most of
the wardens. But there—in Mrs. Broud's chest, and in
Mr. Holiday's—dark, lifeless blots that the green
threads could not touch.

*Ironhearts, Grace. The eye on the black cloth—it's the
symbol of the Raven Cult. Broud and Holiday were
ironhearts, and they made Fulch into one. That's what you
saw that night, that's the memory you locked away. But there
was no way you could have understood, not then, not like you
do now. That's why you came back here—to see this.*

But if that was true, why was she still here? Why
hadn't the flames come?

"I'll take care of the little nit," Mr. Murtaugh
snarled, holding out his big hands, moving toward
Grace.

"No," Mr. Holiday said, stopping the groundsman
with a look. "Leave that to . . . the visitor."

The metallic light grew brighter and the humming
louder, so that Grace thought the sound would
scramble her brains. The black cloth with the symbols
fluttered, then moved aside as something tall, pale, and
impossibly slender drifted through.

The adults fell back to either side. Even Broud and
Holiday looked on with a mixture of fear and hatred.
Grace could not move as the being drifted toward her.

The wraithling was grotesque and beautiful. Its huge
head balanced on a spindly neck, and its eyes were like
great black stones in its mouthless face. The wraithling
drew close, stretching out delicate arms to deliver its

fatal embrace. Grace's breath fogged on the air. The shadow pressed in from all sides.

Don't let it touch you, Grace. Her own voice was dull and distant in her mind. *You've got to make the flames come.*

It was too hard to move. The cold of the wraithling had turned her flesh to clay. She felt the first chilling caress of its slender fingers. The shadow seemed to pulsate with glee. It was going to eat her alive.

No, it isn't, Dr. Beckett. Because you're not going to let it. Don't give up on your patient just because she happens to be you.

Doctor, heal thyself.

Somewhere, deep inside of her, a spark flared to life. It was not anger, nor was it hate. It was simply regret at so many years spent hiding from shadows—years that had kept her from the light as well. But she had escaped them as a girl; as a grown woman she could do the same. They had stolen her life from her once. Grace would not let them do it again.

It was time to banish her shadows.

She lifted a hand, and the air of the room burst into brilliant flames.

The wraithling raised its spindly arms, its head thrown back in a soundless cry of pain as the fire wrapped around it like a shroud.

Grace backed away. The door swung shut before her, muffling but not silencing the crackling of flames and the cries of human pain. There came a scrabbling on the other side of the wood. Grace glanced at the doorknob, and it melted into a shapeless lump. The door rattled but did not open. Black smoke poured from beneath it instead of silver light.

Slowly, calmly, Grace walked down the corridor away from the door. Flames followed in her wake, licking up the walls, dancing on the ceiling like joyful blue ghosts, consuming wood and shadows alike. She paused to pull the handle of a red fire alarm on the wall, and at once a shrill wail split the air. The others— Sarah, Nela, Lisbeth, Mattie, and all the rest—the children would have time to escape. But only the children.

The entire corridor was burning. The last wisps of the shadow burned away like curls of black paper, yet the flames pulled away from Grace like a gleaming curtain as she passed. But it was her fire, was it not? She had called it, and it had come: the first true spell cast by a thirteen-year-old witch.

Grace descended the burning stairs and left the shadow and the sound of screaming behind her.

83.

Travis pushed against the peeling picket gate. Rusting hinges creaked, and the gate lurched inward, sloughing off chips of white paint like flakes of dead skin. He stepped through and started down the weed-choked path. Weeping willows sighed as he passed, and the house glowed in the purple air of the Illinois twilight as if it were made of bones.

Why had he come here? He had never been back to this place, not since the sweltering day he turned twenty, when he left the farmhouse where he had grown up, had turned his face west, and had never looked back.

But that's not true, Travis. You did look back. Every day you looked back.

And now he was here again. But how? He had been in a . . .

But it was so hard to remember where he had been. It was a vague blur, as if everything that had happened to him since he left this place had meant nothing next to what had gone on within these faded clapboard walls. There had been a shadow, that was all he remembered. But maybe it didn't matter now. Maybe all that mattered was that he was back.

Travis walked past the garden—his mother's garden. In his memory it was as neat as her kitchen: everything tucked into its proper place. Now it was a tangle of honeysuckle and clematis and wild zinnias. A few fireflies glowed amid the foliage. They seemed dim and sickly, their time all but spent.

And so is yours, Travis. Why else would you come back here, if it wasn't the end?

He reached the steps to the front porch, started to ascend the rotten wood, then hesitated. He couldn't go in there, not yet. He turned and made his way around the house, to the backyard.

It was even wilder than the front: a commotion of thistles, goldenrod, and milkweed. The white fluff of dandelions floated on the muggy air, drifting back and forth but never finding a place to stop and lay down roots. Travis knew all about drifting. Wasn't that what he had done ever since he left this house? Look for a place that could be his own?

"I guess you never found one," he murmured. "If you did, why would you have come back here?"

For a moment it seemed like a fragment of a memory shone in the darkness of his mind: a place where he *had* settled down. No, not a place. A valley. Then the shadow was there, blotting out the memory.

The house looked in even worse repair from the back. Half the shutters had fallen from the windows, the gutters slumped, and some of the clapboards curled away from the walls like fingernail parings. Why hadn't they kept the place up?

Because they're dead, Travis. Remember? They're dead, and you didn't even go back for their funeral.

The only way he had known about their deaths was from a letter their pastor had written, and which had somehow found its way to him. Travis didn't remember much of what the letter had said. There had been something about cancer, about how it had been advanced by the time they found it, and how his father had followed not two months after from a stroke. All he really remembered was the last line.

God bless them both, for they have joined their beloved Alice at last.

Travis shivered.

The trees whispered her name, the weeds echoed it, the fireflies flashed weakly in time. That was why he had come back to this place. Not for them, but for Alice.

His eyes found it in the gloom: a low mound covered with crown vetch. They had buried her right there in the backyard. Not in the center of the yard, but off to one side, where they must have known he would be able to see from his bedroom window: a constant reminder of what he had done.

Killing is a terrible sin.

It was his father's voice, hoarse and shaking. Travis had crouched at the top of the stairs, listening when he shouldn't have been.

Not when it is done in accident, Mr. Wilder. That was the pastor's voice. Dry but not unkind.

Yes, an accident. His mother, her words as faded as the gingham curtains hanging in the kitchen window. *An accident can't be a sin.*

His father again, lower. *And was it? He was jealous of her. He's always been an idiot. And she was so perfect, so smart . . .*

A warm zephyr brought on the night, unveiling muted stars in the sky and blowing away the words.

But it *had* been an accident. He had loved Alice more than anything—her piping voice, her cheerful blue eyes. He would have done anything for her. But she had been sick; they had left him to take care of her. Only the numbers on the medicine bottle had danced like they always did. He had mixed them up, had given her too many of the pills. Far too many.

A yellow glow touched his cheek. He looked up. The farmhouse was dark and silent—except for one window in the upper story. Someone had turned on a light there, up in her old room.

Before he really thought about it, Travis tried the kitchen door. It was unlocked. He pushed it open, stepped into the house.

Dark, musty air closed around him. How many years had it been since they had lived there? He didn't know. It smelled like a long time. It was hard to see; only a faint starglow filtered through the curtains. Then he moved farther in and saw the dim light falling down the stairs.

He fumbled his way toward the stairs, then climbed to the hallway on the second floor. All the doors were shut except for one. Gold light shone beyond. It drew Travis forward, over the dusty rag carpet, past molding wallpaper. He hesitated at the door, wondering what waited beyond, then stepped through.

It took a moment for the scene to register fully, then he laughed—although it was a bitter sound. Had they done this as their last act—had they left this to wait for him until the day he finally came back?

And it didn't matter. All that was important was that he finally knew what he was supposed to do.

Her room was just as he remembered it. The white shelves were crowded with books and stuffed animals, and more books were piled on a small white desk. A pink canopy covered the bed, matching the pillows and sheets. On the white table next to the bed, beside the clown lamp someone had turned on, were a glass of water and a medicine bottle.

The darkness in the hallway behind Travis gathered

in on itself, taking shape, pushing him forward. But he hardly needed its urging. They had joined Alice. But they could never have loved her like he did.

Travis moved into the room, careful not to knock into any of her things. He was tall and clumsy, and he had to be careful around her because she was small and fragile. That's what his mother always told him.

He crouched beneath the canopy, then lay down on her bed. It was far too small, and he had to bring his knees close to his chest so that he was more sitting than lying, his back to the pillows and the wall. But that was all right. A light, sweet scent rose from the bedspread. Her scent. He breathed it in a moment. Then he turned and took the medicine bottle from the night table. Pills jiggled inside.

Travis looked at the label on the bottle, but the numbers and letters capered about in a mocking dance. He concentrated, but he couldn't follow their movements. Not that it made much difference. He opened the cap and upended the bottle, dumping its contents onto his hand.

A pile of small, purple pills rested on his palm, each one marked by a tiny lightning bolt.

Travis frowned at the pills. They seemed wrong, somehow. Sinister. But what did it matter? Whatever they were, they would do what they had to. They had joined Alice first, but it was his turn now. The shadow poured in through the door, pressing against the little yellow light, hungry. Waiting.

Good night, Big Brother.

'Night, Bug.

He wasn't even sad anymore as he lifted his hand and took all the pills at once into his mouth.

Don't do this, Travis.

He clenched his jaw, holding the pills against his

tongue, as the voice spoke in his mind. It was a woman's voice, smoky and familiar.

Don't swallow them. If you do, it will win.

Confusion filled him. *What will win?*

The shadow. That's why it brought you here.

No, I came here.

The woman's voice was urgent. He felt a presence, like a green-gold light. *No, Travis, you didn't. It brought you to this place, to your past. I know because it did the same thing to me, it tried to destroy me with my memories, but I . . . I resisted. You have to resist, too. If you don't, then everything is lost, everything we've fought for.*

Travis still didn't understand, but the voice seemed so familiar. It was impossible not to listen.

Spit them out, Travis.

The voice was harder, a doctor giving orders. It was so hard to move. The pills had begun to melt into a bitter sludge on his tongue. He must have swallowed some of it, for a heaviness descended over him. The shadow pushed deeper into the room, eating the light.

Please, Travis.

The voice was fading. Travis's eyes started to droop shut. The shadow coiled a dark tendril around his neck, massaging his throat gently, insistently. Travis started to swallow.

Listen to me, Travis! The voice seemed to call from far away. *I know what happened—I can see it all. And she would never have wanted you to do this. Alice loved you. . . .*

Travis's eyes flew open.

Yes, why hadn't he seen it? The voice was right. This is what *they* would have wanted, not Alice. She had forgiven him even before she shut her eyes; she would never have demanded such vengeance. The shadow strangled him, shoved itself against his mouth, trying to force him to swallow.

With a moan of pain, Travis turned his head and spat out the pills. They fell upon the bedspread in a glistening mass. The shadow rose above him, drawing in all its mass to fall back down on him and crush him with its dark weight.

Silver-green light burst into being, tearing the shadow to shreds and flinging them aside.

Travis looked up, into the light. His breath caught in his chest. A small, slight figure stood before him, arm outstretched. A stone rested on her hand. It was from this that the light welled forth.

"Alice?"

She smiled, displaying crooked teeth. "It's me, Big Brother," she said in that voice that always seemed too grown-up despite the slight lisp. "Here. I brought you this." She held up the Stone. Its surface was a mottled gray-green. Sinfathisar.

He stared at her. "But how . . . ?"

She shrugged thin shoulders. "Beats me, Big Brother. But I think you need this, so I brought it to you. Okay?"

Travis reached out a trembling hand, took the Stone from her. "Okay."

He tightened his fingers around the smooth surface of the Stone. Alice looked just as he remembered her, with her brown pigtails, her blue dress that matched her eyes.

"You can't really be here, you know."

Alice smiled again, but the expression was quizzical, and sad as well. She tilted her head to one side. "I love you, too, Travis." Then she turned and walked through the door, vanishing into the dark beyond.

Travis started to get up, to go after her.

You can't follow her, Travis.

The voice was close once more, gentle in his mind.

Fractured memories began to shine in his brain, and he fought to fit them together.

"Grace?" he whispered.

It's me, Travis.

"I have to go after her."

But you can't. She was never really here. None of this is here. I think I finally understand what it's been doing. It's creating the illusion as a way to bind you, as a way to bind all of us until it's strong enough to consume us. You've got to use the Stone to stop it before it's too late.

"Use the Stone to stop what?"

The shadow of the past. . . .

And at last he understood.

Oh, Grace—help me.

For a moment he was horribly alone, suspended in the void between past and present. Then a cool and comforting presence drew near, and green-gold light encapsulated him.

84

Travis woke. This was no illusion.

He sprawled on the floor of the Etherion, a howling wind tearing at him, pelting his face with small stones. A gaping hole had been ripped into the blue dome high above, and in places the walls had collapsed inward. Even as he watched, a nearby row of marble columns bulged and burst outward. However, the rubble did not fall on him. Instead, the chunks of stone began to spiral in a circle thirty feet above his head, like water going down a drain. More chunks of stone moved round the Etherion, drawing closer with each pass to the dark spot that hovered at the very center.

In sharp, painful jabs to his mind, Travis remembered everything. He had followed Sareth, Durge, and Lirith through the gate, and they had found themselves on a crumbling balcony on the edge of the Etherion. A wind had roared around them, tugging violently, and they had gripped what was left of the railing to keep from being snatched into the air.

The demon was there, in the center of the Etherion, and it pulled at every piece of inert matter—marble, wood, cloth—drawing it inward to the center. Each time something reached the demon, there was a flash of light, and the object was no more. So Xemeth had been right. The demon was still weak, waiting for its food to come to it—just as Xemeth and the Scirathi had used the gate to bring the gods to it. But with each piece of matter it consumed, the demon would grow stronger.

It was only when Lirith screamed that Travis saw the sleeping figures that floated on their backs amid the rubble. So it was not only inert matter that was pulled toward the demon. Melia and Falken, Grace and Aryn, Beltan and Vani—all of them seemed to be asleep as they floated around the Etherion, moving closer to the demon with each pass.

There was no sign of Xemeth anywhere. Maybe he had escaped. Or maybe the demon had already consumed him. Certainly the thing had not been bound again. And from the looks of things, Travis had known there were only minutes until the demon consumed the others.

He had turned toward Sareth, Durge, and Lirith, and that was when he had seen them let go of the balcony and rise up into the air, their eyes closed. He had cried out, reaching for them, but he had been too slow. The three had started their inexorable, spiraling trek toward the demon. Then Travis had felt a heaviness come over him. Too weary to resist, he had let go of the railing, and the shadow had wrapped around him, guiding him toward the dark remembrances of the past.

"But you're here now, Travis," he said through clenched teeth.

Alice. Alice had helped him. And Grace.

He stood up, searching for the others. For a terrible moment he thought they were already gone. Then he saw them, floating dangerously near the center of the spiral, their bodies still rigid. Melia and Aryn were the closest. Another turn of the spiral and they would reach the demon. The others were not far behind. But where was Grace?

"Travis!"

The word was nearly lost in the roar of the wind and the groan of fracturing stone. Then he saw her on the other side of the Etherion, staggering over the cracked and heaving floor.

"Grace!" he shouted, taking a step toward her.

Now her voice spoke in his mind. *Hurry, Travis.*

Before he could answer, invisible hands tugged at him with terrible strength. Across the Etherion, Grace flung her arms around a column, but in the center there was nothing for Travis to grab. He felt his body grow terribly light; the toes of his boots skittered on the floor. Then came another tug, and he was rising into the air.

The Stone, Travis! You must use it.

This time it was a different voice that spoke in his mind—the voice of an old friend.

I don't understand, Jack.

You must use Sinfathisar against the demon. The Stone can complete it.

Travis was rising beneath the center of the spiral. There would be no slow roundabout for him. He was hurtling upward, straight toward the demon.

What do you mean, complete it?

Do quit thinking and start listening for a change, Travis. Jack Graystone's voice sounded fiercely in his mind. Travis could almost see the elderly antique dealer's blazing blue eyes. *The Stone of Twilight cannot destroy, not like the demon. That's not its power. The demon is a paradox, a thing of nothingness bound in rock. Sinfathisar can resolve that paradox—it can make the demon one thing or the other. Haven't you learned by now that's the essence of the Stone? Water to wine. Lead to gold. Darkness to light.*

Possibilities, Travis, that's what it's always been. All you have to do is choose what it shall be.

Choose what it shall be. That was what the fairy had said, why it had suffered itself to be brought to Earth to give him Sinfathisar. But what was he supposed to choose?

The wind screamed past his ears. He could see the demon amid the rubble, could see with his new eyes past the haze of shadow that surrounded it. It had no shape, but was rather a blob that roiled like a drop of liquid metal. Except that was just a shell, the thing the sorcerers had used to bind it to Eldh. Inside the shell it was one with the *morndari*, the ravenous spirits that had pursued him in the void between the worlds: a hungry pit of emptiness that would never, could never be filled no matter how much it consumed.

He was ten feet away.

Do it, Travis!

Five feet. A sinuous strand of darkness spun outward from the demon to reel him in. Travis gripped Sinfathisar in his right hand. It shone with fierce light.

But I don't know how, Jack.

Nonsense! Of course you know how. You are a runelord— I made you one myself. The Stone must obey your commands. Now do it!

There was no more time. The tendril reached Travis, coiled around him. He felt his being start to dissolve as everything good that he had ever been was stripped away, leaving only the bare, blackened bones of his darkest memories. Trying to wake up Alice, her skin like ice. Fleeing the Magician's Attic as Jack faced the wraithlings alone. Realizing Max had betrayed him to Duratek.

Finally, he understood. That was how the demon did it, how it drew people to it, and how it finally consumed them. It dug through the layers of their lives, excavating the pits of their souls, exhuming all the worst moments of their lives. And with only such dark remains left to them, who would not wish to surrender to the void?

The black tendril tightened around him, scraping away the last bits of comfort he clung to, leaving only calcified relics of pain. The faded clapboards of the Illinois farmhouse the day he left it forever. The look of madness in Max's fevered eyes as fire took him. Beltan lying motionless in a pool of blood beneath Castle Spardis. The bare patch of freshly turned earth he could see from his bedroom window. . . .

No.

The word was barely a whisper in his mind, but he hearkened to it as if it had been a shout. No, he wouldn't let that be his only memory of her—the tiny form flung into the damp, worm-rich soil on that gray Illinois day. Her crooked smile, her elfin laughter, her small body snuggled in the crook of his lanky arm as they read a book. No matter what had happened afterward, he would not forget those things. He would not.

I love you, Big Brother.

I love you too, Bug.

It was so terribly hard. His fingers were nearly transparent; he was already fading away. With his last spark of will, Travis gripped Sinfathisar, touched it to the dark tendril of the demon, and made his choice.

"Be rock."

It was less than a whisper. However, Jack's voice spoke the words in his mind, and a hundred other voices echoed them in a resounding chorus: the voices of all the Runelords who ever had lived, speaking now as one through him.

BE ROCK!

Brilliant silver-green light blazed into being, burning through his hand. There was a shriek that was not a sound—a shrill *unsound* of agony that pierced his mind before it abruptly ended. The violent wind ceased.

Then, along with a distorted chunk of black stone and everything else in the Etherion, Travis fell toward the marble floor thirty feet below.

85

"Hold!" called out a clear voice of power.

Invisible hands seemed to grip Travis, stopping his descent. Below him, countless tons of stone crashed to the floor of the Etherion with shattering force, along with all the other flotsam that had been caught in the demon's spell. A sound like a hundred peals of thunder combined into one echoed off the remains of the blue dome above.

The thunder faded, and a few remaining pebbles skittered on the rubble below.

Drifting in midair, Travis craned his neck. He saw the others floating as well, their faces as stunned as his own. Lirith, Durge, and Sareth hovered in a knot to one side of Travis, while some distance in the other direction floated Aryn, Beltan, and Vani, as well as Falken and Melia. Melia was glowing a brilliant blue, her hands pressed to her temples, her face lined in concentration.

Panic rose in Travis's throat—last he had seen Grace, she had been on the floor of the Etherion. Then he sighed as he saw her drifting not far beyond Melia, awake and alive. The force of the demon must have pulled her into the air just before the end.

"Very well, Melia," Falken bellowed, spinning slowly head over heels and getting tangled in his faded blue cloak. "You can set us down now. Just do it slowly."

"It's really not quite that simple. I'm either holding you or I'm not. There isn't exactly an in-between."

Falken groaned. "What do you mean there's not an in-between. All I want is to get—"

The word *down* turned into something of a yelp as Falken abruptly dropped a dozen feet, then stopped. A second later the rest of them did the same, and Travis nearly succeeded in biting off his tongue as he jerked to a halt. In several more fits and starts, the rubble-strewn floor grew successively closer. The final drop was no more than five feet, although Travis managed to land rear-first on a decidedly pointy chunk of stone.

He was still in the center of the Etherion, the others about a dozen paces away on either side of him. He didn't know which group to move to first. Then he saw Vani stand, and Beltan helped Grace to her feet, her face smudged with dust. A warmth surged in his chest at the sight of them. They were alive; they were all alive.

"Travis!" Beltan called out.

Grace held on to the big, blond knight for support. She looked up and grinned. Vani stood beside them, hands on hips, her golden eyes gleaming.

Travis wasn't certain of much in his life. He still didn't know why Jack had chosen him, or who Brother Cy really was. For that matter, he didn't usually know right from left. But at that moment he knew beyond any doubt that these three people meant everything to him. Grace was the closest friend he had ever had. And he knew now that it didn't matter whether he *could* love Beltan because he *did*, loved him body and soul. Then there was Vani—and what Travis felt when he gazed at her he didn't know, except that it felt like . . .

It felt like fate.

But you're not supposed to have any fate, isn't that right, Travis?

Chalk that up as one more thing he didn't know. Impossible that he had never really found love in his life, and now he had found it twice. He started to pick his way through the rubble toward the trio.

"No!"

The cry came from behind him, along with the sound of sliding rock. He halted, turned around. Lirith bent over a pile of rubble as Durge hurried to her. The two began pulling at the stones, heaving them aside.

"Goodman Travis," Durge called out, "we require your assistance. Quickly."

Then Travis understood what it was the two were trying to free from the heap of stones.

Sareth had vanished.

Travis shoved Sinfathisar into his pocket and broke into a run, pawing his way over piles of stone.

"What happened?"

Durge's face was grim, white with rock dust. "The heap of stones on which he fell was not stable. It collapsed as he tried to climb down it, covering him. I imagine that the worst has transpired."

Lirith opened her eyes. "No, he's alive. But he doesn't have any air. We've got to get him out."

Durge began heaving stones from the pile with furious efficiency. Lirith pulled at the rubble, hands bleeding. Travis started to push aside a rock, then stopped. There was a better way to do this.

"Stand back," he said.

Knight and witch gaped at him.

"Now!"

He was surprised at the metal in his tone, but there was no time to wonder at it. The two obeyed, and

Travis gathered his will. He laid his right hand on one of the stones, then spoke a word echoed in his mind by a hundred other voices.

"*Sar!*"

The stones knew their name, and they obeyed.

The rocks flew away from the heap, whistling through the air. Lirith and Durge were forced to duck to keep their heads from being knocked off. With resounding crashes, the stones fell harmlessly to the floor dozens of feet away. Where the stones had been, a figure stirred and sat up. Pebbles fell from his clothes, and he blinked dust from his eyes.

"Sareth!"

Lirith flung her arms around him, then seemed to think better of it and moved away. Sareth's dark eyes were suddenly thoughtful in his dusty face.

"But you are not crushed to a pulp at all," Durge said, sounding surprised and perhaps a little disappointed. "Not even your head."

Sareth grinned. "I had something to prop the stones up with."

The Mournish man held up a length of wood, and Travis wondered where he had found the prop. Then Sareth screwed the piece of wood back onto the end of his leg, solving the mystery. Durge helped him to stand.

Sareth grinned at Travis. "Thank you, sorcerer. You are skilled at . . . uncovering things."

Travis winced. He supposed he had just convinced Sareth that he was going to dig up the lost city of Morindu the Dark after all. He opened his mouth to say something—anything—that might discourage the thought, but Lirith spoke first.

"By Yrsaia, what *is* that thing?"

The witch pointed to an oddly clear space amid the

rubble on the floor. In the center of the circle was a lump of black rock the size of Travis's fist. If he squinted, he could almost see what looked like an inhuman face in the rock, the pit of a mouth open in a soundless scream.

Sareth drew close to Lirith. "It is the demon. Or what remains of it. That is the rock the sorcerers of old bound it into."

"Rock or nothing," Travis murmured.

Lirith glanced at him. "What do you mean?"

He slipped his hand in his pocket, drew out the smooth shape of Sinfathisar. "The demon was a rock, and at the same time it was nothing. The Stone let me choose to make it just one."

"It is a marvel," Sareth said.

"Actually," came Melia's clear voice, "the real marvel is that you were able to act at all, Travis."

He turned around. The others were close now, picking their way across the rubble toward the center.

"I'm curious, dear," Melia said. "Even I was not able to resist the spell of the demon. How was it that you were able to use the Stone against it?"

Travis gazed down at the Stone of Twilight, quiescent now, and he thought of the girl who had given it to him in his dream—who had given him what he already had, but what he had been too afraid to accept as his own.

Forgiveness.

I love you, Alice.

But aloud all he said was, "I had a little help from my sister."

Melia cocked her head, but before the lady could ask more, Falken spoke, eyeing the rock that had contained the demon.

"So it's dead?"

Melia nodded. "I can still feel a fraction of its power lingering on the air, like ripples in water. But the ripples are already beginning to fade."

She glanced at Grace and Aryn, both of whom nodded in reply.

"It's over then," Travis said with a sigh.

The demon was no more—as were Xemeth and a large number of the Scirathi, he supposed. But somehow he and his friends were still alive. One more mystery to contemplate. Grace met his eyes and smiled at him. He smiled back, then his eyes moved past her to Beltan and Vani. What was he going to say to them? He didn't know. Maybe he would start with—

A shuddering groan rose on the air. Dust and flakes of stone rained down from the fractured dome.

"I do not like the looks of this," Durge said. "I believe those cracks have grown since I last checked. We should leave this place at once."

"This way," Melia said. "The doors of the Etherion are—"

The sound was like lightning passing inches from Travis's face. The floor gave a violent lurch, and he stumbled back into Durge, Lirith, and Sareth. Grace, Beltan, and Vani fell in the opposite direction, colliding with Aryn, Melia, and Falken. Just as Travis started to regain his balance there was another deafening crack, and the floor shuddered yet again.

Someone screamed—Aryn, he thought—then Travis watched as the solidified demon, along with several heaps of rubble, vanished into a pit of darkness. For a confused moment he thought the demon was not dead after all—if such a thing had ever been alive. Then the pit elongated into a black line, swallowing more rubble as it grew.

The floor of the Etherion was cracking apart.

"Back!" Durge shouted. "You must get back!"

The knight pulled at Travis with strong hands. Lirith and Sareth were already fleeing from the crack. On the opposite side, the others did the same.

Again the floor convulsed, and with terrible speed the crack grew until it was a rift fifteen feet across, cutting the Etherion in half. The edges crumbled, falling into the chasm. Stones crashed down from above.

"Travis!"

It was Beltan. There was fear in his voice, in his eyes. Then Travis understood why.

"We can't get to the exit, can we?" Lirith said.

"Not unless you care to leap that."

"It is far too wide," Durge said.

And it was getting wider. Another tremor, and more of the floor sagged into the abyss. The crack was beginning to reach up the walls.

"Melia!" Falken called out above the din of falling stone. "Can't you retrieve them?"

The lady's face was anguished. "Preventing us all from falling was all I could do. I have no strength left for such a deed." She held out a hand. "Oh, my dear ones."

"We must go," Vani said, glancing at the sagging dome.

"But we can't just leave them!" Aryn cried. She reached out her trembling hand—but it was not Lirith's name she called, nor Travis's. "Durge . . ."

"Do not fear for us, my lady," the knight said, his voice stern but his eyes strangely gentle. "You must go now."

The baroness's face was stricken.

Grace struggled to keep her feet. "Travis, what about your runes?"

He shook his head. If there were any runes that could transport them out of here, he didn't—

Travis smacked his forehead with a hand.

"Sareth, the gate!"

The Mournish man's eyes went wide. "*Ga'dath!* We are fools!" He pulled the gate artifact from his pocket.

Lirith moved close. "Do you still have the scarab, Travis?"

He pulled it from a pocket.

"I would advise making haste," Durge rumbled.

"Vani!" Sareth called out. "We have other means of making our escape. You must get the others out of here. Now!"

Vani's eyes shone with understanding. "I shall see you on the other side, my brother."

Beltan raised a hand. "Travis?"

He grinned and waved back. "I'll see you outside, Beltan!"

The knight smiled at him, then nodded.

"Run," Vani said to the rest of them. "We must run!"

Beltan turned and helped Grace and Aryn scramble across the rubble. Vani moved nimbly over the tumbling stones, guiding Melia and Falken through the maze. The six of them disappeared through an archway and were gone.

Stones tumbled down all around, shattering into sharp fragments. Travis turned to see Sareth squeeze the wriggling scarab. One drop of blood oozed forth and fell into the artifact. That meant there was one drop left. It was good to know they had a backup.

Lirith placed the prism atop the artifact, and instantly the gate sprang into being: a black oval ringed by blue fire.

The gate sizzled and wavered.

Durge eyed the portal. "What is wrong with it? It looks sickly."

"I don't know," Sareth said. "Perhaps some lingering effect of the demon interferes with its magic. But it is open, and we must go through."

As if to punctuate Sareth's words, a full quarter of the blue dome caved in, burying the archway through which their friends had fled moments before. The rest of the dome sagged.

"Now!" Sareth shouted.

Together, the four lunged for the gate.

Travis tripped. The sack he had managed to hang on to through everything—and which held his precious objects—slipped from his shoulder and tumbled to the stones. A glinting object skittered out of the pack, halfway slipping into a crevice. His spectacles, the ones which had once belonged to the gunfighter Tyler Caine.

He jerked his head up. The others had already vanished through the gate. It was sputtering. But he couldn't leave the spectacles—Jack had given them to him. Desperate, he groped into the rocks. His fingers touched wire and glass, then closed around the spectacles.

With a cry, Travis hurled himself forward and fell into the crackling gate.

86.

As stone rained down in the Etherion, something stirred beneath a pile of dust and rubble. A figure unfolded itself, its black robes torn to tatters and gray with dust, its serene golden face dented but intact. The figure was broken and bleeding, but it was not dead.

The rift in the floor stretched like a hungry mouth. The high walls groaned, slumping inward. In a moment it was all going to collapse.

Then the figure saw it not ten paces away: a black oval of nothingness surrounded by blue fire. A gate—they had opened a gate. But it was closing in on itself.

The figure sprang into motion, ignoring pain as it scrabbled over sharp stone. A final, dying groan of rending stone shuddered on the air, then the remains of the dome and the walls all fell inward.

With a cry, shredded robe fluttering, the figure flung itself forward—

—and passed through the shrinking iris of the gate.

Like an eye shutting, the gate blinked out of existence, and the Etherion of Tarras—which had stood in splendor above the city for two thousand years—collapsed, forming its own burial mound as it fell.

87

Grace huddled alongside the others, watching as the great blue dome of the Etherion slumped, sagged inward, and collapsed. Thunder rumbled on the air, and a white plume of dust rose into the sky.

The citizens of Tarras crowded the streets of the Second Circle, pointing and crying out as they watched the collapse of the great edifice. Tarrasian soldiers ran in all directions, barking orders. No one paid any attention to the companions, nor had anyone seen them run from the Etherion, for a cloud of rock dust had billowed forth with them, concealing their escape.

Everyone will think an earthquake brought down the Etherion, Grace. They'll never know about the demon that almost consumed the city and everyone in it.

But maybe it was better that way. Maybe it was better they thought it an act of nature rather than an ancient and ravenous magic. Sometimes it was best not to know what dark things dwelled in the world.

Now the walls of the Etherion fell inward, sending more dust into the sky. Aryn sighed, leaning her head on Grace's shoulder, and Grace wrapped her arm around the young baroness.

It's all right, she spun the words over the Weirding, amazed at how easy it was. *We're safe now, Aryn.*

I know, the young woman replied, and sighed again.

Beltan and Vani stood close to one another, their expressions thoughtful. Grace was suddenly struck by how brilliant the big, blond man was next to the dark-haired assassin. He was like bold, bright day to her deep, secret midnight. She couldn't imagine two people who were greater opposites.

But they have something in common, don't they? They both love Travis. Beltan because that's what his heart tells him, and Vani because of the cards.

"I can't bear to watch it," Melia said softly, tears shining on her coppery cheeks.

She turned away from the destruction, and Falken held her, his faded eyes grim. In her arms the small lady held a tiny black kitten. Grace wondered where it could possibly have come from. The kitten let out a soft *mew* and patted Melia's cheek with a paw.

More soldiers ran into the street, sun glinting off their breastplates, shouting at the onlookers to stay back.

"We should not draw attention to ourselves," Vani said. "There might yet be Scirathi about. We cannot hope all of their number were destroyed in the Etherion."

They moved into the mouth of a narrow street where they could watch the chaos from blue shade. Again came a low rumbling, and more dust rising into the air.

"Xemeth," Vani murmured, her eyes full of pain.

Grace glanced at the assassin and thought maybe she understood. In a way it was because Vani had rejected Xemeth's love that he had allied himself with the Scirathi and freed the demon. All the same, that had been Xemeth's doing, not hers. Grace gently disentangled herself from Aryn and moved to the

T'gol. She hesitated, then laid a hand on Vani's arm.

"It wasn't your fault," she said.

Vani gave a stiff nod but did not reply.

Falken flexed his black-gloved hand. "Now that the demon has been destroyed, I hope the river of time will return to its rightful flow."

Melia had dried her tears. "It already has. Mandu tells me that there are yet a few eddies and ripples, but no more, and that even those are growing calm. We shall not lose ourselves in the past any longer."

Beltan shuddered. "Yes, that's what it was like— getting tangled in the past."

Aryn looked up, her eyes wide. "I thought . . . I thought it was just me."

Grace gazed at the young woman, concerned. "What happened, Aryn?"

"It was horrible." The baroness folded her arm around herself. "Like a bad dream, only so much more real than that. It was Midwinter's Eve again, and I . . ." She drew in a breath and squared her shoulders. "I did something terrible in the dream, something I did once in truth, and of which I am horribly ashamed."

Grace understood. Leothan. Aryn had slain the young lord with a spell. But he had been an ironheart.

"Then a shadow was there. It wanted me to leap from the highest turret of the castle. But I didn't." She looked up, blue eyes shining. "You see, I knew that wasn't the answer, that dying wouldn't undo what was done. I think the shadow was furious. It screamed at me, but I ran."

Grace didn't know what to say. She took Aryn's hand—the right, not the left—and held the pale, folded appendage between her own two hands.

"Your dream is not so different from mine," Beltan said, the knight's face uncharacteristically sober. "Like you, I saw again a dark deed that I once committed. It was . . . a man that I killed. Then the shadow came to me, and it bade me to turn the knife upon myself. I started to push the blade into my own heart. And then . . ."

Grace gazed at him. "Then what, Beltan?"

The big knight shrugged broad shoulders. "Then I realized that, whatever I had done in the past, there was something in my present that made me want to live."

Grace smiled at him; she didn't need to speak the name aloud. *Travis*. But what dark deed could Beltan have possibly done? He said he had killed a man, but he was a warrior. Had he not been forced to slay many men in battle?

Melia touched the blossoms of a *lindara* vine that climbed up the white wall of the lane. "The shadow in your dreams was the demon, I think. That was part of its magic. Had you done the things in your dreams that it wished you to do, then it would have won, and it would have consumed you." She looked up, her amber eyes bright. "But you didn't surrender yourself to the shadow. The ghosts of the past will haunt you no longer."

Grace knew that wasn't entirely true. The shadows of the past were still there. If she shut her eyes and reached out with the Touch, she could still see them as she had once before, attached to the gleaming life thread of each of them.

And yet . . .

The shadows were smaller now, and more distant. Even Grace's own. She thought that, just maybe, she understood the reason. They could never leave their past behind, not completely; like a shadow, it would always trail after them. But also like a shadow, it had no real power, no true form. The dark would always remain, but that did not mean they could not face forward, into the light.

Grace drew in a breath, then she shut her eyes, reached out, and Touched the shimmering web of the Weirding. She did it with abandon, without holding back any fraction of herself, and for the very first time, Grace embraced the glittering threads—embraced the fabric of *life*—without fear.

It was glorious.

Grace?

It was Aryn's voice, speaking in her mind.

Grace, are you all right?

How could she explain?

I am, Aryn, she spun back. *For the first time in my life, I really am all right.*

Doctor, heal thyself.

Grace opened her eyes. The others were looking at her with curious expressions. She grimaced, then laughed.

"Sorry," she said, and left it at that. As Lirith had once taught her, it was all right for a girl to maintain a little mystery.

Her laughter faded then, and she found herself gazing at Vani, and at Melia and Falken. What had each of them dreamed about while caught in the thrall of the demon? Whatever it was, they seemed unwilling to say. Yet Falken's weathered visage was haggard, and Grace thought she could guess what moment the shadow had made him live again: the death of a kingdom.

But Malachor isn't dead, is it, Grace? Not completely, not if you're here.

It was absurd of course. But then, so were the hundred other things that had happened to her since that October night just under a year ago when she journeyed to Eldh. Back to Eldh.

She touched the steel pendant at her throat. *You're a queen, Grace, whether you like it or not. But lucky for you, you're the ruler of a kingdom that doesn't exist anymore. You have to admit, that makes it rather convenient. All of the majesty, none of the burden.*

"What about you, Grace?" Beltan said. "What did you see in the shadow?"

She gripped the necklace, licked her lips. "It was the orphanage, back in Colorado. I was there again, the night the placed burned down. Only I—"

Her heart lurched, and she looked up at the others, cold despite the balmy air. "It was me. I was the one who did it. I didn't remember it that way. I don't . . . I don't think I understood at the time. But now, seeing it again, it was so clear."

Aryn moved toward her. "What was clear, Grace?"

"The fire. I was the one who started the fire that burned down the orphanage. With a spell."

The baroness stared in amazement, and Melia pressed her lips together and nodded.

"I have heard," Melia said, "that sometimes a witch's talent can first manifest in a moment of great duress."

Dizziness swept over Grace. Duress. Yes, that was one word for it. She remembered the stairs, the door opening, and Mrs. Fulch on the chaise, the gaping wound in her chest . . .

She gasped and looked at the bard. "Falken, I have to tell you something I saw. It was so horrible, I must have . . . I must have locked the memory away somewhere inside myself. But now I remember everything. I . . ."

The others gazed at her, concern on their faces.

Falken took her shoulders in his hands and held her firmly but gently.

"What is it, dear one?" the bard said. "You're safe here. You can tell us."

It was so hard to speak. The words tumbled out of her like fragments of glass.

"Ironhearts. At the orphanage on Earth. I saw them making one. Mrs. Fulch. They put it in her chest, the lump of iron, and she woke up. And the other was there. The Pale One. And then I saw it in the wraithling's light—the symbol of the Raven Cult." She shook her head. "But it's not a raven's wing. It was an eye . . . an eye set in a horrible face, and they said they were going to help him get back, to return to his world and rule it all."

Melia's face was ashen. Falken's fingers dug into Grace's flesh, his eyes intent.

"Who, Grace? Who were they trying to help get back to his world?"

Somehow she forced the words out one by one. "The Lord of Nightfall."

Melia gasped, and Falken swore. The bard seemed to realize he was squeezing her brutally and let go.

"Grace, forgive me, I . . ."

She shook her head, laid her hand on his arm. Her mind worked furiously, putting the pieces together, making her terrible diagnosis.

"It's him, isn't it, Falken? I asked you about it once—how if the Little People could come back, why couldn't the Old Gods? And it turns out he's been there all along, on Earth, searching for a way. He's been behind everything—the Pale King, the Raven Cult. Even the Scirathi. I'm sure of it, from what Xemeth said. He's the cause of all of this."

Aryn and Beltan exchanged puzzled looks, and Vani frowned.

"Who do you speak of?" the assassin said. "Who is the master of all these evils you describe?"

Grace licked her lips. "Mohg."

Melia was shaking. "The eye . . . of course. We should have seen it before. Not a raven's wing, but an eye. The eye that was blinded—"

"—and which sees once more," Falken finished.

Melia's face was stricken. She held her arms out to Grace, then pulled them back in. "Oh, my dear one, what did we do to you? We thought to protect you, and instead we sent you into the very hands of darkness. How you suffered because of our deeds. You must hate us."

Grace couldn't bear it. She had not regained her heart only to have it break like this.

"I love you, Melia," she said softly. "I love you and Falken both, so much."

The amber-eyed lady turned back, her face writ with agony and astonishment, as was the bard's.

Grace moved to them. "You fought for the lives of my parents, and for my life as well. How could I do anything but love you both?"

She caught them in a fierce hug. For a moment the bard and the lady were too stunned to move, then they returned her embrace.

"My little Ralena," Melia murmured.

"No," Falken murmured. "Our Grace, all grown up."

At last they stepped back from one another.

Beltan was gazing at them, green eyes hazed with confusion. "I don't understand, Falken. No surprise there, I know. It seems I'm always the last to catch on to these big, world-shaking sorts of things. But why does Mohg want to get back to Eldh?"

Aryn clasped Beltan's hand. "You're not the only one who's slow at catching on, cousin."

"He wants to finish what he began a thousand years ago," Falken said, voice hoarse. "He wants to do what together the Old and New Gods prevented him from doing once before."

"Which is?" Beltan said.

"Mohg wishes to break the First Rune and reforge Eldh in his own image, enslaving it and all of its people forever."

These words left them speechless. Outside the lane, the crash of stone had ceased, and the soldiers had done their work, for the streets of the Second Circle were clearing.

Vani moved with lithe steps and peered out. "I do not like this."

"What is it?" Melia said, drawing closer.

Vani turned around, her gold eyes gleaming. "My brother, Travis, and the others. They should be here by now."

Only as she said this did Grace realize it was true. They had been so caught up in their discoveries they had forgotten about Travis, Sareth, Durge, and Lirith.

Falken scratched his chin. "Doesn't it take some time to go through the gate? I just assumed it did."

"No," the assassin said, her words sharp as knives. "Transport through the gate is instantaneous."

A frown lined Beltan's face. "I don't see what you're getting at."

"What does it mean?" Aryn said.

Vani met each of their gazes in turn, and Grace felt fresh, new dread well up inside of her.

"It means," Vani said, "that something has gone wrong."

88.

This wasn't right. It couldn't be.

Travis blinked as a brisk wind kicked up gritty dust in his face. Tumbleweeds danced and rolled across the broad dirt street that stretched before him. Wooden buildings lined the street, their sharp square fronts jutting up into the blue-quartz sky.

"This does not look like Tarras to me," Durge said in his rumbling voice.

That was an understatement. Travis opened his mouth, but it was too hard to speak. The unnatural cold of their passage still gripped him. As he watched, frost evaporated from their clothes in curls of steam, sublimating under the bright force of the sun—a sun that seemed at once whiter and smaller than the sun that shone above Tarras.

Lirith shook her head, moisture glittering in her black hair. "Sareth, what is this place?"

The Mournish man took a step forward, his wooden leg stirring up more dust. "I do not know, *beshala*. Nothing about it is familiar."

But it is to me, Travis wanted to say. He knew this place. But how? He remembered stepping through the gate, and the freezing gray nothingness of the void. . . .

The void. But there shouldn't have been a void, not

when passing from one place to another in Tarras. The gray emptiness existed only between worlds. . . .

At last understanding cracked through the ice that encased his brain. They weren't in Tarras. They weren't even on Eldh. This was Earth.

Not just Earth, Travis.

Yes, there was McKay's General Store, as well as the opera house, the assay office, and the Mine Shaft Saloon—

The Mine Shaft? But the saloon couldn't possibly be there. He had watched it burn down with his own eyes. Yet it was. Which meant this could only be one place.

"It's Castle City," he murmured.

The others gave him sharp glances.

"You mean your home village, Travis?" Durge said. The knight's brown eyes went wide. "This is your *world*?"

Travis staggered forward. "Yes, it is. But . . ."

But something was wrong.

"What happened to us, Sareth?" Lirith said. The witch laid a hand on his arm, her gaze imploring.

The Mournish man hefted the black stone artifact. "I cannot say. The gate was acting strangely. I suppose some magic of the demon must yet have lingered on the air, distorting the power of the artifact."

"But we have one last drop of the scarab blood," Durge said. "Can we not use it to go back?"

Travis hardly heard them. His brain raced. What was going on here? The storefronts, Elk Street, Castle Peak looming in the distance—all of it looked familiar. But it all looked *wrong*. He took another step forward. . . .

He almost didn't see it in time. A dark shape came rattling around a corner and hurtled down Elk Street. A whip cracked, and horses neighed.

"Travis!"

Durge's strong hands grabbed his shoulders and jerked him back just in time to keep him from being run over. Travis blinked and watched the stagecoach bounce down the rutted swath of Elk Street toward the Silver Palace Hotel.

"That is a most curious sort of wagon," Lirith said. "Is it a common conveyance for your world, Travis?"

Common? Not in the last hundred years or so.

"It can't be," Travis whispered. "This is impossible."

But hadn't the demon distorted the flow of time? Wasn't that part of its power?

A dust devil whirled around them, catching them in a gritty embrace, and a piece of paper struck Travis, clinging to his face. He pawed at the paper, pulled it away, then gazed at the large, black words printed across the top:

THE CASTLE CITY CLARION

He didn't want to look. All the same, he forced his eyes to the small print beneath the masthead, forced the letters to stop swimming. Despite the sickness that flowed into his gut, Travis knew he had not mixed the numbers up:

FINAL EDITION—June 13, 1883

"What is it, Travis?" Lirith said, words breathless.

Even the gate couldn't help them. Not unless they wanted to get back to Tarras over a hundred years before their friends ever arrived there. He looked up from the newspaper and met the eyes of the witch, the knight, and the Mournish man.

"I think we're lost," Travis said.

Here ends *The Dark Remains*, Book Three of *The Last Rune*.
The tales of the companions on both worlds will continue in Book Four, *Blood of Mystery*.

ABOUT THE AUTHOR

MARK ANTHONY learned to love both books and mountains during childhood summers spent in a Colorado ghost town. Later he was trained as a paleo-anthropologist but along the way grew interested in a different sort of human evolution—the symbolic progress reflected in myth and the literature of the fantastic. He undertook this project to explore the idea that reason and wonder need not exist in conflict. Mark Anthony lives and writes in Colorado. Fans of *The Last Rune* can visit the website at http://www.thelastrune.com.